DEMUS
JOSEY WALES
KIM CLARKE
TRISTAN
ALEX
CE
HN K
AS PALMER
RECORDS STEREO
W9-BMX-624

ABOUT THE AUTHOR

MARLON JAMES was born in Jamaica. He is the author of the Man Booker Prize-winning novel, *A Brief History of Seven Killings* (Oneworld 2014), which also won the American Book Award, the Anisfield-Wolf Fiction Prize, was a finalist for the National Book Critics Circle Award, and featured in over twenty best books of the year lists. His debut novel, *John Crow's Devil* (Oneworld, 2015), was a finalist for the *Los Angeles Times* Book Prize, shortlisted for the Commonwealth Writers' Prize, and was a *New York Times* Editors' Choice. His second novel, *The Book of Night Women* (Oneworld, 2009), won the Dayton Literary Peace Prize and the Minnesota Book Award, and was a finalist for the National Book Critics Circle Award. He teaches at Macalester College, Minnesota, USA.

JAMAICA, 1976

Seven gunmen storm Bob Marley's house, machine guns blazing. The reggae superstar survives, but the gunmen are never caught.

From the acclaimed author of *The Book of Night Women* comes a dazzling display of masterful storytelling exploring this near-mythic event. Spanning three decades and crossing continents, *A Brief History of Seven Killings* chronicles the lives of a host of unforgettable characters – slum kids, drug lords, gunmen, journalists, and even the CIA. Gripping and inventive, ambitious and mesmerizing, *A Brief History of Seven Killings* is one of the most remarkable and extraordinary novels of the twenty-first century.

'The most thrilling and radical winner in years.' *Independent*

'It's like a Tarantino remake of "The Harder They Come" but with a soundtrack by Bob Marley and a script by Oliver Stone and William Faulkner.'
New York Times

'A vast, ambitious burning mansion of a book.' *Telegraph*

'A fabulous literary performance – astonishingly energetic line by line, with a whole host of different verbal registers, storytelling moves, moments of tenderness and broad comedy as well as, yes, sex and violence and swearing.'
Evening Standard

'This novel cracks open a world that needs to be known. It's scary and lyrically beautiful – you'll want to read whole pages aloud to strangers.' Russell Banks

'A vivid plunge into a crazed, violent and corrupt world, told through multiple narrators and executed with swaggering aplomb ... The most original novel I've read in years.' Irvine Welsh

'Magnificent ... James has triumphed in capturing the tension, the politics, the heat, chaos, beauty and music of Jamaica.' *Financial Times*

'This is the go-for-broke BIG BOOK of the year, a vast, challenging kaleidoscopic historical novel, as told from the edges of history. Hilary Mantel would approve.' *Chicago Tribune*

'Dazzling.' *GQ*

A NOTE FROM THE AUTHOR

There it stands, like a cornerstone in the middle of the book. If you are reading this, then we're at the beginning, but if you turn to page 458 you'll see where the book really began—the first paragraph I ever wrote, the first character I created and the first scenario from which came this book. Except at the time, a book, a novel, and a novel as large as this one was the furthest thing from my mind.

A Brief History of Seven Killings was supposed to be my shortest novel. Maybe even less than that, and more of a padded novella, much like the short, brutal and brilliant novels I was reading at the time from James M. Cain, Jim Thompson and Jean-Patrick Manchette. Crime novels. It was really very simple: a gay hitman from Chicago on assignment to kill a Jamaican gangster finds himself crippled by anxiety over a possible break up. The Jamaican gangster, fat with crack-cocaine millions, was to be told, right before the kill, "Jah live."

It was supposed to be the novel's 'rosebud,' an in-joke that only Jamaicans and backward-looking conspiracy theorists would guess at. But instead, from those two words a novel exploded in my face. It wasn't the only novella I was writing at the time, but I soon discovered, after my late friend Rachel noticed it first, that all these shorter stories were actually one big story, that could never be just one voice. She pointed me to Faulkner's *As I Lay Dying*, and from there I went on to other great novels with multiple voices, or dealing with multiple characters, such as James Ellroy's *American Tabloid*. Ellroy's gift for throwing center-stage history to marginal characters had a huge impact on me as well.

The problem was really me. For the novel to work I had to get out of the way. It's a novel driven by language and built on voice, and the one voice not needed was my own. And with it, out went my ideas of narrative, plot, and even what the modern novel should be like. In a very real way, this novel could only be created by breaking it down, stretching my idea of prose to the breaking point, risking sentimentality, risking extremity, injecting comedy into the tragedy, and verse into the violence. In short, to build this novel I had to take my idea of everything a novel should be, and destroy it.

Marlon James

A BRIEF HISTORY OF SEVEN KILLINGS

A PLAYLIST BY

Marlon James

1. **World A Music** (5:45)
   Ini Kamoze

2. **Natty Dread** (3:35)
   Bob Marley & The Wailers

3. **King Tubby Meets The Rockers Uptown** (2:32)
   Augustus Pablo

4. **Ark Of The Covenant** (3:46)
   The Congos

5. **Ghetto Funk** (3:12)
   Boris Gardiner

6. **Ma Baker** (4:35)
   Boney M.

7. **Shadow Dancing** (4:35)
   Andy Gibb

8. **Living on the Frontline** (5:57)
   Eddy Grant

9. **Party Next Door** (5:55)
Black Uhuru

10. **Kids In America** (3:24)
Kim Wilde

11. **Rockit** (5:26)
Herbie Hancock

12. **Jam On It** (6:24)
Newcleus

13. **Hip Hop Be Bop – Don't Stop** (5:41)
Man Parrish

14. **White Lines (Don't Do It)** (4:27)
Grandmaster Flash

15. **Electric Avenue** (3:47)
Eddy Grant

16. **Tempo** (3:25)
Anthony Red Rose

17. **Sleng Teng** (3:19)
Wayne Smith

18. **Budda Bye 2014 (feat. Johnny Osbourne) – Vocal Mix** (4:26)
Capitol City Rockers, 6Blocc, Johnny Osbourne

19. **When** (3:36)
Tiger

20. **Ghetto Red Hot** (3:52)
Super Cat

21. **Sound Boy Killing (Remix)** (3:32)
Mega Banton

22. **Higher Than the Sun – A Dub Symphony in Two Parts** (7:37)
Primal Scream, Jah Wobble

23. **Welcome To Jamrock** (3:33)
Damian Marley

A BRIEF HISTORY *of* SEVEN KILLINGS

Marlon James

ONEWORLD

A Oneworld Book

First published in Great Britain and the Commonwealth by
Oneworld Publications, 2014

This special edition published by Oneworld Publications in 2015

A CIP record for this title is available from the British Library

ISBN 978-1-78074-976-1
ISBN 978-1-78074-588-6 (eBook)

Author photograph © Jeffrey Skemp
Printed and bound in Great Britain by Clays Ltd, St Ives plc

Oneworld Publications
10 Bloomsbury Street
London WC1B 3SR
England

CONTENTS

To Maurice James

An extraordinary gentleman in a league of his own.

CAST OF CHARACTERS

GREATER KINGSTON from 1959

Sir Arthur Jennings, former politician, deceased
The Singer, reggae superstar of the world
Peter Nasser, politician, strategist
Nina Burgess, former receptionist, presently unemployed
Kim-Marie Burgess, her sister
Ras Trent, Kim-Marie's lover
Doctor Love / Luis Hernán Rodrigo de las Casas, CIA consultant
Barry Diflorio, CIA station chief, Jamaica
Claire Diflorio, his wife
William Adler, former field officer, CIA, now rogue
Alex Pierce, journalist, *Rolling Stone*
Mark Lansing, filmmaker, son of Richard Lansing, former CIA director
Louis Johnson, field officer, CIA
Mr. Clark, field officer, CIA
Bill Bilson, journalist, the Jamaica *Gleaner*
Sally Q, fixer, informant
Tony McFerson, politician
Officer Watson, police
Officer Nevis, police
Officer Grant, police

Copenhagen City

Papa-Lo / Raymond Clarke, don of Copenhagen City, 1960–1979
Josey Wales, head enforcer, don of Copenhagen City, 1979–1991, leader of the Storm Posse
Weeper, gang enforcer, Storm Posse head enforcer, Manhattan/Brooklyn
Demus, gang member
Heckle, gang member
Bam-Bam, gang member
Funky Chicken, gang member
Renton, gang member
Leggo Beast, gang member
Tony Pavarotti, enforcer, sniper
Priest, messenger, informer
Junior Soul, informer/rumored Eight Lanes spy
The Wang Gang, gang based in Wang Sang Lands, affiliated with Copenhagen City
Copper, gang enforcer
Chinaman, gang leader near Copenhagen City
Treetop, gang member
Bullman, enforcer

The Eight Lanes

Shotta Sherrif / Roland Palmer, don of the Eight Lanes, 1975–1980
Funnyboy, gang enforcer and second-in-command
Buntin-Banton, coleader and don of the Eight Lanes, 1972–1975
Dishrag, coleader and don of the Eight Lanes, 1972–1975

Outside Jamaica, 1976–1979

Donald Casserley, drug trafficker, president, Jamaica Freedom League
Richard Lansing, CIA director, 1973–1976
Lindon Wolfsbricker, American ambassador to Yugoslavia
Admiral Warren Tunney, CIA director, 1977–1981
Roger Theroux, field officer, CIA
Miles Copeland, CIA station chief, Cairo
Edgar Anatolyevich Cheporov, reporter, Novosti News Agency
Freddy Lugo, operative, Alpha 66, United Revolutionary Organizations, AMBLOOD
Hernán Ricardo Lozano, operative, Alpha 66, United Revolutionary Organizations, AMBLOOD
Orlando Bosch, operative Omega 7, United Revolutionary Organizations, AMBLOOD
Gael and Freddy, operatives, Omega 7, United Revolutionary Organizations, AMBLOOD
Sal Resnick, journalist, *New York Times*

Montego Bay, 1979

Kim Clarke, unemployed
Charles/Chuck, engineer, Alcorp Bauxite

Miami and New York, 1985–1991

Storm Posse, Jamaican drug syndicate
Ranking Dons, rival Jamaican drug syndicate
Eubie, head enforcer, Storm Posse, Queens/Bronx
A-Plus, associate of Tristan Phillips
Pig Tails, enforcer, Storm Posse, Queens/Bronx
Ren-Dog, enforcer, Storm Posse, Queens/Bronx

Omar, enforcer, Storm Posse, Manhattan/Brooklyn
Romeo, drug dealer, Storm Posse, Brooklyn
Tristan Phillips, inmate, Rikers, member of Ranking Dons
John-John K, hit man, carjacker
Paco, carjacker
Griselda Blanco, drug lord, Medellín cartel Miami operations
Baxter, enforcer for Griselda Blanco
The Hawaiian Shirts, enforcers for Griselda Blanco
Kenneth Colthirst, New York resident, 5th Avenue
Gaston Colthirst, his son
Gail Colthirst, his daughter-in-law
Dorcas Palmer, caregiver
Millicent Segree, student nurse
Miss Betsy, manager, God Bless Employment Agency
Monifah Thibodeaux, drug addict

Gonna tell the truth about it,
Honey, that's the hardest part

—BONNIE RAITT, *"Tangled and Dark"*

If it no go so, it go near so.

—*Jamaican proverb*

Sir Arthur George Jennings

Listen.

Dead people never stop talking. Maybe because death is not death at all, just a detention after school. You know where you're coming from and you're always returning from it. You know where you're going though you never seem to get there and you're just dead. Dead. It sounds final but it's a word missing an *ing*. You come across men longer dead than you, walking all the time though heading nowhere, and you listen to them howl and hiss because we're all spirits or we think we are all spirits but we're all just dead. Spirits that slip inside other spirits. Sometimes a woman slips inside a man and wails like the memory of making love. They moan and keen loud but it comes through the window like a whistle or a whisper under the bed, and little children think there's a monster. The dead love lying under the living for three reasons. (1) We're lying most of the time. (2) Under the bed looks like the top of a coffin, but (3) There is weight, human weight on top that you can slip into and make heavier, and you listen to the heart beat while you watch it pump and hear the nostrils hiss when their lungs press air and envy even the shortest breath. I have no memory of coffins.

But the dead never stop talking and sometimes the living hear. This is what I wanted to say. When you're dead speech is nothing but tangents and detours and there's nothing to do but stray and wander awhile. Well, that's at least what the others do. My point being that the expired learn from the expired, but that's tricky. I could listen to myself, still claiming to anybody that would hear that I didn't fall, I was pushed over the balcony at the Sunset Beach Hotel in Montego Bay. And I can't say shut your trap, Artie Jennings, because every morning I wake up having to put my pumpkin-smashed head back together. And even as I talk now I can hear how I sounded then, can you dig it, dingledoodies? meaning that the afterlife is just not a happening scene, not a groovy shindig, Daddy-O, see those cool cats on the mat? They could never dig it, and there's nothing to do but wait for the man that killed me, but he won't die, he only gets older and older and trades out wives for younger and younger and breeding a whole brood of slow-witted boys and running the country down into the ground.

Dead people never stop talking and sometimes the living hear. Sometimes he talks back if I catch him right as his eyes start to flicker in his sleep, talks until his wife slaps him. But I'd rather listen to the longer dead. I see men in split breeches and bloody longcoats and they talk, but blood comes out of their mouths and good heavens that slave rebellion was such ghastly business and that queen has of course been of bloody awful use ever since the West India Company began their rather shoddy decline compared to the East and why are there so many negroes taking to sleeping so unsoundly wherever they see fit and confound it all I seem to have misplaced the left half of my face. To be dead is to understand that dead is not gone, you're in the flatness of the deadlands. Time doesn't stop. You watch it move but you are still, like a painting with a Mona Lisa smile. In this space a three-hundred-year-old slit throat and two-minute-old crib death is the same.

If you don't watch how you sleep, you'll find yourself the way the living found you. Me, I'm lying on the floor, my head a smashed pumpkin, with my right leg twisted behind the back and my two arms bent in a way that arms aren't supposed to bend, and from high up, from the balcony, I look like a dead spider. I am up there and down here and from up there I see myself the way my killer saw me. The dead relive a motion, an action, a scream, and they're there again just like that, the train that never stopped running until it ran off the rails, the ledge from that building sixteen floors up, the car trunk that ran out of air. Rudeboys' bodies bursting like pricked balloons, fifty-six bullets.

Nobody falls that way without being pushed. I know. And I know how it feels and looks, a body that falls fighting air all the way down, grabbing on to clumps of nothing and begging once, just once, just goddamn once, Jesus, you sniveling son of a mongrel bitch, just once that air gives a grip.

And you land in a ditch five feet deep or on a marble-tiled floor sixteen feet down, still fighting when the floor rises up and smashes into you because it got tired of waiting for blood. And we're still dead but we wake up, me a crushed spider, him a burned cockroach. I have no memory of coffins.

Listen.

Living people wait and see because they fool themselves that they have time. Dead people see and wait. I once asked my Sunday school teacher, if heaven is the place of eternal life, and hell is the opposite of heaven, what does that make hell? A place for dirty little red boys like you, she said. She's still alive. I see her, at the Eventide Old Folks Home, getting too old and too stupid, not knowing her name and talking in so soft a rasp that nobody can hear that she's scared of nightfall because that's when the rats come for her good toes. I see more than that. Look hard enough or maybe just to the left and you see a country that was the same as I left it. It never changes. Whenever I'm around people they are exactly as I had left them, aging making no difference.

The man who was father of a nation, father to me more than my own, cried like a sudden widow when he heard I had died. You never know when people's dreams are connected to you before you're gone and then there's nothing to do but watch them die in a different way, slow, limb by limb, system by system. Heart condition, diabetes, slow-killing diseases with slow-sounding names. This is the body going over to death with impatience, one part at a time. He will live to see them make him a national hero and he will die the only person thinking he had failed. That's what happens when you personify hopes and dreams in one person. He becomes nothing more than a literary device.

This is a story of several killings, of boys who meant nothing to a world still spinning, but each of them as they pass me carry the sweet-stink scent of the man that killed me.

The first, he screams his tonsils out but the scream stops right at the gate of his teeth because they have gagged him and it tastes like vomit and stone. And someone has tied his hands tight behind his back but they feel loose because all the skin has rubbed off and blood is greasing the rope. He's kicking with both legs because right is tied to left, kicking the dirt rising five feet, then six, and he cannot stand because it's raining mud and dirt and dust to dust and rocks. One rock claps his nose and another bullets his eye and it's erupting and he's screaming but the scream runs right to the tip of his mouth then back down like reflux and the dirt is a flood that's rising and rising and he cannot see his toes. Then he'll wake up and he's still dead and he won't tell me his name.

ORIGINAL ROCKERS

December 2, 1976

Bam-Bam

I *know I was fourteen.* That me know. I also know that too many people talk too much, especially the American, who never shut up, just switch to a laugh every time he talk 'bout you, and it sound strange how he put your name beside people we never hear 'bout, Allende Lumumba, a name that sound like a country that Kunta Kinte come from. The American, most of the time hide him eye with sunglasses like he is a preacher from America come to talk to black people. Him and the Cuban come sometimes together, sometimes on they own, and when one talk the other always quiet. The Cuban don't fuck with guns because guns always need to be needed, him say.

And I know me used to sleep on a cot and I know that my mother was a whore and my father was the last good man in the ghetto. And I know we watched your big house on Hope Road for days now, and at one point you come talk to us like you was Jesus and we was Iscariot and you nod as if to say get on with your business and do what you have to do. But I can't remember if me see you or if somebody told me that him see you so that me think I see it too, you stepping out on the back porch, eating a slice of breadfruit, she coming out of nowhere like she have serious business outside at that time of night and shocked, so shocked that you don't have no clothes on, then she reach for your fruit because she want to eat it even though Rasta don't like when woman loose and you both get to midnight raving, and I grab meself and rave too from either seeing it or hearing it, and then you write a song about it. The boy from Concrete Jungle on the same girly green scooter come by for four days at eight in the morning and four in the evening for the brown envelope until the new security squad start to turn him back. We know about that business too.

In the Eight Lanes and in Copenhagen City all you can do is watch. Sweet-talking voice on the radio say that crime and violence are taking over the country and if change ever going to come then we will have to wait and see, but all we can do down here in the Eight Lanes is see and wait. And I see shit water run free down the street and I wait. And I see my mother take two men for twenty dollars each and one more who pay twenty-five to stay in instead of pull out and I wait. And I watch my father get so sick and tired of her that he beat her like a dog. And I see the zinc on the roof rust itself brown, and then the rain batter hole into it like foreign cheese, and I see seven people in one room and one pregnant and people fucking anyway because people so poor that they can't even afford shame and I wait.

And the little room get smaller and smaller and more sisterbrother-cousin come from country, the city getting bigger and bigger and there be no place to rub-a-dub or cut you shit and no chicken back to curry and even when there is it still cost too much money and that little girl get stab because they know she get lunch money every Tuesday and the boys like me getting older and not in school very regular and can't read Dick and Jane but know Coca-Cola, and want to go to a studio and cut a tune and sing hit songs and ride the riddim out of the ghetto but Copenhagen City and the Eight Lanes both too big and every time you reach the edge, the edge move ahead of you like a shadow until the whole world is a ghetto, and you wait.

I see you hungry and waiting and know that it's just luck, you loafing around the studio and Desmond Dekker telling the man to give you a break, and he give you the break because he hear the hunger in your voice before he even hear you sing. You cut a tune, but not a hit song, too pretty for the ghetto even then, for we past the time when prettiness make anybody's life easy. We see you hustle and trying to talk your way twelve inches taller and we want to see you fail. And we know nobody would want you to be a rude-boy anyway for you look like a schemer.

And when you disappear to Delaware and come back, you try sing the ska, but ska already left the ghetto to take up residence uptown. Ska take the plane to foreign to show white people that it's just like the twist. Maybe that make the Syrian and the Lebanese proud, but when we see them in the newspaper posing with Air Hostess we not proud, just stunned stupid. You make another song, this time a hit. But one hit can't bounce you out of the ghetto when you recording hits for a vampire. One hit can't make you into Skeeter Davis or the man who sing them Gunfighter Ballads.

By the time boy like me drop out of my mother, she give up. Preacher says there is a god-shaped void in everybody life but the only thing ghetto people can fill a void with is void. Nineteen seventy-two is nothing like 1962 and people still whispering for they could never shout that when Artie Jennings dead all of a sudden he take the dream with him. The dream of what I don't know. People stupid. The dream didn't leave, people just don't know a nightmare when they right in the middle of one. More people start moving to the ghetto because Delroy Wilson just sing that "Better Must Come" and the man who would become Prime Minister sing it too. Better Must Come. Man who look like white man but chat bad like naigger when they have to, singing "Better Must Come." Woman who dress like the Queen, who never care about the ghetto before it swell and burst in Kingston singing "Better Must Come."

But worst come first.

We see and wait. Two men bring guns to the ghetto. One man show me how to use it. But ghetto people used to kill each other long before that. With anything we could find: stick, machete, knife, ice pick, soda bottle. Kill for food. Kill for money. Sometimes a man get kill because he look at another man in a way that he didn't like. And killing don't need no reason. This is ghetto. Reason is for rich people. We have madness.

Madness is walking up a good street downtown and seeing a woman dress up in the latest fashion and wanting to go straight up to her and grab her bag, knowing that it's not the bag or the money that we want so much, but the scream, when she see that you jump right into her pretty-up face and you could slap the happy right out of her mouth and punch the joy right out of her eye and kill her right there and rape her before or after you kill her because that is what rudeboys like we do to decent women like her. Madness that make you follow a man in a suit down King Street, where poor people never go and watch him throw away a sandwich, chicken, you smell it and wonder how people can be so rich that they use chicken for just to put between so-so bread, and you pass the garbage and see it, still in the foil, and still fresh, not brown with the other garbage and no fly on it yet and you think maybe, and you think yes and you think you have to, just to see what chicken taste like with no bone. But you say you not no madman, and the madness in you is not crazy people madness but angry madness, because you know the man throw it away because he want you to see. And you promise yourself that one day rudeboy going to start walking with a knife and next time I going jump him and carve sufferah right in him chest.

But he know boy like me can't walk downtown for long before we get pounce on by Babylon. Police only have to see that me don't have no shoes before he say what the bloodcloth you nasty naiggers doing 'round decent people, and give me two choices. Run and he give chase into one of the lanes that cut through the city so that he can shoot me in the private. Plenty shots in the magazine so at least one bullet must hit. Or stand down and get beat up right in front of decent people, him swinging the baton and knocking out my side teeth and cracking my temple so that I can never hear good out of that ear again and saying let that be a lesson to never take you dutty, stinking, ghetto self uptown again. And I see them and I wait.

But then you come back even though nobody know when you leave. Woman want to know why you come back when you can always get nice things like Uncle Ben's rice in America. We wonder if you go there to sing hit songs. Some of we keep watching as you shift through the ghetto like small fish in a big river. Me know your game now but didn't see it then, how you friend up the gunman here, the Rasta with the big sound there and this bad man and that rudeboy and even my father, so that everybody know you enough to like you, but not enough to remember to recruit you. You sing just about anything, anything to get a hit, even stuff that you alone know and nobody else care about. "And I Love Her," because Prince Buster cover "You Won't See Me" and get himself a hit. You use what you have, even a melody that's not yours, and you sing it hard and sing it long and sing yourself straight out of the ghetto. By 1971 you already on TV. By 1971 I shoot my first shot.

I was ten.

And ghetto life don't mean nothing. Is nothing to kill a boy. I remember the last time my father try to save me. He run home from the factory, I remember because my face reach him chest when we both stand and he panting so hard like a dog. The rest of the evening we in the house, on we knee and toe. Is a game he say, too loud and too quick. Who stand up first lose, he said. So me stand up because me is ten and me is big boy and me tired of game but he yell and grab me and thump me in the chest. And me huff and puff and breathing so hard that I want to cry and want to hate him but then the first one slip through like somebody fling gravel and it bounce 'gainst the wall. And then the next and the next. And then they rip right across the wall *pap-pap-pap-pap-pap-pap* except for the last bullet that hit a pot with a bang and then six seven ten twenty blast into the wall like a *chukchukchukchukchukchukchuk*. And he grab me and try to cover my ears but he grab so hard that he don't realize that he's digging into my eye. And I hear the bullet and the *pap-pap-pap-pap-pap-pap* and the *whoooshboom* and feel the floor shake. And woman scream and man scream and boy scream in that way where life cut short and you can hear the scream get lost in blood rushing from the throat up to the mouth a gargle, a choke. And he hold me down and gag my scream and I want to bite him hand so me bite him hand because it also covering my nose and please Papa don't kill me, but he shaking and I wonder if it's death shake and the ground shaking again and feet, feet all around, men running and passing and passing and running and laughing and screaming and shouting that man from the Eight Lanes all going dead. And Daddy push me down flat on the ground and cover me with himself but him so heavy and my nose hurt and he smell of car engine and him knee or something in my back and the floor taste bitter and I know it's the red floor polish and I want him to get up off me and me hate him and everything sound like it covered in stockings. And when he finally get off me, people outside screaming but there's no more papapapapapapap or whooshboom, but he crying and I hate him.

Two day later my mother come back laughing because she know her new dress is the one pretty thing in this whole r'asscloth ghetto and he see her because he didn't go to work, because nobody feel safe to walk the street and he go right after her and grab her and say bombocloth whoring gal, me can smell man stinking cockycheese 'pon you. He grab her by the hair and punch her in the belly and she scream that he not no man since he can't even fuck a flea and him say oh is fuck you want? And he say make me find a cocky big enough for you and he grab her by the hair and drag her into the room and me watching from under the sheet where he put me to hide just in case bad man come in the night and he grab a broomstick and he beat her from head to foot from front to back and she screaming until she whelping and then moaning and he say you want big cocky, make me give you big cocky you fucking pussycloth whoring bitch and he take the broomstick and spread open her legs by kicking them apart. He kick her out of the house and throw her clothes after her and I think that is the last time me going to see my mother but she come back the next day, bandage up like a mummy from the movie that show for thirty cents at Rialto Cinema and three other man with her.

They grab my father the three of them, but my father fight, fight them like a man, even punch them like John Wayne in a movie, like how a real man supposed to fight. But he is one and they is three and soon four. And the fourth one come in only when they beat me father like a smash tomato and he say me name Funnyboy, me next in line to be the don but you know what you name? You know what you name? Me say if you know what you name, pussyhole? and my mother laugh but it come out like a wheeze and Funnyboy say you think because you work in factory you hot? Is me get you the work at factory and me can take it away, pussyhole. You know what your name is, pussyhole? You name informer. And he tell everybody to leave.

And he say you know why them call me Funnyboy? 'Cause me no take nothing fi joke.

Even in the dark Funnyboy lighter than nearly everybody else, but him skin always red, like blood always right under the skin or like white people who in the sun too long and him eye grey like a cat. And Funnyboy tell my father that he going die now, right now, but if he make him feel good he can live like them lion in *Born Free* only he would have to leave the ghetto. And he say only one way you going live and he say other things but he pull down him zip and he take it out and he say you want to live? You want to live? And my father want to live and my father spit and Funnyboy hold the gun right near my father ear. And he tell my father about country and where he can go and he can take him pickney with him and when he say pickney I shake but nobody know that me under the cover. And he say you want to live? You want to live? Over and over and over again like a nagging little girl and he rub my father lips with him gun and my father open him mouth and Funnyboy say if you bite off me head I going shoot you in the neck so you hear yourself dying and he put it in my father mouth and Funnyboy say you might as well lick since you suck like a dead fish. And he groan and groan and groan and fuck my father head then pull himself out and hold my father head steady and fire. *Pap.* Not like the pow in cowboy movie and not like when Harry Callahan fire, but one big sharp *pap* that shake the room. The blood splat on the wall. My gasp and the gunshot go off the same time so nobody know me under the blanket still.

My mother run back in and start to laugh and kick my father and Funnyboy go up to her and shoot her in the face. She fall right on top of me, so when he say find the little boy they look everywhere but under my mother. Funnyboy say, Can you imagine, the little batty boy say him would suck me like some bow cat and mek me feel good if me make him live? Dutty pervert all reach out and grab me wood. Can you imagine that, he say to the men who looking 'round for me, but my mother on top of me and her fingers right by my face and me in a cage looking through her fingers and I don't cry and Funnyboy going on and on about how he know that my father was a battyman, have to be a battyman that must be why him woman was such a whore because how else her pussy going get look after, and then he say don't tell none o' this to Shotta Sherrif.

The house quiet. Me push me mother off and happy that it dark but I can't leave because they might catch me, so I see and wait. As I wait my father on the floor by the door and he get up and come over to me and say English is the best subject in school because even if you get a job as a plumber nobody going give you any work if you chat bad, and chatting good is everything even before learning a trade. And that a man must learn to cook even though that is woman things and he talking and talking and talking too much, just like he always talk too much and sometimes he talk so loud that I wonder if he want the next door to hear and learn from him too, but no he still on the ground and he telling me to run, to run now because they going to come back to take them Clarks shoes off him foot and whatever else in the house that worth anything and they will tear down the house looking for money even though he put all him money in the bank. He over at the door. Me pull the Clarks off but see him head and vomit.

The Clarks too big and I *clupclupclup* to get over to the back of the house, with nothing outside but old railway and bush and me trip over me damn whore mother who jerk like she alive but she not. Me climb up the window and jump. The Clarks too big to run so me take them off and run through bush and broken bottle and wet shit and dry shit and fire not yet put out and the dead railway taking me out of the Eight Lanes and I run and run and hide in the macka bush until the sky go orange, then pink, then grey, and then the sun put out and the moon rise fat. When me see three truck drive pass with nothing but man in them I run until me reach the Garbagelands, nothing but waste and junk and shit stretching for miles. Nothing but what uptown people throw out, rubbish rising high like hill and valley and dunes like a desert and everywhere burning and I still running and I don't stop until me see ghetto again and a roadblock by a truck and I run under the truck and still running and man shouting and woman screaming and the house them look different, closer, tighter, and I running and some man come out with a machine gun but woman scream that is just a boy and he bleeding and something trip me and me fall and start to bawl loud and two man come up to me and one point a gun and me wheezing now like my daddy do in him sleep and the man with the gun come up to me and shout where you from? You smell like one of them Eight Lanes battyman and the other man say a pickney dat and blood 'pon him and the other say if man shoot you, boy? I can't talk, all me can say is Clarks is good shoe, Clarks is good sh . . . and the man with the gun go click and somebody shout how that bloodclaat Josey Wales love fire a gun so! and not everything solve by a bam-bam and both man step away from me but plenty gather including woman. Then they open a space like Moses just part the Red Sea and he step towards me and stop.

Shotta Sherrif killing him own now? Him no know say able-bodied man rationed? he say. Must be Eight Lanes birth control. Everybody laugh. I say Mama and Daddy and can't say anything else but he nod and understand. You want to kill him back? he say and I want to say for my father but not my mother but all I say is y-y-y-y-y and I nod hard like I just get hit and can't talk. He say soon, soon, and call a woman over and she try to pick me up but I grab my Clarks and the man laugh. He is a big man and wearing a white mesh merino that glow in the streetlight and light up him face, most of it hiding in him beard, but not him eyes for them big and almost glow too and he smile so much that you barely notice how thick him lips be or that when he stop smiling and him cheek sink, that him beard cut him face into a sharp V and him eyes stare at you cold. The man say, Let them know that is not ghetto dog that live over here in Copenhagen City, then he look at me like he can talk without saying anything and I know that he see something that he can use. He say get this boy some coconut water and the woman say yes Papa-Lo.

And I live in Copenhagen City from then on and I see the Eight Lanes and I wait for the time. And I see man in Copenhagen City with nothing but a knife, then a cowboy gun, then an M16, then a gun so heavy he can barely carry it himself and I turn twelve or least I think so, since Papa-Lo called the day he find me my birthday and he give me a gun too and he call me Bam-Bam. And I go to the Garbagelands with other boy and learn to fire but the recoil make me trip and they laugh and call me little pussyhole and I say that's what me call your mother last night when me fuck her and they laugh and another man, the man called Josey Wales, put the gun in my hand and show me how to point. I grow up in Copenhagen City and watch the guns change and know they don't come from Papa-Lo. They come from the two men who bring guns to the ghetto and the one man who show me how to use it.

We, the Syrian, the American and Doctor Love out by the shack near the sea.

Barry Diflorio

T*here's only one sign* hanging outside, but it's so big that even inside you can see the yellow curves of the logo tilting off the roof. So huge that one day it's bound to fall, probably when some little kid's running in because school had let out early. So this kid, right, is gonna cross the threshold just as the big logo starts to creak, and he won't even hear it because his little tummy is grumbling so loud, and as he tries to pull the door open it'll all come crashing down. Poor kid's ghost will curse like a fucking sailor when he gets a load of what popped him: King Burger: Home of the Whamperer.

There's also a McDonald's farther down Halfway Tree Road. The logo is blue and the people who work there swear Mr. McDonald is in the back room. But I'm at King Burger, Home of the Whamperer. Nobody here has ever heard of Burger King. Inside, the chairs are plastic and yellow, the tables are fiberglass and red and the menu looks like those letters at the cinema that say *coming soon*. The place is never packed at three p.m., which is of course the reason I come here. People in packs always make me antsy; all you need is the wrong spark and a group turns into a mob. I wonder if that's why outside is all grilled up. I've been in Jamaica since January.

There's a sign behind the cashier that says if your burger isn't ready in fifteen minutes it's free. Two days ago when I touched my watch sixteen minutes later, she said it only applied to cheeseburgers. Yesterday, when my cheeseburger was late, she said it only applied to chicken sandwiches. Poor girl must be running out of burgers to blame. But nobody comes here. One of the things I fucking hate about my fellow Americans: whenever they fly to a foreign country, first thing they do, they try to find as much of America as they can get their hands on, even if it's food in the shitty cafeteria. Sally, who's been here since the Johnson administration, has never had ackee and saltfish ever, despite me being probably the two millionth person to say baby, it's like scrambled eggs but better. My kids love it. My wife, she wished they had Manwich or Ragú, or even Hamburger Helper, but good luck finding that at a supermarket. Good luck finding anything, really.

The first time I had jerk chicken a guy at the intersection of Constant Spring Road and some other road came up to my car and shouted, Boss, you ever have jerk chicken? before I could find that broken-off handle to wind up the window. He was tall and skinny, in a white undershirt, huge Afro, shiny teeth and shiny muscles, too many muscles for one kid, but the man, boy really, smelled like allspice so I got out of the car and followed him back to his shop, a small shack, wood tacked together with a zinc roof and striped in blue, green, yellow, orange and red. The man grabbed the biggest fucking machete I ever saw in my life and sliced off a piece of chicken leg as if he had just cut through warm butter. He handed it to me and as I was about to eat it, he closed his eyes and nodded no. Just like that: firm, peaceful and final. Before I said anything he pointed at a huge jar, kinda translucent like it's been standing there awhile. Hey, I'm nothing if not adventurous, my wife would say crazy. It was a humongous glass jar of mashed pepper paste. I dipped the chicken in and swallowed the piece whole. You know that part in Road Runner where Wile E. Coyote's bomb goes off right after he swallows it, and smoke comes out of his ears and nose? Or that dipstick, first time at the sushi bar, thinking damn right I can swallow a teaspoon of wasabi? That was me. I don't think the man knew that white people could turn so many shades of red. I blinked a teardrop and hiccupped for at least a minute. Somebody had doused my mouth with sugar and gasoline, lit a match and woof. ShitGoddamnmotherfucker-thatfuckingshitisthefucking-blood of life! I remember coughing out.

I asked the cashier at King Burger if they ever thought of a jerk burger. Ghetto food? she said and scoffed in that way Jamaican women do, closed her eyes, lifted her chin and turned away. I'm in here nearly every day and this girl is the same. She says, Can I take your order? A cheeseburger. Would you like a lemonade or a milk shake with your order? No, just a

D&G Grape. Does that complete your order? Yes. Whamperer tastes just like a Whopper, minus the taste. Even the lettuce knows it can do better, so wet and bitter on this burger that I order every day for shits, just so I can tell my kids, You know what I had today? Poppa had a Whamperer, and they think their pop has a stammer.

The sun is jumping ship and evening's coming. But this country needs a good disco. Right now skipping countries every three to five years or so is all that keeps me sane. Though nobody gets to the other end of the Company keeping sane. Some of the craziest bullshit I've ever heard was from my former station chief, well before he got a serious case of the conscience. His son is here, came in on American flight DC301 from New York. He's been here now three days and has no idea I know he's here. Not that he knows me or anything, Bring Your Child to Work Day was not one of the ideas his daddy bounced around. It's not like it's a secret why he's here, but when the son of the former head of the Company suddenly shows up in Jamaica, even a guy on the inside starts to wonder if there was something he missed.

Word was he's a filmmaker, or one of those rich kids with enough money to buy their own camera. He came with a bunch of photographers and film people for this peace concert by that reggae guy who's bigger than sliced bread these days. It's supposed to be big, and though I've only been here since January, even I know the country needs some sort of peace. It's not going to come from that guy in the Prime Minister's office, but still. So the big reggae guy is staging a concert which was organized by the Prime Minister's party, which almost makes big reggae guy a person of interest. The embassy got news that Roberta Flack is flying in and Mick Jagger and Keith Richards are already here. The motherfucking Rolling Stones.

No, I don't listen to big reggae guy. Reggae is monotonous and boring and the drummer must have the laziest job in the world next to King Burger cashier. I prefer ska, I prefer Desmond Dekker. Only yesterday I asked the King Burger cashier if she liked "Ob-La-Di, Ob-La-Da," and she looked at me as if I just asked her to hit me up with some smack. Me no know, she said. I said, Then what do you listen to? What's playing at the jam session? She said Big Youth and Mighty Diamonds. I said yeah, Mighty Diamonds and Big Youth are cool and all, but did either ever get name-checked in a fucking Beatles song, like Desmond Dekker? She said, Please watch your language, sir, this is a law-abiding premises.

How do you construct an accident? Nobody in the Company is indispensable, but sometimes I wonder why don't they just call somebody else. At least they didn't have me groundworking Montevideo. What a goddamn mess that turned out to be. But I like having a job I can't talk about. It makes keeping the other secrets easier. The wife finally came around to the fact that as long as we're married there are just some things she will never know and she had to get used to what all our wives get used to. Knowing two out of every four facts. Five out of every ten trips. One out of every five deaths. I don't think she knows exactly what I do. At least that's the story I'm sticking to this week. I'm in Jamaica and almost everything is moving according to plan. Which is a boneheaded way of saying things are moving so textbook easy that it's actually rather boring to work here. Not surprised at all, Jamaicans tend to react exactly as you think they would. Maybe that's refreshing to some, or maybe just a relief.

So back when I mentioned the jerk chicken guy, that was in May and I wasn't in that area because I suddenly wanted to experience the real Jamaica. I was following a man in a car four cars up. A person of keen interest that a driver picked up at the Constant Spring Hotel. At first I thought I was brought here to shadow him, only to find out that he was shadowing me. He used to work for the Company until he also caught a terminal case of the conscience. This is what happens when top brass still tries to recruit from Ivy League washouts, prep school faggots, American Kim Philbys waiting to come out of the closet if not the cold. By the time I found out that he was in Jamaica he had already found out I was here. I'm not exactly undercover—too late for that. That said, I couldn't have this man talking up a mess that I would then have to clean up. Pity that I didn't have clearance to proceed. It's not even over and I miss the Cold War already.

Bill Adler checked out of the Company in 1969 a very bitter customer. Maybe he was just a disgruntled left-wing commie, but tons of those are still in the Company. Sometimes the good ones are the worst, the mediocre ones are just civil servants with wire-tapping skills. But the good ones either become him or me. And he was sometimes very good. After he was done with Ecuador, a four-year job done with, dare I say it, *brio*, all I had to do was clean up the stray debris. Of course I'd much rather remind him of that lovely mess in Tlatelolco. The boss called me an innovator but I was just following the Adler rulebook. Ceiling mics, like the one he used in Montevideo. Either way, he left the CIA in 1969 with a critical case of conscience and has been making trouble and endangering lives ever since.

Last year he dropped a book, not a very good one but there were explosions in it. We knew it was coming but let it go, thinking well, maybe a diversion with his out-of-date info would actually help us out there doing real work. Turns out his info was very nearly top-notch, and why wouldn't it be, come to think of it. He named names too. Inside the Company. Top brass didn't read it, but Miles Copeland did, another whiny faggot who used to run the Cairo office. He ordered the London office restructured from the ground up. Then Richard Welch got murdered in Athens by 17 November, a second-rate terrorist group that we wouldn't have sent a candy striper to monitor. Killed with his wife and driver too.

But with all that, with knowing all that he was capable of, I still had no idea why Adler was here. He wasn't an official guest of the government; that would have been an irredeemable faux pas on the Prime Minister's behalf, especially after shooting the shit with Kissinger just a few months ago. But the Prime Minister was certainly happy he was here. Meanwhile I'm waiting for orders from head section to neutralize the threat of this man, or at least mute it. The Jamaica Council for Human Rights invited him, forcing me to open a brand-new file on my already crowded desk. Within days the guy was giving speeches, long speeches about all kinds of bullshit, like his name was Castro or something. Saying that people like me were in Latin America with him and he was disgusted by what he saw, especially in Chile when we allowed Pinochet to take power.

He didn't name me, but I knew who he was talking about. Calling us the horsemen of apocalypse, destabilizing any country in our wake. He was dramatic all right, all the time pulling back on how much of this came out of his own rulebook. And that's all this Prime Minister needed, a nice multi-syllable word like destabilization to turn it into a fucking jingle. But he threw us on the defensive in a way that I'll make sure never happens again. Of course the only people listening was *Penthouse* magazine. Goddamn, what does it mean when the conscience of America airbrushes pussy for a living? Guys like Adler, guys who suddenly develop this sense of mission to expose evil America when they're just white guys with a guilty conscience who never know when to quit. And the Company couldn't decide if I should just quit him.

At one point he claimed he had evidence that the Company was behind arson in some tenement they call it on Orange Street, murder of more than a few Cubans in Jamaica and industrial unrest on the wharf. He said he had evidence that the Company was giving the opposition party money, which was just preposterous considering what bad form it would have been, trusting anybody in the Third World with money. I don't know why he didn't just send an article to *Mother Jones* or *Rolling Stone* or something. Before the Company gave me a clear directive of what to do he was gone, my eyes and ears tell me, to Cuba. But the bastard did his damage. He gave the Jamaicans names. Fucking names. Not mine but eleven of the staff at the embassy, blowing the cover of at least seven of them. They had to be shipped back before any realized that they knew them by assumed names. Because of Adler I had to start from scratch. In the middle of September in a year that was doing nobody any favors. Everything from scratch, which already led to problems.

Passing his office I overheard Louis on the phone about a shipment at the wharf that went rogue. I did some checking. Nobody in this office has ordered any shipment of anything, and if they did they certainly wouldn't have had it go through Jamaican customs for two-thirds of it to be stolen. Need-to-know basis serves him as much as it does me, but I don't like when a fucking rogue agent somewhere in Cuba finds out something is gone before I even knew I was supposed to miss it. Means his low-level snoops still have higher clearance than me, and I'm supposed to be running the fucking show. Louis didn't sound too distressed when he was telling all this to God knows who, and I got tired of standing near his doorway like I was trying to get gossip.

The wife called not long ago to tell me she had run out of maraschino cherries again. I tell you, the Cold War isn't even over and I miss it already.

Papa-Lo

Listen to me now. Me warn him y'know, my magnanimous gentlemens. Long time I drop warnings that other people close, friend and enemy was going get him in a whole heap o' trouble. Every one of we know at least one, don't it? Them kinda man who just stay a certain way? Always have a notion but never come up with a single idea. Always working plenty of scheme but never have a plan. That was certain people. Here is my friend the biggest superstar in the world and yet him have some of the smallest mind to come out of the ghetto as friend. Me not going name who but I warn the Singer. I say, You have some people right close to you who going do nothing but take you down, you hear me? Me tired to say that to him. Sick and tired. But him just laugh that laugh, that laugh that swallow the room. That laugh that sound like he already have a plan.

People think me understand everything to the fullness. That is not no lie, wondiferous gentlemens, but Jah know, sometimes I don't learn till too late, and to know something too late? Well, is better you never know, as my mother used to say. Worse, you all present tense and have to deal with sudden past tense all around you. It's like realizing somebody rob you a year late.

So look at me. See all this? From the old cemetery to the west, the harbour to the south and all of the south West Kingston? Me run that. The Eight Lanes is PNP so they watch them own affairs. Then you have the territory in the middle that we have to fight for and sometimes lose. He used to live in Trench Town so some people have him as stooge for the People's National Party. But me will take a bullet for him and him would take one for me too.

But them new boys, them boys who never dance the rocksteady and don't care 'bout niceing up the dance, them boys don't work for nobody. Me enforce for the Jamaica Labour Party in green, and Shotta Sherrif control for the People's National Party in orange, but them new boys enforce for the party in them back pocket. Can't even control them no more.

Earlier this year when he gone on tour, after begging me to come with him to see London town (of course me couldn't go, me so much as sleep and is armagideon down the ghetto), he leave certain brethren at the house. Soon as him gone, them boys call ghetto boys from Jungle, because they have a grand scheme. This one boiciferous, like them big scheme you watch on TV where Hannibal Heyes and Kid Curry stick up a bank and still get the sexy girl who hand them over the money. We try to keep the peace, me and Shotta Sherrif, but whenever things get out of hand, somebody kill a school pickney for her lunch money or rape a woman on her way to church, is usually somebody from somewhere like Jungle, man who born with no light in them eye. Them is the people that get together with the Singer friend on him own premises and scheme.

One week before the Kings Sweepstakes, five man from Jungle drive all the way down to Caymanas Race Course on a training day and wait for the top jockey, who never lose a race, to come out to the parking lot. As soon as he step out, in him riding clothes, two man grab him and one cover him head with a crocus bag. They take him somewhere, I don't know where, and do something, I don't know what, but come that Saturday, he lose the three race he was in, three race he was supposed to win easy, including the sweepstakes. He board a flight to Miami the following Monday, then poof! Gone. Nobody know where he gone, not even him family. Horse fixing is as old as horse race, but a little people make a lot of money too fast. Too fast. The same week the jockey vanish, two man from Jungle also disappear, poof! like they never born in the first place, and certain brethren all of a sudden had to make pilgrimage to Ethiopia. Now me respect Rastafari to the max, and a man have to go to him homeland if that is where he think it be. But somehow all of a sudden when people holding out for money, the brethren with all of it just skip. Who knows what happen to the money.

That was the beginning. From then all sorts bad guzum come to the Singer own house. Con man with con-plan in the same house where music need to vibe off pure spirit. I remember when that was the only place any man, no matter what side you on, could escape a bullet. The only place in Kingston where the only thing that hit you was music. But the fucking people soil it up with bad vibes, better if they did just go into the studio one morning and shit all over the console, me no going say who. By the time the Singer come back from tour, mob from Jungle was already waiting for him. Jamaican man head thick like brick. Never mind that the man was on tour and don't know nothing 'bout no horse race, or that he never cheat no man ever. Jungle man say, The scheme launch 'pon your property so you responsible. Then they take him out to Hellshire Beach, saying he need to eat some fish.

He tell me all this himself. Now he is a man who could talk to God and the devil and make them work out they difference—as long as neither of them have a woman. But that morning they come for him at six o'clock, before he go off to run and exercise, and swim in the river like he do every morning. That was the first sign. Nobody mess up with the Singer's morning, that is when the sun rise to send him message, when the holy spirit tell him what to sing next, when he closest to the most high. Still he go with them. They drive out to Fort Clarence Beach, twenty miles or so from West Kingston but just across the sea and so close that you can see it from across the water. He tell me all this himself. The whole time them was talking they look away, shift from side to side, staring at the ground because they didn't want him to mark they face.

—Your brethren, him gone in a scheme with we, sight? Your brethren come 'round the Jungle 'cause him want bad man fi do him dirty work, sight? Your brethren bring we 'pon your base fi talk business, sight?

—Seen. But me no know 'bout that, my youth, he say to them.

—Oi! Me, me, me no bloodclaat care what you want say, business go down under your roof so is you responsible.

—Brethren, how you see that? After the man is not me, him not me brother, him not me son, how me responsible?

—Oi, you, you hear what we say? Me just say it . . . me mean, me say me just say it, you never hear? It happen under your roof and him gone like some stinking bitch 'cause him get greedy, sight? After we show the jockey and say Yow, you better throw off them three race or we coming for you and the baby in you woman belly. We do we thing, the jockey do him thing, everybody do him thing, but your friend and him friend dash out with the money and leave poor man fi stay poor. How people can so fuck up?

—Me no know, star, him say to the man who was doing the most talking. Short, stubby, and smell like sawdust. I know who him talking 'bout. So they say to him, Yow, hear how it ah go go, sight? We want we money, sight? So every day we a go send a brother 'pon a bike fi pick up two shipment, one in the morning one in the evening, you see me?

Him never tell me how much money them ask for, but me still have eyes and ears. Them tell me say is forty thousand U.S. the scam pay off. And them never see none of it. Them must did demand at least ten thousand out of that, probably more. So now they want to pick up stash of cash every day till they feel they get enough. Him say No, boss, that is con man business, me nah pay that. And how you fi do the I so? Is three thousand of you me pay for every day, send you to school and feed you. Three thousand of you.

That's when the second thing happen, nearly all of them pull gun 'pon him right there at Fort Clarence Beach. Some of them man not even fourteen yet and them pull gun 'pon the one man that understand what them have to deal with. But them man is a new kind a man. They operate in a different stylee. Everybody, grandiloquent gentlemens, everybody in Copenhagen City, the Eight Lanes, Jungle, Rema, uptown and downtown know that nobody ever pull gun on the Singer. Even the weather knew that this was a new thing, some different kind of black cloud that nobody see in the sky before. The Singer have to talk the guns, all seven of them, right back into their back pocket, belt loop and holster. The next day a man on a green Vespa start showing up at the house two time a day, every day.

He tell me this the same day me come 'round to hail him up, smoke two weed and talk 'bout the peace concert. Plenty people say that the concert was not a wise move. Some people already think he support the People's National Party and that only going make it worse. Some of the people say they don't respect him no more because Rasta not supposed to bow. You can't reason with them man, because them never born with the part of the brain that man reason with. I tell him all this, and that he have nothing worry 'bout from me. Truth be, I getting old and want me pickney to see me get so old that them have to carry me. Last week in the market me see a young boy come pick up him old grandfather. He couldn't even walk good without a big cane and him little grandson giving him a shoulder. Me grudge the weak old man so much me nearly start cry right there in the market. I go back home and walk the street and notice something for the first time. Not a single old man in the ghetto.

Me say to him, Friend, you know me, you know Shotta Sherrif from the other side, just call him and tell him to make them Jungle man back off. But he wiser than me, he know that Shotta Sherrif can't help either when man with gun gone freelance stylee. Last month a shipment on the wharf just disappear. Not long after that freelance bad boy have machine gun, M16, M9 and Glock, and nobody can account for where they come from. Woman breed baby, but man can only make Frankenstein.

But when he tell me 'bout the boys from Jungle, he tell me like a father who just tell him son something too big for him to handle. He know even before me know, that me couldn't help him. Me want you understand something good. Me love that man to the max. Me would take a bullet for the Singer. But gentlemens, me can only take one.

Nina Burgess

R*ight after they told me* at the gate that nobody can come in but immediate family and the band, a man rode up right behind me on a lime green scooter. He rode up the same time I walked up and said nothing, just listened to the guard talk to me without shutting off his engine and then took off without talking to the guard himself. Was that a pickup or a delivery? I said to the guard, who didn't see it funny. Ever since news broke about the peace concert, security here tighter than the Prime Minister's motorcade. Or up a nun's panty, my last boyfriend would say. The man at the gate was new. I knew about the peace concert, everybody in Jamaica knew about it, and so I expected guards or police, not these men who looked like the very people you would want to keep out. Things was getting crucial.

Maybe it was a good thing, because as soon as the taxi dropped me off, the part of me that I like to shut off after morning coffee said, What do you think you're doing here, skinny-legged fool? The great thing about a bus is another one is right behind it, ready to sweep you away as soon as you realize you've made a mistake. A taxi just drops you off and it's gone. I would start walking at least, but damn if I could think of a better idea.

Havendale is not no Irish Town, but it's still uptown and if we didn't think it was safe we still didn't think it was sorry. I mean, this is not the ghetto. Babies aren't crying in the street and women aren't getting raped pregnant as what happens every day in the ghetto. I've seen the ghetto, been there with my father. Everybody lives in their own Jamaica and damn if that was ever going to be mine. Last week, somewhere between eleven p.m. and three a.m., three men broke into my father's house. My mother is always looking for signs and wonders and for her the fact that the newspaper last week said gunmen crossed the Half Way Tree line and have started picking off targets uptown was a very bad sign. The curfew was still on and even decent uptown people had to be indoors by a certain hour, six, eight, who knows, or they would be up for grabs. Last month Mr. Jacobs from four houses down was coming home from night service and the police stopped him, threw him in the back of the van and sent him to the Gun Court lockup. He would still be there if Daddy didn't find a judge to tell him that this was straight foolishness when we start to lock up even proper law-abiding people. Neither man mentioned that Mr. Jacobs was too dark-skinned for police to assume he was proper people, even in a gabardine suit. Then gunmen broke into our house. They took my parents' wedding rings, all my mother's figurines from Holland, three hundred dollars, all her costume earrings even though she told them they're worth nothing, and his watch. They punched my father a couple times, and slapped my mother when she asked one of them if his mother knew that he was sinning. I asked her if any of the men had their way with her but said the rosebush was growing wild like a leggo beast, and I pretended I was talking to somebody else. The policeman didn't come until the morning even though they called the station all night. Nine-thirty in the morning, long after I got there (they didn't call me until six), and he took a statement on a yellow pad with a red pen. He had to say *perpetrator* to himself three times just to figure out how to spell it. When he said wuz h'any h'aggressive weapon brawt into play? I burst out laughing and my mother said I should excuse myself.

This country, this goddamn island, is going to kill us. Since the robbery Daddy don't talk. A man likes to think he can protect what's his, but then somebody else comes and takes it and he's not much of a man anymore. I don't think less of him, but Mummy always talks about how at one time he could have bought a house in Norbrook and he turned it down because he already had a safe and sound home with no more mortgage to pay. I'm not calling him a coward. I'm not saying he's stingy. But sometimes when you're too careful it just turns into a different kind of carelessness. It's not that either. He's from a generation that never even expected to get midway up the ladder so when he got there he was too stunned to dare climb higher. That's the problem with midway. Up is everything and down just means all the white people want to party on your street on Sunday night to feel realness. Midway is nowhere.

Back in high school I used to have him stop at the bus stop or pray for the light to go red so that I could get out before he dropped me off at school. Kimmy, who has yet to visit her parents even after they've been robbed and her mother possibly raped, never caught the drift and always cussed when he said you get out too. Fact is Daddy was not a fourteen-year-old girl at the Immaculate Conception High School for girls, trying to act as if she had as much money and as much right to stick her head out and walk like an air hostess as anybody else who showed up in a Volvo. You couldn't just drive up in a Ford Escort in front of those little bitches who were always lying in ambush at the gate just to see who drove up in what. *Did you see Lisa's father drop her off in some jalopy? My boyfriend says it's a Cortina. That's what Daddy have the maid use.* What really boil me blood is that it's not that Daddy didn't have money, but he never could think of a single good reason to spend it. Which is why, in a way, it makes sense that he would be robbed, but it also makes sense that the robber didn't get away with anything much. That's the only thing he would talk about, that the sons of mangy bitches only got three hundred dollars.

Can't play it safe when nowhere safe anymore. Mummy say at one point they held my father by his two hands so that each could kick him in the balls like they playing football. And how he's already refusing to see a doctor even though his stream not as powerful as it was only a week . . . good God, now I sound like my mother. The fact is that if they came once they could come again, and who knows, they might even do something bad enough for Kimmy to call her goddamn parents after they've been robbed and her mother possibly raped.

This socialist Prime Minister's latest ism is runawayism. I must be the only woman in Jamaica who didn't hear the Prime Minister say that there were five flights to Miami for anybody who wanted to leave. Better must come? Better was supposed to come four years ago. Now we have ism this and ism that and Daddy who just loves to talk about politics. That is when he's not wishing he had a son, since men would actually care about the fate of the country and not being a beauty queen. I hate politics. I hate that just because I live here I'm supposed to live politics. And there's nothing you can do. If you don't live politics, politics will live you.

Danny was from Brooklyn. A blond-hair man who came down to do research for his degree in agricultural science. Who knew that the one thing Jamaica created that was the envy of sciencc was a cow? Anyway, we were seeing each other. He would take me around to Mayfair Hotel uptown for a drink and suddenly there would be Caucasians, men, women, old, young, all as if God just waved a wand and poof! White people. I am what they call high brown, but even with my skin colour seeing so many white people was a shock. Somebody must have mistook this for the North Coast for there to be so many tourists. But then one would open his mouth and patois would tumble out. Even after going there too often to remember, I would pick my jaw off the ground every time I overheard a white man chat bad. *Wait! Ho ho ho, is you that, busha? Ho ho ho, can't see you these days, man, you get rich and switch?* They didn't even have a tan!

Danny would listen to really weird music, just noise that he would play loud sometimes to piss me off. Just noise, rock and roll, the Eagles and the Rolling Stones and too many black people who should just stop acting white. But at night he would play a song. We broke up almost four years ago, but every time I look outside the window I sing two lines over and over. *I do believe. If you don't like things you leave.* Funny, it is because of Danny that I met him. Some party that the record label had all the way up in the hills. Bush people and white people are all that live up here, huh? I remember saying. Danny said he never know black people could be racist. I went to get some punch, poured it slow to kill time, then saw Danny talking to the label boss. I was exactly what these workers thought I was, some uppity naigger fucking the American. Right beside Danny and the label boss was him, somebody whom I never thought I would meet. Even my mother liked his last single, though my father despised him. He was shorter than I expected, and me, him and his manager were the only black people there not asking if we would like our drinks freshened up. Standing there he was like a black lion. How the sexy daughter just come 'pon the man so, he said.

Fifteen years of schooling on how to talk proper and that is still the sweetest thing I ever heard come out of a man's mouth.

I didn't see him again until long after Danny went back and I followed my sister Kimmy, who has yet to call her parents after they've been robbed and her mother possibly raped, to a party at his house. He didn't forget me. But wait, you is Kimmy sister? Is where you was hiding? Or you was like Sleeping Beauty, eh, waiting for the man to wake you up? The whole time I'm splitting in two, the part of me that I like to shut off after morning coffee said yes, reason with me, my sexy brethren, the other part going what do you think you're doing with this lice-infested Rasta? Kimmy left after a while, I didn't see her go. I stayed, even after everybody left. I was watching him, me and the moon when he went out on the verandah naked like some night spirit, with a knife to peel an apple. Locks like a lion and muscles all over and shining in the moon. Only two people know that "Midnight Ravers" is about me.

I hate politics. I hate that I'm supposed to know. Daddy says that nobody is driving him out of his own country but he's still thinking gunmen are somebody. I wish I was rich, I wish I was working and not laid off and I hope he would at least remember that night on his balcony with the apple. We have family in Miami. The same place Michael Manley told us to go if we want to leave. We have a place to stay but Daddy don't want to spend any money. Damn it, now the Singer is so big nobody can see him anymore, even a woman that know him better than most women. Actually I don't know what I'm talking about. This is the dumb shit women always think. That you know a man or that you've unlocked some secret just because you let him into your panties. Shit, if anything I know even less now. It's not like he called me after.

I'm across the road, waiting at the bus stop, but so far I've let two pass. Then a third. He hasn't come through the front door. Not once, not for me to run across the road that instant and shout, Remember me? Long time no see. I need your help.

Bam-Bam

T*wo men bring guns* to the ghetto.

One man show me how to use it.

But they bring other things first. Corned beef and Aunt Jemima maple syrup that nobody know what to do with, and white sugar. And Kool-Aid and Pepsi and a big bag of flour and other things nobody in the ghetto can buy and even if you could, nobody would be selling it. The first time I hear Papa-Lo say election coming, he said it cold and low as if thunder and rain was near coming and there was nothing you could do. Other men visit him, none of them look like him, some even redder than Funnyboy, almost white. They come in shiny car and leave and nobody ask but everybody know.

And at the same time, you come back. You bigger than Desmond Dekker, bigger than The Skatalites, bigger than Millie Small and bigger even than white people. And you know Papa-Lo from when neither of you have chest hair and you drive down into the ghetto like a thief in the night, but I see you. Outside my house, the house Papa-Lo put me. I see you drive up, just you and Georgie. And Papa-Lo squeal almost like a girl and run out and hug you with him bigness and you was always small and you have to bawl out for the man to put you down, any more hugging and touching and you going mistake him for Mick Jagger. You turn into the person who talk about a lot of people that nobody know and you talk about how this coke-head who call himself Sly Stone but who really have some girly name like Sylvester give you an opening slot like he throwing a dog a bone and you jump 'pon the stage and mash down the place but some of the black people say what is this slow hippie bullshit? and they don't like you at all, so you say fuck this fuckery, better I do my own tour, and Sly Stone just go off and sniff some more cocaine, leaving you stranded in Las Vegas. We don't know him either, but you're the man who now talk about people we don't know. You say the cokehead's fans couldn't take the real vibration and you leave after just four shows.

But that was just water under the bridge. You tramp through Babylon and the rest of the story Papa-Lo could tell it because everybody know it. So Papa-Lo tell it and you just nod. And then you say you have big things to talk about but it have to wait because now everybody hear that you in Copenhagen City and they come out to give thanks and praise to the sufferah who turn big star, but who don't forget them sufferah who still sufferin' and some thank you for the money for by now you feeding three thousand people, which everybody know but nobody talk about, but your truck look beat up and not what we expect and that make me angry because nothing worse than when a man have money and pretend he don't have none like acting like you poor is some pose. And a woman hug you and say she have some stew peas and you say, Mummy you know me don't touch the pork and she say is ital stew! And it good, y'see? And you say then Mummy run go bring me a big bowl, the biggest bowl in the kitchen, and bring it to Papa-Lo house because me and him have fi talk plenty things. And you and Papa-Lo gone off and none of him deputy, not even Josey Wales, follow him. And I watch Josey Wales as he watch them walk away and he stand there, and he look, and he hiss.

The two men who bring guns to the ghetto watch you sing yourself out of their hands and they not happy at all. Nobody uptown singing thanks and praises for you. Not the man who bring guns to the Eight Lanes, still run by Shotta Sherrif. That man know him party going up for re-election and they need to win, to stay in power, to bring power to the people, all comrades and socialists. Not the Syrian who bring guns to Copenhagen City and who want to win the election so bad that he will move God himself if God in the seat. The American who come with guns know that whoever win Kingston win Jamaica and whoever win West Kingston win Kingston, before any man in the ghetto tell him.

Prime Minister Michael Manley tell everybody on the TV and the radio that he give you your first big break and you wouldn't have become famous were it not for him. And that he always support the voice of the downtrodden, the comrades in the struggle. Then you sing, never let a politician do you a favour or he will want to control you forever, but he didn't think it was about him for by now he is not no politician, he is Joshua.

And the man who bring guns to Copenhagen City so that it can deal with the Eight Lanes problem hear of you talking all the time to Papa-Lo like you two is back in school and up to mischief and scratch him Syrian head and ask Papa-Lo why he talk to you, since you is known as a PNP man because they give you your first big break, and maybe this little Rasta trying to convert Papa-Lo to the PNP. You don't know that from then on people watching you like a hawk, because you talk to Papa-Lo all the time and nowadays Papa-Lo even go uptown to your house to spend the whole day. That weekend when Papa-Lo did gone and nobody know where, rumour was that he did gone to England to watch you in concert. And word reach that you still talk to Shotta Sherrif, the man whose deputy kill me family, and me learn to hate you in a new way, even as me love Papa-Lo. You turning him, you converting him into something and everybody seeing it. Especially Josey Wales. Josey Wales watching you and I watch him watching you and he don't like the way things running and he don't say it too loud, but he say it to who will hear. And a little bird say Papa-Lo getting weak.

But then one day a boy from Copenhagen City rob a woman at gunpoint, a woman who sell pudding and toto by the corner of Princess Street and Harbour Street. She come to Papa-Lo house and point him out, a boy three door from my house who nobody ever like. And the boy mother shout, Lawd! Woi! Tek pity 'pon the boy, Papa. Is 'cause he no have no daddy fi teach him them things! And is lie, she lie, look how she pussy dry up. Josey Wales just hiss because Papa-Lo thinking too much these days, but then Papa rip off the boy clothes and yell out for a machete and beat the boy with the flat side, every whack slapping the air like a thunderclap, every whack slicing the skin a little. The boy bawl and scream but Papa-Lo big as tree and faster than wind. Do, Papa-Lo, lawd, Papa-Lo, but Papa-Lo, is caw she did want me buddy and me never give her, he say, which only make Papa-Lo worse. He kick the boy down and beat the boy back and batty and leg and when he tired of machete he pull off him own belt and beat the boy with the buckle side. And the buckle dig hole into the boy back and chest and forehead. The mother run to him screaming but he lash her one time in the face, and she stagger and run off. People come out to watch. He pull out him gun to shoot, but the mother rush in and cover him and bawl out and beg Papa-Lo, beg the woman who get rob, and Jesus Christ who rest in the hills of Mount Zion. Even Papa-Lo not going step in after Jesus intervene. Then he say, A woman who raise this kind of pussyhole deserve to get shot too and lower the gun right to her forehead, but he walk away.

Jamaica Labour Party rule the country in the sixties but the People's National Party tell the country that better must come and win the election in 1972. Now JLP want the country back and there's no word named can't, there's no word named no. Downtown on lockdown and police already shouting curfew. Some street so quiet that even rat know better than to come out. West Kingston on Fire. People still want to know how JLP lose Kingston when they have Copenhagen City. People reason that it's Rema, that place between JLP and PNP that vote against JLP because PNP promise corned beef, baking flour and more exercise book for the children to take to school. The man who bring guns to the ghetto bring more guns and say he not going be happy until every man, woman and pickney in Rema bleed. But both party stun when a third P rise up, you, and you come on the TV in the chiney shop saying that your life is not for you and if you can't help plenty people then you no want it. And you do something else in the ghetto even though you not there. Me not sure how you do it. Maybe it was the bass, something you can't see but feel and who feels it knows it. But a woman will talk for herself, let her tongue loose in her own backyard, cursing with each wring of the shirt and pant that she washing, saying she tired of the shitstem and the ism and schism and is high time the big tree meet the small axe. But she didn't say it, she sing it so we know that it's you. And plenty in the ghetto, in Copenhagen City, in Rema, and for sure in the Eight Lanes sing it too. The two men who bring guns to the ghetto don't know what to do since when music hit you can't hit it back.

Boy like me don't sing your song. He who feels it knows it, you say, but it's long time since you feel it. We listen other song that ride the Stalag Rhythm, song from people who can't pay for no guitar and don't have a white man to give it to them. And while we listen to people just like we, Josey Wales visit me, and I joke that he is Nicodemus, thief in the night. Thirteen and he give me a present that nearly drop from my fingers because a gun weight is a different kinda weight. Not a heavy weight but a different one, cold, smooth and tough. Gun don't obey your finger unless your hand prove first that it can handle it. I remember the gun drop from my hand, slip out, and Josey Wales jump. Josey Wales don't jump. Last time that happen it blow four toe clean off, him say, and pick it up. I want to ask if that was why he limp. Josey Wales remind me that is him teach me how to use gun to shot up a PNP boy if they try anything and it's soon my time to defend Copenhagen City, especially if the enemy come from home cooking, not outside dessert. Josey Wales never could talk like music, not like Papa-Lo and not like you, so I laugh and he punch me in the cheek. Don't disrespect the Don, he say. I was about to say you not the Don, but I stay quiet. You ready to be a man? he say. I said I was a man but him gun right up at my left temple before I could finish. Click. I remember squeezing myself hard, thinking please don't piss, please don't piss, please don't look like a five-year-old wanting to go piss.

Papa-Lo would have killed me so quick and so sure, that it would be like the idea just come to him. But if Papa-Lo kill you on a Friday, he was thinking about it, weighing, measuring, planning from Monday. Josey Wales different. Josey Wales didn't think, he just shoot. I look at the black O of the gunmouth and know he could kill me right then and tell Papa-Lo anything. Or he wouldn't. Nobody ever bet on what they think Josey Wales would do. Still holding the gun to my temple he grab my pants at the waist and tug until the button pop off. I have only three brief with no more coming, and never wear any unless me leaving the ghetto. Josey Wales grab my pants then let go and watch it drop. He look up then down then back up, up and up then smile. You not no man yet, but soon, soon. I goin' make you, he said. You ready to be a man, he ask, and me did think then that he mean it in a politician way, the way Michael Manley would say, You want a better future, comrade? So I nod yes and he walk off and I follow him down a street that nobody drive on anymore because of too much guntalk, with no house but mound of sand and block, for bigger tenement yard that government not going to build because we is JLP.

I follow him down this street to where it seem to end, on the train line that cut through Kingston from east to west. By the train line, this far south nothing block the view of the sea. Kingston can close in on itself, so much so that you could be right by the sea and forget that you live on the island. That there is a sort of ghetto boy who run to the sea every day just so they can dive into something and forget. I only think of them when I see the sea. The sun was setting but it did still hot and the air taste like fish. Josey Wales turn left, to a small shack, where man long time ago would get up early to close the road so that the train could pass. He never tell me to follow. When I finally go inside he look at me like he was waiting all day.

Inside night fall already and the floor creak and crack. He light a match and I see the skin first, sweaty and shiny. The funny thing about smelling sweat is that you soon smell piss, not fresh, but soak in the floor, piss from not long ago. The boy did in the corner, belly down on the floor. Josey Wales or somebody tie up him hand, then tie the rope to him foot so that he look like a human bow. Josey Wales point to him clothes on the floor, then point at me with the gun and say pick them up, them might be your size. Now you have four brief he say, I don't remember telling no man about how much brief I have. I go to pick them up but Josey Wales fire. The bullet buck the floor and both me and the boy jump. Not yet, pussyhole. You no prove you ah man yet. I look at him, tall with a bald head that him woman shave for him every week. Tall and brown and full of muscle, where Papa-Lo black and thick. When he smile Josey Wales look like a chineyman, but he would shoot you if you say so, because chineyman cocky small like a bump, not like black man cocky.

You see how Rema boy live good? You think you can buy them jeans, yah? Is Fiorucci this you know. You see what thirty pieces of silver can buy a Rema boy? Josey Wales know label. Most of him clothes, him woman get from her job at a factory that make and ship clothes back to America so people could wear them to the disco, which is what people in America do. Everybody know because she tell everybody. You want this, then grow some bombocloth balls. Right now, he say, and shove the gun in my hand. I hear the boy crying. He hail from the Rema and I don't know anybody from there so. Wouldn't know anybody from the Eight Lanes either if me see him now. Right now, Josey Wales say again. Gun weight is a different kind of weight. Or maybe it be something else, a feeling that whenever you hold a gun is really the gun holding you. Now, or me deal with the two of you, Josey Wales say. Me walk right over to the boy and smell him sweat and piss and something else and pull the trigger. The boy don't scream or shout or ungh like when Harry Callahan kill a boy. He just jerk and dead. And the gun jerk my hand hard but the shot didn't sound like when Harry Callahan fire a shot, where the echo going on so long it don't end with the movie. The shot was two boards slap together that push against your ears quick then gone like a lick from a hammer.

When a shot enter a boy you don't hear anything more than a zup. Me did want to kill that Rema boy. Me did want it more than anything. I don't know why. Yes I do. And Josey Wales didn't say a thing. He said shoot him again to make sure, and I did. The body jerk. In the head, fool, he say, and me shoot again. I couldn't see if blood was running on the floor. The gun was lighter and warmer. Me tell meself that it was starting to like me. It really was nothing to kill a boy. Me did know it would be, maybe it was something ghetto boy just know. It was not the death, but the piss and shit and blood that make me vomit when I drag him down to dump in the sea. Three days later the newspaper have as headline *Boy floating in Kingston Harbour: Murder execution style.* Josey Wales smile and say me is big man now, so big that me make news and all of Jamaica 'fraid of me. I don't feel big. I don't feel nothing. Is more of a big thing that I don't feel nothing. No, that's not a big thing neither. He tell me don't tell Papa-Lo or he going kill me himself.

Josey Wales

Weeper taking his own good time as per usual. He and the white men get on real well, real well since one of them show him how to shoot like a man and not a silly ghetto boy. That's what Louis Johnson call him first, just like that. White man have balls, as I would say. Weeper jump up and pull a gun, a little pussy .38 right in front of the white man only to feel a bigger gun rubbing against him nuts. Me can kill you still, Weeper say. You got your gun on my brain and I got my gun on yours, Johnson say, which for a Jamaican is like killing you worse, no true dat? Weeper look at him and laugh and shake his hand, even hug and call him mi bredda. And is when you learn to talk like a yardie? What I remember was that he was wearing Wrangler jeans. American trying to look more American when he leave America. That was in this bar, Lady Pink down on Pechon Street, the last street between Downtown Kingston and Ghetto Kingston, which bring in fresh new girls every Thursday, although last week the new girl was the same girl from two years ago who still dance like a shaking banana tree. Things hard and getting more and more crucial by the day when a nursery worker have to skin out onstage. Weeper like to fuck her too.

Lady Pink open from nine in the morning and only have two things on the jukebox, some nice ska from the sixties and sweet rocksteady, like the Heptones and Ken Lazarus. None of that Rasta reggae fuckery. If I come across one more pussyhole who won't comb their hair and recognize Jesus as their lord and saviour I might send that little fucker to hell. Take that joke and bank it. The wall is too red for pink and too pink for purple and have gold record all over, which the owner himself spray-paint. Lerlette, the skinny girl, is up onstage, she the one who always want to dance to Ma

Baker. One year we provide security when Boney M. come to Jamaica and nobody knew that three woman and one man from the Caribbean could all look like such sodomite. Every time the song end with the chorus, *she knew how to die!* Lerlette split right down on the ground and hold up her two hands in gun pose like she's Jimmy Cliff in *The Harder They Come.* Girl must be putting her pum-pum through all kinda distress. Weeper used to fuck her too.

When she finish her dance, she pull back on her panty and come over to my booth. Me have a rule with woman. If your titty prettier and your body hotter than my woman, I'll deal with you. Otherwise fuck off. Ten years and I still never meet that woman. Dog years it take me to find Winifred, a woman who would breed the kind of boy I would want as son, because a man can't afford to have loose seed around the place. Last week Weeper come around the house with a son from some woman in Jungle, even he can't remember her name right. The boy was either retarded or start smoke the ganja way too early, drooling and panting like a big dog. In Jamaica you have to make sure that you breed properly. Nice little light browning who not too dry up, so that your child will get good milk and have good hair.

—Beg you di bone nuh?

—Dutty gal, move you bombocloth from here so. You no see big man is here?

—Lawd, yuh hard, eh? A weh Weeper deh?

—Me look like Weeper's keeper?

She doesn't answer, just walk away, pulling her panty out of her batty. I know for sure her mother drop her on the head when she was a baby. Twice. If it's one thing I can't stand is when people chat bad. Worse, when they know better. My mother send me all the way to high school. I didn't learn a fucking thing, but I listen to plenty. I listen to the TV, to Bill Mason and *I Dream of Jeannie*, and the radio serial on RJR at ten every morning, even though that was woman business. And I listen to the politicians, not when they're talking to me and pretending like I'm some backward ghetto naigger, but when they talk to each other, or to the white man from America.

Last week my son say, *Daddy you want know say di I? I ah go 'pon di base fi check a beef, sight?* and I slap that little wretch so hard he nearly cry. Don't talk to me like you was born behind cow, I say to him.

Damn boy look at me like I owe him something. That is the problem with these young rudies, they wasn't around for the fall of Balaclava in 1966, but I done talk about that. Everybody talking like they only know ghetto, especially him. See him on TV couple years ago and was never so shame in my life. To think you have all this money, all these gold record, have lipstick print on your cocky from all sort of white woman, and that is how you talk? *If my life is juss fi mi, mi no want it?* Then give it up, pussyhole, I coming right 'round there to take it.

Now Weeper, him different. The first day he come out of prison—not a good day to leave either, he come out right in the middle of war—the man have a big bulge in his back pocket. When he pull it out, there was so much red ink on even the cover that I ask him if he was bleeding from him batty. Turn out to be red ink from the only pen he could thief in prison. I ask if he write another book in the book. No star, he say. Bertrand Russell is the most top of the top ranking, me brethren, me can't outwrite him. Bertrand Russell is a book I still don't read yet. Weeper tell me how thanks to Bertrand Russell he don't believe in no God no more and me have one or two problems with that.

Waiting on Weeper. Now there's a title for a song, a hit record too. Last week I tell him, and the youths Bam-Bam, Demus and Heckle, that every Jamaican man is a man searching for father and if one don't come with the package, he's going to find another one. That's why Papa-Lo call himself Papa-Lo, but he can't be the father of anything anymore. Weeper say the man gone soft, but I say no, you fucking fool, look closer. The man not getting soft, he just reach the age where the person in the mirror is an old man who don't look like him anymore, and he's just thirty-nine. But that's an old age out here, the problem with getting so far is that he don't know what to do with himself. So he start to act like he no longer like the world he himself help create. You can't just play God and say I don't like man no more so make me wipe slate clean with the flood and start again. Papa-Lo start thinking too deep and start thinking that he should be more than what he is. He's the worst kind of fool, the fool who start believing things can get better. Better will come, but not in the way he think. Already, the Colombians start talking to me, they tired of them loco Cubans who sniff too much of what they should only sell, and the Bahamians who are of no use since they teach themselves how to freebase. The first time they ask me if I want to sample the merchandise, I say no, *hermano*, but Weeper say yes. *Brethren, coke was the only way me could fuck in prison*, he say to me, knowing that no man in the ghetto would dare come up to him and call him battyman because of it. That man still send him letters from prison.

People, even people who should know better, start to think that Papa-Lo getting soft, that he don't care about enforcing for the party no more. That he going slip and allow PNP man to move in on territory and that Jungle and Rema, always up for grabs, will soon bleach their green shirts and dye them orange. He not getting soft, he thinking deep, which politicians don't pay him to do. Politicians rise in the east and set in the west and nothing you can change about them. Here is where we go down two different road. He want to forget them. I want to use them. They think he no longer care about the people but the problem is that he starting to care too much and he already dragging the Singer into it.

They call me first, last year. They call me to a meeting out by Green Bay and the first thing I ask was, where's Papa? The black one (almost all of them white, brown and red) said *Enough of the Papa, Papa time gone, new blood time now*, talking like he playing fucking ghetto for *Candid Camera*. At one point the little pussyhole Louis Johnson hold a note upside down, some bullshit on embassy letterhead about some ambassador's reception, and pretend that it was some agency memo, reading and smiling at the others as if he confirming some bullshit that he tell them about me. Papa don't care about the dutty life but what these retarded batty fuckers don't get is that I don't care either. Medellín on line two.

So I let Louis the con man sweet me up with his con-plan. I listen to them tell me with a smile that they don't think they can trust me and pretend I don't understand when they say give us a sign, like this is the Bible.

I act the fool until they tell me what they want plain. Louis Johnson is the only man from the embassy I meet. He maintain the links with black people. Tall, brown hair, and dark glasses to hide him eyes. I tell him that he's in Copenhagen City now, otherwise known as the palm of my hand, and if I feel like it, any minute now I can make a fist. I lift up my shirt and give him the history of 1966. Left chest, bullet almost reaching the heart. Right neck, bullet straight through. Right shoulder, flesh wound. Left thigh, bullet bounce on the bone. Rib cage, bullet rattle the bones. I don't tell him that I about to set up a man in Miami and one in New York. I don't tell him that *yo tengo suficiente español para conocer que eres la más gran broma en Sudamérica.* I chat to him bad like some bush naigger and ask dumb question like, So everybody in America have gun? What kinda bullet American fire? Why you don't transfer Dirty Harry to the Jamaica branch? Hee hee hee.

And they tell me the news, that the Singer's giving money to Papa-Lo and them two thinking big, thinking of some way to eliminate the need for all people like them. I pretend that Papa-Lo didn't already tell me that from the last time he kill a boy in Jungle and regret when he see that he was heading to high school. And I say to the politicians and the Americans sure, to prove that me is the don of all dons I going do what need to be done. The man say let me be clear that the United States government does not support or condone any illegal or disruptive action of any kind in sovereign territories that are her neighbors. They all act as if I don't know that they already planning the double cross, already searching for who in my crew they can meet alone like Nicodemus in the night to tell him to take care of me as soon as I deliver. So I'm here waiting on Weeper, to talk things that only him and I can talk about, because tomorrow I going take care of a few people. The next day I goin' take care of the world.

Nina Burgess

Seventeen buses. Ten minibuses, including one calling itself Revlon Flex that already passed twice. Twenty-one taxis. Three hundred and seventy-six cars, I think. And not once did the man step out of his house. Not even to get some air, not to make sure that the guards are doing their job. Not even to tell the sun, later me brethren, I man have some serious work to do. The man on the lime green scooter came back in the evening and they sent him away again, but not before he got off and spoke to the man at the gate for two minutes and seventeen seconds. I timed him. Danny's watch still works, but it wasn't until lunch one time at the Terranova when I ran into a former schoolmate, breast droop down like a tired goat, but still a stuck-up bitch, that I found out Timex is the same watch *that my daddy gave Hortense last week for fifteen years of meritorious service to the household.* Bitch was calling me cheap. I wanted to tell her how happy she must be as a married woman now that she no longer have to bother with looking attractive, but I smiled and said, I hope your little boy can swim because I just saw him running for the pool.

I wish they would invent phones that you can take with you, or I would have called Kimmy and asked if she's gone to see her poor mother and father yet and what are we going to do about leaving this country before something worse happens. Knowing Kimmy she probably finally showed up in her Ganja University t-shirt and jeans, the one cut off halfway down the backside, calling Mummy her sistren and saying that this is all the plan of Babylon shitstem, and it's not the robber they should be mad at but the shitstem that robbed them first. That's what they say at the Twelve Tribes meeting place in that rough-and-tumble neighbourhood called West Kings House, near the home of the Queen's representative. I really need to get better at this sarcasm business. I might be a snob, but at least I'm not a hypocrite, still coasting around because I have nothing to do now that my life's dream to fuck and breed for Che Guevara blew up in my face. Nor am I hanging out with rich people in West Kings House who now don't wash their hair and calling themselves I-man to upset their parents, when everybody knows in two years they're going right back to their father's shipping company to take it over, and marry whichever Syrian bitch just win Miss Jamaica.

Car three hundred and sixty-seven, sixty-eight, sixty-nine, seventy. Seventy-one, seventy-two. I need to go home. But I'm outside here, waiting on him. You ever feel like home is the one place you can't go back to? It's like you promise yourself when you got out of bed and combed your hair that this evening, when I get back I'll be a different woman in a new place. And now you can't go back because the house expects something from you. A bus stops. I fan it off, trying to tell the driver that I don't want to get on. But the bus is still squatting there, waiting on me. I step back and look down to the road, pretending that people aren't in the bus cussing that they have home to get to and plenty pickney to feed so why that damn woman don't get on the bus. I walk away, far enough for the bus to drive off, but walk right back to the bus stop before the dust settle.

The bass creeps up on me from across the road. It sounds like he's been playing the same song all day. It sounds like another song about me, but there's probably two dozen women in Jamaica right now and another two thousand in the world who think the same thing anytime a song of his come on the radio. But "Midnight Ravers" is about me. One day I'm going to tell Kimmy then and she'll know, won't she, that just because she's the prettiest doesn't mean she get all of them. A white police car with blue stripe going all around parked itself by the gate. I didn't even see it coming. Jamaican police tend to use their siren all the time, just to get people to clear the street so they can reach Kentucky Fried Chicken quicker. I never had any dealings with the police. That's not true.

There was that one time when I was on that No. 83 bus to Spanish Town for an interview because that's 1976 for you, you take a job where you can find it and this was a Bauxite company, when three police cars sirened us down and forced the driver to stop right there on the highway. *H'everybody h'evacuate the ve-HI-cle right at this present moment,* the first policeman said. Right there on the highway. Nothing but a thin stretch of road with swamp on both sides and everybody had to file out. Most of the women started cussing about having to get to work on time, most of the men stood silent because the police only thought twice about shooting women. *Dis h'is a spat searrrrch,* the policeman said. *We h'are gonna do the proceejah of getting all of unu name.*

—And you name what, sweet girl?

—Pardon me?

—You, the hot ting that ah carry the swing. What you name?

—Burgess, Nina Burgess.

—Bond, James Bond. Sound like you h'in movie picture. You carrying a conceal weapon h'under there? Mind me have to search you.

—Mind me have to scream rape.

—And who the r'asscloth going care, eh?

He sent me back over to the other women while another policeman gun-butt one of the men who started to talk about equal rights and justice. Here's a secret about police that no Jamaican will ever say out loud, that is any Jamaican who ever had to deal with one of these assholes. Whenever one get shot, and plenty do, there's a part of me, the part before morning coffee, that smiles a little. I shake the thought out. I wonder if the guard over the gate is telling the police, right at this minute, that I've been at the bus stop all day watching the house. But instead somebody says something, and the fat policeman, there's always one, laughs and it echoes all the way over this side. He leaves to get back in his car, but somebody from inside shouts at him. I know it's you, it has to be you. A car is coming up on my side of the road, ninety feet? I can beat it before it slams into me and I know it's you, I just know it, the car, now forty feet? Run, run right now, don't blow your damn horn at me, son of a bitch, deaf like you damn mother I'm in the median too many damn cars driving down the other side of the road and me in the middle marooned like Ben Gunn and I just want you to see me, it's you, it must be you, remember me, "Midnight Ravers" is about me even though it was after midnight and you might not know what I look like in the day, and I just want a favour, I just need a little help, they robbed my father and raped my mother. No they didn't rape her, no I don't know, but the story sounds more urgent when an old woman's pum-pum get messed with and I know it's you, and the policeman is waiting, good, good wonderful-good he's going to come outside—it's not you. Another guard runs outside to tell him something and the fucking fat policeman laughs again and deposits himself in the car. I'm stuck in the median, traffic blurring past me and lifting up my skirt.

—Hello, I'm here to see—

—No visitor. On-site tours start back next week.

—No, you don't understand. I'm not here for the tour, I'm here to see . . . He's expecting me.

—Ma'am, nobody coming through except immediate family and the band. You him wife?

—What? Of course not. What kind of question—

—You play no instrument?

—I don't see what that have to do with anything, just tell him Nina Burgess is here to see him and it's urgent.

—Lady, you could'a name Scooby Doo, nobody coming inna yah.

—But, but . . . I . . .

—Lady, step 'way from the gate.

—Me pregnant. And is fi him. Him need fi mind him pickney.

The guard look at me for the first time today. I thought he was going to recognize me until I realize that he really was seeing me for the first time. He looked me up and down too, maybe wanting to see what type of woman it takes to breed for a star like him.

—You know how much woman come here since Monday saying the same damn thing you just say? Some of them even have belly to show me. Me say no visitors but family and the band. Come back next week, me sure the baby not running 'way to Miami by then. If there is a—

—Eddie, shut you r'asscloth mouth and guard di gate.

—Then after the woman don't want move.

—Then move her.

I step back quick. I don't want none of these men touching me. They always grab on to ass or crotch first. Behind me a car pulls up and a white man comes out. For just a split second I nearly shout Danny, but this man is only white. His hair brown and long, and a little beard on his chin, the way I used to like it but Danny didn't. A yellow plain t-shirt and tight, bell-bottom blue jeans. Maybe it's the hot weather why you can tell that (1) he's American and (2) American men hate underwear more than American women hate bras.

—Bombocloth. Look here, Taffie, Jesus is risen.

—What? But me no repent yet.

The white man didn't seem to get the joke. I stepped out of the way, maybe making too much of a show of it.

—Hey buddy, Alex Pierce from *Rolling Stone.*

—Wait deh now, tight jeans Jesus, Jehovah know say you lie? Two man from Rolling Stone come here already, one name Keith and one named Mick and none of them look like you.

—But them all resemble still, Eddie.

—True that. True that.

—I'm from *Rolling Stone* magazine. We spoke on the phone.

—You never talk to me on no phone.

—I mean, someone from in the office. His secretary or something I don't know. I'm from the magazine? From the U.S.? We cover everybody from Led Zeppelin to Elton John. I don't understand, the secretary said come December 3 at six p.m. when he's on rehearsal break and here I am.

—Bossman, me don't name sexetary.

—But—

—Look, we get strict orders. Nobody in or out except family and band.

—Oh. Why does everybody have an automatic weapon? You guys police? You don't look like the security guard from last time I was here.

—None of your damn business, you want step off now.

—Eddie, the man still bothering you at the gate?

—Him say him magazine is 'bout Lesbian and Elton John.

—No, Led Zeppelin and—

—Tell him to move off.

—How about me making it easy for you.

The white man takes out his wallet—I only need ten minutes, he says. Damn Americans always thinking we're like them and that everybody is up for sale. Just once I'm glad the guard is such an asshole. But he's looking at the money, he's looking at it long. You can't help it with American money, getting 'round the fact that this piece of paper is more valuable than everything else in your purse. That if you whip out one you change the behaviour of a whole room. It just doesn't seem right, a piece of paper with no colour but green. Lord knows pretty money isn't the only pretty thing that's worthless. The guard takes one last look at the piling bills and walks away, over to the entrance of the house.

I chuckled. When you can't fight temptation, you have to flee, I say. The white man looks at me, annoyed, and I just chuckle more. Doesn't happen every day, a Jamaican who doesn't turn into a yes massa I going do it for you now massa, whenever he sees a white man. Danny used to be appalled by it. Until he started to like it. Hell of a thing when white skin is the ultimate passport. I was a little surprised at how good it felt, me and the white man both being kept outside like beggars. On the same level in that regard at least. You'd think I'd never been around white people, or at least Syrians who think they're white.

—You fly all the way from America just to do a story on the Singer?

—Well, yeah. He's the biggest story right now. The number of stars coming out for this concert, you'd think it was Woodstock.

—Oh.

—Woodstock was a—

—I know what Woodstock was.

—Oh. Well, Jamaica is all over the news this year. And this concert. *New York Times* just did a story that the Jamaican opposition leader was shot at. From the Office of Prime Minister, no less.

—Really? That would be news to the Prime Minister, since the opposition would have no reason to be at his office. Also that's uptown. On this very road. Nobody firing no bullets here.

—That's not what the newspaper said.

—Then it must be true then. Guess if you write shit, then you have to believe every shit you read.

—Aw, come on, don't bust my balls like that. It's not like I'm some goddamn tourist. I know the real Jamaica.

—Good for you. I've lived here all my life and haven't found the real Jamaica yet.

I walk off but the white man is following me. There's only one bus stop, I guess. Maybe by now Kimmy has paid a visit to her goddamn parents, who have been robbed and her mother possibly raped. Yet as soon as I cross over to the other side I want to stay. I don't know. I know I have nothing to go home to, but that's no different from any other day. I only need to remember every headline about some family getting shot, bulletin about the curfew, news report about some woman who get raped or how crime moving like a wave uptown to scare myself stupid. Or my mother and father trying to act as if the gunmen didn't take something that was always between him and her and them alone. The whole day I was with them they never touched each other once.

The white man takes the first bus that comes. I don't and I'm telling myself that it's because I don't want to be on the same bus with him. But I know I'll miss the next one. And the one after that too.

Demus

Somebody need to listen to me and it might as well be you. Somewhere, somehow, somebody going judge the quick and the dead. Somebody goin' write about the judgment of the good and wicked, because I am a sick man and a wicked man and nobody ever wickeder and sicker than me. Somebody, maybe forty years later when God come for all of we, leaving not one. Somebody going write about this, sit down at a table on a Sunday afternoon with wood floor creaking and fridge humming but no ghost around him like they around me all the time and he going write my story. And he won't know what to write, or how to write it because he didn't live it, or know what cordite smell like or how blood taste when it stay stubborn in your mouth no matter how much you spit. He never feel it in the one drop. No coolie duppy ever go to sleep on him and fool him with a wet dream while she suck out him life through him mouth even though me grinding my teeth shut and when me wake up my whole face cover in thick mouth juice like somebody just stick me in Jell-O and put me in the fridge. John the Baptist saw them coming. Now the wicked running.

This is how it begin.

One day, me was in Jungle, outside of me house by the standpipe just to catch an early morning bathe because a man can't stink when him go out looking for work. Me out in the backyard, for only one back in the tenement yard and trying to wash meself with soap and water, when police burst in 'cause some woman, some church lady saying she was only going to offer the Lord's name in prayer, officer, when some stinking ghetto boy from Jungle jump out at me and rape me, officer. You, you boy who a play with him cocky like pervert, come over here now! Me try to reason with the officer for Jah Rastafari say we must reason with the enemy and me say, Officer, you no see that is bathe me a bathe and he come right over and kiss me mouth hard with the rifle butt. Don't come tell me no fuckery, nasty man, he say. A play with youself and love up yourself like some bloodcloth sodomite. Then he say is you rape the church lady on North Street? And me say what? No star, me no rape woman, why when me have plenty girl friend, but he slap me like me is woman and say go outside. Me say, Officer, let me wash off or at least put on me brief, no man, and me hear click. Move, pussyhole, him say, so me move and outside seven more man line up and people watching and some people see me and look away and some look and all me have to stay decent was soap sud. You catch him before him wash off the evidence, another police say.

The police, six I count, say one of you is a nasty rapist who rape church women when they coming back from praising the Lord. And since you is all lying nasty ghetto boy me not even going ask the guilty perpetrator to step forward. We don't know what to do, because if any one of we get called the rapist the police going shoot him before he reach the jail. So the first policeman who talk all the time say, But we know how fi catch you. The whole of you drop to the ground now! We confused so we look around and me look at the soap bubbles popping one by one and exposing me business. The policeman fire two shot in the air and say drop-a-ground now! So we drop. He ask another policeman for a lighter and grab a newspaper rolling down the road. Now listen what me want you all fi do, he say. Me want all of you to fuck the ground good. One of we laugh loud because this just turn into TV comedy and the police kick him in the side two time. Me say fi fuck the dirt, the policeman say. So we hump the ground and keep humping when he say continue. The ground tough and have pebble and bottle and dirt and me hips slamming into it and me skin starting to rub and me stop. Who tell you fi stop, the policeman say, and light the newspaper. Fuck, fuck, fuck, me say fi fuck, the policeman shout, and shove the burning newspaper on me batty. Me scream and he call me a girl. Me say you fi fuck, him say. And then he burn another boy and another boy and all of we fucking the ground.

Then the policeman move up the line saying, You can't fuck, go home.

You can't fuck neither, remove youself. You look like you can fuck, stay. You go, you go. Hold on, hold on now, you move like is you the one who getting the fucking. Batty boy, remove youself, and you, you better stay. He mean me. They grab three of we and throw we in the back of the van and me still naked. I ask for a shirt and the policeman say yeah, man, we'll find a panty for you. My woman come 'round with pants and shirt, a police tell me. But them look too good for ghetto clothes so we keep it, them say. Then one policeman slap her and say go find some ambition and stop fuck with ghetto man. We in jail a week before they let us out. They kick me in the face, beat me with the baton, whip me in me balls, beat me with a cat o' nine like them name buckra massa, and break my brethren right hand. That was the first day when they still feel like treating us nice. The whole time me still naked and they take my nakedness and make joke.

This is what happen on the seventh day. The woman change her mind, say it's Trench Town man that rape her and didn't want no prosecution so they let us go. Nobody talk to me in jail and the police never even say sorry. So the first time me back in the Copenhagen City and a policeman come through, firing his revolver and saying he keeping the peace, me make sure me have a gun. What they didn't know is that in the ghetto me learn to shoot good, like a soldier in *The Dirty Dozen*. Me watch that movie and watch it and watch it and watch it again. By the time the police give up and run away from Jungle I shoot two of them, one in the head and another in the balls because I want him to live with no use for him cocky for the rest of him life.

This is where it happen. The Singer brethren, no not him the other one, drop word that we to come to the Singer house. That alone not regular. Natty gone uptown now and only certain man get invite and all of them is big man or top shotter. But this wasn't the natty, it was the brethren, and he invite Heckle and Heckle say him need five or six other man to come with him. The Singer house was the biggest house me ever see. Me run up and touch the wall just to say me touch it. So much first time in that trip that me can't even remember most of them. First time me ever go uptown. First time me on Hope Road. First time, me see so much woman in pretty clothes walking up and down the street. First time me see the Singer house. First time me see white woman looking like Rasta. First time me see how people who have things live. But the Singer never did there, only the brethren and a whole bunch of people me never see before, even white people. He say it simple. Horse racing is big something in Jamdown, everybody know that. This is how it must go down. The champion jockey might win the race, him might not win, but if you bet against him, high stakes, and him lose, that is more money than you could ever dream of even if you dream two time. Money enough that every man in the ghetto can buy him woman a good Posturepedic mattress at Sealy.

Me no care about the mattress. Me just want to bathe inside not outside and me want to see the Statue of Liberty and me want Lee jeans and not idiot jeans that some thief sew on a Lee patch. No that's not what me want. Me want enough money to stop want money. To bathe outside 'cause me want to fucking bathe outside. To say Sealy mattress is shit, what you don't have none better? To look 'pon America and don't go, but make America know me can go anytime me want. Because me tired of people living like they can waste money and looking at me like me is some animal. I want enough money that when me kill them me have cash and don't give a shit. Kidnap the jockey, reason with him and ting, the brethren say.

Race day was Saturday. Tuesday, Heckle drive me and two other man to Caymanas Park racetrack. Soon as the champion jockey done practise and head to him car we run up 'pon the man, throw pillow over him head, push him in the car and take him away. We take him to an old warehouse downtown that nobody use no more. Heckle shove the gun in the jockey mouth so far that he start to choke.

—Pussyhole, this is wha you going do Saturday, him say.

The jockey lose him three race. Then jump on a plane to Miami and disappear like magic. But then some other people vanish. The four man who collect the money at Caymanas Park, including the brethren. That leave me, Heckle and plenty other man with nothing. Nothing at all. Me think me di vex enough until me see me brethren squeeze a Horlicks bottle so hard it smash and he have to get stitches. By the Saturday we march up to the Singer house 'cause some bloodcloth man was going give we what we have coming. But the Singer on tour. The next time man go up to the Singer house him was there we hear but he already meet with man from Jungle. Nobody tell this to me or Heckle. Man was going samfie we again. Nobody even notice when me and Heckle make one of them boy disappear. But now some people look like them getting money and all now we can't get no share. Me shouldn't have tell me woman nothing, 'cause now me just become another thing keeping her down. When me think of the brethren who gone to foreign with the money I want to burn the whole Hope Road house down. This is how they do it, this is how people keep people poor.

When Josey Wales first find me, he ask if I can use gun. I laugh. Me use gun better than Joe Grind use him cock, me say. Him ask if me have any problem shooting up a boy. I tell him no, but me only shoot Babylon police or man who samfie me. Me shoot three and not stopping till me kill ten. He ask why ten and I say because ten sound like a number even God find heavy. He say soon, soon I will feed you police like how I feed snake rat. I tell him that my leg in pain from the time I was in jail and it don't stop paining for a year now. Him friend Weeper say, I can cure that right now. After that first time, I was sweet for so quick that I beg him almost like a girl for more cocaine since then. And the pain gone, gone like when me use little weed. But weed slow me down. Cocaine make me quick. I said, But wait, this too good. You going to give me white powder, gun and money to kill people that I would kill for free? Today is April 1? Josey Wales say, no me brethren, we going paint Kingston red with police blood. But I want somebody else blood first.

This is what I want to say before the writer say it for me. When the pain was so bad that only strong weed could help me, the only other thing that help was the Singer. They never play him on the radio. A girl that check for me give me a cassette. Is not that music take away the pain, but when it play I don't ride the pain, I ride the rhythm. But when Josey Wales tell me last night who we shooting up I go home and vomit. I wake up in the morning thinking that this must be a stupid and scary dream, until he leave message on me door that me to meet him at the old train shack near the sea. Me is a wicked man, me is a sick man, but me would never join in this if I did know that he want to rub out the Singer. This hurt me brain worse than anything ever hurt me before. All now me don't sleep, I lie in my room with my eye wide open hearing me girl snore in her sleep.

When the moon rise and a light cut through the window and slice my chest I know God coming to judge me. Nobody who kill a police going to hell but is something else to kill the Singer. I let Josey Wales tell me that the Singer is a hypocrite, and he playing both sides taking everybody for idiot. I let Josey Wales tell me that he have bigger plans and is high time we done be ghetto stooge for white man who live uptown and don't care about we until election time. I let Josey Wales tell me that the Singer is a PNP stooge who bow for the Prime Minister. I let Josey Wales tell me to shoot up three more line and I won't care who. I let Josey tell me that the brethren come back. He living in the house too like a fat house rat just dying for me and only me to show him why you don' fuck with a Jungle boy. When morning come and I still awake that is what I hold on to. Is enough. I want to shove the gun up him batty and fuck him a bullet.

I take it through the day sitting in the bed while my girl cuss about nothing around to eat and she going to work because if the PNP win again she won't be able to get a good job. I wait till she leave before I put on a pants and go outside. I don't bathe at the standpipe since the police come for me the last time. Outside, the sun not up and center yet so it bright, green and cool. I walk down the lane barefoot, past zinc fence and board fence and zinc roof that people use stone, building block and garbage to hold down. Those who have a job and those who looking for a job all gone, leaving those who can't find work because this is JLP town and PNP in power. I keep walking. By the time I get to the edge of Jungle, the sun almost noon and I hear music and somebody's radio. Disco. I hear wet squeaking, a woman washing her clothes with her hands around the back of her house, near the standpipe. It's like I don't know nobody or everybody I know gone.

Josey Wales asked me two question when he meet me. I was walking down the road from Jungle to the Garbagelands and he pull up in a white Datsun and stop. Two other man was in the car, Weeper and a man I still don't know. He said he hear me was good with a gun and ask how come, since all ghetto man do is shower people with bullet. I said I was good because unlike them I have certain man in particular to kill. Then he said, You good but plenty man good, what I want know is if you hungry. He didn't have to explain it to me. I did know exactly what he mean. That was a week ago. I meet up with him every night at the train shack. One night a white man show up and said that a shipment at the wharf and nobody watching it and it would be a shame if something happen to it, but this is Jamaica, right? Things go missing all the time.

This is what you need to know. Somebody need to know where me coming from, although that don't really mean nothing. People who say they don't have a choice just too coward to choose. Because it's now six p.m. We go to the Singer house in twenty-four hours.

Alex Pierce

Gig like this got its own juice. I'm in Kingston, somewhere between Studio One and Black Ark, thinking there must be a reason why hippies have such a hard-on for this scene. I mean, a poor boy can't do nothing but sing in a rock and roll band. A rich boy, on the other hand, can stop cutting his hair, call himself a hippie along with some hairy armpit chicks, confuse having the means to tune in and drop out with the conviction to fucking do it and call himself a Rastafarian. Then he goes off to St. Bart's, or Maui, or Negril and Port Maria, sticking it to the man in between rum punches. Always fucking hated hippies. Worse, now you have rich bitch Jamaicans imitating hippies imitating Rastas, what the fuck. But hey, it's Jamaica. At least everybody should be pumping some Big Youth and Jimmy Cliff.

And yet when I get here, first time in a year, the only thing playing on the radio is *More More More, How Do You Like It How Do You Like It*, and I'm thinking this rep is bogus. I flip to another station and it's *Ma Baker She Knew How to Die!* Switch to FM radio and it's *Fly Robin Fly up-up to the Sky!* I asked this busboy at the hotel, So where do I hear some Mighty Diamonds or Dillinger? He looks at me like I just asked to suck his dick and then says not every Jamaican sells the collieweed, sir. Even Abba gets more play than reggae here. I've heard "Dancing Queen" so much I can feel myself turning fag.

I'm at the Skyline, the hotel with a commanding view of . . . the hotel in front. In Kingston you go down this street, there's a black guy and white guy and lots and lots of mixed guys, and they're all at the same hotel, or at the Singer's house or just on the street. Even on TV the weather guy is black. You see black people all the time in the States, right, but you don't really see them, certainly not reading the news. You hear them on the radio all the time, but once the song is over, they vanish. They're on TV but only when somebody just acted like a jive turkey or somebody just made them say dynomite! Jamaica's different.

A Jamaican is on TV. A white woman just won Miss World, but she's from here. She just said that the Singer is her boyfriend and she can't wait to go back home to be with him. No shit. Some stone foxes live in this city, and they can all dance. Out the window even the traffic has music to it. That and people telling people about their bombocloth. In the resorts the Americans say bumperclat, and think they're cooler because they got their head braided by a Girl Friday (not from the movie, this is some Robinson Crusoe black personal slave shit, no kidding, and they looked at me weird when I dropped my drink the first time I heard it) and learned to talk like a real Jamaican, mon.

People let it all hang out here, they move with a kinda swag, but nobody forgets their place. And if you talk to enough people in the hotel, you get the white tone, people being polite to a fault because that's how they were trained to talk to you. And because it's all about race—it fucks up all the time. One time this black guy asked for the busboy to take his bags and the boy just walked off. Guy started shouting that this is some slavery-loving Uncle Tom bullshit right here for them to realize he was American. And even then the boy asked to see his room key. Go out on the street it's the same thing until you walk far enough and the people get realer.

Still, it's Jamaica and this place is kinda ace. Serge Gainsbourg, the ugly French dude who keeps making cheesy records and scoring hot chicks, has a story. So he comes to Jamaica because eez ere to do zee reggae and motherfuckers at the studio just laugh him off, right? Like who the bombocloth this skinny likkle frenchy think he is. Serge says but I am zee biggest pop zinger, they say we don't fucking know you, the only bombocloth French song we know is "Je T'aime." Serge says, "Je T'aime," that iz me. Gainsbourg was a God in Kingston after that, square biz. So I'm at Studio One and ask one of the men here if he could get me a cup of coffee, black no cream, and he says, What? You hand sick? Go get it you bloodcloth self. Classic, man.

I'm supposed to be on Mick Jagger's tail but nobody is going to call *Black and Blue* a misunderstood masterpiece, not in ten years, not in twenty, and I said so in print. Fuck him and Keef anyway and fuck *Rolling Stone* Random Notes gossip bullshit. I'm this close to getting the skinny on something big. "Armagideon Time," square biz. The busiest, most vital music scene in the world is about to blow up and not on the charts. The Singer, he's up to something and it's not just the peace concert. It took putting in a few years uptown and downtown and some convincing to prove to people that I wasn't some stupid white boy waiting for the limbo party for people to start talking to me. The fucking Kingston sissy at the front desk doesn't even know who Don Drummond is, but he keeps telling me that everything I might need is in New Kingston.

There's this too, Jamaicans and not just the ones working at the hotel, but brown and white men who are always drinking rum at the restaurant and who, when they see my camera, first ask if I'm from *Life* magazine, then tell me where not to go. Go where they go and you end up at the Liguanea Club where it's fucking "Disco Duck" and boring rich bitches who've just finished tennis and want to ball. I tell them I'm bailing for the Turntable Club and they look at me in wonder, worse when I don't bother asking for directions, because I know they wouldn't know. I asked the concierge just a few hours ago, Where's the jam session? He says and I quote and kid thee not, "Sir, why would you wanna go mingle wid them element of society?" I was this close to saying dude suck a dick already, it's cool. But this story, it's something.

I'm in the taxi heading to the hotel and the taxi driver asks me if I bet on horses. I'm not a betting man, but he is and who did he see at the tracks a couple weeks ago? The Singer. He was there with two guys, one of them calls himself Papa-Lo. I did some checking around on this Papa-Lo. Racketeering, extortion, five counts of murder, only one reaching trial, acquitted. Runs a shanty town called Copenhagen City. So here is the Singer, along with two hoods from a political party he's supposed to not support and there they are chummy together like old school pals. The next few days, he's seen hanging out with Shotta Sherrif, the godfather of the Eight Lanes, controlled by the other party, the other side. Two top goons in one week, two men who pretty much control the fighting halves of downtown Kingston. Maybe he's just being a peacemaker. I mean, he's just a singer. Thing is I'm catching the drift that nobody is ever just anything in Jamaica. Something's cooking and I'm already smelling it. Did I mention there's an election in two weeks?

And if white boys from New York are catching a whiff, then the trail is already cold. Coming on the same flight with me was that little asshole Mark Lansing, trying extra hard to not see me. No shit. Crappy filmmaker still using Daddy's little bucks to make a movie is here in Jamaica to film the peace concert. He said the record label hired him. Maybe, but when a dim motherfucker like him suddenly shows up in Jamaica to film a concert despite no previous experience doing anything of this magnitude, my brain gets a case of the shits.

My taxi driver is just trying to win enough money so that he can fly out. He thinks that if the People's National Party wins again, Jamaica might become the next communist republic. I don't know about that, but I do know that just about everybody has eyes on the Singer, as if a lot of stuff is riding on what he does next. Poor brother probably just wants to release an album of love songs and call it a day. Maybe he feels it too—everybody is feeling it—that Kingston is on boil. Two nights in a row now, the concierge has slept behind the reception desk. He didn't have to tell me, I could see it in the bags under his eyes. He'd probably say he was dedicated, but I'm betting he's just too scared to go home when it gets late.

In May some guy named William Adler said on local TV that there were eleven CIA operatives working here in the U.S. Embassy. By June seven had left the country. Come on. Meanwhile, the Singer, never one to pull punches, sings Rasta don't work for no CIA. In Jamaica 2 + 2 = 5, but now it's adding up to 7. And all these loose strands knotting around the Singer like a noose. You should have seen his house today, security like Fort Knox, nobody being let in or out. Not the police guarding him either, just a posse of goons I found out are called the Echo Squad. Everybody is squad, posse or guard lately. Some poor chick was waiting out there all day, probably claiming she had his kid or something. Does Lansing have a way in? He said he was filming the concert for the label, he must be doing some behind-the-scenes shit. The only problem is to get any info would mean actually being nice to the fucker, and one can't have that.

I'm trying to not seem so hungry. Twenty-seven years old and six years out of college my mother keeps asking when I'm going to stop being a pinko on the hustle and get a real job. I'm impressed that she's heard of pinkos but I think she got "on the hustle" from my little sister. She also thinks I need the love of a good woman, preferably not black. Maybe she's looking at me and smelling wannabe. I think I'm trying to convince myself that I'm not one of those white boys drifting around trying to find something to belong to, something to fucking mean something because after Nixon and Ford and the Pentagon papers and fucking Carpenters and Tony Orlando and Dawn there's nothing to believe in anymore, God knows not rock and roll. Rolling into West Kingston, the rudies left me alone because they knew I had nothing to lose. Maybe I'm just a stupid kid bitching about the world. I think I got problems but I ain't got no problems.

The first time I came to Jamaica we flew into Montego Bay and drove to Negril, me and a girl whose dad was ex-army. I loved that she had no idea who The Who were, but listened to The Velvet Underground because she grew up with German kids on the army base. After a few days, it wasn't as if I felt I belonged, nothing as cheesy as that, but I did get the feeling, this sensation or maybe it was just a belief that said, You can stop running now. No, that did not make me want to live here. But I remember waking up early one morning, right at the point where the temperature finally dips, and saying, What is your story? Maybe I meant the country, or maybe I meant me.

I'm being obvious. I'm better thinking about what's ticking in this country, right about to boom.

The general election is in two weeks. The CIA is squatting on the city, its lumpy ass leaving the sweat print of the Cold War. The magazine is expecting nothing much from me but some paragraph on whatever the Stones are recording, complete with a stupid pic of Mick or Keef with headphones half on with a Jamaican in the shot for some color. But fuck that. What kind of game is Mark Lansing running? Cocksucker isn't smart enough to pull a total scam all by himself. I should head back to Marley's house tomorrow. I mean, I had an appointment. Like that means anything in Jamaica. Who is this William Adler anyway?

Josey Wales

W*eeper is a man* with a whole heap of stories. All of them start with a laugh, because Weeper is a man who love to joke. And that is how he play fisherman on you because the joke is the hook. But once he hook you the man drag you down the blackest, reddest, hottest pit of hell you could ever imagine. Then he laugh and just hold back to watch you try to climb your way back out. Just don't ask him about the Electric Boogie.

Make sense that I would be in a bar seeing woman dancing, and man watching, and music playing and what I doing? Thinking about Weeper. Jungle never produce a rudie like Weeper before, and not going to again. He is not like any other man who live in Balaclava before the fall of 1966. Weeper's mother send him to school all the way to secondary. Not many people know that Weeper pass three GCE subject, in English, mathematics and technical drawing, and was reading big book even before Babylon send him to prison. Weeper read so hard that he had to start stealing glasses until he find one that work. Now the rudie in glasses make people think there is something behind him face. His baby mother get a good job in the freezone only because she was the only woman in freezone history to send in a real job letter, of course one that Weeper, not she, write.

Now every Weeper story have only one hero, and that is Weeper, except for the man who send him letter still, the man who he love to talk about all the time, this man who did this, this man who said that, this man that teach him this, and with a little coke or even less H, he let the man do that and both of them feel good. Weeper will talk about the man like he couldn't care less what anybody else think, because everybody know Weeper is the fucker that will kill a boy right in front of his father and have the father count his last five breath. Just don't ask him about the Electric Boogie.

Weeper even have a story about the Singer. A man can't pay attention to everybody, especially if he in a place on a mission, but Weeper for some reason take it personally. Nineteen sixty-seven and Weeper was a boy from downtown in Crossroads, the middle ground between uptown and downtown, staying out of trouble, thinking that with Maths, English and Technical Drawing he could apprentice for some architect somewhere. Weeper didn't forget to comb him hair that day. He was wearing the grey shirt and dark blue pants his mother buy for church. Picture Weeper walking through Crossroads like a head cock, rocksteady bouncing in his shoes, looking way too boasty for a boy downtown. Picture Weeper looking different from everybody else, because unlike everybody else he have somewhere to go.

As Weeper make a left to go to Carib Theatre the police draw down in numbers. Two truck full with police, one grabbing him, another butting him with the rifle, another kicking him in the head when he fall down. In Gun Court the police say he resist arrest and wound two officer with intent. Milord says, You are charged with one count of robbery of the Ray Chang Jewellery store in Crossroads along with wounding with intent, how do you plead? Weeper say he don't know nothing about no robbery, but the police say they have witness. Weeper say you don't have nothing, you just round up any black man you see uptown like Marcus Stone from Copenhagen City in jail for a murder that happen forty-eight hours after he was arrested. That made the law look either stupid or corrupt or both. The judge give him the chance to reveal his accomplices. Weeper say there are no accomplices because there was no crime. Weeper was innocent but he couldn't afford a lawyer. The judge give him five years in the General Penitentiary.

The day before prison, police pay Weeper a visit. Boys from Copenhagen City, Jungle, Rema and Waterhouse not friends with the police. But police show him what to expect from prison. Even then, even after the sentencing, Weeper is still holding on to hope, because his mother was still alive and he has three GCE passes and is about to make something of himself. Weeper think it an even match, they with the power, he with being right. He thinking surely a boy wearing glasses can't be a rudie. Weeper thinking even up to that point that God at any minute was going to take Daniel out of the lion's den. Six policemen, one of which say Weeper, we come to give you something. Weeper who up to that point still named William Foster, but the police say him cry like a girl. Weeper, who can never keep a smart word in his mouth where it should stay, tell the man that he kinda pretty but 'round there is only exit not entrance. The first swing of the club didn't break his left hand but the second one did. The policeman says you goin' tell h'us h'all o' you accomplicisties. Weeper bawling from pain but still he can't lock off the smart mouth. Don't you mean accomplice? he says. The police say we know how to make you talk, but they know Weeper have nothing to say, they were the same police who just pick him up because dutty ghetto boy have no right to palaver in decent clothes like him is somebody, and is thief the bloodcloth boy thief the clothes from decent people and nasty naigger must always know them place.

They break the left lens of his glasses, a break Weeper wear even now, when he can afford to change it. They take him to a room in the lockup he never see before. Take off all his clothes, even brief, and tie him down to a cot. The policeman say, You know what them call the Electric Boogie, pussyhole? One of them come 'round with an electric cord they rip out of a toaster. They split the two wires. Mind they call you a battyman one police say when another grab onto Weeper's cock and wrap the first wire 'round the head. Then they plug in the cord. Nothing happen when they do that, but something happen when they take the other cord and touch his fingertips, gums, nose, nipples and asshole. Weeper didn't tell me any of this, but I know.

Weeper was something new to prison. A man that damage before, not after they lock him up. I hear that the first week in prison everybody stay out of his way because a wounded lion was more dangerous than a healthy one. Anybody could take him, but whoever did was going to hell with him. Weeper can carry whole line of conversation with his eyes alone. Still do, another reason why he's the best to work with. He on one side of a grocery shop, I on the other side, and between two winks and a stare we both know that he's taking the back door and I'm taking the counter and shooting anybody who so much as reach down to adjust their pants or go into their handbag. Weeper's gun have five notches on the left side, none on the right. Each notch, a policeman. And—

—Yow! Yow, Josey! Brethren, come back, planet Earth need you.

—Weeper? Is when you get here? Don't think I see you come in.

—I and I come in two minute ago. You think that's a good idea making dream distract you in this bar?

—'Cause why?

—Huh? Nothing, star. Man like you don't have to watch you back anyway when man watching it for you.

—How come you just coming?

—You know me, Josey. Every road must have a roadblock. So is which world you coming back from?

—Pluto, the one far out.

—Seen. Where the woman have one breast but two pussy?

—No, man, more like *Planet of the Apes.*

—Might as well sink down the cock 'pon two monkey, since—

—Don't start with that man come from monkey fuckery again, Weeper.

—Who say that?

—No so your atheist evolution idiot brethren chat 'bout.

—Yeah, man, me and top-ranking Charles Darwin. Brethren, nobody come from monkey. Well, except for Funnyboy, must be some gorilla poom-poom him push out of.

—Weeper, what the bloodcloth.

—What? What?

—Brethren, me pretty sure my beer was more than half.

—Good to know.

—Pussyhole, you drink off me beer?

—Didn't look like you was using it. What Granny used to say? What stay too long serve two master.

—Granny know, say you drink man backwash?

—For serious, is where you did gone?

Weeper even more chatty than usual. Might be because of this bar where liquor loosen every tongue but mine. He know I hate him getting high when we in the middle of business. He going to say that the C take the edge off, but that's just some fuckery he hear from a white man in lockup on narcotics charge until the embassy come for him, or from some movie, he don't know what the fuck it mean. In this state he will pick a fight when there is no fight to pick. And he more paranoid than Judas hiding after he betray Jesus.

—Hey Josey, your Datsun outside? Man over there. Three o'clock.

—What, what the bloodcloth you talking 'bout now? And what it have to do with my Datsun?

—That man, three o'clock.

—How much time I must tell you not to use that American movie bullshit with me?

—Fine then, pussyhole. Man behind you to the right—don't look. Tall, dark not handsome, lip like fish hanging off, at the bar but talking to nobody. Three times now he look over here.

—Maybe him like you.

Weeper look at me hard. For a second I think he going to say something stupid and make me cuss him out. Weeper earn the right to do what he want to do, even if it is some sodomite business. He'll talk about it all the time but sideways like an Aesop fable, or a riddle and rhyme. He can shape and mold it and make it Greek, his word, not mine, I don't know what the fuck he's talking about with that Greek shit. But that don't mean he want anybody to say it back to him. Something happen when somebody tell you something about yourself even if you already know.

—Man, fuck a battyman, he says. I kick my own foot.

—That man watching us.

—That's what the C telling you. Of course he watching us. If I was him in the bar I wouldn't be able to take my eye off me neither. This is what him really dealing. He, like everybody here, recognize me, then he recognize you. He right there thinking, Who in here did they come to cancel and how long before they kill him? And should I just chill out to the max, or should I run like a pussyhole? I don't even have to look, one hand on him drinks, other tapping the bar. Watch him look away quick as I swing around, one, two, three . . . now.

—Haha, man knock over him own drinks. Brethren, maybe is a police.

—Maybe you should stop feeling up you bloodcloth gun. You have twenty-two days of Christmas leave to add couple more notch.

Weeper stare at me hard then laugh. Nothing like a Weeper laugh, it start like a wheeze, then somewhere, and you never know where, it explode into the biggest thing in the room. Who teach this little black man that he can laugh so? It spin off in the whole room and other people start laughing, not knowing why.

—More paranoid than usual these few days.

—That's because you think tomorrow special. No different from any other day. You know why I pick you, Weeper, you know why? Because if it's one thing I can't stand it's a man who can only tell me what he about to do. That's why I don't fucking trust no politician. All he can tell me is what he going to do.

—Never make a politician do you a favour he will want . . . I ever tell you how me run 'pon the Singer?

Ten thousand time but I don't tell him that. There are things Weeper need to say a dozen, a hundred, a thousand time till he no longer have the need to say it.

—No, you never tell me.

—Three year into the service . . .

He always call the years in prison, the service.

—Three years. Them take us out Port Henderson beach.

—They make prisoner swim? I would escape so fast.

—NO, no, no. Them have we out there 'pon a work, have big man chopping down wood. You right, I should have just swing the cutlass and chop off a guard head. Anyway, brethren, we out there a work and the Singer and him friend come out there. The man look 'pon me and say, We everybody out here a fight for you, seen? And me look at the man and hear him a reason with me, right? And him say him fighting for my rights! Me. Then him laugh and walk off. Hate the pussyhole like poison after that.

He hate the Singer for real. But the real story don't have nothing to do with Weeper. He think they talking to him and his heart leap up, Weeper was even about to walk over, despite guards watching. Then he realize the Singer were talking to the man beside him, not him. For some reason, even after cat o' nine, gun butt and piss in the rice when he get too testy with a guard, this is the thing that hurt him the most. The thing that make him blood boil. And it never even happen, but something in Weeper need it to happen, need it to end this way. I don't care, this is what drawing him to pull the gun when I need him to.

—Them waiting by the shack right now, time to go, I say. —Everybody but Bam-Bam. Take my car and pick him up. He watching the house all day.

—For real, brethren, for real.

Bam-Bam

Is a hell of a thing when a gun come home to live with you. The people who live with you notice it first. The woman I live with talk to me different. Everybody talk to you different when them see a new bulge in you pants. No, is not that at all. When a gun come to live in the house it's the gun, not even the person who keep it, that have the last word. It come between man and woman talk, not just serious reasoning but even a little thing.

—Dinner ready, she say.

—Me no hungry.

—Okay.

—I going need it warm when me finally hungry.

—Yes sah.

When a gun come to live in the house the woman you live with treat you different, not cold, but now she weigh word, measure it before talking to you. But a gun talk to the owner too, telling him first that you can never own this, that outside is plenty people who don't have a gun but know you do, and one night they going come like Nicodemus and take it. Nobody ever own a gun. You don't know that until you own one. If somebody give it to you, that somebody can take it back. Another man can think is for him even when he seeing that is you control it. And he don't sleep until he get it 'cause he can't sleep. Gun hunger worse than woman hunger for at least maybe a woman might hungry for you back. At night me don't sleep. Me stay up in the dark shadow, looking at it, rubbing it, seeing and waiting.

Two days after he leave, we hear that Papa-Lo was in England watching the Singer on tour. Rumour was that Funnyboy was in England the same time, but nobody could say if that was true or untrue since they crucify the last informer right in the Garbagelands. The man who bring guns to the ghetto tell we of more waiting in the night in a container marked Peace Concert. When we three get to the wharf it empty like Clint Eastwood just ride off. No crane working, no floodlight on, no people, only water slapping the dock. The crate was open and ready. Weeper drive right up in Josey Wales' Datsun. Me, him and Heckle load the trunk and backseat with so much ammo that neither me nor Heckle could fit in the car when Weeper drive back. He give we money for taxi, but no taxi going to ghetto, worse during curfew, so we take the money and buy Kentucky Fried Chicken, watching the cashier waiting on we to leave so they can lock up but too 'fraid to tell we to leave.

That night the same white man who joke with Frouser teach we how to shoot. Plenty man come from the ghetto and when he see one of them he smile and say, What's shaking, Tony? But Tony don't answer. He say to nobody that Tony and him go way back to our little school in Fort Benning, but nobody know about this Tony going to no school. He set up target and ask me to shoot. Then the man who bring guns to the ghetto look at me and smile. Weeper telling the white man that Papa-Lo get soft but the white man don't understand much of what Weeper saying. He just nod and laugh and say I gotcha! then look at Josey Wales to repeat everything slower but he still laugh too loud at what wasn't no joke. This make Josey Wales' face even more cross because everybody know that he proud that he can speak good. The white man say we're fighting for freedom from totalitarianism, terrorism and tyranny, but nobody know what he mean.

I look at the other boys, two younger than me, five older including Demus and Weeper. We all dark, we all hate to comb our hair. We all wearing khaki or gabardine or jeans pants with the right leg rolled up right under the knee and a rag sticking out of the left back pocket because this look carrying the swing. Some of we wearing tam but some of we don't because tam is for Rastas and Rastas look like they turning socialist. Socialism is another ism and even the Singer so sick of ism that he write a song about it. Then the white man talk about how some people trying to use smooth talk to win people over and how totalitarianism always happens with consent and we nod like we understand. He say chaos nine time. He say how the country will thanks us one day and we nod like we understand.

But Josey Wales want something more than this party business. I think of how he always smell kinda off even though him woman dress him. A smell like garlic and sulphur. And after they show us how to shoot again, Josey Wales say we going to Rema because naiggers 'roun' dere acting a way. You got yourself some uppity niggers, the white man say and laugh as he leave in a jeep. There was Rema again, between JLP and PNP, between capitalist and socialist. Josey Wales tell the white man that he not an ist for anybody, he just smarter than all of them and he will do what they want if they leave him alone in Miami. The white man say he doesn't know what Josey Wales was yapping about but then smile like he and the devil have a secret. Word was that Rema people were grumbling that JLP put money and corned beef and sewage system in Copenhagen City but don't do nothing for them and maybe it's time they join with the PNP for real, and turn the Eight Lanes into Nine Lanes. All this Weeper tell we when we go back to shack by the train line. He still telling we while he mix white C with ether and heat it with a lighter. Then he suck up the coke through him nose and give some to me first.

We coming up to Rema in the Datsun. I grab the door but it feel soft the air peeling through me hair like two hundred woman fingers brushing past my nipples and this must be how woman feel when you suck them titties my head feel lumpy clear gone like I'm walking around without a head and then my head is back but now it's a balloon and the dark street getting darker the yellow streetlight yellower and that girl in the house across the street make me so horny but the seam won't pop pop pop in my pants and fuck fuck fuck I have to fuck fuck fuck every woman in the world and I will fuck the shit out of Miss Jamaica and when the baby come out of her pussy I will fuck her too and I going pull this trigger and kill the world. But I want to fuck and it not hard. It not hard! It not hard! Is the freebase. It must be the C. Or maybe H. Me no know. Me don't bombocloth know and this car need to reach where it going and stop being a snail and I want to swing the car door open and jump out and run all the way and run back and run again and run so fast that I fly and I want to fuck fuck fuck but it's not hard! It's not hard! And the radio in my head playing a killer tune that it never play on the radio right now rhythm hold I, rhythm wild! and the other boys in the car feel it and know it too and I look at Weeper who look at me and know and I could kiss him with tongue and shoot him for being a batty boy and laugh and laugh again and the truck hit a hill and we feel like we going up to heaven no, yes heaven, the Datsun flying and my head turn into a balloon and then I think of Rema and how man who live there must learn a lesson and I want them to learn it so hard that I grab and clutch the M16, but I really want to grab a little boy on the street and wring his neck around and around and around until it pop off and then I'll scoop up some blood and rub it on my face and say who under heavy manners now pussyhole and I want to fuck fuck fuck but it not getting hard! It not getting hard! and the Datsun screech. And before Weeper say anything we jump out and run down a street and the street is wet and the street is a sea and no, the street is air and I'm flying through it and I can hear my footstep as if it's somebody's footstep that clap the pavement like gunshots and then I'm at state theatre with Josey Wales because Harry Callahan is back with *Enforcer*, and the other bad man because boy with gun is man not boy, and every time Clint Eastwood shoot up a boy Josey Wales sing people are you ready? we sing Bow! Oh Lord, and shoot up the screen till all we see is hole and smoke. And everybody would have run out of the theatre but they know they better keep rolling the film or we'll come up into the screen room and enforce. And before I fire again at the screen I remember me in Rema fields not the movie theatre and we firing up a house and a shop still open and people running and screaming, *Yes, pusssyhole, run run 'cause gunman ah come chil-li-li-boom-boom-eh!* but we not to shoot anybody well not to kill them and this make me really really mad and I still want to fuck fuck fuck and I don't know why I want to fuck so bad but can't get no cock-stand so I run down one of the girls and shout I goin' kill you and a grab her and I want to but Weeper grab me and butt me in the face with him gun and say what the fuck take you? This is warning nothing else and I want to kill him too, but he already signaling that we leave because though Rema man can't afford anything, one or two of them have guns too, but who care 'bout Rema pussyhole? Bullet bounce off me like Superman. Me take the S off of Superman chest and the B off Batman belly. We see a boy and chase after him, but he disappear like a mouse in a hole that spring up only for mouse and I shout out for the battyman to come out and die like real man, I want to kill him so bad, I want to kill kill kill then a dog come out and I run after the dog because I want to kill this dog, I need to kill the dog, I going to kill this dog, I kill this dog! Josey Wales and the others running to the truck and they catch a boy and kick him in the back and in the shin and in the batty and say that this be for all Rema pussyhole who think they can switch to PNP just so, you better remember say we have the gun and know where you stand, and they kick the boy again and he run off and I go to shoot him and Weeper look at me and I want to shoot him, I want to shoot him bad and I want to shoot him now now now but Weeper say get you pussycloth backside in the fucking car or every man here going full you up of so much bullet that you goin' whistle in the breeze and I don't know because when I want to fuck, I want to fuck fuck fuck and when I want to kill, I want to kill kill kill and now that I don't want to die, I 'fraid 'fraid 'fraid and I never 'fraid like that ever and my heart beating real real bad. But I jump in the backseat and I think of the shooting and how it feel better than good and how I feel better than good but also how just as I started to think I feel better than good I started to not feel so good. Leaving that fish town without killing somebody make me feel like how some people feel when a person dead and I don't know why. It's not something to feel anything about and yet still. And the darkness was never so dark and the drive was never so long even though it wasn't far and I knew that Weeper was mad at me but I thought he was going to kill me and kill everybody and the entire Copenhagen City grey and rusty and dirty and I hate it and don't know why since it was all I know and all I can think is that when I smoke that thing everything look good and every road was pretty and every woman I wanted to fuck now and when I fired that gun I could kill anybody and it would be the greatest killing ever and now I didn't have that greatest killing ever and now red wasn't the reddest red and blue wasn't the bluest blue and the rhythm wasn't the sweetest rhythm and all these things made me sad but also something that I can't describe and I want one thing. To feel good again and right now. Right now.

And Papa-Lo come out raging like a madman saying who give Josey Wales and Weeper permission to chuck badness on Rema, who the fuck give it to him and he says a man bigger than you and Papa-Lo looked like he was going to hit Josey Wales but then he see we, he see me and he see the guns and I don't know what he think but it must be something heavy because he walk away. But not before he said to anybody, everybody and nobody that one day we all goin' run out of people to kill. Josey Wales hiss and go off to fuck him woman or play with him pickney. The woman I was living with look at me as if she never see me before. She right. She never see nothing like me before.

Nineteen seventy-six come and bring an election with it. The man who bring guns to the ghetto made it clear that there is no way that socialist government should win again. They will bring down hellfire and damnation first. They send us to shoot up two of the Eight Lanes at first but then they send us to do more. At the Coronation Market we walk up to a seller woman and a woman who dress stoosh, as if she come from uptown, and shoot them both. The next day we go to Crossroads, right where downtown rub up against uptown, and break into a Chinese shop and shoot it up. The next day we stop a bus passing through West Kingston on the way to St. Catherine. We stop to rob and scare the people but a woman police shout out Stop, like she is Starsky or Hutch. She couldn't get her gun out in time so we drag her off the bus and the bus drive off. In the wild bush to the side of the road we shoot her six time while cars pass. Her body do the bullet dance when we shoot her, but is what Josey Wales do before that make me swallow back down me own vomit. Papa-Lo would never allow that. Josey wave him gun in front of us promising judgment if we tell.

The woman I live with look at how I change but I don't care about anything as long as I get a smoke. And soon Weeper make it known that what stand between me and one big whiff of smoke was them pussyholes that need to get dead. I need to get rewarded, something anything to stop the downpression. That is what happen now, either you're smoking or you're dreaming about smoking and you grieve like somebody dead and not coming back.

News spread in Jamaica that crime is out of control, the country is going to the dogs, not even uptown is safe and PNP is losing control of the country. Is two weeks before the election, and Papa-Lo send us to every house to remind people how to vote. One of the boys say he don't take orders from Papa-Lo. Josey Wales might hiss and grumble and say something with double meaning but Josey Wales never forget that Papa-Lo became Papa by being the toughest and most brutal man in the ghetto. Papa-Lo walk right up to the little boy and ask him age. Seventeen, he said. Look like age eighteen lock off, Papa-Lo say and shoot him in the foot. The boy scream and hop and scream again. People getting testy 'round here, he shout. People forgetting who is top ranking 'round here! You! You forget? he say and point him gun at another one of the boys. The boy jump and tremble out no-no-no Papa-Lo you is the don, the don of the dons, and Papa-Lo laugh as the boy start to piss up himself. Lick it up, Papa-Lo say, and the boy look stupid for a second until Papa-Lo fire his gun and say either you clean up the piss or we clean up you blood, and the boy, seeing that Papa-Lo not joking, crouch down and start to lap up his pee-pee like a cat gone crazy.

And so we go into the street and knock on the open door and kick down the locked one and one person, old and almost mad, say he not voting for anybody, so we drag him out of him house and take out all him clothes and burn them and then we strip him naked and burn those clothes too and kick him two time and say he better know how him going vote or we start burning things in the house, and the woman I live with ask if they coming for her too since JLP and PNP is both shit and I say that we might and she didn't say a word to me again. But when the white man come and when the man who bring guns to the ghetto come, they talk to Josey Wales, not Papa-Lo. Papa not even in the ghetto that much anymore. Spending too much time with the Singer.

Night. December supposed to be cool by now. The Singer in him house. Living and singing and playing. All Jamaica and in the ghetto talking about how he decide to do the Smile Jamaica Peace Concert even though it's PNP propaganda and night and day that the Echo Squad, bad man on PNP payroll, guarding him house. No police except for one car that stop early in the night. Nobody getting in and few people coming out. I watch car pass by and I watch room light go on and off and on again. I watch the stubby manager go and come and the white man with brown hair. He say one time that him life don't mean nothing if he couldn't help plenty people, and he help plenty people but he keep giving people what they need and young people don't need nothing, they just want everything. We sing other songs, songs from youth who can't afford to make song so we ride the real rock rhythm and skank because only women dance. And we sing song that we make up in our sleep that if you ride like lightning you going crash like thunder. And the Singer think Johnny was, but Johnny is, Johnny change and Johnny coming to get him. Before this night I see him smoking weed with Papa-Lo, and then give envelope to man who run with Shotta Sherrif and even people bigger than me wondering what the r'asscloth this Natty Dread up to. This Singer think because he come from where we come from that he understand how we live. But he don't understand nothing. Everybody think the way him think when they leave and come back. That everything was exactly how they leave it. But we different. We harder than him and we don't care. He flee before you turn into something like we.

And we? We be top-ranking bad man. Heckle mother come out one day when we controlling the street corner and playing domino saying 'bout *how she can smell all sort of nastiness in him room* so he slap her in the face and say don't disrespect the bad man when him out'a street. The woman I live with ask if is so I goin' treat her too but I say nothing. I don't want to beat no woman. I just want some free C. That is all I want. That is all I need. Two day ago I walk past some woman house and see Weeper walk out naked to the standpipe 'round the back. He pull the condom off him buddy, fling it away and bathe himself. Everybody know that condom and birth control was white man scheme to kill off black people, but he don't care. I watch him take off him glasses and scrub everywhere with rag and soap as if the standpipe and the tree build for him alone even though it wasn't even his regular woman house. I didn't want to fuck him, none of that nasty batty boy business, I just wanted to go inside him like a duppy and move when he move and buck when he buck and wind when he wind and feel myself pull out little by little by little and ram back in hard then soft, fast then slow. Then I wanted to be the woman. I just need to fucking breathe.

Tonight I watching the Singer house alone, but other times I watch with company. The short man with the big mouth that manage him, he thought we was just another set of boys coming looking for either money, weed or a chance to cut a big tune, but he look at we different. And we go back to the ghetto and the white man who seem to know him tell us about every room in him house. *That everybody have their price, even the people right under him, and at the right time they will take a nice little break, no a nice long break, a good funky disco nap like funky Kingston I gotcha!* That there is only one way in and one way out. That he take a break usually at around nine, nine-fifteen, and go to the kitchen, alone, since the children not there and everybody else still in the studio or about to leave. That the steps leading up to the kitchen give a clear view but we should just shower the place to make sure. That two should drive, two go inside and four case the grounds. We don't know what he mean, so Josey Wales say he mean take the guns around out of the case, which sound stupid. The American go red again and the man who bring guns to the ghetto says he means surround the place. They show us picture. The Singer in the kitchen, him and the white man who manage the label, him in the studio with eyes bursting out of him head from good weed, him and the new guitarist straight from America, him fucking one girl, him fucking her sister, him leaning against the stove like even the Singer now tired of the Singer. All of Jamaica waiting for the Smile Jamaica Concert. Even some people in the ghetto going because Papa-Lo say we should go for Bob, even though it's PNP propaganda. All I could think of was one more night and I would stop being hungry. One more night and I was going to take the S off Superman chest and the B off Batman belly.

Alex Pierce

There's a reason *why the story of the ghetto should never come with a photo. The Third World slum is a nightmare that defies beliefs or facts, even the ones staring right at you. A vision of hell that twists and turns on itself and grooves to its own soundtrack. Normal rules do not apply here. Imagination then, dream, fantasy. You visit a ghetto, particularly a ghetto in West Kingston, and it immediately leaves the real to become this sort of grotesque, something out of Dante or the infernal painting of Hieronymus Bosch. It's a rusty red chamber of hell that cannot be described so I will not try to describe it. It cannot be photographed because some parts of West Kingston, such as Rema, are in the grip of such bleak and unremitting repulsiveness that the inherent beauty of the photographic process will lie to you about just how ugly it really is. Beauty has infinite range but so does wretchedness and the only way to accurately grasp the full, unending vortex of ugly that is Trench Town is to imagine it. You could describe it in colors, red and dead like old blood, brown like dirt, clay or shit, white like soapy water running loose down a too narrow street. Shiny like new zinc holding up a roof or a fence right beside old zinc, the material itself a living history of when last the politician did the ghetto a favor. Zinc in the Eight Lanes shines like nickel. Zinc in Jungle is riddled with bullet holes and rusted the color of Jamaican rural dirt. To understand the ghetto, to make it real, one should forget seeing it. Ghetto is a smell. Sometimes it's something sweet: baby powder women wear on their chests. Old Spice, English Leather and Brut cologne. The rawness of recently slaughtered goat, the pepper and pimento in goat's head soup. Sour chemicals in the detergent, cocoa butter, carbolic acid, lavender in the soap, fermenting pee and aging shit running down the side of the road. Pimento again in jerk chicken. Cordite from a recently fired gun, poop in baby baggies, the iron in blood congealed from street kill, still there after the body has been removed. Smell carries the memory of sound and there's that as well. Reggae, smooth and sexy but also brutal and spare like super poor and super pure delta blues. From this stew of pimento, gunshot blood, running water and sweet Rhythms comes the Singer, a sound in the air but also a living breathing sufferah who is always where he's from no matter where he's at.*

Fucking hell. Shit sounds like I'm writing for ladies who lunch on Fifth Avenue. *Unending vortex of ugly*? Holy sensationalism, Batman! Who the fuck am I writing for? I could move in closer, get to the real Singer, but I'll just fail like every other journalist before me because, shit, there is no real Singer. That's the clincher there, that's the real motherfucker right there, that he is something else now that he's in the Billboard Top Ten. An allegory kinda, he exists when some girl passes by the hotel window singing that she's sick and tired of the ism and schism. When boys in the street sing them belly full but them hungry, trailing off before the next line and knowing there's a greater threat in not singing what everybody knows.

Out the window streetlights glow orange all the way to the harbor like these matches popping off, one, two, three. Then just as you notice them, the yellow of some, the white of others, the lights really do pop off, block by block. I blink and my room goes dark. Kingston shuts itself off for the third time since I've been here, but the moon is full and for a while the city is silver and blue and the sky is this sweet indigo, as if the town just turned country. The moon hits buildings on the side and walls of shiny gray rise out of the ground. The only lights come from cars.

There's a hum from below. I'm on the tenth floor or eleventh, can never remember, and the light comes back on, this time with a buzz. My hotel switches itself on and then the hotel in front of me and then another and the fake light brings back the orange which kills our silver. But downtown is still in darkness. Blackout's probably going to last all night. I've been downtown once, following Lee Scratch Perry when the lights quit. This is what every reporter hears of, the Arma in the Gideon, the point where every single criminal element in the city explodes into lawlessness. And yet it was so quiet that Kingston became a ghost town. For the first time ever I heard the waves hit the harbor.

I don't know what I want. I'm in over my head. Who wants to be a music writer when rock and roll is dead? Maybe there's something to the punks or maybe it all just means rock is sick and living in London. Maybe this band the Ramones are onto something, maybe rock and roll has to keep rebirthing itself by going back to Chuck Berry. Fucking hell, Alexander Pierce, the only way to write about music is to talk like a fucking rock critic? Wenner thinks, he hopes, he hopes desperately that any second now Mick and Keef are going to wake up, put down the heroin, deep-six those shits padding the band and make *Let It Bleed* again, not sludgy shit like *Goats Head Soup* and good sweet Jesus, no reggae. Instead they're here doing exactly that, barreling through this song of theirs near nineteen times now in shitty one-drop. I came to this country knowing I would find something. And I think I have, I know I have, but damn if I know what it is.

The lights go off and come back on, minus the hum. No shit. I don't think anybody was expecting that. I imagine outside the city just got caught off guard. In flagrante delicto. What was Mark Lansing doing before the lights came back on? Who does he know here anyway? The guy who told me about how the ghettos run used to be a rudeboy himself until he went to prison, and came out changed, thanks to books. *Autobiography of Malcolm X* I expected, and even I have checked out Eldridge Cleaver. But Bertrand Russell's *The Problems of Philosophy*? They leave him alone because he's an old-school former rudie who runs a youth group and mediates between the gangs, but also because nobody expects much from a coolie.

Sometimes I envy Vietnam vets because they at least had a belief in themselves to lose. You ever want to leave somewhere so bad that the fact that you don't have a reason why is all the more reason to go?

In 1971 I couldn't leave Minnesota fast enough.

Every Jamaican can sing and every Jamaican learned to sing from the same songbook. Marty Robbins's Gunfighter Ballads. *Grab the collar of even the most top-ranking rudie and say El Paso, and he'll follow up in a perfect croon;*

El Paso citeeee, by the Rio Grandeeeeheeee. It's the Homo erectus of Jamaican guntalk, where anything you want to know about Kingston's green versus orange war, everything you ever need to know about the rudeboy-cum-gunman is not in Bob Marley's lyrics or in Peter Tosh's but in Marty Robbins's "Big Iron."

> He's an outlaw on the loose came the whisper from each lip
> And he's here to do some business
> With the big iron on his hip

This is the story of the gunmen of Wild, Wild West Kingston. A western needs a hero for the white hat and a villain for the black, but the truth, ghetto wisdom is close to what Paul McCartney said about Pink Floyd's Dark Side of the Moon. *It's all dark. Every sufferah is a cowboy without a house and every street has gun battle written in blood in a song somewhere. Spend one day in West Kingston and it makes perfect sense that a Top Ranking calls himself Josey Wales. It's not just the lawlessness. It's the grabbing of a myth and making it theirs, like a reggae singer dropping new lyrics 'pon di old version. And if a western needs an O.K. Corral, an O.K. Corral needs a Dodge City. Kingston, where bodies sometimes drop like flies, fits the description a little too well. Word is that downtown is so lawless that the Prime Minister hasn't been lower than Crossroads in years and even that intersection is up for grabs. Because come on, once the white and well-spoken Prime Minister says something like Democratic Socialism, within days you're going to see a sudden influx of American men in suits all called Smith or something. Even I can smell a Cold War and it's not even a missile crisis. Locals are either catching a flight out or getting killed. Either way everybody is getting the fuck out'a Dodge.*

Better, I guess. Try not to be Hunter, try not to be Hunter. Fuck Thompson and fuck the Beats anyway. My story needs a narrative line. It needs a hero, a villain, and a Cassandra. I'm feeling that it's moving to climax resolution, denouement or catastrophe without me. In *Miami and the Siege of Chicago*, Norman Mailer dropped his own bad self into an event, posing as Ronald Bedtime for fucking Bonzo Reagan's security detail move to get into a GOP Banquet, which would never have fucking invited him. It's a thought, only that.

The Singer meets the top goons, warring goons within the space of one week. Guns that are not supposed to be in a shipment at the wharf disappear, according to my philosophy-reading snitch. An election in two weeks. Let's not even talk about Mark Lansing. Meanwhile the entire country seems frozen in a game of wait. Maybe what I really need to know is why William Adler was in Jamaica some months ago, what does he know, and how the Singer, the people, hell, the country are going to make it through the next two weeks. And then I'll write a motherfucker and give it to *Time* or *Newsweek* or *The New Yorker,* because, well, fuck *Rolling Stone.* Because I know he knows. I just fucking know it. He just has to.

Papa-Lo

They think my mind is a ship that sail far away. Some of those people in my own district. I see them in the corner of my eye. After I help them grow, they thinking me is the one now blocking progress. So they treat me like old man already, and think I don't notice when a sentence cut short because the rest of it not meant for me. That I don't notice that phones come to the ghetto for talking, but not to me. That I don't notice they leave me alone.

Man in the ghetto making power move because politician now have a different vision. Word seem to get out that I don't like the sight of blood no more. Two years ago two thing happen to me in one week. First I shoot up a little upstart in Jungle. Word was that certain boy was getting uppity again, selling their own weed and partying with PNP boy like we sign peace treaty or something. We grab a rudie to make an example but the rudie wasn't dress in khaki because he was tougher than tough or some brigadista back from Cuba. The boy was on him way to Ardenne High School. Boy fall on one knee then sideways and roll on him back before I see the school tie.

I don't remember how much man fall because of me and I don't care too much either, but that one. Is one thing when you kill a man and he just dead. Is another thing when he too close when you shoot him and he grab you and you see him the way he looking at you, him eye frighten as fuck because death is the scariest monster, scarier than anything you dream up as a pickney and you can feel it like a demon, swallowing you slow, big mouth swallowing your toes first and the toes go cold, then the feet and the feet go cold, then the knee, then the thigh, then the waist, and the little boy grab me shirt and bawling no, no, no, it coming up on me, no, no, no . . . and he grab you hard, harder than he ever gripped anything because maybe if he put all the strength, all the will in just those ten fingers on a living thing, maybe he can hold on to life. And he inhale like he sucking in the world and scared of breathing out more than anything because if he exhale he might breathe out all the life he got left. Shoot the boy again, Josey Wales say, but I couldn't do nothing but look. Josey walk over to me, put the gun to him forehead and pow.

That cause a new 'ruption. Everybody know that Papa-Lo hard, especially if you thief, or rape woman, but nobody ever call me wicked before, not like the boy mother who walk all the way to the front of me house screaming 'bout how her boy was a good boy who love him mother and go to school where he just pass six GCE subject and was going to get scholarship to University. She say that when God come he going have a special punishment for a little naigger hitler like me. She scream for her son and for Jesus to intervene before Josey Wales gun-butt her in the back of the head and leave her in the road, her skirt flying up every time the wind blow.

One time the Singer say to me, Papa, how you get to be top ranking when you worry so much? I didn't tell him that be on top is to worry. Once you climb to the peak of the mountain, the whole world can take a shot.

I know the Singer know that plenty people hate him, but I wonder if he know what shape that hate take. Every man have something to say, but the real haters blacker than him. Bossman in the court say him read every single thing ever written by Eldridge Cleaver and gone and get himself a big fucking degree only to have that little half-white shortass become the voice of black liberation. This is who is the Jamaican public face number one? Him can read? Bossman who just come back from New York and Miami say what a public relations disaster for the country. Customs stop him twice asking if he in a reggae band and what's that smell coming from his suitcase, gawn-ja? Bossman who own a hotel on the North Coast say that fucking white bitch drinking a daiquiri with an umbrella in her glass just ask him how often he wash him hair, and if every Jamaican is a Rasta, even though him clearly have good hair that him comb every day. Then she leave fifty dollars on his desk and her room key. I tell the Singer one time, that I don't think I ever sense in the spirit, so many bad forces with so much power line up against one man as the forces lined up against you and he say, The devil no got no power over me. The devil come, and me shake hands with the devil. Devil has his part to play. Devil is a good friend too, because when you don't know him, that's the time he can mash you down. I say to him, Brethren, you're like Robin Hood. He say, But me never rob from a man in me life. I say, brethren, neither did Robin Hood.

But evil force and samfie force rising in the night. The Singer smart. Him is friend with me and him is friend with Shotta Sherrif. The Singer reason with me and he reason with Shotta, not together, that would still be madness, but he reason with we the same way. If puss and dog can live together, why we can't love one another? No so Jah say? But puss and dog don't want to live together, me tell him. But then me think 'bout it hard and come with another reasoning. When dog kill puss, and puss kill dog, the only one happy is the john-crow. And the john-crow been waiting for this all it life. The vulture with him red head and white feather chest and black wings. The john-crow in Jamaica House. The john-crow at the Constant Spring golf club, who want to invite him to them pretty party, now that he too big to look away from, and push roast pork in him face, and tell him how they *been thinking 'bout doing the reggae* like the reggae is the bombocloth twist, and ask him if he meet a real star yet, like Engelbert Humperdinck.

Still evil force and samfie force rising in the night. Especially a hot night like this, too hot for December, all certain man can think 'bout is who have and who have not. Me on the verandah with no light on. I look out from my house and the road quiet, nothing but lovers rock coming from the bar further down the road. One slam, then two, then three, somebody just win a domino game. I see the calm and hear the calm and know the calm can't last. Not for me, not for him, not for Kingston, not for Jamaica.

For three month now, two white man come to the ghetto, along with Peter Nasser. One speak only English, one speak too much Spanish. They come to see Josey Wales, not me. A man can be top ranking all he want, when the politician make a new friend, that be the one they come to. I wonder what Josey say he will do that they me want. Josey is him own man, never tried to control him then or now, not since the fall of Balaclava. Copenhagen City is a palace with four or five prince. Nobody ever wanted to be king before. But when the two new white men come to the ghetto, they come to my house to pay respects but they leave with Josey Wales, and at the boundary when I expect Josey to wave them off, he get in their car and say nothing about it when he come back.

Josey go check him woman at six-thirty and leave her house in new ganzie and pants she get from the freezone. Then he leave. Me not his mother or his keeper, he don't have to tell me where him going. Shipment of guns gone missing on the wharf on a night he was missing too. Man in America sing give peace a chance, but he not the American living here. I think, I know Josey rounding up men to wipe out Rema once and for all. He don't know that I know that he burn down that tenement on Orange Street with the people in it and shoot anybody who tried to put it out, including two fireman.

Nineteen sixty-six. No man who enter 1966 leave the way he come in. The fall of Balaclava take plenty, even those who support it. I did support, not quiet but loud. Balaclava was a piece of shit that make you beg for the richness of a tenement yard. Balaclava was where woman would dodge murder, robbery and rape only to get killed by a cup of water. Balaclava get bulldozed down so that Copenhagen City could rise, and when the politicians come in after the bulldozers with their promises they also demand that we drive all PNP man out. Before 1966, man from Denham Town and man from Jungle didn't really like each other, but they fight each other on the football field and the cricket pitch and even when two boy get rowdy and a mouth get punched bloody, there was no war or rumour of war. But then politician come. Me welcome them because surely better must come for we too.

Nineteen sixty-six. All this happen on the Sabbath day. Josey walking back to him yard from Mr. Miller locksmith shop where he learning a skill. He coming home through a street that never declare colours before. He didn't know that on the Friday before, politician come through saying close your mouth and fire your gun. They shoot him five time. Fifth shot he fall down on him face right in a puddle of nasty water. Everybody run, and those who didn't, see and wait until a man come up on a bike and grab him and put him in front and try to hold him from slumping down while he ride to the clinic. A different man come out of that clinic three weeks later.

Evil force and samfie force rising in the night. The Singer tell me a story. How back when reggae was something only few people know, how white rock and roll star was him friend. You reggae dudes are far out, man, pretty neat, you got any gawn-ja? But as soon as the Natty Dread sing hit songs and break the Babylon top 100, everybody start to treat him a way. They like him better when he was the poor cousin that they can feel good for taking notice. I tell him that politician do the same thing to me when they realize me can read. In 1966 they carve up Kingston and never ask we what slice we want. So every land that hit midway on the boundary, Rema, Jungle, Rose Town, Lizard Town, they leave it to we to fight over. Me fight hard until me get tired. I raise the men who now run with Josey Wales and nobody ever badder than me. I swell Copenhagen City two times it size and eradicate robbery and rape from the community. This is election year and nothing left now but war and rumour of war. But tonight I look from my verandah and the night keeping secret close. The verandah is wood and is long time it don't paint. My woman snore like a kicked donkey, but you grow to like the few things that never change. Tomorrow some youths coming over here to talk about their own peace concert, since this one is PNP propaganda. The whole night almost gone and the police eradication squad don't make one sweep yet. This make the night strange, for ghetto people not used to full night sleep. Somewhere, somehow, especially a night hot like this, somebody going pay for it.

Barry Diflorio

W*haddiya have for lunch* today, Pop, a Whampererererer?

—Sure thing, sweetie.

—Pop, stop calling me that.

—Calling you what?

—Sweetie. I'm not a girl.

—You're not, huh? Don't have any girly parts?

—Nope, nope nope. So I can't be a sweetie.

—You're my sweetie though.

—Nope. Boys aren't sweet. That's girls. Girls are sweet. And icky.

Kinda hard to argue with such rock-solid logic. I could write an article on the things I knew at six that I don't fucking know at thirty-six.

—They are kinda icky, aren't they? But when you're thirteen you're going to wanna be with them all the time.

—Noooooooo.

—Yeahhhhhh.

—Will they like playing with my frogs then?

—Something like that. Anyway, it's a school night, honey.

—Pop.

—Sorry, I forgot that you're a little man now. It's a school night, buddy, so off you go. You too, Timmy.

—Aw, man. Babylon business this.

—Excuse me?

—Aw . . . nothing, Dad.

—That's what I thought. Go to bed, guys. Gee, neither of you kiss your pop anymore?

—They're grown men now.

—I noticed. Make sure you brush your teeth, both of you.

My wife follows them.

—Where are you going?

—To brush my teeth too. Very long day. Then again every day in Kingston is kinda long, isn't it?

I knew what she was doing. Amazing how women can use any opportunity to start up an argument, but especially moments like this when you don't want to fight, but not fighting makes it seem like you don't care, so you say something nice or compliment her, which just makes her say that you're patronizing her, which of course just leads to the fight anyway.

—I'll be up—

The phone rings.

—In a minute.

She goes up the stairs muttering something about the phone ringing when I'm home. Considering I forbid anybody calling here, not for business or pleasure, this is weird.

—Hello?

—Ten million dollars and all you have to show for it is some occasional crap you have that faggot Sal Resnick write in the *New York Times*?

—William Adler. Bill. How's it hanging, Bill?

—To the left last time I wore boxers.

—They probably ration that shit where you are, huh?

—Really? Where am I?

—Some socialist Utopia, somewhere. Freedom worth the world's best piña colada?

—What, like in Cuba? You really think I'm in Cuba? That's your info? Don't make my respect for you sink any lower, Barry.

—So where are you?

—You're not going to ask how I got your number?

—Nope.

—Don't pretend it doesn't bother you.

—Buddy, I've got a bedtime story to read to my kids. This date of ours going somewhere good?

—What's your favorite seat at the circus?

—Know what I hate, Bill? People who answer a question with a question. The Jamaicans do it all the fucking time.

—Then put a trace on the call. I'll wait.

—No need. You might be overestimating your pull.

—Nah, I think I estimated my pull just about right.

—You're killing me, man. What do you want, Bill? Fetching some shit for Fidel?

—Maybe. But why would I call you? You haven't had access to good info since Montevideo.

—You seem to have nothing but good info these days.

—I guess. Pity about those seven guys you had to send back. I mean, the company was always sloppy as wet shit, but Jesus.

—You endangered lives, son of a bitch.

—I endangered a ten-million budget. An awful lot of money for a little country like Jamaica.

—How're book sales going?

—Can't complain.

—Made the fiction best-sellers list yet? I've been watching.

—Nope, racing up the How-to Advice list though.

—Nice. Listen, Bill, as much as I like this Bogie 'n' Bacall thing we got going here, I'm actually really tired, so what do you want?

—A few things. One, either call off the dipshits you've got tracking me or get better people to do it.

—Nobody is following you far as I know. Besides had I, wouldn't I know where you are?

—Call them off. Or stop insulting me by being so obvious. By the way, you might want to send some manpower out to Guantanamo to pick them up before the Cubans do. I'll leave you to guess where they are. Two, you might want to reconsider putting all that ten million behind the JLP to deliver us from communism. Most of that is going to go into guns, the rest in—

—Want me to deliver peace in the Middle East while we're at it?

—Oh, stick to your limited range of talents, Barry. Three. If you think those gunmen that you have Louis teaching to shoot are too stupid to shoot you, you're kidding yourself. Figured that'd be the only reason Louis Johnson would be in Jamaica. Blowback can be a motherfucker, buddy.

—Are you kidding? They were like little kids with Fisher-Price: My first real gun.

—So you are out there training boys? I wasn't quite sure. Sloppy, Barry, even for a by-the-book hack like you.

—I don't know what you're talking about. As for Louis, he's his own man so you'll have to take up that business with him. What you got cooked up this time? I'm surprised you aren't somewhere where people are always on the up-and-up, like East Germany. What secret war do you have us hatching? Angola? Maybe we're starting something in Nicaragua. I hear Papua New Guinea is ripe for a socialist takeover any second now.

—You don't even know what socialism is. You're a trained monkey set for point and shoot. That said, I'm wondering. What's Richard Lansing's son doing there? Trying to help you spite Daddy?

—I don't know what you're talking about.

—This is a secure line, Barry, cut the bullshit. A Prime Minister that gives Kissinger the shits because he's on Castro's dick is about to be re-elected.

—You sure about that?

—As sure as I know which school you send your kids to.

—Bill, don't fuck—

—Shut the fuck up, Barry. As I was saying, a Prime Minister who seems a little too ignorant that he's about to enter the Cold War, is about to be re-elected. Puts on a concert where the biggest star in the world, who just happens to be Jamaican, is performing. And of all the people in the world who should come down to film the whole thing, Richard Lansing's own son. I'm no fan of either guy, but you gotta admit how neat it all seems.

—Nice little conspiracy theory you've got cooking there. And just who was on the grassy knoll? You're forgetting something, aren't you?

—What's that?

—That Lansing resigned. In many ways, he's just a classier version of you. Both of you having a sudden attack of the liberal schoolboy conscience.

—I thought I was serving my country.

—No, you thought you were serving an idea. You wouldn't know how a real country works, even with written instructions.

—You trying to turn this into a class debate, Barry? How socialist of you.

—I'm not trying to start anything. I just want to go to bed. Instead I'm stuck on the phone with either a man without a country or a man without a point.

—I just don't get how you guys think. Socialism is not fucking communism.

—It's an ism though, that's for sure. Your problem, and it has always been your problem, Bill, is that you think you're hired to think. Or that anybody gives a shit what you think.

—Lots of Jamaicans did.

—Yeah, I was here for your two-week residency back in June, remember? Jamaicans don't give a shit about CIA policy, they don't even know the difference between the CIA and the FBI. No, lots of Jamaicans went batshit for a white man who let them off the hook, because *Roots* just came on and surely nothing is ever their fault, with evil whiteys running around. Give me a fucking break. Spoke to Nancy Welch lately?

—Why would I speak to Nancy Welch?

—Can't blame you. I mean, whaddya say? Gee, Nancy, awful business me getting your brother and his wife offed in Greece.

—Hold the fucking line, you think I got the Welches killed?

—You and your little exposé, your little trashy novel.

—He's not in the fucking book, you idiot.

—Not like I'm ever gonna read it.

—Really? You think I'm to be blamed for Welch? I overestimated you, Barry. I thought the company trusted you with more info than you've clearly got. I must be talking to the wrong man.

—Really? You're not the only one who's estimating just right.

—Louis Johnson is in West Kingston teaching young terrorists how to use automatic weapons. Same weapons that never arrived at the Kingston wharf so they were never stolen afterwards.

—You have no proof of that.

—The only man who ever had use for Louis was me in Chile. He wouldn't have been in the country for any other reason. Or Brian Harris, or whatever Oliver Patton is calling himself these days. You guys never smell blowback until it hits you in the face. Fucking Ivy Leaguers who never had to deal with people. My question is why the fuck is the Singer on your radar? What could he possibly do?

—Good night, Bill. Or *hasta mañana* or *luego* or whatever.

—I mean, really, what can he fucking d—

—Don't call me again, son of a bitch.

—Who's the son of a bitch calling you? my wife says. I didn't hear her come back in and don't know how long she's been there. She sits down on the couch that I'm standing behind, not looking at me or saying anything, but expecting an answer. I plug out the phone and go over to the bar where a half-empty Smirnoff and a bottle of tonic are waiting.

—You wanna drink?

—Just brushed my teeth.

—That's a no, then.

—Sounds like you wanna continue that little fight with me.

She rubs her neck and takes off the necklace. If Jamaica wasn't so hot she would never have cut her hair above her neck. Haven't seen her neck in years and I miss kissing it. It's funny that she would hate being here so much, because until Jamaica I was so fucking afraid that she had become that woman I can't fucking stand, the one who doesn't feel any need to look attractive anymore. It's not that she was ever unattractive, or that I've ever been sorry, or that I've ever cheated on the woman, not even in Brazil, but not long ago I toyed with leaving her, just to see if it would get her to wear lipstick again. She bitches about the country every day, every minute, more than likely in a minute or two, but she's wearing mini shirts and cut her hair like a pageboy and is tanned like a Florida heiress. Maybe she's fucking somebody. I heard that Singer gets around.

—Kids asleep?

—Pretending at least.

—Haha.

I sit down beside her. This is the thing about redheads, isn't it? No matter how long you've lived with them, you're always surprised when they turn and look straight at you.

—You've cut your hair.

—The heat here is unbearable.

—It's nice.

—It's growing back. I cut it two weeks ago, Barry.

—Should I go upstairs and tuck them in?

—It's ninety degrees, Barry.

—Good point.

—And it's December.

—I know.

—Nineteen seventy-six, Barry.

—That I know too.

—You said we'd only be here for a year, if not less, Barry.

—Baby, please, I cannot have two fights in the space of two minutes.

—I'm not fighting you. I'm barely talking to you as it is.

—If we leave—

—*If* we leave? What the hell, Barry, when did that change from a when?

—I'm sorry. When we leave, are you going to be happy anywhere else but Vermont? Maybe I should retire and live on your salary.

—Funny. I'm not having a fight with you. I'm just reminding you that a year is twelve months and this is month twelve.

—The kids will miss their friends.

—The kids don't have any friends. Barry?

—Yes, sweetheart.

—Don't overestimate how many choices you think you have.

—You have no idea how fucking tired I am of that goddamn word.

She's not going to ask what I mean, preferring to let her sentence hang like that. Work? Marriage? She's not being specific because if she were, it would reduce the threat. I could ask what she means and then she'll (1) explain it to me like I'm some retard, slow on the uptake, and (2) use it as a way to start a fight. I don't know how she thought her life was going to turn out, but I'm sick and tired of explaining it to her like I'm on some fucking TV show that has to bring the audience up to speed every week. In the preceding stoooooooory, our erstwhile hero, Barry Diflorio, the intrepid, dashing, charming and hung hero, took his wife to the concrete Jungle of Jamaica, on a mission of sun, sea, sex and secrets. Barry Diflorio was on the job but his wife—

—Stop that.

—Stop what?

—Humming the words that you're thinking. You don't even realize when you do it.

—What am I thinking now?

—Oh for Pete's sake. It was bad enough raising three children in Vermont.

Takes a while for me to realize she said three. —You're so pretty when you're angry, I say, anticipating the look before I get it. Except I don't get it. She doesn't even look at me, right beside her, trying to grab her hand. I think about repeating it, but don't.

Nina Burgess

B*us 42 drove past* and didn't even stop, trying to get home before turning back into a pumpkin, I suppose. Except it was six o'clock. The curfew started at seven, but this was uptown so there wasn't any police around to enforce it. Can't imagine them stopping a Mercedes-Benz, the man might turn out to be in the Prime Minister's Cabinet. The last bus was a minibus with Irie Ites painted on the side in blue, not red, green and gold. Bigger buses passed too, the green public JOS bus run by the government, small buses that I have to crouch to get into (and stay crouched the whole ride), most of them on their way to Bull Bay or Buff Bay or some other bay, meaning coastline, meaning country. Irie Ites left me behind at six p.m. I heard the last bass note at ten forty-five. It's now eleven-fifteen.

The buses kept passing and I kept not taking them. Two cars pulled up too. Illegal taxis both of them, both with two in the front seat and four in the back, including a man with dollar bills between his fingers shouting, You want reach Spanish Town, baby? At first I thought it was the same car. I stepped back and looked away, long enough for the car to drive off, then did it again.

I have finally gone mad. Must be, waiting outside the gate in the hope that some man will remember having sex with me and hoping I was most memorable out of all the women he has had sex with, maybe even having sex with this minute. And if he remembered the sex maybe he would pull some strings and get me and my family out of this country and hopefully pay for it too. It made so much more sense at seven in the morning after I saw my father trying to act like younger men didn't just make him feel like the oldest man in the world. Maybe they didn't rape my mother, maybe they just hit her, or use something to mess with her pussy and then have him watch them do it. Maybe they said no bitch you too old fi fuck, that deh pussy for Jesus now. Or maybe this is just me at near midnight, standing here in stupid high heels, my feet killing me because I spent all day killing my feet. And all I can do is listen to my mind go crazy. The son of a bitch didn't come out once. Not even once. Maybe I have it wrong. Maybe I was memorable, too memorable, and he saw me from a window and sent a message not to let that girl in. Maybe I was a lousy lay or too good a lay, something about me that said to him, Boy, you better stay inside and don't get involved with that one, that Nina Burgess. Maybe he even remembered my name. Or maybe not. My heels and my feet are covered in dust.

By around two or three the pain in my feet moved up to my shins then my knees, which felt better only because the ache was being shared. At some point you lose all ache until you realize, maybe an hour later, that you didn't lose the ache at all. It had just spread all over until your whole body becomes ache. Maybe I'm not a madwoman, but I am something. The two women who passed me an hour ago knew something. I saw them from who knows, a mile up the road, when they were moving white dots, until they were barely twenty feet from me, two dark women in white church dresses and hats.

—But that is what me telling you, Mavis. No weapon formed against almighty Jesus shall prosper, the one on the left said.

They both looked at me at the same time and went quiet. They didn't even wait until they were past me before one whispered to the other. It's ten p.m. I know what they were whispering.

—Me just fuck your man for twenty dollar, I say.

They speed up their walk trying so hard to get away that the left one nearly trips. Nobody has walked past me since. It's not that Hope Road goes to sleep. Behind me are apartments and in front is his house. Lights are on everywhere. The people don't go to sleep, they shut themselves off from the road. It's like an entire city turning its back to you, the way those church women did. I think about it, being a hooker, jumping in the last Benz or Volvo heading way up Hope Road, to Irish Town maybe. A businessman or a diplomat who lives in New Kingston who'll rape me because he'll get away with it. If I just stand here under the orange streetlight and lift up my skirt so that the light hits my bush, maybe somebody would stop. I'm hungry and I need to piss. The light in the top room of his house just went out.

The night that Kimmy took me here and then left, I didn't plan on sleeping with him. I did want to see him naked but not like that. I heard he got up every morning at five and drove to Bull Bay and bathed in the waterfall. Something about it sounded so holy and so sexy at once. I've been imagining him rising out of the falls, naked because it was early enough. I've been imagining river water being the saddest thing in the world because sooner or later it had to slide off his body. When I saw him out on his balcony naked eating fruit I thought the moon must be sad too, knowing he would soon go inside. Thought is stretching it. I didn't think. Thinking would have stopped me from going out on the balcony. Thinking would have stopped me from taking off my clothes just in case me clothed and him naked would have made him self-conscious, as if he had a self-conscious bone in his entire body. He said *Me know you*, which might have been true. A woman likes being remembered, I guess. Or maybe he just knows how to make a woman feel like she was missed.

After the music stopped a few people left. It was the first time that gate opened. Couple cars, one jeep, not his truck. He was still there, him and probably half the band too. I thought about running in, taking off the heels and sprinting fast enough that the guards wouldn't have caught me until I was inside. By the time they grabbed me they would see that I was brown and leave me alone and I would shout his name and he would come downstairs. But I stayed on my side of the road, by the streetlight and bus stop. A light from a room on the right just went out. My father keeps saying that nobody is going to drive him out of his own country, but some months before the attack he sat me down in the kitchen and read me an article in the *Gleaner*. I was visiting and didn't plan to stay long. He wouldn't let me read it myself, he had to hear himself tell me. The article was called "If He Fails," he being the Prime Minister. Daddy, that article was from January. You hold on to it all this time? I said. My mother then told me he reads it every week. That would be forty-seven times so far. The light in a room downstairs left goes off. There's a curfew and I'm not supposed to be out here. I have no explanation for the police should a car pass by. I have no explanation for myself.

Kimmy was home when he read the article to me. This was the second time for her and she was not going to sit down to hear no CIA samfie bullshit. Not before hissing, yawning and groaning like she was six years old and we had to sit through adult church. This is just JLP right wing propaganda, she said before he finished the last sentence. Total propaganda. How can you have a JLP chairman writing an article like him is a journalist? Is just more politricks and samfie bloodcleet business this. What about free education for everybody all the way up to bachelor's degree? What about the equal rights for women act? What about all those bauxite companies who now at least have to pay a fee before they rape us? My mother gave her the that-is-not-how-I-brought-you-up look.

Me, I was just happy that she didn't show up with Ras Trent, bass player in *African Herbsman*, otherwise known as the son of the Minister of Tourism. My mother called them an item even though he called Kimmy the Babylon princess to her face. Even though as the Minister's son he would reach thirty before visiting all the rooms in his father's four houses. But Kimmy needed that somebody who could knock her off whatever platform Daddy placed her, so that she could make a new daddy out of him, and as I said, Che Guevara was dead. Mummy, who never takes a side in the discussion, much less talk, said that she was thinking that we needed a home guard. The Prime Minister himself had been talking about it, what with the crime rate skyrocketing and the people having to take it on themselves to shoulder the burden of safety. The three of us never agree on anything but we all looked at her like she was mad, in fact that's just what she said, Don't you all look at me like me mad. My father said there is no way he hiring no Ton-Ton Macoute in him own country.

He asked me what I thought. Kimmy looked at me as if our relationship would hinge on anything that came out of my mouth. When I said that I don't think anything, they were both disappointed. I prefer to remember than to think. If I think, sooner or later I'm going to have to ask myself questions, like why did I sleep with him, and why did I run when it was over, and why am I out here now and why did I stay out here all day. And what does it say that I can pass the entire day doing nothing. If it means I'm one of those girls that serve no damn purpose. The thing about staying out here all day, the really scary part of this, is just how easy it is. My mother sings *One day at a time sweet Jesus*, and even Daddy likes to say that, one day at a time, as if it's some strategy for living. And yet the quickest way to not live at all is to take life one day at a time. It's the way I've discovered to not do a damn thing. If you can break a day down into quarters, then hours, then half hours, then minutes, you can chew down any stretch of time to bite size. It's like dealing with losing a man. If you can bear it for one minute, then you can swallow two, then five, then another five and on and on. If I don't want to think about my life, I don't have to think about life at all, just hold for one minute, then two, then five, then another five, before you know it, a month can pass and you don't even notice because you've only been counting minutes.

I'm outside his house counting minutes, not even realizing that an entire day just ran away from me. Just like that. The light in the room, top left, just went back on.

The thing I should have said, the thing I wanted to say, is that it's not the crime that bothers me. I mean, it bothers me like it bothers anybody. Like how inflation bothers me, I don't really experience it but I know it's affecting me. It's not the actual crime that makes me want to leave, it's the possibility that it can happen any time, any second now, even in the next minute. That it might never happen at all, but I'll think it will happen any second now for the next ten years. Even if it never comes, the point is I'll be waiting for it and the wait is just as bad because you can't do anything else in Jamaica but wait for something to happen to you. This applies to good stuff too. It never happens. All you have is the waiting for it.

Waiting. The son of a bitch didn't even come out to his verandah. But should he come out right now, what? I don't know if I could move. I don't know if I could run across the street and shout from his gate. My dirty feet are telling me that I've been waiting for so long that wait is all there is. The one time I didn't wait was when I saw him on the back balcony. I didn't wait afterwards either. I thought about telling Kimmy. She wouldn't have expected it of me. Which is why I wanted to tell her that I got closer to Che Guevara than she ever would, the Babylon princess.

Across the road, but a good fifty feet or so from the gate, a car just pulled up. A white sportscar that I didn't even see coming. I didn't see the man either, jumping off the wall on my side of the road and walking over to the car. I clutched my bag even though he was already in the car. I don't know how long was he there, standing by the wall in the dark, only a few feet away from me, watching. I didn't even see him or hear him, he could have been there for hours too watching me all this time. The white car turned into his driveway and stopped at the gate. I'm pretty sure it's a Datsun. The driver got out and I can't tell if he's light or dark but he's wearing a white merino. He walks to the side of the gate, to talk to security, I guess. When he turned to get back in the car his eyes flashed. Glasses. I watch the car drive off.

I need to leave. Not just Jamaica, but this place, right now. I need to run, so I do. The house doesn't look at me but shadows do, up the road and down, shadows moving like people. Men maybe. Men change at eleven when there's some defenceless woman around. Part of me is thinking that is bullshit and maybe I just need something to get frightened over. My high school teacher used to warn us not to dress like sluts and fear rape all the time. We wrote a note in left-hand writing with crayon one day and slipped it in her desk drawer. It was months before she found it and read, *As if even a blind man would rape*—before she realized she was reading out loud.

Running is relative. In high heels you can only skip real fast, barely bending your knee. I don't know how long I've been skipping, but I can hear my feet tap tap tapping and my head decides to laugh at how stupid I must look and Wee Willie Winkle runs through the town, Upstairs, downstairs, in his nightgown jumps into my head and stays there. Tapping at the window, crying through the lock, Are the children in their beds? It's now eight o'clock! Wee willie—cho r'asscloth.

Broke a heel. And the damn shoes was not cheap. Shit r'ass—

—Then hi, a wah dis deh 'pon we? Coolie duppy?

—It h'are the pretty-hest coolie duppy h'eye h'ever see.

—H'is where you coming from little girl, did you just perpetrate a crime?

—Maybe she about to bring her gun into play?

Police. Fucking police, in their fucking police voice. I made it as far down as the Waterloo Road intersection. Devon House, looking like a haunted mansion, is to the left. The traffic light just went green, but three police cars block the road. Six policemen leaning against the cars, some have a red seam down their pants, some have blue.

—Yow, lady, you know say we h'inna curfew?

—I . . . Me . . . did have to work late, officer, and lose track of time.

—Time not the only thing you lose. One of you foot longer than one or you break a heel?

—What? Oh cho r'asscloth. Sorry, officer.

—Haha.

They all laugh. Police in their fucking police voice.

—You see h'any bus or taxi running? How you was going get home?

—I . . . I . . .

—You h'is going walk?

—I don't know.

—Miss, you better get h'in the car.

—I can reach home, I say. I want to say that neither in, any, or is, is spelt with an H, but they can probably pick up when a woman is being rude.

—Where h'is 'ome, the next block?

—Havendale.

—Ha ha ha ha.

Police and their police laugh.

—No bus coming pass 'ere for the rest of the night. You going walk?

—Yes.

—With one 'eel?

—Yes.

—H'in a curfew? You know what sort of man h'on the street with you this time of night, lady? You the only woman who don't watch news come nighttime? Scum of the earth deh 'pon the street. Which one of them word you can't spell?

—I was just—

—You was just being a damn idiot. Better you did stay at the work till morning when bus start run. Get in the car.

—I don't need—

—Lady, go inna the bloodcloth car. You breaking the law. Either you going 'ome or you going to lockup.

I get in the car. Two policemen get in the front, leaving the two cars and four policemen behind. At the stoplight a right turn takes you to Havendale. They turn left.

—Shortcut, they both say.

Demus

This is the house by the sea. It only have one room and is not a house, but it used to be a home. The man who close the road to let the train pass, me no know him name but he dead in 1972 and nobody take him place. The train stop passing when West Kingston turn into the Wild West and every man turn into cowboy. I wanted to be Jim West, but him pants too tight. The TV in the chiney shop black and white but I guess that him pants is blue, a girl blue. This is the house that is one room and the man who used to live here sleep on a sponge and shit in a bucket that he wash out in the sea. Nobody remember him name. When they find him body all the water boil out of him but he wasn't a skeleton yet. This house have two window. One look out at the sea and one look out at the tracks. When the train stop running, ghetto people try to steal the tracks, but don't have no tool to break up something that heavy.

This is the colour of the room. The room paint in five colour that cut short. Red from floor to the bottom of the window. Green from the bottom of the window to the ceiling. Blue on the next wall reach the ceiling, but run out before it reach the corner. Pink that start the third wall and cover it. Green at the bottom of the fourth wall stopping in the middle with hard brushstroke, like he was begging and pleading and forcing the paint to stretch further. This is what it must be like for a man to grow old without a woman. Do he forget him parts and sad every time he have to piss for that remind him, or do he play with himself like some pervert? This is the one chair in the room, a red chair with dainty legs. Dainty is a word from a poem we learn in school. Love dainty Spanish needle with your yellow flower and white. Dew bedecked and softly sleeping, do you think of me tonight?

This is the first mistake God make. Time. God was a fool to create time. It's the one thing that even he run out of. But me beyond time. Me in the now, which is now which is also then. Then is also soon and soon might as well be if. Two man just come in the house, making seven nine. One from Rema, two from Trench Town, three from Jungle, three from Copenhagen City.

This is the list of the men in the room.

Josey Wales, also known as Franklin Aloysius, also known as Ba-bye, who just come in with

Bam-Bam, who love to hold the gun but don't know where to shoot.

Weeper, the police killer who have Babylon on the run. When he talk like a Jamaican he talk all coarse and evil. When he talk like a white man, he sound like he reading a book with big word. There is one thing about Weeper that no man who want to live talk about.

Heckle, who used to move with Jeckle until a bullet from PNP turn Jeckle from is to was.

Renton from Trench Town.

Matic from Trench Town.

Funky Chicken, who have the heroin shakes before they give him cocaine.

Two man from Jungle, one fat, one skinny, that I don't know. The skinny one not even a man, not even a boy that much, him shirt open wide but no chest hair growing.

And me.

This is how ten man turn into nine. Three night ago. Matic from Trench Town try to light the C the way the Weeper show him, but he forget how and Weeper wasn't there. A night with no moon and we with no flashlight to show the way to and from the house. Matic thinking he know the freebase and that a spoon full of C, is a spoon full of C, is a spoon full of C. Matic think that Weeper would leave C just anywhere and so he search the floor, in the corner, inside two cupboard near the window and in the ash of the coal stove near the door. He look and look and the other boys start looking too, feeling the C itch even though C don't leave an itch, that is H. Matic find some white and when the other try to move in for him to share it, he pull out him gun. He use him own lighter and cook powder. He remember to heat the C in water and adding the baking soda he see in the cupboard. He smile like a pro while the other men look at him like a hungry tiger. But Matic forget the rest. He forget the other liquid that Weeper use, the ether. He was also stupid enough to think that Weeper would leave a stash in the house. The C wouldn't burn, it wouldn't change. No smoke was coming for him to smoke it, so he lick it. Lick the fire-hot spoon so hard that we hear him tongue sizzle. Freebase hit with a quick kick and the kick takes eight. Seven. Six. Five. Four. Three. Two. One. Nothing. Fuckery this, Matic, then fall frontway him face slamming into the floor with a bam and him mouth start to froth. Nobody touch him until Weeper come and laugh and ask if we didn't think it funny that a dirty, nasty shack like this don't have no rat.

This is how nine man become eight. Last night Josey Wales tell we what we going do. Renton from Trench Town say him cut a hit tune and he not pulling no gun like that boy in the Heptones who in prison when white man put him song in a movie. He say that him baby mother go to the Singer record studio and they give her money for the baby and her mother and her whole family. And he know that she is just one of more than hundred people that get help from the Singer and what goin' happen if that stop? Josey Wales say that don't make him better that make him worse because all him doing is giving poor people fish to eat because now that he reach he don't want nobody else learn how to catch fish for himself. Some of we receive that reasoning but not Renton from Trench Town. Weeper take out him gun to shoot the bitch right deh so. Josey Wales say no, man, listen to the man and understand him reasoning. Then Josey Wales say that one has to know the factors. We don't know what he mean, so he say kinetic energy: $KE = mv^2/2$ (where m is mass and v is velocity). Yaw. Deformation. Fragmentation. Bleeding. Hypovolemic shock. Exsanguination. Hypoxia. Pneumothorax, heart failure and brain damage. Bang. Him skull stopped the bullet but blood still splash on Weeper chest. Not me Starsky and Hutch t-shirt! Weeper say as the man body fall and he wipe brains off him chest. Josey Wales put the gun back in him holster.

This is how the white man teach we how to load an M16A1, an M16A2 and an M16A4.

Point the rifle muzzle in a safe direction.

Cock the rifle and open the bolt.

Return the charging handle to the forward position.

Place the selector lever on SAFE.

Check the chamber to ensure it is clear.

Insert the magazine, pushing it upward until the magazine catch engages and holds the magazine.

Tap upward on the bottom of the magazine to ensure it is seated.

Depress the upper portion of the bolt catch to release the bolt.

Tap the forward assist to ensure that the bolt is fully forward and locked.

You won't need to put it back on SAFE.

This is what you get when you have man from Jungle. Them hot for the C so they freebase and freebase thanks to Weeper. Josey Wales leave we but warn that anybody leave him get shot, and we remember that they used to call him Ba-bye. As he and Weeper close the door they lock it and we hear a click. The house getting smaller and hotter and I think about the guard I going to kill, the police. The Babylon.

Seven man. Twenty-one gun. Eight hundred and forty bullet. I think of one man and one man only and is not the Singer. I think of him running into a wall and balling high voice like a little girl. I think of him saying is not me you come for who you come for downstairs because he must be a pussyhole like that. I think about man who cheat and get away and man whose luck run out. I look at him and say this is what death going to look like.

Sir Arthur George Jennings

And now we are in the time of dying. The year surrenders in three weeks. Gone, the season of wet hot summer, ninety-six degrees in the shade, May and October rains that swelled rivers, killed cows and spread sickness. Men growing fat on pork, boys' bellies swelling with poison. Fourteen men lost in the bush while bodies explode, three, four, five. Many more will have to suffer. Many more will have to die. I stole those words from a living man who already has death walking with him, killing him from the toe up.

I look down on my hands and see my story. A hotel on the south coast, a future my country could taste. Sleepwalking, they said when they found me, and so they build a picture from hearsay of my two hands held out in front and stiff like Frankenstein, my eyes closed, my legs stomping in a communist march, over the banister, three, two, one. They found me naked, my eyes alert but washed of their brown, my neck floppy and the back of my skull smashed, my penis at attention, something the hotel workers saw first. Hidden in my blood was dirt from a man's push.

There are things about death that the dead cannot tell you. The vulgarity of it. Death changes where you die into a room where the body shames itself. Death makes you cough, piss, death makes you shit, death makes you stink from inside vapors. My body rots but my nails still grow into claws as I see and wait.

I heard that a rich man in America, a man with money and power written in his name, died inside a woman that was not his wife. An enormous boat of a man crushing the woman with his deadweight, a man who was burned eighteen hours later by his wife because she couldn't bear to smell another woman on his body.

I was inside a woman whose name I cannot remember but she stopped me complaining of thirst. But there's wine right here. Can you get some ice? Who puts ice in wine? I do, and there are other things I'll do too if only you'll get some ice. I run out naked, and giggling, it's five in the morning. Tiptoe down the corridor like Wee Willie Winkle. The dead have a smell but so does the killer. My death took two, one to demand it and the other to make it so. Before I flew over the banister there was lemongrass and wet dirt, the crunch of a footstep on floors clean as mirrors.

I am in the house of the man that killed me. I have never smelled myself on his hands, just the linger of old death, not a stench but the memory of it, the iron tinge in the blood of stale kill, the sweet stinking lure of a body dead five days. In the world of the living he is a mature man now, not caring that he smells like he stumbled upon somebody else's money, like expensive suits that used to belong to somebody else. Except he is not wearing a suit. I was naked when they found me and he is naked as I find him. His belly is rounder, his back ripples fat as he thrusts up and down and he'll have to dye the back of his head again. His body hits hers in a sweaty slap, slap, slap. He grunts on top of her, the first runner-up he married. The white bed is a whirlpool. She notices that he is not stopping and taps him on the shoulder. His head is in the pillow but he's holding her down, she's in jail and knows it so she taps him again. He grunts and she pushes him *You know I don't want to get pregnant you son of a bitch.* He plops his weight on her until he comes and blows his breath all out in the room. Jamaicans need to know that them leaders can work it, he says. It's the first time in years that I'm hearing his voice, except it's not years. I'm stunned that it hasn't changed, still sounding improper even when he speaks correctly. I am in the wrong place and so is she. She is the first runner-up he married when he failed to get the Miss Jamaica. Her father wanted her to marry full white. Dry shit come of me batty before me make some Syrian with a Lebanese haberdashery marry my bloodcloth daughter, he said.

The woman whom I was inside I cannot remember her name. I never see her, not that I would know where to look. Maybe there was love but ghosts haunt out of longing and I have no longing. Maybe it was not love or maybe I am not a ghost. Or maybe my longing isn't for her. Who asks for ice in wine? Did she know that he was outside the door waiting on me? Someone called me a mangled spider with a cock on top. Not one of the hotel staff, they would have no knowledge of words like mangled. Maybe someone who was already happy to see me gone. I have no memory of his face.

The first runner-up pushes him off and hisses *Is a good thing I didn't forget the foam.* Don't . . . you . . . know . . . he pants the rest of it out . . . that birth control is a plot to kill black people? . . . and laughs. He rolls over and plays with himself. I want to slip inside him, to pretend that I would feel what he feels, but even at the foot of this bed I smell over a hundred dead men. A glass shatters and they both jump. Her nightie had been pulled over her breast so she pulls it down. You and that fucking cat, he says and gets up. I watch his belly settle itself and his cheeks go sallow, not even this, not even sex ruffles his hair, packed tight like the tin man. He makes me miss living, swinging, sagging. The bedroom has furniture she picked out, with knobs and curves and carvings of grapevines. A mosquito net hangs from the ceiling. A television hides in the corner, the door to the bathroom open but the doorway dark. He always thought that men who had any sense of style or beauty were perverts. I remember him saying this about another party member as he drove away. I never shared his hate because I saw Noel Coward every summer and called him uncle. He and his traveling companion.

The man who had me killed reaches for his gun, lying in wait on the bedside table, and leaves his pants on the floor. Thc first runner-up points to the pants and he makes a joke about never dressing up just to meet loose pussy as he goes through the door. I want to stay with her for a while, curious about how she regains a peace in herself, but I follow him.

In the living room is a man I can't remember if I know. The living room is a cemetery, rank with dead smell. Some of it coming from the man. He is black one second, a hint of chinaman the next or maybe he shifts with shadow. I can already smell how he dies. He is coughing in a glass, saying,

—Me did think this was water.

—You don't know what white rum bottle look like, or you can't spell rum?

—Smell? I gulp before I smell.

— Spell. S-p-e-l-l.

—Oh. Hearing not too good. Too much pow pow pow, y'know?

—How the r'asscloth you mistake that for water?

—I don't know, water that come in a special bottle sounds like rich people things. Rahtid brethren, is so you gallivant 'bout the place?

—You expecting modesty in me own house? Or you seeing something you never see before?

—Ah, this is how rich people chuck it.

—Poor people wash them buddy by standpipe and you want to turn this into a class issue? How the bloodcloth you get in me house?

—Walk through the front door.

—How you—

—Enough with how. How you ask how so much?

—You rather why? Okay, make we talk 'bout why. Why the bloodcloth you in me house at . . . hold on . . . three in the morning? What we say 'bout you and me not to seen together in public?

—Never know that you bedroom public. How the mistress? Sound like she was doing good just a while ago. Real good.

—Man, what you want?

—You know what day today is?

—Hmmmm. Hmmmm. I going go with December third. That is the day that follow December second.

—Oi! Enough with your no manners, you better know who you talking to.

—No you better fucking remember who you talking to. Come into my house like some pussycloth house rat. You lucky Rawhide on leave tonight or you would be dead already, you hear me? Dead.

—Good thing for me then.

—I going back to bed. Leave the way you came.

—I was doing some thinking.

—Don't hurt yourself.

—What?

—You were thinking.

—I need some money.

—You need some money.

—After tomorrow.

—Tomorrow's already today.

—After later.

—I told you already that I don't know what you talking about. I don't know about it, I don't endorse it, and I don't even know you that well. Papa-Lo is the only man down there I know.

—Down there? Down there? Is down there you call it now? Artie Jennings never talked like you.

—You and Arthur talk good? 'Cause I have it on good authority that he not talking much these days.

The first runner-up steps into the room wearing the bedsheet.

—Peter, what is all the commotion? And oh my G—

—Jesus Christ, bitch, stop you screaming and go back to bed. Not every naigger is thief.

—Well, in this one case maybe your wife a little correct.

—Peter?

—Go to bed!

—What a slam. Me think the house just shake. Pum-pum lock off for the rest of the night?

—You learned about woman the same place you learned about gun? She slam the door so that we won't think she still there listening. I said, SHE SLAM THE DOOR SO THAT WE WON'T THINK SHE STILL THERE LISTENING.

Now she gone.

—You's a bad motherf—

—Shut yo mouth.

—This day done write down. Nothing you can change about it now, even if you did want—

—I tell you already. I don't know what you talking about. And I certainly don't know what you talking about needing money when you same Josey Wales fly to Miami only two weeks ago. But you know how I know you don't need no fucking money? You fly up for just the day. Come back, what, seven o'clock?

—That was a little business.

—Nothing little about you. Or your other little trip, to the Bahamas. Every man who about him business in this country have a fucking secret.

—The Singer meeting with Papa-Lo and Shotta Sherrif same time.

—Tell me something I don't know.

—Papa-Lo plan to meet up with Shotta Sherrif talk serious things where nobody can hear them. They both stop eating pork, by the way.

—Oh. That I didn't know. What the fuck them two up to? Seriously, what could they possibly have to talk about? And what you mean they both stop eat pork? They turning Rasta? Is this the Singer doing? Is him getting them to talk?

—You really need help to answer that question?

—You talk too much fucking step with me, naigger boy.

—Boy in your fucking brief. The price gone up.

—Take that shit to CIA.

—Rasta don't work for the CIA.

—And Josey Wales, I don't fucking work for you. Take my foolish advice and use the door. And don't come here again.

—Me taking the rum.

—Take two glass while you at it and teach yourself some fucking class.

—Haha. You is something else. Even the devil look 'pon you and go, You is something else.

The man leaves, not closing a single door.

There is another man I see around these dead lands who I don't know. A dead man who died wrong, a fireman who would have gone in peace had he died in a fire. He is in the room as well, he came in with the man named Josey Wales. He walks around him, walks through him at times which Wales mistakes for a shiver. He tries to strike but goes right through him. I used to do that with the man who had me killed, tried to strike, punch, slap and cut and the most I ever did was make him shiver. The rage goes if not the memory. I would say you live with it but the irony is too bitter. I know his story too since he cries it every time. He's crying it now, not seeing that I'm the only person in the room bearing witness. Running to the fire on Orange Street, him fireman number seven. A fire set in a two-story tenement, the flames a mad snake looping through the windows, five children already dead, two shot before the fire. He grabs the hose, knowing the water will only sputter, and runs through the gate. His cheek burns on the right and his temple explodes on the left. The second bullet hits him in the chest. The third grazes the neck of the fireman behind. Now he follows the man who sent him to be with people like me. Josey Wales leaves through the window. The fireman follows. The day is young but is already dead.

AMBUSH IN THE NIGHT

December 3, 1976

Nina Burgess

You can't really know how it feels, just knowing deep down that in a few minutes these men will rape you. God take you make fool, this Cassandra from Greek mythology in history class who nobody listens to, who can't even hear herself. The men haven't touched you yet but you've already blamed yourself, you stupid naïve little bitch this is how man in uniform rape a woman, when you still think they are there to take your cat out of a tree, like this is a Dick and Dora story. The first thing you realize is how fucked up this is, that word wait. And now that you're waiting all you can think is how the hell did you trip and fall and land under some man? They haven't raped you yet but you know they're going to, the threat of it in the third time you catch one looking through the rearview mirror without smiling or laughing and his hand adjusting his crotch like he's playing with, not fixing, himself.

It's the slowness that gets you, the feeling that there is still time to do something, to get out, to run, to close your eyes and think of Treasure Beach. You have all the time in the world. Because when this happens it's your fault. Why didn't you get out? Why didn't you leave? The policeman hears my mind and stomps the gas, raising the stakes. Why don't you get out? Why don't you leave? If you open the door and jump out, just grab your knees and roll until you stop. Then just run to the right, into the bush, over somebody's fence, yes you'll probably have broken something but adrenaline can get you far, very far, I also learned that in class. I might bruise a shoulder, I might break a wrist. The policeman drives through his fourth stoplight. Is kill you want kill we, the other one says and laughs.

I heard a story about a woman who went to the police to report a rape but they didn't believe her so they raped her again. You are afraid and you can smell your sweat and you hope sweat doesn't mean they think you were digging it. You cut your nails only two days ago because this glamour business is damn expensive and now, because you have no nails to scratch the sons of bitches, you hope that no scratch doesn't mean you were digging it. But more than anything else, the one thing that makes you blame and judge yourself and acquit them even before this reaches a court of men who probably discipline their wives with a punch before leaving for court, is that you don't have any panties on. Not only are you the slut your mother talked about but even she will look at you with that you-got-what-you-were-looking-for look. And I'm thinking oh really? Well who told you to be a woman when three gunman came calling? Your rape is your fault too. After a while you realize you're shaking not from fear, but from fury. I take off my right heel, the one that's still there, and grab the shoe tight. As soon as they open the door, one of those bastards will never see out of one eye again, I don't care which. He can kick me, shoot me, rape me in the ass, he's going to have to live with knowing that this pussy he had to pay for.

I can't imagine anything worse than waiting for a rape. If you had time to wait on it, you must have had time to stop it. If you're not for sale, don't advertise, my high school principal is saying at this very moment.

You're already thinking past the rape, to the longer dresses you will buy, the stocking that will reach just above the knee and make you look old, dresses with frilly collars like I'm in the opening credits for *Little House on the fucking Prairie.* I'll stop processing my hair and shaving my legs and armpits. Stop wearing lipstick. Go back to shoes with no heels and marry a man from Swallowfield Church who is willing to be patient with me, a dark man who will balance everything against my giving him light-skinned children and still think he got himself a bargain. You want to scream stop the fucking car and take the fucking pussy and be done with it, because that sounds tough, like it's almost tough enough to scare them a little, but you know words like that could never come from a mouth like yours. It's not that you have the decency, not a r'ass, it's that you don't have the nerve. And that just makes you hate these goddamn police even more, the way they treat you like a bird to their cat. Maybe this is like a man digging his own grave, seeing the end already and just waiting on the middle, the it, the thing that supposed to happen.

I don't know what the fuck I'm talking about, but I'm definitely saying fuck way too much. Any more cussing and I might as well call myself Kim-Marie Burgess. She should be the one in this car right now, she and her freeloving ways. No. That is a wicked thing to think. Except me can't stop thinking it. Nobody deserve this. But she deserve it more than me. They were supposed to turn left, heading to Havendale. Instead they turned right, heading to downtown claiming it's a shortcut. Two of them, one of them saying he never see nothing like that yet, Prime Minister calling election in just two weeks. Sound like some samfie business, he says. But that shouldn't mean nothing to you, you no longtime socialist, says the other one.

—A who you ah call bloodcloth socialist? Better you did call me coolie, or Rasta.

—And you, sweet sugar dumpling, you like socialist or Rasta?

—Haha, says the other one.

—Oi, you in the backseat like coolie duppy.

I want to say sorry, I'm too busy thinking about how woman in 1976 either get herself fucked or fucked over by a man but instead I say,

—Excuse me?

—Rasta or socialist? We waiting on you answer.

—How much longer is this shortcut?

—Longer if you don't cool youself and act right. And . . . what the bloodcloth? How much time me fi tell you me no like no bombocloth cigarette ash 'pon mc uniform?

—Then brush it off.

—To r'asscloth.

—Stop the car then. Engine need a break anyway.

So they stop the car. I don't bother to say I need to get home. I know what they are thinking. Any woman walking with one shoe on Hope Road after midnight couldn't possibly need to get anywhere. Maybe this election was called a little too quick. Maybe communism isn't so bad, I hear there is no such thing as a sick Cuban or a Cuban with bad teeth. And maybe it's a sign that we getting sophisticated or something that every now and then the news is read in Spanish. I don't know. I don't know anything except that even I am getting bored waiting on these police to leave me in a ditch somewhere. I wish I was afraid. A part of me knows that I am supposed to be afraid and wishes it; after all, what does it say about the kind of woman I am if I'm not? They are both leaning on the car, blocking my door. I could get out on the other side right now and run, but I don't. Maybe they are not going to rape me. Maybe they are going to do something and that thing, good or bad, maybe even good, sure beats the nothing that I have been doing all day and all night. This is morning though. This is his fault, his security guard's fault, this whole goddamn peace concert's fault. The country. God. Whatever beyond God, goddamn I wish they would get over with it already.

—Starsky and Hutch wicked last night. That episode top the chart! So Starsky get inject with this secret poison, right? And the brother have only twenty-four hours to find who inject him before him kaput and—

—Me never know who is Starsky and who is Hutch. And why them have to be so touchy-touchy so, like sodomite?

—Man, everything for you is battyman this, sodomite that. Man even have one woman, you think is 'cause him is battyman. A big-time show that. But me still don't know how that car can jump so high and so far.

—You want we to try it out?

—And kill the sweet thing in the back?

Hearing them mention me I ask,

—We going to Havendale or should I get out and continue walking?

—Ha, you know where you deh?

—Kingston is Kingston.

—Eh-eh! Who tell you that you in Kingston? So sweet cheeks, which one of we cuter, me or me brethren? Eh? Which one of we going be you boyfriend?

—If you going rape me, rape me already and leave me in whichever ditch you leave woman. Just stop bore me with your r'asscloth mouth.

The cigarette falls out of the policeman's mouth. They look at each other, but don't say nothing for a long time. So long that I can't even count it, more than minutes. More than five minutes. They're not just quiet with me, but with each other, like what I said took away anything they would want to say to each other or to me. I don't say sorry, after all what was a woman to think when two strange men drive her to some place she doesn't know and didn't ask to go? At midnight where all she can do is hope that when she scream the dark don't suck it out.

They take me home. The one who was smoking says, next time if is rape you looking for, tell we early so we can drive off and leave you where we find you. They drive off.

That was four hours ago and I still can't sleep. I'm in bed, still in the clothes I've been wearing all day, ignoring that my feet still burn and the dirt is soiling the bedsheets. I'm hungry, but I don't move. I want to scratch me feet but I don't move. I want to piss, to shower, to wash off a day that is already gone, but I don't move. I haven't eaten anything since yesterday morning and that was just grapefruit cut in half and drenched in syrup and sugar, exactly the way my mother told me would lead to early diabetes. My mother is so afraid of trouble that trouble sticks to her close just because he never gets tired of proving a point. Tomorrow is the peace concert and all it will take is one shot, just one shot, even a warning shot in the air for all hell to break loose. Earlier this year at the stadium, rain started to drizzle and the spectators panicked. It only took fifteen minutes to kill eleven people, stomped to death. Nobody is going to take a shot at him, nobody would dare, but they don't have to. Hell, if I knew that such a big PNP thing was going to happen in little over twelve hours I would take out my gun too.

This country has been swinging into anarchy for so long that the whole thing is going to be an anti-climax. I don't even sound like myself saying that. Jesus Christ, I sound like Kimmy, or her other boyfriend, the communist, not the Rasta. JLP goons are going to drive down on the park, just a small section, maybe by the Marcus Garvey monument, and shoot somebody. They only need to shoot one. They'll get away but the crowd will burn down half of Kingston. Copenhagen City will put up a fight but the crowd will be too huge then, when they step I'll feel the tremor from all the way up in Havendale. They will burn Copenhagen City down to the ground killing them all and people from Copenhagen City will burn down the Eight Lanes killing them all and a big tidal wave will rise up from the harbour and wash all those bodies and all that blood, and all the music and all that ghetto bullshit out to sea and maybe, just maybe, finally my mother can stop wrapping up her body like a mummy just to keep nasty men out of her vagina, and keep sane and sleep in peace.

Papa-Lo

One more thing, ostentatious gentlemens. Never turn your back 'pon a white bwoi. After a hot night with no moon all you can think of is that something out to betray you, maybe God, maybe man, but never turn your back 'pon a white bwoi. Turn your back 'pon a white bwoi who drink your mannish water and blush red from the spice and he go back to America and write about how the natives gave him goat's head soup to drink, and the flavour come from blood. Turn your back 'pon a white bwoi when he say he come to the ghetto to look for the Rhythm and he go back to England with your 45s and him get rich while you stay poor. Turn you back 'pon a white bwoi and he will say that is he that shot the Sherrif, ennit? and make you the deputy then go onstage and say the black wogs and coons and Arabs and fucking Jamaicans and fucking blah blah blah don't belong here, we don't want them here. This is England, this is a white country, because he think naigger boy never going read the *Melody Maker.* The Singer learn this in peculiar fashion only a few weeks ago at the Hope Road house, when he rehearsing for the peace concert.

This was only few weeks ago. Maybe just two. The Singer and the band rehearsing from early morning right into the night. Judy just go call him aside to tell him that that line he singing, *under heavy manners,* is a slogan for the PNP and if he sing it that will mean he siding with the PNP, which too many people already suspect. They running through the song again when there is the white bwoi. He just appear out of nowhere like magic trick—poof!

—A where you come from, boss? say the drummer.

—Outside.

—You with Chris?

—No.

—You the boy from *Rolling Stone*?

—No.

—*Melody Maker*?

—No.

—*New Music Express*?

—No.

—Old massa plantation?

—Huh? No.

—Keef Richards send you with weed? That man get better weed than anybody in Jamdown.

—No.

The Singer go to find out who this white bwoi be that just show up in the studio, not even out in the grounds where white people usually swarm like ants, usually with long hair in imitation dread and sunglasses and tie-die t-shirts and saying you reggae dudes are far out, man, got any gawn-ja? But this white man didn't dress like he running from something or looking for something else. The Singer go to demand a name but the band didn't wait and he go right back into rehearsal. The white bwoi fan away ganja smoke like it be a swarm of mosquito, he look like he was holding his breath. Every now and then he nod to the beat, but behind the beat, like most white people. He look like he was waiting for everybody to finish. The band ignore him, but when they finish the song the man gone.

About that time, the Singer go to the kitchen like he always do, to get himself an orange or a grapefruit, and there like he waiting is the white bwoi. He look up but not at the Singer and ask, What's a Crazy Ballhead? Before he get an answer, he start to sing it, dem crazy, dem crazay, like he have to feel the words to know the words. You heard that stuff Eric Clapton said about you some months ago? Real piece of work, that man, so he gets onstage and says, Keep Britain white. Chase all the wogs out and all the Arabs and all the fucking Jamaicans, can you believe that? He actually said all the fucking Jamaicans! Wow. Didn't he cover a song of yours? Just goes to show that you never know who your friends are, huh? The Singer tell him that he always know exactly who is friend and who is enemy, but the white bwoi continue like he talking to himself. Two of the band come into the kitchen and them stunned too that the man appear again, like magic. Yow, brethren, look like the tour bus leave you, one of them say, but he didn't smile, he didn't even do that out of breath heh-heh-heh-heh laugh that white people do when them don't know for sure if you make a joke.

—God. God. God. You know what's God's problem, the man say. I mean, Jehovah, Jesus, Yahweh, Allah, Jah, whatever bullshit you want to call him—

—Don't blaspheme against His Imperial Majesty.

—But the thing about God, is that he needs the fame, you know? Fine, the attention, the notice, the recognition. He said it himself, in all your ways acknowledge me. If you stop paying attention or call his name out he kinda ceases to exist.

—Brethren—

—Now the devil, he doesn't need acknowledgment, in fact, the more hush-hush the better.

—Bossman, what you—

—Meaning he doesn't need to be name-checked, identified, or even remembered. The way I see it, the devil could be anyone around you.

—Yow, the last tour bus leave so you going have to go find a taxi. Now.

—I can get around.

—But we rehearsing and . . . hold on. But no tour bus come here today. Where the fuck you come from?

All this time the Singer saying nothing. Is the band that asking questions. The man walking around the kitchen, looking out the window, at the stove, and pick up a grapefruit. He examine it, throw it up in the air two times, then put it back down.

—So what's this Crazy Baldhead about?

—Brethren, Crazy Baldhead is about Crazy Baldhead. If the man have to explain him song him would'a write explanation, not song.

—Touché.

—What?

—And congo bongo I? "Natty Dread" congo bongo I. I mean, I get "I Shot the Sheriff," that's a metaphor, right? Ism and Schism? What I want to know is what happened to the man who sung sweet little songs like "Stir It Up." Is it because the other two left you? What happened to the love everybody vibes? "Burning and Looting"? Is that like "Dancing in the Street"? You know, angry nigger music.

Black man who live in Jamaica all him life don't see much trouble in the word nigger. Black man who come from America is a different story. One man say what the fuck, but it trail off into a mumble. It say something that the white bwoi strut like peacock in what is not him territory, without muscle or gun, like he still own it. Like of course nobody going touch him, he is a white bwoi. I know things. I know this come from slavery. Jamaicans love to talk 'bout how they was the most rebellious negroes in the world, but truth be that slave master would go off in the forest with six or twelve man slave, some of who he whip only a few day before, and not one nigger do a damn thing.

—New album looks like it's heading to number one with a bullet. You're all booked out, Sweden, Germany, Hammersmith Odeon, New York City. You listen to American radio at all? I mean, I personally got nothing against black people, you know, Jimi Hendrix, right? But you know what? Jimi's dead and rock and roll right now is rock and roll, Deep Purple, Bachman-Turner Overdrive, *Brain Salad Surgery*. They don't need anybody coming on masquerading, pretending to be rock stars . . . "My Boy Lollipop," that was a good song, good song, good beat, that's what I like, she went in, got herself a hit, then got out. You make my heart giddyup, hah!

By now, the man stepping back 'cause he see they circling him. But he don't look nervous, he only talking all over the place and nobody understand him. The Singer say nothing.

—America? We're in a tough time. Really tough time. We have to pull things together. Last thing we need is a rabble-rouser setting off the wrong element. Rock and roll is rock and roll and it has its fans it doesn't need . . . Look, I'm trying to tell you people this nicely. But rock, well, rock is for real Americans. And you all need to stop trying to cultivate an audience . . .

Mainstream America doesn't need your kind of message so think real hard about these tours . . . maybe you should stick to the coasts. Stop trying to reach mainstream America.

He say the point over and over, from one direction then the next, with new words and the same words until he figure they get him point. But as usual, white bwoi think black man stupid. Them get the message from he come through the door. Stop mess with white people.

The man don't look at nobody while him message sink in but he wait for it to sink. He say something about not wanting to come back here again. Then he say something about all these performance visas sitting on some overworked embassy clerk's desk. The Singer say nothing. —My Boy Lollipop, now there's a song. There's a song, he say and leave through the kitchen door. The room stay quiet for a minute until somebody shout 'bout the bombocloth white bwoi and follow him through the door, but outside he vanish. Poof.

Some people take that as visitation from the devil himself. But this is December 1976 and if Rasta don't work for the CIA then somebody else do. I ask how the guards let the man in, but them tell him that he just walk past them like he have bigger business than they could overstand. Is not that. Me know and the Singer know. Nobody going be the man, with skin like we, to touch a man with skin like that. The Singer suspicious of everybody from that point, even me I think. My name mix with the JLP and everybody already think that is the JLP that work for the CIA especially when a shipment of don't-call-them-guns just vanish from the wharf. Poof. But this white bwoi didn't warn or threaten him to quit the peace concert, and as for the others, who call the phone with heavy breathing, or send telegram, or leave note with the guard or fire shot in the air then they ride past the house on their bikes, the Singer don't 'fraid of nobody who 'fraid to show him face.

But he don't say what I also 'fraid to say. That this all come back to me. Me the baddest man in Copenhagen City. But badness don't mean nothing anymore. Bad can't compete against scheming. Bad can't compete against wicked. I see and a watch them putting me out to pasture, because politics is a new game now and take a different kind of man to play it. Politician come in the late night to talk to Josey Wales, not me. I know Josey Wales. I was there in 1966 when they take a big chunk out of Josey soul, but only he know what he put there in it place.

As for other people, the white bwoi from America and the white bwoi in Jamaica who not white but an Arab, who fuck English blonde to make they children full free, now they too sending threat to the Singer. All this because natty want to sing hit songs and speak him mind. Even now, nobody know where the white bwoi come from and nobody see him again, not at the embassy, or the Mayfair, or the Jamaica Club, or the Liguanea Club or the Polo Club or wherever foreign white mix with local white. Maybe he don't even live here, just fly in for that one mission. Since then, they double the guard at the gate, but one day them guards get replace by the Echo Squad. Any squad better than the police, but I don't trust no squad from the PNP.

A man who know him have enemy must be on guard at all times. A man who know him have enemy must sleep with one eye open. But when a man have too many enemies he soon flatten them all down to one level, forget how to tell them apart and start to think every enemy is the same enemy. The Singer don't think 'bout the white bwoi much, but I think 'bout him all the time. I ask him what the white bwoi look like and he draw a blank.

Like a white bwoi, him say.

Josey Wales

Even on a night so hot, near morning now, even with a curfew on because this bogus government can't control shit, across the road from the Singer house you have a whore working Hope Road. Maybe is not even a whore. Maybe is just another lost woman, plenty of that in Kingston, who think the Singer has something she looking for all her life. I tell you, if birth control is a plot to kill black people, then the Singer must be the plot to breed them back. Even respectable parents from Irish Town, August Town or whichever rich people town now sending down daughter to consort with the Rastaman and breed a rich baby. But this one, the one I see from when I turn on to Hope Road to pick up Bam-Bam, just stand still like a scarecrow. Like she not selling nothing. Maybe she was a ghost. Something tempt me to walk over and ask, So how much for you and is that the Curfew special, but Bam-Bam was with me and I don't like having him in my car as it is. Stay with him too long and he start to ask questions, like if I did know his father and is whose Clarks shoes that he find in that house he live in. Plus, playing pretty word game is Weeper's thing not mine.

Weeper is with me. Just as I was about to drive off I realize I was about to send this loose cannon to pop off in my Datsun and shout after him to wait for me. I still let him drive. We drive back to Copenhagen City, right past Papa-Lo's house with him sitting outside like Uncle Remus. Sooner or later he going to want to talk to me about things, which is usually him going on and on about nothing at all. That man is not the same man since he start to think. Me in the house for two hours now, maybe three. Something tell me that nobody is sleeping this night. I don't like it. Weeper think everything cool. I don't like working with pickney, but Weeper think everything fine. Then again, Weeper is kind of a pickney too. Right now he high and fucking some girl from Lady Pink in my car. Yes, the man have me swing 'round the club to pick her up after we lock those boys in the train shack. That same slow brain girl name Lerlette who rumour have it was the only girl at Ardenne High School to get enroll and expel on her first day. Don't ask how I know, of course Weeper tell me. I tell him that there was no way you taking that whoring gal up in the same house I raise my children. He say, Brethren, me no have problem with car.

So now I'm by the window listening to my Datsun creak. I should be asleep. If I don't sleep I going to be sleepy tomorrow and bad man can't afford to be sleepy, especially tomorrow. Between Weeper fucking in my car and Peter Nasser going on like a pussyhole to show off to him skinny wife, too much trouble going on in my head for me to sleep. I should shout out the window for Weeper to stop him fucking coming and come but that would turn me into his big brother, or father, or worse, his mother.

And that pussyhole Peter Nasser. If there's one thing I can't stand is when a man think he hot enough already. Think he know everything just because when he talk, certain people in the party listen. But I never join any party. He strut into the ghetto chucking badness because he have no fear of me. I don't want politician to be afraid, I just want them to recognize that I not playing. The girl in the car screaming out for him to *go inna it, nuh baby yeah fuck me nuh work the pussy nuh, like you ah mash potato.* This is not going to be the second time in one night that I have to listen to another man fuck. I step away from the window.

Nobody have to touch a man to hurt a man. All these white people who think they can spend time sinning with the devil, then when the time come, slip away without a mark. I remember when Peter Nasser first come to the ghetto wearing shades so that nobody could tell what was going on in the eyes. How he almost chat as bad as naigger, but still sound like he do schooling in America. Still you can never trust a man who look at everybody as replaceable, from wife to gunman enforcer. He already contact

Weeper and Tony Pavarotti about replacing me when things get too big, or too heavy, or too sophisticated for a man who didn't go to secondary school.

This is his constituency and he have the vote and the local woman to prove it. But he starting to confuse representing people with owning them, and soon even he going need a reckoning. Not by me, but by somebody. People like me don't need secondary school because we graduate already. Before man like Peter Nasser start to visit us late in the night with a car trunk full of gun. Before man like Peter Nasser realize that it better for him that Copenhagen City and the Eight Lanes keep warring than make peace. Make them both burn down in judgment is what I say. By then the house in Miami finish build and man like Peter Nasser start to choke on him own growth.

Fucking Weeper. At least he not sending more letter to that damn man in prison. He not telling me who but I'll soon find out. And when I do,

—Well that was a wheel and come and tumble down . . . whooo!

—You want a rag to clean up?

—Nah brethren, everything evatoprate, he say, rubbing his smash-up glasses and squinting.

—Evaporate.

—What?

—How the girl getting home?

—Her foot sick?

—You is the Don of all dons, Weeper.

—No star, that is you. You so Don them should call you Donavon.

—Donovan.

—No that me say? Anyway, me did think you was going sleep. Instead you up and whining like Godmother.

—Don't make no damn sense sleeping now. Too many things to keep me up.

—No damn thing to keep you awake. Keep this up and you soon become like the old man we just drive past sitting on him verandah like house rat.

—You know why I'm not going to sleep? Something don't sit right about those boys.

—The boys can aim a gun and pull the trigger. Stop being the mother.

—I tell you I don't like working with so much man I can't trust.

—You recruit them.

—No, I recruit them and wait for you to nod yes or no. You're the one that pick nothing but boy. I tell you is no problem to link up TEC-9, to telegram Chinaman in New York.

—No, man.

—Bullman, Tony Pavarotti, Johnny W—

—No, man! Stop chat like a fucking idiot! You can't control them man. Give them the chance fucking half would run 'way when the time come, the other half try to kill you. And you supposed to be the thinker of Copenhagen City? You can't control man. You never go to prison yet you still don't know how to run man. We need boy who when I point left they go left and who when I point right they go right. Boy just do it, man spend too much time thinking about, just like you a do right now. You turn a boy, and you work a boy and you drug a boy until the only thing, the only thing that fucker want to do is anything you say.

—Learn that in prison too? You think I don't know about the type of boy you talking about? That kinda boy you can use only one time, you hear. One time and them finish.

—Who say we going use them twice? Ah wah? Bam-Bam is you boy now?

—Me no have no r'asscloth boy.

—Make them stew in the shack. Make them sweat it out. Make them crawl in a corner and cry for some white. Yow, when me reach back.

—You want gunman or zombie?

—Make them boy stay. Make them cook. By the time we go back, them boy going shoot God.

—Don't bloodcloth blaspheme in me fucking house, Weeper!

—Or God will come down 'pon me with lightning and thunder?

—Or me take this bombocloth gun and shoot you meself.

—Whoa. Brethren, just cool. Just cool now. Is joke me a joke.

—Them bloodcloth joke no funny.

—Brethren, put down the gun. Is me this, is Weeper. Brethren, me no like when people pull gun 'pon me, you know, even when them ah make joke.

—Me look like me ah make joke?

—Josey.

—No, tell me. Tell me one fucking joke you ever hear me make.

—Brethren, alright, no more God business in you house. Just cool, man.

—Don't bring none of that monkey man bullshit in me house.

—Yes, Josey, alright, brethren, alright.

—And don't think I won't shoot you and do this meself.

—Yes, brethren.

—Now go sit down and relax youself. Me would a say go to sleep, but me and you know that you not sleeping for at least three day. So cease and settle—

—You look you need to settle too.

—Settle!

Weeper fling himself on the couch and was about to put up him foot until he see my face. He take off his shoes, put his glasses on the side table and then stretch out. He is quiet for a long time. I rub the gun in my hands. Then he start to giggle like a little girl. Then he giggle more. And more. Soon he is laughing out loud.

—What the fuck you take make joke now?

—Then no must you? You is the fucking joke.

I rub the gun in my hands, slipping the index finger behind the trigger.

—You ever notice how bad you chat when you temperature heat up? The hotter you get, the worse you chat. I should draw out you tongue some more, just to find the Josey Wales me grow up with.

He laugh for so long that I start laughing too, even though me and Weeper never grow up together. He roll over into the sofa, back now to me and pants slipping down showing his red brief. Every time he fuck a woman

I hope that this is the woman that fix him. Because some disease lick him in prison, something that make him not normal. Then just like that he start snoring, like somebody out of a TV comedy. That son of a bitch who sleeping on my own damn couch call me a fucking idiot. Weeper mad as fuck but everything he say tonight make a crazy sorta sense. This is a messy job, the real work come with the cleanup. Can't bring in a man like Tony Pavarotti. Man with those skills rare and you have to use them again and again. Some tool make for repeated use. And some tool, you use once then destroy.

Barry Diflorio

Seven-fifteen. We've been stuck behind a Ford Escort farting black smoke for ten minutes. This car is going nowhere and my oldest son Timmy is humming what sounds like "Layla," I swear to God. He's in the front seat singing and mediating an all-out world war between Superman and Batman because the wife told him he could play with his toys all the way up to the school gate but then he would have to leave them in the car. Jesus H Christ, Third World traffic jams are the worst, all these cars and no goddamn road. Daddy, what's goddamn, my youngest Aiden says from the back, the first time I realize that I've been thinking out loud. Read your book, honey, I say. I mean buddy, or would you rather little man? Now I'm just perplexing the kid. Asserting your masculinity shouldn't seem so complicated at four.

We're in Barbican, a roundabout there for no reason it seems other than to direct traffic to a supermarket with the unfortunate name Masters. The roads are congested with rich people taking their kids to school, quite a few of them heading in my direction to the Hillel Academy. I make a left turn and pass women selling bananas and mangoes, out of season, and men selling sugarcane. And weed if you know how to ask. Not that I ever ask for it. You have to get to the point where you know how the country works better than the people who live here. Then you leave. The Company suggested I read a book from V. S. Naipaul before coming here, *The Middle Passage.* It amazed me how he could land in some country, be there for mere days and nail exactly what was wrong with it. I went to that beach he wrote about, Frenchman's Cove, expecting lazy white women and men in sunglasses and Bermuda shorts, attended to by cabana boys. But even the cove got hit by a wave of democratic socialism.

We turn right. Traffic disappears and we're going uphill, past huge two- and three-story houses, quite a few of them closed up, not in a left-for-the-day way with a few windows open, but as if the owners have all gotten the fuck out'a Dodge, probably waiting out the election elsewhere. Hillel is right at the foot of the mountains. Sooner or later the wife is going to ask again, Why do we live all the way down in New Kingston when our children go to school all the way up in the mountains? She has a point, but it's too damn early for her to be right. My oldest jumps out of the door the instant the car stops at the gate. At first I'm thinking of course, my car's not cool enough, but then it hits me. He almost makes it through the gate.

—Timothy Diflorio, you stop right there.

Busted and he knows it. Here it comes, his *You mean me?* face.

—Wha'appen, Daddy?

—Batman. He's really lonely here on this seat. Where did Superman go?

—Maybe he fell.

—Hand it over, little man. Or I'll walk you to your classroom myself. And I'll hold your hand the entire way.

That did it, the fate worse than death. He looks at his younger brother, who, God bless him, still thinks his pop holding his hand is the greatest idea in the world. Timmy throws Superman in the car.

—Babylon business this.

—Hey!

—I'm sorry, Dad.

—Your mom's in the car too.

—Sorry, Mom, can I go now?

I wave him off.

—Have a great Christmas party, honey!

The scowl on his face is worth the whole trip. She harrumphs 'round the back. Mrs. Diflorio. I thought she would have said something by now, but she was transfixed by some article in *Vogue Patterns*, some shit that she'll bring to her crocheting circle so she can add a new collar to the red dress she loves wearing so much. I'm being cruel. It's a book club, not a crocheting circle. Except I never see her with a book. She doesn't bother to come up to the front seat. Instead she says,

—Maybe they'll have a Santa with red cartridge paper on his head and a pillowcase full of cheap candy, and he'll just say no problem mon, instead of ho ho ho.

—Well, take a look at Daddy's little bigot.

—Don't give me that shit, Barry, I have more black friends than you.

—Don't know if Nelly Matar would like to know you call her black behind her back.

—You're missing the point. Last Christmas was supposed to be the last Christmas I spend, we spend, in a foreign country.

—Good Lord, here I thought I had stashed away this broken record.

—I promised Mom we would be in Vermont for Christmas.

—No you didn't, come off it, Claire. And you forget that your mom likes me a whole lot more than she likes you.

—You bastard, why would you say something like that?

—What is it with you women? You just never know, do you? Ever occur to you that nagging on and on about a point might not be the best way to make it?

—Oh I'm sorry, you must be mistaking me for your Stepford wife. Maybe we can swing back to the house and pick her up.

—Well, we're headed that way.

—Screw you, Barry.

I think of at least ten ways to respond to this, including mentioning that we had sex only last night. Maybe it would defuse her, or maybe she would accuse me of patronizing, or changing the subject. Mind you, she doesn't have a fucking subject. It's December 3 and I have way too much to think about right now for this woman to be coming at me again and again. Every response I can think of I've said over a dozen times so I shut up. I already know where this will fucking lead. In silence we drive all the way down to the intersection of Lady Musgrave Road and Hope Road. At the stoplight she gets out and jumps into the front seat. I turn left.

—What's Aiden doing?

—Nodding off between two pages of *The Lorax*.

—Oh.

—Well?

—Well what? I'm driving, honey.

—You know, Barry, men like you ask a lot of their wives, a whole lot. And we do it. You know why we do it? Because you've convinced us that it's temporary. We even go along when temporary means every two years we have to find new friends just so we don't die of boredom. We even go along with the poor way of raising children, uprooting them for no reason just at the point when they finally build connections—

—Connections, huh?

—Let me finish. Yes, connections you never had disrupted when you were a kid.

—What are you talking about? My dad moved us all the time.

—Well, no wonder you have no idea what a friend is. I guess I should just be happy that we're in an English-speaking country for a change. For a while I couldn't understand my own son.

She can go on and on about the marriage, or the kids, or the job, or Ecuador or this fucking country and I wouldn't care. It's stuff like this that pisses me off, makes me really fucking hate her.

—Because you promised an end, you promised us something at the end of it that would be worth it, even if it means more time for your family. But you know what you are, Barry? You're a liar. Just a big liar to your wife and your children, all for a job that who knows what you do? You're probably not even good at it since you never seem to get a good desk. You're just such a fucking liar.

—Please, enough.

—Enough?

—Lay off. I've had enough, Claire.

—Enough what, or you'll what, Barry? Sign us up for more years, in where, Angola this time? Maybe the Balkans, Morocco? I swear to God if we go to Morocco I'll sunbathe topless.

—Enough, Claire.

—Enough or what?

—Enough or I'll shove this fucking fist between your two fucking eyes so fast that it'll burst through the back of your fucking skull and shatter this fucking glass.

She sits there like she's not looking at me, but not staring out at the road either. It doesn't happen often, a reminder that maybe her husband has killed for a living so all bets are off. I could leave her like this, at least it would give me some fucking peace. This is punching below the belt, tapping into the fear that every company wife has for her husband. If I were a wife beater she would be suffering in silence for the rest of her life and not even her fucking father would care. But then not only would she be afraid of me but she would teach that fear to my kids. Then I'll become just like the others, like Louis Johnson, who I hear actually does hit his wife. I give her an in to come back out on top.

—Sunbathe topless, my ass. That just makes you a WASP chick that sucks dick. Catnip for the fucking Moroccans.

—Wonderful, now you're whoring out your own wife.

—Well, you do have that sexy new haircut, I say, but she's gone off.

Nothing gets her going more than the sense that she is being ignored. I can hear her volume increase. I'm tempted to say you're welcome, instead I turn around and see it, just popping out of nowhere. His house. I drive past this house all the time and yet I don't think I have ever looked at it. It's one of those houses that must tell you that it's had a long past. I heard that Lady Musgrave Road happened because she was so horrified that a black man had built a mansion on her route that she had her own road built. Racism here is sour and sticky, but it goes down so smooth that you're tempted to be racist with a Jamaican just to see if they would even get it. But the Singer's house is just standing there.

—You giving him a lift somewhere?

—What? Who?

—We've been idling at his house for over a minute now. What are you waiting for, Barry?

—I don't know what you're talking about. And how do you know whose house this is?

—Every now and then I climb out from under that rock where you put me.

—Didn't think you'd care for someone so, so wild, so unkempt.

—Christ, you really are my mother. I quite like wild and unkempt. He's like Byron. Byron's a—

—Stop treating me like I'm a goddamn idiot, Claire.

—Wild and unkempt. He's like a black lion. Wish I had some wildness. Instead I got Yale. Nelly thinks he wears leather pants really well. Really well.

—Trying to make me jealous, sweetheart? It's been a while.

—Honey, I've not tried to make you anything in four years. Come to think of it, Nelly did say there was a reception for the peace concert tonight and she—

—Don't fucking go over there tonight!

—What? Why wouldn't I? . . . I don't take orders from . . . wait a minute. What did you say?

—Don't go over there.

—No. You said don't go over there tonight. You're up to something, Barry Diflorio.

—I said I don't know what you're talking about.

—I wasn't asking a question. As for the part where you get all spooky again to make me mind my own business, let me save you the trouble by not caring. Barry—

—What? What now, Claire? What the fuck now?

—You missed the left turn for the hairdresser.

The wife thinks she's the only one who wants to go home. I want that too. I want it so fucking bad I can taste it. The difference is I already know that there's no place we can go back to, no home in that sense anymore. Neither of us remembers that little Aiden is still in the car.

Alex Pierce

The weird thing is, you try to sleep, you try so hard that you realize soon enough that you're actually working at falling asleep, and will never really fall asleep because then it's not sleep anymore, it's work. Pretty soon you need a break from work.

I open the slide door and let traffic in. The problem with New Kingston is that reggae is too far away. I never had this problem when I stayed downtown where music, some jam session or some concert, always bubbled up. But damn brother, this is 1976, almost 1977. People from the embassy who I don't even know started telling me to not go below Crossroads after a certain time, people who've lived here for five years, and yet still sweat before noon. You can't trust somebody who tells you how much they loved your column about The Moody Blues. I've never written any column about The Moody fucking Blues. And even if I did, it would never be something some asshole getting fucked by the man would like.

Couldn't sleep so I put my jeans and t-shirt on and went downstairs. I need to blow this joint. The woman at the front desk was snoring so I slipped by before she gave the customary heads-up to all white people leaving locked doors at night. Outside the heat is fucking dancing around me. The curfew is still on so all you get is the feeling that trouble might want to hang out, but no real trouble at all. Here's the skinny on the rest of the night: I see a taxi driver, reading the *Star* in his car parked in the parking lot and ask if he could take me to somewhere that's still jumping. He looks at me like he sorta knew the type, but maybe the jeans were too tight, hair too long or legs too skinny, and I wasn't some fat fucker in a Jamaican Me Crazy t-shirt who came down here to ball with his little dick.

—I think, Mayfair Hotel lock up, pardner, the taxi driver says and I don't blame him.

—Wasn't thinking of somewhere white folks go to run away from the black folks, buddy. Hook me up with some real action?

He looks at me good and even folds the newspaper. I'd be a liar if I said this isn't one of the greatest feelings in the world—when the normally unflappable Jamaican just got his ass flapped. He looks at me like it's the first time he's seeing me tonight. Of course this is the point where 99.9 percent of Americans fuck it up by getting too excited that a Jamdowner thinks they're cool without passing the can-you-bubble-to-the-reggae-riddim test first.

—What make you think anywhere open? Curfew, me brother, everywhere under heavy manners.

—Come on. In Funky Kingston? Not even curfew puts this city on lockdown.

—You looking for trouble.

—Nah, running away from it most likely.

—Wasn't asking no question.

—Ha. So come on, somewhere must be jumping, curfew or no curfew. You're telling me all of this city is locked up tight? On a Friday night? That's some crazy jive, mister.

—Friday morning.

He looks me down again. I'm tempted to say yeah, bud, I only *look* like a stupid tourist.

—Jump in and let see what we can find, he said. We going to have to stay off main road so Babylon don't stop we.

—Rock 'n' roll.

—That's what you going say when you see these roads, he says.

I want to say buddy, I've been to Rose Town but that's just white people mistake number ten: being proud about visiting somewhere Jamaicans would never be proud to visit. He took me to the Turntable Club up Red Hills Road, another one of those streets that the hotel concierge gives a strict time limit on how long a person of caucasoid extraction (her words, not mine, swear to God) should consider himself safe. We passed a line of boys roasting chicken in oil drums with the smoke hazing straight across the road. Men and women sitting in cars, standing by the roadside, eating pan chicken and soft white bread, closing their eyes with big grins, as if nobody should be getting this kind of bliss at three in the morning. Seems nobody here heard there's a curfew. Funny that we should end up at the Turntable Club because the last time I was here I was trailing Mick Jagger. Dude was going batshit crazy over all the stone-ass foxes in the club and all his favourite colour, black. The driver asks me if I've ever been to Turntable and as much as I don't want to be a smartass, I hate when they think I'm just some ignorant cracker.

—Breezed through a couple times. Hey, whatever happened to Top Hat? And didn't Tit For Tat used to be just down the street? Saw some dude get fucking clobbered for hitting up some pot in the bathroom. Bud, just between me and you? I always liked Neptune better. Turntable gets too mellow, man. And they play too much fucking disco.

He spent so much time staring me down in the rearview mirror that it's a wonder we didn't crash.

—You know your Kingston, he says.

And it weirds me out. I never even liked Neptune and was only guessing at Top Hat, I could have sworn it was called Tip-Top. Without Mick or Keith to tail, the Turntable Club became just any other club with too much red light. Thick with people like this curfew was somebody else's business, not theirs. I got a beer and somebody tapped my shoulder.

—I goin' keep talking to you while you try your hardest to remember my name, she said.

—You always such a smartass?

—No, just making it easy for you. Whole heap of black women in here.

—Give yourself some more credit.

—I give myself plenty credit. You, on the other hand. You buying me a Heineken or what?

And so it goes, I wake up before the sun comes out and she's in the bed beside me, not snoring but breathing heavy. I wonder if this how every Jamaican breathes, you know, just out of pressure or necessity. Can't remember when she wrapped herself into the covers tight, like I did something that she doesn't want me to do again. I want to wake her up and go sweetie I know the deal with Jamaican women, hell with any foreign women. They have to take the lead and it's cool city, really. Pete from *Creem* landed in jail two years back when a Bermuda groupie started screaming rape, because according to him, he only suggested they French fuck. I remembered her. Jamaican girl who said she went to Brooklyn whenever she wanted to experience ghetto life. I remember that made me laugh out loud. Dark, dark skin, straight, straight hair and voice that's never tender, ever. Of course we slept together that night, both of us were at the Supersoul concert being bored by the Temptations trying to phone it in, and neither of us was having any fun. Truth be told I was happy to see her at the Turntable. It had been a year. Figured out the name yet? she said as we went back to the taxi that I didn't know waited for me. The driver nodded but I couldn't tell if it was in approval.

—Me say if you remember my name yet?

—No, but you look an awful lot like a girl I know named Aisha.

—Driver, is which hotel him staying?

—Skyline, miss.

—Oh. Clean sheets then.

She's fast asleep in bed and I'm totally naked and looking at my belly in the mirror. When did it get so soft? Mick Jagger never gets a belly. I turn on the radio and the Prime Minister just announced a general election in two weeks. Damn, that's hard to core right there. I wonder what the Singer thinks, if the government set him up to piggyback on the good vibes from his upcoming concert. What else could it have been, Third World leaders kinda revel in a sorta obviousness, I hear. It just seems so awfully convenient.

I'm supposed to have lunch, or rather coffee, with Mark Lansing. Ran into him in the Pegasus Hotel lobby last night, after another powercut. Went downstairs looking for smokes but the gift shop was already closed, so I walked over to the Pegasus and who should I see in the lobby like he was just waiting for somebody to see him? How'd the Antonioni shoot go? I said and he snickered twice, not sure if he should answer or find it funny. Too busy with my own stuff, though there has been offers, he says. I'd ask Mark Lansing what he thinks about this sudden election announcement, but he'd be so stunned that I asked him a serious question about politics that he'll just give me a shitty answer and ask why do I need to know since I only write for a music magazine, the same one he once said he read every week.

At some point I must have mentioned how much I've been trying to get thirty minutes with the Singer or he must have heard from someone, because now he felt that I needed something from him. I remember it, him saying the exact words *poor guy maybe there is something I can do for you.* I did not tell this asshole to go fuck himself because, funnily, in that one split second I felt sorry for him. Loser has been waiting to have something over somebody for years. Now I'm having lunch with him later, so he can tell me how fricking awesome he is for getting to film the Singer with his expensive camera, and he'll use the word fricking. He told me it was expensive but never told me the brand, thinking I wouldn't know anyway. Fucking idiot probably went to bed with a stupid grin on his face, saying to himself, Look at me, motherfucker, I'm finally cooler than you. I need to get me some coffee real quick before I start to totally spazz out and freak the fuck out of Aisha. She's still asleep.

Papa-Lo

P*eople like me* love to talk, everybody know that. Me par with the Singer because he love to talk too, even when he pick up the guitar and making ism rhyme with schism he still talking. And even when he rhyming ism with schism he still expect you to talk back, for is conversation we having, people. The reggae is nothing more than a man talking, reasoning with another man, conversating to and fro, as I would say.

But check this. Some man don't talk. And just as how man who love to talk par with man who also love to talk, man who keep quiet par with man who keep quiet. Man who keep secret par with man who keep secret. You go to certain party, certain meeting, and you see Josey Wales go up to certain man, or they go up to him, and together they keep quiet. But last night was a hot night with no moon and today barely born. Me sleep for one hour and wake up with restlessness in the spirit. For too long now, way too long, something trap up in my head that must come down out my mouth. If I was a writing man it would have come down on the paper. If I was a Catholic it would come out all over the confession booth.

My woman gone to the kitchen to boil tea, and cook corned pork and yam. She know what me like and laugh when me cuss her out 'bout her donkey hee-hawing in the night. You don't complain when me make other sound in the night, she say and take her jiggly backside to the kitchen. I slap it before she gone far and she look at me and say mind me tell you singing friend that you still eating pork 'pon the quiet. For a second I think she mean it, then she laugh and walk off singing "Girl I've Got a Date." Some man never get the woman who cure them from looking for other woman. But even she can't do nothing 'bout the restlessness in the spirit. She can make the food sweeter, and rub my head down softer, and she know when to tell the man them don't come 'round the house today, but she know there be nothing she can do or say to put the spirit at ease.

Maybe because is December. After all, only when we come to Revelation that we take stock of Genesis, right? Going to December make me think about January. And not just because the PNP fucked up the country. Everybody know that communist done infiltrate Jamaica. More and more Cubans coming here, but nobody know that more and more Jamaicans going there. And when they come back, they can work an AK-47 like them born to control it. True thing, a school getting build over in St. Catherine and not one man on the job speak English. Then before even God can say, But wait a minute is what this? every doctor in the hospital now name Ernesto and Pablo. But January take something from me and give it to Josey Wales. And right now, everybody know.

Early in December before he give we any work or any money or any goodwill package for Christmas, Peter Nasser give me a message. He say tell your people that come this season and afterwards to boil more banana, and roast more yam, fry more potato and dig up more dasheen, but forget dumpling or fritters or cake or anything that need flour. I don't even notice what he say too good, don't even remember passing on the message to the community or even how it spread, unless me did tell me woman.

December 30 was the first one. January 2 end with three more. Then on January 22, God leave St. Thomas. Thirteen people, family and friend, start have headache, fits, vomiting and a few go blind. They shit and shit and couldn't stop shit, they faint and wake up and faint and shake like God striking each of them with lightning. And even after them dead, they couldn't stop shit and shake. All of them dead the same day from the same lunch. Rumour burst open like polio in 1964 and many man and woman lock up themself 'cause they frighten. It in the flour, it in the flour, it in the flour, they say. The flour have death write in it and death make a mark on seventeen people heart. The next day the health minister say that the counter flour that come over to Jamaica on a German ship did poison with a plant killer they call Mother-in-Law poison. But Jamaica know the poison, we ban it from before *Ocean's Eleven.*

Peter Nasser show himself in January. Again, he come hug me, but ask Josey Wales how the car working with the new battery, and me wonder how that become him business. But he talk to me in way he don't talk to Josey Wales. Telling me 'bout how IMF should really stand for Is Manley Fault, he can't save the country, can't protect it, can't even control it. Funny how he talk to Josey Wales 'bout car battery and girl and invite him to shoot clay pigeon on Tuesday, but he talk to me about politics. Me tell Josey Wales, and Chinaman, and Weeper and more, that some white businessman and politician was coming down to get convince that the Prime Minister can run the country. By the time we done, them shouldn't even believe he can run Kingston.

Me never need convincing, PNP never do nothing for anybody but the PNP. Is JLP that come to the ghetto without we having to beg first, come in the fifties when me reach as far as me going with school and turn the nasty shit run place into building like them building on *Good Times* TV show. Then they build Copenhagen City and for the first time in my mother life she bathe in private. Them talk they talk, but is not PNP come to the ghetto, they only come after Copenhagen City build and set up some hurry come up piece of shit place that call the Eight Lanes. They pack them little lanes with nothing but PNP people to antagonize we, but any fool can shoot.

But who win West Kingston win Kingston and who win Kingston win Jamaica, and in 1974, the PNP unleash two beast from out of Jungle, a man called Buntin-Banton and another named Dishrag. PNP was never going win West Kingston, a fact then and a fact now, so they pull a jim-screachy, they create a whole new district and call it Central Kingston, and pile they people in it. Who they have run it? Buntin-Banton and Dishrag. Before them two, war in the ghetto was a war of knife. They gang did number thirty strong cutting through Kingston on red and black motorcycle, buzz buzz buzzing like an army of bees. When the Buntin-Banton Dishrag gang attack we at a funeral me know right there that the game done have new rule now. People think it way past the time when anybody can remember who start things first, but don't get the history of the ghetto twist up, decent people. Buntin-Banton and Dishrag start it first. And when PNP win the 1972 election all hell break loose.

First they drive we out of the jobs we get only four years before. Then them two boy start drive we out of town, like we is varmint and they is Wyatt Earp. They even attack their own, chopping up union man connected to they own party because he tell workers to go on strike. Then near this time last year, a white van pull up outside JLP headquarters on Retirement Road and just stop. The van block the view so they come out of nowhere, attack of the killer bees, Banton/Dishrag gang buzzing in on them bike. They mash up furniture, tear up documents, kick up man, beat up woman, rape two then leave. And here is the thing: during the whole time not one of them say a single word.

But the gang was nothing but coward. They never dare come to Copenhagen City, never touch the head, so they chop the fingers and toes and keep chopping up until I tell Peter Nasser that is time for this sleeping giant to wake up. When we done with them Lane Number Six burn down and every woman start bawl because they never have to scoop brain back into a dead son head before. When we done with Lane Number Seven the only thing left that could move was lizard.

But them two start to think they run the PNP. The party take them on trip to Cuba. Dishrag, who get the name because him was a Rastafarian and him dreadlocks look ragged, land in Cuba and gone to party with Fidel Castro himself. Nobody never tell the brethren that the national dish was pork. He lose him temper like he was Jesus in the temple that day the Jews turn it into market. He kick over even Castro table. Dishrag turn into a problem for him own party. That's when a man call a man, who call Priest, the only man allow to walk in both JLP and PNP territory, and Priest call me. Me go after that pussyhole meself, tell Chinaman just go to Stanton Bar, quiet-like, and head wherever the girls them running from, cussing and clutching they batty, or titty or poom-poom. Chinaman skill enough to put away a boy with one shot, so when he walk up behind him and say yow pussyhole and fire in the back of him head, the woman them 'round him table didn't even scream until the third shot go in, this one through the same hole the first one make, and blood splatter all over them. After six shot Chinaman disappear like an afterthought.

Then in March 1975, Shotta Sherrif drop a message in a church lady Bible where Buntin-Banton was going be. Right out on Darling Street, on him way to check on him woman, just three more block from the sea, Josey and four man draw down right beside him car and shower the pussyhole until even the car engine dead. Buntin-Banton funeral was the biggest thing, word was that twenty thousand people go. I don't know 'bout that number but I do know that the Prime Minister, the deputy Prime Minister and the Minister of Labour all go.

But that was 1975, and this be December 1976 and one year might as well be one different century. Because every man who fight monster become a monster too, and there be at least one woman in Kingston who think me is the killer of all things name hope. People think me lose it because it bother me that me kill the school boy by mistake, but don't realize that me losing it because it supposed to bother me but don't. But now my woman calling me, saying, Bigger-boss, come eat you food.

Nina Burgess

Hello?

—Well praise almighty Jah-Jah, it seem you finally wake up. Is the third time me a call the sistren.

My sister Kimmy. Two sentences in and she already playing ghetto. I wonder if the sun is up yet. I don't know if I'm up for either it or her this morning.

—I was really tired.

—Too much party last night. You hear me? I said you had too much party last night. You not going ask me what you must take for it?

—I already know.

—You already know what you must take?

—No, I already know you're about to tell me.

—Oh. What a way you facety this morning, sistren. Not used to you being so smart. Must be the morning air.

Kimmy makes a point out of never calling me, ever since she took up with Ras Trent who told her to keep her communication with people still trapped in the Babylon shitstem as little as possible. He escapes such communication by flying out to New York every six weeks or so. Kimmy's still waiting on a visa to go with him. You'd think that Ras Trent, son of the Minister of Foreign Affairs, could arrange a visa for his queen woman. You'd think the same queen woman would read something into him not even offering to try. But everything in Jamaica is up for sale, even an American visa, and I have things to do today.

—How can I help you, Kimmy?

—I was thinking the other day. What you know about Garveyism?

—You call me at, at—

—Eight forty-five. Eight forty-five a.m., Nina. Is soon nine.

—Nine. Shit, I have to go to work.

—You don't have no job.

—Still have to shower.

—What you know about Garveyism?

—Is this a radio quiz? Am I 'pon de air?

—Stop take things make joke.

—Then what else could this be, you calling me so early in the morning for no reason other than a civics lesson?

—My point exactly. That you wouldn't see it as important. That's why the white man just downpress you so, when me say Garvey you ears should'a prick up like dog.

—You talk to your mother today?

—She fine.

—That's what she'd said?

—Mummy need livicate her life to the struggle. Only then she can truly escape our downpression as a people.

Kimmy learning from Ras Trent to take the words English people gave her as a tool of oppression and spit them back in their face. Rastaman don't deal with negativity so oppression is now downpression even though there is no up in the word. Dedicate is livicate, I and I, well God knows what that means, but it sounds like somebody trying for their own holy trinity but forgetting the name of the third person. All a load of shit if you ask me. And too much work to remember. But nothing Kimmy likes more than been given too much work to do. Especially when Ras Trent looking for probably another woman, not a queen like her but a woman who will suck his cock and maybe eat out his ass, so that his no, no, no turns into oh, oh, oh, a bowcat that he doesn't have to respect. Kimmy wants something specific, but she'll never ask, preferring to fish it out. This morning who knows? Maybe she just wants to feel better than somebody and my number is one of the few eight digits she can remember.

—He's a national hero, I say.

—At least you know that.

—He wanted black people to eventually go back to Africa.

—Well, in a way. But good, good.

—He was a thief, who buy a ship that couldn't sail anywhere, but probably not the only national hero who was a thief.

—See it deh know, who tell you that him is thief? This is why black people can't progress you know, they call they own people thief.

—I didn't know Marcus Garvey real name is Burgess? Or is our real name Garvey?

—This is exactly what T say. This is exactly what him say people like you would say.

—People like me.

—Then no mus' people like you. People in darkness. Come out of the dark and come into the light, sistren.

I could try to shut her up, but like Ras Trent, Kimmy's not really talking to you. She only needs a witness, not an audience.

—And why call me, since I'm sure I'm not the only person you know who's in darkness. Call one of your Immaculate High School friends or something.

—Sistren, if the revolution ever going to happen, it must, you hear me, it must begin in the home first.

—Trent's home free already?

—Everything is not about T, Nina. I have my own life too.

—Of course. Everything is about Marcus Garvey.

—Where you think you life going? All you black people running around like headless chicken and don't even know why you direction-less. You read *Soul On Ice*? How much I can bet that you never read *Soledad Brother*? *How Europe Underdeveloped Africa*?

—You were always the bookish one.

—Well, book is for wisdom. Also for foolishness.

—The problem with a book is that you never know what it's planning to do to you until you're too far into it. I really need to take a shower.

—For why? You don't have nowhere a go.

And why you don't go fuck yourself, Miss, I couldn't fuck and breed for

Che Guevara so I going take whatever revolution I can ride with my vagina? It reaches the very tip of my tongue and vanishes, like a little sugar pill. I tell myself that I tolerate Kimmy because she could never survive me even once talking to her the way she talks to me. I hate people like that, people you have to protect while they keep hurting you. Deep down she's still the same girl who wants more than anything for people to like her, the only thing she wants more than that is to go back and be born poor and struggling so she can feel entitled to hate everybody who lives in Norbrook. But one day she is going to push me either too far or not far enough. I keep telling myself I don't have time for her, but I went with her to one of those twelve tribes' Rasta gatherings, can't remember when, might be the same week we went to the party at the Singer's house.

The whole trip on the way there she's talking loud, shouting over the engine of a Volkswagen about what I'm supposed to do and what I'm not supposed to do and how I better not embarrass her with any Babylon fuckery. She shouted about how when I reach I going get swallowed by the positive vibration and livicate myself to the struggle for black liberation, the struggle for Africa and the struggle for His Imperial Majesty. Or maybe me already too trapped in iniquity to get swallowed by anything positive, because Rastafari must first begin with a fire, a fire deep down inside you that you can't quench with a glass of water, and you can't wait till it seep out your pores like sweat, you have to tear your mind open and let it rage out.

—That might be heartburn, I say, the last joke of the night. She gave me that I-expected-just-a-little-more-from-you look that she either inherited or studied from Mummy.

—Is a good thing you dress like a righteous woman at least, she said at the most boring outfit I could find, a long purple skirt that brushed against my ankles when I walk and a white shirt that I tucked in. Slippers because I can't imagine Rastafarians liking their women to be in high heels. I couldn't even remember why I agreed to go, far as I know I didn't, but Kimmy was acting as if she had a quota to fill, like those church cult boys on the University campus who act as if they're going to get whipped if they don't get X number of converts a day. But people funny, boy. When we get to this gathering, on Hope Road in a house that looked like slaves used to get whipped right outside, two floors, all wood, French windows and a verandah, Kimmy is quiet.

The whole ride over she couldn't stop yapping, and once she was there she turn into a nun with a silence vow. Ras Trent was already there talking to a woman, excuse me, dawta, and smiling more than he was talking, stroking his beard and tilting his head left then right while the girl, white but with a Rasta cap, clasps her hands and look like she's saying a heavy American version of I'm SO happy to be here. Me? I'm SO happy to watch Kimmy make sense of it all, to watch her fidget and lean on one leg, then the next, then the first as if she doesn't know if she should walk over there, or leave, or wait for him to notice her. All the time she's silent. All the women were silent except the white one talking to Trent. If it wasn't for the red, green and gold and that the skirts are often denim, I'd think I was surrounded by Muslim women.

Far off in the corner three women are lit up by the bonfire they have going, cooking some ital food whatever. I'm stiff, a lighthouse with only my head moving, sweeping left to right and back. I couldn't help it, I'm already looking for boys and especially girls from my high school, who found the true light of Rasta, but are really here just to give their uptown parents grief. There's just so much sex you can have with a man who doesn't use deodorant or a woman who doesn't shave her armpits or legs. Maybe to be a real Rasta you have to be into man musk and woman fish. A lot of women but they are all moving. It takes me a while to see that they are all getting something to give to the men, food, a stool, water, matches for their weed, more food, juice from big Igloos. Livication and liberation my ass, if I wanted to live in a Victorian novel I at least want men who know how to get a decent haircut.

Kimmy was still beside me, still fidgeting, a different woman from the one who just spent an entire car ride talking like she's better than me. Sorta like what she's doing with this phone call, but I haven't heard anything she's said for the past seven minutes. I know, I glanced at the clock above my door.

—Channeling emotional energies towards constructive racial interests. Mass sacrificial work. Through education in science and industry and character building, stress mass education, and, and, you listening to a word that I saying?

—Huh? What? Sorry, trying to swat a fly.

—A fly? What kind of nastiness swirling inside your bed?

—I'm not in bed, Kimmy. Should I even be calling you that? Thought Ras Trent would have given you something other than your slave name by now.

—Him, him call me Mariama. But this is just between him, me and whoever free.

—Oh.

—That don't mean you until you choose to be free, sistren.

—So now that you're free you going back to Africa?

—Typical. Same thing T said. Back to Africa is not even the chief aspect of the Garvey Philosophy.

Kimmy would never use words like chief aspect. Come to think of it, neither would Ras Trent, who probably spells daughter "dawta" in order to use fewer letters. Amazing that she brings such a bitch out of me, but it always reaches right above my skin or inside my mouth and never comes out. The more Kimmy dances around an issue, the more it must be truly bugging her.

—You call me for some reason other than the history, Kimmy?

—What you talking about? I tell you revolution have to start in the home first.

—Not the bed?

—Same thing.

I want to tell her that I'm sick of being the one person she feels she can talk down to. I really do. And then she says,

—You is a dutty little hypocrite.

Finally.

—Pardon?

—You, you fuck him?

—What are you talking about?

—You think nobody wasn't going see you? Lay-lay 'round him house like some groupie?

—I still don't know what you talking about.

—Shelly Moo-Young said she was sure she drive past a woman that look like you, hanging outside him gate yesterday afternoon when she went to pick up her kids.

—Brown girl in uptown. Of course, nobody else look like me.

—When she pass back with the children, she see you again.

—You spoke to your mother?

—Me know that you fuck him.

—Fuck who?

—Him.

—That is none of your—

—So is true. Now you laywaiting him like prostitute.

—Kimmy, you don't have other things to do? Like tell your mother that is the shitstem that beat up her husband and rape her?

—Nobody rape Mummy.

—That what Rasta Trent tell you? Or him tell you that is Babylon rape her? Go on, tell me. Tell me what him tell you because you sure as shit don't have an opinion for yourself.

—Wh-what? What? What? Nobody rape Mummy. Nobody rape . . .

—Considering that I'm sure Ras Trent just hold down and take way with you, how the fuck would you know?

—Him, him, him was only trying you out, you know.

—Trying me out.

—Trying you out because he still can't forget me.

—Oh Kimmy, most people forget you within minutes of meeting you.

—Is a pity Mummy and Daddy don't know you is such a fucking bitch.

—No, but them probably know that you don't wash you pussy no more because you turning Rasta. I have to work.

—You don't have no fucking job.

—But you do, and why you don't get back to it? Ras Trent shit-up batty probably need to wipe.

—You is a wicked bitch. You is a wicked bitch.

Usually I let her berate me until she runs out of breath, but I went too far this time. I shut up because I know I want to go further. She doesn't see me holding my lips shut.

—And, and, and the only reason him fuck you was to see if good loving run in the family.

—So him going after Mummy next?

—T tell me about you.

—T tell you about everything. You haven't had a single thought for yourself in two years. You hear yourself? Calling me about bombocloth Marcus Garvey like you is a history teacher. Ras Trent sit you down like a fucking four-year-old and tell you little history then you think hmmm, who can I talk down to and make me feel bigger than somebody, and as usual you call me. Well, I don't care about your history lesson, I don't care about Garvey and I don't care about your fucking Rasta boyfriend who probably sucking pussy when he go to New York. And another thing, if you think that red skin asshole ever going to help you get a visa so you can find out what he really does in New York, you're even more stupid than that Ganja University t-shirt you always wear.

I want to go on. I have things to do, but I go on. I have two parents who are sitting ducks, just waiting to be attacked again, from the same bastards who'll probably come back for what couldn't fit on their bikes the last time. I'm so ready to go that I don't care if I start burning bridges even before I cross them, even if it's my fucking sister. I want to go back to Hope Road to just stand there by the gate and scream and scream and scream until he either opens the gate or calls the police. And if he calls the police I'll just spend the night in jail and come back out and scream and scream again. He's going to help me, damn it, because if I could help myself I wouldn't give a fuck about him and his "Midnight Ravers" song either. And he's going to give me money, enough money so that I would shut the fuck up, enough money that I can go to the U.S. Embassy through the back door and leave with three visas because Kimmy won't want one and fuck her. Fuck her. Fuck her. Fuck her. There's at least ten more years stuck in the back of my mouth that I'm finally letting out and fuck all who don't care. I want to spit in her goddamn face and explode all over her bombopussy r'asscloth ears. But she hung up.

Josey Wales

I *have an appointment* with Doctor Love. The day was just starting when the phone in the living room ring. I was up already, moving about my house like a morning ghost. Before he say hello, I say, You really have a fuck-up sense of timing, Doctor Love. He wanted to know how I know it was him. I said he was the only man who would risk getting a bullet in the head for bothering me before morning tea. He laugh, say see you by the usual place and hang up. Weeper still snoring on the couch even though the ringer was set to loud.

Peter Nasser introduce me to him on day he come also with the American, Louis Johnson, then both men make the mistake of thinking they could control all communication between me and this Cuban. But a church pastor say to me one time that man might not know man, but spirit know spirit. He was using it to explain how faggot find each other. I couldn't care less about that shit, but what he say stick with me forever, I even use it as a judge. Yes, you can tell me all sorts of word, I already know the power of word, but will spirit know spirit? So when I first meet Doctor Love most of what we say to each other we didn't use words.

Peter Nasser, in one of his rare trip to the ghetto in broad daylight, pull up in his Volvo one day in November 1975 saying he brought an early Christmas present. I look at him thinking what a fucking fool this stocky Syrian clump of dog shit is, and I look at the Cuban to dismiss him too but could read when he roll him eye that he was thinking something close. Peter Nasser never shut up, even when him fucking, so I notice when a man don't talk.

At first I think that since he was from Cuba, he didn't know enough English, until I realize that he only talk when he have to. Tall man, skinny too, with a beard he scratch too much and curly black hair too long for a doctor. Instead he look like Che Guevara, who was a doctor too. Except Doctor Love try to kill Che at least four time. *That little* maricón*, that little* putito *es not even Cuban,* he say when I point out that the two of them was in medicine and they both leave it behind to pick up gun. Part of what draw me to the man is just to know a thing or two. How you go from saving life to taking life? Doctor Love say doctors take life too, *hombre.* Every fucking day. The day Peter Nasser bring him here, he say to me, This man going take you to a whole new level.

Here is the thing now. Louis Johnson did try to tell me foreign policy in that low draw-out way that white people talk when they think you're too stupid to understand. Louis Johnson know Doctor Love because they both was in the Bay of Pigs, Kennedy's little poppy show to try and kidnap Cuba that flop in everybody face. Doctor Love is to Bay of Pigs what 1966 is to me. I look at him and I know. While Peter Nasser and Louis Johnson walk off because Louis Johnson promise him that he would try cow cod soup since, according to Nasser, he fuck his wife like a sixteen-year-old boy after that, the Cuban stay behind. Luis, he said,

—Luis Hernán Rodrigo de las Casas, but everybody calls me Doctor Love.

—Why?

—Because counter-revolution is an act of love, *hermano*, not war. I'm here to teach you things.

—Already learn enough things from Johnson. And why the fuck you people always assume black people so stupid you need to teach them things?

—Whoa, *muchacho*, I didn't mean to offend. But you offend me as well.

—Me? Offend you? I don't even know you.

—And already you're lumping me with the *americano.* I see it in your face.

—You man take two different bus come here?

—*Hermano*, it's because of that man and men like him why things fucked-up to shit in Bay of Pigs, him and every dumb Yankee fucker who got involved. Don't put me in him.

—With him.

—Ay.

—So what is your claim to fame then?

—You heard of this Carlos the Jackal, no?

—No.

—Funny, he's heard about you. He's been hiding out here for a good while, ever since shit went down in a major, how do you say . . . fiasco with OPEC. Even fucking a few of your women, I am sure of this. I taught him a few things because truth be told, he's shitty excuse of a terrorist. Catholic school boys all wanting to be fucking revolutionaries, I tell you the whole thing makes me sick.

—You a real doctor?

—You sick, *hombre*?

—No. You don't sound Cuban.

—I did my schooling in Oslo, *muchacho*.

—You see any boy here?

—Ha. My mistake. *Pero todo es un error en este país de mierda.*

—Not half a mistake as the stupid country you're coming from.

—¿Por Dios, hablas español?

I nod yes.

—CIA *hombre*, he knows you think?

I nod no.

—Want to hear something? Act as if you are deaf, you understand this, as if you are deaf.

—¿Louis, por qué me has sacado de mi propio jodido país para hablar mierda con ese hijo de puta?

—Luis, Luis, nada más enséñale al negrito de mierda alguna bobería como una carta bomba. O préstale el libro de cocina del anarquista, qué sé yo. Él y sus muchachos son unos comemierdas, pero son útiles. Por lo menos por ahora. He's saying he likes you, Josey.

—Me no know. He don't sound too friendly.

Doctor Love laugh. He look at me and smile. Always good to know who your friends are, isn't that so? he say. Anyway, I think you wanna know my claim to fame, no? Meet me at Kingston Harbour tomorrow and I will show you, my friend.

—Me done learn enough tricks from the CIA.

—But CIA didn't send me, *amigo.* I bring greetings from Medellín.

This was right before Christmas season, after a whole year of PNP boys chucking badness all over Kingston. The next day I meet him at Kingston Harbour, downtown out by the dock. The morning was lazy, not too much people out yet but car line the road right around the harbour. People working early, must be, I can't imagine anybody leaving their car down here overnight—even though funny enough that would be the safest place in Kingston to leave it. And even more funny, some people still live down here and live good too. I didn't see him for a while and think this was joke. Bad enough that I was downtown with no back-up in territory where Buntin-Banton gang still move. Down by the harbour almost all the building look like from a TV show set in New York. Bank of Jamaica, Bank of Nova Scotia, two hotels that must did think a different kind of Kingston was going to happen before Manley take over with his socialism-communism bullshit. Anyway, I didn't see him since he was coming up behind me. He tap my shoulder then put his finger on his lip to tell me to stay quiet even though he was smiling the whole time.

He take off his knapsack and jog down almost to the end of the road. He go from car to car, pausing at some, frowning at others. Some of them he even stoop down but I couldn't tell if he was checking tire, fender, whatever the fuck he was looking for. I wonder why I come out in the first place. He hop from a red Volkswagen, to a white Cortina, to a white Escort and a black Camaro. He keep stooping down but he was on the other side of the car. I couldn't tell what he was doing. If he did think me wake up early to come down in war territory just to see how Norway-educated Cuban rob car or slash tire he was about to deal with one very mad Jamaican. He jump up from the last one and trot over to me like some school girl. He tie his hair back into a ponytail and have on dark glasses and t-shirt saying Welcome Back Kotter.

—*Amigo*, I have a word for you.

—What? What word? What the fuck you talking—

—Duck.

—What?

—Duck, he said and push me down.

The red Volkswagen roof blow off right up into the sky before the rest of the car explode sideways. The road start shaking like an earthquake—waves in the road like wind fucking up sea—then the Cortina explode. The Escort explode with two booms which lift it up straight into the sky, where it flip back on what did leave of the Cortina. The Camaro had to sit there while its face blow off, tire in the sky like flying saucer.

Doctor Love laugh at each explosion, yelling like a little boy with each boom. I couldn't tell if people get kill, but I don't think so. Glass all around shatter and people screaming. The whole time I'm flat in the road with this laughing Cuban on top of me.

—You impressed yet, *amigo*?

—If anybody see me, them going think is me behind this, fool.

—Then let them think it. You want to impress Medellín or not? You John the Baptist? Let me know quick so I can go search for Jesus.

Luis Hernán Rodrigo de las Casas. Doctor Love. Two month ago in Barbados a Cubana plane take off from Sewell Airport heading for Jamaica. Twelve minutes and eighteen thousand feet later two bomb explode. Plane crash killing everybody including the entire Cuban fencing team and five people from North Korea. There are things that Doctor Love learn from the CIA ever since he join Coordination of United Revolutionary Organizations, another one of those group that seem to form every month to get rid of Castro. Give the Doctor this, he was the first man not to arch an eyebrow when he realize that I know all this shit. Louis Johnson still don't really believe I can read, which might be why he keep showing me grocery list upside down and saying it's a classified document. Anyway, Doctor Love learn a lot of things from The School of the Americas, one was to blow things to kingdom come. And then he start teaching it. He said he wasn't even in Barbados when the Cubana blow up, but here. And now he back again, probably because somebody in Colombia need an extra set of eye in Jamaica today.

I leave Weeper on the couch, him sleeping in his red brief. I leave him now sleeping on his back, hand resting on balls, which just make sense. I want to pick up his glasses and put them on, maybe see the world how he see it, but something stop me and no, I'm not even going to think that it was fear. I pick up his pants because my woman not tolerating such facetiness on her floor and feel a bulge in the back pocket. A book with no cover and no back pages. I wonder if they was plain like in most book and Weeper was writing letters on them to the man in prison. I turn a few pages and there the title be: Bertrand Russell, *The Problems of Philosophy*. I ask Doctor Love if he ever read Bertrand Russell. He say yes, but after Heidegger, Russell is just a pansy with a Nobel prize. I don't know what the fuck he's talking about, but I know I'm waiting for the moment to spring that on Weeper. Anyway, he was fast asleep when I leave him, good too because I didn't want him to follow.

When you come into the real truth about yourself, you realize that the only person equipped to handle it is you. Some men can't even handle that, which is why Bellevue always full. Some men can't handle knowing what they are capable of. I thought I know it until Doctor Love teach me, not even a year ago. Orange Street, the tenement yard full of nothing but PNP pussyhole.

—You want to impress bigger . . . how you say this, shark?

—Bigger fish.

—Yes, this is so. Bigger fish than Peter Nasser?

—You mean the head, I already—

—Bigger than that. Bigger than this country, *chico*. We've been using the Puerto Ricans and the Bahamians, but both are full of shitters.

—Don't know what you talking about, Luis.

—Yes, you do. But let us say it is as you say, you don't know. That gift that you don't know about that America needs so much, that gift from Bogotá needs a new how do you say it? Santa Claus. Because the Santa in

Puerto Rico got too fat the fuck, and the ones in Bahamas too stupid. Besides, our efforts to liberate Cuba from that impotent Catholic school boy, *hijo de puta*, stand best to succeed if it comes from here, because Jamaica and Cuba kissing cousins, no?

Peter Nasser think the CIA send Doctor Love to teach me how to better serve him. Peter Nasser is the kind of man who don't know the difference between fucking his wife good and not caring if he fuck her bad. The CIA look like they know too much, but maybe they just don't care. I like a man who don't care what his enemy's enemy do as long as he remain his enemy's enemy. Doctor Love come to Jamaica on the CIA plane ticket but with order from Medellín. That night at the Orange Street tenement he showed me what to do with C-4.

—*Hola, mi amigo.*

—Josef! Long time my friend!

He say even though it's only two months since I see him last. It didn't take long to drive to Half Moon Bay, but you have to look for it to find it. An old dock use by first the Spaniard, then the British in slavery days, even the pirates at one time. It's one of those place where things can come in or ship out and is nobody business. I can see him from up here on the top of the cliff. By the time I get down to the shore Doctor Love run up to me and kiss me on the cheek. That's what these Latino men do so I don't take it no way, though if somebody else was around that would be a different story. Louis Johnson off in the bush doing a fuck-up job of keeping his green Ford Cortina out of sight. Or out of sound since he don't switch the engine off. Good thing he staying in the car. I wonder if Doctor Love have been saying too much. This is a *hermano* who love to fucking chat.

—Things are tighter than a fat woman's asshole, *mi amigo*, he says.

—Serious business in Barbados.

—*Madre de Dios*. Though from technical standpoint it was already international waters. The struggle for liberation cannot proceed without sacrifice, *chico*.

—Was that to impress Medellín?

—Nah, one bomb was to impress Medellín, two was to impress myself. But what do I know, I was in Venezuela at the time, ha.

—Magic.

—You need to do the same, *hermano.*

—I need to blow up a plane?

—I told you I know nothing about no blowing up of planes.

—What do I need to do?

—You need to make it so that you don't call them, they call you. Don't make me doubt you, Josef.

—Nobody doubting me after tonight.

—Impress them, *hermano.*

—Brethren, I goin' impress the world. How long you staying?

—For as long as the threat of communism is real and approaching, Josef.

—The man said he was a democratic socialist.

—Socialism is theory, communism is practice. You need some kabooms, *hermano.* Those boys are watching.

—Not looking to take down all of Hope Road with—

—Don't want to know. But I have some presents in the car, *hermano*, just three or four C-4s. I already taught you.

—No bombocloth bomb, Luis. How much time me to tell you that?

—I'm just laying it on the table, Josef.

—Him know you have bombs in him car?

—That idiot doesn't know if he shit through his dick or piss through his ass.

—Anyway, I prefer one on one. That pussyhole going see where judgment coming from when I come give it.

—Never did like up close and personal. I stay over here and take you down, no? Do what you have to do, my brother. I'll call you tomorrow. We'll drink mojitos and spit on the picture of that impotent Catholic school boy.

—Call me the day after. Going be too busy tomorrow.

Barry Diflorio

I *had no idea* that fucking Cuban was in Jamaica. And just after that shit he pulled in Barbados two months ago, I have to say the bastard has nerve. I'll bet this was Louis Johnson's idea. Ever since he left Chile to join me in Ecuador he has a convenient way of forgetting he works for me.

It was only twenty minutes or so from the Singer's house to the hairdresser in Mona, but thanks to the wife it felt like two hours. Now I'm at my office at the embassy waiting for the events of December 3, 1976, to happen. Today is the day we revoke the Singer's visa because he's suspected of trafficking drugs into the United States of America. Shouldn't be hard to prove really, just check his back pocket. We're supposed to make a big, public show of it, a sign that we, as a friend of Jamaica, will not sit by and allow lawlessness to take control of our gracious ally. I already wrote the press release, signed off by higher up. We also have proof that he has consorted with known drug traffickers in Miami and New York and has aligned himself with men of questionable character in Jamaica and abroad, including at least two local terrorists. This has already been documented. One of them, calling himself Shotta Sherrif, twice tried for murder, is even closely linked to the present government.

Documents in order, arrangements made, pretty much all of them myself, especially after that son of a bitch Bill Adler started singing with that two-faced mouth of his. I mean, really, the nerve of that fucking guy. It's one thing to disavow everything you ever did—I get it, you're just one of those fags who signed on for something you couldn't handle. But don't fucking act like half the stuff you wrote about you didn't fucking cause. At least I didn't pick up his shitty technique for bugging a place. He's probably still joking in whichever country will have him about that time in Ecuador, when the Villa Hilda Hotel maids walked in on him on top of that dinner table trying to bug Manuel Araujo. Or the time he tried to convince those Indian guards at the Czechoslovakian embassy that yes, *hombres*, repairmen do show up at five a.m., even in Latin America.

Anyway, because of his facilitating a quick exit for ten on the ground, seven more had to step in, pronto. We didn't even have time for full clearance, or else I would have never okayed Louis Johnson, not when he and the Cuban came as a package deal. The island is swarming with fucking Cubans, and I'm not even talking the communists.

Yes, I can imagine why he would be here, even on his own. What I don't get is why he's making such a public spectacle of it—public for us anyway, unlike Carlos the Jackal, who's been here too, laying low, rubbing his belly while whores suck him off. Those two have a history. I'm paid to know these things. Word was that Luis Hernán Rodrigo de las Casas taught Carlos how to use C-4. Dynamite too, but las Casas always had a serious hard-on for C-4. This is not his first trip to Jamaica this year. In both cases, as soon as he got here things started to blow up.

My office has four walls and one window with a view of an empty lot across the road where Jamaicans huddle before joining the line at six a.m. for visas. Manley told them there were six flights to Miami every day and everybody has been getting a move on with that. The line has been lapping around the entire block ever since Pan Am suspended services between Kingston and the mainland. Weak gesture right on the same level as Jamaica's women vowing to hold back their sexual services until the government made concrete changes. But you try to teach people little gestures and hope they seed big ones.

This file on Luis Hernán Rodrigo de las Casas is a short one. Short is of course relative. To really read up on Casas you have to access five files, not one. I pick one up from my desk, having asked Sally for it the second I saw him walking off with Louis Johnson. The folder is blue. I open it and recognize so many names. Freddy Lugo, Hernán Ricardo Lozano from Alpha 66, Orlando Bosch, a shifty Venezuelan asshole of no mean order, two men known only as Gael and Freddy, possibly from Omega 7, and de las Casas.

All from the Coordination of United Revolutionary Organizations, all AMBLOOD agents and all Bay of Pigs alum. They have had a busy year, beginning with them all coming together in the Dominican Republic to form this *Coordination*, a meeting of which the Company of course has no knowledge.

In July a red suitcase for a BWIA flight leaving Kingston's airport for Cuba explodes on the tarmac. Offices of the BWIA in Barbados, Air Panama in Colombia, Iberia and Nanaco Line in Costa Rica, all with links to Cubana, are all bombed. A Cuban official in Mexico and two in Argentina are murdered. Then in September Orlando Letelier is assassinated in D.C. Pinochet's DINA in that case, but there are those names, those same fucking names, which come up whenever the topic is Latin America. Then there was that fire in Guyana, that only destroyed Cuban fishing equipment. In June this year, the fourteenth actually, the Peruvian ambassador Fernando Rodriguez was stabbed in his living room, this before this Jamaican government declared a state of emergency.

Crime here is out of control, it has been for most of the year, but the trick about Jamaican crime is that it is localized for the most part. Every time it travels uptown you get the sense somebody is trying to make a very unsubtle point. I've met people on both parties, dozens of bulls let loose in a china shop. But even by their standards, even by gunmen standards, hell, even by Chilean secret police standards, Rodriguez's death was just a little too planned, too meticulous, too strained to appear random for it to be so. Explosives are the Cuban's MO, everybody knows that, but something about that death stinks of him, it just fucking stinks. Of course the United States government to our best knowledge was not aware of any action to terminate the ambassador but hopes the perpetrators of this unspeakable crime and the powers that be that encourages, provides for or protects them will be brought to justice.

Jesus, I'm starting to sound like Henry Kissinger more and more every day.

—Sally?

—Yes, sir.

—Can you check where Louis Johnson went?

—At once, sir.

I release the intercom and look at my desk. My wife has never set foot in my office but Kissinger has, so she can kiss my ass. January, days after we moved here, my first job is to babysit Heinrich, which everybody calls him behind his back, who was not having a good week in Jamaica. But today, on the way to the hairdresser after the don't-call-it-a-fight fight, the wife did something really strange. She looked at me. Well, I think she was looking at me. I was staring at the road in front of me the whole time, heading up Hope Road to Mona, but by now I sure as hell know when a person is staring at me. Anyway, she looked at me and said,

—You know which word I've found that I like, that I like quite a bit, well, maybe not like but does make me chuckle when I hear it, Barry?

—No, dear.

—Scurrilous. Scur-ri-lous. It's one of those words certain people like you use. I never noticed it before, how I'm such an intimate companion to scurrilous. Not a day goes by when I'm not confronted or just annoyed by something scurrilous.

—We get our own dictionary as a goodbye gift from Yale.

—Well, you get your own something. But you know something, Barry, I always burst out laughing as soon as one of you say that word, especially in an interview.

—Kissinger was on TV again or something?

—No, much closer to home, the ambassador that I don't like. Said it to Nelly Matar's husband at some business meeting last Tuesday. Said, "The allegations of destabilization are scurrilous and false."

—I had no idea you lunching ladies talked politics.

—Well, what else are we going to talk about? None of you have any penis size to speak of.

—Excuse me?

—So you *are* paying attention. Ha. Seriously, what the hell are you doing here anyway? Talk to me seriously for once, Barry. I'd ask Louis Johnson's wife but poor girl fell down and hit her face again, and—

—We go where the U.S. government sends us.

—Oh I didn't say we, darling, I said you. I'm here wasting my time and kidding myself. What are you doing here? What have you been doing this past month? I swear to God I would have preferred if you had a mistress.

—Me too.

—Don't flatter yourself, Barry. Those days are way past you.

—*Fuck you too, woman.*

—What are you doing here? Give me the blow by blow.

—The blow by blow, huh?

—Well, the traffic isn't going anywhere. And you haven't said anything interesting to me in weeks.

—You're asking me to reveal classified information?

—Barry, you can either tell me, or sleep with one eye open for the next three years because believe me, I'll find out. You know how I get when I set my mind to something.

—Would you like me to recite the memo?

—I'm one of the ones who can understand big words, remember?

I have a theory that while a man might not always get the wife he wants or needs, he always gets the wife he deserves. I'm not sure the wife feels the same way. But in a perverse way, this was something I always liked about her. I say perverse because any reasonable man, even a passive one, would have slapped her silly by now.

—What do you think we were doing in Ecuador?

—Jesus Christ, Barry, I know the CIA—

—The Company.

—Sheesh. The Company. I know the Company is not some foreign aid division of the White House. If you're in a country you're probably up to no good.

—Excuse me?

—Excuse yourself. You're not the one who always has to pack up the children in a rush.

—Child. We didn't have Aiden in Ecuador.

—But we did in Argentina. So what were you doing there then, and what the hell does it have to do with your boss telling bullshit to Nelly Matar's husband?

—He's not my boss.

—That's not what he would say.

—You really wanna know?

—Yes, Barry, I really want to know.

—CIA-related Missions directive for Ecuador.

—Uh-huh.

—Priority A.

—Christ, you really are going to recite the memo.

—Priority A: Collect and report intelligence on strength and intentions of communist and other hostile political organizations, including international support, influence in Ecuadoran government. Priority B: Collect and report intelligence on stability of Ecuador on government, strength and intentions of dissident political groups. Maintain high-level agents in government, security, ruling political and opposition political parties, especially opposition military leaders.

—I've really heard enough, Barry.

—Priority C: Propaganda and psychological warfare: disseminate information to counteract anti-U.S. propaganda, neutralize communist influence in mass organizations, establish alternative organizations. Support democratic leaders.

—I married an automaton. What has any of this got to do with Jamaica?

—The Company has only one rule book, dear. One size fits all. Maybe you should take a closer look around you.

—I am looking around. That's why I don't believe you.

—What do you mean?

—None of that stuff explains what's going on here.

—On January 12, the *Wall Street Journal* called Michael Manley's PNP the most inept of all Western governments. February *Miami Herald*: Jamaica is building up to showdown. March, Sal Resnick in the *New York Times* writes that the Jamaican government is allowing Cuba to train its police force and align itself with Black Power elements. July: *U.S. News & World*

Report says Jamaica's Prime Minister Michael Manley has moved closer to communist Cuba. August, *Newsweek* says there are three thousand Cubans in Jamaica. Resnick—

—Good Lord, enough about your lapdog Sal Resnick. As for Cubans, I don't see any Cubans. Mexicans and Venezuelans, sure, but no Cubans.

—The man asked for a hundred million in trade credit then thinks he can just shit in our faces by kissing up to communists? Then don't ask for any fucking credit. Hell, don't ask for anything. If only he'd shut his mouth about socialism.

—Sweden's socialist.

—You know too fucking much, dear.

—You pick the weirdest times to swear, *dear.*

—All ism's lead to communism.

—Is that what they taught you in Death to Commies 101 at Yale? I've been married to you a long time, Barry. A long time. And I know you. When you can't shoot straight, which is most of the time, you befuddle with bullshit.

—Excuse me?

—Some of it, some of what you're saying makes some . . . some sorta sense. I guess. But this . . . no. No. Either there's some stuff going on you're not telling me, or there's some stuff nobody's telling you. Jesus, you're such a desk clerk.

—What do you mean, some stuff?

—Something more than that. All of that is economic, and yes, all that adds up, but we've only been here ten months, Barry, and your little game takes at least three years, six if you add up all the time in South America. No, there's something else. Something in the air. A natural mystic.

—What the fuck does that mean?

—It wouldn't even make sense to explain it to you. We're here.

Papa-Lo

The sun rise up and squat down on the sky like it no have nowhere to go. This too, though is barely ten o'clock, heat already creeping into the house. First through the kitchen that nearest to outside, then the living room, east to west, chair by chair, so that when me sit down in the settee by the window me almost jump up fast. I still restless. Preacher said man like me will never know peace and I accept that. But something 'bout today feel specially off and it have something to do with Josey Wales. Election in two weeks and Josey meeting with Peter Nasser and the American and the Cuban who I don't see since January. But the JLP need to win the country and they will do anything to make it happen.

I think I know what that mean. Josey planning something they think me don't have the gumption to do. Gentlepeople, they is right. Plenty things happen in 1976. Yes, when that school boy run into me bullet, that was it, but truth be told me get tired of the taste of blood long time ago. Me never even like it to begin with. Don't make no mistake, it don't take nothing to kill a man and even less to not care that him dead. Certain parts of town you let the baby walk the street and you leave him when he play in the shit water. And when him get sick so that he is just a ballooning, bursting screaming belly that used to be a baby, you take your time to go to clinic which too packed anyway and the baby dead while you waiting in the line, or maybe you take pity and cover the baby with your pillow the night before, and either way, you see and wait, because death is the best thing you could do for him.

Is only two weeks before election and people bussing gunshot every day. Me and Shotta Sherrif both claim that we want peace, but it only take one shot, from a gang like Enforcers in Spanish Town, or the Wang Gang who say they didn't sign no bloodcloth treaty. It only take one shot. And even if we want peace, man like Peter Nasser need him party to win and don't care how. I usually don't care how either. But how come a little election in a little country become such a big thing? Why America care about we so much all of a sudden? This is not 'bout territory, this is not 'bout statement. I think of Josey and I think of all these Americans and I think of Peter Nasser, and I think of Copenhagen City and the Eight Lanes and Kingston and Jamaica and the world, and wonder what kind of bad boy statement would make the whole world look? And just like so it hit me like Revelation. I know what Josey going to do. Me shake in me bones, the orange juice slip out of me hand and drop on the floor. Glass, but it hit my foot first and didn't break. Orange juice sweep across the floor slow, like blood.

—Jesus Christ, Papa, you don't think I have enough to do today?

She down on the floor with a rag and a pail before I even realize what going on. Go outside and put yourself to some use, she say. Outside make me glad that I wearing only a mesh shirt. Josey. If the Orange Street tenement fire wasn't big enough a statement even Jesus would drop him orange juice over what him, them, must be planning. Something that don't involve me. What can be so big and so dark that it too dark for Papa-Lo?

Me don't know what to do, but me legs start walking to Josey Wales' house. Something about the seeing this Cuban with him fuckery name, Doctor Love, make me think serious thoughts. Last time he was here in January, he and Josey Wales go downtown near PNP territory and blow up four car by the harbour, one after the other. He do it just to show off and nobody get kill but he seed something in Josey Wales that growing still. Me legs moving forwards but me mind moving backwards. Back to last December and January and every month till now. You look at certain things and they is just certain things. Look at them another way and certain things add up to one big thing, one terrible thing, all the more terrible because you never add them up before.

January was the last time Peter Nasser call me. Now him call Josey Wales. He call me to say the IMF coming for meeting. The IMF being some group of big man from rich country all over the world who deciding whether to give Jamaica money to haul itself out of the doo-doo pit. That is exactly what Peter Nasser say, since he still think he have to break serious matters down to basic school lyrics for the ghetto boy to understand it. Me was this close to tell him fuck off, me know the difference between ostentatious and loquacious and neither word describe him even when other man write him speech. This is what Peter Nasser also say, that if Michael Manley convince the IMF to give the country money, then he going use it to plunge the country into the darkness of communism.

Doctor Love was there to tell everybody about communism. How Fidel Castro take over from the great leader Batista and just move in him house and kill everybody from before. How he tear down all these capitalist things like school and shop but keep the gogo club Tropicana even though rumour be that the commandante can't get him little sergeant up for years now. How soon they start to just round up men and lock them up, just like the PNP for this whole state of emergency. Doctor Love talk about when he was in lockup and how some man in jail for no reason, but them was doctor, or lawyer or civil servant which mean they was against communism. He lock up even woman and children. One day him best friend escape to the side wall of the prison thinking it was just ten feet drop to the road, but it was a fifty-foot drop and he jump anyway thinking he would miss the ground and land in the sea. That brother didn't land in the sea. People, this was what Michael Manley wanted to bring to Jamaica and the IMF was going to give him money to do it. IMF stand for Is Manley Fault, Peter Nasser say.

January barely born and we set to work. The American show up with a case full of things the Cuban have to teach we how to use. Wish we had these during Bay of Pigs, *muchachos*, he say plenty time. Him already know Josey when me meet him but me never have time to remark 'bout that. Them guns not like guns from 1966 or 1972. Them gun you have to brace on your shoulder, put in one charge and fire. Our best gun can knock down a man even as the bullet tear through the heart. This bazooka can knock down a wall. I pick up an M1 and don't put it down. Josey hold on to his old gun, but he don't tell the American that is an AK-47 though me sure the Cuban recognize it. We take the Cuban to the Garbagelands out far west for him to teach the boys. January 5 me lead a mission to Jonestown while Josey go after Trench Town where the Singer used to live. Trench Town think that make them untouchable but them not.

Learn this, all nice and decent people. An election year commence as soon as the first gunshot buss. A ghetto always on guard but Jonestown sleeping, like they don't know that this is 1976 and everybody have to sleep with one eye open. I almost feel to shoot them up just for their carelessness. We in five car, all the better since nobody in Jonestown have a good enough car to follow we. We don't have time to think, just dash through, shower the place with plenty bullet and dash out. But in the back of the truck is our man with the bazooka. He fire at a bar, but the truck hit a pothole and he slip just as it bust, and little zinc house explode. The road shake. I shout for them to stop the truck to fire, but they taking too long to reload. Jonestown coming out and firing with them simple six-shooter gun and what sound like an AK. But we have new gun, gun that can seek and destroy, gun for people like Tony Pavarotti who take him time, aim, fire and never waste a bullet. Me driving the car with my M1 in me lap. I slam the brakes and burst out fire at a bunch of darkness running away from me. The bunch of darkness all fall down, but more bullet ratatat from the east and hit one or two of we, me not sure. Me shout at them to pull out, but not before the bazooka fire again. The fool miss again, but he hit the bus stop. Steel and zinc explode, flying everywhere and smashing into everything like when a tornado spit on TV. We pull out.

Josey Wales set out for Trench Town with just one man and Doctor Love. I shout out that he mad to go with so few but things now at the place where even when I shout Josey Wales don't hear me. They set off in Josey's white Datsun. One day later, is Josey that make the news. Two tenement yard in Trench Town blow up with explosive, seven house, a bar and a shop burn to the ground from fire. Peter Nasser call me and read a story about it from the *New York Times* on the phone then cuss because me wasn't laughing as loud as him. He hang up and I know where him phone ring next. I still can't remember when Josey Wales get phone.

January 6, police buss in on the Wang Gang because they live on Wang Sang Lands, a ghetto that is JLP but not controlled by we. Them boys have plans, and diagram and chart. And explosive. Two of them know the Cuban by him other name, Doctor Love, and the rest even talk about how they get gun from America. Me cuss 'bout all them little upstarts that nobody controlling will turn out to be a bigger problem than Shotta Sherrif. Still me picture Shotta Sherrif over in the Eight Lanes with him eye trying hard to stay open, just like me.

January 7, six boy from here buss 'pon a construction site on Marcus Garvey Drive and kill two policeman. I only know because I hear them laughing when they drive past me on the way back. Me lose me cool right away.

—Who the bloodcloth send you out to go shoot up construction site? me say, but the first boy start laugh at me. My bullet bust through him right eye and leave through the back of him head before he finish laugh.

—Who send you out, I say again and point me gun at another boy. Then something happen that me didn't have a pen to mark with so me mark it by scratching me gun with a stone later. The rest of the boy pull them gun at me. Me couldn't believe it. Me stand there watching them watching me and don't say nothing. Then one of the boys looking at me burst blood from the top of him head and all down flat. The rest of them drop them guns and start to bawl and cry like they just remember that none of them reach seventeen yet. I turn 'round and there is Tony Pavarotti, holding him rifle and looking into the viewer and beside him Josey Wales. Both then turn and walk away. The same day, the Wang Gang attack a construction site on Marcus Garvey Drive and kill two policeman. The day after, this idiot government make a new law: anybody them find with a gun get send to prison for life.

Peter Nasser tell we to put more pressure 'pon PNP communities so we put more pressure. More than Shotta Sherrif can handle with no Buntin-Banton and Dishrag to back him up. The Prime Minister then come up with idea that the people hire Home Guard to guard they house and street.

People like Peter Nasser come on TV and say, Jamaica, I only have three words for that kind of measure: Ton Ton Macoutes. He call me to read some article from a newspaper in America name the *Wall Street Journal.*

—"Jamaica is not going communist. It is merely going bananas," ha ha ha, you nah laugh, busha? It funny, man, it funny nuh bombocloth.

Then January 24. Seventeen people dead from counter flour.

February 10. Josey and Doctor Love and Tony Pavarotti leave out. In Jonestown and Trench Town, plenty bomb go off. Same month Wang Gang bust in on a youth club dance in Duhaney Park and kill five. Eight wounded.

March. Can't remember which day. Police see Josey's white Datsun and follow him all the way into Copenhagen City. The police demand that he get out of the car 'cause they plan to impound it. Copenhagen people come down on them like judgment with bottle, stone, stick, whatever and the police almost die like whore in the Bible. I remember two thing. The party leader himself have to come down to save the policemen. And two, Josey is a man of the people now.

All nice and decent people, me tell you a lie still. You think me stop like how blood taste when me kill that high school boy, but that was just part of it. And just because me stop like use gun don't mean me did have a problem with how Josey did want to use him own, or even Tony Pavarotti, who never waste a bullet. But that Cuban man, that damn Cuban Doctor Love.

May 19. No, me don't forget the date. He and Josey Wales go to the Orange Lane tenement, sneaking around like rat. But this time they take me. Maybe they did think there was something for me to see and it wasn't just the boom. All the Cuban had with him was some white putty and some wire. But he find the one gas cylinder in the yard and stick the white putty on it. Or white bubble gum, and the second I think it's bubble gum me wonder what is this little pickney shit and why Josey Wales like it so bad that he almost jump up and down like school girl and, as the Cuban say, blow we cover. Then he stick two wire in the putty, two wire that is part of a coil that reel it out far over the fence.

When the place explode, one whole wall blow apart, and what don't blow apart catch fire from all the gas that spray. Josey had him gun ready for anybody who try to run out and for any fireman who try to run in. Me run from me hear the boom. I wonder if certain man look at me as a coward after that.

May, June and July, plenty tribulation did 'pon the city, brethren and sistren. War in Babylon spread to Spanish Town. The police learn a secret that did shut so tight that is the first time me telling all of you. We in Copenhagen City have we own hospital. We have it for years. The PNP didn't know. Shotta Sherrif didn't know, he did just think that Copenhagen City man hard to dead, that we invincible. Truth be that fi we hospital better than the rich people hospital up in Mona. Me no know who bust it, but the police find it in June. Them never know say we could treat gunshot better than any doctor in Jamaica. Me still don't find out yet who bust the secret, but he better hope me find him before Josey Wales. At least me will give him six hours to run. But here is something me didn't know until the damn newspaper tell me.

June was the first time in a long time police come right 'round to where me be and drag all of we out of jail. Me woman go to the door, but they kick it open and strike her in the face with a baton. Me about to say whoever do that dead tomorrow, but that would just give them reason to kill and they hungry for that reason for years now. Me only hear the door bust off the hinge and me woman scream. I run out of the bathroom to see fifteen machine gun already pointing at me. *Every single gun here hungry for a gunman, so give we a reason, pussyhole,* one of them say. This wasn't no police, this was soldier.

Soldier in brown-green uniform with plenty pockets and shiny black boots. Soldier don't act like we is crime and them is order, soldier act like we is enemy and this is war. They go through every one of the tenements and yards and even the community center and the reason is this: 'round the same time they find we hospital in Copenhagen, they find two cell in Rema that they use as prison. Rema gunman who supposed to answer to me, kidnap two man from the Eight Lanes and hold them for nine hours and beat them. That is what they tell the police who raid Rema and find the cell. Then they raid we and drag we out of we house, some of we still in brief, some of we cover up in nothing but towel. Me no mind Rema having cell to deal with a PNP youth who think him bad. And understand me again, me no want no ism or schism named communism in this yah country. Me no want no socialism, or communism or tribalism where PNP boy move in and take we space. But me have big problem with not knowing shit 'bout it.

The police take we to jail and lock we up for three days, long enough for we to overrun the cell with we own shit and manstink. One window in the cell and me sit by it but never say nothing. Not to Josey, not to Weeper, not to anybody. Me just see and wait. While me in jail two bombs explode in Elysium Gardens.

Doctor Love.

Alex Pierce

So this source, right? Tells me that the Singer might have been involved in a horse-racing scam at Caymanas Park some months ago. In Jamaica people have a way of saying that if shit didn't go down a certain way, then the truth is probably not far from it. *If it no go so it go near so.* I don't believe for a second that the Singer could be involved in any kind of scam, that's just fucking crazy. But I'm pretty sure someone is taking a shit and stinking up his own house. My source even told me that one afternoon, maybe couple weeks ago, the Singer came back from Fort Clarence Beach, which already made no sense since even I, a white man and the embodiment of Babylon, knows that he goes to Buff Bay every morning, like clockwork. Few people seemed to know why he went to Fort Clarence, which is curious. He went with some people who came for him, and only one of them did his own people recognize. Then he comes back home three hours later, so furious that his face was red the rest of the day.

Aisha left almost four hours ago, I think. I'm in the hotel room still on the bed and still looking at my belly. This whole fucking trip is a bust. I don't know what I'm doing here. I mean, I know what I'm doing here. I'm the equivalent of the *National Enquirer* scandal hunter for the rag that scooped the Daniel Ellsberg interview. But I'm worse than that, I'm the little lowlife that captions the photo of what some fuck with only one hit song was wearing in the studio. This whole job is just plain bogus. But maybe I should stop looking at my belly and focus. Besides, feeling sorry for oneself is so 1975. Something is coming, I can feel it. Maybe it's something in music, I don't know. I'm on my bed, smelling Aisha's perfume in the sheets and looking at the sun hitting the window when the phone rings.

—In the middle of something . . . or somebody? he says.

—Nice. Been working on that delivery all morning, huh?

—Haha. Fuck you too, Pierce.

Mark Lansing. At some point I need to find out how this cunt knew how to reach me.

—Nice day, isn't it? Isn't it a nice day?

—Looks like any other from this hotel window if you ask me.

—Hold the fucking mayo. You're still in bed? Working girl must have been one hot bitch. You, my man, need to have a better outlook on life.

For the life of me, I don't know if it's because I'm the only American here he knows or if he's under the seriously mistaken idea that we're buddies.

—What's shaking, Lansing?

—I was thinking about you this morning.

—To what do I owe that act of charity?

—Well, lots of things. I mean, you're pathetic, but I'm your friend, so I get to tell you that.

I want to tell him he's not my friend, that I wouldn't befriend him if he was all that could stop me from being buttfucked raw by Satan and his ten big-dicked demons, but he's in that one mode where he's actually interesting. When he needs you for something but is way too arrogant to ever come out and say it.

—So yesterday evening I'm in this room with the Singer—

—What room? What the fuck are you talking about, Lansing?

—I'd be much better able to talk about it without you fucking interrupting me, Pierce. What, your mom didn't have any Emily Post books when you were growing up?

—Raised by wolves, Lansing. Raised by wolves.

I'm tempted now to go way off topic, far into fucking space, because I know how much it annoys him when I don't pay attention to what he says.

—In fact I was only just now reflecting on how my mother did it, catching and killing her own meat. Seriously, speaking of Emily Post, I had an ex-girlfr—

—What the fuck, Pierce. I don't give a fuck about your fucking mother. Or your ex-girlfriend.

—You should. She was fine. Not your type, though.

Seriously, I could do this all day. I wish I was right in front of him to see his face get red.

—Pierce, seriously what the fuck, *hombre*?

Hombre? That's new. I should use it so that he'll think he just started some new slang or something, because "hold the mayo" is going fucking nowhere.

—You were saying about this morning. Your thoughts ran on me for some reason?

—What? Oh. Yeah. Yeah, this morning. Here I was, with some guy from *Newsweek*, yeah? And some chick from *Billboard*, and some other chick, yeah? I think she introduced herself as *Melody Maker*, yeah. They're all asking the Singer some questions about this peace concert, though his manager did most of the talking. Yeah, it was a conference at his house.

He's fucking lying. There's no way he could have had a press conference this morning without me knowing about it. And why is Lansing speaking cockney all of a sudden?

—Yeah, it was pretty quick so they probably didn't have time to contact you. But don't worry, my man. Some guy from *Rolling Stone* was there, or at least he said he was from *Rolling Stone*, which was odd. I mean, don't you work for those guys?

—This guy from *Rolling Stone*, did he say who he was?

—Fuck if I remember. The second I heard *Rolling Stone*, I immediately thought of my good buddy Alex Pierce.

—How nice of you. Buddy.

I'm trying to think of a polite way to get this asswipe off the phone so I can call my fucking boss to see if it's true. I could say that it's just like this turd Lansing to pull some shit like this. Like somebody with no friends, he never could gauge when a joke went too far or just wasn't fucking funny. But if this is true, it would be a new low for this fucking magazine, I swear to God. Shit. Fucking shit. So they leave the real journalism to . . . who the fuck knows? Robert Palmer? DeCurtis? Meanwhile they send me off to write about fucking Bianca Jagger filing her nails, while her husband records some reggae shit. I mean, if that's all they want from me, why not just send the fucking photographer, who by the way, I've yet to meet. Fuck this. Seriously, fuck this.

—And here I was thinking, this must blow for my buddy Alex, he just can't seem to get a break.

—What do you want, Lansing?

—To be called Mark, for one.

—Lansing, what do you want?

—I was thinking more about what *you* want, Pierce.

Thirty minutes later I'm under an umbrella by the poolside of the Jamaica Pegasus. White men in bikinis by the pool are fatter, and their wives are tanner, both of which means richer, especially given how many of these women are younger. I don't know who they are since Kingston is not really a touristy kinda place and everybody here is here on business. Lansing was so convinced he had something I wanted that I was sorta convinced too. Now I'm here wavering between *what the fuck, Alex,* and *maybe he actually has something I want.* Either way I'm curious.

And I'm waiting at the poolside of this hotel watching a man not paying attention to his two fat kids as they leap off into the pool belly first. The older one just hit the water with a slap that fucking echoed. I watch him wobbling to the side of the pool, wanting to cry so bad, his mouth twisting into it and he's huffing through his nose, but he looks around and sees me. Bad enough to cry while a stranger watches, but there's no way the little fat fuck is going to cry in front of his brother. I want to laugh at the little motherfucker but figure he should catch a break. Besides, I'm here waiting on this prick, thinking about what happened thirty minutes ago. Eleven a.m. December 3, 1976. The exact half hour I got fired from *Rolling Stone.* At least I think I was fired. It was like this. I got a phone call.

—Hello?

—What the fuck are you doing down there, Pierce?

—Hi, bossman. How's it shaking? The kids?

—You seem to overestimate the closeness of our relationship, Pierce.

—Sorry, boss. What can I do for you?

—You also seem to think I like wasting phone calls. Where's my fucking story?

—I'm working on it.

—Two hundred words on whether Mick fucking Jagger flew in to Jamaica with or without Bianca and you still can't get me a fucking story? How is this hard?

—I'm working an angle, boss.

—You're working an angle. Let me make sure I heard you right; you're working an angle. I didn't send you down there to run a fucking con, Pierce. I sent you down to put some shit together for a fucking photo essay that should have been on my desk days ago.

—Hey, boss, please listen to me. I'm, well, I'm sitting on something big here. Really big. Square biz, man.

—Quit with the fucking jive talk, Pierce, you're from Minnesota.

—That wounds me, seriously. But it's major. Some serious shit surrounding the Tuff G—

—Do you read the magazine you work for? We already did a story on him in March. I suggest you read it.

—With all due respect, boss, that story was a fucking piece of shit. I mean, come on, the guy was getting off on his fucking self. There's nothing in it about the Singer or what's really going on here. I'm meeting the son of the CIA boss in thirty minutes. Yeah, I just said CIA. I mean, some major Cold War shit is about to blow, boss, and—

—Did you hear a single thing I just said? One sec. Not Helvetica, anything but Helvetica, and for God's sake that pic of Carly Simon looks like Steven Tyler about to give a blow job. Alex?

—I'm here, boss.

—I said we already did him, and we already did Jamaica. If you wanna keep up with that shit and not do what I sent you down there to do, maybe you should give *Creem* a call.

—Oh, so it's like that. Well, well, maybe I will.

—Don't fuck with me, Pierce. Jackson says you haven't even spoken to him yet.

—Jackson?

—The fucking photographer, dipshit.

—Did you send somebody else down here?

—What are you talking about?

—You heard me. There's someone else here from *Rolling Stone.*

—Not on my watch, Pierce.

—Really, you wouldn't be sending some *real* journalist out here, now that you smell a story, would you?

—Jamaica has no fucking story. If somebody wants to go write a story on their own and not on my payroll, that's their fucking business. You, on the other hand, I'm paying for.

—So it's not a case of, this looks too big for Pierce, he's too green, so send in the pros.

—Green is not the color I think of when I think of you, Pierce.

—Really. What color would that be?

—A story with photos of Jagger squeezing some bitch's tits on my desk in two days or consider yourself fired.

—You know what? You know what? Maybe you should consider this to mean I quit.

—Not when I'm the one paying for your fucking trip, Pierce. But don't worry: as soon as you bring your corn-fed ass back to New York, I'll do myself the pleasure of firing you.

Then he hung up. So technically I'm fired, or at least I'm going to be. I'm still not sure how I feel about that. Jagger brought his wife with him? Or that blonde he's fucking around with? How's that gonna work with his manhunt for black pussy? It's weird, in all this I see Mark Lansing coming towards me. He's right over there looking exactly like that white man on the cover of the *How to Speak Jamaican Handbook.* Olive green cargo pants rolled up to the calf, black sneakers, and a red, green and gold wife beater that's already inched up off his belly button. Judging from how the wind keeps blowing it, a rag's hanging out of his back pocket. Jesus Christ, a Rasta tam on his head, with blond bangs hanging out. He looks like he just joined Fags Against Babylon or something. I really wished it bothered me more that I was out of a job.

—Earth to Alex Pierce.

Somehow he managed to throw himself into the chaise longue beside me, pull off his pants to show purple bikini trunks and order a mai tai without me even noticing a thing.

—A pack of smokes too, Jimbo. Marlboro, none of that Craven "A" shit.

—Sure thing right now, Mr. Brando.

The waiter skipped off. I try not to think that he's confirming my suspicion that every man in Jamaican tourism sucks cock.

—Alex, my boy.

—Lansing.

—That must have been some poontang you got last night if you're still daydreaming about it, mon. I yelled out your name three time, mon.

—Distracted.

—I'll say.

The waiter came back with his cigarettes.

—Hey, Jimbo, I asked for Marlboros. What's this Benson and Hedges shit? I look like some British fag to you?

—No, sir, magnificent apologies, sir, yes, sir, no Marlboros, sir.

—Fuck, I'm not paying for this shit.

—Yes, sir, Mr. Brando.

—Damn straight. And freshen up this fucking drink while you're at it. Taste like water with a hint of mai tai.

—Right away at once, apologies, Mr. Brando.

The waiter scooped up the mai tai and skipped off. Lansing turned around and smiled at me with this finally-we're-alone look.

—So, Lansing.

—Mark to my friends.

—Mark. Who the fuck is Brando?

—Who?

—Brando. That's the third time he called you that.

—I didn't notice.

—You didn't notice a man calling you the wrong name three times?

—Who the fuck can understand what these guys say half the time, right?

—Right.

Given who he is, the fact that he's using a fake name should have sent my conspiracy theory instinct into overdrive. But this is Mark Lansing. He's probably only now hearing of James Bond.

—So what's this about a press conference?

—More like a press briefing, really. I really thought I would see you there.

—Guess I'm not enough of a big shot.

—You'll get there.

Fuck you, purple-bikini-wearing asshole.

—Who's the dude from *Rolling Stone* that was there?

—Dunno. But he was asking a whole lot of questions about gangs and stuff. Like anybody wants to hear about that from the Singer.

—Gangs?

—Gangs. About some shoot-out in Kingston or some shit like that. I mean, seriously. Then he asked him how close he was to the Prime Minister.

—Really.

—Uh-huh. All I kept thinking is where is my buddy Alex?

—Nice of you.

—That's me. Nice. I can get you in. In fact I've been with him nearly every day this week. I'm so high that even a kite would go goddamn, Dicky. Met him a month ago when his label boss hired me to get a crew together to film this concert. Even brought him a pair of cowboy boots. A big shiny pair of brick red ones from Frye. Cuz you know, these Jamaicans, they love their cowboy movies. Fucking boots cost a fortune too, I hear.

—You didn't buy them?

—Fuck no.

—Who?

—So we got the exclusive rights to film the concert.

—They hired you to film the concert? Didn't know you were a cinematographer.

—There's lots about me you don't know.

—Clearly.

—You want a mai tai? It's a piece of shit but it's free.

—Nah, I'm fine. So what's the favor you're gonna do for me? And what do you want?

—You always this crass? Hey, where's my fucking drink? Look, buddy, I only want to help you out. Here's the thing. You want to get in with the Singer, right? You wanna be so up and close that it's only you and him?

—Well, yeah.

—I can make you part of my crew. You'll be the journalist or some shit.

—I am a journalist.

—See? You'll play along just fine. Brother, I have unprecedented access to the Singer. Nobody ever had that before and nobody ever will again, certainly no film crew. Hired by the label boss himself and we're to film everything. Hell, we could probably film him taking a shit or fucking that Libyan princess he's supposed to be schooling on mandingo sex. I'll film some of your interview for the doc, but you can use it for whatever you want.

—Wow. That sounds really cool, Mark, but why?

—You travel light, Pierce?

—Always. Easier to run.

—I got some extra luggage that I need someone to take back to New York.

—Why not just pay the extra money?

—I need it to get there before me.

—What?

—Look. I make you part of my crew. When you fly back to New York, you take one of my bags for me. Simple.

—Except nothing is ever simple. What's in the bag?

—Film stuff.

—You're giving me the Singer in exchange for a baggage tag.

—Yup.

—Appearances are deceiving, Lansing, I swear I only look like an idiot. Cocaine or heroin?

—Neither.

—Pot? You're shitting me.

—What? No, what the fuck, Alex? There'll be somebody to take that bag from you at JFK.

—What are you, the spy who came in from the cold?

—Rasta don't work for the CIA.

—Haha.

—Been watching too much James Bond, have we? The bag will contain footage.

—Of what?

—What the fuck you mean, of what? Of the doc. This thing is on rush order, buddy. His boss wants it to air the day after it's filmed. Right now as soon as we film it, we ship it.

—I see.

—I hope so. I don't trust strangers and those fuckers in customs will expose that film like the fucking idiots they are, unless somebody white explains it to them very carefully. You wanna come to 56 Hope Road tonight?

—What? Fuck yes.

—I can either pick you up or you can meet me at the gate.

—Pick me up. What time?

—Seven.

—Cool. Thanks, Mark. Really.

—No problemo. When you supposed to leave?

—End of the week, but I was planning on staying a little longer.

—Don't do that. Leave.

—Huh?

—Leave.

Nina Burgess

Three-thirty p.m. I checked the Timex. Just as I was about to leave the house for Hope Road, my mother dials me to say to come at once to the house. That's exactly what she said, come at once to the house. For some reason it made me think of Danny. Somewhere in the U.S. with a wife by now or at least a girlfriend who knows where he's coming from and who didn't give a moment's pause the first time he brought up oral sex. He must be married by now. I don't know what that means, the man that got away. One time I was cleaning up my parents' house because they went on a trip and I thought to surprise them. I'm arranging my father's fishing equipment in the back room when his tackle box fell. Inside it was a letter he wrote in red ink on yellow legal paper. *It took me thirty years to write this letter*, that's how he started it. The woman that got away is what I was thinking. Then I wondered if everybody has that person that haunts them, the one that got away.

On the radio news at twelve, the Women's Crisis Center was threatening to stage another walk for peace all dressed in black and carrying a coffin. Upper-middle-class women here love to feel they can cause drama, but they're just looking for shit to do. I'm not sure why I'm thinking all this stuff and it's way too early to try to find some big cosmic Carlos Castañeda thing to tie it all together. I was still shaking from cussing out my sister. I didn't shower even though I couldn't remember if I took one when I got home last night, excuse me, this morning.

I took a taxi to my parents' house thinking about what the embassy said when they turned down my visa a month ago. I didn't have enough ties, nothing in the bank account, no dependents, no gainful employment—yes they said "gainful"—nothing to reassure the American government that I won't disappear once I land in the big old USA. As I was leaving the embassy this fat man wearing a yellow shirt and a brown tie came up to me like he knew the look on my face. Before I could imagine the countless pathetic women who have come out of this same embassy with that same face, he asked me if I want a visa. I usually don't listen to that shit, until he opened his passport and I saw not only a visa but stamps from Miami and Fort Lauderdale airports. Him know a man who know a man who know one American in the embassy who could fetch me a visa for five thousand dollars. That was salary for half a year. I didn't have to give him the money until I saw the visa, only a passport-size photo, which I already had in my bag. I think about the news report a month ago about ten people shot. I don't know why I believed him but I did.

I didn't get to my parents' house until about one p.m. Kimmy opened the door. Wearing a dress. Except it wasn't one of her dawta jeans dresses or long skirts with dust all over the hem. A she-not-joking-good-girl purple dress with no sleeves, a sheath they call it, as if she's just about to do the interview section of a beauty contest. No shoes. She behaving like the little girl in the house. She didn't say a thing to me and I certainly wasn't about to say anything to her, even though I had to bite my lip to not ask if Ras Trent deh 'pon the premises. She opened the door looking away the whole time, as if she was only letting in a cool breeze. She can kiss me ass, is what me thinking. And it's getting easier and easier to think it. Let's hope this is just my mother asking me to go get her prescription at the pharmacist who dishes out an extra few pills or something, one of those things she never asks Kimmy to do.

My mother is usually crocheting or cooking whenever I visit. But today she's sitting in the red velvet armchair my father sits in whenever *Dad's Army* is on. She's looking away from me even though I said hello twice.

—Mummy, you tell me to come over here. What can't wait?

She still isn't looking at me, just pressing her knuckles into her lips. Kimmy is at the window walking back and forth, not looking at me either. I'm surprised she didn't just jump at me saying that it's not like Mummy is taking me away from anything important. There's a new crochet on the coffee table, probably from Mummy working all night. Pink thread and my mother hates pink. She also usually crochets into some animal-shaped thing and this doesn't look like anything I recognise. She crochets mostly when she's nervous now and I wonder if something happened. Maybe she saw one of the men who attacked her, maybe it was the gardener next door and maybe they feel somebody is watching the house. Maybe they came back and stole something and threatened my parents to not say shit to the police. I don't know, but her being nervous is making me nervous and Kimmy hovering around like she couldn't do anything about it until I came makes it feel even worse. I look around right then to see if anything is out of place. Not that I would know if it was. Kimmy is pacing and pacing.

—Kimmy, stop moving up and down like some damn monkey, my mother says.

—Yes Mummy, she says. I want to repeat it like a teasing six-year-old. Yes Mummy my ass. The way Kimmy jumps back ten years to make her parents baby her, you'd almost think she was a son and not a daughter.

—And my own daughter. Jesus Christ. Jesus Christ.

—Mummy?

—Talk to your father.

—About what?

—I said talk to your father.

—Talk to Daddy about what? I say that to her, but I look at Kimmy, who is now making a show of not looking at me.

—Even a coolie would have been better but . . . My God . . . it's so nasty I can smell it on you.

—What you talking about, Mummy?

—Don't you dare raise your voice at me! Don't you dare raise your voice in this house. All those years of bathing and I still couldn't wash the slut out of you. Maybe you should have get more beating. Maybe I should have just beat it out of you.

I'm standing now. I still don't know what you talking about, I say. She is still not looking at me. Kimmy finally looks around and tries to give me a blank stare, but she can't hold it. She looks away.

—So you're a whore now or just his whore?

—I'm not a whore. What the hell—

—Don't swear in my damn house. I heard all about you being the whore for that damn singer in his house. How much he paying you? All these months you not having decent work I'm here wondering, How is Nina getting by without gainful employment? How, since she not asking for money and she don't have any friends—

—I have plenty friends—

—Don't interrupt me in me damn house. I buy this damn thing with me and Mr. Burgess' money.

—Yes, Mummy.

—Pay for it cash with no damn mortgage either, so don't think you can back talk me in my own house.

My hands are trembling like I just spent three hours in a deep freeze. Kimmy starts to walk to the door.

—Kim-Marie Burgess, you keep your backside quiet. Tell your sister how it's the big news clearly that she's debasing herself with that, that Rasta.

—Debasing myself? Debasing myself. Kimmy has a Rasta boyfriend.

—You comparing him with what you're wasting your privates on? At least he's from a good family. And he's going through a phase. A phase.

—A phase? Like what Kimmy is going through.

—I swear every time I think of you and that singer, in some nasty bed smoking weed and getting pregnant, I want to vomit. You hear me, I want to vomit. You is such a nasty little girl, I bet you just bring all sort of head lice into my house.

—Mummy.

—All those years of schooling to become what? One of him woman? That is what high school education provide for these days?

Now she's sounding like Daddy and I wonder where he is. Kimmy. She did it. My mother is shaking so hard that when she gets up she falls back down in the chair. Kimmy rushes to help her like a good daughter. She told them. She told them something. And she knows me too. She knows I'm not going to tell them about her because one bad daughter would depress my mother, but two would finish her off. She's counting on me to be the good daughter who will take anything and she's right. I'm almost impressed by the bitch.

—All I can think of is you bringing that ganja smell and frowsy arm into my house. I can smell him on you. Disgusting. Disgusting.

—Oh? And you can't smell it on your other daughter?

—Don't bring poor Kimmy into this.

—Poor Kimmy? So she can sleep with Rasta.

—Don't you dare get impertinent in here! This is a God-fearing house.

—God know that is nothing but hypocrite in here? Kimmy get to mess with Rasta—

—He is not a Rasta.

—Go tell him that. In fact go tell your daughter that and see if she stay with him.

—From when you were a young girl you always going after your sister. All this hatred and envy for what? We never treat one of you better than the other. And yet you just have that nasty streak in you. I should have beat it out, that's what I should have do, beat it out.

—Oh yeah. And when nasty man was beating that jewellery and savings out of you, you did like that?

—Don't talk to my mother like that, Kimmy say.

—You shut you r'asscloth, you little bitch. Like say you good.

—Don't talk to your sister like that.

—You always take her side.

—Well, I need one daughter who is not a slut. Even a coolie wouldn't be so bad.

—Your damn daughter fucking a Rasta too!

—Morris! Morris, come down here and talk to your daughter. Get her out of my house! Morris! Morris!

—Yeah, you call Daddy. Call him so that I can tell him 'bout your little favourite little girl right here.

—You shut up, Nina. You already do this family enough damage.

—I'm the one saving this damn family.

—I don't remember asking any of my children to save anything. I don't want no damn room in some Rasta compound with no wife sharing and little children smoking ganja. Morris!

I want to grab something and fling it at Kimmy who still has not looked at me once. You're probably already carrying one of his children already, my mother says. She sounds like she's crying but no tears are running down. Kimmy is rubbing her back. She's thanking Kimmy for helping her poor mother through all of this. I'm done. There is nothing left to say. There is nothing to do but wait for my mother to say something. I thought I would want to just go over there and grab Kimmy by the neck but I watch her rubbing my mother's and feel sorry for both of them. But then she says,

—Mummy, tell her about the waiting outside his gate.

—What? Oh my God, now she's waiting outside his house like some lady of the night. Even he now realizes she's trash. Lord, look what me family coming to.

—You fucking bitch, I say to Kimmy, who looks at me blank.

—I said I don't want such language in my house. If you can't helping being a damn slut at least try to not talk like one when you're in my house.

I want to say, And what about the slut that's now rubbing your back? How no matter what Kimmy fucking says or do, they always have an excuse or justification for it as if they have been back-stocking on excuses from the day she was born and can pull one without a second's notice? I want to say it, but I don't. Kimmy knows I won't. Kimmy knows I'm the good daughter who'll stay good even when it's worse for me. I'm almost impressed by how much I underestimated her. I'm almost impressed by how far she has gone and will more likely still go. I want to say that at least no man will ever beat me and leave me to think it's just a strike for the struggle but I don't. Instead my heart is pumping and I can only think of grabbing a knife, a dull one, a dinner knife, and walking to her with it in my hands, not stabbing her or cutting her, just have her see me coming and there is nothing she can do about it. Here I was in this fucking house with people I spent all day with yesterday, standing like a goddamn fool for something that I don't even want to do anymore. I bet Kimmy is happy. She gets to take goody goody Nina down a peg.

—Down there not scratching you with all that lice? It not biting you down there? How can you even stand there? Dear Lord, what kind of nasty daughter me have? I want to vomit. Kimmy, I want to vomit.

—Is alright, Mummy. I'm sure she don't have no lice.

—How you know? Them Rastaman nasty you know. I don't care how much money he think him have. They is all just nasty and chupid. Stand twenty feet away you can smell them coming.

—No, it not scratching with lice. Him did smell better than baby powder, I say and regret before the last syllable comes out of my mouth. I want to grab Kimmy and just shake her. Just shake her hard like a damn baby who won't be quiet.

—Morris! Morris! I don't want no damn nasty Rasta bastard pickney, you hear me? I don't want no Rasta pickney in me house.

I look at Kimmy and wonder if this is what she wanted, if she didn't realise it would get like this. My parents get attacked and she stays aways, not because she can't deal with them being attacked but she can't deal with any situation that she's not the center of, even tragedy. Well, good for her. She wins. She knows I'm not going to say that she fucked him too. She knows I will trying to keep the sanity she's dead set on taking away from her mother. I almost admire just how devious the bitch is. I want her to look at me and smile just to show that she knows that I know that she knows. My mother keeps shouting, Morris! Morris! Like it's a magic spell where he supposed to appear.

The leather strap tears across my back, the tip landing at my neck like a scorpion just stung me. I scream but the strap slice across my back again and then two times on the back of my leg and I fall. My father grabs my left ankle and yanks me to him, my skirt pulls up and my panties are showing. He grabs me with his left hand and beat me with his belt. I'm screaming and Mummy's screaming and Kimmy's screaming. And he's beating me like I'm ten. And I screaming for Daddy to stop and all he's saying is damn girl need discipline I going discipline you in the bombocloth house no Daddy please Daddy discipline discipline and he beats my bottom and beat it again again and I twist and the belt cuts my right thigh and he's swinging and don't care where he hit my knuckle when I try to grab the big leather belt with all the rivet because he love cowboy belts and I can smell my welts and screaming Daddy Daddy Daddy and Mummy screaming Morris Morris Morris and Kimmy just screaming and the belt cutting all over me I twist and it hit me right in me pussy and I scream and Daddy saying discipline and discipline and discipline and he kicked me I know he kick me and he's swinging and I'm struggling let go of me foot let go off me foot let go off me foot and I swing 'round and my right foot kicks him in the chest and it feel like an old man chest and he falls right back and coughs but it's only the air not the sound and I still screaming no words just naaaaaah naaaah naaah and I grab the belt and I go over him and I swing it on his legs and I beat him beat the son of a bitch, beat him beat him beat naaaah naaaah naaah naaaaah and my mother scream again don't kill me husband don't kill me husband and he's coughing and I see that I was beating him with the buckle not the strap and turn and I tighten the belt around my knuckles and I look at Kimmy.

Barry Diflorio

My *secretary came back* to me saying that Louis Johnson's secretary had no idea where he went, which was her code for saying that she wasn't telling. I had to get up from my own damn chair and walk down the corridor to this woman's desk to ask if she enjoyed working here and plans to do so in the future. And should she plan to, then it was best to remember that she works for the Federal Government of the United States of America, not Louis Johnson. I could see her eyes widen even within the huge frames of her pink Batgirl glasses, and her forehead wrinkle even though that severe, car-grease ponytail didn't fucking budge. Takes years in the embassy to learn to not look scared and she was almost there, almost, but you could tell she hadn't quite yet figured out how to gauge the level of threat lying in the passive-aggressive remark from a superior. She couldn't tell if I was fucking with her or not. Liguanea Club, Knutsford Boulevard.

I've been there of course. Reminded me of the Gentlemen's Rodeo Club in Buenos Aires and certain clubs in Ecuador, Barbados and South Africa. Liguanea Club at the very least had dark-skinned people and quite a few Arabs doing the let's-pretend-we're-white thing which just never gets old. I leave the office and drive straight out onto Oxford Road where people are still waiting, in the sun, for visas, and head west. At the intersection of Oxford Road and Knutsford Boulevard I turn right, heading north. The guard at the gate takes a look at the white man in the car and doesn't ask questions. The green Cortina is at the end of the parking lot. I park at the other end, even though I'm sure that Louis doesn't know what car I drive.

Inside, the dining room was packed with white men dressed in suits on lunch break and beautiful brown women in tennis skirts drinking rum and Cokes. I heard them before I saw them, Louis throwing his head back then slapping de las Casas. Of course it was him. At first I wanted to go over there and ask Louis what the fuck was up, and do it in front of de las Casas. God, I hate that guy. He has this thing about him I only see in beauty queens and politicians. This "of all my mother's kids I love me best" kinda thing. He thinks he's a revolutionary, but he's really just an opportunist. Louis and Luis, now there's a comedy sketch waiting to happen.

I'm at the far end of the bar trying to not look like I'm looking over. Somewhere, someone is writing a spoof of a spy novel and I'm the idiot at the bar trying to be James Bond. Hell, if I'm going to do this maybe I should order a martini. They both get up and I suddenly realize that they may have to pass me to get to the parking lot. Johnson walks over to the open archway a few feet from his table and the Cuban follows. Outside in the lot his car driving out. I'm on the road in seconds, his car still only a couple hundred feet away. Thank God rush hour is rush hour everywhere in the world.

I haven't had to follow a car since working with Adler in Ecuador. Yes I'm too old for adrenaline, but damn if it doesn't take you over anyway. I really like this. I mean, I really, really like this. Maybe I should translate all this energy down to my cock and fuck, well, somebody.

Louis makes a left on Trafalgar Road into more traffic, then turns left again. A hundred or so yards down on a road I don't know. Then he goes south, cuts across Half Way Tree Road, and before I know it, I'm in the ghetto. Or at least, the houses have gotten smaller and the road more narrow, and more and more roofs are just zinc sheets held down with bricks. Cement walls have turned to zinc with graffiti about the fuckery PNP, blackheart men, "Under Heavy Manners" and Rastafari. If I focus on them, on the green Cortina, I never have to think about how fucking bonkers this is, me a white man driving through what must be the blackest ghetto in Kingston. Half Way Tree is rough too, but I have never seen this. The thought comes that I might not know my way back, but I swallow it. They've picked up speed, I want to kick the gas but some little girl in a blue uniform might run out into the road at any minute.

Louis knows these roads. He's come down here before. He comes down here a lot, I think. I didn't even notice that my foot had pressed down on the gas, but I can hear my own car, see my hand twist the steering all of a sudden and the car swinging left, then first right, then over an exposed manhole. The car is hopping over bumps, jumping, tearing, screeching. The green car in sight, out of sight, vanishing around a corner only to appear when I skate around, behind three or four cars. God, I hope he's not trying to lose me. I almost said "give me the slip." I could feel it coming but I didn't.

We're on some sort of highway now, another stretch I have never seen. The houses are even smaller, zincer, poorer, and the people outside are heading where the green car is going. They look like hills rising on both sides of the road. It's not until twenty or so feet away that I see what they are. Mountains and mountains of garbage—not mountains, dunes and dunes like the Sahara just switched out sand for junk and smoke. The smoke is sour and thick, like animals are burning as well. People are climbing all over the garbage dunes, even the burning ones, digging through the junk and stuffing whatever in black plastic bags. I almost forget the green car.

Minutes pass. The garbage dunes go on forever, and the trail of people stuff junk into their black bags. The green car has disappeared. I stop the car, not quite knowing what to do. Two boys with bags run across the road right in front of me and my right hand reaches for the dashboard. Maybe I should take the gun out, at least keep it in my lap. My heart should stop pounding in a few. What the fuck am I doing here? Then two more boys pass, then a woman, then several women, then a trail of men and women and boys and girls passing in front and behind the car, the men and women shuffling, the boys and girls skipping and jumping, everybody carrying black bags to the other side. Someone bumps the car and I jump, punching the glove compartment so that the lid drops open and I can grab the gun.

God knows how many minutes had passed before I hit the gas again. The road is still clear, but it's the highway, with nothing but rocks to one side of the road and sea to the other. Only one car passes, a white Datsun with a driver who sticks his head out when he sees me, a black man with Chinese-looking eyes. I could have sworn he scowled, which is weird since I don't know the man from Adam. I don't get past a turn on the left before the green car shoots out of nowhere and rams straight into me. My forehead hits the steering wheel and my neck whiplashes into the headrest. The Cuban is out first, at least I think it's the Cuban. He races over to my car, his gun drawn, and shoves it right under my jaw.

—Wait, I know him. He's one of yours, he says.

—Who the fuck? Diflorio? What the fuck? Diflorio, what's the big idea following me?

They insist on taking me to the hospital even though there is nothing wrong with me. At Kingston Public Hospital, the doctor stitches up my forehead as I try to ignore the crowd of people inside and the streaks of blood and whatever else on the floor. The doctor didn't bother to take his surgical mask off. I really want to leave, but I have no memory of how I got there, not even after I see Louis Johnson out by reception sitting beside an old black woman and reading the paper.

—Where's my car?

—Sweetie all stitched up? Baby all better?

—My car, Johnson.

—Dunno, back in the ghetto somewhere. They probably scrapped it totally by now.

—Funny, Johnson. Real funny.

—Las Casas drove behind me, took it to the embassy. It's fine. You'll have some explaining to do to the wife, but it's not totaled or anything.

—What the fuck, Johnson.

—What can I say, sweetie, I see I'm being followed, I decide that I don't dig that kind of shit. And next time, should you decide on this course of action again, at least do a better fucking job of it. Not a lot of Volvos come charging through the ghetto. Did you even know where you were? Let's go.

We're heading back to the embassy on roads I don't recognize. At least I think we're heading back to the embassy. I wish I had my gun.

—You told some black guy to look out for me? I say.

—No, but Luis probably did. White Datsun?

—Yeah.

—Same one.

—Who is he?

—You know, Diflorio, I respect what you do.

—Really now.

—Yeah, that shit Adler and you pulled off in Ecuador was pretty neat. Slow as shitting molasses, but neat all the same.

—You don't know shit about what I did in Ecuador.

—Not only do I know what shit got down in Quito, I also know this is not fucking Quito.

—Meaning?

—Your silly little letter-writing campaign doesn't count for jack shit in a country where most people can't fucking spell communist.

By letter writing he means the letters that I fed the press warning people about the communist threat in Ecuador. And the ones from the "communist party" endorsing the Rector of Quito Central University, to scare people away from voting for him, a success. By letter writing he means the flyers I created for the Young People Liberation Front, a communist organization I created by simply taking out a half-page ad in the newspaper, and having two youngish-looking agents who spoke Spanish set up as leftist exiles from Bolivia, in case anybody wanted to meet. We eventually demoralized the Student Communist movement by tipping the military police every time they met. By letter writing he means the Anti-Communist Front that I created and the 340 people I recruited for training back home on how to recognize and defuse the communist menace, because I've been to Hungary and it is a fucking communist menace. By letter writing he's talking about what it took to get Arosemana elected as well as thrown out once he became the inevitable nuisance Latin Americans become when you give them just a hint of power. All the while keeping this shit out of the *New York Times* when men like Johnson and Carlucci were fucking up the Congo. He has some fucking nerve.

—Don't think I don't respect your soft tactics, Diflorio, or you for that matter. But this ain't Ecuador. Not even close.

—Soft tactics. Could've used some softness in the Congo.

—Congo is fine.

—Congo's a mess. It's not even the Congo.

—It's not communist.

—Of course.

—You a patriot, Diflorio?

—What? Of course. What a fucking question.

—Well. That makes one of us. I just get the job done.

—Is this the part where you tell me that it's for the thrill of it? That you would do it for free?

—No, the pay's pretty good too. Patriot. Shit. Your problem is that you believe the bullshit from your own government.

—You think you have me all figured out, don't you? Every single letter that comes to Jamaica from Cuba, China or the Soviet Union, and every letter from here that goes out there hits my desk first. I've got a man in every leftist organization in this fucking country that even fucking Bill Adler couldn't fish out. You're no different from the twelve fucking idiots he called out.

—How so?

—All you do is fuck up. If guys like you didn't fuck up, guys like me wouldn't be needed in the first place. Right now I just compiled a Subversive Control Watch List that just made Bush very happy. How's your report card, Johnson? I see you got the fucking-around-with-terrorists part down pat.

—Haha, Doctor Love told me about you.

—Oh, that's what he's calling himself these days? He and his dumb-asshit Cuban rich boys who thought they could start some counter-revolution just because their papas could buy them little guns. Had they left Cuba to people like me instead of people like him, there'd be a McDonald's in Havana by now.

—Bravo. Except for one thing, Diflorio. You're under the impression that you can do this alone. You and your kind, the fucking accountants. Motherfuckers like you don't know shit about what happens at ground level. And that's fine. Just stop kidding yourself that you don't need men like me.

—Remarkable.

—And what's your last big project, Diflorio? A fucking coloring book, that's what. A fucking coloring book that—

—Gotta start them young, asshole.

—Page six: My daddy says we're in democracy and not totalitarian state, now color the letters CCCP.

—Fuck you.

—Hey, I for one think anti-communist coloring books are the bee's knees. Just perfect for a country where most of the population can't read.

—That was a fucking stoplight, Johnson.

—Scared?

—Annoyed. Tired too. Where are you going?

—Figured you'd want to go home.

—Take me back to the office.

He looks at me and laughs.

—Maybe you should go home. I still can't figure you guys out, Diflorio. You're just like Carlucci. You and him, the Kissinger boys.

—Don't tell me what to do, Johnson. Seriously, you're something else.

—This the part where you tell me I'm a loose cannon?

—No, this is the part where I tell you to keep your eyes on the road and not on me.

—What do you know, Diflorio?

—More than you think, Johnson.

—Did you know that certain cultural elements here are trying to form their own party? Not the leftists, not the Jamericans, not the church, not the communists. A group totally different. This country is going to end the year in fucking chaos unless somebody does something. By chaos I mean as defined by your boss Kissinger.

—Kissinger is not my boss.

—And Jesus isn't the way, the truth, and the light. You're bookkeeping, Diflorio. You're here for the corner office, and that's fine. Somebody's gotta balance the books and print pretty coloring books, but that's not what gets things done on the ground. Did you know we nearly had him two days ago? Almost had the fucker on a slab of concrete? Almost got the commie motherfucker.

—What stopped you from getting him?

—Don't pretend you know who I'm talking about.

—Who then, Johnson?

—Shit. You really don't know shit. The Prime Minister.

—Don't shit me, asshole.

—The Prime Minister Michael Joshua fucking Manley. We almost got him. Wednesday, probably about four-ish. The PNP sets up this meeting in Old Harbour, you know where that is, right? Anyway, it's just another of their meetings about the violence problem, because these fuckers just love to meet. By the way, we're still waiting on the transcript, but word was Manley was taking phone calls from Stokely Carmichael and Eldridge Cleaver all week. Anyway, for some reason, an argument breaks out and this army guy—we need to get his name—fucking decks the party secretary. Straight punch right in the face. So Mr. Prime Minister finally moseys in and tries to question the officer who basically tells him to kiss his ass. Manley doesn't want to back down but before he knows it he's surrounded by soldiers, every single one pointing a loaded weapon. There they were in Old Harbour, soldiers drawing guns on the Prime Minister of the fucking country. But of course they backed down and nobody took the shot.

—Wow. That's a pretty amazing story. Throw in a love interest and you've got Hollywood gold. Explain to me why we Americans would have wanted to get him? There's no directive to terminate the Prime Minister or any other politician in this country. This isn't Chile, Johnson. I may be a bookkeeper, but you're just a plain thug. Your tactics always amount to shit that men like me then have to mop up.

—Whatever works—

—Listen, you're under no directive to terminate anybody, do you hear me?

—I'm not terminating anybody, Diflorio. The Company does not, has not and will never work with nor condone the acts of any terrorist individual or organization. Besides, as you've said, this isn't Chile.

I want to say that I'm glad he sees it that way, and that these are delicate matters that have to be handled delicately so as to leave as little trace or collateral damage as possible, but then he says,

—Nope, not Chile, but it's sure gonna be like Guatemala in a few days, mark my word.

—What? What did you say?

—You heard me.

—No.

—Yep. This one's bigger than you, I'm afraid, bigger than the Company, so don't tell me about your fucking orders.

—No.

—Yep.

—Jesus Christ. You forget they sent me to Guatemala for a few months to observe the election. Around the same time those pocket psychopaths with our ammo started killing everything in their midst. How long have you been training them?

—Not in the training biz. But unconfirmed reports would say a year.

—The Cuban. He's—

—You're not as slow on the uptake as people make you out.

—How many?

—Come on, Diflorio.

—How many, you son of a bitch.

—I'm not in the intel business, Diflorio. But if I were, I would guess more than ten, less than two hundred? Got another team of patriots in Virginia. Remember Donald Casserley?

—Jamaica Freedom League. Hit us up for cash once, for his little organization. Which we refused to pay because he's a fucking dope dealer. What's this? Second chance for Bay of Pigs flunkies? And with an election in thirteen days.

—Diflorio taking the long view. Look at that. It's not like Guatemala, since they're smart, and it's not like Brazil, since they have no desire to rule the fucking country.

—Who the fuck is your target?

—I don't know what you're talking about, Diflorio. If a bunch of men want to, say, get their feet wet, say, today, it's not my business to interfere in domestic affairs.

—Holy shit, you mean today?

—Not privy to that kind of intel, Barry, but if I were—

—Call them off, Johnson. Do it now, for God's sake.

—I wouldn't know who to call, sorry. My educated guess would be that it's too late anyway. Besides, it's the policy of the federal government of the United States to—

—Blow it out of your fucking ass, Johnson.

—I'll take you home to your beautiful wife.

—Louis, listen to me. I don't know if you're NSA, WRO or whoever the fuck it is you work for, but step the fuck back and let diplomacy run its course.

—Bang-up job in Ecuador, by the way.

—Shut the fuck up and listen to me. We've already invested, damn it. This administration knows it. The CIA director knows it. Seriously, who the fuck are you talking to? We've invested over ten million a full year before this election. Sal at the *New York Times*, the thirty fat fucks in the JLP, Jesus Christ, the Private Sector Organisation of Jamaica.

—Why are you schooling me on this, Barry? We're two sides of the same coin.

—I'm nothing like you.

—Even if those two sides never see each other.

—We're so fucking close, you son of a bitch.

—I'm not the son of a bitch you need to be telling this to, Diflorio, that would be your little boyfriend Georgie Bush. Besides, it's too fucking late, that's what I'm telling you. Go home, go watch *Starsky & Hutch*. Go watch the news tonight. Gonna be something.

Papa-Lo

Me can't remember when last me walking so fast and get anywhere so slow. Maybe is the sun working against me, she's one cantankerous burning bitch today. When me ask Josey if him did know anything about Operation Werewolf, he did shake him head and say no. But Wang Gang have explosive and only two people work with the Cuban. Them and Josey.

Here is what me was thinking. With him controlling the east and me carrying the swing in the west and maybe Tony Pavarotti keep him gun aiming at the north and the sea to the south, then we well protected. But with every man scatter to points like a map, right hand start to not know what left hand done do. Me thinking this is my fault. It have to be my fault. If the body sick, the head should did know first. No so the story go? Me and Josey stop talk. No is not that. A man, no, certain men come between all of we, man who use we then throw we out like rubbish. Me getting tired of the wicked game, and Shotta Sherrif getting tired of it too. What a funny thing that me sure of the mind of Shotta Sherrif more than me sure of the mind of Josey Wales. Me is ninety yard from Josey house.

The world now feeling like the seven seals breaking one after the other. Hataclaps or ill feeling, something in the air. Two sevens clash in less than thirty days. I walking to Josey house and I forget what my woman looks like. Is only a minute it take me to remember but it scare me that I forget her face. But then I remember a little girl, that look like she, but we don't have no pickney yet, even though plenty woman out there saying they boy and girl answer to my surname. I walking up the road and passing yard after yard. One tenement then the next tenement then the next, all four floors high, fence high enough to hide the ground floor, one building pink then the next green then the next the colour of bone I can't even remember who make we go with them colours, maybe the woman them. Me is seventy yard from Josey house.

When a father turn away from him son, he can't act shock when the son don't know him no more. Not that Josey is me son, he would shoot me if me even call him boy. But is my fault, me turn away from him because me carrying things that I used to think he can't carry. That some people do nothing but dream and some people do nothing but act and that both good and bad. People like Josey have no vision, people like me have no drive. I've been thinking and I've been talking and I've been showing people a new reasoning that is just about we and only we. No politician and no government. A different kinda system better than the shitstem, where gun too heavy to carry so nobody carry any and where my woman and him woman and everybody woman don't work no more just to get they boss richer. You wake up wanting new because old is so old that it don't even stink anymore, it just blowing away like dry rot. Fifty yard from Josey house.

I want to leave him house with me and him of the same mind. Nice and decent people, the Rastafarian show me the way. The first way Babylon fool we is to get we to think we have future in the Babylon shitstem. And me tired of that and Shotta Sherrif tired of that and the Singer tired of that. Every time me go to the Singer house and me see that man from Copenhagen City and man from the Eight Lanes can par and reason, I just start to think that a triangle have three side, but everybody always only look at two. Forty yard from Josey house.

I know what Josey planning. Plenty people going dead before it happen for real. Josey and Doctor Love. Josey and the American. Josey and Peter Nasser. There is no way the PNP can get 'way with this election. A PNP win is hataclaps for the island. The American say that we is all that stand between peace and chaos, plenty and starvation. But Jamaicans can be fool, they can be really fool. Poor people already know suffering. If PNP win, then PNP-bad become PNP-worse. But still. Still I have to wonder 'bout the level of bangarang a man going to perpetrate when he won't even tell me about it. When too many people in the mix don't look like and don't sound like we. Twenty yard from Josey house.

Ten yard from Josey house a line of bullet blast across the dirt one two three four five six seven eight and cut me off. Three jeep jump out of the lanes and drive around me and kick up dirt like white people tornado. The dust rise and rise and thicken and tighten. The trucks still driving 'round and 'round but me can only hear them, the dust making me blind. Is not before it clear when me see that all of them already jump out of the truck, policeman and army man, all with machine gun draw, some pointing at me, some aiming at the street, searching up and down for one idiot to scratch the itch to fire. I searching too. This never happen, even the baddest of Babylon know that the only way to get into Copenhagen City is to sneak through a loose gap or a uncork hole, like the sewage. Police know better than to set foot in here. Especially after what them get the last time. Soldier prefer to go back at a vantage where they can pick we off one by one like fly. I searching too, because my men supposed to be out with firepower ready long before any jeep reach Copenhagen City. But every house door shut. Josey not coming out. Josey not there. Tony Pavarotti not guarding the north. The place look like them town in Clint Eastwood movie that bandits empty out.

Two soldier in green and two policeman, one in blue and the other in khaki and sunglasses, walk towards me.

—What the bombocloth this is, eh? me say to the khaki police.

—H'is your name Papa-Lo? him say. He tall and his belly plumb out front like a pregnant lady.

—Who the r'asscloth?

—Oi, me look like hi love fi repeat when me h'address known criminal element? Hi's say h'if you be the man them call Papa-Lo.

—You sound like you don't know.

—Yow, me look like hi 'ave no time for no stinking ghetto boy?

He look right past me and nod two time. I catch it too late to duck before the soldier behind me ram the rifle butt in me head back. Him must did hit me again, because I hear two clap and me head get woozy, I can't hold on to even the next word that was about to come out of me mouth. My knees drop me. I didn't want them to, me fight for them to stand back up but they wouldn't stand me back up. The police and soldiers move in 'pon me. Them kick up so much dust that me never see the boots coming before they an inch from me face. Them kick up me face and work down to me belly and batty and balls before somebody yell that they need him alive.

Two time me wake up, two time them knock me back out. Third time me wake up, me rise from a cot and see the three stone wall of a jail cell.

Alex Pierce

F*or some reason* it just gives me the willies, riding shotgun down Hope Road with Mark Lansing. Motherfucker can't drive to save his life, at least not in Jamaica. So we made it all the way to Hope Road from New Kingston driving in the center of the street because he just couldn't hang left. Still, he's got balls of a brass monkey telling all these Jamaicans to go fuck themselves when they honked at him. Me, I just sunk in the seat, half not wanting anybody to see me in a car with Mark Lansing—not that anybody would recognize me—and half hoping that if anybody shoots the slug will hit him first. It's seven p.m. Work is over for most of Kingston, and the road is packed bumper to bumper, horns screaming like they're continuing the cussing match everybody was having before they got into their cars.

A siren suddenly goes off and everybody but Mark swerves out of the way.

—Get out of the way, Mark.

—Fuck that shit, let them swerve.

—Mark, without going into the history lesson why some Jamaicans would only be too happy to kick a white man's ass.

—They can try—

—Move the fuck over, Lansing.

—Fine, fine, sheesh, you really need to chillax, brother.

I'm in the car with Greg fucking Brady. The sad thing is Mark probably learned this lame shit from Greg Brady. Every single thing this guy does just screams little penis.

The ambulance dashes past and in a move that is shocking one second then absolutely inevitable less than a second later, Mark swings out and dashes after it. I like to keep track of the moments when I'm genuinely speechless and not when I just say that for dramatic effect. He's grinning like an idiot too, stunned that he hit on a brilliant idea. Four cars are behind us with the same idea. I see us coming to the Singer's huge double gate. I mean, I don't see it, but I know it's just a block away. Lansing grabs the wheel and swerves into the driveway, making such a sharp right that the tires screech and the car behind him shouts *Suck yuh mother.*

—Up yours, brother.

We're outside the Singer's gate. It's too dusky but I can see a tree out front, almost blocking the front door. The top floor looks like it's standing on top of the tree from here. Lansing honks twice and goes to honk a third time when I put my hand over the damn horn. He scowls, gets out of the car and walks over to the side of the gate to get the guard's attention. The guard doesn't even bother to get up. I'm not sure he's even talking until I hear Lansing say that he's supposed to fucking park inside, what the fuck do you mean do you know who you're talking to I'm shooting the big man right now today and fuck you if you think I'm not coming in. The guard isn't nearly as loud, in fact it still looks like he's not saying anything.

—Assholes. They're not letting any cars in unless you're family or band. Motherfuckers.

Lansing drives over to the apartment building facing the Singer's house and parks in somebody's clearly marked parking space. I get out of the car with him, not even bothering to point it out. He's not taking his camera. This is funny, watching him stomp and fume like he's about to give somebody a good talking-to. Jamaicans are so unflappable, they might as well be Minnesotans. They're probably laughing all the way till he gets to the gate.

—Happy now? he says to the guard. I'd say I don't recognize him, but honestly I can't tell these guards apart. The guard gives him a look from toe to head and opens the gate.

—Not you, only one, he says to me and I step back.

—Just wait there, Pierce. I'll get clearance from the big guy.

—Yeah. It's been real, Mark.

—Just wait there.

He heads for the front door then turns left and disappears. I can't see where he went. The guard looks at me and I look at him. I light a Rothmans and hand him the pack. He takes one and hands it back to me. Neither of us is taking this as some sort of connection. But at least he doesn't mind me leaning against the gate. I can hear the band stopping and starting, guitar most of all. Damn me for stereotypes, but I thought I would have heard bass and drums first. I heard that the new guys in the band were pushing the Singer towards rock. I'd say away from his roots but then I'd become just another white man who has the presumption to think he can school black people on their roots.

Not much to see from the gate. The Singer's beat-up truck under a shed. Trees, wild grass, part of the west side of the house and guards, at least I'm assuming they're guards, about ten or so scoping the grounds. For the first time I'm noticing all the buildings around me. The apartment complex in front where Lansing parked, the set of townhouses one gate over, cars now cruising up and down Hope Road. I haven't even thought about what question I'd ask him first. What do you think about the predictions of when the two sevens clash? Bunny Wailer's new album? Does this concert mean he's endorsing the PNP? If Rasta don't work for the CIA, does he know who?

I take a pad out of my knapsack and look at the empty page. You'd think I would have written down a million questions to ask him when Lansing told me he had an in. Now I'm at his gate and I'm all out of things to say. I know there's a story and I know I want to know it, but now I'm wondering if this is what I want. I can't figure out if I just got a sudden case of the chickenshits or if I am slowly realizing that even though the Singer is the center of the story, it really isn't his story. Like there's a version of this story that's not really about him, but about the people around him, the ones who come and go that might actually provide a bigger picture than me asking him why he smokes ganja. Damn if I'm not fooling myself I'm Gay Talese again.

Cars are speeding up. I'm watching them for so long that I don't know for how long the guard had left his post. But I do know my watch is saying that Lansing has been in there fifteen minutes. I walk right up to the gate and push my head against the bars.

—Hello? Hello? Anybody there?

I don't know where the guard went. It's just a little latch on the fucking gate. I only need to lift and I'm inside. Can we say unauthorized access? Fuck Hunter S. Thompson, I'm Kitty Kelley. I almost touch it when another guard shows up. He's not the guy who was here before. Lighter skinned, with a scar on his right cheek like a telephone. I beat myself up inside for drawing conclusions. No I don't, not really. It's pretty obvious that these guys aren't police, or even a decent class of security guard either, even if they are all carrying machine guns. Maybe the Singer just hired some boys from the ghetto. I really should have known better than to trust Lansing. He's probably looking out from some window inside, getting off on leaving his good buddy Alexander Pierce to wait in the heat. I'd almost think he has the Singer by the window laughing too, but I can't imagine somebody so cool wasting any time with a prick like Lansing, no matter what he's there to do. Still.

The gate opens only wide enough for his BMW to slip through. My heart jumps, I swear I'm a teenage girl. But it's not him. Somebody else is driving it, a thin Rasta with a woman who looks like one of the back-up singers in the right seat and another guy in the back. The driver's pissed, glancing behind him and then at her, then at me, then driving off. Only when he's driving off do I realize he's heading off into serious darkness. Headlights roll past on the street. I forgot that it's past eight. They've turned on lights on the second floor. The gate closes. I'm kinda sure that I've been waiting outside this gate forty-five minutes now but honestly I've lost count. Do you know where my friend is? I say to empty space. The guard left his post and I think about slipping in again. It would be so easy. Well, up to the point I actually enter and ten guards throw down on me before they ask questions.

A Red F100 truck slams its brakes and makes a hard right up the driveway. I jump out of the way. Inside are two men, both dark and both wearing shades even though it's night. The driver stares at me and I try with every fucking thing I've got to stay looking at him. The other guy is tapping the side of the truck. The engine is still running. Then the gate opens only three feet or so and seven men, in jeans, khakis, bell-bottoms and all carrying guns and rifles, head for the truck, jumping in the back. The last, a short man with dreadlocks and a red, green and gold tank top, glances at me for a second but does not stop running. The truck backs into traffic without looking and heads left. The gate opens wider and I'm jumping out of the way of a blue Escort that shoots down the driveway, packed with four or five men sticking their guns out the window. I was too busy rolling on the pavement to count. The car makes a left on Hope Road and other cars slam their brakes. I pick myself up and look over at the guard post. Nobody closes the gate. I think they're all gone.

It's the first time I'm on his property. Is it his home? I don't even know. The full driveway is a roundabout with a set of trees in the center that take you to an entrance with four pillars, and a doorway with a double door that looks half open. Two floors and all the windows are rusty colored and open. The band is still playing but everybody outside is gone. I walk left, over to his beaten-up truck. My dad had one of these, not the same truck but an old beat-up one that he loved more than his kids. I think he loved the truck so much because it was the only thing that could get old but would never die. Well, that was until it did. So fucking weird, but there's music clearly coming from inside and yet outside is quiet. It doesn't sound quiet, not with the stop-start keyboards and drums and the traffic, but it feels quiet, which is starting to bug me. I don't know how else to explain. I can't believe that son of a bitch Lansing just left me out here. Maybe he's really standing me up. Maybe it's the dark crouching all around me. Does anybody inside know that the guards have all left with the gate wide open? Shift change? New guys running on Jamaica time?

Fuck this. And fuck him. I should have known. Maybe he was getting back at me for all the stuff I've said behind his back, because now I feel like a fucking fool. Except that Mark Lansing is just not somebody I would talk about ever, not even to say some shit about him. And who would I say it to?

Fuck this son of a bitch and you know what, fuck this whole place. Maybe I'm kidding myself. Again. Maybe I better get a fix on Mick Jagger's whereabouts just so that I can keep my fucking job, or at least rendezvous with this photographer that I still haven't met. Come to think of it, I'm not even sure he's still in the country.

I turn and walk out the gate. Hope Road is busy. I don't have a thing in Lansing's car so I keep walking. Cars keep moving along and I see a white Escort that looks like a taxi. Well, the driver has his arm out the window, which usually means he's waving folded dollar bills in between each finger from collecting the fare himself. I wave him down and he stops. I open the door to get in, look up the road and see a blue car turning into the driveway.

Nina Burgess

Evening catch me. I've been walking for hours. Yes buses pass me up and down and some of them even stopped, but I've been walking for hours. I've been walking from Duhaney Park where my parents live, call it north-west from His house, if you call His house the center. Kimmy thought I was coming after her so she ran. She thought I was coming at her with the belt held wrong, strap in my hand, buckle hanging waiting to whip an eye out of one of her fucking sockets. She ran like she was the bitch in *Black Christmas* who dies first. She even stumbled over the vacuum that Mummy forgot to pack up because she was just so distraught over how her oldest daughter turn into some stinking pum-pum, Rasta-loving slut.

But I wasn't going after Kimmy. Just like her to want to be the screaming girl in an evil movie, it makes her the center of attention again. I'll bet she probably thinks this thing backfired, not because my father was on the floor catching his breath and my mother was screaming for me to get out with me ignoring her, and not even because this didn't play out anywhere near she was hoping. It was because she couldn't find a way to make all this about her. I should have ran after her and dropped at least two solid welts on her back. But when your mother keeps screaming about how you're a demon from the black pit of Gehenna and it must have been because she didn't give up anything for Lent why the devil slipped inside her and replaced her sweet baby with a devil, you can either tell her that she needs to watch better movies or you just leave. And that is what I was doing. Kimmy just happened to be in the way of the door. She kept screaming all the way to her bedroom, sorry, former bedroom, and shut the door.

I dropped the belt and went outside. As soon as the sunset touch me I started to run. Six o'clock already come and gone. When Mummy called it sounded like an emergency, so I pulled on green track shoes that I hadn't worn since Danny, who bought them because track shoes is foolishness after all. I haven't run track since high school so why would I need them? At some point I stopped running from my parents' house, maybe when I ran out in the road and that first car slammed the brakes and told me about me bombocloth. Or maybe when I kept running in the middle of the road and another car slammed the brakes and said that bitch mad as shad. Or maybe when I got on the bus that took me to Crossroads even though I didn't want to go to Crossroads and couldn't remember when I got on the bus.

The visa is a ticket. That is all it is. I don't know why I am the only one who sees that. The visa is a ticket out of the hell that this fucking PNP going bring on the country. You have to watch news to know. You don't have to wait till one of Mummy's horsemen of apocalypse shows up or whatever the r'asscloth that means. She who love to go to church to hear about signs and wonders and how we're living in the last days. Ungrateful wretches the two of them, don't they see this is the . . . this is the . . . shit, I don't know what this is, or why I'm in Crossroads when I need to be at Hope Road. Shouldn't talk, I should just show. I should just get the visa and the plane tickets and shove it to them before they have time to talk or have fucking Kimmy convince them out of it, like her parents are supposed to wait and see for when the shitstem supposedly right itself. I get off the fucking bus.

I left before I heard my father catch a breath. Serve him right. Serve everybody right. I'm getting just a little sick and tired of every man including now my damn father feeling that as soon as they see me, they get license to be on their worst behaviour. Great, now I sound like me mother and kiss my r'ass if that's who I want to turn out like. My daddy beat me like I was a little girl. Like me was a bloodcloth pickney and is Kimmy fault. No is not her fault. She is just a damn jackass who worth whatever man tell her she worth, including Daddy. No, is the Singer fault. If he didn't fuck me, me wouldn't have anything to do with him and if the embassy did just give me the bombopussy r'asscloth visa and don't tell me no fucking shit 'bout me don't have no bombocloth ties like me would want to run away to the fucking country where Son of Sam shooting people in the head and big man raping little boys and white people still calling people nigger and trying to stab them with a flagpole in Boston and not caring who take a photo, they have another fucking thing coming.

Jesus bloodcloth Christ I hate when I chat bad. I also realize that for the entire little rant I was also chatting it aloud and the school girl who just happened to be walking right beside me take foot and run across the street. Pity car never lick you down, I want to say. It reach the tip of my tongue but I don't say it. Instead I walk east of Crossroad and all the buses and people and school girls in blue uniforms and green uniforms and boys in khaki uniforms growing up too quick, and head for Marescaux Road.

On the bus my heart is pumping hard again, harder than before when I hit Daddy. And it won't stop. I'm on the bus with suitcases, handbags, knapsacks, shiny oxford shoes and modest heels. Everybody leaving school and work to go home, but not me. I don't even have a job. And my damn feet are scratching me because of these damn track shoes. I catch a woman on the left, four seats to the back, looking at me and wonder if something is wrong with me. My hair doesn't look too mad, I think. And my t-shirt is back in my jeans and I certainly don't look like I begged a free ride from the bus conductor. I wait for her to look up again from her newspaper and when she does I glare at her. She looks away quick. But the damn woman made me miss my stop. I come off when the bus stops and realize that I was wrong. The woman made me miss plenty stops, at least five or six. That's when I started walking. I didn't even think about it, or how long it would take or just how far off I was. Lady Musgrave is one long road.

My legs must know why I'm doing this because my head doesn't have a clue. Maybe there's nothing else to do, maybe there's nothing else but it. Is this what a job is supposed to do, fill this space that I think I'm feeling now that I need to fill with an it? Such bullshit. I don't know what I'm talking about. My parents don't even want to be my parents anymore. Maybe I'll just stand there, outside his gate, until something moves me or I find something to do. Maybe whether they want to move is beside the point and all that matters is that I get these fucking visas and they can do whatever they want with them. I tried, yes their disgusting Rasta fucking daughter. Maybe I should have asked what irked them more, the Rasta part or the fucking.

At the intersection I stop. I want to lie down in the grass on the sidewalk and I want to run and keep running. I open my handbag and pull out my compact, but I swear to God I can't remember when I had a handbag. I know for some woman it's like an eleventh finger and you don't even think about it, even if you change every day. But I can't remember the handbag either. Who can run with a handbag? I must be going crazy. I'm going to the Singer's house to get money for something for people who don't want it or me, but I'm going anyway. Because, well because. Somehow I feel as if this is the first time I'm looking at myself today. Seems I've been lying to myself about my hair, which is a madwoman mess. It looks like I pulled the rollers out but did nothing after that. One big curl is jutting out of the top left of my head and another big curl is down past my right brow. My lipstick looks like it was put on by a blind baby. Shit. I would run from me.

I choke up. Damn r'asscloth, I'm not crying right now. You hear me Nina Burgess, I'm not crying right now. But the grass looks so good, I want to just stoop down and bawl, loud enough that people will know to leave the madwoman alone. What kind of a wretched woman I must be, just like my mother thinks. Maybe it's the walking that's driving me mad. Who else would be walking anywhere right now? Last night I actually thought I was going to walk home all the way to Havendale, like an idiot. Does any woman my age, any woman I went to school with, have any purpose? Why don't I have a man? What was I thinking, hoping to move back to America with Danny? He was here to score some local pussy, so mission complete. This message will self-destruct in three years. I really should have beat the shit out of Kimmy. Or at least given her one kick.

Between the walk and the stopping that's when evening crept up on me.

—Excuse me, sir, what time you have?

—What time you want?

I look at this fat son of a bitch, clearly walking home even though he's wearing a tie and say nothing. I just look.

—Eight-thirty, he says.

—Thank you.

—That would be p.m., he says and grins. I put every single bad word and ugly thought I can think of into the stare I give him back. He walks off. I stand there watching, yes, for the first and second time he turns around. You know something? All man is fuckery. Yes every woman know this, but we forget it every day. But leave it to providence, sooner or later in the stretch of a day some man will remind you. My heart is pumping again. Pumping hard. That might be because I can finally see Hope Road. Cars and buses cut across my view, east to west, west to east. I'm running again. Hope Road can't hit and run me fast enough. I don't know why, but I just have to run, I have to run now. Maybe his car is driving out, maybe he's set to go to Buff Bay, maybe somebody coming to see him and will take up his time, maybe he just finished rehearsing "Midnight Ravers" and is finally, finally remembering what I look like. I just have to get there now. That one year running track did not come back and it's my lungs that feel like it's going to burst, not my heart. But I can't stop, I almost run into Hope Road, making a sharp right and going still. Your mother and father won't want it, another me is saying and it's slowing me down. Fuck her. She can kiss me r'ass.

One block away from his gate and the streetlights are all on and traffic is moving smooth, not too fast, not too slow. Two white cars shot it past the intersecting and race down. The first turns into his gate so fast that I can hear the screech. The second swerve in as well. My feet stop running and start to walk. I hope these aren't people taking him away from the only chance I've got. There's just this, I'm doing this because that is all I can do now and there is nothing else—this will work, it don't have to make no sense. Not even Christmas yet, barely December, and somebody is already bursting firecrackers. I run and run and run again, then hop, then walk right up to just ten or so feet from the gate.

Demus

T*his is how bad man* wake up. Shaking first, hungry second, scratching and itching third, with you cocky burning to explode. This is what you do: shake off the shake with a head nod, scratch the itch till your black skin turn red and go off into the darkest corner of the shack and pull down you zipper. Others say to you, What the bombocloth you ah do boy? but you don't listen because right now, to let go that piss is the sweetest thing. But the shaking continue and won't leave until Weeper come back. In the morning the shack seem bigger, even with six man in it trying to sleep the bad man sleep.

This is how bad man wake up: never go to sleep. I wasn't sleeping when Funky Chicken with the heroin shakes start to walk in him sleep saying Leviticus, Leviticus, Leviticus, over and over. Me never did sleep neither when Heckle run over to the window and try to push himself out. Bam-Bam sleeping but he sitting on the floor and leaning against the wall and the whole night he didn't move. Me dream awake, about the brethren who leave me poor on Caymanas racetrack. Me make the heat rise up in me like a fever then take it back down and make it rise again. You can do that the whole night. Last night Josey take me aside for a second and say the pussyhole come back from Ethiopia two night ago. This is how you can make a thing you lust for keep you awake.

This is how you know most man in the room too young. Not an hour after they fall asleep they start moaning and mumbling and if you is the fat man from Jungle, you call out a woman name three time. Dorcas or Dora, me can't remember. Only young man get wet dream. Heckle in the corner sinning with him hand down him pants. Only young man can sleep even with all the burden crushing down on two shoulder like God just get tired of carrying burden and throw it on you.

I didn't sleep. I not even sleepy. Flies in the room even at night. Nobody have no watch for me to tell the time, but in what feel like deep night, the skinny man from Jungle try to push him way out the door. Nobody wake up, but me wasn't asleep. I hear him saying what kind of fuckery this for them to lock up big man like him in pigsty and I want to say you better relax yourself because Josey Wales is man who love to discipline a boy, but I stay in my corner, lying flat on my back, closing my eyes every time somebody look over this way at me.

But that was hours ago, me think. Now everybody in room going mad and ting. Bam-Bam scream out over and over. Me sight the two man from Jungle pace and pace and every time they run into each other they break out into a fight. Heckle searching every corner, every crevice, every empty juice box and soft drink bottle, the top of the house and the bottom for some cocaine. I know that be what he looking for, even though the last time a man do that, he take industrial-strength rat poison. Funky Chicken can't take it no more so he go off into the corner where we piss and sit down in it and scratch him chest through the shirt with a *tch tch tch*. Bullshit this, you hear me, Heckle say. Yow who going help me push down this bloodcloth door? Josey Wales would come after we, another one say, but he say it quiet, like Josey is horseman from the Book of Revelations.

When me take a stop Bam-Bam screaming like a fucking girl. I say shut up, pussyhole, but he keep screaming like he sleeping with night terror. I kick him like thunder and he jump like lightning. A punch at least would make him feel like a man, but a slap make him feel like a girl. Outside the window gone from grey to yellow and sunlight cut through and land on the floor. There be nothing to do but watch it retreat, from the wall, down to floor, backways across the floor, and then gone like it reverse out the window. No sunray coming in but the room hot like fire. Must be noon.

Now five man roaming about the room and working up a stinking sweat. Now Funky Chicken screaming. Bam-Bam staring into the wall and

Heckle staring at the window like he thinking he can fit through it. I know he thinking that if he back far enough and run with him hand stretch out like Superman, he can fly right through just like that. Or maybe that is what me thinking, because the heat wet and sticky and ting, and me can smell man all around me. Only the two man from Jungle look like they still have sense. They stop walking into each other and start walking together. But one walk past Heckle and brush him foot and Heckle say, Weh di bloodcloth you ah kick me for, star? and jump up and push. The two man from Jungle take set 'pon him double. One grab him right hand, the other grab him left and slam him into the wall making the shack shake. They about to double punch him when Funky Chicken say, You hear a car?

A car coming but it drive past, vrrrroooOOOOOOMmmm and gone. Funky Chicken start to sing that *when the right time come some ah go bawl fi murder.* Bam-Bam up and skipping on the spot, saying must be like a soldier, must be like a soldier, which is not what I expect from him at all. The four walls squeezing in and me is the only one that see it. I can smell five man and all of them stink, and all of them hot, and all of them have that fear smell which is to say all of them sour. Me smell piss too. And sulphur. And camphor ball and wet rat and old wood that termite eat out. The room squeezing in and Josey Wales and Weeper take all of the guns so that me can't shoot no hole in the wall.

The room getting cooler and first me think it was the sea breeze reach we finally but it was the sun going away. Them going lock we up from night to night. There must be a stick, a column, a pipe, a hammer, a mop, a post, a lamp, a knife, a Coca-Cola bottle, a wrench, a stone, a rock, something to hit them two with when they come back. Something to hit them quick and kill them. Kill anybody. There must be something in this shack to kill whoever walk through that door, because me no care no more, me just want to get out. Heckle in the corner with him hand down him pants. He look 'round the room to see if we looking and take it out and rub it till he make a girl sound and kick the wall. Bam-Bam in him sleep dreaming about Funnyboy and saying over and over, Don't touch me Clarks.

This is how you stop a screaming man. Punch him in the face if you want him to feel like a man or slap him across the cheek if you want him to feel like a girl. Josey Wales lift Bam-Bam off the ground with left hand and slap him with the right. Slap east to west then slap west to east and east to west again, like the man is him woman. Me scratch me head because me can't think about how a wet slap must feel like, for me can't remember when Josey Wales and Weeper come back. One blink they not here, another blink they appear like magic. Like Obeah. Josey still slapping Bam-Bam, telling him to stop cry like bitch before he really give him something to cry 'bout. The two man from Jungle say go suck your mother, and turn to rush him but Weeper whip out two gun like a cowboy gunslinger and say settle yourself, brethren.

Josey open a big box and plenty gun come out, most of them M16. Weeper open a little box and plenty white powder come out and Funky Chicken and me swarm the table, with Bam-Bam whimpering me me me. Weeper chop up a pile into umpteen skinny line. So he go first, then Funky Chicken, then me, then Weeper again, which make Josey Wales shout at him that he did say that he going to let go off that fuckery. Weeper say, Everything kriss, my youth, everything kriss. One of the boy from Jungle put him nose down on the table but the other boy say no. Weeper point him gun at the boy face and say don't think me can't shoot you and still find use for you body. He point the gun at the boy but the boy didn't flinch. Weeper pull 'way the gun and laugh. I watch Josey Wales watching the whole thing. Josey Wales don't take no line.

Midway through the third line of coke I gone further than where thinking can take me. Dillinger playing on a transistor radio, I didn't know the shack have a radio but coo deh, a radio, and Dillinger *gonna lick the chalice inna Buckingham Palace and chase Mr. Wallace.* The railroad shack hot and stink with piss and ting. I done three line but Weeper keep cutting and the lines so thin that as soon as you sniff it gone. The two man from Jungle laughing loud and crying and singing the tune and waving him gun. And Weeper cut me a line and I sniff it in and it burn but sweet burn like a pepper burn and the shadows starting to jump off the wall and dance. Heckle and Funky Chicken look like fool but not me. I beyond wise and fool.

Little things can fill up a long hour. So Josey Wales say hold on, Joe, and I say me no name so, but me can't remember my name so I take the name Joe, and I say just call me Joe, and it's the sweetest name, sweeter than sweet. Ten minutes pass, fifteen minutes, one hour, one day, five year. I don't care, whatever time pass too long and Weeper cut me another line, but say I not getting it unless I show him how to handle the gun. I tell him even a dumb pussyhole who come out of a batty can fire gun and he slap me, but I don't feel anything. And is just so it happen. I don't feel no slap, no pain and no bullet. I don't tell Josey Wales. And when the shadows start to dance they tell me that we have to kill him, we have to kill the thiefing friend and him too, for he and the thief is brethren. And that make him just like the thief. I don't know how much time passed, but the radio in my head sweet like fuck. He ask if me ready and me say how you mean? Nobody can touch me now, and my eyes see so far and so deep that me in Josey Wales' brain then out and he didn't even know. I know how they going to tell this story even now. I know which part get keep and which part get lost.

This is how it feel when you know that you could kill God and fuck the devil. Josey Wales say we set out soon, but I feel like we should set out now and ah grab me gun and think how I want to kill kill kill this pussyhole and nobody going get to kill him but me and I want to kill kill kill and it just feel so good, so raasclaat sweet every time I say Kill kill kill that the echo in the room sweet too. Josey Wales say time to go. Outside is two white Datsuns. Josey Wales tell we right before we leave how you playing both sides but you still a PNP stooge. And how you about to record a song that say under heavy manners and everybody know that is PNP slogan. And that you never change, but after this things goin' change big.

This is how much time those two go over what we eight going do: three. Me forget the first time and the last time because me feeling this high different. Not that me used to any form of cocaine, but still me know this high different. Funky Chicken already acting bummy. I feel cold, and is not because the sun gone and early night already black and thick. Josey check him watch and cuss, we late to r'asscloth him say. Two white Datsun outside. Josey, Weeper, Bam-Bam and me get in the first. The rest get in the second.

Uptown. Uptown always say the same things to me when I come up here. Green light. We coming coming coming like lightning and thunder. I want another line, just one more line and I fly. A blue car come in front of we and seem to be going where we going. The car is the Piper and we is the rat. We follow the short manager all the way up to 56 Hope Road. Red light say stop but green light say go.

Bam-Bam

Josey Wales said no more line for you, work to do,
We in the car, the big beat jumping bass
No music in the stereo, naigger
Don't need music for the S90 Skank, naigger
The short stump manager
Swerve out boasty on the road
Road Killer, coulda shoulda full ya full o'
Lead. Eight boys two Datsuns white
Like duppy jump out in broad daylight
Weeper notice him first
We laugh
Man leading we to him own judgment
Pied Piper, Weeper say
Don't know what him mean, me ask what
Weeper mean
Nobody say but everybody laugh
Gun in my lap rubbing me, rubbing me,
And I want to fuck fuck fuck
Fuck this
In the middle of uptown
Running from Babylon
Uptown jam
Car on top of car on top of car on top of car
Kingston jam
Make we jam it right here and kill this pussyhole
Weeper look at me a way

He can see it
Nobody move
We so close to the stumpy manager we nearly touch
We should bump him, touch him
So that when time run out he
Would see we was coming
Two Datsuns white
Boys behind boys behind the man leading us to you
I rub the gun but this feel fool
Gun is not buddy, gun is just a gun
And I want to fuck fuck fuck
Fifteen and never fuck a ting
Bad man fuck from ten
Bust the cherry cherry bust
One day I saw my father fuck my mother
White Datsun number two in the back
Red car running up the rear
Two cars on two side, blue Cortina, no Ford Escort
Pink Volkswagen
Pink battyman in pink Volkswagen
And nobody moving
It not going to happen
It need to happen this need to happen I take two line
Three line four line
This going to happen
I think to grab the gun and start shooting
That would make people start moving
Weeper start looking
At me, you, 'low the bombocloth gun
Says something about cokehead
You is the cokehead, cokehead
Want to tell him what this fucking cokehead going
Do next but is cool runnings

Cool runnings, cool like a dead idea
Pink battyman in pink Volkswagen looking at we
Four men in a Datsun white
We off to kill, pervert, not to fuck
Point this gun to you pink pussyface
And boom sha-ka-la-ka
The riddim in me head crazy louder
Bam bam stylee
This car need to bloodcloth go!
And then it going
And the manager gone
Peel out like the rooster running
From sixty sexy chicken
Poof zip swoosh
He getting away
We going the same place, Weeper say
Demus not saying nothing
I don't like Demus
He look at you too long
Like he writing something about you in him head
Coming up Hope Road we see the manager turn in
We stop.
We see and wait.
Echo Squad not standing guard
Echo Squad is PNP
Echo Squad know only one P:
Pay me
Dark come on sudden like it do when you not looking
Sky red then redder
Orange, then oranger
Black, then blacker
I want another hit
I want another hit

I want another hit
It's because of you
You stand between me and it
And now we coming for you
And we screech through the gate
Fi we car first ride right up to the door.
Second car block the gate
Four man jump out of the car
Like Starsky and Hutch
On the one, on the four
Weeper head for the front door
The master's door, the estate
This must be a place white man whip slave to death
Kill kill kill
You 'round the back, in the kitchen up the steps
Vibes and weed, we follow your trail but
Josey beat me to the bang
He driving the car yet still jump out first and with purpose
Your wife she ran out I didn't care
She and some pickney I didn't care
My bullet buck her in head
She fly clear off the ground
And land flat
I move over to finish the bitch
But she flat and blood a rush out her head
I run fast to get you, to see you, to put you down but
But Josey beat me to the bang
Bam bam, wife dead
And your brethren
And your sistren
And anybody that play guitar
I hear the bam bam bam bam on the ground
And reach up and push my feet

Echo in my head, bam bam
Blood rushing beat bam bam
Bomboclaat fuckery, I wanted to shoot you first
Nobody goin' forget the man that shoot you
'Round the back won't stand still even when I stop running.
I run up to the kitchen and cock the hammer
Them going write song 'bout me!
Riddim beating in my head
Beating louder
My father singing
One two three four
Colón man ah come
With him brass chain ah lick him belly
Bam bam bam
But Josey run in first
Josey bombocloth Josey
He run in on you and lift the M16
But the manager run in, right into you
Right into the way
I moving fast but everything slow
I jump on the last step but the sound stretch and the
Faster I lift the gun the slower it feel
I push my head in and see you, before I see Josey
You don't know you stand between me and it
Short stumpy manager run right into it
Chatting shit, monkey business
Bam bam bam bam bam
From Josey gun
Josey riddle him thigh, shower him back
He scream and I scream and all you say is
Selassie I Jah Rastafari
And all fall down

Bang a pot, blam a can, wake up dust and burst through
The window
Pow
Josey don't aim for the head
Like the Cuban tell we
Aim for the head
Make it blast open like a blender
You look straight at me
You drop your grapefruit
You look at me
And I want you to shout and scream and sniff and tear
Piss you pants, jerk and fall
But you just look, you didn't blink
And I and I
BamBam
Jah Rastafari shot you in the heart
You call out Selassie
You get him? I say to Josey
Yeah
Me get the wife too
Go 'round the front
Straight through the head with one shot
Bitch fly and crash on the ground
'Bout she was going make a clean getaway
Who the bitch think she be, Jill, Kelly or Sabrina
Don't call the man's queen, bitch
So you get him?
You get him?
You get him?
Yeah
We run to the front
Brothers was Swiss cheesing the house

Demus run through the front door
Past a girl hiding behind it
And empty a clip that hit the organ
Make a do re fa me so
People inside shuffle and scream
A girl scream out for Seeco
People inside quiet like a mouse
You drop your grapefruit and look straight at me
Like Jesus telling Judas
To get it done already
Me is you, Pilate me is you, Roman soldier
You don't even know who your Judas was
Demus goin' be mad that the Judas wasn't here too
Think he did want him more than he want you
You just happen to be in the way
A brawta, and extra, extra sauce for the dish
Heckle run past Demus down the hallway
And make him gun rip a man in half
Cut a line 'cross the belly
Each shot a blood burst
We shower the place again
And just like so I want to
Make sure you dead
Is me should a make you dead
Me hate bombocloth Josey Wales
Me want to go back 'round the kitchen
And if you dead
Make you deader
Coming to the front Funky Chicken nearly shoot me
You get the wife?
Yeah me get the wife
She did a run to the

Volkswagen
Another man on the floor
The house quiet and shake
Whoop-whoop, sound of the police
Babylon beast
We run
But then me take a stop
As we running out a girl walking in
Angel don't know she stepping into hell
Brown skin and pretty and look like
She don't 'fraid to walk
In her sexy jeans and pretty blouse
She come for him me know it
Brown skin and pretty hair
And I did want to fuck fuck fuck
She see we and just stand there
Don't run don't back 'way, she just stand there
Maybe she crying or her eye just red
She don't move
Siren getting nearer and me raise me gun
She must be one of them, me raise me gun
But Josey get to her first.
Josey walk right up to her, right up to her face
Right up to her face and sniff
He sniff and she jump and start weep
That quiet crying that big woman do
Me want her to piss herself
Me want to do it to her but Josey again
He get in me way again I going shoot him
Josey get inna the bomboclaat car!
The first car gone already
Demus Weeper Josey Heckle me

Weeper press the gas
The woman still standing there like she is Lot wife
That look back
Salt
Three gunshot and the back our window explode
And I want to kill kill kill
And fuck fuck fuck
But I scream scream scream
We dip over and swerve in the left
Into car oncoming
We dead now
Car screech and honk
Police coming in hot
Whooop-whoop
Babylon bussing a bang
Cars swerve out of the way, one crash then two
Down Hope Road other cars hear we coming
Police on the backside rushing we down
Move out ah the bloodcloth way
Bam! Make a right on East Kings House Road
Run red light
Screech screech tire soon bust
Whoop whoop
Fucking police
Bloodclaat Babylon
My head getting bigger and heart pumping
Boom boom boom
And you looking at me
Look up and a car coming straight for my head
Stop scream like a pussyhole, pussyhole!
Weeper say and slam the brake
My head clap the dash
He twist the wheel and slam the gas and, and, and

Demus

And the Datsun dash down another road that I don't know and then another road then left down another road a boy jump out of the way but we still hear a bump nobody talking but everybody screaming Weeper say shut up, pussyhole, shut up, pussyhole, we turn again turn turn and dash down a lane so narrow that we scrape house on both side sparks burst off and somebody scream inside outside of the car don't know then we drop into one pothole two three the car just bouncing up and down and then we skid a right past a bar playing HIS song a bar with a Pepsi sign and a sign with the old man from Schweppes Heckle say fling 'way di gun throw 'way di gun and so he fling 'way him gun Weeper say you is a bombocloth fool but keep driving and we turn right the road small no streetlight headlight dog we hit a dog then left then right and nobody know where we is I know I don't know I can feel me head coming down already I not going get a hit now this coming down getting sadder and sadder vomit coming up my mouth send it back down we turn down one empty lane and another lane and end up on a wide road that cut a valley between the Garbagelands before I see that the police not following we anymore right now me is a boy and me want me woman the woman me leave this morning knowing that me might not come back but not thinking it I want me woman but nobody in the car making a sound until Heckle say dog going nyam we supper we going roast in hellfire them goin' fuck we up them going put we under heavy manners they going eradicate we he start to cry and Weeper stop the car and come out and what the bloodcloth you a do Josey say but Weeper pull out him revolver and pull open the back door on the left *get out of the bloodcloth car, you batty boy* he say to Heckle but Heckle say him nah go nowhere Weeper fire a gunshot in the air me thinking Jesus Christ people surely goin' come now but Weeper put the gun right near Heckle head and say to me *Brethren, you betta shift 'cause brains going splash over you* and Heckle start bawl me coming out me coming out me gone he climb out of the car and Weeper grab the M16 from him and throw it on a garbage hill and point his gun and say you better run 'cause me no business with you and as the boy turn Weeper kick him in the bottom he stagger get up and run and Weeper get back in the car *anybody who want to join him better come out of the fucking car now* nobody want to come out I just want to go somewhere a cave 'round the beach or some hole I want just want one more line I just want one more line one more line before me dead just then I reason that they will kill me because they must and I goin' be one of the man who kill HIM which is like the man who kill Jesus I wish me woman could sing to me I wish me did dead from ghetto sickness from polio or scurvy or dropsy or whatever poor people die from Weeper start the car and we drive through the Garbagelands who have the time how long we going keep driving if we never stop why we can't reach Copenhagen City and in the gully outside Trench Town Weeper stop get out of the car and run he just run leaving three of we he just up and run and disappear in the bush like it swallow him up I wait for it to burp and Josey Wales in the front seat look at Bam-Bam and Bam-Bam run and disappear in the west and Josey Wales look at me and say fucking fool it was almost you, it was you until you sniff Weeper shit and I say what the bombocloth you talking 'bout but he run off east into the bush that swallow him up I think to wait for another burp thinking of a burp make me want to laugh but there is nothing to laugh about not this time so I start to cry nobody watching or at least I can't see nobody watching me I want to cry louder I want my woman I want a line 'cause I hate coming down I hate it I hate it worse than I hate thinking of them shooting me and is not even a month but me start sniffling turning into madman on the street with the cocaine hunger I going mad me brain must be gone somewhere that it never coming back but nothing coming back now not a single thing something brush the bush at the top of the gully and the bush burst with light like hair on fire like burning bush in Exodus the light mean a car coming this way to use the gully as a shortcut it's the police I know it's the police I feel it's the police run run run trip over a stone smack knee hiss bombocloth get up try to run but left leg only limp like the killer in *Dirty Harry* now Harry after me no no no right there is a clump of weed so high it hide me like a tiny chair can hide a big wabbit which way did the wabbit go which way did he go but I'm not the rabbit I'm Foghorn Leghorn and I'm a gonna hide I say I'm a gonna hide behind this here weed see that what I gonna do that's a joke . . . I say, that's a joke, son tee hee hee giggle giggle giggle the car pass by I can't stop giggle they're going to catch me tee hee hee and kill me tee hee hee I don't know why I can't stop laughing shut up mouth I clamp my mouth shut the car pass with a rattle and roll and splash in the nasty water running down the gully waking up the rats so many rats I want to scream and aieeeeeeeeeeeeeeeeee nobody 'round to hear me aieeeeeeeee like a girl now me gun missing I can't find it the rats took it they going tear me skin off and eat my toes and so much garbage in the gully: Brillo box, corn flakes box, FAB detergent, reconstituted flour enriched flour plastic bags dead rat trapped in plastic bags live rats coming out of milk boxes biscuit boxes running over soft drink bottles cooking oil bottles Palmolive dishwashing liquid I think it's Palmolive *you're soaking in it* so many bottles like rats and rats in bottle that can't come out have to run have to run now forget the gun just forget it they're coming to kill you I don't want to die have to beg Jesus have to beg Papa-Lo have to beg Copenhagen City but is not Papa-Lo send we is Josey Wales but Josey Wales can't do anything without Papa-Lo saying yes no maybe so right I trying to think in a straight line but line means white means coke I need a hit hit hit and I shot up HIM place and now it's something that I don't think of all the time but something that run in and out of my head like when I not wearing brief I know that Josey Wales was supposed to make a lot of money from this or he wouldn't do it politics don't mean nothing to a man like that everybody know and there was no police and no guard no guard at all which is like they know we was coming but Josey promise I would get at least one police to deal with and no guard at the gate we just run in but we could have walk I think all I kill was a piano I need to get back to Copenhagen City because this look like PNP area why Weeper leave we in a PNP area when we just kill PNP most famous sufferah and whoever find me going kill me till me dead I don't know where this place lead and the road breaking up and the rats rats rats rats rats rats I run out and it must be late because this first street empty and I don't know where I am this place two bars the sign say closed two sleeping dogs one creeping cat a burned-out car shell blocking the road a sign that say Rose Town Walk Ride Drive and Arrive Alive another one saying Slow: School both sign bursting with old bullet hole every hole I see I hear a blam or a bok or a pow like Harry Callahan *did he fire six shots or only five* and my gun gone and maybe I leave it in the garbage fields dunes fields dunes and *in all the confusion to tell you the truth I forgot myself in all this excitement but being this is a .44 Magnum, the most powerful handgun in the world and will blow you head clean off, you've gotta ask yourself a question do I feel lucky well, do ya punk* and Harry blam blam blam hands stop shaking stop shaking please stop shaking nobody love me nobody care my head don't think them ways it must be the coming down from the drugs why when you come down you just go down and down and downer and a high is nothing but a peak from which you just come down and down you fall and never stop and I going down lower lower soon sink into the road under the road into hell nobody going see me running through the night run faster make the world move slower but everything moving faster than me and road popping potholes and zinc fence blocking me from seeing the houses run run run right into people who I didn't hear before I see quick behind this bush they playing dominoes somebody must did see me somebody must be behind me no they all under the streetlight four man at the table three man watching two woman the man at the head leaning back on the fence slamming down one domino then another then another they bang hard and the table shake the women scream and laugh and the radio *love to love but my baby he loves to dance he wants to dance he loves to dance he's got to dance* but nobody around I hate them for ghetto people not supposed to be happy nobody should laugh everybody should be in misery me never laugh must be two time my entire life and saying my entire life make me feel like me old even though twenty birthday don't come yet and all me have is me woman and she be a good woman and me running back to her but me not running back to her and I just want to get away just crawl with left knee then right then left right left right somebody water this hedge mud on me knee and in me fist God Hallelujah Jesus don't make there be no dog but I crawling like a dog in somebody yard this must be a PNP area because every wall orange and them people too fucking happy I should have me gun them people don't know what it really mean to kill Jesus fucking Christ rockstone in the mud ow ow ow ow bloodcloth oh shit the woman hear, the woman who not playing where me gun where me gun where me gun but then she laugh again and say stray dog over deh so and me crawl and crawl until me can't hear no domino no more then me run run run until I run into the main road a car scream and I aieeee back and run across the road to the banking I don't know how only God know how or maybe Satan know but now I'm on the railroad track the track push me and pull me and lead me back to the shack somebody sing *take me back to the track jack* but is the radio in my head taking me right back to whatever start all of this and will people think that is because of something political but it is political the white man don't care 'bout no horse race I remember when the white man and the Cuban say know the difference between pointing a gun and shooting it and now me here on the racetrack but it too dark to know if it's really a racetrack but one plank of wood follow another it must be so no train coming this time of night but one pass by early in the morning before cock crow maybe I should just lie down right here go to sleep on the tracks and wake up in hell no that's not me talking it's the comedown Jesus I hope Weeper is back at the shack with some lines but there is no shack just a railroad going everywhere this could be taking me back to country or even a PNP area but at least I smell the sea them probably take him to the hospital now a hospital that scorn Rasta but you're there now in emergency with plenty of white doctor around you the nurse says he's lost a lot of blood doctor and the doctor says I need blah blah blah for blah blah blah on the blah blah blah stat then grab two paddles says clear and jumpshock your chest the music come up not pretty music but music that make the back of my neck sweat the nurse look away first and the doctor say we've lost him everybody turn black if only my head would stop traveling and leave my feet to do it alone because they going nowhere but here the moon half but orange the sky black and red and bombopussyr'asscloth me ankle broken bottle rat and shit on the railtrack Daddy say that train toilet flush right out on the track and which worse, broken bottle or dry shit I don't know there's the shack I can roll out a towel and sleep please for this is not a house but is my house now closer closer who looking who watching who set trap closer closer now the door not supposed to open so easy I don't know I say I don't know need a line need a hit fucking pussyhole Weeper give me a hit the shack never look so small the window look out into nothing but black and inside getting darker and darker than black then I wake up drowning until I touch wood. I smell a raw man in here with me but can't see nobody.

—Oi, you can't stay here. Pussyhole, me say you can't stay yah so. Yow. Yow!

—Haffi wait for Weeper. Haffi wait for Josey Wales.

—Clint Eastwood coming? Who behind him, Francis the talking mule?

—First. Is me come here first.

—No brethren me see you from last night. You not first or last.

—When you . . . You was in the second Datsun or first? Bam-Bam? So tired, so—

[CLICK]

—Hear that, pussyhole? You know click? You can tell difference between click and tick?

—Second Datsun or first? Me know you name? You is . . . you is . . .

—Like what you hear a second ago. Click or tick?

—Is not a second ago. Weeper? Tell Bam-Bam to stop chuck badness with me.

—Pussyhole, the click from a click ago. Me give you nothing to laugh 'bout?

—Me never hear no click. Heckle?

—After tick come tock. You know what come after click?

—Me never hear no click.

—Never hear the click? Well after the click come the fucking bang, want to bet say you hear that?

—Chitty chitty bang sitting on a fence.

—Boy you coked up?

—Trying to make a dollar out'a fifteen cents.

—Them make you smoke lizard tail weed?

—She twist, she twist, she twist like this.

—How much line them make you sniff?

—You know Josey Wales? You know Weeper? You know if him coming?

—You is a cokehead, pussyhole. Better if you was a battyman.

—Me not no cokehead, me just want a line. Just a line. Weeper coming and when he come he going give me a line.

—Cokehead.

—Just tell Weeper—

—Nobody name Weeper come 'round here.

—He coming and when he come he going tell you who can and who can't come 'round here. Is fi him house this! You going see. You going see.

—House? You see any house here?

Bush. No wood, no floor, no window, just bush. On the ground, under a tree hanging tamarind and bats. Tamarind in the dirt. Tamarind in the grass from one to another, tamarind to tamarind to tamarind to broken dish to Pepsi bottle to doll's head to grass to weed to zinc fence. A yard, somebody's yard. Somebody who scream as soon as I see that I'm lying in the grass in somebody's yard. She screaming and screaming and I can see who it is.

—You can't come back here.

—How you mean? But me come back.

I looking for wood and stone and nail and dried blood but this is not the shack, this is not even inside and the woman is the woman I live with, the woman whose name I can't call out. I say is me.

—Madman, come out of me yard!

But me is not no madman. Me is the man who live with you like you is the mummy and me is the daddy. And just then I realize that I can't remember what she look like and don't see her face but I know that me in her house. My house. The red house on Smitherson Lane fourth from the crossroad, the house with an inside kitchen that most people around here don't have and have to cook outdoors.

—But me live here as you man.

—Man? Me no have no man. My man dead. Him dead to me. Get out now.

She done talk. She pick up a stone. The first one miss and the second one but the third hit right in the middle of me back.

—Wha the bloodcloth do you?

—Come out of my pussycloth yard! Rape! Rape! Rapery in me house! Lawd me pussy ah get trample! Rapery!

If there's one thing that Papa-Lo simply can't abide by is a rapist. Better you murder ten woman than rape one. The woman me live with stoning me and I running left and right like a ground lizard. She scream again and the sun shine down on me like a spotlight. See him there. The sun send demons after me, just as he send demons after Judas Iscariot.

Come out, she say, and I turn around to see her raise her hand to throw another stone. I look at her straight, and don't blink. She drop the stone and run into the little bedroom that me and she make wet so much that she have to hang out the mattress to dry. On the other side of the fence I don't see or hear them but I know them coming. I look out from the fence and see Josey Wales with three men behind him that me seen before. One is Tony Pavarotti but the other two me don't know them name. I want to shout out is what kinda a fuckery this after all the brethren never did even at the house. Before I can shout that it's me pap pap pap go off in the distance then bang bang bang on the zinc fence, the last bang just missing my right ear. I don't know why but I look out again so that Josey Wales can see that it's me and not some rapist but he look straight at me as he running and fire again. Four bullets bust through the fence and two zip-zip right past me. I run around to the back of the house and jump the fence but don't land when I thought I was going to. Not a road, but a gully deep like the way to hell. I can't stop falling. I try to roll like Starsky or Hutch would do but my right knee land first and drive into the ground. No time for aieeeee. Running left would take me deeper into Copenhagen City and running right would take me downtown.

In downtown buses on the street with no time to wait. The sun is so high that it hit only the tip of building. Boys younger than me run past with stack of newspapers on them head. The Singer Shot! Manager Critical! Rita treated and sent home!

Jah live.

No.

Bam-Bam

D*on't hide* in plain sight, don't hide in plain sight, pussyhole. That shit come from movie and gunman only see what in front of them. Don't hide in no crowd either 'cause all you need for crowd to change to mob is one See him there! No him dat? and we become me and them. But he was with them, and from them and everybody now against me. I want my daddy to come back and my mother to not be a whore and Josey Wales to not try to find me. Last night, man, last night. Weeper jump out first, then Josey Wales and me no know, me just jump. Me no wait 'pon Demus. No, star. But then me no get far when bullet start chase after me, brap brap brap. Me run thinking police deh 'pon me. Me turn left and bullet turn left. Me turn right and bullet turn right. Me run until me back in the Garbagelands and bullet still a follow me. Me dive into a big pile of garbage that smell like shit and piss and rotten egg, and it wet. Wet and stink, and the wet and stink drip in me hair and on me lip. Me don't move. The stink garbage shelter me, hide when them pass. Not police.

Josey Wales and Weeper both with gun cocked.

—You think you get him? Weeper say.

—How you mean if me get him? Me look like me ever miss?

Weeper laugh and wait. A red car drive up and them get in. Now me can't go back home. Me stay in garbage until the wet stink dry on me. Me don't move until me know all of downtown Kingston gone to sleep. Me run out of the Garbagelands and through the empty marketplace. Near here is where Shotta Sherrif live. Me sight a shop that either didn't close or just opening up since is curfew. All me hear on the transistor radio is treated and sent home, but will he perform? And me know Josey miss. The dutty stinking pussyhole miss, me know me should a go back and finish him meself. Me know me should a gone back and make sure. Eight r'asscloth bullet the man fire and still miss. And now him after me.

Me need coke, even half a line, even one third of a line. Last night, in the middle of the night somebody splash something in my face and I couldn't breathe. Not water, water run off quick, this stay on me face then run down slow, into my nose and mouth even though I blow and blow. Like saliva. Like God go to sleep on top of me and drool all over my face. I wake up choking and he still on me breathing his hot stink breath into my nose, no, a dog. A dog was licking my face. Me jump up and yell and kick the dog and watch it yelp and run away on three legs. Now me deh 'pon a park bench in National Heroes Park. They say he coming, they say it right there on the wall, that poster with the Singer pointing to the sky, Smile Jamaica a public concert, Sunday December 5 at five p.m. He beat death like Lazarus, like Jesus. People in the park talking, already people coming, walking right past me, the madman on the bench, and saying that they hope police going deal with me so that decent people don't have to abide by no stinking madman. They come from early in the morning, people waiting for him. I blink and see them running in and out of the people and coming for me. They look like babies but one have three eyes and one have teeth so long they hang out of it mouth and one have two eye but no mouth and one have bat wings. Last night after me get 'way from Josey Wales somebody start chase me again. They chase me all the way up Duke Street to the park. No, last night me catch a sleep 'pon the railroad tracks. No, last night me did fall asleep in the Garbagelands because Josey Wales was shooting at me and me only wake up because somebody set my heap on fire. I don't know if this is two nights since I shoot him or one. But the newspaper wouldn't take two days to tell the world that the Singer get shot and live. That not even gunman can silence him. Everything is one day, no two. Me know we go after him on December 3. But people coming into the park two by two and four by four, so it must be December 5.

Josey Wales pop in my head and I remember running from him and I remember that I was telling myself don't cry, don't cry, don't cry, you little battyman, but I cry anyway because I didn't understand and I don't understand why he was shooting at me when he send we out and then for the first time my mind run on the others and I wonder where they be. Or if Josey Wales shoot all of them already and is only me left. And I don't know if this make sense to big people, but it don't make sense to me. I didn't stop running even after I couldn't hear Josey Wales no more. I take foot from the Garbagelands and run and run and run all the way downtown, on Tower Street going east to west past haberdashery and Syrian shop and Lebanese supermarket all closed until the general election pass. Tower Street cut 'cross Princess Street and them beggarman, Orange Street and them higglerwoman, King Street and them tradesman and Duke Street and them lawyer lawyer. I turn up Duke Street and run into darkness. And I realize it's not Josey Wales coming after me, or Papa-Lo or Shotta Sherrif, it's him. He beat death and he coming after me. He not even coming, but sitting back maybe on some hill somewhere and setting a trap knowing that people like me born fool, and going fly straight into it. National Heroes Park. Is him park today and he own every single man who will set foot in it. All of Kingston. All of Jamaica.

Thick juice like saliva on my face, in my eye and in my nose. Me wake up choking on bench in the park with bird shit on my shoulder. Me don't know if me drop asleep again and wake up, or if the last time me wake up was a dream. People are already in the park to wait and see. I see and wait. For them, for the police, for JLP gunman, for PNP gunman, for you. By four o'clock there must be thousand more, all of them waiting but something different. These people are not JLP or PNP or any other P, they're just man and woman and brother and sister and cousin and mother and bredren and sistren and sufferah and I don't know these people. I get up and walk and move past them, in between them, around them like a duppy. Nobody touch me, they don't step out of my way, they just don't see me at all. I don't know people who don't pick side. I don't know what they look like, what run in their head before they say something, people who never wear Jamaica Labour Party green or People's National Party orange. And these people getting bigger and bigger and the crowd bigger and the belt around the park about to burst and spill but they waiting on him and they sing him songs until you come.

The crowd is one. Them going know me no one of them, sooner, later, sooner. Sooner or later one of them lambs going say see him deh! See the wolf. Me no know how them going know but them going know. But them don't care about me. Me is a bug, a fly, a flea, less than that. Third World Band playing, surrounded by every policeman in Jamaica and the prettiest woman on the stage talk like she is John the Baptist and the Singer is Jesus, and she make the crowd ooh and ahh and yay and her dress red and orange and flow down to the ground like she is Moses burning bush, but she not talking to them, she talking to me, saying hey, little idiot, who are you to think you can take down the Tuff Gong.

The crowd rush forward and roll back. East swing to west and west swing back and I trying not to look and I trying to not make anybody look at me, and two boy pass by, one of them looking at me too long, but the other drop a newspaper. It's dark but the streetlight hit the people and sometimes hit the ground. Jamaica *Daily News*. The Singer Shot. Gunmen's night raid leaves Wailers Manager Don Taylor—I-Thr—somebody step on it, then another, then another, the crowd suck it up and the paper is gone.

I look up and he—

Not he. You.

You look right at me.

You're onstage fifty, a hundred yards aways, not even feet but yards and you look at me. You see me long before I see you. But you not looking at me. The only light now is on the stage and I lost in the darkness.

You wrap tight in a black shirt like you coming out of hell and I can't see your pants, I don't know if it's jeans or the leather one that make the woman who I live with breathe heavy. You spin and the light flash through you whipping up your locks. Blue jeans. So many people on the stage that you can't even dance like you used to. The pretty woman, your John the Baptist, have her arms folded but she feeling the music. Then on the left me see a duppy and try to run. Me run into a chest. I say sorry but the man don't even feel me, he only feeling the positive vibration. Me look back and the duppy not a duppy, but your woman dressed in white. The horn blow and you stand still. I not hearing you, I hearing the people and they hearing you and I can see you but you lock me out like I must be deaf and I wonder how this night would play for deaf people and if you really starting a revolution if they can't join.

You.

You say that you always knew, always knew that you were confident in the ultimate victory of good over evil. You not talking about me. Me know you nah drop prophecy 'bout me. You ah idiot. You forget that you is the lion and me be the hunter. You flash your dread again. Then I forget that though you be the lion and me is the hunter, me inna fi you jungle. Concrete Jungle. Me turn fi vanish but there nobody move, nobody get hurt. The crowd stand still then push forward. Then they start to jump and I stop. One foot crush my toe and another and another and if I don't start jumping they all going stomp till one by one they trample me down.

You doing it.

You telling them to close in and stomp down Babylon. Now me jumping to you singing to them 'bout me. You is the lion and now you is the cowboy, going to chase those Crazy Baldheads Out of Town. I look at the ground but the bass about to push me down so that the people can trample me. And the guitar coming through the crowd like a spear straight for me heart. Me did think it was one day since we shoot you but when me take a stop is two and me don't know if me did sleep in the Garbagelands, or Duke Street, or the park and when evening turn to morning and then evening again for two days. And where me did gone for a whole day that me can't remember. But me can't think nothing right now 'cause you just ah attack me and everywhere me look to run the people just ah block me and maybe they should block me because Josey Wales must be here too, and Papa-Lo and me see that this is what you plan all along.

I look up and people still in the tree and one of them must have a gun aiming at me head. *Now you got what you want, do you want more?* you say and is me you a say it to, ah me you ah chat 'bout, and only me know what you really mean. *You think you bad, pussyhole? You think you can come take this bombocloth? You think you can kill off the Tuff Gong? You think you can just snuff out His Imperial Majesty either? Jah Live, pussyhole, and Jah coming to cut out you bombocloth heart. Jah going point him finger like lightning to strike and burn you down to pile of ash good for nothing but for a mangy dog to lift him left leg and piss 'pon you so you wash 'way down drain.*

Now you get what you want, do you want more? No. Me no want no more because me see them, the baby with bat wings, and the baby with two eyes but no mouth and more burning blue flame, and taking their time walking through the crowd and I want to shout people you no see them? You no see the demon them? But the people looking at you, only at you. Something slither over my foot and rub scales against my ankle. And then do it again and I scream but the guitar scream the same time and suck mine out. Maybe if me no run but try to walk me can leave. So me take foot, cut through, but everybody jumping and waving and grinding and singing and to the left is uptown, to the left me sight Wolmer's Boys' School and nobody would see me, so I head left but people keep singing and moving and singing and jumping so much me can't see but me walking and walking and every time I think something, that I finally reach the end of the park another voice say *You not going nowhere, pussyhole* and then you sing *So Jah say* and make it official.

I going to make it to the east.

No.

So Jah say.

No bombocloth duppy going catch me.

Yes, them going catch you.

So Jah say.

Josey Wales going find me and then he going kill me but he goin' kill me quick because me know. Or maybe Papa-Lo going find me and he going kill me slow so that all bad man would know.

Yes.

So Jah say.

Nobody can kill the Tuff Gong.

So Jah say.

Me take foot. Me walking, me foot moving faster, but you getting louder, louder, louder, and me take a stop and look and you nearer than before. Loosen the line to trick the fish. And then you look at me and me can't move. And the babies with bat wings and blue flame coming closer, me can't see them but feel them and me can't run from them because you looking at me. And you better stop. You hear me? You better stop. Was not my scheme to kill you, I don't even care if you live or die. Leave me alone, leave me alone, fucking head-lice-infested natty-head Rasta. You looking at me, I know, *so Jah say.* So many people in the stage that you can't even move, police chief in khaki, white man with camera, the Prime Minister standing 'pon top of a Volkswagen, black people so plenty and so black they look like shadow wearing clothes and dancing and skanking in the dark. And you singing and your ghost wife singing and everybody singing and the crowd singing and your real voice slip under all that.

I look at you and see your mouth moving, singing one thing but talking something else. *Look up here Babylon boy, think you can come 'gainst the livication of His Imperial Majesty King Haile Selassie. His foundation is in the holy mountains. Jah loves the gates of Zion more than all the dwellings of Jacob. Glorious things have been spoken of thee, oh city of God. I'll make mention of Rahab and Babylon to them that know I. Behold Philistia and Tyre and with Ethiopia it shall be said that this man was born there and the highest himself shall establish the earth, Jah! Rastafari. Look up here so boy.*

I look. But you not looking at me. You don't need to look at me for the same reason God don't look at man. For one look and man eye would burn out of him skull, burn to nothing, not even a speck, not a dot, less than that. That is not me talking, but you. Me not me no more, me don't sound like me only you and no people deh 'bout, only shadow and no sound dropping through the speaker, only the deep end of the riddim. And you hold the mic up in the air like a torch and cover your eyes again, but you seeing all. They think you dancing but you signifying, your word not mine. My sweat run cold and it won't stop, it run down my back like a cold finger right down the split between me bottom.

Then you move your hand and you flash your dread and lock your stare on me. Through me, inside me, behind me, you reach straight into my heart and grab it. You say watch the work of Rastafari. Watch him turn lion into hunter and hunter into hunted. You know I lost my gun, the gun that nearly take you. You know that even if I did have the gun I couldn't shoot. You know that me is nothing, me is a dead man. You know my heartbeat the snake around me feet, you know you can will the crowd to push me down and swallow me up. You in the jungle, the bush, and you step out in the clearing for audience with His Imperial Majesty. You step forward and roll up your sleeve. Babylon try to smite you through the hand, but fail. You pull the first button on your shirt, then the second, then the third, then puff out your chest like Superman. You point to the wound on your arm and the wound in your chest. You do the war dance of victory and you relive the hunt and everybody see but only I know. My sweat cold. You point to your wound like Jesus pointing to his side to show the work of the spear. More people on the stage now and the pretty woman take back the mic but not before the wind blow and the cock crow and you pull two pistol fast from your holster like the Cisco Kid. Like Marty Robbins. Like, like, like the Man With No Name. You throw back your head and laugh so long that the laugh don't even need a mic. You laugh at me then stop quick and fierce and look straight at me, you eye two fire. I shut my eye tight until I feel you not looking and when I open them you gone. And me know me dead, I can only run when I see that you leave.

But the baby with bat wings flying after me. People shoving, people pushing, and something or somebody hit me straight in the face. Then another hit, straight in the belly, and I think I going vomit but I piss myself. Me not crying. Me not going cry. I can't stop anything that going to happen to me right now, not even my own piss. It run down me foot and people hitting and slapping and punching and passing and running and running and passing. I make out of the park, before people realize that you gone and not coming back, so the street dark and empty and I don't know any of the building across the street. I don't even notice Josey Wales' man Tony Pavarotti until he right in front of me, until him knuckle charge straight for my face.

Demus

Me run all day into the night. Two nights ago I was running down a dream.

A gully so stink with garbage that even the rat them don't come 'round too much. I run from Duke Street up to South Parade and jump on the first bus leaving. Me can't remember if me pay the conductor the five cents. Only four people did was on the bus and only one behind me. Me head start to hurt me, not a big hurt but that nagging one, like a buzzing mosquito fly through your earhole and now he moving up to the top of your head. The buzz that make you feel somebody eyes on your back. I turn around and it's a school boy. Take off the uniform he not older than me, me think. But he not looking at me. Or he only looking at me when I turn my back. I turn around again. I want to walk up to him and cut a telephone mark on him right cheek with my switchblade. I want to smash him head for going to school 'cause me didn't have no chance to go to no pretty school in any pretty khaki uniform. But he is just one boy. I turn my back again and I hear horsefoot. I hear horsefoot getting louder and louder and I know it's the ratatatat of this old bus old engine but I hear horses coming. That's when I jump off the bus in Barbican and climb down from a little bridge down to a gully underneath and stay there.

When me wake up, a hand 'pon me balls. A hand grabbing my pants hard making me jump. All I can see is the hand stretch out from a pile of garbage, a garbage monster made out of newspaper and cloth and plastic bag and spoil food and shit. I yell and kick the monster straight with my foot and it fall back and scream. Some of the newspaper fall away and a woman head pop out. She black like tar with her hair crust up with dirt and paper and two pink hairclip and when she scream again I see only three teeth, one so long and yellow, that she must be vampire covering up herself with newspaper. She still screaming when I look around and find a rock-stone and threaten to fling. She jump up quick, I forget how mad people can be fit and bouncy and ready to run, which she do, down the gully screaming until she get so far that she just a blip, a dot, nothing.

I can't tell the last time me eat food. The last time me bathe. And I was hoping that if me didn't think about a line me wouldn't want a line but now me think about it and is all me can do to stop it. But then me hear horse hoof again. Me heart start to beat fast, boom boom boom with the horse foot clap clap clap and me hand and foot feel cold and getting colder. Me head saying run fool run and the gully shake. But is a truck passing over the bridge. I have to stay hungry. If I stay hungry I think about food. If I stay hungry for a line I think about a line. Because if I think about how hungry me be then I never have to think about Josey Wales *fucking fool it was almost you, it was you until you sniff Weeper shit.* I don't have to think about this bridge and how me only did want to show the brethren not the Singer to never fuck with Demus. How me sick and fucking tired of man using me, first the brethren, then Josey Wales *fucking fool it was almost you, it was you until you sniff Weeper shit*, and before that every man in the fucking ghetto who only think about what they want and how to use me to get it. Something must be on my head that say: use him, for him fool enough, and it must be true. Under the gully you just never know how the stink can drive a man mad. How he can think crazy shit and wicked shit and nasty shit, kill a baby shit or fuck a little girl shit or shit in church shit because the stink so stink all you can think is that the stink must be easing into you like water through a strainer and now you must be stink too. And I just want to wash it off, I just want to wash the whole thing off but the water running through the gully stink too. No. Now I have to think straight. I have to think like a thinking man. I have to get out of Kingston. I have to go. I have to go somewhere, somewhere people never talk about, somewhere like Hanover, who the r'asscloth know what going on in Hanover? Hanover so far from the rest of Jamaica that I can bet they don't even vote in no election. Go to Hanover and take a name like Everton or Courtney or Fitzharold, a name that sound like both mother and father raise me. I hear the horse hoofs again and get up and run. I run in the same direction that the madwoman run me must be mad too hearing horse hoof like me is some naked runaway slave with the mass hot on me trail while me go to the land of Maroons. That must be it, maybe I should run to the maroons—who run to the maroons in 1976? But who going look for me there? This sound like reasoning. It sound like solid reasoning. Like me still have sense. At least me still have sense. It almost make me laugh, me running through the gully, watching it go dark every time me run under a bridge then back into the light when me run out from under it. I run and run and run until the air start to taste salty and me know me soon near the sea. I run and run until the sun reach the top and bake me back, then slide down and down and down until it shock the sky one last time with orange, then sink. And I don't stop, not even when me see that me don't have on no shoes and the water me splashing in start to get cleaner.

I run to a burnout car and almost stop to go in and hide until me turn into bones, but me keep running. Nothing hurt me unless me think about it, so when me think about food, hunger stagger me so bad that me fall down and roll. So me stop thinking about food. Running make me think that surely it soon be curfew so me can climb out of the gully and go somewhere where they be food to thief or water to drink, but me cuss 'cause there me was thinking about food again and me belly groan and cut me up with pain. Is true, you do feel better about things the further you run from it.

I pass the skeleton of a truck next and is not till me pass the skeleton of a boat that me see that me not in the gully no more. But me not in the sea either even though me tasting the salt and smelling the waves. Me toes digging in sand and mud and all around thick with tree, yellow tree that look like plastic with branch the bend smooth and vines hanging down and curling on the ground like snake. The sand cold and wet in one patch, then dry and hot in the other. I walk past a wet patch and a little hole open up and all sort of crab rush out. I stoop down and watch them, the light going out and sea getting louder. I look up and right there in front of me is a plane. It look like it fall and try to fly again but get trap in a spiderweb. The plane still struggling but the bushweb winning. It upright like a cross but the belly still silver and shiny. Half of the left wing gone and the tail sink into the sand. Sea bush and sea flower pushing through the cockpit and out the windows as if bush was the real passenger. Crab running all around it. Part of me want to fly open the door and look if a real skeleton inside and part of me want to sit in the seat and wait for the plane to pull itself free and fly away. The bush rustle and branches crack like wild pig tromping through the bush. I turn around and five six seven eight Rastaman surround me, all of them in white.

—What the bloodcl—

Bam-Bam

M*e a scream out lawd!* Woi! Nononononononono! screaming but me can't scream 'cause the gag block me mouth and me tongue can't push it out and me vomit come up and me can't swallow it back down and me coughing and choking. Josey Wales pull off me own ganzie them was using to blindfold me and all me can see is torch and shadow of man and shadow on tree that look like big giant hand stretching out from the ground but everything blurry. It dark and me try to run but me foot tie together and me hands too. Me can't do nothing but hop so me hop and Josey Wales laugh. I can't see him, me just hear the laugh. But then he nod and come out from behind the tree and I see that he is a man and not a shadow. And Weeper and Tony Pavarotti grab me and lift me up and me can't do nothing, me can't punch them, or thump them, or stab them, or kick them, me can only look at them real fierce, look at them like just once, just once pussyhole Jesus Christ give me the superpower me begging for since me was twelve. Make me stare them with heat energy power that slice them in two. Jesus! Jesus! They grab me and lift me and swing with a one, with a two, with a three and let me go and me fall right down in the grave landing 'pon me stomach with me face right in the mud. Mud cake in me right eye and it burn and it hurt and me can't blink all the dirt out. Me roll over and they just watching me from up top and Josey Wales look down grinning and me mouth taste like vomit and stone and nooooooooooo noooooooo nooooooo me hand a burn and the skin won't come off! The skin won't come off! The skin won't come off so that the blood would loosen the rope and free me hand. Weeper just shoot me, just shoot me please just shoot me, shoot me you bloodcloth wicked pussyhole, shoot me! Shoot me! Josey come up to edge and piss down on me. Me hand behind me back I hearing earthworms and ants I hearing ants they going bite and Pavarotti start filling up the grave nooooo nooooo noooooo mud raining dirt raining kicking and kicking and kicking five feet not six feet under can't get up can't get up mud and dirt and dust to dust and rocks and one rock break me nose and rock bullet me eye and no more toe and noooo sweep with you head sweep it off sweep off the dirt blow hard blow hard blow hard no no no no no no no no no no no no no blow hard can't blow gag Jesus Superman Spiderman Captain America stare hard and superpower goin' come superpower and me don't have a little finger and me pull and pull and pull the rope over the stump of the little finger and free! Free! But the dirt raining and rising and me can't look up but me hear them digging and throwing and dirt and dirt and stone clap forehead, can't think superstare pow wap zip zooo zooom zooooooom pow them take this make joke see I can kick 'way dirt with two foot at the same time can kick 'way dirt like football, like you no like football kick 'way see it deh me bad me bad me tired me tired the dirt keep landing wetter and heavy like God pushing me down no no nuh nuh n—dirt in me left eye can't shut it can't blink can't blink Weeper laugh more dirt more people more more more wiggle! Wiggle! Wiggle! Wiggle foot foot stuck then rock! Rock! Rock side to side no side only dirt turn over turn over 'bout turn over and crouch like baby crouch and so you have air I should have fuck the woman I live with no not her some other girl the girl two door down some other girl white girl charlie's angel pussy pink pussy is pink me see in daddy secret book under the bed which he take out when he think me sleep and go off by himself and make man sound jesus me hard could fuck the ground must fuck the ground fuck fuck fuck want pussy no don't want pussy fuck fuck fuck bend her over and rub the cunt and hoist up the battyhole and sink down the cock and it tight feel like piece of liver wrap 'round you cocky big big like daddy cocky when he fuck me whore mother her back to him she didn't care who sleep and who wake and when she raise up herself daddy cocky like flagpole she raise and raise and couldn't come off but she don't want to come off she slide back down and yelp like puppy pussy cocky balls balls and me never see me father naked and me never see him fuck me mother maybe some other man maybe Funnyboy no he is battyman who make man suck him cocky then shoot them and shoot them dead and me never reach Cuba and me never go to Barbados and never take the S off Superman chest and can't cry through the left eye it full with dirt so breathe in short not deep air scarce air scarce can't feel new dirt dump on me only hear it so dark and wet and heavy, the dirt heavy and can't more no no no no no no no no stop stop breathe breathe short save save what? Dig dig dig dig chuck chuck chuck dead you going dead you going dead make me dead quick no live no dead you going dead take another breath don't use up the air the air feel wet and hard and tight somebody hand over me nose it feel like somebody hand over me nose ah ah ah ah ah hhhhhhhhh Jesus! Jesus! Jeeeees one breath breath breath 1 breath 2 breath 3 breathe 4 breathe breath breathe fi fi fi fi fiiiiiiiiiiiive breath six breath se se se se sevennnnnnnneight br nnnnnnn huhhhhhuhhhuh hhuh hhuhh breeeeeeeeeee-huh huh huh hh hhh hhhhhh h h h h h h nine! Niiiiiiiine nuhhhh nuhhhhhhhh nuhhhh huhhhh hhhhhhh hhhh h h hhhh h daddy no not the yellow fire engine the red one the yellow one can't be real daddy no daddy I want a kisko pop and and lollipop and a tootsie pop and all kinda pop and a purple crayon and red too pink no pink is for girls pink is for girls HubbaBubba chewing gum don't stick even when you blow a big big bubble biggest and bubblest ring around the rosie pocket full of posie aw shucks aw shucks we—

Sir Arthur George Jennings

G*od puts earth* far away from heaven because even he can't stand the smell of dead flesh. Death is not a soul catcher or a spirit, it's a wind with no warmth, a crawling sickness. I will be there when they kill Tony McFerson. I will be there when the Eventide Old Folks home goes up in fire and smoke. Nobody tries to save himself. I will be there when the boy buried alive crosses over but still thinks he's not dead and I'll follow him when he walks to the house of the reggae Singer. I will be there when they come for the last one in the old city. When three run into rough justice. When the Singer dancing with his undead toe falls in Pennsylvania and his locks drop and scatter.

Those who are about to die can see the dead. That is what I'm telling you now but you can't hear me. You can see me following you, you wonder if I'm walking then why does it look like I am not touching the ground even though I walking behind you, behind them? They followed you all the way down to where the swamp meets the sea, you didn't even notice until they were all around you, right by the still shiny plane with the dead man in it surrounded by sacks of white powder. They were seven and you thought they were horsemen from Revelations but they were just men with cutlasses who could smell you out by your fear, men who didn't pursue you at all, but waited until you fell right into place. I can see that you see me. This is not good for you.

You woke up with it on you, demon spit clumped around your face like someone held you by the feet and dipped your head in gelatin. You scooped some off and thought it was a dream, but it was already in you, you breathed it in like a fish. You and the boy buried alive and the rest of them that will never notice that they now sleep on their backs.

Is the white man that don't make no sense, no sense at all you're thinking. I'm following you like the widow in a funeral procession. Your pants snag on a half-buried rock and rip your left pocket. These men pull you like a fish and with each pull the noose around your wrists gets tighter. They've been pulling you for miles and you twist and turn but the last time you twisted you rolled onto your belly and the rocks felt worse, slicing lines down your belly, a jagged red one cracking your right kneecap. They've been dragging you over secret roads, forgotten lanes, weed-ambushed paths and hidden rivers, through the cave that leads deep into the Kingston that only dead slaves know. Only one of them is dragging you and not making much effort to do so, he never yanks, he tugs you like you're a pillow full of nothing but feather, sponge and air. You're not heavy at all: nobody under twenty is heavy. I try to bow my head in reverence as we march, but my head falls whenever I nod and my neck snaps. You roll again and wet grass cuts your face. You've been screaming for miles but the scream dies in a gag, but I will be there to listen.

Rasta avengers all in white smell of ganja smoke and iron in the blood. Seven men with nothing to say, seven men, one pulling you by rope through the bush, up this hill, down this valley, then up another hill while the bloody moon pays no attention. I wonder how their pants stay so white in the bush. Three of the seven have wrapped their head in white, like African tribal women. You can see me. You're hoping that I read eyes. I can and *they don't care when me roll and me face and nose and mouth full with dirt and grass it bitter it bitter it bitter nuh fuck where we going where them going me face going scrape right off and me head going look like the bloody moon and the moon be bleeding and the grass slice through me skin with every step and they all moving through the bush like they not walking nobody walking everybody walking on this air gliding through bush the bush blade cut ow.* But you're not the man I'm waiting for. I thought so because I smelled his scent on you, faint, but there, and I almost thought it was him until I saw that it was you. Many more will have to suffer. Many more will have to die.

These men sing no songs as they drag you through the bush. My skin is as white as their clothes but I have no clothes on. You can't stop yourself from trying to scream. You're wondering if I am with them or not, if they can see me or not, and if I am not real then this is not real, and even a procession towards death is just a metaphor for something else. You have never heard the word metaphor.

But you have it in you, something I did not have. An understanding of the men taking you up. Maybe after so many miles of being dragged you've separated them, id and superego, your mind that knew you had it coming and your heart that could never accept it. It's the irrational side of man that clutched the straw, that tried everything to stay alive, that grabbed clumps of air in the midst of a fall over a balcony, screaming to God for a grip. I have no understanding of the man who killed me. You look at me, and even in the dark I can see your red eyes blink fierce.

He right there. He looking at me and at them. He marching at the back, left right left right, plenty step behind them and he looking at them and at me and at the sky like he crying and he don't talk to them help me help me police murder stop don't walk like you don't see blood and you not no witness. I don't know if that make more sense than that he be a white man so white man say something nuh? Scream run come back with gun scream run don't just walk and no me nah look 'pon you when them pulling me through the bush me pull back no twist spin 'round 'pon me back the bush underneath me rope around me hand burning roll over back on stomach no back no side no stomach and see them two no three no four we on a hill must be 'cause the rope pulling me harder and it hurt and the white man looking but then he head gone and me can't see 'cause is deep bush and the bush thorn cut bombocloth jeeezas the white man gone but then he back see him there still behind but him head gone, no, it swing like he no have no neck then he use him hand what him doing? He putting him head back on he screwing it tight Jeeesaz Christ Jeeesaz Christ, bombocloth is not man is rolling calf but he look like a man but him eye not on fire and me go through a bush and stuck stop pulling stop pulling me scream into the gag stop pulling and he stop pulling and two come 'round me no don't kick me and other one set him foot on me side no don't kick me and push to roll me over and the two of them is Rasta they dreadlocks alive like is snake, no smoke, no snake and they in white and both have machete in left hand, no right hand forehead booming don't chop me do please don't chop me and it cold where me little toe suppose to be the left one, no the right me woman crying she crying right now she find other man to mind her the pussycloth whoring bitch no she crying she gone to Josey Wales and ask where me man deh? What you do with him? Josey Wales get her too he fuck her he fuck her and turn her into fool or him give her money you hear that? Me have judas woman too white man, me too, and the Rasta in white kick me and roll me out of the bush the moon white it not bleeding no more r'asscloth me wrist burning they pulling me over a rock in the middle of me back cutting scraping down it hook me pants they pulling and pulling stop stop stop they pull rip tear they pulling me up the hill and bye-bye pants behind wet grass cutting through the white man gone they pulling me bump me head bump asphalt road they drag me across a road scraping stop stop stop gravel dig into me bottom gravel stuck in me back digging digging my bottom wet, wet bottom blood know is blood sticky iron smell blood white man is blood for true answer me pussyhole where you deh? Them pull me 'cross the road into bush still up the hill Josey Wales me going kill Josey Wales me oh God Jesus Christ Jesus Christ Lord Jesus me no want to dead lawd Poppa Jesus Woi Jesus do me no want to dead the white man come back the white man is Jesus no why you don't say nothing look blood running down him face.

I say too much. I'm the man nobody listens to. And soon you will be too. They pull you up the steepest the hill has been, your body snapping twigs and crushing leaves and even I am wondering why the moon won't pick a side. They pull you onto a trail that runs along a dark river rustling, I have some memory of this place but I don't know if it's my own. They drag you along the path for minutes, and then stop. I look ahead while you try to swing around and do the same. When you see what I see your mouth will exclaim so wide that the gag nearly falls out.

A line, a gate, a fortress wall of Rastamen, most in white but some in colours hidden by moonlight, all in a line, side by side, with cutlasses and knives in hand, machine guns strapped across backs, as far as anyone can see. Man beside man, and beside him, men all the way across right, all the way across left, stretching so far that the lines disappear around the bends of the hill and continues. A band of men in a circle around a mountain that I know of, but cannot remember. I cannot stop looking at them. I forget about you. I want to run around the hill and see if the line ever breaks but I know it does not. They have sealed the top of the mountain from the country. But they let through the seven Rastas pulling you. Not a single man speaks except for your screaming mumble. They pull you along the path fifty feet then veer off, all of them, like the sudden turn of birds. The bush reaches waist-high, there is no path but they seem to know where to go. I see the tree before you do.

They stop. The man pulling you lets the rope loose while two help you up by the arms. They position you to stand but you see the tree spread out above you and collapse. They grab you before you fall. You wait for them to let you go and try to hop away. They do not follow or even raise alarm, just wait for you to fall. The large one who pulled you all this way grabs you by the belt and you're in the air. He carries you like a doll. Only one man on this hill has run out of time. He holds you in place. The noose was already there. Already waiting. He tries to put it around your neck but you jerk left to right, north to south, screaming into the gag. You wiggle, you shake, you turn and look at me. Even in the dark I can see you blinking. You've been screaming for minutes but I'm the only one who knows that you have been screaming at me. With one hand the big Rastaman holds your neck in place and slips over the noose. Tightens. I thought they would have put you on a drum and kicked your life away. But your neck is in a noose at the end of a rope that shoots up and over a strong branch then down the tree into the grip of two Rastas who wrap it in their hands and tug. I wonder if you find this as obscene as I do that they are so quiet, as if this is work. There will be no last words. I wonder if you are crying now. I wonder if you hope somehow the Singer will hear you begging for mercy.

But you should know this.

The living, they never listen.

SHADOW DANCIN’

February 15, 1979

Kim Clarke

E*very time I get* on the bus there's this point where I know it's going to blow up. The thing is I always think it will explode from the rear and because of that I sit up front. As if sitting up front is going to make any difference. Maybe it was because of the bombing of that restaurant in London in February—I stopped watching the news for months then turned on the TV only to see that shit. Chuck says *you worry too much, babykins, just don't take the bus.* Jesus Christ I hate babykins, hate it, can't stand it, pull out a gun and shoot it, which makes him like calling me that all the more. He says it's because he can see my eyebrow arch before I feel myself arching it. Chuck says then babykins just don't take the bus if you hate being packed like a sardine. I don't tell him that is not what I hate.

You know I can feel it, my back getting straighter and straighter as I walk home. Something about it, walking home. I like people seeing me walking to that home, but I don't like them watching me. They don't see me as me, but me as a woman walking to that house near the beach that looks like somebody up and plucked it out of *Hawaii Five-O.* A house that looks like it have no business there and people will wonder why this black woman think she have reason to go deh so with her head held high like she own it. First they will see me as *a woman* who go there once and have to leave in the morning with whatever was my rate. Then they'll see me as *that woman* who go there plenty and must be sweeting that white boy good, or at least being discreet about it. Then they'll see me as maybe him woman who leave at any hour. Then they will see me leaving and coming and carrying paper shopping bag and think, maybe she have something to do with the house, like the maid. Then they will see that I leave in not good clothes and return, or go on a jog which is the new white people thing in

America, and only then start to think maybe she live there for true. She and the white man. No, the white man and she. Afternoon to you too, sir, Mr. Let-me-push-my-handcart-slow-so-that-me-can-spy-into-people-private-business—move on, master. Broke my good heel on this road last week—road my ass, this is a trail, up the hill then down again, to the little cliff near the beach where only people like Chuck would think to live. Or Errol Flynn.

Chuck. How much wood would a woodchuck chuck, I said when he came up to me at Mantana's Bar where all the expatriates and people who work for Alcorp Bauxite go, because it's the only place where the hamburgers don't taste like the Jamaicans really believe they are made out of ham. And he took his hat off too like he was some cowboy and said, *Howdy I'm Chuck.* You're sure you not Bill from Sales who howdy'd me only three nights ago? I thought but didn't say. Chuck. It's like Chip, Pat, Buck or Jack. I just love these one-punch American names, they sound like apple pie and easy money and you utter them once with so little effort and you're done. You get a yup, a howdy, a what's shaking lil' lady and suddenly you feel the need to tell them that no, this is not one of those local ladies who is not wearing a panty underneath her dress for your convenience, but thanks for the scotch which I'm not going to drink. Don't know which I relive more, counting down hours and reducing them to minutes in Mantana's waiting for HIM or when Chuck said howdy and I thought, well you'll do.

Home. Watch it, Miss Kim, you're calling the place something not even Chuck calls it. I'm going to walk into the living room right now thinking about exploding buses and say, Chuck, and he's going to say *Yep? What's shakin' honeybun?* and I'll feel like a rabbit safe in a hole. No I'm not. That's some stupid shit from a stupid book for God's sake stop thinking, Kim Clarke. Late day at work, usually he's home by now. Usually I would have cooked dinner by now, the shit you can get away with when you're making it up as you go along, *damn, babykins, I didn't know Jamaican rice had pepper in it,* he said last night. Look where that thinking shit has gotten you, now gulls are out the window. Now I'm the woman who lives close to seagulls. I hate gulls. Little bitches plopping down their little shitty batties like unwanted guests every afternoon and taking over my own damn terrace saying move bitch is fi we terrace now. I don't know why they keep coming, there's no food outside and I sure as shit am never going to feed them. And they're so damn loud and nasty and only fly away when they see Chuck. They couldn't care a r'asscloth about me. I know what they're thinking. They're thinking we was here first, long before you start shack up with man and we was here before him too. Screaming like they know stuff about me—get away from my window or my American Chuck will pull out his American gun and bang bang Quick Draw McGraw and put a lead one through your head, see? Jesus Christ, when did I start watching cartoons?

Today I will love his hair. I will think about his hair and how it's brown but never one colour brown and red when it gets near his cheek and how he likes it short like a soldier but now he's growing it long because I said honey you'd make a nice pirate thinking the sentence would vanish to the same idle place it came from but he loved it so now he's my sexy pirate—I never called him sexy. Must be because I said honey.

Sexy.

Sexy is John—what's his name? What is his name? *Dukes of Hazzard*, General Lee, not the brown hair one he's too husband-looking, the John one, damnit shit his name is John.

Sexy. Luke Duke sliding off the car trunk lifting one leg into car and squeezing his snake down the other leg, do other women see this or only me? Kim Clarke, you pervert, you nasty girl. He never wears a brief, that John. Schneider. *Dukes of Hazzard*'s showing this week on the satellite dish, the only satellite dish I know is the big one outside the JBC TV station back in Kingston but Chuck put one up on his roof.

Yes, today I will think of how I love what he is about to do with his hair. Yesterday, I loved how he always took his cap off when he came through the door, *yes ma'am*. Any door. The day before, I loved how he calls me Miss Kim anytime I go on top when we fuck, no I don't like it, don't like it at all, the Miss Kim not the fucking, but I like that he likes it so much, of course he likes it the black bitch that finally makes him go wild—he must have heard the story about Jamaican girls two years before he even landed with a technical drawing kit and a cock-stand. Americans call cock-stands hard-ons, which makes no sense. No. He's sweet. The man sweet, and nice so till, and he lifts me up with his two hands like me make out of paper but hands so soft so sweet and he lifts me up and put me on the kitchen counter and smiles and says *hey babykins miss me?* and I think about it more than once that yes, I did miss you, I did miss you because when you're not here it's just me and thoughts and I hate thinking, I fucking hate it gone to hell.

Leave the thinking to Chuck.

Leave the moving to Chuck. Leave the deciding what to take with and what to leave behind to Chuck. I like the second half of that thought much more than the first and ohshitjesuschrist.

Oh wait,

it's a muffler.

It's a blast from a muffler.

Jesus Christ breathe, Kim Clarke. Breathe in, out, in, out, in, out. That's the third time I called myself Kim Clarke without thinking right before that I need to call myself Kim Clarke, or after saying look at that I called myself Kim Clarke. Even this thinking about Kim Clarke is about me reaching the point where I don't even have to think about it anymore, or that other name. Fuck that person. See? I say fuck like an American, like Chuck who still says darn it—cute. Chuck and his *motherfucker*, every time he watched Monday night football it was about *motherfucker this* or *motherfucker that* or *it's called a spread offense, motherfucker.* Nobody in the game uses their feet, but it's football. I love how Americans can just claim something to be whatever they feel it is, despite clear evidence it's not. Like a football game with nobody using any feet that takes forever. Last time he had me sit through that shit I said baby only sex should last this long and he called me his *sexy little slut.* I didn't like that either, it was one of the two hundred mistakes men make every day with women they live with, and it made me wonder just how many women has he actually had sex with. I mean, he's not bad looking. No, he's cute. No, he's handsome. Look, right now three thousand Jamaican women probably hate me because I'm with him. I have what you want, you pussyholes. Me, Kim Clarke. Come and get it if you bad.

Lie that. I know for a fact that Jamaican women not out there looking for a white man from foreign. Most of them can't even figure out what they would look like naked. They think white men are all balls no cocky, which only prove that they've never seen a blue movie. Coming home in the sun, three p.m., Montego Bay feels like Miami, you never been to Miami, Kim Clarke. But still, coming home, going home I hope Chuck isn't there. That was harsh. Uncalled for he would say, which he's been saying a lot these days, making me think that everything that come out of me mouth tainted with something. That is not what I want to think, I just want some me time. There I go again talking like a hurry-come-up American for so long that now I can't drop the Yankee talk even in my own head. Straight thinking please! I just hope he's not there because I just want to sit in the settee and hear my own breathing and watch *Wok with Yan* on TV and just put the brain on rest because all of this, this living, this walking, this talking, this sitting in space that is still not my space is fucking hard work. Existing is hard work. No it's not. It's the living that's bombocloth hard. I swear sometimes.

Are these gulls hearing what I think? Is that what they are doing outside? Listening to my thoughts and laughing. Does fly and roach spray work on birds? Maybe they would rip my skin apart and eat it. Fucking hate the damn birds. Fucking don't know what to do with all these Chuck-isms I speaking lately. It just happens doesn't it, some point where a man just start living all over you.

Chuck isn't home. This couch feels nice. I fall asleep in the couch all the time but never fall asleep in the bed. Most nights I just lie on Chuck's bushy chest to listen if his heart ever skips.

I really need to clean this house even if we're leaving. Even if we're leaving at the end of next month. Would have given anything to have cut this place loose in December. I want a white Christmas. I've been dreaming of a white Christmas. No, I've been dreaming of a faraway Christmas. The quicker I can get away from this godforsaken country, the better. When Chuck told me he was from Arkansas I think I asked him if that was near Alaska. He asked if I just love polar bears or lumberjacks. Whatever that meant. I rubbed his belly and said I have the big bear I love but he didn't think that was so funny. American men are strange. Can't take a little joke, but then find the most fucked-up shit funny. There I go, thinking like an American again, fucked-up shit, thinking like him. Today I shall love his hair. I will sink into this settee and close my eye and think about his hair. And what to pack.

They've had enough, really they've had just about enough from this comic opera of a government. Funny, this house is far from the road, right by the sea that's roaring all the time with those white feather bitches cawing outside my window and yet traffic sounds still find a way to get down here. Like that damn horn interrupting my thoughts. But they've had enough really, he said they said. Time to cut this fucking place loose, his boss said. Enough of this government and this Michael Manley wanting to suck cash from the bauxite companies like they don't already do enough to help this country. *Shit, Alcoa transformed this fucking backwater island, sure they didn't build the railway but they certainly put it to profitable use. And other things: schools, modern buildings, running water, toilets, it was a slap in the face really, demanding a levy on top of all we do for this country. And that slap in the face was the first shot heard around the world for Jamaica's entry into communism, mark my words. Nationalization is always the first step, how these fucking people voted the PNP back into office is a fucking mystery to me, babykins.* He's said this little rant so often that I can almost recite it verbatim, even the mixed metaphors. So what about that pitch-lake you guys left that's only good for gunmen to dump bodies in so that they will disintegrate without a trace? I say. Sometimes I have to remind even him that three feet north of this vagina is a brain. Still, even an American man don't like when a woman's too smart, especially a Third World woman whom it is his duty to educate. This couch is softer than I remember.

Two years since the election. Jamaica never gets worse or better, it just finds new ways to stay the same. You can't change the country, but maybe you can change yourself. I don't know who's thinking that. I'm done with thinking, quite frankly. Every time I think it takes me to a bus exploding or me looking down the barrel of a gun. Shit, all that shaking is me, not the couch. I mean, settee. Goddamn, that man is changing me. I like to act like I don't like it. But I don't think I fool him. He looks at it as some kind of victory every time he gets somewhere with me, because truth be told I don't let him get very far. That sounds harsh. I hope I'm not harsh. I can't even remember how we went from howdy to him taking me out, his term not mine.

Figuring things out is a dangerous thing. It makes you look backward and that's also dangerous. You keep doing it you find yourself right back at the thing, the one thing that pushed you forward in the first place. I don't know and I swore I put myself on the damn couch to stop the fucking thinking. I wish he was home. Silly girl you just wished he wasn't. Barely five minutes ago, girl, I was with you I heard every word. Can people do that? Can people want to be with someone all the time, okay most of the time, and yet also wish they were alone? And not in little compartments but at once? At the same time? All the time? I want to be alone but I need to not be. I wished Chuck was one of the men I thought that would make sense to. Usually I just turn on the radio and let it fill the house, noise, people, music, company that I don't have to acknowledge or respond to but I know they are there. I wish I could do that with people. I wish people would do that with me. Where's the man who I can be with who doesn't need me to need him? I don't know what I'm talking about. Need is the only reason I'm right here, right now in this room. No. Jesus, what a bitch. Today I shall love his hair.

Tonight I shall love all the sounds he makes when he sleeps. The heehaw, the whistle when one of his nostrils blocks. The half of a sentence. The mumble. The flap flap flap flap snore. The groan. The American fart. That part of the night, three-ish, four-ish, when I can ask a question and he'll answer, which is how I know he's not really sure how his family will react to meeting a woman like me, though his mom is just the sweetest gal, really just the sweetest. I know all his sounds because I never sleep. Up all night, sleep all day, there are names for women like me. Women like me don't sleep. We know that the night is no friend of us. Night does things, brings people, swallows you up. Night never makes you forget but it enters dreams to make you remember. Night is a game where I wait, I count off until I see the little pink streak cut through our window and I go outside to see the sun rise over the sea. And congratulate myself for making it, because I swear, every night. Every night.

Last night I realized I could kill anybody, even a child. Maybe a boy. Don't know about a girl. Just because you don't sleep doesn't mean you don't dream, there's something my mother never told me. Last night I could have killed a kid. There was this gate and it was just some rusty gate but I knew I had to get through it. The only way forward is through. Who said that? I had to get through it, if I didn't I would die, get cut open, sliced with a knife from the neck right down to labia with me screaming all the time, I just had to get through the fucking gate. And there was this kid at the gate, one of those children you see in movies where you can't tell if it's a boy or a girl. Maybe he was white but white like linen not skin. And the whole time I could see the white alarm clock about to hit two a.m. and the four walls around me, two glass windows, even the sky outside, but I could also see the gate, and I could hear Chuck snoring but I could also see the kid and I could look down and see slashed-up flesh where my feet was supposed to be. I had run my feet off. And I wanted to go through the gate and this kid was blocking it with this look, not threatening but confident, smarmy, cocky—Chuck would have said cocky. And I took this knife that I had and grabbed him by the hair and lifted him up and drove the knife in his heart and because the blood was blue I didn't feel bad about stabbing him again and again and every time the knife went through his skin it's like his flesh was too tough and the knife bent in a different direction than where I aimed and the kid was screaming and laughing and screaming and the only thing to do was pull out the knife and saw his head off and throw it away. And scream as I ran to the gate. Then I woke up. But I wasn't asleep.

Maybe I should bathe or something. When Chuck was going off to work he asked what am I up to today? Shouldn't have told him nothing because I went out. Maybe I should take off these clothes or at least these shoes. Even a man who loves to say *babykins, I don't know about this fashion shit*, knows the clothes I wear to go out is not the clothes I wear to buy bread. And if he sees his woman in the good clothes he would know she was trying to impress a man and might have succeeded, but that man is not him. I really should at least take off this blouse. Or lie down until the gulls fly away. Maybe if he asks I can say I was dressing up for him, hoping we would go out. *But babykins, nowhere's safe outside*, he's going to say. *Not even in Montego.* I'll say that Jamaicans shorten Montego Bay by saying Mobay, not Montego. I'll say I want to go out, I want to dance and he'll say *but I dance better than you* and I'll pretend that last one didn't sting. The truth is I don't want to go dancing. Every time I ask I hope he says no. I just want him to believe that I'm interested in doing everything with him. Maybe he'll come home with friends again and I'll have a reason to keep these clothes on. The last time he brought home four men from work, all of them looking like shorter and taller versions of him, all of them with the same burnt white skin. The short blond one, I swear his name was Buck, but it was close to Chuck, said *well, you're as fine looking a squaw as I've ever seen.* And here I was getting upset when Jamaican man call me beef. Tonight I going love the way him sleep. I going to lie on him big chest and lick him hair and I going to hold tight so that he can't go without me. There's this memory I have of waiting for my sister to sleep then grabbing the tail of her nightie and wrapping it 'round and 'round my hand so that if the duppy come to snatch me away he would pull her too and wake us up. Except I don't have a sister.

Shit. Damn it, ackee, how did you get under me for me to roll on you? I must be getting old or mad to walk in the house with a shopping bag full of ackees and not even remember it. Old and mad. Maybe mad and old. Chuck loves ackees. He keeps asking for *that thing, hon, that scrambled egg thing, you know what I mean, that grows on trees and is really sweet to boot.* Bought two dozen from this woman who was listening on her transistor radio to an American preacher with a cowboy accent who kept saying it's the end times. *Do you know we're in the last days?* the higgler said to me. No, but I do know it's 1979, I said to her even though I was thinking about the Preacher, sweating like a red hog and rubbing his forehead with a handkerchief, shifting his toupee. Not the answer she was looking for, so she punished me by adding on fifty cents to the price. I think I said, You know what, babylove?

Have it. Take it, for in a few weeks the only thing Jamaica money would be good for would be to wipe me batty. I like that. It sounded Jamaican. I didn't say any of that. I would never call anybody babylove.

Damn place too quiet but I just can't handle the radio. I don't want to hear any news. Ever since I stopped listening to news, reading newspapers and watching TV, my life just seems so much happier. Happy feels like something you can take out and sell. I just don't want to know the news and I don't want people to tell me anything. All my news comes from Chuck and I still don't like it. But his news is different. His is the news of somebody leaving. He's leaving. We're leaving. Has he bought tickets? Will we need tickets? Is a helicopter coming like this is war and just airlift we out? It will just land outside and Chuck will say *babykins, there's no time to grab anything just come now* and he'll look really sad and not know that this is exactly what I want, to take nothing, not even a towel, nothing that will remind me of anything I'm leaving behind, because fuck all of it, really, fuck all of it, I want to get to America as blank a slate as slate can be with no memory of anything behind me. I want to teach myself to write something new on my skin and say howdy to people I don't know. And the helicopter won't land until we're somewhere far, like Buffalo, New York, or Alaska, somewhere that I'll never hear wha'appen ever again. Ever again.

Something good must be on the damn radio. FM: more music, less talk. Wish Chuck was here. He can dance much better than me, the disgrace to the black race. It's something when a white man can dance. He took us to the club for our anniversary—six months already. He wanted to celebrate our six-month anniversary. And they say woman is the cornier sex. But still. Sixth was dancing. Fifth was earrings. Fourth he tried to cook chicken and failed. My mother would have said that means he's not a homosexual, dear. I don't know, but sometimes there's just too much Chuck. I'm starting to like him more when he's at work. No. That's not true. Right now I'm loving his hair and tonight I will love how he sleeps.

Back at Mantana's when I met him I was at the point where that inner voice said whatever it is, God, let it happen now please. I was so sick and tired of being sick and tired. I was so ready to go. My boss put his hand on my knee the same day, second time? No, third, and asked me how much I liked working here. And how he could tell that this job was a make-or-breaker, a last resort. Like selling cheap as shit jewellery from some over-glorified coolie shop calling itself Taj Mahal was the best I could do. Except it was, Kim Clarke. All you needed to take the job was to know that they wouldn't have wasted a second to look for somebody else. Montego Bay just had to work. It had to, there was no going back to Kingston.

I don't think of Kingston. I want to think about Andy Gibb. Almost as cute as John from *Dukes of Hazzard.* Andy Gibb: hair, chest, hair, chains, hair, teeth, hair, hair. John the Duke smile, hair, jeans, hair like a girl, *I just want to be your everything*, Luke Duke's big white duke down the left leg of his pants, Jesus Christ girl you must be the one woman in Montego Bay with such a dirty mind. But it's not "I Just Want to Be Your Everything" on the radio. *Do it light, take me through the night, shadow dancin'*. I know what I want. One night where I don't think of Luke Duke when Chuck inside me, on top of me. No I didn't think that. Yes I did. I should go cook his ackee. He likes it for breakfast. He won't mind it for dinner. I will think about how I love his hair.

Sooner or later he's going to know. Kim Clarke, you think you're so smart. That man bound to find out if he don't know already. This morning I only took ten dollars. It was the most in one shot. Last Friday, five. Four days before that six, no five, no it was a five-dollar bill and two one-dollars. I never touch the U.S. Look, he just going to think it's cute. Which wife doesn't take from her husband's wallet? I'm not his wife. I'm going to be his wife. No you're living together. It's what people do in the modern age, this is 1979. I really need to cook. I'm sure he doesn't know. I mean, what kind of man counts how much money he has in his wallet?

An American man.

All of them come through Mantana's. White men, that is. If the man is French he thinks that he gets away with saying cunt but saying you cohnnnt, because we bush bitches will never catch his drift. As soon as he sees you he will throw the keys at your feet saying you, park my car *maintenant*! *Dépêche-toi!* I take the keys and say yes massa, then go around to the women's bathroom and flush it down the shittiest toilet. If he's British, and under thirty, then his teeth are still hanging on and he'll be charming enough to get you upstairs but too drunk to do anything. He won't care and you won't either, unless he vomits on you and leaves a few pounds on the dresser because that was such dreadful, dreadful business. If he's British and over thirty, you spend the whole time watching the stereotypes pile up, from the letttttt meeeee sssssspeeeeeakkk toooo youuuuu slowwwwlyyyyy, dahhhhhhhling beccauuuuuse youuuuuuu're jussssst a liiiiiiitle blaaaaack, speed of their speech to the horrible teeth, coming from that cup of cocoa right before bed. If he's German he will be thin and he will know how to fuck, well in a car piston kind of way, but he will stop early because nobody can make German sound sexy. If he's Italian, he'll know how to fuck too, but he probably didn't bathe before, thinks there's such a thing as an affectionate face slap and will leave money even though you told him that you're not a prostitute. If he's Australian, he'll just lie back and let you do all the work because even us blokes in Sydney heard about you Jamaican girls. If he's Irish, he'll make you laugh and he'll make the dirtiest things sound sexy. But the longer you stay the longer he drinks, and the longer he drinks, well for each of those seven days you get seven different kinds of monster.

But Americans. Most of them spend a very long time, or an awful long time, trying to convince you just how like everybody else they are. I'm just an Okie from Muskogee. Even Chuck introduced himself by saying that he was *just a regular guy from Little Rock.* When I said why would anybody want to be just a regular guy, he didn't know how to answer the question. There's something though about a man saying upfront that what you see is what you get, nothing less but certainly nothing more. Maybe my standards are low. Maybe I just liked that there was one man who said it like it was. I don't even think he found me that cute. Well of course he did, he came over and said *howdy*, and perfect timing too, right after the Frenchman was thrown out for shouting where are my car keys, you cohhnt, and the Italian went over to dance with some stupid American woman who flew here all alone because she saved up for twenty-six months and damn it, this big fat bitch is going to F.U.C.K. The Italian wasn't the black, bulging, big-cocked mandingo that she had read about in *Mistress of Falconhurst*, but his skin was a little dark so he'd do.

Of course I was there every night. I moved to Montego Bay in January, right into a one-bedroom side of a house with a shared kitchen that a retired couple used to rent to boarding school students. But I lived at Mantana's. From the first day on the job I heard about the night club. Well, overheard at work since none of those coolie bitches at the jewellery store talked to any black employee, other than to remind us that they knew the police and should just one pendant go missing we will spend the entire weekend getting raped in jail. Anyway, I overheard that Mantana's *was the place that was carrying the swing, and they only let you in if you had the right look, which thank the Lord wasn't black.* Who knew then that black would turn out to be the right look? Two weeks after moving here, wearing nothing but a white t-shirt, Fiorucci jeans and high heels, they let me in. Walked right past one of the coolies, the hook-nosed, long-haired one who almost called at me before she saw me looking and knew that she would never be able to live with herself. I came this close to saying that sometimes they want chocolate, not curry.

But once inside with the music everything that I thought it would be, it wasn't. The DJ kept playing "Fly Robin Fly" and the white people were dancing like white people. And the non-white people, almost all women, looked at each other with a scowl because only a scowl could hide that we all had the same damn look. The white man please come over here and save me because I have nowhere left to go look. I feel like I pushed myself to the very tip of the country and all that's left was to tip over. Or fly away. Who am I going to be in America? Samantha on *Bewitched*? That bawling woman on *One Day at a Time*? I want to run right into the middle of a city and throw my hat up in the air like Mary Tyler Moore you're gonna make it after all. Jesus Christ I'm so ready to go.

I am so ready to go.

I almost forgot it. I rubbed my hands on it three times in the sun, feeling each groove of the stamp. The stamp makes it real. The stamp made it smell good, yes I smelled it. Seeing it never made it real. Touching it made it real, but the smell made it realer. My fingers smell like American paper, like chemicals waiting to evaporate. I almost forgot it. Kim, try to forget everything around it. And stop smiling like that, it makes your cheeks hurt. But if you don't smile you cry.

You smell. Have to wash the stink out. Wash the ink off you damn finger. How could I have forgotten? He'll be home in a few hours and I haven't washed the stink out. Girl, go wash the . . . enough. This is what I will do. This is what will work. I will go bathe. I will cook the man his ackee. He will take me upstairs and he will fuck me. No, we will fuck each other. And we will wake up together, and he will—no, we will not leave for at least three weeks. I will pack. Go girl, wash the stink out.

Each day he takes home something from the office. Part of it seems like how these Americans grew up. They collect things. So Tony Curtis or Tony Orlando will show up at Mantana's and they all ask him for this autograph business, which is him signing his name on a napkin. And they cling to it, and collect it like they'll never see Tony Curtis again. Now Chuck is taking things home, collecting them like he had to make sure they were safe. I don't know what he has to protect a coffee cup from. Or five boxes of rubber bands, a picture of Farrah Fawcett, a picture of President Carter or a box full of liquor as if they don't have liquor in America. Or a sculpture of a Rastaman grabbing on to his erect penis, the head bigger than his actual head. The man must think he is Noah saving a statue of a Rasta with a huge cock for his ark. If he's saving that fucking sculpture and don't plan to save me I swear to God I will kill him.

I'll go bathe and then I'll go cook ackee and saltfish. No, ackee and corned pork, no saltfish. And tomatoes. Kim Clarke, go wash the stink out. Don't think, just leave these in the kitchen and go wash. And brush your teeth. And swallow just a little Listerine. Maybe it's just the same for men. It is? Maybe, I don't know. Insert whatever I'm supposed to be feeling right here:_________________ so I can feel it. I don't feel anything. Maybe I should feel something about not feeling anything but I don't feel that either. What kind of a woman are you, Kim Clarke? Every time you lick your lips, you smell and/or taste him. Wash him out of your mouth at least, nasty girl.

I can see him kicking me out. It will be like in a movie where everybody is talking Italian. He's dragging me out of my house—his house—the house and me on the floor screaming and begging and crawling and bawling Chuck do, no kick me out, do, no kick me out, me beg you. Me will walk on all fours fi you. Me will cook you food and breed you pickney and suck you cocky even when you don't wash it first, Do! Do! And he will look at me and ask what the fuck you mean by do? What kind of ignorant bushbaby bullshit is it when do means the same thing as please? A cock is a cock is a cock to you, he will say because it sounds savage, like he didn't spend any time to think it up, so then he can be angry and still be smart while me on the floor whimpering do, do, do, and wonder if I can just be like in *Dallas* and say it's not what it looks like, honey.

I should bathe, brush my teeth, wash it out with soap. But then won't I be too clean? Then I'm so clean that it's suspicious. We at the stage where I don't have to comb my hair or wear lipstick and perfume, and don't care if he catches me scratching my batty and stirring the pot with the same hand. He now bursts a fart whenever he wishes, which I really don't like. American farts are stinker, they smell like they eat too much meat. Careful what you wish for when you finally make a man feel comfortable around you. You realize how much of this courting bullshit was just show. Not show, performance. How long would he have kept the act going, and if it was longer than he bargained for would he have just cut me loose and move on to the next local girl staring into her drink? Thank God that black skin don't show. A black woman can hide the traces on her. Maybe that's why man think it easier to beat a black woman. You can track the relationship between a man and a white woman on her skin. Stupid girl, then just make him not want you tonight. Give yourself a headache, say you on your menses, he especially hates when you call it menses, says it sounds like pussy measles.

Do I have any passport photos left over?

Do they have hot water in America?

Dumb bitch, of course they have hot water. And they don't have to turn on the heater and wait either. Maybe I should put a capful of Pine-Sol in the water. Jesus Christ, Kim Clarke, you have his sweat on you, not pus. Look, boss, that is all the money I have, you have my watch, you even have the chain he gave me last week. Now I'm going to have to say that it fell down the drain or something. Give me the damn passport. What you mean me have one more valuable thing? I don't know what you're talking about.

Oh.

I tell you, you could be from the South Pole or south St. Catherine you man is all the same *Don't back-talk to the man, Kim, just get it done.* Here? In your office? People outside *of course people outside. He wants everybody outside to hear and know.* How do I know you going to hand it over afterwards? *Don't aggravate the man, silly cunt you been waiting two years, almost two years but still a long time, and he can tear everything up right in front of you—do I have any more passport photos—I really don't like when people take pictures of me, do I have the negatives? Pictures all over the wall, naked white women, two black, squeezing their titties together.* Oh don't take off my dress? Jesus Christ wait nuh, I can pull down my own panty thank you. *Kim stop looking at calendars and remember to act like it's a big hataclaps when he pushes himself in you, he'll* Ooh, ooh, oh God you never tell me you was so big *Big like a rotten banana, don't you agree Miss December? You see him taking it out all the time to every woman who comes through that door that needing something they're not supposed to have. Will I have time to buy ackees after this and still wash him out? Maybe I can go over to the hotel across the street and slip in their bathroom and wipe this son of a bitch off me. Hush, Kim Clarke, close your eyes and think of Arkansas.* Uh huh uh huh uh huh. *On his door is NOTARY PUBLIC and JUSTICE OF THE PEACE in reverse. When a man behind you can never tell what he have coming. Shit, didn't even notice that me frigging finger was in the stamp pad. Great, purple ink on fingertips while this man keep working me from behind and all I can hear is skin flapping and slapping. Maybe I should steal these fake stamps just in case I need another passport.* You soon come? *One year, five months, seventeen days, eleven hours, thirty minutes and this is what you come to. This is what it takes to finally get it, the passport, the visa, the ticket out of bombor'asscloth Babylon—I hope to God this man comes soon. Just close your eyes and think of tumbleweed, Kim Clarke. Arkansas, no Arkansaw, I love it. We're going to pull up in a wagon on top of a hill and Laura Ingalls and Mary Ingalls and the little one who keeps falling in the grass are going run towards us for by now we have three children all girls, okay maybe a boy, but only one. God, good thing I'm on the pill. Maybe this son of a bitch won't give me gonorrhea. I hear people in his office stopping to listen. No finger has struck a typewriter key in seven minutes, I've been tapping the seconds and watching the clock on the wall. And Miss April, Miss May, Miss September and Miss August, not pressing her titties but spreading her—maybe if I get on like a blue movie girl this would finish quicker—Chuck, does he know that I know that he keeps all the* Hustler *magazines under the cash box in the hidden drawer at the back of his desk in the study?* Screw *behind the golf bag?* Penthouse *in the same box as his ties because he wants me to find that one so that I can get tips from The Happy Hooker?* This always goes on longer than you think it will go. Funny how it's the sex that brings me back to thinking in Jamaican, *no, Kim Clarke, you will not now think about what that makes you.* The son of a bitch was fucking me for seven more minutes. Nobody outside typed a single letter. He gives me the passport and I open it again to look at me looking at me with a visa stamped across my head. It's B1B2. I was going to cuss that I had paid for a green card, but then thought maybe I should take what I get and let Chuck do the rest—who knows what this son of a bitch would want me to do for a green card.

Kim Clarke, you lie.

You're lying now. A lot of that really happened. But you said nothing to the man, you didn't even grunt. You just raised your skirt and pulled down your panties and prayed that the man didn't have syphilis. And he was almost nervous, so much so that it was then that you realize that you were probably the first woman that fell for the threat and he couldn't believe his luck. You weren't tapping to seconds, you were tapping his back just so he could get a rhythm and maybe not think about his wife, and when he finally came you felt sorry for him, because he knew you had to walk through the door past his staff. And you haven't looked at the passport since because if you do even the shitty photo will make you ask yourself if it was worth it. Was it worth it, Kim Clarke? Yes, yes, yes damn it, and don't ask me again.

Me would fuck him again and put him cocky in me mouth. Me will even lick him battyhole, this is 1978. Is nineteen seventy fucking eight and a woman must know that sometimes the only way forward is through. When I landed in Montego Bay I knew that whether on a plane or in a box, I was going to leave this place. You almost think you did get me don't it, Jamaica? You almost think you did get me. Well kiss my bombocloth ass. Shit, purple thumbprints all over the fridge—how much washing this going take before it's gone?

Waiting for the water again. Standing under the showerhead listening to the drain hack a cough. This fucking country. Every day water goes at the precise time you need to use it. I wish there was a river behind the house so I could go wash like a country woman. Just fucking fabulous, the one afternoon I need a shower. Get this man off me before my man comes home. Why can't I feel more? Why don't I feel more? My heart beats faster when I'm experimenting with a new dish. Maybe if I punch it hard enough or long enough blood will fill up where conscience supposed to be. Don't you understand, I WANT to feel something. I want my heart to pump because guilt riding it hard and won't jump off. Guilt would mean something. How many times should I wipe before it's clean? What I would give for water to come back right now. Please, right before he comes home. No? Then fuck you then. As soon as he comes in I'll have dinner ready and then I'll play with his hair like I'm not even thinking about it and he will love that. Maybe I will sing "Dancing Queen," he knows how much I love that song, or maybe Andy Gibb. Maybe "Shadow Dancing" will come back on the radio and I will pull him from the chair and say dance with me, baby, and he will say Kim Clarke, no, babykins you sure you're okay? And I will just show him the visa.

No. That's a terrible idea. You already told him you had a visa, fool, and it's not like he asked. Show him now and he will see that it was stamped only last week. And he still hasn't said beyond a shadow of a doubt that you were going with him. But why would he have to say it? We can't be living together for him to just up and go. Is he practicing to see which goodbye will cause the least tears? Which one won't make me try to kill him? Is he doing it in front of a mirror? Kim Clarke, if you had sense you would have gotten yourself pregnant by now. If I stop taking the pill today will I be pregnant by the time he's setting to leave? Today I will love his hair, and ask when I need to pack.

Kim Clarke, you make a wrong move. Kim Clarke, shut up and get out of this shower. I need to cream my hair. Should I do that here or in America? It's coming down to that with everything. Should I do it here or when I go to America? Jesus Christ, the day when I get bored with thirteen channels, what will I do? The day I get bored with corn flakes, no not corn flakes, Frosted Flakes. The day I get bored with looking up and seeing buildings that clouds hit and run into. The day I get bored with throwing out bread because it's been there four days and I want a new loaf. The day I get bored with Twinkies, Halston, Lip Smackers, L'eggs and anything by Revlon. The day I get bored with sleeping straight from night to morning and waking up to the smell of coffee and the sound of birds and have Chuck say, Did you have a good night's sleep, babykins? And I'll say yes I did, sweetheart—instead of watching the dark all night, and listening to the damn clock tick, because once I fall asleep things come after me. I thought we were going to stop this thinking business, Kim Clarke. Seriously, thought is one tricky bitch. Because all thoughts take you back to that one thought and you will never go back to that one thought, you hear me? Never go back. Only stupid women ever walk backwards.

—I love this country. You people have got it so good and don't even know it. But you got a shit for brains Prime Minister, how come you people voted for him again?

—You want to stop using "you people"?

—Sorry, babykins, you know what I mean.

—No I don't know what you mean. I didn't vote for him.

—But—

—Stop the "you people" like I'm the rep for all the people of Jamaica.

—Sheesh, it's just an expression.

—Then express yourself better.

—Damn, what got your panties in a bunch this morning?

—You know us people, every day is that day of the month.

—I quit. I'm going to work.

You, girl in the mirror. You, girl, Kim Clarke, admit that it was easier to do it when you made yourself mad at him. But what did you do, stupid bitch? You never get mad, you never give him reason to even think about going away and leaving you behind. You never become the difficult bitch, that's the white woman's territory.

—Well, hopefully you're in a better mood when I get back.

—Hopefully you stop chatting shit when you get back.

Sometimes I think he likes me feisty. I don't know. A woman supposed to know when to shut up and make a man think he won. I don't even know what that means. I used to think I knew what American men want. When he takes you out for Kentucky Fried Chicken it a "date." But if he only comes around every now and then for sex then he's "seeing" me. Or I'm "sleeping" with him. Crazy business, if he is only coming around for sex the last thing I want him to do is sleep with me. Can you make a man love you harder?

The company is pulling out after thirty years in Jamaica, he says on the "date" last week. Alcorp mining finally get their bauxite belly full and now packing up to go. Chuck says *it's because of this bauxite levy, which is just step-one towards nationalization, which is in itself step-one towards communism.* I said you Yankees are afraid of communism the way old country women are afraid of rolling calf. *What's that?* he said. The boogieman I said. He laughed that loud laugh.

—Gotta get out before this becomes the capital of Cuba.

I laughed that loud laugh.

—I might know something you don't, Kim.

—No, you might have heard some things I haven't heard. Not the same thing.

—Damn, that mouth on you—

—You don't complain when you're inside it.

—Babykins, you're one sexy bitch, you know that?

Do men marry their sexy bitches? I need to take him someplace where he'd have to introduce me, just so that I can hear what he calls me, see where I stand. Right, like I really want to know that. Kim Clarke, your life is nothing more than a series of plan B's. I must be glad that I have a man who likes to rub my feet. A big man, a tall man, a mountain. Six feet four? Must be at least that. Grey eyes, lip so thin that it looks like somebody just cut a slit open. His hair is curly, now that he's growing it out. Big chest and arms, he used to work with his hands before he started to work and eat at a desk. Brown hair on his head, but red above his penis and sprouting from his balls. Sometimes you have to just stop and look at it.

—What are you doing?

—Not doing a thing.

—If you keep staring at it like that, it will shrink away from you.

—I just waiting for it to burst into flames.

—Black men don't have pubic hair?

—How would I know?

—Dunno. I mean, you're a modern woman, right?

—Modern woman meaning slut?

—No, modern woman meaning you've been going to Mantana's for months. And having fun.

—How you know what kind of fun I've been happening?

—I was scoping out the scene in Mantana's long before you took a look at me, Kim. Seriously though, you've never slept with a black man? Not even with a Jamaican?

Mind, do a check of what situations this man calls me babykins and what situations this man calls me Kim. This is important, Kim Clarke. Men marry their babykins. Yes they do. Maybe I should be glad the man hasn't called me sexy bitch in a while. When last? Can't remember. Think harder. No, I can't remember. I need him to move from I love you, but only enough for a tearful goodbye to I love you so much let's get married right now, right here, so that you fly back to Arkansas as Mrs. Chuck. Isn't Arkansas one of the places that hate black people? If I can get him to marry me, can I get him to move to New York, or Boston? Not Miami, I want to see snow. Yesterday I stuck my hand in the freezer for as long as maybe four minutes to feel what winter must feel like, and almost stick my head in as well. I grabbed a clump of frost and squeezed until the cold started to burn and the ache reached all the way to my head. I rolled the clump into a ball and threw it at the window. The ball stuck for a second then dropped and I cried.

—Baby, I never leave anything up to chance.

I wonder if that means me. He wasn't about to risk me leaving and never coming back to Mantana's, even though I was there every night. Looking. Or if it means that he has already bought tickets or the company has given him tickets back to America. Tickets. Ticket. They gave him only one to come here, why should they give him two to leave? *Charles, Charles, we can't be giving extra tickets to every man who falls in love with the local wildlife, what do you think this is,* South Pacific*?* Oh stop thinking, Kim Clarke, believe you me, you're going to drive yourself crazy. Back in church youth group they used to say that worry is sinful meditation because you are choosing not to trust God. I used to think that if nothing else, the one thing I knew in high school was that at least I was going to heaven and not all those nasty girls who let boys feel them up because they said their titties were growing fast and the boys said we don't believe you. Had to move all the way to Montego Bay to make sure I never ran into any of those bitches again (no that's not why, stop lying, like it matters now). At least I didn't have no fucking child making my titties drag down to my kneecaps, Jesus Christ I used to hate those bitches.

Should I pack? Do it . . . Kim, yes, Kim Clarke. Do it, I dare you. Pack your suitcase, that same purple one you took with you to Montego Bay. Pack it now. I really should buy a new suitcase for America. I wonder if he will want to take the towels. I only bought them last week. Fuck the towels, we should leave everything behind and don't look back. Don't go turning into Lot's wife, Kim Clarke.

Do it light, do it through the night. This deejay not letting Andy Gibb go. I want to hear "You Should Be Dancing" right now. That's what I want to hear. Baby let's go dancing, I will say once he comes through the door. We'll go dancing, not at Mantana's, maybe Club8, and when we get him drunk I will say, Baby I know you didn't ask me yet, but I started packing to save us both the trouble. What you Americans call it? Pro-active. See, I was being pro-active because you men always wait until it's near too late to do anything, including propose. No, I won't say propose. No man wants to feel tricked into a marriage. And when he ifs and buts I'll take out his cock and show him that I learned exactly what I was supposed to learn when he put on the reel of *The Opening of Misty Beethoven.*

—I dunno, I didn't expect Jamaican women to be like black American women.

—You weren't expecting us to be black too?

—No silly, I didn't expect you to be so sexually conservative. I swear, growing up in Arkansas you get the wrong idea.

—Why do you always use plural when you talk about me?

—Maybe I have a thing for black women.

—Uh-huh. I must be the black woman delegate.

—I hear Mick Jagger does too.

—You hear me talking to you?

—But I have all that jazz, right, babe?

—What you talking 'bout?

Come to think of it the only other man to put his mouth anywhere near my pussy was a white man. And American too. And, no I can't think about that. Something scared the gulls away. How long have they been gone? Didn't even realize I was thinking out loud. They wouldn't be gone unless . . . better check the living room.

—Oh, hi hon.

—Uh. Oh, Chuck.

He answers with a wide grin.

—I didn't know you were here. I didn't even hear you come in.

—Yeah? Sounded like you had company in there. Was taking my shoes off to come in and join—

—I'm alone.

—Oh really? Talking to yourself like some crazy chick?

—Thinking out loud.

—Oooh. About me?

—Can't believe you came in the house and I didn't hear you.

—It's my house, baby, I don't have to make a scene just because I entered it.

No that didn't sting, brush it off, Kim Clarke.

—I was about to cook dinner.

—Love how Jamaicans say cook dinner instead of make dinner.

—What's the difference?

—Well, you could just boil some mac and cheese, and there, you've made dinner.

—You want mac and cheese?

—What? No, baby. I want whatever you're cooking. What is it that you're cooking?

—I can't believe you just came in like that.

—It's bothering you? Rest assured, darling, nobody is going to come all the way down here to assault you. What's for dinner?

—Ackee.

—Lordy.

—With corned pork this time.

—What's corned pork?

—Like thick pieces of bacon.

—I love me some bacon. Well, you go back to that, and I'll go back to this *Star* newspaper I was reading. I swear this shit is a riot, not at all the bummer that's the *Daily News*.

I hope he doesn't start telling me what's in the paper. Getting harder and harder every day to dodge him telling me the news. It sweet him so to tell it back to me, more than it sweet him to read it in the first place. Last Tuesday I saw him coming to me in the kitchen and said I already read the paper, thinking that would shut him up, but the whole thing backfired. As soon as he heard that, the man wanted to *discuss* things. I really can't stand the news. Most times I don't even want to know what day it is. I swear the second I hear of something, or if I realize I'm about to hear something, my heart just starts to pound and I want to do nothing more than run to my bedroom, cover my face with a pillow and scream. Even in the market all I need is one higgler saying, Then you no hear 'bout Miss so and so? and I start walking away without stopping. Without buying a single thing. I don't want to hear nothing. I don't want no fucking news. Ignorance is bliss. I know him, he's going to walk through that door—get the oil hot, get it hot, Kim Clarke, so hot that as he steps in just drop the onion and the skellion and the PSSSSSSHHHHH will drown out what he says. I'll say whaaaaat? And he'll say it again, and I'll say whaaaaaat? and drip some water so that the oil pops loud and scares him and he'll forget the subject, maybe. I wish the gulls were still here because then he would rush outside to drive them away and I could ask one of those dumb questions like do they have gulls in America? One of those questions that make white men just love to smile, nod a little and answer. Do they have bicycles in your country? Do they ride on the highway? Do you watch *The Munsters* in America? Do you watch *Wonder Woman*? How tall is the Statue of Liberty? Do you have a dual carriageway?

Take a deep breath, Kim Clarke. Cool runnings. You're happy.

—Funny thing in the *Star* today, he says, walking in.

—Honey, you sure you don't want to change out of your good clothes?

—You're my mother now?

He smiles.

—Is you scare away the gulls?

—They were bothering you again?

—Not any more than usual. What kind of gulls you have in Arkansas?

—The same gulls I told you about three days ago.

—Oh. My brain is like a sieve. As soon as information go in I strain it right back out.

—Sounds more like a rectum than a sieve.

—But what a way you bright though, eh?

—Love it when you curse me in Jamaican.

—Ha ha. Well, if any of this oil splash on you I going tell you that you get what you was bloodcloth looking for.

—More.

—Pass the onion and skellion.

—Where?

—That basket on the cupboard by the door beside you . . . watch your step, I just shine the floor . . . slippery.

—I'm a nimble guy.

—Uh-huh.

—Man, you chop that thing really fast. Does every Jamaican woman know how to cook?

—Yes. Well, all the women who not worthless. So no, no Jamaican woman in Montego Bay can cook.

—You trying to get me to stop going to Mantana's?

—Ha.

—Hey, babykins, I gotta tell you something.

—Honey, I can't deal with anything in that newspaper right now. That *Star* is nothing but shame and scandal and white girl on page three showing her titties. What you steal from work today?

—I didn't steal. A jar, just a jar, but it's a green one, like emerald, I guess.

—You should buy me an emerald.

—Kim.

—I mean, I was born in November and that's actually topaz, but you're the one that started with emerald and—

—What the fuck, Kim.

—I don't want to hear no shit about nothing in the r'asscloth *Star*, Chuck.

—What? I wasn't talking about the *Star*. I was talking about Alcorp.

—What about Alcorp?

—We got a memo today. The company is winding down operations at a faster timetable than was originally anticipated—I mean, projected.

—You want to translate that memo?

—We're flying out next week.

—Oh. Oh shit. Is good thing.

—It's kinda fucked-up, really.

—No. Is a good thing the garage already cleaned out! So much stuff to do! But what the hell, right, as you would say? What can't pack just get left, eh?

—We means the company, Kim.

—Of course no ackee in America so you better eat this up when me finish.

—We meaning the staff and crew.

—I better make it extra good since it's the last supper, haha, sorry Jesus, me borrowing that one.

—I gotta pack.

—Pack, yes, to think, you're going to think is funny, I was looking at that ugly purple grip just a while ago.

—My stuff, all this shit from the office, I don't really have a place for any of it.

—I wonder if I should pack jeans. I really was thinking what if I should pack jeans. I mean, I know I'm not going to pack towels and rags because that is just ghetto people behaviour. But jeans? I mean, you know how much I love the Halston, or rather how much you love how I wear the Halston.

—So much stuff to leave behind.

—But to pack a towel, what kinda butu business is that? Is not like we flying to Mocho. It's like packing a toothbrush. I want to brush my teeth fresh in America. I know that sounds stupid.

—Oh Lord, Kim.

—And toothpaste. You Americans get gel toothpaste, in the big family pack that had a pump cap.

—I didn't think it would come down to this.

—Will I have time to do my hair? To Rahtid, the deejay playing Andy Gibb again? The song just reach number one or something? You just call in and request it?

—Kim.

—Fine, no hairdo then, well, if I look like a madwoman on the plane is your fault. You better speak up for me.

—Okay, okay, Kim.

—Before customs cart me off.

—Kim.

—Jesus Christ, you sure know how to spring something on a woman. At least nobody going say we eloped.

—What we—

—Bedsheets, pack or leave?

—Huh?

—I swear, man, don't serve no damn use.

—They're not going to—

—We leave all the white ones, except the Egyptian cotton. That one we're taking, you hear me? Come to think of it, you better make me pack your belongings because you men don't know how to pack either.

—It's all your Manley's fault. He's fucking up everything with this . . . with this . . .

—I think you should pack all your gabardine pants, but none of the Kariba suits, don't want nobody in America thinking their son turn into socialist.

—And now—

—And that blue shirt for when we go dancing. Is there a Studio 54 in Arkansas?

—Not going to Arkansas. Never going back to Arkansas.

—Oh. Okay. Well, wherever then. Ha, I was just about to say, wherever as long as I am with you until I remembered that I heard that same damn line in a movie last week. Or maybe it was on *Dallas*. You think it was *Dallas*? Pamela Barnes would say some shit like that.

—Fucking hell, it's like a troops pullout. I said to Jackman, it's Montego Bay, not Saigon, motherfucker.

—Should I tell the jewellery store? You know, I didn't really resign, I just stopped working.

—They actually chartered a jet.

—Fuck them, no fuck 'em, as you would say. I mean, I didn't even quit, I just stopped, remember? You thought it was so funny—

—Chartered a fucking jet like it's going to be an airlift.

—I know, why contact them now? I'll just have to put up with all those other wives on the plane but fuck 'em, right? I love it when you say fuck 'em.

—Kim—

—So much to do. I can't believe you just spring this on me. Can't believe they spring this on you.

—Kim—

—But hey, is so it go. When—

—KIM!

—WHAT?

—Oh baby. Babykins, what we had here was really swell, but . . .

—What.

—I'll send you some money, as much as you need, anything you need.

—What.

—You can stay here as long as you like. It's paid up for the rest of the year.

—What.

—I thought. I mean, surely. I mean, this was swell, baby, it really was, but surely you didn't think—

—What.

—You knew. I mean, you know I can't . . . Baby—

—Fine, do your airlift without me. Leave the ticket so I can come to America through the back door. No that doesn't piss me off. Much.

—Baby, no—

—Stop the baby and say what you're saying, damn it.

—I've been saying it for the past five minutes.

—Saying what? What Chuck? What?

—You're not. You're . . . you're not coming with me.

—I'm not coming with you.

—No, you're not. I mean, you must have known.

—I must have known. I must have known. Right, I must have known. No wait, make me say it like you, I must have knowwwwwnnnn.

—Jesus Christ, Kim, the stove!

—I must have known.

—Kim!

The man shoves past me and turns off the stove. Smoke all around. All I can see is him, back to me, smoke shooting east and shooting west like they coming out of his ears, like a Bugs Bunny cartoon.

—What's so funny? What's so funny?

Kim. Kim. Kim, you must have known.

—Stop fucking laughing at me. Jesus Christ, Kim, I didn't even take the ring off. I just don't understand why you would think, why you would assume . . . I mean, you hang out at Mantana's. Everybody knows about Mantana's. Everybody. I mean, I never even took my ring off. Oh, man, fuck, now look, dinner, it's all ruined.

—Dinner's ruined.

—It's okay.

—Dinner's ruined?

—It's okay.

The ring, the ring, the fucking ring like a Cracker Jack ring in a box, a free toy inside.

—Baby, you know how fond I am of you.

—What's her name, your white wife?

—What?

—The white wife, the woman you cheating on to get some black pum-pum 'pon the side.

—She's not white.

—I need a cigarette.

—You don't smoke.

—I want a cigarette.

—Babykins—

—I say I want a fucking cigarette, so give me a bombor'asscloth cigarette!

—Okay, okay, babyki—

—Don't fucking call me that, don't ever call me that pussycloth name.

—Sorry, here's you cig—

—You expect me to rub it 'gainst me battyhole to light it?

—This lighter, well, it was my father's.

—Me look like me want to thief you fucking lighter?

—Kim, I'm so sorry.

—Everybody sorry. Everybody so fucking sorry. You know what? I tired of everybody sorry. I wish you wasn't sorry. I wish you would say you not sorry, that me is an idiot. That we were playing dolly house because it was cute and now you have to go back to your American white wife now.

—She's not white.

—I need to lie down.

—Of course, baby, take your time, take your—

—Stop talking like you is my fucking doctor. Poor Chuck, didn't think this was how it was going to turn out, did you? How many times you rehearse this? Two? Three? On the way over here? I at least deserve four rehearsals.

—Kim—

—Stop calling me that name. How about we shake hands right now and say nice doing business.

—Now look, there's no call—

—You prefer to write a cheque and leave it on the breakfront?

—I never once called you a prostitute.

—Of course you were so fond of me. Bombocloth white man bullshit.

—This is not about white or black, my wife—

—Oh I've grown so fond of you. We've grown oh so very fond of you my dear, so very fond—

—She's blacker than you.

—What is this then, black pussy contest?

—Kim.

—Shut up! You don't get to tell me what there is no bombocloth cause for in anything.

—What? You're not making any sense.

—Just take me to foreign.

—What?

—Just take me to foreign.

—What are you saying?

—Just take me to foreign, to r'asscloth. Leave me at the nearest bus stop.

—Kim, you're not making any sense.

—Look, I just got to go. I just got to fucking go. I'm so ready to go. Chuck, please I'll do anything. I'm so ready to go. I'm so ready to fucking go I'm so ready to go—

—Go where? I don't understand what you're saying, Kim, let go of my shirt, what the fuck? What has gotten over you? Kim, Kim, let go. Kim. Let. Go. Fucking hell!

—Ugh—

—I'm sorry. I'm sorry. I'm . . . look what you made me do. Kim, it's your—

—Just shut up please.

—But you might be bleeding. Let me—

—Don't fucking touch me. Just give me the damn paper.

—But you never read the *Star*, you hate the news.

—Stop talking like you know me. You don't know me, you hear me? You don't know me. Makes me want to vomit. This half boyfriend, half daddy, paternal fuckmate bullshit. That's what it does, it makes me want to vomit right here on your fucking floor. I don't even like ackee. Give me that paper or, or, or I will start screaming.

—Baby—

—Please, please, please, please, please shut up. Just shut up. I'm going to go find my head.

I take his paper and I go into the bedroom and I slam it. Ring on his finger. Like me never see no ring on him finger. I did well and see ring on him finger. No I didn't see it. I didn't want to see it. The fucking son of a bitch.

—You is a fucking son of a bitch.

Calm down, Kim Clarke. Calm down. You couldn't even shout that out because you know you've got no cause. Remember why God lead you to this house. Remember why God lead you to this room and go back out there and love his hair. Tell him you don't have to be his wife, you can be his whatever you like woman. Is distance him want? You're a Jamaican woman, you know how to give him distance. Go out there and say, Yes, baby, I understand. You have this world here and that world there, but those two worlds can't mix, you know that. But look at us, look at us, we make two world work all the time and we don't even live in a land as big as yours. Mr. Big has a wife in the hills and a woman in the clubs. The wife will never come down, the woman will never step up, so the man stays level. I can show you. And I don't have to fly back on no Alcorp plane. I don't have to live in Arkansas. I don't have to set up no home. . . . We don't have to, oh shut the fuck up woman. 'Bout you can adapt. That doesn't make you a woman, it makes you a bacteria. The man samfie you. Steal from a thief and God laughs. The man samfie you good. Like you wanted to set up no fucking dolly house in Arkansas. You just want a way. You just want a light. You just wanted a piggyback to jump off and everybody in this room right now know it. Go out there and love his hair. You already have passport and visa. But with him I would have had a . . . a what? Girl, you need to get the fuck out of this simmering pot before time run out. You think you're safe, but look underneath your dress and you'll see concentric circles all leading to one bull's-eye. You think that your forehead don't still have the mark? You think they not still looking for you? . . . No. I will go out there and I will love his hair. Tonight was the night I was supposed to love his hair. But you spoil the ackee. You know how much he loves ackee and you spoiled the ackee. Maybe you should go out dancing, tell him it's one last time before he goes. We go. You were going to land in God's land with this man and just suck up the American colour.

You know what—

Shut up

Just shut up

You sound like two black American brats in a TV comedy, "you shut up."

Shit, I don't even smoke.

—Kim, you okay in there?

—Don't come in here.

—Have you put a bandage on your cheek yet?

—Don't come in here.

I should have known. What the r'asscloth him think this is, that every woman in Mantana's rehearse this day from the day they set foot in that club? Clearly every woman but me. I can't remember any other man in the club. I mean, I can remember them but I can't remember their fingers. Poor Kim Clarke, by the time you got to Mantana's your purpose already blinded you. Poor Kim Clarke, Mummy and Daddy weren't there to teach you about the time when woman and man come to the crossroads with cross purposes and if you give a man a free hand he will rub it all over you. Poor Kim Clarke. You knew Alcorp was closing shop and setting to go from before you met Chuck. Alcorp was setting to go and you had set your sights. On somebody. Everybody. Anybody. How do you make a man love you harder? Did every man in Mantana's have a wedding ring or the mark of one on the fourth finger? Think on your feet, Kim. Think on your feet.

—Kim.

—I am alright. Just don't come in here.

—Okay.

Stand still. Stand still and know peace. I swear now is when Sunday school turn out to serve some use. No you will not think about God right now. Maybe I will read the newspaper after all, maybe I will read the *Star*, The People's Paper. I don't know why he reads this every day other than to remind himself how stupid Jamaican people can be, is that it? And yet I have heard of what happened in Little Rock. This stupid girl paid attention in history class when they talked about civil rights and Martin Luther King.

Three The Hard Way: Body Guard, Home Guard and Security Guard in Love Triangle. The Star *understands . . . Twins for Miss Jamaica . . . Our Page 3 Girl Pulchritudinous Pamela, our luscious buxom beauty is training to be an air hostess and loves the long arm of the law . . . Counter Flour Shortage in Hanover. The* Star *understands that shopkeepers have been "marrying" Baygon insect spray, insisting that customer purchase one spray for every two pounds of flour. . . . Dupply Slaps Graveworker in May Pen Cemetery. Eulalee Legister was minding her business when . . . Return of Communist Menace Through St. Mary? . . . Eliminations and sashing of contestants for Miss Jamaica 1979. Shelly Samuda, Miss Marzouca, Arlene Sanguinetty, Miss Bobcat, Jacqueline*

Parchment, Miss Hunter Security, Bridget Palmer, Miss Sovereign Supermarket, Kim-Marie Burgess, Miss Ammar's

Kim-Marie Burgess, Miss Ammar's

Kim-Marie Burgess, Miss Ammar's

Kim-Marie Burgess, Miss Ammar's

Stacey Barracat, Miss River Road Cleaners. Beauty Contest is foolishness. *Domestic Violence end in wounding with intent. Justice Patrick Shields in a ruling today . . . Four Killed in Shootout in Jonestown . . . April 20, Your Birthday Horoscope. You are an Aries on the cusp of Taurus and you will be guided by your emotions . . .* This is what you have been missing for almost two years. Turn the page.

FROM CONCERT TO COMMUNITY BUILDING ONE YEAR LATER

. . . back from fourteen-month exile after the attempt on his life, December 3, 1976. The concert was opened by HRH Asafa Wosen, the Crown Prince of Ethiopia . . . this was the reaping of two years of careful workings, said JLP political activist Raymond "Papa-Lo" Clarke. Too much war and tribulation in the street, time for unification. Proceeds from the concert will go towards all sort of projects in the community, first thing first a good public sanitary convenience and a new room for the West Kingston Clinic, said top PNP activist Roland "Shotta Sherrif" Palmer. Central to the effort was the reggae superstar who flew home to the island after a nearly two-year absence.

Enough. Stop reading, Kim Clarke.

Since the beginning of this year there has been three hundred murders that have been rumoured to be politically motivated.

Stop reading, Kim Clarke.

Photo inset: Political activists shake hands over concert proceeds.

Don't look, Kim Clarke.

Left to Right: Minister of Youth and Sports Mr. ________________, JLP political activist Raymond Papa-Lo Clarke, PNP political activist Roland Shotta Sherrif Palmer. Kim Clarke, stop looking, stop reading, stop searching. Don't look: Papa-Lo in his white top, his pecs popping like women's breasts. Don't look: Shotta Sherrif's khaki pants, like a student's, like a soldier's. A black-and-white photo but you know it's khaki. Don't snake your eyes from face to face, to faces looking in the camera, faces looking away and faces looking beyond anything in this damn photo. Beside Papa-Lo is a woman. Beside the woman is a man. Behind the man is another man wearing sunglasses. You know the look, don't you? He's not hiding from you, you're hiding from him. Close the newspaper now, Kim Clarke. There he is at the back not smiling, not looking, not agreeing to no bombocloth peace. He's not looking at peace, he's looking at you. Two years on the run and him find you. You is a fool. Him find you.

—Kim, what's going on?

Kim?

Kim?

Two years of running in a straight line that turns into a circle. Walk up to the gate. Nothing stopping you now. Nothing pushing you but you walk right up to the gate anyway because what else was there to do, not walk forward? Walk up to the gate and rub your belly like you're pregnant. Ignore the firecrackers even though this is way too early in December for firecrackers. Look at the man, face already going dark in the eight o'clock but coming towards you and you can't move. He's looking at you, undressing you, auditioning you. Listen to screams coming from the back and police siren coming from up the road and the gun right in front of your face. Once you started running you never stopped. You packed a purple suitcase and ran away from December 3, 1976, because fuck that day that the Lord had made and everything was terrible in it. You think you're going to run to America, but the man has already worked out right down to the last rent cheque how he will soon run away from you. And this man, the man in the photo. He walked right up to you from the edge of this newspaper. He has a name—don't read it.

Silly woman. You never ran from December 3, 1976, you ran right into the middle of it. You've never known December 4, you do not know April 20, you only know December 3. That day will never close until he comes to close it. December 3 is coming back for you, this picture is saying. We have unfinished business, this picture is saying. Montego Bay couldn't stop it and neither can America. I coming for you, Nin—don't call her by that name, don't ever call that fucking name. That is a dead name of a dead woman in a dead city. Keep running because she's dead. Now light the cigarette with his lighter that he wants back and don't give it back unless he asks. Light the cigarette and take a drag. Cough, cough longer, cough louder. Take another drag. Drag until your heart goes back to beating so slow that if you touch your chest you can count the beats. Now take the cigarette and burn out his head. Stub through to the back page, burn until you flick a flame brilliant with the paper and throw it on the bed.

—Kim, what the hell is going on?

Burn a way through the white man's knocking and shouting and screaming and rapping and ramming down the door that won't budge, and the cackling pillows and the hissing silk sheets and the laughing polyester curtains, watch the flame shoot up like under a skirt and expose the screaming window.

Burn a way to safe passage. The only way forward is through.

Barry Diflorio

Shit just blew up in Iran. Well, it blew up back in January, but fallout's just reaching us now. Shit is blowing up all over the world. Chaos and disorder, disorder and chaos, I say them over and over like they have anything to do with each other, Sodom and Gomorrah, Gomorrah and Sodom. All these family pics go in my bag—not the briefcase, take them out of the briefcase and that folder I should give Sally to shred, but should I take some shots first? Jesus Christ, I think I've caught some Nixon fever. I spend so much time telling people that life is not like fucking 007 that I miss the times when it really is. What I really want to do is sit back in this chair, take my shoes and socks off and guess where shit will start flying first. Meanwhile, shit of a totally different kind blew the fuck up in Yugoslavia. And NATO boy didn't even know. He's the head of the fucking CIA and he didn't even know.

Lindon Wolfsbricker. Now there's a name where you knew the parents spent an awful long time trying to figure out what the fuck can precede Wolfsbricker. Seriously, it sounds like something you'd call a Nazi fetishist. Wolfsbricker the American ambassador to Yugoslavia. Don't ask me how he got it but somehow Mr. Ambassador comes across a directive from within the Company. A directive from Clandestine Service to station chiefs worldwide to keep all major operations secret from all ambassadors. First thing I thought was, come on. I mean, it really makes sense. Some ambassadors get the gig because the President likes them, and a good gig in a good locale where you make a name for yourself, like say Cyprus, will set you up for senator, governor or vice president. Some get the gig because the President can't stand the fucker and what better way to get you and your potential threat out of the way than to post you in the Soviet Union or some place nobody gives a fuck about, like Papua New Guinea? Either way, an ambitious jackass on a power trip is not someone who should be kept in the loop about anything ever, because more than anything else, he's a major pain in the ass. And here is Wolfsbricker, the shit-kicker on the phone, with Admiral Tunney, mad as hell that info is being kept from him, in violation of standing presidential orders going back seventeen years by the way.

So Wolfsbricker sends a message to the admiral that the CIA is out of business in Yugoslavia until the order is rescinded and he wasn't kidding. He said nobody was to come to the office or conduct any business in Belgrade or anywhere else in Yugoslavia. Mr. Ambassador was piiiiiiissed. Worse, he was cursing the director about something he didn't have a fucking clue about. I heard the admiral was so furious he spilled his hot water and lemon all over his pants. Calls went out all over the world to find out who knew about the directive and who authorized it. Of course when they called me I just said that the Company was in transition between Mr. Bush and Admiral Tunney and I followed orders. From whom? Not from Clandestine, sirs, if that's what you're asking. I don't create policy, I make sure it's carried out. Funny I knew the second I said it that I was never going to make the corner office, something that will piss off the wife far more than me.

But good God, 1979 and Jamaica is for a pleasant change the only place not going to shit. Well, not going to shit today. Flight to Argentina is next week and Claire is happy for the first time in years. *Do we have to learn Spanish now?* says my little one and just then I remember that we haven't been in a Spanish-speaking country in three years. Judging by the number of calls she's been making this month totally in Spanish, it seems she's alerting all her fellow bitches that the eagle is about to land. Funny how for someone who couldn't stop bitching about how much she hated this country and wanted to go back to Vermont, she hasn't mentioned Vermont even once. I wonder if the new guy will want this paperweight. God knows I don't want . . . or maybe I do. So distracted today. Shit, what was I thinking about? Wolfsbricker. Yugoslavia. The admiral catching a fit. I mean, shit, the Company was in effect breaking the law.

My son could use this sharpener. Fucking office is not going to miss one sharpener, and even if they do who gives a flying fuck? Like anybody in Jamaica is keeping any records. Sloppiest fucking place I've ever . . . actually that's not true, Ecuador was far, far worse. I'm definitely getting angrier and I don't know why. Maybe it's because we're going back to fucking Argentina. I really don't hate Argentina, and it will be nice to actually eat at an outside café and watch sexy Argentinian women for a change. It's just this country. Shit. I'm not going to be the ten thousandth white man to fall for this country. I'm not falling for it. Or at least if I'm going to I should at least waste my life smoking pot in Treasure Beach with all the other washed-up hippies.

A quiet evening in Jamaica, the only place in the world right now that's actually quiet. Because Iran, good fucking Christ, to think that's where we were once headed to. And this fucking aw shucks heehaw president. Louis told me that not long after riding his redneck ass into office by tearing the Company a new one and calling us a national disgrace he's already given us more orders than Ford and almost as many as Nixon. Of course he wouldn't see it that way. A permanent attack of the conscience, this one. This guy wants to save some black people abroad, who knows, because he can't do squat for the niggers in his own country. Let's undermine apartheid, sure, because all you need are a pair of red shoes with heels to click. Undermine it for what? ANC has been funded by the Soviets for years because guess what, for all its shit, communism is more socially progressive than us. He wants to pump a lethal injection into apartheid and get rid of that Nazi maniac Ian Smith in Rhodesia. I know two of the guys working with BOSS, both of whom got their clumsy asses caught by the fucking Rhodesian Secret Police. It takes a whole new level of incompetence to get caught by an African secret police. Three of us caught by those morons and the fourth guy given up by BOSS itself. Boy were those South Africans pleased with themselves. We shouldn't even be in fucking Africa, leave that to the fucking limeys and the fucking Belgians and the goddamn Portuguese, still so fucking bad at colonialism after all these years. Jesus Christ, Barry, somebody overhearing you might think you were turning liberal. Credit Louis at the very least to waking me up to how things really fucking go. Or maybe it was William Adler.

Sally is wondering if they will reassign her too. My secretary's developed a little crush on me. It's great to know somebody has. The wife is already teaching Aiden Spanish. Timothy doesn't even remember speaking it. Boy was he mad when he heard we were leaving. Eediot business this, he said and threw his fork on his plate. Bad enough that he now refuses to eat American food and only wants crab and yellow-yam and corned pork and breadfruit. I had to remind the little bastard who was the man around here. Poor kid, he thinks I don't know about his little Jamaican girlfriend, hell, I knew it from the second he told Aiden that superhero toys were eediot business—mind you, they were his toys. Damn kid thinking he knows what love is. Love is settling, that's really all it is. Fucking settling.

Louis Johnson, my little compadre in '76, got sent back to Central America, I'm guessing the School for the Americas needed some hand-holding this year. Gotta keep building that army to vanquish the forces of socialism and communism, and whatever ism washes up next week. Funny how we never liked each other, actually I couldn't stand the wife-beating scumbag, but now he calls me all the time. Some shit about just needing to hear more than one sentence in English. I could have said, Well, if you stopped beating the crap out of your wife, you might actually have somebody to talk to, but that might have been tacky. But we're talking about Clandestine, which he's a part of and I'm not, and who really fucked things up. He thinks it's Admiral Tunney, a man who even on a good day has just a cursory knowledge of how things work in the Company. Tunney's a pencil pusher, I told him. He's just biding time. Besides, who trusts a man who drinks hot water with lime instead of whiskey or even coffee? What next, peeing sitting down? No sir, Nixon's the one who really fucked up the CIA. He never trusted the Company to begin with. Still you gotta admire the simplicity of his worldview, that the world is populated by people with him or against him, and shit, I've never even met the guy.

Because here was the problem with the weasel. You can't go whole hog, downright creating a fucking culture of surveillance and then gripe when stuff gets leaked. Means you have so many people watching that you can't even keep tabs on who's watching who. Worse, to give the job to a fucking

Bay of Pigs alum—and we know how competent they are. Say this about Louis, he pretty much knows and refuses to keep anything secret. The Defense secretary snooping on Kissinger or so I heard. Hard to believe Kissinger wouldn't know about it. White House and Camp David bugged. Kissinger himself tapping his own aides and people, including me, I'm assuming, to contain leaks, and yet the leaks keep on coming. The problem is they picked somebody both me and Louis knew really well, hell, when Louis called me he was hiccupping in the phone how he couldn't stop laughing. Chip Hunt. *Holy fucking horseshit, Diflorio, here's a fuckup that makes a fuckup go holy fuck, now that's a fuckup. Jesus Christ, man, how does he do it? The man single-handedly ruined Uruguay. You think Tricky Dicky picked him because he's reading Chip's little spy novels?* Anyway, that was all she wrote, besides it was over eight years ago and Nixie's own little culture gave him a major fuck in the ass. And when he went down he took nearly everyone with him.

Funny, when Bill Adler called me that time in '76 I blamed him for Richard Welch's death in Greece. Said some bullshit about him leaking names of company people and jeopardizing their safety, but it was all bullshit. He knew and I knew it, I just had to say it. Fucking Nixon killed Richard Welch. Telling us to spread all sorts of shit in Greece that just blew up the war in Turkey over Cyprus. And then worse, letting that crap get leaked. Next thing you know Richard Welch and his poor wife—all killed. All fucking dead. Jesus Christ, a station chief. Fucking Nixon tried to ruin the FBI too as soon as Hoover croaked. And hell, who gives a shit in 1979?

Did I think that or say it out loud? Nobody's here and it's a quiet Kingston evening. I really need to go home. Claire's bitching about having to move one second, then calling all her friends in Buenos Aires as if they're really her friends to ask if the American school has gone to the dogs. Meanwhile I'm trying to think who do I know still in Argentina and who would I actually want to talk to? God, maybe we can just go back to simpler times where I meet with whoever is there to make sure the president's hands don't get dirty, brief them about what's going on in their world, slip them some cash and promise these itchy-fingered bastards that sure I can look into the procurement of some new toys. And if they were especially good, we'd even organize a nice little holiday at Fort Bragg.

Lord, it's a hell of a thing to miss days when work actually worked. Me in Argentina, hearing from an agent in La Paz that we finally got Che. I don't even know why I'm thinking about Che Guevara. I was thinking about Argentina and how much it's changed since 1967. Claire, the way she is on the phone you'd think she's just slipping back into a space her friends kept warm for her. That's my wife, always assuming everything is exactly as she left it. I think she's just happy to get the fuck out of Jamaica. When she told me that she and Nelly Matar had had words, boy was she pissed off when I added *finally*. Such fucking hypocrites these Syrians in Jamaica, and all so goddamn vulgar. I mean, I know they were shopkeepers, but at least the Chinese are never like that.

—I merely asked if Matar's Cash and Carry Downtown was her family's place. I mean, nothing's wrong with an honest business. For some reason she took great, great offense.

—Can't imagine why.

—Oh please, Barry. Either you're a shopkeeper or you're a snob. You can't be both. Besides, if I had to tell her one more time that the kinds of hats she wears are only meant for days at the races I would have just yanked the damn thing off her head.

Always thinking about the other person, that's my wife. I am an accountant. An efficiency guy. This is why the strangest bunch of fucking people think they can unload whatever shit on me. I mean, I get it—nobody seeking crucial info would ever think to ask Barry Diflorio. One other thing the Mrs. doesn't seem to know. Argentina is still in the middle of a fucking shit show.

The Egyptians used to strip their rabble-rousers buck naked, bolt them down on all fours, cover them in bitch piss and let a bunch of dogs loose that would mistake them for bitches in heat and butt-fuck the poor losers. And this Shah was worse. Yet four days into February shit hit the fan. Roger Theroux called me. Bill Adler was at best a fucking mediocre agent but Roger was the real deal, maybe the best we got that was actually American.

I knew somebody in Washington who knew both Roger and me, asked if I wanted to see his report on Iran. Theroux said something way different from what the Company told Carter. He was right there, on the ground, and said that it was like Cuba in 1959, only worse because this was all religious.

I can see why a report like this wouldn't make sense to Carter, or anybody. Religion? Revolution is liberals, hippies, communists, Baader-Meinhof bullshit, and the thing driving this was religion? Come on, it's nineteen seventy fucking nine. Half of these Saudi and Iranian kids were living in Paris, wearing tight jeans, getting butt-fucked more than the average American fairy—how did religion rise again? And then Roger Theroux got kidnapped.

They roughed him up pretty bad. Accused him right away that he was CIA, set up some sham court, convicted him and sentenced him to death all in less than a month. Thank God or Allah, I guess, that Roger knew his Koran. When I finally spoke to him he said, Barry, I demanded to see that fucking Mullah. When the fucker finally showed up, because believe me he took his time, I said, look, you can go through it and go through it again, but nowhere in the Koran is this kind of action sanctioned. And if you do this you go against the will of your own God and Prophet. They let him go. And even with all that, two days ago still came like a fucking surprise to Washington. You gotta wonder: How does something manage to be surprising and inevitable at the same time?

I don't think she's read anything about Argentina. Probably best to leave that alone for now, besides I'm sure that things haven't affected her friends much. Will she at least miss the house? She certainly put a lot into it, but she was always like that. Even if she was staying in a hotel for two days she had to rearrange it, make it hers. I'm trying to think of what I'll miss, other than jerk chicken. What the fuck, Barry Diflorio, three years and you sound like you were visiting via the Love Boat. Maybe I should tell her. That neither of the poets she used to invite over for dinner has been heard of since 1977. Or the dancer, or that white-haired homosexual Umberto she thought was so charmingly communist. I can see him wearing white, head to toe, right up to the very last.

When that bomb blasted its way through that Buenos Aires apartment building in '78, for a second I thought it was de las Casas. But he's back here in Jamaica, probably to finish what he couldn't in 1976 and Lord knows what that will be. I do know that he is not to be touched. Worse, he knows it. And nobody is replacing me, though somebody is definitely replacing Louis. Far as I know he was even supposed to have landed a few days ago. I don't know if my not even knowing his name is Clandestine being efficient or the agency being incompetent. At least somebody thinks it's not wise to close the book on Jamaica just yet. You never know with this country, these people. Sometimes it sounds like I'm talking about the Philippines.

I still want to know who wrote that damn report and who authorized it, or how fucking soft is this president that they would need to goose up that report so badly. *Not in a revolutionary or even a prerevolutionary situation.* Jesus Christ. Then three days ago, the rebels finally overwhelm the Shah's troops and everybody is looking on stunned. Everybody but Roger Theroux.

And I'm looking at an office that I won't have to ever see again, wondering how much I tell the wife. Umberto is going to hit her the most, she's been calling their home for weeks now, convinced that they have either moved or she must have written down the wrong number. At one point she even asked me if they gave her a wrong number on purpose, and I really didn't know what the hell to answer. The weirdest thing is that when she asks her other friends about him they have nothing to say. I mean, it's so strange that none of them say anything. Not even the Figueroas, who live only five doors down. Even if they don't know what specifically happened to him, they know something happened.

Politics shape policy. That's been on my mind all week. That and Bill Adler. He called me again two days ago, funnily enough, both him and Louis. He was feeling particularly pissed off about being finally kicked out of the U.K.

—Come on, Bill. As small as America's dick is, those limeys will stretch across the Atlantic to suck it.

—Good point. I knew I was biding time, but was kinda hoping, you know.

—Bad form, even for an ex-agent.

—Not ex. Fired.

—Tomato, tomahto. How's Santiago?

—I hear it's sunny in the summer. Really, Diflorio, Brzezinski won't find this conversation half as interesting as Kissinger did.

—Maybe not, but didn't you hear? We're cutting costs all around. Anybody waiting for their phones to be debugged is shit out o' luck. Speaking of cutting costs, how's—

—How's that broken record you can't seem to fucking fix?

—Touchy.

—It's one motherfucker of a February in case you haven't been paying attention. Everybody's touchy.

—What do you want, Adler?

—What makes you think I want something?

—Aw, honey, you called because you're all lonely?

—Never met a guy in the field who wasn't, Diflorio. Then again, you're an—

—Accountant. You know, if we're going to be friends, you really have to stop calling me—

—Accountant?

—No, Diflorio.

—Don't be so smarmy, Diflorio, it doesn't suit you.

—If you knew what suited me you'd call me Bar, or Barry, or Bernard, like my mother-in-law. Now for the second time, what can I do for you?

—Did you see all that stuff about Iran?

—Does disco suck?

—Just making chat.

—No, you're making small talk. I heard John Barron's writing a sequel to his KGB book.

—Might as well, Lord knows we have to ferret out those KGB sleeper agents.

—And the traitors who support them.

—Who would that be? The Bill in his book? I read that I'm an alcoholic skirt chaser who's constantly broke.

—So you've read it?

—Of course I've read it. I'm surprised that you're taking this wannabe agent so seriously.

—His book is at the very least as entertaining as yours.

—Fuck you. Have another book coming, by the way.

—Of course you do. You have at least a thousand more lives to fuck up. By the way, how's your buddy Cheporov?

—Who?

—Nifty. Very skillful. But shit, Adler, even the *Daily Mail* knows you've been talking to Cheporov.

—Don't know who—

—Edgar Anatolyevich Cheporov, Novosti News Agency in London. He's KGB. Go ahead. I'll just sit here while you act all aghast that you didn't know. Mind you, aghast is hard to pull off without me seeing your face.

—Cheporov isn't KGB.

—And I wear briefs, not boxers. You've been in contact with him since 1974 at least.

—I don't know anybody at Novosti News.

—My dear Bill, you will simply have to do better. First you say you don't know him, then you say he isn't KGB. Should we pause while you get your thoughts together? If you didn't know Cheporov was KGB, you're either very stupid or very gullible, or maybe you just need some money. How much did Cuban intelligence pay you? A million?

—A million? You don't know Cuba.

—Lord knows you do. What do you want, you fucker?

—Information.

—How much? A treasure trove? Wasn't that your exact words to the KGB when you tried to whore yourself out?

—I'm not asking for information, prick, I'm giving it. Some of it might even concern you, fucking Yale boy.

—Hey, don't shoot me because you swam out of Tacoma, Florida. Whatever you're selling I'm sure as hell not buying. This conversation is being recorded.

—We've already established that.

—No worries, it'll all be evidence for later.

—For when I turn myself in?

—For when we fucking catch you.

—You accountants can't catch a breath.

—This from the case officer who got caught trying to bug an embassy at five a.m.

—Did you know you were in the *Horrors* book?

—What's the *Horrors* book?

—Can't confirm that's what they're calling it, if they're calling it anything at all. My biggest regret in life, I swear, is to have put my book out before this shit broke.

—I don't know what you're talking about. And one day we're gonna find your fucking leak.

—One day soon?

—Sooner than you think. This is an awfully long phone call. You sure you can afford it? I really have to close up shop, Bill.

—Oh yeah, all that packing and saying goodbye. Wonderful. Poor President Ford. He was on the fucking Warren Commission and didn't know we didn't tell him everything.

—What are you going on about now?

—The *Horrors* book. Who gave it that name? You gotta wonder.

—No I don't. I swear sometimes, Adler, you're not talking to me at all. It's like we're two girls and you're talking about some boy just so the boy can overhear you. Few years out of the Company and you're like those crackpots thinking aliens abducted you just to stick a dildo up your ass. Jeez.

—Maybe it's not a book exactly. Maybe it's a file.

—A file. In the CIA. The CIA has a file, and top secret to boot. How did you ever get this job?

—Don't insult my intelligence, Diflorio.

—I don't fucking have to.

—I'm telling you about a file Schlesinger compiled for Kissinger, the same report he presented to Ford on Christmas Day 1974.

—You're talking to me about 1974. Dude, I hate to break it to you, but we've got a new President, and even he's not going to be President much longer if today gets any worse. Iran's blowing up all over the world press and poor William Adler, just now passing shit that everybody else shat in 1974.

—Kissinger presented a version that dressed up the really juicy stuff. Schlesinger's original file is still floating out there and I hear it's a doozy.

—Well, you've already had my opinion on your opinions, Adler. Running out of writing material, buddy?

—You're a garbage man, Diflorio. The only reason you're not interested is that you're not high enough to be interested. Schlesinger's little memo has it all: all the little things that the average American thinks some spy novelist cooked up. The breakdown of Tom Hayden's last shit. Who Bill Cosby's fucking. Mind control after LSD. Assassinations all over the place, Lumumba in the Congo, for example, lots of stuff on your buddy Mobutu—

—Correction: Frank's buddy.

—Well, you, him and Larry Devlin are interchangeable, you Latin American African boys.

—The number of assassination attempts on Castro authorized by Bobby Kennedy himself.

—Did you know that Haviland's being pushed to retire?

—Who?

—Haviland. The man who trained you and me. Sorry, I forgot you trained yourself.

—You realize if the American public or even Carter got hold of that book it would be the end of the Company? Your job would go down in fucking flames.

—I swear at times I don't know if you're a fucking idiot or if you're just pretending to be one on TV. What kind of world do you think this is, Adler? You are the one agent who doesn't seem to know what's going on on this fucking planet. You think your buddies in the KGB are on some humanitarian mission, is that what you think?

—Ex-agent, remember. And you don't know what I think.

—Oh, I know exactly what you think. Originality is not one of the things you got going for you.

—I should have known you wouldn't have given a shit about this *Horrors* book. You're the worst of the lot. It's one thing if you approved of what your government is doing, but you don't even care. Just punch the clock and cash the check.

—I love how you assume you have me figured out. It's one of your worst shortcomings, Adler, thinking you can read people when you can't read shit.

—Oh really?

—Yes really. You know why? Because in all this talking about your *Horrors* book, in your breaking it to poor me that my government has been engaged in all sorts of fucked-up shit, in all your failure to spark my interest even once, it never occurred to you that maybe I'm not interested because I wrote the motherfucker.

—What? What did you say? Are you fucking shitting me?

—Do I sound like I'm remotely interested in shitting you? Yes, you fucker, this little bookkeeper wrote it. What, you think the secretary of defense wrote the damn thing himself? You know, at first I felt kinda slighted that I didn't appear in your book even once. Then I realized you really don't have a fucking clue what I do, do you? You have no fucking idea. Because if you did, you wouldn't have wasted my time for the past six and a half minutes. Instead you'd have fallen out of your fucking hammock and while you're on the floor, thank your commie God that I'm not the son of a bitch they sent after you. By the way, your Sunbeam Coffeemaster's broke and the view from your new apartment fucking sucks. Tell Fidel you want an ocean view.

Of course the son of a bitch hung up. And he hasn't called back. I suspect that he'll never call me again.

Fuck this desk. Fuck this office. Fuck this country. Fuck this year already. I'm going home.

Papa-Lo

Kidnap Mick Jagger and make two million. Me and Tony Pavarotti we out in a car, riding up and down a road that twist and turn like river, riding right up next to the windy wavy sea. Josey Wales didn't come. Racing for the curb, the Ford Cortina. Swerve left then swerve right, a wave just burst on rock and froth splash and hit the windshield. This is how close to the road is the sea, how close we is to the sea and Pavarotti still driving, cooler than coolness' mother.

Tony Pavarotti with his nose like a Pavarotti. Can't remember him mother nor father, can't remember him growing up or doing the things boys do when growing up or getting into crosses boys get into. It's like he be the sidekick in the movie, the baaaaaaaaad *hombre* who just show up in the middle and start walk and talk like we was waiting for him all this time. Tony Pavarotti just is, and you think hard about what you need before you call him. And he will lie and wait in an old building window all day, or up in the tree on the hill all night, or in the wall of garbage in the Garbage-lands or behind a door for as long as it take for him to become a complete shadow and take out your enemy from three hundred feet away. He do work for Josey Wales but not even Josey had whatever it take to keep Tony at him side permanent and plenty people side with Josey permanent these days. We don't talk. When I stay home I stay inside, and when I go I leave the country. I don't go to him doorstep. But Tony Pavarotti is man who serve every man and no man and today all day he in my employ, in the left seat driving and hugging the thin road, too narrow for such an angry sea.

Learn this: Jail is the ghetto man university. Slam clink slam. Babylon come for me two years ago—is it two years yet? I try to not forget any time Babylon encroach 'pon the I. In the truck to take me to jail a policeman spit in me face (him new), and one, when I say, Pussyhole, you spit smell like bubblegum, gun-butt me between the head so hard that is when they throw water on me in the jail I wake up. Both police dead before 1978 thanks to the man beside me who carry them to me as soon as me come out. Learn this all nice and decent people, Mama-Lo didn't raise no son who walk with he back straight to get spit on like mangy dog. And this here Papa-Lo never ever forget. Man, like we don't forget, we collect. We take them to the end of Copenhagen City where only John Crow live and rich man shit drain into the sea and one start to wah wah wah 'bout how him wife not working and he have three pickney and me say all the worse for them now they have a dead pussyhole for a daddy.

But back to when them send me to jail. And even if you could jim-screechy, slip through the system you can't slip through the iron. Iron is iron, and iron stronger than lion and steel don't budge. The bars say, There's no way out, just cease and settle and if you ever plan to travel you better tap inside your head and tell it to start traveling. This must be how man end up reading book they otherwise wouldn't read, and write book too. But the bars also say, Nobody can come in and stop the learning, so maybe a learning is a visitation in your head and maybe a jail make you still in the spirit so that you ready to hear it, because, gentlemens, nobody—and I mean nobody—can learn nothing if them not ready to listen.

The car hit a bump but Tony Pavarotti don't notice. I wish I didn't jump like a man who can't drive a car. He the only man I know who drive with glove, they cover him palm but show him finger with a cut-out for each knuckle and the back of him hand. Brown leather. The sun running away before we get to the bay. It don't have what it take to witness when man get dark. The moon now, the moon is better company especially when it full and fat and deep like it just rise out of blood. You ever see a moonrise? I want to ask Tony Pavarotti but I don't think he would answer. You don't ask a man like this them kind o' question.

I pull two cigarette out of my pocket and give him one. He stick it in him mouth and me light it. Palisadoes strip, past the airport, on the stretch to Port Royal where James Bond drive the man off the road in *Dr. No.* We drive along until we reach a fort that build from before man like me come over on the slave ship. 1907 Earthquake—half of it sink into the sand but if you drive fast it look like the fort was just now rising out of it. You see cannon peeking out of sand and you wonder how tall and proud it must did look when Nelson hop on him hob-leg all around it. Nelson we learn about in high school along with Admiral Rodney who save Jamaica from the French. Who going save Jamaica now?

Farther down this road is Port Royal and Fort Charles that everybody done know. But few people know the beach bush hide two more forts including this one. I stick my head out the window and watch the last sun streak turn orange, then pink, then nothing and I can hear the sea growing wild even over the car engine. Me and Tony Pavarotti driving to the lost fort in between the sinking sun and the rising moon and the disappearing shadow. We make a sharp left through prickle bush and swing over a rough bump. Me hold the door like a man that can't drive. We ride over a mound, that look like a mountain top, because from the top is a steep drop right down to the beach. Bumpy ride down, swing to the left then right, pull you hand into the car before the prickle bush slash the window—my hand would be bleeding right now. Down, down, down. The car swing left, again then right, then jump—we going roll over right now, have to, how this bloodcloth man can so calm and don't say nothing but grip the steering wheel like race car driver? The car skidding down, me about to shout out hey! But then we brake. Tony Pavarotti slow the car down to crawl as we come the thin strip of beach up to the entrance of the fort. No gate so we drive in. Kingston is a now place across the sea.

The car stop. Tony wind down him window and climb out in one swing, like is the style. Him on the right, me on the left, we both reach the trunk the same time. He stick the key in and fly it open. If the first boy could scream he would scream at the weak light, this is for sure the most brightness them see in three hours. It did take all me rage to push the last two in the trunk meself for me would a deal with them from long before, almost two year before, but by now me no have none of that left, nothing left to pull the first one out but two hands. Him light like a feather when me grab him by the collar. The handcuff behind him back stain sticky with blood and his wrist white where black skin supposed to be. He smell like shit and iron. Boy bawling over tears so him cheek and eyes red and him nose have booger running down over booger. The man Tony Pavarotti pull out just the same, both of them stink and also wet from them own pee-pee.

On the way over here me did all set to ask them, You remember the beach, pussyhole? You remember when you pull gun 'pon the Singer 'cause other man fuck up your samfie business but you want him fi pay for it? You did know then that him mark you face? You did know you was dead from the second you pull gun 'pon the man? You might as well did pull gun 'pon God. Me did have all them things fi say to the two but now, in the fort where Spanish man and British man and Jamaican man dead over years and years, reminding me that one day me too soon dead, me don't have nothing to say. And Tony Pavarotti never ever say nothing.

But them saying plenty. Even with the gag me can make out letter and word and sentence. Each blink of their red eye fierce and squeezing out tears. Beg you, Papa do, me never did involve, look how me still poor. Beg you, Papa do, the Singer did already gimme mercy. Beg you, Papa do, all me know 'bout is the horse race, me no know 'bout the ambush in the night. Beg you, Papa do, make me go out to sea and me will swim 'way like mermaid to Cuba and never come back to Jamrock again. But me don't care. There is a bunch of man who ambush the Singer in the night. There is a bunch of man that pull gun on him at the beach 'cause they drag him into horse race con-plan fuckery him never have nothing to do with. A wind in the air say them was one and same man. Another wind say them be two different entity. But even to that me run out words to say. Me just don't care. Them drive a gash between me and the Singer, a cut that heal but leave a scar. Man must get punish for drawing gun and man must get punish for firing it too. The devil who standing waiting at the gate of hell can do all the sorting out. All this me think to say to the two, but don't. Me, Papa-Lo, the biggest most magnificentest man in the ghetto. Me might as well be Tony Pavarotti. He already dragging the first one through the bush, out onto the black sand beach.

The trick, the whole thing is, the whole reason was to bring him back, not for good but to knock down the first domino. To bring him back for this concert though we already talking things bigger than that. Better than that. Things, boy, I don't know, Jamaica, you ready for it? My head hopeful but not at ease, it so uneasy that the only thing that put it to rest is remembering that poor Papa-Lo heart never at ease. I mean, what make sense in England don't must make sense here. England is England and London is London and when you in a city so big you also start to think big and talk big and you foretell grand tidings and then you come back to Jamdown and you wonder if your head did swell TOO large.

Plenty people even in the middle of sufferation going pick the bad they know over the good they can only dream about, because who dream but madman and fool? Sometimes war stop because you forget why you fight, sometimes you tired of warring, sometimes people who dead come back to you in you sleep and you can't remember them name, and sometimes you come to see that who you supposed to fight not even your enemy. Look 'pon Shotta Sherrif.

The beach is sand until it reach the sea. There it change to rock that roll and tumble with the waves and cackle like a woman duppy when more waves rush in. *Kekekekekekeke.* Tony Pavarotti drag the boy right down to where sea hit sand and kick the back of him knee so that he fall like he about to pray. And then he do. Quick and wild, like he can't get one word out before he rushing out the next. *Kekekekekekeke.* The boy in him white brief that yellow in the front, brown in the back. Tony Pavarotti in navy blue—soldier shirt with epaulette and plenty pocket and gabardine pants roll up over him soldier boots right above the calf. Him steady the boy head slow with both hand, almost soft, almost like he taking care. The boy mistaking the soft touch for mercy. He crying again and him head shaking too much. Tony still him head again. *Kekekekekekeke*—pow.

The boy in my hand scream into the gag, but he also go weak and I have to drag him to the beach. Water don't reach him pants yet so I know the new wet is fresh piss. Tony leave the car on and I can swear I hear the radio, but is probably just the rock. *Kekekekekekeke.* I drag this boy right beside the other body and push him down on him knee. I did make him keep on him green shorts. I steady him head but he turn just as I pull the trigger. Pow. Pow through the side of him temple and an eye pop out. *Kekekekekekeke.* He twitch and fall. Tony Pavarotti point to the sea, and I say no, leave them.

Lockdown remind you that what make you brothers is not blood but sufferation. And when as brothers you suffer together you also get new wisdom together. Because I pick up a new wisdom the same time as Shotta Sherrif and when we take a stop and realize say we really of the same mind we take the reasoning to England and realize the Singer have the same wisdom too. In fact he wiser since him did run him own house under that wisdom where for a long time enemy used to meet as friend, even when we fight like wild animal everywhere else. People think this is about a concert or is about white man from the PNP shaking hands with white man from the JLP, like you can fix cancer with a vaccine. Even me did know this concert was nothing and me was the one who pull up Seaga onstage meself.

Shotta Sherrif was on the stage but then him jump and start follow around Mick Jagger who was walking up and down and reasoning with the people and vibing with the rhythm like he don't know the grounds swarming with bad man. Every minute he flashing that big teeth grin. *Make we kidnap Mick Jagger and hold him for two million dollars*, Shotta Sherrif say as joke but then he watch Mick Jagger dip in and out of the crowd and I know he start to think it for real. For white boy let loose and grin like rich politician pickney talking 'bout them trip to Mi-yah-mi. Shotta chase off what he say with a hahahaha but the Singer did hear him and shoot him a look Moses only wish him did have in *Ten Commandments.* Anyway, make them think he come back just to sing pretty song 'bout love just 'cause him make pretty album. Make him go to sleep while we work like Nicodemus. Because when me and Shotta Sherrif done talk 'bout planning the concert, we didn't stop talk, and we still talking now. The sun setting.

Tony Pavarotti driving the car and a song come on the radio. *Do it light, do it through the night, shadow dancing.* I know this song. My woman love it, say is some man named Gibb sing it. Me ask her how she know and she shoot back, *So you think me is ignorant woman?* I laugh because me been dancing with shadow in the dawn and in the night. Even in broad, bright daylight we searching for dark. It take four day to round up all the man from the horse racing con-plan who pull gun 'pon the Singer. One night to put them in the cell that up to few years ago me, the don of all dons, was the only man in Copenhagen City who didn't know 'bout it. Josey Wales have yet to explain that one to me.

Early morning we take the first two out, only because them jump in front and was making the most noise, the first man 'bout how the naked man duppy with blue flame drape around him skin and long shark teeth was eating they flesh all night and covering they mouth so they couldn't scream. The duppies slap them across the cheek and punch them in the face one two three four times like a jackhammer. Both man eyes did swell and wet for true. The first man point to him chest saying the duppy eat out him heart even though him chest have no mark. The second one didn't stop bawling 'bout the snake eating a way out through him head until it crawl out of him left eye, see the hole, he say while pointing to him eye. All of them blabbering about the devil spit on they face when they wake up. The two wouldn't stop so we stuff they mouth with calico cloth and throw them in the car trunk. When we drag them out to the car they don't even struggle. We take them to a part of Hellshire Beach that now closed off with a No Trespassing sign. They walk of they own free will, which bother me. Me no like see people so ready for what come next, so me push one with the snake in him head and he stumble. And he still don't say nothing, just get up and keep walking.

Tony Pavarotti put him hand on the first one shoulder to push him down but they both kneel down fast and close them eyes, whispering what sound like prayers. When the snake in the head man open him eyes they wet and he nod again like he saying do it now, do it right now, I can't wait any longer. Tony Pavarotti walk behind them and shoot both quick. Even the baddest gunman bawl like baby for him life, but them boys quiet. Me wonder what them life come to, when a man could be so ready to dead. Duppy dressed in blue fire, to shit. I wonder what going wake me up in the middle of the night?

When evening come we take out the other two. Time is coming, passing and running, and I know it leaving me behind, but damn. But damn if Josey going make that happen to him. He going run ahead of time and say, Look, pussyhole, me reach before you, me beat you just like you beat me in 1966. He leave all this to me, for he still never give no damn 'bout the Singer. Josey taking meetings with the Cuban who back again even though for all him bombing and dynamite couldn't make JLP win in 1976.

Many more will have to suffer. Many more will have to die. When Babylon come for me and take me out of the way so man can shoot up the Singer without me trying to stop it, Babylon also come for Shotta Sherrif. People from both sides start to think that we the don of dons no longer have any use. Put puss with dog and just bring a bucket for the blood. They think if them put all of we, man from Copenhagen City and man from the Eight Lanes, in the same lockup and throw away the key then we bound to kill each other. But something did die in jail, something die for real.

The first day we circle each other like lion and tiger who get stuck in one jungle. Me sit in a cell in the east and find man loyal and ready, since at all times a good number of man from the ghetto reside in jail. Shotta Sherrif rest in the west with man loyal to him. Both of we get news of the other whereabouts and roundabouts and nobody fall asleep without at least two eye watching. Didn't take long for man to hatch a plan. A man on my side act on him own and try to cut down one of Shotta man. Shotta Sherrif send message he going cease one of my man in retaliation. Me send message that me never attack him so why him going attack me? He send message that one of my man pull out a dinner knife and cut a mark like a telephone in another man face when them go out for exercise. Me send message to Shotta Sherrif saying he should name the man.

Treetop. That who it be in the message that come back. The next time we go out in the open me walk up to Treetop meself and say, My youth, a long time me a check you still fi move up in the ranks, make me see you knife.

—Papa, then no must, him say.

—Me going need you to prove to me what you can do by cutting a PNP pussyhole, me say while me holding him knife and testing how it sharp.

—Papa, him say—me more previous than that. Tuesday me done mark a youth. You want me deal with Shotta Sherrif case?

—What a way you eager, eh? No my youth, you no need to do that, but learn this, me say and ram the knife right through him neck and up him throat. Then me ram him again three time in the side of the neck while my men make a wall. Then we all break away leaving the little pussyhole spraying blood on the ground and jerking like headless chicken.

Shotta Sherrif send message later, saying is true time we fi talk. When puss and dog kill one another the only one who win is Babylon. Me take this reasoning and me reason 'pon it more. Babylon is a country, Babylon is a shitstem, Babylon is oppressor and Babylon infiltrate with police. Babylon get tired of waiting so he put head puss and head dog in lockup for them to kill each other quick, but a different vibration come down 'pon the lockup. A positive vibration.

Me and Shotta Sherrif play domino all the time after that while Babylon hovering outside, and the only eye him got is the police. I hear him reasoning, he hear my reasoning and the two of we make a new reasoning. Me release from jail first, and in January them release Shotta Sherrif. First thing him do is find me. That night, January 9, 1978, people with me and people with him put down gun, light candle and start sing we ain't gonna study war no more. That night Jacob Miller come through with a new tune, a boomshot from the natty, a hit song named the "Peace Treaty Special," which shoot up to number one. Positive vibration. But learn this all nice and decent people, you walk into every situation with an injection needle or a gun. Some things you heal, and some things you shoot.

For lo and behold all nice and decent people: the last movements of Babylon. January 5, four day before we light candle and sing. Me feeling good because it too early in the year to feel the heaviness of it come down on you. But the new year reach the Wang Gang with no gun. Fool like fuck, the Wang Gang. A Peter Nasser idea he couldn't control once outside of

Copenhagen City. Yeah they still was about, and still taking no instruction from the likes of me or even Josey. But by end of 1977 Wang Gang didn't have no gun, since even Peter Nasser realize you shouldn't arm man you can't control. Somebody tell them if they promise to use them to mow down some PNP youths in two of the Eight Lanes and weaken the center, then Wang Gang can keep a shipment of guns that was to magically appear at this old bay in St. Catherine.

This somebody was just going to leave a car trunk full of guns and all them have to do is pick them up, start some ruckus in a PNP territory and they can keep the guns. As usual Wang Gang don't take seek no counsel. They start to think big, since this somebody who inform them have personal connection in the Defence Force. They even get promised of some real work at the wharf, mostly security, where they could put them guns to use. Nobody ride for free in Jamdown, but the gang agree and in the early morning two army ambulance come down to Wang Gang Lands and pick up fourteen boy.

Two ambulance take them east of West Kingston, over past Port Henderson, across the bridge, past the four beaches of Portmore and up into the hilly cliff. When them reach Green Bay, the driver tell them to come out of the ambulance and wait right there. Another truck was going come with the guns—none of them remember the army did say a car was coming not a truck. Them boys see and wait. A soldier come up and start talk to the boy in charge. He and the soldier go into the bush when the other boys hear a single shot, like the start of a race. And then, hataclaps.

Jamaica Defence Force man come down 'pon them from afar and open fire. Soldier rush down 'pon the boys and start fire machine gun while one big one hiding in the bush push through and start ratatatatatatatat like this was war. Boy who manage to run, run into other soldier, boy head blow off and drop, man dash straight into thorn bush that rip off him skin until he reach the sea. Five shot to death, more wounded and one or two dive into the sea and get save by fisherman. The rest scatter. The soldier come on TV and say them boys trespass 'pon them firing range in the middle of a shooting practice in the evening. Coming 'pon the TV and talking over the radio, the minister say, "No saints were killed in Green Bay." Three days before the concert, we launch a protest about how people in the ghetto still shit and eat in the same place when down swoop Babylon police force and kill three people including a woman. The same minister again,

"If one policeman is killed this year, the people who did it will be hunted down like dogs."

Many more will have to suffer. Many more will have to die. My first week in lockup Babylon beat me 'round the clock. They wasn't searching for no news, they wasn't trying to turn me into no informer. They was just all taking they turn to show me who is the bigger boss. The police never come one at a time, not after the first one come after me and me give him a kick that send him balls right up into him brain. Afterwards they come two by two, three by three, one time even four. Is like them was in contest, who make me bawl out first win. The first three, me mark them name, Watson, Grant, and Nevis, almost sneak in late at night. But as me hear the clang of the gate they set 'pon me with baton. This is for what you do to Roderick, one say. And him widow. Then it must burn you that if you kill me somebody going deal with you, me say and spit out my back tooth. Probably black from cavity anyway. After that new police come nearly every night for a week, always with one of the first three as tour guide.

The last night the four come, two hold down my face in the floor which smell of me own piss. They fold over a towel and put bath soap in it. Then they take turn beating me in me back singing one potato, two potato, three potato, four. Me getting tired of this shit so me tell Grant and Nevis to back off before me really get mad. They shocked me know them name but that make them set 'pon me worse. Two day later both men ask for a few days' leave. Grant wife might never use her left eye again and Nevis' son arm and leg break. Nevis come to me cell saying he personally going kill me. I tell him I feel real bad 'bout him son but now he have to take special care him little thirteen-year-old daughter hymen don't get burst from the wrong man infiltrating it. Is always funny when a black man go white. When they finally let me out into the general area with me own men waiting for me, everybody around me hush and in gloom. At first me did think they hear about Nevis' son and think that was going too far, or they was just showing me proper respect. But then me grab a newspaper from one of them and there on the front page was the Singer.

Evening. Me and Pavarotti late. I don't have a watch but I can count when time ticking away. Could do it from me was a boy. Plus me grandfather teach me how to tell time like a Colon man. Hold on, him wasn't me grandfather, no man in the ghetto have grandfather. He was just an old man unlucky to be the only man who live to old age, singing the Colon man song. *One two three four Colon man a come. One two three four Colon man a come. One two three four Colon man a come, with him brass chain ah like him belly bam bam bam. Ask him the time and him look up in the sun with him brass chain a lick him belly bam bam bam.*

Pavarotti look at me blank—I didn't realize me was singing it out loud. So evening, maybe seven-thirty, but we near the sea so nothing blocking the sun as it run away. Tony Pavarotti driving slow and me not telling him to drive fast and the disco music fulling the space where otherwise two man would have to talk. First me think it was a batty boy vibe but then the lyrics penetrate. Shadow dance for true. We shadow dancing as soon as light set to go. What done in darkness can never come back to light.

We riding against the sea in peace and I thinking about how the second peace concert born in England. Because 1977 was nothing but war. The concert was calling for one love, and we charge two dollar for the "togetherness section," five dollar for the "love" section and eight dollar for the "peace" section, that way if rich burn-skin white man and woman want to come they can come too with no fear, although there was no way in hell that was going to happen. Burn-skin white man don't want peace, he want Jamaica to become the USA state number fifty-one, shit, he would settle for just a colony.

We do the concert because whether you green or you orange, some place still don't have no toilet and we have pickneys surviving stick, stone and bullet only to get kill by a drink of water. We do the concert because one in every three never have no work, and that was not just in the ghetto. We do the concert because Babylon was coming for all of we. The Singer come back but things did change in him. Where before he would grab you before he even see you, now he wait one-two second and nod or grab him chin and smile. Where he would finish a sentence you start, now he wait for you to finish, look right through you and don't say nothing. Understand this, me didn't have nothing to do with December 1976, but I know he now sleep with one eye open and that eye sometimes 'pon me. Me and Tony Pavarotti leaving the sea and turning for McGregor Gully.

The concert. Me never get to see the peace concert in 1976. But me get to see the war right after. So April 22 me at this concert. Me on the stage. Me watch Seaga and Manley form steeple over the Singer head. People always looking for signs and wonders, but signs signal nothing and nothing in a wonder to wonder about. The man me never going forget is Tosh. First me think this man come shit 'pon we concert. That man just had a thing for rubbing me the wrong way until me figure him out. And even when me figure him out and think we have an understanding, him still a little fuck-up, maybe because more than the other two, him is the one Babylon fuck with the most, especially Babylon police. Just a month before the Singer come back, the customs officer stop Tosh at the airport and hold him for long. Here is what the officer whisper to him: *Me looking for a reason to shoot you.* Me didn't even want him too much because a man like that never feel the positive vibration. Is the Singer who did want him and convince him to come. Me no get between family and them affairs. Almost a month now and is still Tosh me remember. Tosh was the one who make sure nobody ever forget. Right before the concert he say he *not playing no bombocloth concert because every man involve in that concert going end up dead.* Man come on the stage in the still hot evening wearing black from head to foot, like him official, like is CIA work for Rasta. The first thing he do is tell man to lock off them bombocloth camera. *Is word sound and power that break down the barriers of oppression and drive away transgression and rule equality. Well right now you have a system or a shitstem wha' go on in this country fi a long ages and 'imes. Four hundred years and the same bucky massa business and black inferiority and brown superiority and white superiority rule this little black country here fi a long 'imes. Well I and I come with Earth-*

quake Lightning and Thunder to break down these barriers of oppression, drive away transgression and rule equality between humble black people.

Me stun like little boy when him first see a dead shotta. Even with the Rastaman vibration moving through me head, me never once think 'bout the black, even when me drive past plantation still standing. The last thing him say,

If unu want go ah heaven a fi unu business I will be here a billion years.

Mick Jagger prancing like a drunk goat, looking on like proud daddy. Me and Tony Pavarotti driving down the road. How much minute me just miss? I feel like when me fall asleep and wake up and the plane still in the air. Tony Pavarotti saying nothing.

—We turn for McGregor Gully yet?

Him nod yes, just as I remember. Maybe me just tired. Making things right is hard work. Harder than crime. McGregor Gully always smell like shit and factory chemical run loose. People live 'round here but me send message from two day ago that they better clear out when me coming. They can come back when we gone.

Police wasn't going find none of them boy but I was. Two years me see and wait. See them a hide like pussyhole while me wait for the Singer to come back to deal with them for real. One man hide in Jungle and there be a mother to blame. Damn them and they motherlove. Plenty woman-killer remember Mother's Day. So mama hide son in her cupboard for over one year until even she get tired of it. Leggo Beast, crouched in cupboard with bread and roach and cheese and mouse for over a year. Come out only at night like him name Count Dracula. The little pussyhole never learn say if you want to hide in plain sight, then don't be a fool and get your mother to buy cocaine for you. Josey is the one who tip me off.

Seven forty-five in the morning. Babylon still asleep, like it always asleep when it come to justice. Me send word that is time to deal with that little pussyhole. Fucking idiot. Me send two man to pull him out of the cupboard and bring him and the mother too. Me hear her scream 'bout nobody deh yah even though nobody ask her anything. Good Lord, woman can fool. When they bring the boy and him mother to me, right at me gate, the boy blinking from too much sunlight and him skin white from head to toe. Me don't want neither of them disgrace me premises with they presence so me come out to the road. The mother bawling do no take me boy, do no take me boy. Me don't have no words for either. But me want the boy to see how much what him do cost, and how he was going pay. The year in cupboard make him stop grow. He nothing but bone and skin and he look at me all shifty, like lizard, then stare back at the ground. This from the boy them call Leggo Beast. I look at him mesh sleeveless and him jeans shorts, which cut off too high and the scab on him right shoulder. Leggo Beast look at me again and me take him in good, size him up nice then ball a quick, tight fist and punch straight in the mother face.

She stagger back and he yell. I grab her in the front of her dress before she stagger back too far then one two three more punch straight in her face. Her lip burst like tomato and her knees buckle and me let her sink into the road. Put me finger together and slap her right cheek with a strike, then left, then right again, then left. Leggo Beast bawling out for him mother, me point one finger and my man take him gun butt and clap him in the balls. People coming to watch. Let them watch. Let them remember how Papa-Lo discipline work. I slap her again, left, right, left. A woman scream out do Papa show her mercy and me drop the fucking bitch and walk over to my man and take him gun. I walk right up to the woman and put the gun 'pon her forehead and say, You want mercy? Make me show you bombocloth mercy. Me will show her mercy if you come take her punishment. The woman back 'way.

I walk back to the woman and kick her two time. Then me grab her left hand and drag her backside all the way back to her yard while the people follow. The boy bawl out for him mother. She not moving so me tell a woman to bring a bombocloth bucket of water now. She run and bring it back quick. Me dump the bucket 'pon the woman and she nod and cough and scream. Me grab her hair and pull her head up so she can see me face.

—You have half hour to leave yah so, seen? And me never want to see, smell or hear 'bout you again, seen? Me see you, me kill you, you brother, you mother, and you daddy and all you other pickney, seen? Thirty minutes and get out of me bombocloth territory, or me'll make you watch me fucking kill him.

Then me turn to the people.

—And hear this. Any one of you help her, any one of you even talk to this bitch, watch how fast me send you packing too.

Me put the damn boy in the cell with the other men who shoot up the Singer. One of them gone mad already, talking to himself and shit him pants while him talk 'bout how the radio in him head won't believe him dead. Him talk day and night, and in the morning he talk about how the naked man duppy with blue fire wrap around him skin and long shark teeth was eating him flesh all night and covering him mouth so he couldn't scream. And when the duppy done eat, he just open him mouth and cover him face with spit so thick is like Jell-O. Me say, pussyhole, you know why you life going get cut short? And him just say Jah live, Jah live, Jah live.

Three p.m. me tell the people set 'pon the mother house take out everything and burn it right in the street. Leggo Beast in the jail begging and pleading and weeping and wailing and saying is Josey Wales recruit him and the white man who train them was CIA. CIA man wearing brown pants and shades even at night take them into the high bush up in St. Mary, *it must be St. Mary because we go east and up in the hills, and he show we how to load and cock an M16 and an M9. Point the rifle muzzle in a safe direction. Cock the bolt and open the rifle, no, cock the rifle and open the bolt. Return the charging handle to the forward position. Place the SAFE level on selector—no, place the selector lever on SAFE. Check the chamber to ensure it is clear. Insert the magazine, push it upward until the magazine catch engages and holds the magazine. Tap upward on the bottom of the magazine to ensure it is seated. Depress the upper portion of the bolt catch to release the bolt. Tap the forward assist to ensure the bolt is fully forward and locked. The man who talk like Speedy Gonzales show we what to do with a C-4, see? You mold it like a piece of putty, no? Like so and you put this wire in the putty and the mechanical sinting, the blasting cap and then have a long wire to make it explode and you click then boom,* hombre. *And since they give me cocaine and heroin it make me want to kill people and fuck woman, man and dog but if is heroin you cocky won't stand up even though you want to breed a gal so bad. Some night them lock we up in a room tight and make we sweat because you fucking Jamaicans have no drive, no soul, no dedication, you're nothing like the Bolivians or the fucking Paraguayans who learned a lot more in the space of two fucking weeks than you fucking jackasses will do in two years. And the Jamaican who fly down from Wilmington the third week with two big army-splotchy suitcase touch the white man shoulder and say, Easy pardner, chillax my brother, is revolution we building, while he go off with Josey and Speedy Gonzales who only talk English when he want we to know he still mad about the Pigs of the Bay. Josey talk Spanish with him. Yeah he can talk the Spanish, is truth, is truth, me hear him. Don't believe what him say, all of we hear him. And is one month we training, day and night in soldier uniform and one night Josey walk in the room and just shoot a boy in the head because him say him nah do it. Josey go off with Speedy Gonzales and the two of them reasoning for a long time. After them done reasoning we go out after midnight to take a cart off the wharf, which did full of more gun, including gun that me see you have now, Papa. You have gun from that shipment too. And the white man saying you guys're all that's saving Jamaica from chaos so you gotta do God's work. Save order from Chaos. Save order from Chaos.*

Save order from Chaos
Save order from Chaos
Save order from Chaos
Save order from Chaos
Save order from Chaos

Tony Pavarotti gun-butt him.

The first time they give me the cocaine them turn me into man that want it so bad, Jah know, me would open up me battyhole and make white man fuck me in it for another line. Jah know. Tell that to the jury me say to him to cut him off with all that batty fucking business, but me mark how him perplex me. Half of what come out of him mouth, not just what him say, but also how him say it didn't originate in Copenhagen City.

This CIA business—stupidness, especially since me see all the white man who come here with Peter Nasser and none of them say them was with no CIA. But that sorta lie seem like them no have no mental skill to think up something like that. Is like when a little boy open him mouth but what flow out sound like TV. This make me think deeper for a while, after all the Singer did sing that Rasta don't work for the CIA. All me know 'bout the CIA is they from America and would like JLP to win more than PNP because communism so bad in Cuba that mother already killing they baby.

But why would the CIA take it so serious that they would try to kill him? After all, him is not no politician and him don't have no government. Why not send James Bond or them special agent instead of three ignorant fool from the ghetto? Me ask Josey Wales what the bombocloth them a talk about, and he say if me too stupid to not know that when boy drowning he will clutch any straw, which sound like something me would say, and then he drive out, like this is pickney business he too big for. Me decide to not talk 'bout how him just call me stupid, as if is not me did pull him out of 1966 with my own hand. And how him always boasty but lately he getting just a little too big with me, like me 'fraid to cut his bad-breed part-chiney self back down to size. Me look 'pon him and think it but me don't say it. Me ask how can me be sure he really don't have nothing to do with the shooting since so much man say him involve and he say, Brethren, if me was trying to kill the Singer, the pussyhole would be dead now.

Believe him or don't believe him, me don't know. Plenty black man don't like the Singer, but they mostly wear shirt and tie and work on Duke Street. What don't sit right with me is the new thing in him face, and the hissing teeth saying whether I believe or not he don't care. Me scratch me head trying to find it, the year, the month, the day, the hour when this man pass me out and think him badder than me. And when a good number of rudies in the ghetto notice. Me is the last to know that rudie don't call themselves rudie no more. Now them is shotta. And they not no gang no more, now them is posse. And them answer phone call from America. Few nights ago me send message with Tony Pavarotti to the Singer and the manager. Meet we at McGregor Gully, me say, and make we once and for all do justice.

We deep in McGregor Gully, so deep the stink change. Leggo Beast and the two man tie up with the madman mouth in a gag because me can't stand to hear him talk. Tony Pavarotti kick each man in the back of the knee and they fall to ground. Two other man stand with Pavarotti. On the other side three woman and three man who answer to me. Verdict leave to them, judgment leave to me. Then we hear the sound of two vehicle coming to a stop before the four lights shut off. My two man come out of their car first. The Singer and him manager follow.

And the world say people must have justice, so we going give them justice even though in the world is nothing but Babylon justice that treat we like animal. McGregor Gully is a hole. Is a passage beneath ghetto that rainwater supposed to pass through to prevent flood, but since Babylon don't send garbage truck to the ghetto, everybody throw garbage in the gully so when rain fall the same ghetto people get flood with water, rubbish and shit. So much rubbish it turn into a wall of garbage. At first me did think the court would say they verdict quick just to get out from the rat and the shit but these man and woman sit down on rock and tree trunk and they stern. Me study them face and they study me. They don't even look 'pon the Singer and him manager. As soon as Leggo Beast see the Singer, him start whoop and wail and holler like him in the spirit and me tell Tony Pavarotti to silence him so he gun-butt him again.

—Them three man was descended 'pon Hope Road and try fi commit murder, me say.

—Is no me Papa, is no me is—

—You boy, shut you shit. People see them, and we have man who is witness. But me is a beneficent man. Me nah take justice for meself. Babylon court is fuckery so we set up we own court. You people is the court. You people judging, that way is judgment by the people for the people and nobody can say Papa-Lo just bring down hataclaps 'pon people like he name old testament God. We doing this proper. Babylon don't have no justice, ladies and gentlepeople. Babylon don't catch a single one of them 'cause Babylon on a different mission. But hear me now. Right now, you listen to the witness and you listen to the accused for even them have a right to give account for themselves, after all this is where we prove a man guilty, not where a man have to prove himself innocent. Is more than they deserve and is more than what they will get from the Babylon shitstem named Gun Court. If it even reach court. Police would ah shoot them and kill them long before them reach court. After all next thing we know, behind the trigger is Babylon for real. You, Mr. Manager, tell we what happen 'pon that evening.

—Well, I must say that right now I am in view of one of them. But some crucial fellows I don't see. I don't see at all.

—Who you don't see?

—He's not here.

—Who?

—But this one was there. And this one. And . . . hold him up to the light. Him, too.

—The Singer have anything to say?

—I speak for the Singer and for me, since only he and I were in the kitchen.

—I see.

—It is interesting to note what the young man just said.

—What him say? Go on.

—Well, as you may not know, I was a soldier in the U.S. Army. Served from 1966 to 1967. That was when the Vietnam crisis was in full swing.

—Jimmy Cliff did do one song name "Vietnam."

—Huh? Well, yes I'm sure. As I was saying, so I know all about the full workings of the CIA. So I know that should you see any attaché, consultant, embassy employee, any white man in a suit who's too far from the New Kingston, he is most certainly CIA. In fact if I were you I wouldn't trust any white man you see anywhere but Negril or Ocho Rios. So anyway, on the day in question—

—Nobody questioning the day.

—It's an expression. It's . . . anyway, I was pursuing some much needed relaxation at a Jamaican establishment, when I had to leave to catch a flight to Miami on some business. I returned the following day, this would be what, December 6? Yes, I think that is correct. So let's see. First I went back to the establishment to check on things. Then I went over to House of Chen for some curry goat—

—What this have to do with—

—I'm getting to that, gentlemen. And lady. Ladies. So I went to House of Chen on Knutsford Boulevard for some fine curry goat. From there I went to the Sheraton to pick up the head of the label, but he wasn't there. I returned the car for it was a rental and made my own way in my car to 56 Hope Road. I always park my car under the alcove so that's what I did. I could hear the band rehearsing so of course I looked in for him, but he wasn't there, he was in the kitchen. So in the kitchen I went and there he was, eating a grapefruit. Anyway, he and I had matters to discuss, and, well, I haven't had grapefruit in God only knows. So, I said I would love a piece of grapefruit, and he waved me over. As soon as I reach out to grab it we both hear a sound like a firecracker. Of course gentlemen and lady. Ladies. This was the Christmas season so of course I paid scant attention to what we both thought were firecrackers. I think he said something like who the bloodcloth bursting firecrackers in my yard? Something like that. But before he could even finish, next thing we know, more ratatatatat. All of a sudden I just felt this burst of a burn. Then another one, then another so fast that it almost felt like just one burst. I didn't even realise that I was shot. You don't feel like you're being shot, you just feel your legs burn, then give out, and still have time to wonder why. All I know is that I fell forward on him and then he said, Selassie I Jah Rastafari. It was just all so fast. So, so fast.

—Then if you get shoot in the back how you know who shoot you? one of the woman say.

—I think I passed out. When I regained consciousness I was still in the kitchen. They shoot me. I'm dead or something, I hear people saying. Since they thought I was dead none of them wanted to pick me up since, as you know, Rastafarians don't touch dead bodies. Everybody kept assuming I was dead. The police threw me in the backseat of a car because they thought I was dead. At the hospital the nurse actually looked at me and said, This one dead. They actually started wheeling me to the morgue, all this time I could see everybody saying these things about me and couldn't do a thing. Imagine that. Thank God for Bahamians. This Bahamian doctor passing by just said let me check and told them I was still alive. Four shots, gentlemen.

One near the base of my spine—it's a miracle I'm walking today, thanks to doctors in Miami. Well, it was a miracle I didn't settle for what Jamaican doctors and nurses told me.

—The Singer have anything to add to this here proceed—

—I speak for the Singer.

—Him know who try to kill him?

—Of course he knows. He knows some of them personally.

—Who fire the shot?

—Shots.

—Shots. Him see who fire the shots here?

—Three of them, sure. But where are the others?

—The others dead.

—Dead?

—Dead.

—Surely that's not the case. I saw at least two of them at the peace concert. One was even near the stage.

—Me don't know what you talking about. We have three here and them all confess.

—Even this one with the gag in him mouth?

—The other two say him involve.

—Them force me, skipper! Leggo Beast say.

—Them and Josey Wales and the CIA and them use powder fi, fi hypnotise me! Them threaten fi kill me.

—Can I hear from the one with the gag? the manager say.

—That idea, it not too good.

—I'm afraid I must insist.

—Insist? What that mean?

—It means we both leave if we don't hear what he has to say.

—Tony, pull that thing out ah him mouth.

Tony pull the gag off. The boy just drool and look straight on in the evening like him blind.

—Young youth, what you have to say for yourself? You. You boy. You no see we giving you chance?

Fool-fool boy. Him look at the manager and say,

—Me can see right through me. Me can see right through, right through, Leviticus and Numbers and Deuteronomy.

—Nothing good going come out that one mouth, me say and motion Tony Pavarotti to put the gag back on.

—So any of them man you see?

—We saw the one at the back, who not saying nothing, the manager say.

—This one, him mother was hiding him for a year. Right under we nose.

—The CIA con we. Me can't even remember nothing. Is when me mother tell me say me shoot . . . is only then me know and me still don't remember, Jah know.

—Hold on a minute. I am acquainted with this one. They call him Leggo Beast. He's from Jungle. Not far from where we all grew up. He used to come around an awful lot, so much so that even I recognize him and I was rarely around there.

—Is the CIA, the CIA and Josey Wales, and the other man who sound like Jamaica and America. Like you. Why nobody believe me?

—Tony, shut up this pussyhole. Leggo Beast? You see him 'round the house?

—Once or twice, never inside the house, but outside the gate, or in the gateway, once we even went out to talk to him and his brethrens.

—We?

—Us. We who you see here. Went outside to reason with him and his friend, but they said they were from Jungle and they have business with the friend, not the Singer.

—I see. 'Cause me know me never authorize nobody to go bother the Singer. Nobody go 'round to him house without my permission. Worse if they begging him anything.

—I don't think it was that.

—That me tell you! We never come for him! We never come for the Singer! Me personally did come for the friend. Me an' Demus.

—Tony, me never tell you to gag that boy? Who name Demus?

—He one of we. And Weeper. And Jeckle, no Heckle. And Josey.

—Shut the man up.

—Josey? the manager say.

—Enough, me done with talking, me say.

—Is time for more witness. Miss Tibbs?

One of the woman jump up.

—You have the lady as jury and witness? the manager say. Him seem to love chat. And laugh when him not supposed to laugh.

—Miss Tibbs? I say and she stand up and look around twice, but not at the Singer.

—Is was ten, no the eleven o'clock hour. Me just done say me devotional, praise the king, and look through me window and see white Datsun just screech up. Me see four man come out, include that one there at the back. Yes me sees it through me window with me owner eye. They's come out of the white Datsun and run in all direction like when you sudden shine light 'pon roach. Somebody ask that one, the one behind Leggo Beast, not the mad one, him. Somebody ask him where him gun deh? And him say him no know, he must did drop it when them was driving out of Hope Road. Me hear him say Hope Road with me own ears. The next day him girlfriend leave the premises and me never see she again.

The next one don't wait for me to tell him to stand up. He rise and say, You all know me as a man allow to walk through Copenhagen City and the Eight Lanes too. Me was the one who go to Shotta Sherrif and say, them man here who shoot up the Singer, nobody in Copenhagen City responsible for them. Papa-Lo would have never authorize them kinda fuckery—

—Watch you language.

—Them kinda sinting, me mean. Me say, So Shotta, you know them not in no JLP territory no more. So look through you own territory or beyond and sniff them out. Is them find this mad one, a hide in the bush all the way in St. Thomas. Man did have him gun in him brief. Me ask Shotta men how they find him, they say police did know where him be from, he jump 'pon a minibus and head out to country.

—What about the one who shot him personally? The same goon who shot me as well?

—Him dead, me tell you.

—The man who shot me four times?

—Dead.

—I most sincerely beg to differ. He was at the con—

The Singer touch the manager shoulder.

—Oh. I see. Perhaps that is for the best. Carry on then.

The manager shut up. Me did think the Singer was going talk. Me was hoping him did talk. But him already say enough to me. He know who shoot him. I know who shoot him.

Josey Wales.

Every other man in the two car was, brawta, extra, parts of the body, neither the heart nor head. We don't talk but we say plenty. I look 'pon him and disappoint him again. But surely he must know the world and the sky and the planets and that they not the only things bigger than just an ordinary man from the ghetto trying to make wrong right.

Josey Wales.

But wrong six feet taller than right, I want to tell him. If you can't catch Harry, catch him shirt and hold on to that at least, I want to tell him. Me is an old man and when you get old all your guns fire blanks, I want to tell him. Him looking at me and seeing the man who did aim for his heart.

Josey Wales. I was hoping the man was among these three even though me did know that wasn't going to be so. Surely a man know the man who try to kill him even if only in the spirit. The manager get shot from behind, but the Singer get a bullet in the chest. But even that perplex me. Why anybody would want to shoot the Singer? Even the boys who get con from the horse race scam had a writ against the friend, not the Singer. He look 'pon me and me look 'pon him and we both know that on certain man neither of we can look. I want to kill Leggo Beast, bring him back to life and kill him again. At least seven time until the Singer satisfied. But that won't satisfy nothing. And this court is already a joke. Me want to leave even before he want to leave.

—Me never shoot him. Me shoot the wife, Leggo Beast say.

Even the manager quiet after that one. The whole gully quiet while we all look at Leggo Beast hard. Him say it like it supposed to be something, that this is the only straw leave to clutch. Me mind run 'pon it right then, the man who once say to me, Papa, me never kill that woman, me did just rape her. The man beside him start laugh.

—Bam-Bam shoot the wife, not you, him say.

—No, is me did shoot her.

—Where? me say.

—Then no must in the bombocloth head. Yeah, inna the head.

The other one, not the mad one, start to laugh. Deep down, way past me heart, me did almost want to laugh too.

—You shoot the wife in the head and still couldn't kill her? CIA train you for almost two months and you couldn't even kill one woman? What happen to all them thing we see in movie? What kinda fuckery training that be when eight or nine man all with machine gun couldn't kill one man? One unarmed man? Ten sitting duck in the studio?

Then me woman say, But Papa, you is a thinking man.

I look and think I see her standing at the top of the gully, but is nothing, not even a tree. Cold breeze sweep down into the passage. I swear I could see it hanging above we for a second then dive down, though breeze don't have no colour. That song jump out of the radio and dive down in the gully too. *Do it light. Do it through the night. Shadow.* Me and Tony Pavarotti driving in the car. No, me in the taxi with three man but none is Tony Pavarotti. No, Tony Pavarotti gone. No he right beside me. No he over there behind the three jury. We in McGregor Gully, and him right there. He looking in the dark, we not in a car. The Singer is right there, him and the manager. Talk, manager, say something boasty and out of turn so I know you still there. Me didn't shoot the Singer, me shoot the wife, Leggo Beast still saying. Me feel like me was outside and just walk right back into a discussion which gone far from where it was when me leave. But me never go anywhere. Me is right here and up above the wind swooping up and down like a ghost and I can see it and I can't see it and I wonder if me is the only one seeing it and not seeing it, the wind rising above the gully like spirit about to fly.

—Enough with this r'ass. How unu find them? Guilty or innocent?

Guilty pop off all over the gully. I look around from the first to the last and count them off. One . . . three . . . five . . . seven . . . eight . . . nine. Nine? I look again and see eight. Me blink and between the blink and the open eye me sure me see nine and the ninth look like Jesus. No, like Superman. No, like CIA? Blink Papa, blink it again, blink it out. Just blink it out and pass judgment.

—This court find—

—This not no bloodcloth court.

—This court find you guilty.

—You not no bloodcloth court. Me want justice.

—This court find you guilty.

—The whole of unu a fuckery. You and him and him, too. Force people to do what you want then—

—You all sentence to death. This is a civilized court.

—Top man get 'way and poor man suffer.

—Everybody suffer now 'cause o' you.

—Him not suffering. Him is like lion in Zion now.

—Tony, bring that r'asscloth man here.

Tony shove the gag back in Leggo Beast mouth and drag him over. He didn't even bother make him walk, just drag him by the shirt like him is corpse already, him legs scuffling on the road. He pulling him towards me but me nod towards the Singer. Me did think the women was going leave but them stay and look. I walk up to the Singer for the first time. He know what me going to do. He can say yes or no with just a nod, but he need to tell me. The man who justice wronged is the man who must choose how we going to right it. The manager step out of the way, for this is between me and the Singer. He look at me, me look at him for a second, me see a flash and hear a boom and pow and a hiss. Me on the road with three man, but not Pavarotti. The Singer switch in and out like a bad signal from a TV and his eye flash fire. I shake it out. I don't feel the breeze on me. Cool breeze like we at sea. I shake it out. I look at him and he look at me. Behind me back and shoved in me pants, the gun, I pull the gun from behind me and hold it by the nozzle and hand it to the Singer. I wait for him to take the gun in him hand. I look at Leggo Beast and at the Singer. Him hand don't even flinch. He don't even nod no. He turn and walk away with the manager hopping right behind him. I don't want him to leave before knowing that for this man Papa-Lo will see him get justice. He stop for one second when me squeeze the trigger. Someplace at some session the DJ just say *People, are you rea-eh-dy?* The Singer don't turn around when Leggo Beast body fall flat on the ground and I shove the gun back in me pants. Leggo Beast flat on the ground, the hole in the back of him head gurgling blood like baby vomit. The wind spinning 'round and 'round like American tornado.

We by the beach, I can smell the salt in the sea. But McGregor Gully not by no sea. The Singer and the manager gone. When him drive away? Me blink and they gone. I shake me head out again. I look and see him on a bed in the white man country and room in a house with a long road that go up in the mountains, a place that look like it come out of a fairy tale book. And me blink again and another man coming towards me, no is not the Singer, this man near all bones and him black. He come right up to me and him breath smell of weed and food and it stink and he saying *Where the ring? Where His Imperial Majesty's ring? I know you see it. I know you see him wearing it. Where him put the bombo r'asscloth ring? I want it now, it can't go back down in the Earth with him, you hear me? I want the bombo-cloth ring. Me have a right to it, me have a right to the livication of His Imperial Highness King Menelik son of Solomon who reign in Israel and send the fire of creation back down in the Queen of Sheba belly*, he say and he come right up to me and me looking past him and the wind blowing colder and louder and harder like a storm, but is not the storm, is the sea and I shake real, real hard and it all go and is McGregor Gully looking clear again. My gun rubbing my back, still warm from the shot, the barrel down right below the belt, two man who was just jury lasso the other two man like they is both cow they dragging back to the ranch and still the women stay, and watch. I watch them watching it. I want to know what would make a woman watch the evil man do. Maybe if woman don't witness judgment then judgment didn't happen.

But Papa, you is a thinking man, me woman say.

Me hear her but me can't see her. They lasso the two man and take them into bush. No beat, no ceremony, no music. They throw the other end of the rope over two brand of the same tree. Why is a white man here? Why he behind them, looking at them, and why he turn around and look at me? When he look at me the breeze get cold. The two man standing on two tall stool, they trembling and they screaming. They trembling too hard and shifting the stool, but every time the stool shift they scream. The not-mad one thinking he just need to tense up him neck, just stiffen up every muscle and when the stool fall he won't dead. I don't know why I know what him thinking but that is exactly what him thinking and me know. But the white man looking at them, he looking up and down the rope and he looking at me and me want to jump and shout, Who you, white man? Who you be? You was following the Singer? How you get this far? But me can't talk, me can't say a word 'cause nobody else going on like white man suddenly deh 'pon them. Nobody don't see him. Me don't know but he look at them and stare at me. Tony Pavarotti don't wait. The women watch. Maybe him is a duppy.

Tony Pavarotti kick 'way the first stool, the man drop one foot, two feet maybe. The man jerking and gagging and swing so hard and wild he knock the other man stool and then he fall to him death too. They swinging and jerking and the rope creaking and me look at them and me look between them at the white man and me neck start to burn and cut and bleed and blood in the skull pumping like a balloon filling with more and more water. They still jerking. This is cowboy movie fault. People thinking a hanging death happen as soon as the music stop. But hanging where the neck don't snap can take a long, long time. It taking too long, and the women start to walk away backwards into the dark. The two men head swelling packing full with blood. The lungs give up from air hunger and both of them stop jerk. And neither of them dead yet. I know. I don't know how I know, but I know. I know from feeling it inside them and outside them, and just watching they neck.

The white man is still there. The white duppy. I blink and he in the car with me. Me and the two other man who I know but I can't remember, and we on a road, a bridge over the sea, but is not Pavarotti driving, is another man. I know him because he making joke about the idiot horse me buy a year ago and it still can't win no race. And that don't make no sense for me only buy the horse one week ago. But when me talk nobody hear me because me also talking in the car, and me can see meself talking in the car, me can hear what me saying 'bout the horse and me telling meself you only buy the horse one week ago.

The bodies now swaying with the breeze but still otherwise. Everybody gone, the women gone, the man them gone, nighttime gone, the sky grey and seagulls screaming. And me can't see the white man. We in the car. Now we in the car but the car stop long time ago. We going to McGregor Gully. No, we coming from the football match, me only thinking horse race because Lloyd in the car and him train horse. No, is April 22, 1978. Me never forget the day of a hanging. No, is February 5, 1979, me never forget the day of that idiot football match because me was talking to Lloyd about how he training me horse.

No, wait. Roll back the tape. Me head not sitting right.

Clouds grey and heavy, rain about to fall.

Trevor, why you always drive so bombocloth fast once you reach the damn causeway, is daylight you running from?

You know him, boss. Him can't wait fi leave Portmore.

Can't wait, eh? What this one name Claudette or Dorcas?

Haha, you how it be boss, them Portmore girl is nothing but vampire.

Stop giving them your neck and spend 'pon you pickney for a change. How 'bout that?

Good one, boss! Good one.

All this talk 'bout woman, how come is nothing but man in this car? Cho!

We can turn back and go check two thing, name Claudette and Dorcas, boss.

No sah, me no want Trevor what-left. Them gal there mash up. Serve no use now.

Woi, boss, you give too much joke.

Papa how you ah do me so? And is Lerlene and Millicent, not Claudette and Dorcas.

Claudene and Dorcent.

Lerlent and Millicene.

Haha.

The whole of unu mad. Lloyd, talk some sense to me.

Pussycloth. Boss. Papa.

Brethren, wha we a slow down for?

Boss . . . look.

A wha the r'asscloth this?

Four of them, boss. Babylon. Three bike park and four police. Red seam too. Stop?

No. Any of you see any parked car that we pass? Somebody must be coming up from the back soon.

Me nuh remember no car.

Then is what behind we? Cho r'asscloth. Lloyd, how far we be from the zinc factory?

'Bout a hundred yard, boss.

But we can't take foot nowhere.

The car behind we stop, boss.

How much police? Not them three, how much coming out of the car?

Nobody coming out of the car. We stopping?

Slow down little bit. Shit r'asscloth shit.

If you don't stop them going shower this car with bullet.

Is just four man on three bike.

Four man with AK, Papa.

Reverse and swing 'round.

Them would catch we easy, boss.

Catch we for what? After we nah hold nothing in the car.

Anything we do them going full we o' lead, boss, that one have megaphone.

Hold on. Me know him.

Stop the cyar h'an come out with your 'ands h'up.

Trevor, Trevor stop the car. But don't turn off the engine.

This h'is a routine spot check. Come h'out of the cyar with you 'ands them h'up.

Papa, don't come out the car. Don't come out of the car.

This h'is a routine spot check. Come h'out of the bombocloth cyar with you 'ands them h'up.

Papa, me no like it, star. Don't come out of the car.

Look, we not going tell you four time, come h'out of the bloodcloth cyar, Papa-Lo.

I-is what this, Officer?

Papa, them know is you?

Officer, is what this?

Does me look like me h'in h'any conversating with you? You h'and your personnel need to make h'an evacuation from the cyar.

Brethren, throw the car inna reverse.

Right into the car behind we? You ah idiot or what? Papa, what you want to do?

Who in here have a piece? Me have me .38.

Not me.

Me neither.

Me train horse, boss.

Shit.

Papa, you not going like it h'if me 'ave fi tell you fi come h'out again.

Papa?

Come out of the car. We coming out, Officer. See we—

Not talking to the likes of you. Come h'out and stand right there so by the bush. Yes the bush across the road, eediot.

Easy no, pardner.

Me not you pardner, pussyhole. You think me 'fraid of you?

You should be frai—

Trevor, shut you mouth. Where you want we, Officer?

You h'is a bombocloth deaf man or what? You want me say it slow? Re-

move from the vicinity of the cyar so that we can search the cyar. Move h'over to the left and keep walking till you is in front of the wild bush by the side of the road.

Papa, Papa you think them—

Shut up, Lloyd, just ease yourself.

You, Mr. Papa-Lo, you want to know why we stop you this h'evening?

Me no business with anything Babylon want.

Well, we certainly have to teach you some manners before the h'evening h'is through.

Suit yourself, Officer.

Sergeant, you wouldn't believe what in here.

H'in the cyar?

H'in the cyar. Them owner radio.

A radio? In ghetto man cyar? How that work? Turn it on. Hold on deh, turn it up . . . louder. What a thing. Then Corporal you know how fi dance the disco? Spoon it right, spoon it through the night, shadow dancing.

Haha, after the song nuh go so, Sergeant.

You ah tell me how the song go? Is you and me did go to Turntable Club last night?

Last night? But we deh 'pon curfew, Sergeant.

Kibba you mouth. Inspector, in the mean time you want to give them four man a little search? Make it quick and pad down the cocky and batty, since them ghetto boy think we too fool to check it. Search Papa-Lo first. Yes man, spoon it right, spoon it through the night, shadow dancing, blah blah blah bla-blah, spoon it more, spoon it more-more-more, shadow danceeeeeeeng blah blah blah bla-blah. Yeah, man, is when you can do them disco moves that the girl them love you. Inspector, any of them over there doing the shadow dance?

No, Sergeant, but if you blink you might catch them do the hustle.

Corporal, anything else in the car?

Not a thing, Sergeant. Not a thing. Not a thing but this .38 revolver some-body think them was going hide under the passenger seat.

But what the bombocloth. .38? 'Pon the floor? Not you, Papa? Not a fine upstanding son of the soil lacka you. Is who fer gun fi real, your mother's? Inspector, go take a look at the gun, while me and the constable watch them four. Is a real .38?

Real like me wife pregnant belly, Sergeant.

Kiss me neck. .38. Here is what me wondering now, Officers. This .38 we have here. This here .38. I wonder if is the same .38 Papa-Lo and him cronies use to fire at the police.

Hard to tell, Inspector.

Yeah, man, yo nuh remember? When Papa-Lo and him three cronies fire 'pon the police in what was only supposed to be a simple spot check? You four, keep you hands up.

Me no remember that.

Think 'bout it good and hard. Inspector, I see you already feeling what me talking 'bout. You nuh remember when Papa-Lo open fire 'pon the police? Fire from this same .38 and the poor police them did have no choice but to fire back?

When him do that?

Right now. Fire!

He fire from me own .38 and bullet burst a hole through me lip and blast away two teeth graze burn the tongue and the back of my head let air rush in and my blood rush out but we was just hanging two man, yes we hanging two man and the prophet Gad asking me where is the bloodcloth ring like me know anything about the Singer's hands bullet YKK a zipper down me chest one two three four five six seven eight and there in him house is Peter Tosh on him knees after one bullet go through a woman mouth and blast 'way her teeth and Leppo push the gun 'gainst Tosh forehead and pow and pow again two more bullet for the man on the radio one bullet for the next man right in him back where it staying forever but is me getting shot me forming river of blood and piss between me legs and Carlton me see you, Carlton 'pon the rhythm while the wife behind you wrapping her pussy 'round the man who going kill you, Carlton! And the Singer have no hair anymore the Singer on a bed the Singer getting a needle from a white man who have a German Hitler sign burning in him forehead bullet pop me finger off and mark me like Jesus Christ in my left palm no pain just quick burn me body have two dozen little fires but air rushing through me hear me body whistle Trevor and Lloyd doing the bullet dance they whip whip whip and turn and jerk and scream and cough and shake like they have fits bullets make them jump and me jumping too and me skipping gun shot like firecrackers from far away me neck speaking blood me mouth can't open the angel of death sitting on the Singer shoulder the angel is a white man me see him already me know that now see him standing on a stage like Seaga and Manley and promise poor people sweet thing and then me neck crack me seeing meself doing the bullet dance like me watch theatre from a seat upstairs rising higher and higher, high over the causeway and sea and high above the seven cars coming and they all swarm down like flies the police all come out and they all walk up and fire one two three shots me down on the ground sinking into the asphalt and another police fire two shot take that pussyhole you not so bad now and another police and another police and another one pow pow pow get up and shoot we now nuh pussy-hole gunman and police on the walkie-talkie saying guess who fer case we just deal with and more police come and everybody paying them tribute and this one aim for me neck pow and this one aim for me kneecap pow and this one aim for me balls pow and how come no car passing no car but police them block the road from far off they knew me was coming somebody in the ghetto is informer and tell them me was coming and Trevor face eat off and Lloyd chest and belly burst open and my head split open and me heart still pumping and another policeman stoop down and say this is for Sebert and fire straight through the heart and the heart burst and dead then he get up and go back to him car and the other policeman go back to them car and me rising higher and higher but me still on the road and I can see them all in a line the police cars they leave me and they driving with they sirens on so people shift out of the way and they drive as one animal a siren snake all the way up to the block that have the Minister of Security office and they circle the block 'round and 'round and 'round all the while laughing loud and me can see everything around and above and below and what happen ten year ago Peter Nasser with the first gun 1966 when me take in

Josey Wales and when me kill that school boy by mistake and what happening in a grey place as if me can do something and change it if I shout loud enough cut off the toe skip cut off the toe don't listen to no bombocloth idiot Rasta who just sucking your blood through the chillum pipe cut off the toe and don't make no Nazi touch you but the white man standing across the road the white man I know and I don't know and he looking over through the bush right by the road the little swamp and in the swamp the driver swimming no blood from the shot good so no crocodile going after him and he swim and swim and swim and a fishing boat see him and motor over to pick him up and he climb in and shaking and bawling that all him do is drive taxi and the fisherman sail away and me not in the gully no more proclaiming judgment me wasn't in the gully at all that was over a year ago and everything was over a year ago and all that take place between the shot to my head and the shot to my heart in one blip all the last things me do in me life play out at once happening then and happening now and happening one after the other and also all at once but there is Trevor spooling blood still and Lloyd with death rattling in him throat and there is me, gentlemens. There is me.

Alex Pierce

D*o it light,* do it through the night. Shit's gotta work. Cut that fucking song loose goddamn it, what the fuck. Keep this shit up and you're gonna move, you're gonna jerk or you're gonna—I don't know, I don't fucking know—it's going to make him know and you'll end up a fucking murder scene, chalk line baby dig it, because you woke up with that fucking song shaking its polyester sweating ass in your head. Sooner or later, a cracker's gotta pay for being the one white man who can move. Right side of my brain's saying at least you bit it for a greater cause than "Disco Duck." At least I might be still asleep. I must be. Tapping my fingers one by one against the pillow, four means dream, five means real. One two three four five.

Motherfucker.

But what if I'm dreaming this is real? What if I'm dreaming in a dream? I read somewhere that this is what happens when you die. Freaky shit, Jesus Christ. Breathe slow. Don't breathe at all. No, breathe slow. Stop breathing. No, he will feel it, he will know you're not asleep. I know what this is. I mean, gotta be, man, you're just tripping off bad shit. You're just crashing hard off bad shit, this is what you get for hitting C anywhere but 42nd and 8th, that's where the steerer on 41st and 5th sent me. But hold up, I'm not tripping. I never trip in Jamaica. Jamaica is a trip all by itself, and Jesus Christ stop thinking so hard. Keep this shit up and you'll start to think out loud—have I said anything? Jesus Christ, Jesus Christ, Jeezuzchriiiiiist, stop it, stop it, fucking stop it, Alex Pierce. Chill out right now, chill the F.U.C.K. out. Close your eyes and try to catch up to that dream that got away from you, go off and catch that dream, and when you wake up there will be no man sitting on the edge of your bed. Better yet, there will be no man opening your door, walking in just as you're waking up, because you never really went to sleep and couldn't really sleep on this torture-chamber bed. No man walking in, going over to the window to pull in the drapes, reaching in his shirt for—don't look, don't fucking look, and sitting on your bed. No series of clicks and clacks and ticks and locks. Close your eyes. Simple as that, this will work, THIS WILL WORK.

I am at the Skyline hotel. I got in two days ago, though I've been in Kingston five months and Jamaica for eight. Eight months since Lynn gave me an ultimatum, Jamaica or her. Fucking woman, I didn't expect her to understand my work but I at least hoped for some respect for what I had to do. It's not that she didn't like it. Hell, I could have dealt with her hating it. Hating it at least is something. But she was just so fucking indifferent it drove me batshit, worse she was giving me an ultimatum over something that she really didn't give a shit about. Yeah, I'm finding a way to take all this shit out on her. But honest to God I think she said the book or me as a fucking fact-finding mission, just to see what I would say.

And here's the fucked-up part: either answer would have been satisfactory. So right now? Yeah, I kinda hate her for not hating me. I hate her for walking into my study back in Brooklyn, fine, my bedroom with the saddle horse desk, and saying, It's your lucky day, honey. You get to choose between this Jamaica book of yours that is going nowhere or this relationship that is going nowhere, because one of the two has gotta get somewhere. I said, Jesus H. Christ, have you been listening to *Slow Train Coming*? because you couldn't have picked a lousier time to become a Dylan fan. She called me a patronizing jerk who should answer the question. I said I've been reading a lot of new stuff on psychology recently and that is what they're now calling emotional blackmail, so I refuse to answer the question. She looks at me and says, Well, there's your answer then, and walked out of my bedroom, our bedroom. Jesus Christ, I would have given anything for a slap, maybe I should have slapped her.

I don't know what I'm thinking. I should have chosen her, fine, happiness would have turned into an act of will and we would have waited another two years to finally admit that we're bored out of our skulls but maybe that's what I deserve, to be a bored content house-husband working on a sympathy pregnancy belly, maybe then I wouldn't have woken up to a man sitting on the side of my bed staring at the floor. Bored in Brooklyn—that's funny. Hey, Dear Abby, I've got myself a handle even before I got myself a problem.

Truth is I went back to New York knowing that there was some Third World–sized hole in me that I already knew she wouldn't fill but I tried to make her fill it anyway. And maybe I resented that she didn't try, give me the drama about how she can't be Superwoman and break up with me with a bucket of tears and writing some bad Carly Simon song about me. Instead I got a girl who treated me the same way Jamaica, my other girl, treats me, meaning what we have may be good, but you're kidding yourself if you think I'm ever going to care beyond a certain point. Maybe I fell for her for the same reason I fall all the time for Jamaica. I knew from the get-go that it wouldn't work but that doesn't stop me from going after it anyway. Why? I don't fucking know. Would I still be doing it if I knew why? Shit, probably.

Meanwhile there's a man sitting on the side… on the left side of my bed looking down on the floor. I feel he's looking down on the floor. I only lifted my head once and freaked the fuck out when I did it as soon as I did—surely he must have felt it. Maybe he didn't. There's a man sitting on my bed so light that I barely feel the dip in the bed except that he's on top of the sheets which are now tight and trapping my right leg right behind his back. God knows where my left leg is, just don't move it. Just don't. You'll be fine. Dude, you were supposed to go back to sleep, remember that was the plan. Fine, just close your eyes, pretend to go to sleep until you're asleep for real and when you wake up he'll be gone. Stop thinking it won't work, spazz, you haven't tried it yet. Just close your eyes. Close them so hard you'll squeeze a tear out. Close hard and count the seconds, 12345—too fast, too fucking fast—1 . . . 2 . . . 3 . . . 4 . . . 5 . . . 6 . . .—slower, slower and when you open your eyes he will be gone. He'll be gone—nope, still here.

He is still here. Look at him with your eyes ¾ closed. Did he turn a light on? The fucker turned the light on? Who the hell turns the light on? No, don't look. Black pants, no navy blue, I'm sure it's navy blue and blue shirt? Is his head bald? Is he holding his head with his hands? White guy? Light brown? Is he resting his head in his hands? Who wears matching navy blue shirt and pants—don't look. If I snore will he go away? Shit. I should roll. Everybody rolls, if I don't he'll know I'm not sleeping. But what if rolling spooks the fucker and he does something? Jeans still on the chair by the desk, the desk where I'm getting no work done. Wallet almost falling out of the pocket. Bus ticket, condom, thirty bucks no fifty bucks why am I viewfinding my fucking wallet? Empty box of Kentucky Fried Chicken, a fucking food cult in Jamdown, where's my fucking bag? Does he have it at his feet? Is that what he's doing, looking through it? Alex Pierce, you fucking coward, just get up and say what the fuck brethren, does this look like your fucking room?

Say what? Oh shit, buddy, I thought this was my room.

Does this look like your room?

We're in a hotel, bro-ski, what do you think?

You got me there.

Man, I got myself wasted last night, ooh boy, I don't even know how I made it upstairs and it's your fault anyway for leaving your door unlocked so that a drunk fuck like me could just mosey on in. Good thing you ain't a fox or you'd have woken up with my cock in ya all the way up to Sunday.

Good thing I ain't a fox.

Ain't that the truth.

You gonna get out—holy shit, who am I talking to? Did I think it or say it? He didn't move. He's not moving. He's still not moving.

Get your shit together, man. Just get your shit. Breathe slow, breathe slow. Maybe if I kicked him just a little. I mean, this is a secure hotel. Maybe he's in room 423, a simple mistake really and maybe I did leave the door open, or maybe the hotel was being a cheap shits and gave every door the same key thinking we'd never have a reason to find out, because Lord knows white men hunting for good times with no questions asked in a Third World country could never ever end up drunk.

God, I wish I could stop thinking. Just go back to sleep, man, go back and when you wake up for real he won't be here. It's like, it's like, you know what it's like? Leaving a window open when you see a lizard in the room.

Close your eyes please. Beside the Colonel Sanders box, the banged-up typewriter that's too fucking heavy. Maybe I can just mutter under my breath how much money it's worth and he'll take it and go? Just like a writer to think the thief gives two shits about books. Jesus Christ. Mannix would have grabbed this lamp and swung it by now. Just grab the base and swing right for the back of the head. Life doesn't move at twenty-four frames per second. Barnaby Jones would have tried something. Police Woman would have tried something and she never does anything.

On my left is the desk, on my right the bathroom and between us is the man. Bathroom, five feet. Six feet, can't be more than eight feet away. Door's open. Was there a key, there has to be a key, every bathroom door has a key, no they don't. I'll just jump from this bed, pull my foot out from almost under him and leap out, maybe scram for the doorway—I could be in the bathroom before he gets the jump on me. Or maybe it would be two steps, three steps tops. Carpet on the floor so I won't slip. It's right there, the fucking bathroom door is right there and all I have to do is run to it and slam the door, hold the knob tight if there is no key and there is a key, there has to be a key, there must or else I will fucking . . . I'll do what, exactly?

I'll get up to run just as he leans back and pins my fucking foot under his butt and he'll have just enough time to swing that cutlass because Lord knows he must be Jamaican so motherfucker must be holding a cutlass, just enough time to chop me in the thigh so I can't run and he'll hit that artery I heard about, the one where if it's cut you bleed to death in seconds and there's nothing not a damn thing anybody can do—please don't roll back on my foot, you son of a bitch. Maybe I could just leap up like I just woke up from a nightmare in a horror flick and kick him hard in the back, well, side, and while he tries to do whatever it is hoods do, collect himself, reach for the gun, whatever, I run straight for the door at twelve o'clock, which will be open since he came in, run straight out in these tighty-whities and just start yelling rape murder police anything because here's the deal: he couldn't be here for me.

Brethren, you ah hear me? Is time fi the I fi think 'bout getting a piece.

Piece?

Piece. You look like a Beretta sorta man.

What the fuck? No, Priest, I don't want any fucking gun. You know what happens with guns? People get killed.

Then that no the point, brethren.

The wrong people.

Depend on who in front and who behind the trigger.

What am I doing with a gun? Hell, why do I need a gun?

Better you ask how quick the I can get a gun and how easy it going be to use it.

Fine, how quick could I get a gun then?

Right now.

Holy sh—

Take this.

What? No. Fuck no.

Brethren, take the piece.

Priest—

Take the piece me ah tell you.

Priest—

Brethren, hold this and control this.

No, Priest, I don't want any fucking gun, Jesus Christ.

Me say anyting 'bout want?

Jamaican men and their talking in riddles. One day I just want to say to him, Look, Priest, all that cryptic bullshit doesn't make you smart one bit. But then I'd lose the most useful informer in Kingston.

How much year me know you now?

Dunno, two, three years?

Me ever tell you anything that don't make no sense?

No.

Then get a gun. Or a knife, get something, brethren.

Why?

Because after Tuesday come Wednesday. And what you do on Tuesday change the type of Wednesday that going come to you.

Jesus Christ, Priest, can you give me a straight sentence for once?

You think me wouldn't find out? Is me tell you everything that going on, remember? Me know everything that going on about everybody. Even you.

Don't sink further in the bed please, don't roll, don't touch my leg, is he crossing his legs? Nobody crosses their legs, only British faggots cross their legs. He's looking at me now, I can feel it, that thing, when the back of your neck tingles because you know somebody is looking at you. Now it's twitching and it won't fucking stop. How is he looking at me? Tilting his neck like a dog thinking how come you look so funny like those Jamaican kids who do a double take when they see me and wonder if Jesus was actually coming would he be wearing tight jeans? Is he going to reach and grab my balls? Can he see me through the sheets?

Brethren, you know say you frig it up? You know how much you frig it up? Right now me nuh even want talk to the I.

What now? Come upstairs, brother, it's raining. I'll ring front desk to leave you alone.

Me like when Jah decide to bathe me.

You're being ridiculous, Priest. It's nine-thirty in the night. I can't even hear you above the fucking thunder.

Last Monday you come talk to me, you say, Priest, me just want to ask the man one question. Me say to you, you can go ask it but one, him don't have to answer you and two, if him answer you, you not going like the answer. You remember that?

Of course I remember it, I'm the one you said it to, you said watch what you ask Papa-Lo.

Ah no Papa-Lo me a talk 'bout. Him not the only man you question them past day.

Huh? You mean Shotta Sherrif? You didn't set that up, I did.

Me talking 'bout the JLP man them, brethren. You talk to Josey Wales.

Yeah. And what of it? He was there. I asked if I could shoot the shit for a bit, he said yes, so I asked.

Me also tell the man that my mouth soon have to zip up because them start to smell informer 'pon me. Brethren, all me doing is telling the truth, me no even like informer.

You're not an informer, I get it. Come inside, brother.

Me also tell you that don't think everybody in Jamdown turn idiot when them see white man. Don't go to the ghetto without you ghetto passport.

Priest—

Don't go without you ghetto passport me tell you.

Priest, don't you think that is some bullshit right there.

Me tell you don't go into certain territory before me make certain people know. Me tell you don't go into certain territory unless me come with you.

Fucking Priest, it took me a while to realize that he wasn't quite what he said he was. But then I guess the only way you can access info from the top is if you're a bottom-feeder. Figures, informers are the lowest no matter where you go. You don't think they would be the same, exact kinda guy in every country you fly to. One-third weasel, one-third liar, one-third just a pathetic loser with a limp who knows he's only important for as long as he says he is. Especially this one spouting stuff like he wrote Deuteronomy all by himself. Street passport my ass, the guys in the Eight Lanes I ended up talking to thought he was the biggest bombocloth joke of the ghetto. *Priest think him chat mean shit in the Eight Lanes? You think you could'a just come down here because Priest send you or come with you? You know why them call him Priest?*

He told me it was because he's the only man that can walk through Copenhagen City and the Eight Lanes.

Kiss me r'ass, ah that him tell you? Yow, you hear what Priest tell him, brethren?

Not true?

Nah, man, that deh part true, but is not 'cause him have no Jesus power, pussycloth idiot always a gwaan like him about to give you five loaf and two fish.

Huh?

Priest walk through ghetto because he the only man in the ghetto that not even puss 'fraid of. Why you think man call him Priest?

Well, he . . .

Learn this, white boy. Is long time Priest want to be big shotta. Long time.

Every day him asking the don, Don, man, gimme a gun nuh? Gimme a gun nuh? You no see me born fi turn rudie? Well Shotta Sherrif get tired of him ah yap-yap like them little pussyhole and give him gun. You no know what the boy do? My youth shove the gun in him brief and right deh so, all of a sudden kapow! Him shoot off him cocky. Is a wonder how him never dead.

One time me ask Shotta if he did take the safety off on purpose but all now him no answer me.

Is a wonder how him never kill himself after that. I mean, if you can't ram out the pussy, wha you ah live for?

Brother's still gotta tongue.

Wha you just say?

The Eight Lanes. It's true, Priest didn't do shit to set me up with the Eight Lanes. I just asked the nervous lady at Jamaica Council of Churches if I can talk to some of the people behind this peace treaty. She made a call and next thing I knew she said you can go down there tomorrow. Jamaicans, they never leave their prepositions out. It's always either up here or down there, up there or down here. Nothing like Copenhagen City, that's for sure. You veer through the market and if you're not dizzy enough from all *that* stuff, wood stalls full of bananas and mangoes and ackee and grapefruit and jackfruit and frill dresses and gabardine cloth for pants and—blink you'll miss it, rolling papers, and reggae bumping, always bumping, you're never going to hear that shit on the radio, then you almost walk past Lane Number One of the Eight Lanes.

But every lane has a corner and every one has four to six guys on the corner standing on the verge of getting it on. They left me alone so I figured that by now, thanks to the Singer, they're used to white people strolling into their territory. Better answer: nobody moves without the don's say-so. Nothing like four hungry boys waiting to pounce being held back by an invisible leash. Priest was so busy warning me about Copenhagen City that it didn't even cross his mind I might go to the Eight Lanes. He said it only the day before I came down here. Priest also thinks I'm working on his clock. He also thinks I'm some stupid American who is still alive only because of him. But Lord knows coming down here might have been a stupid thing to do.

To think I try so hard not to be lumped with those fuckers on the North Coast wearing Jamaican Me Crazy t-shirts, but how many times can you say, Brother, I've been to the real Jamaica. I was down here with the Stones when they were recording *Goats Head Soup* at Dynamic Sounds though I got nothing to do with the record being an absolute piece of shit. And in the years since 1976 Peter Tosh can actually see me in the same room without insisting I leave. And you should have been there when I told the Singer that his version of "And I Love Her" was Paul McCartney's favorite Beatles cover ever.

So no, I'm not scared to go deep into Kingston. But sweet Jesus, there's deep and there's this. And it's the kind you've never seen before despite the hundred times you've seen it. I tried drawing parallels before but you just can't when you're there. You pass the boys on the corner and it never occurs to you to look up, to get a sweep of the place. So you pass the boys and the men playing dominoes. The man facing me had swung his hand far back to whirlwind slam it on the table and win probably so I could see his smirk, but he sees you and his hand slows down and he just places the domino on the board all delicate like the play itself is so lame that he's ashamed that a white man was around to see it.

You continue and you wonder if you've just become the show. You expect people to look at you, even stare, but you just never expect it, the movie thing. Where everything grinds to a slo-mo and your ears pick up silence like it's at full volume and you wonder if somewhere music just stopped, or a glass just shattered or two women just gasped or if it was quiet all along. And you pass the first house, no, not a house, somebody's home maybe, but definitely not a house and you try to not stare past the three children in the doorway. But you do anyway and you wonder how come it's so well lit? Is it a corridor between houses or is the roof gone? But the wall is blue and deep and you wonder who is it that thought to take care of the place.

The little boy, wearing a yellow Starsky and Hutch t-shirt that reaches his knee, smiles, but the two girls, both bigger, have already been taught not to. The one on the lowest step, almost down in the road, lifts her dress up to show her jeans shorts underneath. The door behind them is so weathered it's driftwood, but I try to not look at that either because just two feet or so down a woman is on the steps combing the hair of a bigger girl on the step right below. And between the three kids and the woman—mother?—is a brick wall with so many bricks dug out that it's a checkers pattern. Somebody started painting it white but gave up. It kinda throws you for a loop because the PNP won the election and this is PNP turf. You'd think their own slum would have come off looking better, but it's worse than the JLP area. And worse is always relative each day in Kingston and—what the fuck, there is a fucking man sitting on the side of my fucking bed and I'm thinking about a fucking ghetto that is fucking ten miles away.

Oh shit, dude, sit up straight, don't sink further into the bed. Come on, you've been here, what now, ten minutes? Are you asleep? I've done that, resting my forehead in my hands with my elbows on my knees, but usually I'm not asleep, I'm tripping. I don't know. Fuck it, I'm going to roll. What's the worst that could happen? Him panicking for a little before he realizes I'm still asleep. It's only natural I should roll, he'd think it weird if I didn't roll a little. Wouldn't he? I want to see his fucking face. He rubs the back of his head, bald, I see that now, and his hands reddish brown? Maybe it's blood rushing? I'm going to roll over and kick him in the back. Yes, that is what I'm going to do.

No. I just want to get up in my own fucking hotel room and order a fucking cup of joe, which will suck because this is a cheap-ass hotel that thinks Americans are too stupid to know what real coffee is supposed to taste like which is kinda true if you always drink shit to the last drop, but I'll drink it anyway, because I just need to keep my mouth busy while I transcribe this fucking tape from yesterday that might not even have anything juicy on it.

And then I can grab my knapsack and pull on my jeans and jump on a bus and look at people thinking holy shit, there's a white dude on the bus, except they won't think it that way and I'll just mind my own damn business and get off at the bus stop in front of the *Gleaner* and talk to Bill Bilson even though he's a fucking stooge for the JLP and the American government who's always feeding that guy at the *New York Times* some horseshit.

But he's essentially a good guy and he's always good for an anonymous quote or two and all I want to do is ask him if Josey Wales couldn't remember what day it was when the Singer got shot (but what a tragedy it was), how come he could tell me they shot him just as he was about to hand his manager some grapefruit even though nobody knew this little fact other than the Singer, his manager and me, since I'm the only person they have spoken to about it. I mean, it's not like it's a secret or anything but it's the kind of detail that only slips loose after you've done the long hard work of making an interview subject comfortable.

Of course I'm not going to mention the grapefruit, only that this don seems to have a really intimate knowledge of the ins and outs of this assassination attempt, which by the way I'm not allowed to call it. The last time I asked the Singer who tried to kill him, he looked at me, smiled and said that is a top secret. I didn't bring this up with Josey Wales either because I dunno, last time I checked I didn't have FUCKING PANSY tattooed on my forehead.

Shit, I can't keep my thoughts straight. This is not what happened. I mean, this hadn't happened yet, I'm still at the edge of the Eight Lanes looking for Shotta Sherrif, not Josey Wales. Why the fuck am I thinking about Josey Wales? He's not even the kind of guy that anybody's mind runs on and I'll bet anything he prefers it that way. Josey Wales is Copenhagen City. That was afterward, Alex Pierce. What you learned in the Eight Lanes sent you to Copenhagen City just to clear shit up. But first I was in the Eight Lanes. And if I was in the Eight Lanes I was there to see Shotta Sherrif. I wanted to know if the peace treaty was still on, given the outburst of killings on Orange Street and Pechon Street last week, where a JLP youth shot a PNP youth over his girlfriend. And that last showdown with the police where the boys in black and red recovered a stash of guns and ammo the likes of which you can't even find in the U.S. National Guard.

Of course I could never ask a question like that. After passing the welcoming committee that gave me the skinny on Priest, I found him sitting under a street lamp waiting for me. In fact, that's what he said, Brethren, me did a wait 'pon the I long time. The I meaning you, meaning me. Ghetto communiqué, more backward and more forward than the phone. He was just sitting there on a steel barstool from an actual bar, thirty feet from the corner where I came in, smoking a cigarette, drinking a Heineken and watching the domino game play itself out. He looked like the kind of man you go up to and ask, Hey, you seen this dude named Shotta Sherrif?

—You know that's not the place one expects to see a shiny barstool.

—Or the second coming of Jesus. With a tape recorder.

—I get that a lot.

—You get what?

—Never mind.

He also knew I came to talk about the peace treaty. Turns out he and Papa-Lo ended up in the slammer the same time, right about when goons tried to take out the Singer, and like any group of reasonable men who happen to be thrown together they started to reason. Next thing you know, there's a peace treaty with even singer Jacob Miller writing a song about it—okay, not great—and the Singer coming back to seal the deal with another concert. I wanted to know what really kicked off the treaty and if the future of it's already gone to shit. I asked him about the night before the army killed those boys at Green Bay, the thing that kicked off this peace treaty in the first place. Had he heard of Junior Soul? You can't trust that a gunman with a name like a doo-wop singer actually exists, but surely if he did, Shotta Sherrif must have heard about him. I mean, he's crucial to the birth of this peace treaty too, well, in a fucked-up kinda way.

—No, star, me no know a who that? And that nuh JLP business?

—They said Junior Soul was a PNP goon.

—Goon?

—Shady character.

—Shady?

—Never mind. So he wasn't from around here?

—Nobody from here ever name so, Jesus boy.

That was pretty much all she wrote with Shotta Sherrif. Before I asked him if I could speak to anybody else he grabbed me, looked around to see if anybody was watching and said, This yah treaty have fi work, my youth.

It have to. He was almost pleading. I asked his men some silly questions about if they knew that the "More More More" singer was actually a porn star and left.

Priest found me somebody even more useful days before. He took me down some really scummy, shit-leaking lane in the JLP half of Kingston to meet one of the men who got away from Green Bay, my first time meeting a guy from the actual Wang Gang. He took me to a bar less than twenty feet away and just started talking. Word was this Junior Soul guy had slipped himself into Southside, a JLP area, making pals with the Wang Gang, letting slip that the army was short on men to guard a work site out in Green Bay. Junior Soul linked them up with a Mata-Hari from the Kingston hotel who told the boys they would get guns soon, along with three hundred U.S. bucks each, then fucked three or four of them to seal the deal. Priest told me about Junior Soul but the survivor told me about Sally Q, such an un-Jamaican handle. Poor kid, probably not even seventeen yet, but kinda old for a Jamdown kid to be first tasting pussy.

So this Junior Soul guy shows up January 14, he remembers, well, he remembered after I gave him my pack of Marlboros, seventy bucks and the Gerry Rafferty cassette I didn't even remember I had in my knapsack. He showed up with two ambulances *it did look kinda suspicious* the kid says, but to tell a young shotta that there're guns for the taking if you only come and get it, it's like telling a junkie there's some horse in a dumpster down the alley with nobody's name on it. He said something and it was crucial motherfucking info and I can't remember what. Have to check my notes. *Most of we was Rastas, you know, not labourites.* That's it. *We never did inna the politics and the politricks, seen? Not in nobody pocket so we work for either side, seen?* But it was January, right after Christmas, and everybody knew that nobody in the ghetto would have any money, worse, the Wang Gang had burned all bridges with the other gangs in Kingston.

So new housing site go up and them looking for yardie to guard it, but them not giving you no gun so you have to find you own gun. Me know it never sound too right, but when baby mother up north tell a man she need baby feed'n and baby mother down south say you pickney need school uniform, you just don't think certain things. Anyway, this man with gun did link with the soldier and me no know, soldier not so Quick Draw McGraw with them trigger, you understand. If it was police me would a tell Junior Soul 'bout him bombocloth and beat him up too. But we never have no need to worry 'bout soldier as long as we stay out of them way. As me say, we never did inna the politics thing. But me no know, from the soldier say that all of we should stand up over there, by the target, I just, I just drop like me faint, drop, even right before they start to fire. Me crawl through macka bush, and me did barefoot too. Don't think me breathe till me get 'way from that army land and into the cane piece. The man them did all have helicopter to search for we. Is a wonder how them no find we since all that macka cut up me foot so bad that me leave a trail of bloody footprint all the way to safety. But me did know Green Bay. Is me save four man by leading them out of the bush, into the cane piece, thank Jesus that the cane did grow tall enough to hide we from the helicopter, and all the way to downtown to Sister Benedict school. One of we manage to make out the other way to the sea and two fisherman pull him out of the water. For once we call police. More time them would be only glad to kill we, but if is one thing that make them blood run cold is when soldier get to do it first, since the only thing police hate worse than gunman is soldier. You believe it, me brethren? Police is who come and protect we!

The more I gave the man booze, the more he kept talking, and the more clear he got, the more things didn't add up. The Jamaica Defence Force haven't exactly been tight-lipped about the whole thing. In fact I met the army officer in charge who seems like a nice enough man, if not a little too rough around the edges. The men were all Wang Gang or ex–Wang Gang members and associates who infiltrated the Green Bay JDF training range where they opened fire on the few soldiers who were there that morning for target practice. Maybe they had planned revenge to get back at them for patrolling their community with too much heavy manners. Or maybe they heard there was a lightly guarded arsenal of new weapons for the taking. Either way they got what they deserved *coming down in high noon, like they was cowboy.* Except . . . except, you can't come guns blazing if you don't have any guns, hell, if you were coming to pick guns up.

Back at Bill Bilson's office when I told him I ran into one of the men who escaped from Green Bay he suddenly got super interested in knowing who he was. Just a guy, I said. You know how it is, after a while they all look the same, I said. Bigoted bullshit, I know, but since Jamaicans believe deep down every white man is kinda racist anyway it was convincing enough to throw him off track. Anyway, so he showed me these pics he said some guy just left in his mail slot. Some guy? Now who's being shifty, I almost said, but didn't. Instead I looked at five dead bodies sprawled out in the sand. Two in one shot, two in another and all five in one shot with nothing but shadows of the soldiers looking over them, no actual soldier in any shot. Only one of the dead men wearing any shoes. Little blood, maybe it all just sunk in the sand, I don't know. It's not like it's the first time I'm seeing a dead body in Jamaica.

—Hey, Bill, so what's the deal with this? Does the JDF know that you've got them?

—Them must by now. Me can't say for sure that is not them leak it in the first place.

—Oh yeah? So what's the story?

—What is your story?

—Huh? No, brother, you first. Surely there had been an official statement. I mean, this was nearly a year ago.

—Statement? Soldier don't release no statement. But your friend the major—

—Not my friend, buddy.

—You going want to tell certain gunman that. Anyway, the major didn't release no statement but him did say that a group of assailants tried to attack a contingent of JDF officers at their target practice facility in Green Bay. The gunmen maybe was thinking that if is shooting range they call it, people must have gun somewhere.

—Who says they were gunmen?

—Every single man was from West Kingston.

—That line from him or you?

—Haha. You not easy at all, boy. Anyway, him say them just draw down on the premises in the middle of the day like them name cowboy. The JDF had no choice but to return fire.

—Don't you need to be fired on to return fire?

—What you mean?

—Nothing, buddy. Just shooting the shit. So these guys attacked at noon, right? He said noon?

—Eehi.

—Huh. But . . .

I didn't get it. I mean, come on, the shit was spread out in front of me like a fat stripper. Maybe he's either that dumb or he's doing that hear-no-evil-see-no-evil thing Jamaicans do when they find themselves smack dab in the middle of politricks. The major gives this statement saying the gang attacked them at noon and they returned fire. But I'm looking at the shot, looking at the shadows in the photo, and every single shadow is long and stretched out. There're no long shadows at noon. This shit happened in the morning, any half-blind, senile, semi-retarded old fart could see that. But I looked at them too long, the pics. He noticed that I stared too long and he wasn't about to forget that I cut my own question in half. Jamaicans have a way of looking at you when they finally dig that you're the kind of white boy who catches on quick. They hold the look too, because then they're wondering for just how long have you been catching on and have they been saying too much. If it's one thing Jamaicans are still pretty proud of is their genius for keeping their guard, not letting anything slip. Not giving away anything even if they want to fuck you right here and can't bear to wait.

Okay, don't know how Aisha came into this. Maybe because I'm in bed. Maybe because I'm in a bed with a fucking man sitting on the side of it. I wish I still slept with my watch on. Brother, can't you just steal something and fucking go? Who the fuck, in the midst of robbing a joint, takes a breather? Oh Jesus, don't, don't please don't please don't sit, Jesus, he's gonna sit on my . . . he's on my foot. The bastard has his bony ass on my foot. He's turning, holy shit. Now it's dark. Red darkness, the light forcing itself through my eyelids. Open slow . . . no, you fucking idiot. Do I want to see him shoot me quick? Maybe it's better if he blows a fucking hole in the middle of my sentence. Maybe I should die thinking something smart. Is this the part where I think about heaven and shit like that? My Lutheran mom would be proud. Does he think I'm asleep? Where's the second pillow? Is he going to cover my head with it and fire? I'm such a coward, I'm such a coward, such a motherfucking coward. Goddamn it. Open, motherfucking eyes. He's not looking at me. He's still looking at the ground. Shit, damn, motherfucker, what is he looking at? Some stain on the carpet that looks like Jesus? I thought only ceilings had that shit. Cum stains from the nasty fuckers who slept in this room before me? I really hope they cleaned the sheets before. You can never tell with a hotel off Half Way Tree Road.

If you go two blocks down and make a left on Chelsea, walk just up to the bend where there's the Chelsea Hotel, there's a sign right up front that says under no circumstances will two adult men be rented a room. I guess if you're a pedophile, on the other hand, that's cool city. I don't know why I'm thinking that, I don't know why all of a sudden I really wish these were well-laundered sheets. Sheets that make me want to use words like laundered. No, well-laundered. Jesus Christ, motherfucker, leave already. At least I won't remember how I was a fucking coward in all of this, lying down in my bed, hoping shit doesn't fall out of my bag or that my left foot would stop trembling, or maybe it's just tingling from having fallen asleep, how am I supposed to make a mad dash for the bathroom if me leg is asleep? Me leg. Now I'm worrying in Jamaican. Brother, can't you just be a pervert? Can't you just grab my nuts then go?

So a soldier shooting some kids in Green Bay early 1978 leads to the birth of the peace treaty. A police shooting downtown less than a year later and people are already talking like it's the end. Usually when a gunman is moving in neutral space and the police or the army is suddenly on the scene with guns, it's a set-up, sometimes within the gunman's own party. That's what happened to a couple of PNP goons years ago (so Priest says) and what might have happened to this guy I tried to ask Papa-Lo about. This meeting Priest did set up, though God only knows what they thought of me, since I was there as some loser who knew Priest. I couldn't even figure out this killing anyway, since Priest told me one of the terms of the peace treaty was that nobody gave anybody up to the police.

Hell, the minister himself kinda laughed when I brought up the whole thing to him. He said *off the record* before I started taping the whole thing, like he heard some jerk say it in a movie last week, but then just repeated what he already said in the press, that these men would be hunted down like dogs. Mind you, dogs are usually doing the hunting, not being the hunted, but I guess one gets similes wherever one can find them. He was smart enough to notice I was being a smartass and that was all she wrote with that interview. Minister was a piece of bullshit anyway, with his stupid nappy hair brushed back so hard it actually became straight.

I'm rambling. The point is that a big part of this peace treaty, according to Priest, was that nobody gave up names to people like the minister anymore. And yet here we had a dead man, a gunman, sorry, political activist, and having been smack dab in the middle of criminal intelligence, I knew there was just no fucking way Babylon found that man by themselves. Jamaican police wouldn't find a billboard in the middle of Half Way Tree with a naked woman spread out fingering her pussy and saying look up here, Babylon, unless somebody told them where to look. Like Priest, this man could slip into JLP and PNP territories. Unlike Priest, this man had real clout, being Papa Lo's number two or three. It was something though, wasn't it? That Kingston got to the point where such a top ranking could go get drunk with men whose friends he might have even killed. You talk to Bill Bilson, John Hearne, just about any journalist, intellectual, light-skinned person who lived above Crossroads and they all try to find new ways to ask how long will it last, not from concern though. That loud sigh and head nod is trying to say I'm so exasperated, but it's really saying that not even this would make us give a fuck. Why am I going on about the fucking peace treaty? It wasn't even a real document anyway. Except both Papa-Lo and Shotta Sherrif flew to London to meet with the Singer about it. Not like any of that is news, but how things go from hopeful to hopeless in just one year, who the fuck knows.

Actually I know. Papa-Lo knows but he's not telling. Shotta Sherrif knows, but you know when somebody stops telling you a joke or a story because he figured you already know the end? Except I really don't know.

There's a man in navy blue sitting on the edge of my bed. I've met Papa-Lo before. Right before this peace concert I went to the Copenhagen City with Priest. There was a big man making himself even bigger by spreading his arms wide and hugging everybody, and I'm not a brother to be taken aback, but even I was kinda thrown off by the big man's bear hug. Everybody safe here! Is peace and love vibes we ah deal with! he would say, then he would ask where Mick Jagger was, maybe him did lock down with more black pum-pum than him can deal with. Took me all of two minutes to realize the glimmer twin's rep stretched beyond Studio 54.

—You've heard *Some Girls*? It's a return to form for them.

—Me hear plenty girls.

That was all she wrote on that one. Flash forward to just a few days ago and I've never seen a big man look so small. He didn't even have the energy to tell Priest 'bout him bombocloth for bringing the white bwoi back again. He didn't want to talk about the guy the police shot. He didn't want to talk about the police. He was doing that thing, that thing old people do, when they know too much or maybe they're finally past the age where you just figured the whole world out. You figure out shit between people and why we are all so base and vile and disgusting and how we're just fucking beasts really, and it's a wisdom people get at a certain age. And it doesn't have to be an old age because really Papa-Lo isn't so old, nobody gets old in the ghetto. It's the age where you learn something, I don't know, but something big and something gray and you just know there's no use in trying anymore. But as I was saying, in just one year he had the look, and it was making him exhausted. No, not exhausted, weary.

—Why did the police kill your number two?

—Why rose red and violets blue?

—I don't understand.

—Y is a crooked letter with a long tail. Cut off the tail and you get V. V is for vagabond, and you is a vagabond.

—How did they manage to kill him?

—With two or three gun, me hear.

—You think the PNP gave up your guy?

—What?

—PNP. That they tipped off your boy? And why wouldn't the police respect the treaty?

—White boy, you full of joke. Who tell you that policeman sign treaty? And what you mean with this PNP tip-off business?

—You may be right.

—Haha, white boy, you going tell me if me right or not.

He was right. Shotta Sherrif looked at me when I brought up the death of number two. He looked at me exactly as Papa-Lo.

—Bad times is good times for somebody, me boy. Bad times is good times for somebody.

—Who tipped off the police about number two?

—You see Josey Wales since you come here?

—I've only met him once.

—He live down the other end. Ask him about the number two.

—Josey Wales?

—Me don't know nothing 'bout the street anymore. The peace over.

—The peace between who? Can I ask you what you mean? Can I ask a few more questions? Papa?

Guess not. Didn't have to find Josey Wales, he found me. Just as I was leaving Papa-Lo's gate, don't ask me why I was walking backward as I left Papa-Lo but I was and backed right into two guys. The bald-headed one didn't say anything, didn't even look at me even as he was holding my arm and taking me down the street. The don going to talk to you right now, said the other guy, bigger, fatter, with baby dreadlocks. But isn't Papa-Lo the don? A question I did not ask. Bald guy in blue, dreadlock guy in red, moving at my sides in perfect step, this must be a cartoon. And the people in the street just looking away. When we were passing, they just looked away, and I mean nearly everybody. Everybody looked away, only two women and one man holding eye contact, staring, like they weren't even looking at me really.

Like I was a ghost, or a stranger being driven out of town. Every Jamaican village is a one-horse town. They took me to Josey Wales' place, let me in through the front door, but nobody told me where to sit. An Esso calendar tacked itself to the first of three big windows in the living room. The only windows I've seen that have not been shot out. Curtains on each window, red and yellow floral pattern, he has a woman living with him.

—Nice curtains.

—Plenty of questions you're asking, white boy.

—Huh, I haven't . . .

—Palavering around the place with your little black notebook. Do you write everything in that?

I've heard about Josey Wales' high opinion of his English.

—Where did you learn to speak like that?

—Where did you learn to shit?

—Huh?

—You saving the intelligent questions for last?

—I'm sorry, I . . . I . . . I—

—You . . . you . . . you . . .

All this time I'm seeing nothing but a head wrapped in a towel on a person sitting in a couch not facing me. A don, man, with a girl who just sits there and keeps quiet. Where the fuck was his voice coming from?

—You smart mouth run out of fast. Sit down, white boy.

I sit down on the dining chair by the front door.

—They don't sit in the living room in your country?

I move over to the living room, if that's what you could call it since it was as small as a doctor's waiting room. In fact the couch was gray with the clear plastic covering still on it. Not a girl just sitting there, I see the mesh vest first, then the big hands pulling the towel off his head. He rubs his hair a couple more times then tosses it behind him. Maybe he's got the kind of woman who picks up after him. Josey Wales. He really is a big man, lighter than Papa-Lo, but his eyes are narrower than you expect, almost like a Chinese guy's eyes. His belly is starting to push against the mesh vest, ghetto youth uniform though I'm guessing he only wears this in the house. When a Jamaican bad man ascends it's noticeable in his wardrobe first. Once he steps out of the house he is always in a shirt, I hear, as if at any minute he might end up in court.

—You have your pen ready all the time?

—Yes.

—I know some men who behave like that with a gun. Two of them standing outside my house right now.

—Not you?

—Nothing good ever come out of a gun mouth. You need to improve on that thing about you?

—Say what?

—Move faster. Get better reflexes, I think they call it.

—I don't understand.

—Just a while ago, just as I was saying that nothing good ever come out of a gun mouth.

—I heard you, Mr. Wales.

—Only the judge calls me Mr. Wales. Josey.

—Okay.

—Just as I was saying nothing good ever come out of a gun mouth—

—I heard you.

—Something sticking you up your asshole, why you keep interrupting me? As I was saying, just as I was saying nothing good ever come out of a gun mouth. Me see you jerk. Your eye blink open wide, like you never expect something like that to come out the don's mouth.

—I didn't—

—You did, brethren. But it was only like a second, so fast that most people would miss it. But none of my three names is most people. You probably didn't even notice it.

—No I didn't, and it's my body.

—People like you don't see much. Always putting down little note in your little book. Before you even step off the plane you already write the story. Now you just looking for any loose shit to add and say, See it there America, this is the Jamaica runnings.

—You know, not everybody, not every journalist is like that.

—You from the *Melody Maker*?

—*Rolling Stone.*

—So what you doing here almost one year now? Black pussy that sweet?

—What? No, no. I'm working on a story.

—You need one year to write on a story on Copper?

—Copper?

—Copper. You don't even know the name of the man you asking all sorts of questions about. Copper, the man who misread the treaty.

—There's a document?

—You not the brightest boy *Rolling Stone* send here.

—Well, I'm not stupid.

—Why *Rolling Stone* would send man out here for over a year? Which story could be so hot and ready?

—Ah, they didn't actually send me.

—True that. In fact, you don't work for no damn *Rolling Stone.* Or *Melody Maker* or any of them for that matter. *New York Times*, yeah they would station a reporter out here for a year, but not a magazine that love to put batty boys on their cover. I think you just here for the black pussy. How is that Aisha girl? Treating you good? Still have the P U S S Y with the tight needle eye?

—Oh my G—

—Look like I know more about you than you know about me, white boy.

—Aisha, she's . . . she's not my girlfriend.

—Of course not. White boy like you, you don't have black woman for that particular use.

—I don't have any woman for that particular use.

Josey Wales laughs like a wheeze, like it's gritting through his teeth. Not like Papa-Lo, who throws his head back and pushes it out from deep within his big belly.

—That answer wicked, my youth. Wicked and wild.

—I'm here all week.

—No, you leaving today.

—It was a joke? I'm here all week? I say something that makes you laugh, you laugh and I say I'll be here with more jokes all week? It's from a stand-up . . . never mind.

—Why you going 'round asking about Copper?

—Well, I—

—You even ask that short-ass idiot, Shotta Sherrif.

—He didn't really say much.

—Why would the man have anything to say? He didn't even know him that good.

—Were you two friends?

—Josey Wales love everybody.

—I mean Copper, not Shotta Sherrif. He was really involved in the Central Peace Council, wasn't he?

—Eh, what do you really think you know about the Central Peace Council? I bet you didn't know that it was a joke. Peace. Only one kind of peace can ever come down the ghetto. It's really simple, so simple even a retarded man can catch the drift. Even a white man. The second you say peace this and peace that, and let's talk about peace, is the second gunman put down their guns. But guess what, white boy. As soon as you put down your gun the policeman pull out his gun. Dangerous thing, peace. Peace make you stupid. You forget that not everybody sign peace treaty. Good times bad for somebody.

—Huh. I could have sworn I heard . . . You saying the peace treaty is a bad idea?

—No. You just say that.

—So whatchu saying?

—Copper come from Wareika Hills, almost country. He didn't understand how Kingston work. So he come down to Copenhagen to his good friend, Papa-Lo, then he walk over to drink rum with his other good friend, Shotta Sherrif, and everything sweet and safe as long as he in JLP or PNP territory.

—But then last May he go to Caymanas Park, which is—

—No man territory.

—Worse, he go by himself.

—Peace vibes turn him into a damn fool. That's the problem with peace. Peace make you careless.

—How did the police know he was there?

—You think it's that hard to find a gunman?

—But there was a swarm of them, not just two random dirty cops betting on a fixed race.

—Ambush. You like cowboy movies?

—I usually say fuck 'em, quite frankly. I'm part Sioux.

—Sue?

—Sioux, like Cherokee. Like Apache.

—You an Indian?

—Part.

—Seen.

—You know who set him up? Copper, that is.

—Maybe he set him own self up.

—But some of the men here said that he was Papa-Lo's number two, maybe even number one, one day.

—A man who didn't even live in Copenhagen City because him 'fraid of bullet? Who said that?

—People. And with him gone . . .

—By—look at that, the same fucking bullet him was hiding from. So what if him gone? You can replace any man in the ghetto. Even me.

—I see. How do you think the Singer will react to all this?

—Me look like the Singer keeper?

—No, I mean . . . No love lost between you and him?

—Don't know what you mean by that, but that man gone through plenty. People just need to make him rest. Just 'low him, make him rest.

—He must be dedicated to the cause though, to come back again to do another concert, especially after what happened the last time.

—Haha. Nobody going to make a move on the Singer again.

—I'll bet nobody thought anybody would have made a move on him the first time.

—The last time friend allow friend to run horse race con in him house. Him not allowing that shit again. Nobody shooting him in the chest this time because nobody stabbing him in the back.

—Hold up, you think they were out for the Singer's friend? What's this about a con?

—I don't have anything to say about the Singer.

—But you were talking about his friend, not the Singer.

—Certain tree get pruned a long time ago.

—Now you sound like Papa-Lo.

—That's what happen when people fade. They live on in your memory.

—I sometimes sound like my dad.

—I sometimes discipline like my daddy.

—Oh. Really?

—Yes, white boy. Some men in the ghetto actually know their father. Some of them were even married to their mother.

—I wasn't saying.

—All the important things you saying so far not coming out of your mouth.

—Oh.

—Papa-Lo is the reason why we living fine in the ghetto. Papa-Lo is the reason that when I flush that toilet I never have to look at shit again. You take that for granted, eh, white boy? That once you press a lever you never have to think about your shit again. Yes, thanks to Papa-Lo ghetto people living fine indeed. Papa-Lo and the Singer is the same. Same thing going happen to the Singer.

—Excuse me?

—Excuse yourself.

—Not a fan, I gather.

—Rather check for Dennis Brown.

—He seems to have believed in this truce.

—You ever get locked up in jail, white boy?

—No.

—Good. Because once them put you in jail, police beat everything out of you. Is not just the beat in the face with the baton or the kick in the back or the punching out two good teeth so you can't eat good and nearly slice off your own tongue. Is not even when they put two electric cord, one around your balls and the other on your cock-head and plug in the socket. That's just the first day and not even the worst thing that happen in jail. The worst thing about jail is how they separate your own time, your own date, even your own birthday. Is a hell of a thing when you can no longer tell if it's Wednesday or Saturday. You lose sense. You lose grip on what really goin' on outside in the world. You know what happen when you don't know night any better than day?

—Tell me.

—Black turn into white. Up turn into down. Puss and dog turn friend. You ask yourself, This peace treaty? Was it between two communities or just two man in jail too long?

—What do you think about—

—I not here to think.

—No, I mean about the Singer.

—You keep thinking I supposed to be thinking about the Singer.

—No, I mean the second concert for peace last year. Maybe he thinks he has big stakes in this peace process.

—The first concert was for peace. This one was for a toilet.

—Huh?

—You work for a magazine and don't know nothing at all? Maybe you work for a Jamaican newspaper.

—Still, to come back after two years, after they nearly killed him.

—They who?

—I . . . I . . . I don't know. The assassins.

—Like a Bruce Lee movie.

—The killers.

—Like a Clint Eastwood movie.

—I, I don't know who they were.

—Ha, Papa-Lo seem to know. I have a question for you about the Singer, maybe only you, being a foreign man, and you educated?

—Yes.

—That only an educated man can answer. You know what they mean by literary device?

—Yes.

—So when the Singer get shot in the chest with a bullet that was meaning for his heart, you think him take that as just a shot in the chest like any other shot, or he take it to mean something more than that? A literary device.

—Device. You mean a symbol?

—Something like that.

—You mean if he thought being nearly shot in the heart might mean . . .

—All the things that shot in the heart can mean.

—How do you know he was nearly shot in the heart?

—So I hear.

—From who?

—From the natural mystic blowing through the air.

When I told Priest that I spoke to Josey Wales he was standing in the rain and refused to come in. You know how even in the dark you can tell how a person is looking at you?

There's a man in blue sitting on the edge of my bed. Sid Vicious died two days ago. Nobody knows shit, but word was that his mother just fed the fucker heroin and right after coming out of detox. Rock is sick and dead in New York City. Found him sprawled out naked in bed with a probably also naked actress. Twenty-one. Fuck punk anyway. The only thing we agree on is *Two Sevens Clash*. My mom would be proud, Lord knows it wasn't the greatest idea being an audiophile when the band du jour was Hawkwind. But Sid Vicious died two days ago. And months after killing his girlfriend. Dead men, all these dead men. Only four people know the Singer nearly got shot in the heart. The Singer, his manager, his surgeon and me, because I caught him on a lucky day when he didn't try to kick my ass for following him all over London. Only three people know he was eating quarter of a grapefruit, having cut off half to give to the manager. Only two people know that the Singer said Selassie I Jah Rastafari and I only know because I caught him on a lucky day in London.

There's a fucking man in fucking blue sitting on the fucking edge of my fucking bed. And I'm starting to feel like I'm the murdered character in the game Live about to tell the murderer to grab his fucking weapon and fucking get on with it already. Just fucking get on with it.

My left leg has gone to sleep. I'm seeing some black men and more black men and they are merging into one black man and no black man at all. There is a bald-headed man in blue sitting on the side of my bed, rubbing his head, rubbing his shiny sweaty light brown head. His shirt is navy blue. Fucking left leg has gone to sleep behind his sinking ass. Stare at the ceiling, Alex Pierce. Count grooves in the stucco, look for Jesus. There's Jesus. Look for a cross. Look for Italy, look for a shoe, look for a woman's face. The man on my bed holy shit a gun he has a gun motherfucker has a fucking gun waving it he's waving it at his temple at me at his temple he's about to pull a fucking Hemingway why would he sneak into my room to off himself motherfucker I'm not going to be your audience fucking Christ don't fucking pop off that shit and splat your brain all over my clean sheets dirty sheet fucking scum fuck cum-encrusted pubic-hair-littered sheets but they're mine and I don't want your fucking blood and brains all over them oh he's not going to shoot himself he's going to shoot me he's going to shoot me fucking heart stop pumping he's going to hear, nobody can hear a heart pump yes he can he's going to hear you oh fuck oh fuck oh fuck he's spinning it he's dangling it he's a cowboy and this is his six-shooter *High Noon Liberty Valance Sons of Katie fucking Elder* at least I'm gonna die like a true Jamaican that is not funny it's not fucking funny fuck this I'm not going to die today I'm not going to fucking die today stop spinning the gun like a motherfucking gunslinger like you just picked up the worn-out copy of *Gunfighter Ballads* that's in every fucking Jamaican's house I'm not going to die today my mother is not going to be left standing out at Minneapolis–St. Paul Airport sorting out a fucking coffin box, or worse, putting up posters all over Kingston saying MISSING HAVE YOU SEEN THIS MAN? Coming on Dick Cavett to talk about her poor son and the horrible bureaucracy in Jamaica who won't assist her and it's a conspiracy, really it is, or at least a cover-up, maybe it's just really bad incompetence that took her son and she knows something was up, somebody did something and she'll move heaven and earth to find out the truth even if the police, the minister, and even the ambassador won't lift a finger to help, I'll become a story and she'll become one of those haggard old women whose other children will desert her (she was the world's greatest mom before she became obsessed with a ghost) and will have nothing but cigarettes and the mission left, the mission to uncover the truth. She'll also do *60 Minutes* and more Cavett and when everybody starts to forget she'll . . . I don't know what she'll do.

Jesus Christ, please make him go away. Please let it be that I'll close my eyes, I'll close them for as long as you want, and when I open them he'll be gone. Do you want me to pray? Because I will, I swear to God. Swear to God. Swear to you. Oh fuck this. I will not think what heaven is like. Who the fuck does that? I will not do it. I'll just say to him that if you kill me now right here I'll look you in the eye and stain myself in your head for as long as you live. I swear I'd haunt you like a motherfucker so hard that an exorcist would look at you and say goddamn, my son, there's really no help for you. I'll come with that crucifix fucker Linda Blair and that sister fucking mass-murdering motherfucker from Amityville and I'll cut out one chunk of your brain so that all three of us can live there and then we'll eat you from the inside out, like cancer. I'll fucking haunt you, motherfucker. I'll make you scream devil deh 'pon you in church and I'll make you see blind and fuck your sister and I'll make you talk to yourself everywhere because only you and I will know you're talking to me. And I'll drive you off the causeway into the fucking sea and you still won't die because I won't make you die, I'll make you live a hundred years to haunt you forever and I'll write my name in the mirror every time you take a shower and one day you will read *get ready to suck cocks in hell* on the ceiling and I'll make your bed shake and elbows itch and you'll scratch so hard everybody will come looking for the heroin and no dog will go anywhere near you because they can sense when a spirit is living rent-free in your head, so you better turn away, you better get up and walk out of this room right now or I swear to God I will. I will. I will.

Phone rings.

He jumps.

I jump.

Gun in mid-spin, gun drops.

He looks at me look at him.

Bends down for gun kick him kick him.

Kicked him in the back and again in the back of the head.

Roll now, climb out of bed—he grabs my foot.

Get the fuck off me get the fuck off he's climbing.

Punch he catches my hand won't give it back.

Pulling off the bed screeeeeee—hand around my neck.

Squeeze. I'm red I'm red I'm getting redder a fat red goose where are your eyes. Cough cough hand grip my neck squeeze crushing Adam's apple he don't care can't punch can't kick scratch scratch he's not even trying to stop me scratch his cheek scratch his face he slaps me away like I'm a bitch a fucking bitch cough he sitting on my chest I can't breathe I can't breathe vise grip Jesus Christ Jesus Christ he grabs my right hand like I'm a silly little bitch such a silly bitch such a silly bitch I'm a fucking silly bitch can't move pinned my neck burning head bursting head light head dark no I need to tell her tell her that I knew she was going to leave from the day I met her fuck this life flashing business any time now relax the feet first, relax the feet first let them find me at least in peace what the fuck the phone is ringing I jump and he jumps not on my neck too slow turns back his hand on my hand slap my hand on his hand slap his hand my face knuckle punch I slap if I'm a girl I'll be a girl he's not saying anything my fingers are slippery his hand on my neck not a strangle a pindown he's looking for it oh fucking shit the gun the gun the gun he looks I look at the lamp the fucking heavy lamp the crochet the Gideon Bible Jesus fucking Christ the letter opener compliments of the hotel on the stationery he turns around back to me back to hand it to me gun? No gun? Can't see the gun can't remember when I grabbed it sharp end dark end why won't he say anything he's about to squeeze my neck I squeeze the letter opener he in mid-squeeze I'm in mid-swing straight for his neck, my knuckle slam right under his chin feels like a punching, my finger slips off fuck no, it's gone in deep. He looks at me through high eyebrows eyes wide he's not touching it, the letter opener in his neck blood trickles then spurts then spurts more like tap just burst his eyes are doing that thing like they can't believe what the rest of the body is doing. Not speaking, he's not speaking he's jerking, he's rolling off me, he's on the bed, he's off the bed, he walking to the door right knee buckles stand up straight right knee buckles he's on the ground.

Josey Wales

I *already know:* there are three things that should never come back. One is the spoken word. Two I forget in 1966. Three is a secret. But if I was going to add a number four, that would be him. How many bullets need to miss your heart and lodge in your arm before you reason that home is not home anymore? The bullet in the arm no doctor would remove because they know if they touch it you would never play guitar again. I just sit down in the nice chair my woman just polished until the phone ring. How many bullets? Maybe fifty-seven? they say he said, but nobody can tell me when or to who, that for the fifty-six bullets fired at the house, the said culprit shall also die by fifty-six bullets. Now that kind of prophecy need a new sort of reasoning. Is that fifty-six for each man, fifty-six multiply by eight? Or fifty-six divided by eight, which would take long division and I don't have time to be that smart.

Or maybe he thinking fifty-six for the man behind the plan, the top ranking, the Don Dada. Ask me just how sick and tired I getting from all this witchdoctor Obeahman fortune-teller fuckery. If a man call himself Rasta today, by next week that is him speaking prophecy. He don't have to be too smart either, just know one or two hellfire and brimstone verse from the Bible. Or just claim it come from Leviticus since nobody ever read Leviticus. This is how you know. Nobody who get to the end of Leviticus can still take that book seriously. Even in a book full of it, that book is mad as shit. Don't lie with man as with woman, sure I can run with that reasoning. But don't eat crab? Not even with the nice, soft, sweet roast yam? And why kill a man for that? And trust me, the last thing any man who rape my daughter going get to do is marry her. How, when I slice him up piece by piece, keeping him alive for all of it and have him watch me feed him foot to stray dog?

I remember last year at these peace treaty parties that spring up in West Kingston like head lice, a Rasta trying to give me a reasoning about who is carrying the mark of the beast. Nothing set a Rasta on fire more than talk of "Armagideon." So the Rasta say,

—Yow me no buy nothing that no fresh, brethren, because everything in package now carry the mark of the beast. You know, them code number in the white box with the black line.

I was trying to watch this man who was checking out my woman, looking warm under the streetlight while people dancing around her, some man from the Eight Lanes who didn't know that this woman's ring finger marked. No need to worry—she already know how to deal with that kind of man—she deal with them harder than me. But that's the thing about Rasta reasoning. Even when you know it's total fuckery from the start to end, it still have a hook to it.

—Barcode? I say. But barcode have whole heap of different number, and me sure me never see 666 yet.

—You saying you look?

—No, but—

—But is for ram goat, brethren. Check the reasoning. Nobody in Jamaica have the power of the beast. Them just nyam wha the beast feed. You no notice that all the time the number start with zero zero zero? That be some decimal science. Whole number and natural number and double number. That mean all the number on all the code in all the world add up to 666.

I walk away from the man because the worst part of all this was that it was starting to make some kind of sense. And nothing at this peace party was making any damn sense. Not the Twelve Tribes branch of Rastafari, who skin colour was getting lighter every month, not JLP and PNP palavering, Copenhagen City and the Eight Lanes playing domino and hugging and kissing and lovey-doving like I didn't kill your brother, father and grandfather three years ago. What is peace? Peace is my blowing a little breeze on my daughter forehead when she sweat in her sleep. This don't name peace, this name stalemate. I learn that word from Doctor Love.

Doctor Love just fly to Miami saying he has a president to get elected. Where I just send Weeper. Who know what those two up to since they both realise that they love book more than woman. Doctor Love say, Hermano *them motherfuckers from Medellín are going to test you, yes test you again, what did you expect,* muchacho? *Last week they stole a dead baby from the morgue, gut it out like a fish, stuffed the little shit with cocaine and had some girl fly with it to Fort Lauderdale—just a day after her* quinceañera. *Hardcore like a porno, no?* Me, I starting to get just a little tired of testing. They know and I know that December 3 was just a stupid test. I give them a message but they say they want a body. A dead body is a dead body, I don't care. But I do care about some bombocloth Spanish-speaking pussyhole thinking that this is some little boy 'prentice that they can just test and re-test.

December 1976, the Singer just do the concert in the park and I wasting time at fucking Jamintel Communications because I need to make an international phone call only to hear Doctor Love and some idiot cursing out in Spanish, but not Cuban Spanish so I didn't understand most of it, but I know he was mad. And I'm thinking who the fuck this pussyhole think he talking to, as if I don't know what *hijo de puta* mean? What he think I was going to do, start cry and say I'm so sorry, bossman, next time I'll do better I promise? Like some whore who need discipline from her pimp? Was about to tell this *maricón* about him bombocloth when Doctor Love say to me, Just finish the job, *muchacho*, just finish it. So the Jamaican Syrian, the Cuban and the Colombian all want a body yet none of them realise that I gave them something better than a body. Same week Peter Nasser call me with,

—What the bombocloth wrong with the whole of you fucking ghetto people?

—This is not the first time I hear you with "you people."

—I didn't say you people, I said you fucking ghetto people. What the bombocloth wrong with you? Nine man?

—Eight.

—Eight man storm into O.K. Corral with, what, fourteen gun? And yet not a single man can shoot straight?

—Man can shoot straight enough.

—How you manage being the first man in history to shoot somebody in the head and not kill them? Answer that, master.

—I don't know who you mean by you. Or you so fucking fool you think phone can't tap?

—What? This look like spy movie? Who the r'ass want to tap you?

—Even so I don't know who you mean by you, but I'm sure him, whoever he is, didn't aim for anybody head.

—He, whoever him is, didn't aim for nothing but wall and sky, it look like. No busha, that kind of slackness and poppy-show only happen in comedy. Imagine hundreds of bullet and they couldn't take out one fucking man. Is a fucking machine gun, how r'asscloth hard can it be to shoot? I thought Louis taught you people how to deal with these things.

—I don't know no Louis and I sure don't know no "you people."

—Don't draw me tongue, Josey Wales. I told him you know, don't make sense trying to teach ghetto naiggers anything that will take any kinda intelligence, they bound to fuck it up. My blind grandmother could hit a target better than you. All eight of you. I don't know why I even bother to call you.

—I don't know either since none of those people you keep talking 'bout live here.

—Why me even running up me phone bill, eh? Tell me.

—I don't know why either, busha.

—What? You know who you talking to? You know who you bombocloth talking to, you little—

—Little? You must did drop your pants and look again.

I hang up the phone. It's a bitch of a thing when you realise that though you are the only one who didn't go to a top-class school and foreign college, you is the only man in the room with any sense. I really wanted to educate this ignorant, bad-chatting, Syrian shithouse. That it's bad enough that plenty man and woman have the Singer off as a prophet, but kill him and the man graduate to martyr. This way the whole world know that guess what, the prophet is just a man like any other man, he can get shot like any other man—and like any other man in this country, not even he safe. I shoot that man off the pedestal and he fall back down to man size. I didn't tell Peter Nasser any of that. You have to look past a man, below the skin to the real skin to know that for all the whiteness (in the face of a man who don't go to beach because even a tan looks black), Peter Nasser is just another ignorant as shit naigger. But at least he was calling me busha these days. I must ask my woman when exactly I change into a white man who drink at Mayfair Hotel. Cho bombocloth man, I hate when a man get me so mad that I start to cuss. Only ignorant man cuss.

I say to Doctor Love, who also call me that night, that I done deal with proving things to people from 1966 and if they really think this is prep school where they feel they must test and test, then Medellín can go right back to using those batty boys in Bahamas. But then, to use the Rasta own words, I get hit with another reasoning. If the Singer did turn into a martyr it would be a big problem, for sure, but it would be their problem, not mine. Peter Nasser would be so busy shitting himself trying to kill a legend that he won't have time to bother me with his fuckery, because truth be told, both he and I know that I long past the days when politician say jump and I say how high. Now when politician say jump, my woman say he can't come to the phone right now but I will take a message. Talk about fool, what do you think was going to happen once you give a man with a head a gun, that he was going to return it? Even Papa-Lo wasn't so fool.

So I decide to let my mind work on this new reasoning. December 8, 1976, news just come that he and everybody survive. Too much Babylon at the hospital and besides, by that time I grab Tony Pavarotti, because Weeper was not the man for anything that need that kind of skill. But at the emergency room they already treat him and send him home. Only the manager was still in the hospital and there was not much use to finishing him off. So me and Pavarotti drive down to 56 Hope Road, expecting police. Police mean nothing when all you need is one shot. Besides, I make one phone call and they would disappear in sixty seconds. Except 56 was a ghost town. Empty driveway and darkness in every window. Not a single police. I laugh and Pavarotti look at me like he was about to ask a question. Meanwhile Peter Nasser getting so sloppy that it look like a TV show on how much mistake one man can make. The stupid piece of dog shit leave a message, a goddamn message with my woman that *if the sage go onstage it going make the page and he'll be the rage.* One of the few times in my life I ever hear Tony Pavarotti laugh was when I read that note out loud. My woman didn't know what the r'asscloth was going on about so she leave the two of us in the living room. With Tony Pavarotti in the room I wonder if I made a mistake picking Weeper, who I send to clean up what we just do. Instead of doing it himself he just call the Rastas like some girl who always afraid. Worse, he did it on my phone. I make a phone call.

—Where the bird flying to?

—Brethren, weh you ah call me for?

—I don't like repeating questions.

—He gone. They leave the manager at the hospital and take him up the white man hill.

—Police?

—One in the car with them, few more back at the place. Twelve Tribes on the watch all over the hill. And a white boy—

—A white boy?

—White boy with a camera. Nobody know where he come from, but him say him is with the film crew. Anyway, me done talk.

—No you no don't done talk yet, Inspector.

—Me done sing this sankey.

—Done, canary you just ah start.

—Not even Jesus getting up that hill tonight.

—What about the concert?

—Full police escort to and from.

—The next day?

—I don't know.

—Talk, pussyhole.

—The next day he supposed to fly out. Them have him on a private jet.

—When?

—Five-thirty or six.

—Morning or evening?

—What you think?

—To where?

—Nobody know.

—Jet going take off and nobody know where it going? Boss, you taking ghetto man for idiot again?

—Mister, me say nobody nuh know. Not even the commissioner know. He don't even know that the Singer plan to fly out.

—Is a top secret?

—More secret than the colour of the queen panty. We only know because our man in the car with them pretend that he gone to sleep and listen to them talk. Him white manager tell him up the hill that as soon as he done with the concert—

—So it official. He going do the concert?

—No, nothing no official. Them just putting things in place just in case. Anyway, the manager say that as soon as the concert done him setting up a plane for him at the airport but early, before the airport even open.

—Norman Manley Airport or Tinson Pen?

—Manley.

—Overseas.

—You can radio the police up the hill.

—Yeah, man, but why would I want to—

—Radio your police up the hill. Right now.

Six in the morning and the airport looking like the first reel of a cowboy movie. Only thing missing was whistling wind and tumbleweed. Pink sky. Me and Tony Pavarotti waiting in the stairway leading up to the waving gallery. Somebody thought it was a good idea making this wall like some checker pattern with open space to stick a rifle through. Checker pattern shadow leave we in the dark. Pavarotti was shifting and moving, he wasn't feeling for this angle at all. But the plane was already out on the runway, waiting. Pavarotti quiet, his right hand gripping the trigger and his left eye in the rifle lens.

Way at the end of the runway, two jeep hang back lazy, Jamaica Defence Force, with four or five soldier positioned behind them, two with binoculars. See them from the second I went out to the waving gallery. Seeing soldiers on the lookout made me think of the Singer coming down from the white man hill. The look on his face when he wake up and see no police. He probably send two or three Rasta brethren ahead to see if the road safe, which mean he and his right-hand man was coming down the hill all alone. With no soldier watching through binoculars. You can always assume one or two things about the police: (1) make a deposit to a bank account or a back pocket and anything can happen and (2) that they always come cheap. But with soldier you never know. They hang back, standing watch maybe, but just as likely that they just waiting. I wonder if the pilot expect them to come over.

—Make sure you take him out before the soldier them drive over.

Pavarotti nod.

6:02. Everybody but the sun waiting for the Singer. For a second it feels like I waiting for a parade, like that grainy newsreel that come on TV every November about Kennedy in Dallas. Everybody waiting on the Singer. Not just me, not just the soldiers, not just Tony Pavarotti or the plane, but Peter Nasser, Doctor Love, and a phone number for the Medellín cartel that I never use myself. But then I wonder. Everybody waiting to see his next move or mine? Who is the real dancing monkey in this episode? Who people watching to see the next move? And if people say jump and you manage to jump high, do they stop telling you to jump, or disrespect you forever because you didn't act like a man and say, Fuck you, bad man don't jump for nobody. The problem with proving something is that instead of leaving you alone people never stop giving new things to prove, harder things. Bullshit things until it become a TV comedy. Or just a joke.

Tony Pavarotti tap my shoulder. He is here. He and another Rasta walking to the plane. Nothing moving but the dust they kick up. The airport is still empty and not waking up till seven. They look around while walking, moving slow, stopping one second then moving again. The Singer look to the plane, scanning left and right, with the other Rasta walking backwards making sure nothing behind them. Both of them see the army jeep and stop. The Singer look at the jeep and look at the plane. Nobody move. Tony Pavarotti turning the gun to aim, following them. His finger slip around the trigger. The Singer looking at the soldiers and say something to the Rasta. They start moving again but slower, stopping right in front of the plane. Maybe they waiting for somebody to come out. I remember that Tony Pavarotti don't need orders from me. I hear a click.

—Stop.

Pavarotti look at me, look at the two of them running to the plane now.

—No bother with it.

They run to the plane and have to close the door themselves.

When I get two phone call the next day I cut both short with the same line. You want him dead so much, you kill him.

Now I'm sitting down in my living room waiting for the phone to ring. This phone better ring soon. Soon as it start ringing I can stop thinking. Time for action, no time for thinking. I wonder if she pay the phone bill? The phone is supposed to ring three times before I go to bed. Not even tomorrow coming before my phone ring. Sitting down, waiting for the phone, the Singer enter my head again and I want to cuss. That man will never know how I come to near finish him twice. How I let him go because I knew that once he board that plane he will never come back. And yet in 1978, coming off the plane and even causing fuss in customs is he. In two years Peter Nasser know better than to come to me like a barking dog and to speak to me like a man. He even take to calling me busha all the time, which make me check if this carbolic soap was bleaching my skin. Me all stop using it, which made my woman very happy since she didn't feel like she was sleeping in a hospital ward anymore. I don't know what surprise him more, that the Singer was coming back to do yet another concert or that I know from before and tell him so.

—All this fucking peace treaty business, you have anything to do with this fuckery?

We're at Lady Pink Go-Go Club, which he is liking just a little too much. None of the whores that Weeper used to deal with seem to be here anymore. Look like they lose interest in fucking Pepsi bottles onstage as soon as he lose interest in them. But the new lot include a light-skinned girl so of course the place packed. The head woman put the two of us in a room upstairs and ask if we want we cocky clean or batty wash. I said not tonight, but Peter Nasser wasn't going to pass up the chance for a ghetto vacuum, as he himself call it, and look around as if it was going to catch on. He want to talk business even as the whore was sucking him juice out. I say, Brethren, two man can't have cocky expose in the same room, is what you be? Last thing he want is man to call him battyman, so before he ask, I say I going outside. I said look for me in fifteen minutes but when I come back in eight she already walking out, spitting and cussing 'bout the bloodcloth white man who bust himself in her mouth.

—You know what me tired of? All this shit 'bout the peace treaty. Now Jacob Miller write a song about it? You hear it yet? Want me to sing it?

—No.

—Peace treaty to r'asscloth.

—Next time tell the soldiers don't shoot.

—Soldiers? What you mean, Green Bay? All of this is because of Green Bay? You no hear the news, no saints were killed in Green Bay.

—Funny thing, eh? Don't all of them come from your constituency? One of them even tell me that it was some man name Junior Soul who come to your lands telling them they can get free gun.

—I don't know anything 'bout no Junior Soul.

—But everybody did seem to think I know. I ask people, Who from the ghetto would have a name like that? Sound like some singer out of Motown.

—Is what you know 'bout . . . never mind.

—Maybe he was something in the air.

—A natural mystic?

—You know that him coming back? Now because of all this peace treaty fuckery he of all people coming back.

—He was just here for this damn peace concert. Wasn't that enough?

Isn't he a Londoner now? Maybe he want install all those ghetto toilet himself?

—So if you did give the ghetto toilets, he wouldn't have a reason to come back then.

—Of course Josey Wales, because my party is in power. You seem—busha, what the fuck you finding funny?

"Ma Baker" was playing out on the floor. I could hear it even over the crowd yelling and joking and cussing and screaming for the woman to spread out di meat. I didn't bother tell him why "Ma Baker" makes me laugh.

—Nothing, busha. You really think the Singer coming back again for a toilet?

—Well, not a toilet exactly but fixtures and fittings, or whatever you call it that ghetto people bawling that they need now. They can continue bawl, who tell them to vote for this bombocloth socialist government. Twice. You have to ask, How far can a cocky go up you battyhole before you realise a battyman is fucking you?

—The Singer not coming to fix no damn toilet.

—So he's coming again because of this fucking peace business. I hope you know this is making people further up very concerned. Very concerned. You know how many Cubans fly into Jamaica last week? And now that fuckery ambassador Erik Estrada parading around like he own the place.

—The Singer meet with Papa-Lo and Shotta Sherrif the same time.

—Who the r'asscloth don't know that? Everybody mix-up-mix-up at 56 Hope Road, even your fucking Prime Minister used to act like he work there.

—The three meet up in England right before the peace concert.

—So? And the peace concert come and gone almost a year ago. So?

—You think three biggest men to come out of downtown Kingston only meeting about a peace concert?

—Seem to be as much as those three could handle.

—Peace concert was just the fringe benefit.

—I'm going to take it for granted that you know what that means.

—For real. Just as I take it for granted that your financial wizard boss know what really causes inflation.

There it is again. Peter Nasser doing the double take with just his eyes, so I don't notice it. Syrians.

—What this little mongrel pussyhole doing, starting a third party? What serious things?

—You didn't seem like you want to know a minute ago.

—Busha, talk the fucking things, man. Cho.

—There's a program after the peace concert. A plan, call it an agenda.

—What kind of agenda?

—You ready for this type of news? A Rasta government.

—Wha? What the bombocloth you just say?

—This is how you going know, when a bunch of Rasta from England all of a sudden fly down here. Some land already. Hold on, my boy, you don't know say even Papa-Lo turning Rasta? He stop eat pork months ago. Twelve Tribes meeting? Regular thing that for him now.

—Me'll believe it when him stop comb him hair.

—Who tell you say all Rasta have dreadlocks? Jesus Christ.

Have to remind myself to not make him look too stupid.

—How you mean—

—Anyway, you want to hear what Rasta and honorary Rasta was reasoning in England or not?

—Me all ears, busha.

—So one of them, me not sure who, say, The idea is to involve the Rasta in society, politics and grass roots.

—Those actual words?

—Me look like receptionist?

—Whoopee. So they meet for the peace concert and start talking about government. Just like every man on every verandah in every home in Jamaica. This is the news?

—No, brethren. They meet about new government then start talking about a peace concert.

—What?

—You don't know what clock ah strike. You didn't even know that the clock was Big Ben. Hear the plan: to set up a new opposition from both sides of the ghetto, party truly for the people to get rid of the whole of you in the name of Rasta.

—Some Jamdown Mau-Mau?

—What?

—But Rasta want to go to bombocloth Ethiopia. Why them don't just splash red, black and green paint on some fucking boat and fuck off? Call it Black Star Liner 2 or some fuckery.

—You think London Rasta know shit about Ethiopia? London dread know Rasta through reggae, busha. Wherever is the home of reggae is the real home of Rasta. All of a sudden Rastaman in England going to business school and running for London Parliament and sending them children to get all sort of education, even the girls. What you think all of that is for? England don't want them. Where you think they going go?

—Shit.

—Downtown divide up, master. You should know, you divide it.

—Me never divide nothing.

—You cutting yourself out of your party now? The two of you divide it. Me? I just enforce it. But what you think was going to happen after the peace concert? What happen when people come together?

—No more divide.

—That's just first phase, sah. People come together in peace, means people soon come together in politics. Already people picking out which don can be an MP of which area. That means no more you.

—And all this happen at this meeting in London?

—For real.

—But busha, that meeting was one year ago.

—So it go.

—You wait one year to tell me this?

—Didn't think you need to know.

—You didn't think I need to know. Josey Wales, me ever hire you to bombocloth think? Does it look like when I need thinking done, I call the naigger man to do it? Answer me that.

—Mind you get an answer you don't like, I say and watch the eye-only double-take again.

—Bombo pussy r'asscloth. Motherfucking dripping cunt bitch. You mean all now some fucking secret Rasta sect migrating back even when so many people right now flying out? You know how much could be here right now? You did think about that?

—No busha, when thinking need to be done, I leave that to you.

—Shit, shit, fucking shit. Election is only next year. Is only next r'asscloth year. What the bombo r'asscloth. You know how much people I have to call now? Can't believe you wait a year to tell me this. Me not going forget this, Josey Fucking Wales.

—Good. Because you all love to forget when it suit you. Because of forgetting why Papa-Lo run things in the first place. But that is between you and Papa-Lo.

—Of course, because you all about your little trips to Miami now. You think the ministry don't have eyes? Well, before you think you too big for people, just remember that you still in an appointed position.

—What that mean?

—You say you want to think? Figure it out.

But I figure it out long before he had to ask me any question. I figure it out from December 8, 1976. I figure it out from before the Singer get on that plane that if he was going to come back, he was going come with new reasoning and new power. Ignorant little-cocky Syrian don't realise that certain dog sniffing a different master now, and even that master already mistake him for servant.

I look at this hook-nose idiot and realise something I learn from Bible school long ago. This man already receive his reward in full. Nowhere leave for him to go, not even down. Think he can raise voice because some people still think white skin give him the authority to speak to anybody any way he feel like, especially man who don't know word like authority. Good for him that right now, I feeling a wave of good Samaritan-ness. Doctor Love tell me a stale thing a year ago, to keep my friends close and my enemies closer. Stale as dog shit, yes, but every time you take a step higher that tip turn fresh. After all, the hunter don't shoot the bird that fly low.

Peter Nasser pay off three men at the airport to be on the lookout for any cockney-speaking Rastafarian landing at Norman Manley airport, especially at night. For some reason he didn't think the Rasta revolution would be coming in through Montego Bay. He was even having them run to the one pay phone in the airport to call him every two hours. Then he want me to go, or send my best man to London to find the Singer and do something wherever he was on tour or recording. I ask him if he think this was a James Bond movie and should I also take out the beauty queen he was with, because that would be a shame to take out the most beautiful woman in the world. I laugh over the phone because otherwise I would be cussing that yet again this man wasting my time. Besides, the Singer really was good as gone. Send a man to near death and you do more than almost kill him. You unroot him, tear him from home so that he can never live anywhere in peace again. The only way the Singer was coming back for good was in coffin.

But that was 1978 and I done with 1978. When the old American leave for Argentina in January, a new one come and take the spot. New American song, same old lyrics. He call himself Mr. Clark. Just that, Mr. Clark. *Clark, just ditch the E.* He think it was funny so he say it every time we meet up. *Clark, just ditch the E.* He already know Doctor Love, but then it seem every American who walked around in Kingston in a sweaty white shirt with the tie open know Luis Hernán Rodrigo de las Casas. April 1978 and we're at Morgan's Harbour, the hotel for white people over in Port Royal. We're looking over at Kingston from the almost empty restaurant, well, they were looking. I was watching. Me with two foreigner, who already feeling the pirate spirit taking over them from head to cock. It is a thing to watch, the kind of feeling that take up a white man every time you take him to Port Royal. You wonder if this is the same spirit that leap up in them as soon as they land on any rock. I'm betting it is so, from as far back as Columbus and slavery. Something about landing from sea that make a white man feel free to say and do as he please.

—Did Blackbeard ever pillage and plunder these parts, matey?

—Me only know 'bout Henry Morgan, sah. Also in Jamaica matey is a woman that a man keep that is not him wife.

—Oh. Oops.

It was the long time since I chat bad on purpose, so much so that Doctor Love have to translate two times. At least this one wasn't like Louis Johnson, holding that memo upside down and pretending to show white people that naigger can't read, something I still remember. But then he say,

—You poor, precious people don't even know that you're on the very verge of anarchy.

—Me no understand. If we precious how we must be poor? Diamond precious.

—But that's what you are, my boy, a diamond in the rough. So rough this island. So roughly cut and beautiful. And so precarious. By precarious I mean that you're teetering on the edge. By that I mean—

—Precarious?

—Yes. *Exactamente. Exactamente*, isn't that right, Luis? Luis and I go back a ways. Too far back, it seems. A few *estados latinos* before this one, eh?

—You part of that Bay of Pigs flop show too?

—What? Huh? No, no. That was before my time. Way before my time.

—Well maybe one day you people going find a poison that really work on Castro.

—He-he-he-he, you're a perceptive one, cunning even, eh? Has Luis been feeding you the news?

—No. The news have been feeding me the news.

Hold on now, Josey Wales. Nothing throw these Americans off more than when they realize that they were wrong about you. Remember to say at least one *no problem, mon,* and vibrate the mon like this: mohhhhhnnnn, before he drive away, just so he leave thinking he find the right man. For the first time I wish I had dreadlocks or know how to break into the jogging on the spot landing on the one foot hop that Rasta do, even when there is no rhythm to dance to. Because I spend the whole time watching Doctor Love nodding at everything this man say, I almost forget that for most of the time he was trying to tell me that Jamaica is at war. A bigger war than 1976 he say, the first time he say 1976.

The Cold War, he say.

—Do you know what we mean by Cold War?

—War don't have no temperature.

—What? Oh no, son. Cold War is a term, a figure of . . . it's just a name for what's happening here. You know what? I've got something right here . . . Here, look at this.

The white man take out a colouring book. When you keep playing fool with Americans you learn to expect anything, but this one throw even me off.

—A wha this?

I had it upside down because who need to flip around a cover to read the *Democracy Is for US!* title. The American look at me holding the book wrong and I know exactly what he was thinking. *Look Luis, compadre, I know you know what you're talking about but you sure we've got the right guy?*

—It's a breakdown, that's what it is. Luis, does he know what . . . I mean . . . look. May I have it for a second? Thanks. Let's see, let's see, let's see . . . Ah! Pages six and seven. See on page six? This is the world in a democracy. See? People in the park. Children running down the ice cream truck, maybe somebody over there is grabbing a Twinkie. Look, see that guy reading a newspaper? And watch that chick, hot, right? Wearing that miniskirt. Who knows what those kids are learning, but they go to school. And every adult in this pic? They can vote. They decide who should leave, I mean lead, the country. Oh yeah, look at the tall buildings. That's because of progress, markets, freedom. That's the free market, son. And if anybody in this picture doesn't like what's going on they can say so.

—You want me to colour this picture, boss?

—What? No, No. I'll tell you what. Say I give you a couple dozen for the school you've got. We have to get the word out to the young, before these fucking pinko commies recruit them. Fucking freaks, these commies, you know why so many of them are faggots? Because normal people like me and you, we reproduce. Commies? They're just like homos, they recruit.

Or like any American church that comes here, I think, but don't say. Instead I say,

—True thing that, boss, true thing.

—Good, good. You're a good man, Mr. Wales. I feel I can share things with you. I'll tell you what, this, what you're about to hear is classified intel. Even Kissinger hasn't been briefed yet. Even Luis is about to hear this for the first time. Hey Luis, bet you couldn't guess what is the biggest industry in East Berlin right now? Late-term abortions. Yup, you heard me right, some butcher pulls the baby out of a five, seven, sometimes nine months pregnant chick and slashes its throat just as the neck comes out of her pussy. Can you believe that shit? Things are so bad that a woman will decide to kill her kid rather than let it be born in East Germany. People in East Germany, they line up for everything, just like in the book, Mr. Wales. Line up for fucking soap. You know what they do with the soap? Sell it for food. Poor little bastards can't even score up a decent cup of coffee so the fucking government mixes that shit with chicory and rye and beet and then calls the whole thing, Michkaffee. Sounds like mischief, eh? I thought I heard everything. Boggles the fucking mind, I tell you. Boggles the fucking mind. You drink coffee, Mr. Wales?

—Me is a tea drinker, sah.

—Good for you, my boy, good for you. But this precious little country you see here? It'll be Cuba, or worse, East Germany in less than two years if that process isn't reversed right now. I saw it nearly happen in Chile. I saw it nearly happen in Paraguay. And Lord only knows what's going to happen to the Dominican Republic.

Some of this is in some way true. But they can't resist it, these men from the CIA. Once they think you believe them it's like lying turn into a drug. No, not a drug, a sport. Now let's see how far I can go with this ignorant naigger. From the corner of my eye I watch him watching me, thinking that I was just the man he expect me to be. By the time Louis Johnson leave he was so impressed that a man who couldn't read much was so smart. Of course smart in the way a good trained dog was smart, or a good monkey, talking to me about aliens to see if I would, as he say, buy it. But here Mr. Clark get so serious that I look up in the sky to see if it was going to turn grey just to add mood to the story.

—What I'm trying to say is that your country is at a crossroads. The next two years are going to be crucial. Can we count on you?

I don't know what kind of fuckery answer the man was looking for. What was he expecting me to say, that me coming on board? Maybe I should say aye-aye Cap'n since we're in Port Royal? Doctor Love shoot me a look, then close his eyes and nod up and down. His way of saying just tell the idiot what he wants to hear, *muchacho.*

—Me on board ship, sah.

—Glad to hear it. Fucking ace.

Mr. Clark get up to leave, saying that his car will take him back to the Mayfair Hotel where he's crashing until his apartment is ready. He leave ten dollars U.S. on the table and start to walk, but then turn back and bend down right to my left ear.

—By the way. I've noticed you're making a few trips to Miami and Costa Rica lately. Busy little bee, aren't you? Of course, the U.S. government has no interest in activities between Jamaica and the members of its diaspora. Assist us in any regard and we will honor that arrangement. Translate that for him, will you, Luis?

—Walk good, Mr. Clark.

—Clark, just ditch—

—The E, I say.

—Hasta la vista!

I look at Doctor Love.

—Him real name Clark?

—My real name Doctor Love?

—He says I instead of we.

—I noticed too, *hombre.*

—That something I should pay attention to?

—Fuck if I know. Just keep on truckin', man. You guys unpack your box of good-goods yet?

—I think Americans say goodies.

—Do I look like a fucking Yankee?

—How you want me to answer that, Dr. Lee dungarees? Anyway, that box unpack long time.

He's talking about another shipment, that come the same way that last one come in December 1976. In a big box marked Audio Equipment/Peace Concert, left out on the wharf for me, Weeper, Tony Pavarotti and two more man empty it. Seventy-five of the M16s we keep. Twenty-five we sell to man in Wang Sang Lands who seem to be itching for firepower lately. We keep all the ammunition, Weeper's idea. Let them make them own bullet, he say.

It look like we planning for war, even though everybody else was planning for peace. Papa-Lo himself bounce back out of that grey cloud he put himself in ever since the Singer get shot. Just like him to put the entire blame on himself, since taking all the blame is just the flip side of taking all the credit. Telling the Singer that is 'cause him was in lockup why things happen or they would never have happened at all. Papa-Lo take a rocket ship and fly off this planet a long time ago, he might as well join Pigs in Space. Trouble is every day more people boarding that flight. Peace treaty fever take over the ghetto so much that the man who kill my cousin come up to me at the end of the first Unity Dance with his arm open like he was expecting a hug. I call him a battyman and walk off.

Peace treaty fever reach as far as Wareika Hill where man like Copper come down for the first time in years, as if he forget that every single policeman in Jamaica have a bullet in the chamber with his name on it. When even Copper come down the hills to eat, drink and make merry, it's time I start scope out another country.

Papa-Lo even come to my house asking why I not jamming to the new peace riddim, and that is high time black people listen to what Marcus Garvey did plan for us all this time. I didn't bother ask if he know any fucking thing about Marcus Garvey or if this was reasoning that some damn Rasta from London was feeding him. But then his eyes, when I look at them, was wet. Pleading. And I realize something about this man and what he was doing. He was already seeing far beyond the clouds, far beyond the ghetto, far beyond time and his place in the world. That man was thinking about what would write on his gravestone. What people will say about him long after the last chunk of flesh rotten off his bone. Forget the seven time he go to jail for murder and attempted murder to walk out every time. Forget that before the white man and Doctor Love come along, he was the one who teach every man how to shoot. Forget that both him and Shotta Sherrif operate in boundaries that they mark off. He want his gravestone to say he unite the ghetto.

People think that I have animosity towards Papa-Lo. Me have nothing but love for the man and I would say the same to anybody who ask. But this is ghetto. In the ghetto there is no such thing as peace. There is only this fact. Your power to kill me can only be stop by my power to kill you. You have people living in the ghetto who can only see within it. From me was a young boy all I could see was outside it. I wake up looking out, I go to school and spend the whole day looking out the window, I go up to Marescеaux Road and stand right at the fence that separate Wolmer's Boys' School from Mico College, just a zinc fence that most people don't know separate Kingston from St. Andrew, uptown from downtown, those who have it and those who don't. People with no plan wait and see. People with a plan see and wait for the right time. The world is not a ghetto and a ghetto is not the world. People in the ghetto suffer because there be people who live for making them suffer. Good time is bad time for somebody too.

That's why neither the JLP nor the PNP fucking with the peace treaty. Peace can't happen when too much to gain in war. And who want peace anyway when all that mean is that you still poor? This is what I thought Papa-Lo understand. You can lead a man to peace all you want. You can fly out the Singer and make him sing for money to build a new toilet in the ghetto. You can go wind your waste in Rae Town or in Jungle and par with man who only last year kill your brother. But a man can only move so far before the leash pull him back. Before the master say, Enough of that shit, that's not where we going. The leash of Babylon, the leash of the police code, the leash of Gun Court, the leash of the twenty-three families that run Jamaica. That leash get pull two weeks ago, when the Syrian pussyhole Peter Nasser try to talk to me in code. That leash get pull one week ago, when the American and the Cuban come with a colouring book to teach me about anarchy.

These three men leave me a busy man. Mr. Clark talk about Cuba like a man who can't accept that him woman don't want him no more. And he not letting that happen to Jamaica, whatever he think that might mean. Strange how a man wants to fuck with a country him never live in before. Maybe he should wait a year and then ask himself if this country really worth buying a Valentine's card for. I tell you, move with these white men long enough and you start to talk like them. Maybe that's why Peter Nasser now calling me busha. One vulgar politician waiting every day for a phone call from the airport about the coming Rasta apocalypse. One American who answer to an American who answer to an American who just want to step on this country to jump over to Cuba. And one Cuban, living in Venezuela, who want this Jamaican to help the Colombian ship his cocaine to Miami and move it on the street in New York, because the Bahamians was a bunch of battymen who started to freebase off their own supply and selling that shit local. Worse, those little pussies don't like how blood taste. Three men who want this fourth one, me, to shape 1979 for them. Me, I'm getting tired of doing what men want, including Papa-Lo.

But Papa-Lo energize himself for the mission of justice though. It run through him like a Flintstone vitamin. You'd think he was doing fifty-six acts of penance for the fifty-six bullets fired at Hope Road. Right before the second peace concert, I feed him Leggo Beast. Tell him that Leggo Beast was hiding in his mother cupboard just five house down from him, but didn't tell him that he was hiding there for two year now. The man take the news by sucking in the air. Couldn't tell if it was a wince or a sigh. He and Tony Pavarotti and some other man march down to the house like he was Jesus about to clean out the temple. He was going to turn it into a show, for the people, the ghetto and for even the Singer to see that he was taking revenge nobody ask him to take. Drag the boy and his mother out of the house and proceed to beat the poor woman who already past forty right in public.

Say what you want about a boy who try to kill the Singer, but it's a different story when is a mother trying to keep her only boy alive. But Papa-Lo must have people seeing him do something. Like he making a difference on something that already gone and done and can't change. He try to make an example out of her, burn down her entire life and kick her out with him own boot, but all he do was make an example out of himself. Like some naigger being extra wicked to impress the massa.

Then Leggo Beast start to scream that is the CIA that make him do it. The CIA and people from Cuba, which don't make no sense since everybody know that Cubans are communist and would not have any dealings with anybody from America. As if Papa-Lo knew anything more about the CIA than any Jamaican. Then Leggo Beast start to scream how this was my idea. I watch Papa-Lo watching me to see if I blink. Leggo Beast scream it for so long that he started to wonder if he should believe it, after all in Jamaica what don't go so, go near so. In fact that is exactly what he say to me when he come knocking on my door the day after I tell him where to look, with two youths so young that their gun was sliding down into their brief. I look at the two of them hard and both look away, the one on Papa's left fidgeting like some nervous girl. The other turn back and try to look. I mark him. Papa-Lo tapping his foot like he already annoyed.

—What no go so, go near so, he say.

—What Leggo Beast think him saying now? You don't know the proverb about the drowning man?

—Drowning man don't have time to make up a story with so much iration to it.

I squeeze my knuckles to stop myself from telling him that iration is not a word.

—And I don't have time to bring to the light why you can't trust an idiot like Leggo Beast. Two years to get as far away as a man could go, and the furthest he could reach was his mother cupboard?

—But you did know where to find him though, me brethren.

—The mother go shopping every week and always coming back with a big bag from the market. Why so much food when is only she one live there? You think she running a Salvation Army? The real question is how come you, the don of all dons, didn't even notice?

—Can't have eye in every nook and cranny, me good brother. That no be what me have you for?

—Oh. Well, don't ask me no idiot question 'bout the Singer when you know the answer already.

—True? So give me the answer quick then nuh? Since you—

—If it was me trying to kill the Singer, not one of those fifty-six bullets would have missed.

Always speak proper English when you want a man know that this argument is over. Papa-Lo walk away with the little boys hopping behind him. Little after that he taking Leggo Beast to a kangaroo court on McGregor Gully to prove to himself that he can still ration out rough justice. Some people say that the Singer himself show up to watch it, which strike me as a strange thing to do with the world watching him every move, but the only person whose word I would trust is Tony Pavarotti and he not saying nothing. Then he find some of the men involve in that horse-racing con and take them out to the old fort to turn them into fish food. Thing I want to ask: how all this blood on your hands work when you're on a mission for peace?

My living room is getting dark. I'm waiting for three phone calls. My big son walks past me holding a chicken leg. He's already looking so much like me that I had to rub my belly just to make sure that I'm the one with one.

—Boy, what you doing here and not by your mother? Hey, I talking to you.

—Cho man, Daddy. Me can't deal with her sometime, no lie.

—What you do to upset the poor woman now?

—She never like something me say 'bout you.

—Something I said about you. And it's didn't like.

—Cho man, Daddy.

—What you tell your mother?

—Haha, that even bad man can cook better than she.

—Hahahahahaha, boy, you not easy at all. But is true, though. I never know a woman who was such an enemy of the kitchen. Might be why I didn't stay with her too long. You lucky she never shoot you.

—Wha? Mama know what to do with a gun?

—You forget who her man used to be? What you think? Anyway, it too late for you to be walking 'round my house like duppy.

—But you awake. You always awake this late.

—Oh? What you doing, watching your father?

—No . . .

—Your lying about as good as your mother cooking.

Don't know how I didn't see this coming. I watch the boy, just one year in high school and not even twelve yet. He trying to be brave, looking straight at me, eye to eye and frowning a little because he don't know yet that you have to age into a stone face. It's the first time he doing it, he know and I know, the son trying to stare down the father. But boy is a boy and not a man. He can't hold it, not yet. He look aways first and just as quick turn on the stare again, but he just lose the round and he know it.

—I waiting on a phone call. Go bother your brother, I say and watch him walk off. The time soon come when it is me who must watch him.

One day, my son, you will know enough and see enough that you can get the last word. But not tonight. One phone call I don't want bothering me in the night is Peter Nasser. Is two months now since I first clue him in on the Rasta Apocalypse and he still either sweating blood or giving some stupid girl at Lady Pink the sloppiest seven minutes of her life. The point about the Singer was already proven, to him, to Jamaica, to Medellín—and Cali, but he wouldn't let it go. Why? Because even if the Singer wasn't going to be the voice of this new party, movement, whatever you want to call it, he was going to be something else far more important: the money. By now three thousand family see a little money every month because of the Singer, even the family of the boy who shoot him. Speaking of shooting up, even I get the shock of my life, the next time I see a picture of him in the *Gleaner.* There right beside him was Heckle.

Back on that night when Weeper stop the car near the Garbagelands and throw Heckle out, me never see head or tail of him again. Another one of those men I didn't realise was smarter than Weeper, if not braver, smart enough to make me think very carefully who I was keeping alive. So smart that he was the only one who catch the drift that after doing what we do there was not coming back. I like when a man can read writing on the wall. But Heckle should have known that he have nothing to worry about, retribution was coming for the stupid, not the smart. If I spoke to him I would have tell him, Brethren, don't fret. The world smarter with you still in it. Still he catch where the wind was blowing quick and flee, jumping out of the car like a dog let loose. Garbagelands wasn't even supposed to be his stop. Weeper sniff out where most of the men run off to, and those he couldn't find, the Rastas did. Nobody saying nothing about them, since the only evidence that Rastas was on the hunt was Demus swinging from a tree in the John Crow Mountains, the john-crows already gone with his eyes and lips. But nobody could say where to find Heckle. Not even him woman, not even after slapping her three time and grabbing her by the neck, almost strangling her. I tell you, that make me admire him even more, a man who was a genuine disappearer.

But then almost one year later, Papa-Lo come stomping to my house more mad than usual. Not just mad, but so perplexed his eyes almost crossed.

—He take the pussyhole on tour with him? You can imagine that? Him get this man a bombocloth visa.

—Calm down nuh, man, you no see say is five?

It really was evening, and peaceful in the ghetto.

—Me no understand it at all. Maybe he really is like the prophet. Me don't even know if Jesus would ever do such madness, and him did love to confound the wise.

—Who the Singer get visa for now?

It could only be the Singer he was talking about.

—Me never believe it until me see the little pussyhole hiding behind him like frighten fowl. Heckle. Heckle, me say.

—Heckle? For real?

Who knows where Heckle was hiding for almost two years? South Coast with the hippies? Cuba? Wherever he was, he just plant himself at 56 the third day after the Singer come back for the second concert. No gun, no shoes on and stinking of bush. Of course the Singer know exactly who he was even though I am sure he never see anybody. I don't know what to admire more, his bravery or his stupidity, but the man just walk up to Hope Road, walk past security when they see how him look like death, throw himself at the Singer feet when he come out of the house and beg forgiveness. Kill me or save me, what I hear him say. Of course every single living soul on that compound wanted to kill him. They wouldn't even need to worry what to do with the body.

Maybe it was lucky for Heckle that Papa-Lo wasn't there. Or maybe he was lucky that by now, the Singer only take the long view. Or maybe the Singer think that any man with hollow-out eyes like he smoked lizard tail weed, a smell like cow shit and bush, with shoes that give up once the first big toe burst out, couldn't get any lower. Or maybe he really is a prophet. The Singer not only forgive him, but move him quick into his inner circle, even taking the man with him when he leave Jamaica. Papa-Lo didn't find out until he see that picture in the *Gleaner.*

For the first time in years I have to rethink the Singer. Papa-Lo cussing about another situation over which he have no power. After the Singer bless which man would dare curse? Heckle turn untouchable. He never return to Copenhagen City either, or Jungle, or Rose Lane, but take up residence in the same house where he try to kill the people who live there. When he wasn't there he was all over the world.

Now it getting late and I'm still at the phone waiting for it to ring three times. These people know how I feel about being on time. I can't stand late and I hate early. On time means on time. One man has four minutes. The other have eight. The other have twelve.

—Kiss me neck, is all me children haunted tonight?

My youngest, the girl, is in the doorway yawning and rubbing her eyes. She's standing on one foot and rubbing her calf with the other. Her little Wonder Woman t-shirt pop out even in the dark. Her mother had plait her hair in two before bed, and I can bet she would be very mad if she see this little girl walking around late in the night, pulling her panty like they itch. She's not going to lose those cheeks, just as her mother never did. At least she light like her mother. No future for no dark girl in Jamaica, despite black power bullshit. I mean, look who just win Miss World.

—Duppy seal your mouth shut, little girl?

She don't say a thing. Instead she walk over to me, still pulling at her panty, and stop right at my knee. My girl rubs her eyes again and look at me long as if she's making sure it's me. Still quiet she grab my pants and pull herself up, climb up my knees and gone off to sleep in my lap. Did she get all this liberty taking from her mother or from me?

How did bad man business get done before the phone? Even I already forget how news used to come and go. First call in three minutes. Another phone call pop up in my head. Of course I know why. It's what Doctor Love call déjà vu. Right about when every sensible man get tired of this whole peace and love fuckery. About the time when Copper come down from the hill, as if people, meaning me, would forget what a pussyhole he was before the peace, raping woman after he killed their man. Even Papa-Lo, Mr. I-kill-any-man-that-rape-a-woman, let Copper slide and climb up Wareika Hills. Good times was bad times for somebody and the people about to experience bad times reach what the new American called critical mass. The critical mass realise what a woman whose man beat her also realise. Sure things bad, but don't mess with it if it working for you. This type of bad we know. Good? Sure good is good, but good is something that nobody know. Good is a ghost. You can't get pocket money from good. Jamaica better off bad, because that type of bad work. So when certain people find themselves going almost into panic from all this good vibes threatening the next election, especially when they seeing what was bound to come out of it, my phone start ringing. My woman took a message and it was only one word.

—Copper.

—Anything else? He said anything else?

—No, just Copper.

No problem for me, I hate the fat belly piece of fuckery from day one, but the peace didn't turn Copper into an idiot. He was safe up the hill and safe in Copenhagen City, even in the Eight Lanes. But he wasn't safe from the police. Copper didn't play in any pen he didn't know. So at the jam session in Rae Town one Sunday I say to him, You know, Copper, man like you who live in the hills, when last you taste fry fish?

—Woi, man, fi tell the I true, a long time me nuh nyam dem sinting deh.

—What? No, star, that not right. Tomorrow, tomorrow we going straight to the beach to get some fry fish and festival.

—Woi. Festival for true? Them fry it in the fish oil? What you is, di devil out fi tempt the I?

—Some roast yellow yam, roast corn with dry coconut, ten bammy, five steam with pepper, five frying in the same oil they frying the fish.

—Lawd, man.

—Have some of your man drive down to Fort Clarence.

—The stoosh beach? Ah wha you ah say?

—Me'll leave you name with security. Go on, act like you don't like it. Plenty fish and festival, you get to tramp down Babylon beach and no police nowhere.

—Man, if you was a woman me would drop down to me knee and married you. But brethren, me can't do that shit. Soon as me hit causeway three police would dress down 'pon me. And them not saying put your hands up.

—Brethren, use your head. Police think them smart. You think them don't know say bad man would try trick them by going by the back road.

—Well—

—Well nothing. Best way to hide is in plain sight.

—That sound like one fuckery idea.

—Me look like me ever come up with a fuckery idea my entire life? You want police to find you, take the dyke. Take Trench Town, take Maxfield Park Avenue. You want get to the beach in peace, drive on the very same road you 'fraid to drive on. Check this, after all these years you don't know how police think? Never in a million years they expect you to drive down Harbour Street in broad daylight. That's why they not going patrol it.

A glutton in one thing always turn out to be a glutton in everything. I tell Copper to ask for Miss Jeanie, a coolie woman with her own fish shack on the beach. She have two ripe half-coolie daughters named Betsy and Patsy. Take either of them back to your car and she will give you dessert. That same night I wake up the inspector with a phone call. Copper never reach the beach.

One minute.

Forty-five seconds.

Twenty seconds.

Five.

I grab the phone on the first ring. Too eager.

—Yeah?

—You mother never teach you manners? Decent people say hello.

—And?

—It is finished.

—Jesus know that you thiefing his words?

—Lord God, Josey Wales, don't tell me you're a God-fearing man.

—No, me only like Luke. Where?

—Causeway.

—Fifty-six time?

—What the bombocloth me look like, boss, the Count 'pon *Sesame Street*?

—Make sure somebody leak to the newspaper that it was fifty-six bullets. You hear me?

—Me hear you, sah.

—Fifty-six.

—Fifty-six. One more thing, I—

I hang up. Damn call was taking up all of the four minutes. He's not going to call back tonight.

Forty-three seconds.

Thirty-five seconds.

Twelve.

One.

Minus five.

Minus ten.

Minus a minute.

—You late.

—Sorry, boss.

—And.

—Boss. Boy, me no know how fi tell you.

—The best way would be to tell me.

—The man vanish, boss.

—Man don't vanish. Man don't disappear unless you disappear them.

—Him gone, boss.

—What the fuck you talking 'bout, idiot? How him just gone? Him have visa?

—Me don't know, boss, but we check everywhere. Home, him woman home, him second woman home, the Rae Town Community Center where him work some day, even the Singer house where he have office for the council. We lay-waiting him on every road since yesterday.

—And?

—Nothing. When we check back his house, everything there but one chest of drawers that totally clean out. Clean clean clean, not even cobweb.

—You telling me that one idiot Rasta manage to slip away from ten bad man? Just like that? What, you send word that you was coming for him?

—No, boss.

—Well, you better find him.

—Yes, boss.

—One more thing.

—Boss?

—Find out who leak this to him and kill him. And brethren: If you don't find him in three days, I will kill you.

I wait for him to hang up.

Bombo r'asscloth.

Shit.

I don't know if I say it or think it. But she still sleeping, my right knee soaking with drool. Tristan Phillips, the Rasta who was actually drawing up peace map and chairing the Unity council, just disappear. Just like that. Add him to man like Heckle. Dead or not dead, the man clearly gone. And given how dumb he is already, Peter Nasser not going to be none the wiser. I just realise that I miss a call that didn't come. From a man who is never late. Never ever.

Five minutes late.

Seven minutes.

Ten minutes late.

Fifteen.

Twenty.

Tony Pavarotti. I pick up the phone and hear tone, but I put it down and it rings.

—Tony?

—No, is me, Weeper.

—What you want, Weeper?

—Yow is which ants in your panty tonight?

—How you know I would be awake?

—Everybody know that you don't sleep. You at the level now.

—What? You know what, it's too late to ask what that mean. Anyway, come off the line, I expecting a call.

—From who?

—Pavarotti.

—When him supposed to call?

—Eleven o'clock.

—Him nah call you, star. If it was eleven the bredda woulda call you at eleven. You know how him stay.

—I was thinking the same thing.

—Why you have him calling you so late?

—Sent him to clean up some business at the Four Seasons.

—Minor matter like that and him don't call you back yet? Me surprised you don't send two man to check him—

—Don't tell me what to do, Weeper.

—Man, you really itching in your panty.

—I don't like when the one dependable man in Copenhagen City, I can't depend on.

—Ouch.

—Ouch? You pick up that from your new American friends?

—Maybe. Look. Maybe something happen and he have to lay low. You know him, he not going call you until the job done good. Not before.

—I don't know.

—I do. Anyway, how come everybody seem to know plans was changing but me? Me almost look like an idiot in front of that Colombian bitch.

—Brethren, how much me must tell you don't discuss them things over me phone?

—Cho r'asscloth man, Josey. We deal with the bush. You tell me when you send me here that we must deal with the bush, you never tell me nothing 'bout the white wife.

—Brethren, I tell you this four time already. Bush is too much trouble and take up too much damn space. Besides, Yankee growing their own bush now and don't needs ours. The white wife take up less space and make seven times more money.

—Me no know, man. Me just don't like them Cubans, man. The communists was bad enough, but them in American worse to r'ass. And none of them can drive.

—Cubans or Colombians? Weeper, me really can't deal with you and them right now.

—Especially that woman, you know she mad, right? She who running the whole thing. She mad no r'ass. Brethren, she lick pussy all night then kill the girl the next day.

—Who tell you that?

—Me know that.

—Weeper, I'll call you tomorrow from Jamintel. Night like this, one phone can have two ears. In the meantime go somewhere and enjoy yourself. Plenty enjoyment for men like you.

—Oy, what that mean?

—It mean what me bombocloth say it mean. And nothing like that shit you do in Miramar last week.

—Yow what you expect me fi do? The man grab me—

—What you think I should do about Pavarotti?

—Give him till morning. If you don't hear from him, you'll hear about him soon enough.

—Good night, Weeper. And don't trust that Colombian bitch. Only last week I realise that she's only a pit stop to where we really going.

—Ah. So where that is, my youth?

—New York.

Sir Arthur George Jennings

Now *something* new is blowing through the air, an ill wind. A malaria. Still more will have to suffer, and many more will have to die, two, three, a hundred, eight hundred and eighty-nine. Meanwhile I see you whirling like a dervish, under the rhythm and above it, jumping up and down the stage, always landing on your Brutus toe. Years before on the football field, a player wearing running spikes—who plays football in running spikes?—stomped on your cleats and slashed the toe. When you were still a boy you nearly sliced it in two with a hoe. A cancer is a rebellion, a cell gone rogue against the body with turncoats turning the other way and seducing parts of you to do the same. I will divide your parts and conquer. I will shut down your limbs one by one, and spill poison in your bones because look, there is nothing in me but blackness. No matter how many times your mother wrapped it in gauze and sprinkled it with Gold Bond medicated powder, your toe was never going to heal.

And now something new is blowing. Three white men have knocked on your door. Five years before the first warned you not to leave. Deep into 1978, the third—they always knew where to find you—warned you not to come back. The second came bearing gifts. You can't even remember him now, but he came like one of the three Wise Men, with a box wrapped like Christmas. You opened it and jumped—somebody knew that every man in the ghetto wished he was The Man That Shot Liberty Valance. Brown boots, snakeskin, flirting with red; somebody knew you loved boots almost as much as you loved brown leather pants. You pulled on the right boot and screamed like that boy who chopped his foot trying to split a coconut. You pulled off the boot, flung it aside and watched your big toe spurt blood with every pump of your pulse. Gilly and Georgie, they had knives handy. An incision in the stitch, flaying the skin of the boot, and there it was, a thin pointed copper wire, a straight and perfect needle that made you think of Sleeping Beauty.

Something new is blowing. At the foot of Wareika Hills, the man called Copper leaves the house and closes the gate. Navy blue night is running and passing, passing and running. He makes two steps and doesn't make a third. The man called Copper drops and spits the little blood that doesn't rush out of his chest and belly. The gunman drops the M1, changes his mind, picks it up, then runs to the car already on the move.

You are in the studio with the band making a new tune. Clocks tick by in Jamaica time. Watchers take two hits of the collieweed and pass on the left. Two guitar leads wrap around each other coiling tight like a snake fight. The new guitarist with shorter dreads, the rocker who loves Hendrix plugs out. You shoot him a quick look with eyes wide open.

—Don' leave! Me don't have much time.

Something new is blowing. The don called Papa-Lo rides home from the races in a taxi cruising down the causeway with the windows rolled down. Somebody makes a joke and the sea salt wind snatches his wide laugh. The road does not bend, just curves into a bridge rising up then leading down into three police cars blocking the road. He knows they know who he is even before his driver stops. They know he knows they know, even before they shout ROUTINE SPOT CHECK. He knows before they arrive, that there will be more cars creeping up behind him. Police number one says remove from the vicinity of the cyar so that we can search the cyar. Move h'over to the left and keep walking till you is in front of the wild bush by the side of the road. Police number two finds his .38. Police number 3, 4, 5, 6, 7, 8, 9, 10, 11, 12, 13, 14, 15 and 16 fire. Some will say forty-four, some will say fifty-six bullets, the exact number of shells found at 56 Hope Road that week in December 1976.

You're playing football in Paris, in the green field below the Eiffel Tower. You play with anyone up for a game. Starstruck white boys and that man from the French national team. Your crew, even after years of touring, never get used to it, cities that never sleep. They are sluggish, even though it's afternoon. The French do not play like the British. None of this single player peacock business. These boys move like a unit even though most have not even met before. One of them makes a bad play, steps hard on your right toe and tears the nail off.

Something new is blowing. The man who had me killed pays the Wang Gang sixty dollars a day to shoot up on two of the Eight Lanes. The two lanes nearest the sea. Lanes run wild with rusting zinc fences and corrosive shit water. The gang drives up at random lulls in the day, opening fire with all guns in a total sweep. A torrent of bullets. A shower.

You are in London. Cut off that toe, cut it off right now, the doctor says without looking you in the face. Stuff those boots with tissue, with cotton, with putty and mum's the word. The room smells of antiseptic thrown on shit to mask it. And of iron, as if somebody in the next ward is scouring steel pots. But Rasta already think a lame toe is a curse from God, what do you think they'll make of an amputated one? You are in Miami. The doctor cuts out the spot and grafts skin from the left foot. It's a success, he says, but not with those words, you can't remember the words exactly. But he says your cancer is gone, you have no cancer. And every night that you stomp down Babylon from the stage, your right boot fills near the brim with blood.

Something new is blowing. Tony McFerson, the PNP member of Parliament, and his bodyguard are trapped in August Town. Gunmen from the hills but allied with Copenhagen City descend on the two and open fire. They fire back. Gunmen blast holes in the car door, the window, and bullets bounce off the windshield. The gunmen shell heavy, but stay far back behind fence and bush reined in with barbwire. Sirens, police, the gunmen's footsteps in a mad retreat that fades with each step. Car wheels whip up gravel and spin until they grip the road. Sirens cut off, boots hit the ground, the police are getting closer, louder. Tony McFerson stands up first with a wide smile on his face, a heave and a sigh of relief one could see from four hundred feet away. The third bullet goes through his neck sideways, explodes the medulla and kills everything below the neck before his brain realizes he's dead.

You are in New York. It's September 21. Everybody knows you were always the first to wake and the last to go to sleep, especially in the studio. Nobody notices you haven't done either in a year. You wake up burning, the mattress has sucked two pounds of water from your skin but you can hear the air conditioner humming somewhere near you. You think of the pain on the right side of your head and it's there. Now you wonder if the pain was just a thought until you thought about it. Or maybe the pain was in you for so long that it became an unseen part of the body, a mole hidden between toes. Or maybe you did speak a curse into being, like the old women up in the hills would say. You do not know it's September 21, you have no memory of the second show the night before, you have no idea where you are or who is here with you, but at least you know this is New York.

Something new is blowing. Icylda says to Christopher make sure you eat up all your food, you think chicken back cheap? Her boy swallows three bites in one gulp and makes a dash for the door. He halts and grabs the vinyl on the counter, a hot dub pressed that day. You just remember you have work tomorrow, Icylda says, but laughs and shoos him out the door. The cha-cha boys on Gold Street are dressed to impress in gabardine pants and polyester shirts and the sexy gals them hot and ready in tight jeans, halter top and ting. The sound system done playing Tamlins and just drop brand-new wax, the new Michigan & Smiley, but Christopher has something new from Black Uhuru that goin' murda di dance. Boys and girls press tight, winding up on each other while the bass jumps on the chest and sits there. But who bring firecrackers to the party? Not firecrackers but heavy rain bang bang banging on the zinc. But nobody getting wet, Jacqueline says out loud just as two bullets blow a hole in her right breast. Her scream vanishes in the middle of everybody. She looks back once, shadows coming from the sea, the five-point blast of light when a machine gun fires. The Selecter takes one through the neck and falls. People are running and screaming, and stampeding over fallen girls. Dropping one two three. More men come from the sea but wearing night colours and lights. They fan out and sweep. Jacqueline jumps over the zinc fences slicing behind her knees, she runs down Ladd Lane with screams still following her. She forgets that blood is shooting from her breast, falls in the middle of the lane. Two hands pick her up and drag her away.

Gunfire raining on zinc, Gold Street men have only two guns. More men arrive from the sea, some by land, all three exits closed off. Gunfire like rain wake up the sleeping policemen a few hundred feet away who grab their guns and run to a padlocked door. The Rastafarian has nowhere to run and the men are coming. Behind people fall down in a slow wave. Fat Earl on the ground just bubbling blood. The Rastafarian throws himself on Fat Earl, not yet dead, and rolls all over him to pick up the blood. By the time the gunmen get to him, they think he's the one really dead and shoot Fat Earl. The gunmen retreat to the sea.

You are jogging around a pond at Central Park South. Different country, same crew, and for a second you feel as if you're back in Bull Bay before sunrise. A run on the black sand beach, a dip in the waterfalls, maybe some football, working up a healthy appetite for breakfast all cooked by Gilly and waiting for you to get back. But you're still in New York and humidity is already sweeping in. You lift your left leg high, widening your stride before it hits the dirt but your right leg refuses to move. Your hip swings—is wah kinda fuckery this?—but your right leg just won't move. Lift it without thinking. That doesn't work. Lift it with thinking. That doesn't work either. And now your left won't move. Both legs stall even after you've commanded them to with three bombocloths. Your friend is coming up behind and you turn to call out, but your neck twists about a half inch and locks. No nodding yes, no nodding no. A scream vanishes on the way from your throat to your lips. Your body is leaning and you can't stop it. No it's not leaning but toppling and you cannot stretch your arms to break the fall. The ground slams into you, face first.

You wake up in the Essex House. Hands and feet recover but the fear lingers. Too weak to leave the bed, you don't know they lied to your wife only minutes before and turned her away. You wake up and smell sex, smoke and whiskey. You see and wait but nobody listens, nobody looks, nobody comes. Your ears wake up to friends running up charges to the room, friends snorting foot after foot of white, friends fucking groupies, friends fucking whores, friends fucking friends, Rastaman on freebase raping the sacred chillum pipe. Men in suits, men on the make, businessmen drinking your wine; your room a temple waiting for Jesus to scour. Or some prophet. Or any prophet. But you sink in the bed thankful that at least you can move your neck. Brooklyn boys pass by with guns, Brooklyn boys with dicks, Rasta fire all doused out. You have no strength to stand, no lips to curse so you whisper *please close the door.* But nobody hears and when Essex House bloats and bursts, the friends spill into 7th Avenue.

Something new is blowing. A reverse evolution. Men, women and children in the Rose Town ghetto start by standing and walking, sometimes running from school to home, home to shop, shop to rum bar. By noon everybody sits, to play dominoes, to eat lunch, to do homework, to gossip about the slut on Hog Shit Lane. By afternoon everybody stoops down on the house floor. By evening they crawl from room to room and eat dinner on the floor like bottom-feeders. By night everybody is flat on the linoleum but nobody is asleep. Children lie on their backs and wait for the burst of bullets on zinc like hail. Bullets in traffic with bullets, zipping through windows, across ceilings, bursting holes in walls, mirrors, overhead lights and any fool that stands up. Meanwhile the man who killed me is on TV; Michael Manley and the PNP need to call the election date now.

You collapse in Pittsburgh. It's never a good thing hearing doctors talk using a word that ends with oma. The oma has hopped, skipped and jumped from your foot to your liver, lungs and brain. In Manhattan they blast you with radium and your locks drop and scatter. You go to Miami, then Mexico to the clinic that couldn't save Steve McQueen.

November 4. Your wife arranges a baptism in the Ethiopian Orthodox Church. Nobody knows that your name is now Berhane Selassie. You are a Christian now.

Something new is blowing. On a downtown Kingston wall: IMF—Is Manley Fault. General election called for October 30, 1980.

Somebody is driving you through Bavaria, near the Austrian border. A hospital sprouting out of the forest like magic. Hills in the background tipped with snow like cake icing. You meet the tall and frosty Bavarian, the man who helps the hopeless. He smiles but his eyes are set too far back and they vanish in the shadow of his brow. Cancer is a red alert that the whole body is in danger, he says. Thank God the food he forbids, Rastafari had forbidden long time. A sunrise is a promise.

Something new is blowing. November 1980. A new party wins the general election and the man who killed me steps up to the podium with his brothers to take over the country. He has been waiting for so long he leaps up the stairs and trips.

The Bavarian bows out. Nobody speaks of hope, nobody speaks of anything. You are in Miami with no memory of the flight. May 11, eyes open, you're the first one up (just like old times), but all you see are old woman's hands overrun with black veins and bony, jutting kneecaps. A plastic machine with veins pushed into your skin, doing all the living for you. You already feel like sleep, probably from all the drugs, but this one comes on like a creeper and you already know that wherever you go this time, there is no coming back. Something coming from out the window sounding like that Stevie Wonder tune "Master Blaster"? In New York City and in Kingston, both skies blazing bright with noon white, thunder breaks out and a lightning bolt slashes through the clouds. Summer lightning, three months too early. The woman waking up in Manhattan and the woman sitting on the porch in Kingston both know. You're gone.

WHITE LINES / KIDS IN AMERICA

August 14, 1985

Dorcas Palmer

You *know how* them girl stay, come all the way to America and still going on like them is some dutty whore from Gully. Me tired of them girl so till. Me just tell one nasty slut who was working with Miz Colthirst. Nasty slut, me say, as long as you working for this here job and living under that there roof, you better lock up that pum-pum, you understand me? Lock up the pum-pum. Of course the bitch never listen so now she pregnant. Of course Miz Colthirst have to let her go—on my recommendation of course. Can you imagine? Some little stinking bottom naigger pickney a run rapid 'round the place? On 5th Avenue? No, baba. The white people would have one of them white people things, a conniption to rahtid.

—So does she go by Miss Colthirst or Ms. Colthirst?

—*So does she go by Miss Colthirst or Miz Colthirst*? What a way you stocious. Them going like you quick. Boy sometime not even me know which. Soon as she start read some magazine name *Ms.*, she say she name Miz Colthirst, me love. Me just say ma'am.

—Ma'am? Like some slavery thing?

For once she looked like she didn't know what to answer. Is three years now I'm with God Bless Employment Agency and every time I come in here, she has a brand-new story about some ghetto slut who got pregnant on her watch. What I don't understand is why she always feels I'm the person to tell these things to. I'm not trying to be understanding or empathetic, I just want a fucking job so that my slum lord doesn't kick me out of my top-class fifth-floor walk-up with a toilet that makes all sorts of murder sounds when you flush it, and rats that now feel they can just sit up on the couch and watch TV with me.

—Try no use them slavery word around the Colthirst. New York people who live on Park Avenue very antsy about them kinda remark.

—Oh.

—At least you have one of them Bible names they love on a Jamaican. Me even get a man one of them jobs last week—can you imagine? Probably because he name Hezekiah. Who knows? Maybe them think that nobody with name from the good book going thief from them. You not no thiefing girl?

She asks me this every week I come to pick up my pay, even though I've been here three years. But now she looks at me like she really wants an answer. The Colthirsts aren't the usual clients clearly. Where is my tenth-grade teacher now for me to tell her what doors I've opened in life just from knowing how to speak correctly. Miss Betsy is looking at me. Some jealousy sure, but every woman have that in them. Some envy too because I have what beauty contestants call deportment, after all I am a high school–educated girl from Havendale St. Andrew. Pride, of course, because she have somebody she can finally use to impress the Colthirsts, so much so that she probably trump up some false bullshit on the last girl just to get her fired. But pity too, that one most definitely. She's wondering how a girl like me come to this.

—No, Miss Betsy.

—Good, good, wonderful good.

Don't ask me why I was walking on Broadway past 55th because not a damn thing was going on, on that street or in my life. But sometimes, I don't know, walking down a New York street . . . well it doesn't make your problems easier or manageable but it does make you feel you can just walk. Not that I have problems. Actually I don't have a thing. And I'll bet anybody that my nothing is bigger than their nothing any day of the week. Sometimes having nothing to worry about makes me worry, but that would be some psychological bullshit to make me feel busy. Maybe I'm just bored. People here with three jobs and looking for a fourth and I wasn't even working.

And that meant walking. Even I know it don't make no sense, though it explains why these people never stop walking, even to somewhere you can get to on the subway. You really do wonder if anybody works in this city. Why are there so many people in the street? So I was walking down Broadway from 120th. I don't know, there comes a point when you're walking that you've walked too far and there's really nothing to do but continue. Until what, I don't know. I always forget until I find myself walking again. And besides it was only a few blocks before Times Square and Lord knows you only need ten minutes in Times Square to miss a quaint charming little place like West Kingston. Not like I'd be caught dead in West Kingston. Anyway, walking down Broadway past 55th Street and looking out for freaks, flashers and everything I always saw on TV but never see here (except for bums and none of them ever look like Gary Sandy undercover). The little sign was failing to stick out between two Chinese restaurants on 51st. God Bless Employment Agency, which was enough to make it clear Jamaicans run it, but if that didn't do it, then the proverb at the bottom of the sign, "*A Soft Answer Turneth Away Wrath*," which didn't have a fucking thing to do with anything, certainly did. The only thing left was to add INTERNATIONAL in the title. But I had some nerve thinking I could talk down to a place that existed to help losers like me, after all there was only so many times you could call your American ex in Arkansas and ask for money to help before he said, Fine, I'll send you some cash, but if you ever call my house again and threaten to talk to my wife I'll just make a little call to the INS and you'll see if you don't find your conniving nigger ass on the next fucking flight back to Jamaica clutching one of those clear plastic bags they give deportees so all of JFK airport knows which brand of panty shields you use. I didn't want to tell him that the word nigger didn't quite have the kick he was counting on, nor bitch, nor cunt, since Jamaican girl don't response to none of them things. But yeah, I was in no position to walk past anywhere called Employment Agency. His last gift was running out.

—You know why me giving you the job? 'Cause you is the first girl to come in here with some manners.

—Really, Miss Betsy?

We've also had this conversation before. She runs an employment agency that places mostly black women, mostly immigrants, into these posh houses to take care of their very young children or very old parents who, news to me, have the very same needs. In exchange for us putting up with whatever shit, sometimes literally shit, they don't ask questions about immigration or employment status. So everybody wins. Well two people win, I just collect the money. I don't know. It's one thing when you ask your boss for cash, but it's something else when the employer is only too happy to give it to you.

The first client she sent me to was a white middle-aged couple in Gramercy, too busy to notice their weak mother smelling like cat shit and talking about those poor boys on the USS *Arizona.* She was in a room by herself with the thermostat set at fifty degrees at all times. The first time I met the couple the wife didn't look at me at all and the husband looked at me too long. Both wore all black and the same black round glasses, like John Lennon. She just said to the wall beside me, She's in there, do what must be done. For a split second, I wondered if they expected me to kill the woman. And what woman? In the room was nothing but pillows and a bedsheet heaped up on the bed. I had to come in closer to see that there was a little old woman in the middle of the bed. The piss and shit nearly made me walk out, until I remembered the money orders were done coming from Arkansas.

Anyway, I lasted three months, and it wasn't the shit. There always comes a point when you living in a house with a man when he start to think he can walk around with no clothes on. The first time he do it, I could tell he was really hoping I would be taken aback, but I just saw another old person to nurse. The fifth time, he said the wife was gone to her Mother of Veterans meeting and I said, So you need me to figure out where you misplace your drawers? The seventh time he jiggled it in front of me and I start laughing so loud I hiccupped. The mother in the room started shouting what was the joke and I told her. Hey, I didn't care. She laughed too, saying his father was just the same, always putting on a show even when nobody bought any seats. From that day the mother was always sharp around me, she even developed a little sass. Too much sass for cocky jiggler. I quit before he fired me, and told Miss Betsy that while I will scoop up any load of shit, I'll have nothing to do with a withered white penis. She was impressed that I managed to stay in standard English the whole time, even when I asked if this was a whorehouse with granny care as a fringe benefit.

—Is must be Immaculate High School you come from, she said.

—Holy Childhood, I said.

—Same difference, she said.

The day John Lennon was killed I was walking my second job in the park. Another old woman, whose forgetfulness didn't yet reach the point where she forgot that she forgets. I had already taken her to the park, and was about to go to bed, when she suddenly said she wanted to go to the Dakota and would not shut up about it. It was either us walking or she flying into hysterics, which usually ended with her screaming that these strange people and a negro had kidnapped her.

—I want to go, damn it, you can't stop me, she said. Her daughter looked at me like I was hiding her Valium. Then she just fanned the two of us off. Spent the entire night outside the Dakota with her and maybe two thousand other people. I think we sang "Give Peace a Chance" all night. At some point I started singing too and even started crying. She died two weeks later.

The next week I went to a Jamaican club in Brooklyn called Star Track. Don't ask me why, I don't like reggae and I don't dance. And Lord knows I've never had any use for this community. But I felt like I just had to since I couldn't get those deaths out of my head. The place was some old building with three floors, almost a brownstone. As I walked in Gregory Isaacs' "Night Nurse" was playing. Some men and women looked at me like it was their job to sum up who came through the door, as if this was some western or something. Every now and then there was a whiff of either ganja or cigar smoke. If I stayed here long enough somebody from Jamaica was bound to think she recognized me, which just felt like the worst thing ever. Because at some point that bitch would ask me what was I doing, and before I answer, would tell me about what she's been doing and where she's living and who got totally fat and who's just breeding like a fucking rabbit.

At some point the Rasta eyeing me since I came in slid up to me at the bar and told me I needed a back rub. This was the part where they taught you that if you ignore men they would go away. Except boys were always in the same class. At least let's look at the man, somebody in my head who sounded a lot like me said. Dreads yes, but clearly groomed by a hairdresser. Light skin, almost a coolie, and lips thick but still too pink even after years of cigarettes trying to blacken them. What's Yannick Noah doing here, I would have asked if I thought he knew who that was. He asked me if I thought the Singer was going to recover because it really doesn't look too good. I came this close to asking what type of Jamaican uses a phrase like doesn't look too good. I really don't want to talk about the Singer, I said. I really don't. He kept talking with the little Jamaican accent he got from his parents or maybe his neighbors. I didn't have to hear him shorten Montego Bay to Montego, instead of Mobay, to know he wasn't a real Jamaican. He gave himself away the second he asked me if I had cum. He left his number on the dresser when I was asleep. Part of me was prepared to be offended if I saw money under the note, but part of me kinda was hoping it was at least fifty bucks.

It's 1985 and I don't want to think I've been fucking no-commitment Jamericans and wiping old ass for four years, but work is work and a life is a life. Anyway, so the ma'am put me up with the Colthirsts who for a change had an old man to take care of. I don't know. It's one thing to have to clean woman parts but man parts was another thing entirely. Yeah, a body is a body, but no part of a woman body can get stiff and poke me dress. But then who was I fooling? The man probably hadn't poked anything since Nixon wasn't a crook. Still it was a man.

First day, August 14. Eighty West 86th Street, between Madison and Park. Fifteenth floor. I knocked on the door and this man looking like Lyle Waggoner opens it. I just stood there looking like an idiot.

—You must be the new girl they hired to wipe my ass, he says.

Weeper

S*omebody pull* the sheet off. Looking at myself, my chest puffing in, my chest puffing out, some hair, two nipples, cock gone to sleep on me belly. Look left at him, he wrapped himself around in the sheet tight like caterpillar three days before butterfly. Not cold weather just cool morning. He lying there like somebody agree to let him stay or get too tired to disagree. First I thought him was just a spic with blond hair dye but he said he was a hundred percent honky juice, cousin. Morning, so say the clock by the bed, on his side. Outside the window, nothing in the sky proving morning right. Brooklyn navy blue. Streetlight throwing darkness in alleyway where man get kill, woman get rape and pitiful fool get mug with two bitch-slaps, the tax for being a sucker.

Three weeks ago, Saturday night, check the scene. Walking home the short way, the white trick, skinny muscle tight inside the cut-off t-shirt, not gym ripped but crackhead ripped and walking step behind like a Muslim wife. None of we saying nothing but Deniece Williams singing *Let's hear it for the boy* behind a glass window two floors up with a line of panty hanging on the fire escape. *Scope this ill faggot-ass bullshit* this nigger say, popping out of the alley wall like him was a jigsaw piece. You two fudgepackers pick the wrong ghetto to get on with that nasty-ass shit. White crackhead inched back and I said stop. He's still inching so I turn me head and look at him. Stop, I say. White boy make a sound like a snake hiss, something say the nigger about to get the drop on you. I quick-dodge the knife-carrying hand to the left, pull him down with me left hand, swing 'round my back to him and flick up my right hand. Knuckle right in the nose. Nigger yelling, but not before I knee him balls, take 'way the knife, then grab him left wrist, push against a board-up window and crucify the motherfucker. Nigger now screaming when I say to the white boy, *Now you can run.* Him laughing hard. We running, and grabbing, and laughing, and hardening, and stopping and a tongue in me mouth before I say I don't use tongue. By the time we get to me walk-up, we leaping step two by two. Last flight of step, belt buckle pull, pants drop to the floor, brief down to the knee and battyhole up. You're not worried about the gay cancer? He spit and push it in. No, I say.

Three week now.

Today.

So morning. Foot already on the ground. Sun soon coming one way or another. East north east. Pull this end of the cover and roll him out. Him going fall on the floor but at least that going stop the snoring. Boy wrap up himself tight like is protection, against what? Pull, tug, pull, tug, yank, pull, tug and in all of this the fucking boy didn't even wake up. Try to remember him face. Brown hair, red beard, scruff. Red scruff all over kid-white chest. Oh you're a bad boy, huh? he say every time he push in deep. Finally roll him out of the covers and he now on him back. Not even that wake him. Sleep perchance he dead. Yesterday the Strand didn't have no Bertrand Russell. Not many people know I'm a thinking man. Maybe open a window. Maybe get back in bed and rub him hairy chest and nipples and put my tongue in him navel, move down and suck him awake. Last night he was another mind who find out something new. Don't think the man getting fucked must be the bitch. I shut him mouth and show him what my hole was for. I love you—I don't mean that, I said.

Kick him foot and kick him out.

Leave him and he might be here when you get back.

Leave him there and come back to a house so clean empty that he even move off with the cockroach. Kick him foot and kick him out.

Leave him here and share a line when you come back. He didn't ask for money.

In the sky a pink spot, east north east. Sun definitely coming on now. The spic rolls over on his side then back on his back. Think like a movie.

This part you put on your clothes, boy wake up (but boy would be a girl) and one of you say babe, I gotta go. Or stay in bed and do the whatever, the sheet at the man waist but right at the woman breast. Never going to be a movie with a scene like this bedroom ever. Don' know. Could go back in bed right now, move in under him right arm and stay there for five days. Yes. Do it. Do it now. Today can be the one day that can go by without me. Do it. Is not a boy this, is a man this. In the bed spread out now like he welcoming everything and not worried about nothing. Lookin' at what just went up in me last night. Bad man don't take no cock. But me not bad, me worse. Bad man don't make a man know he fucking him good, because then he will realize a man on the top. Better to stand up or bend over so he come from behind and invade. Moan a little, hiss, say work it harder, fucker, like a white girl getting black cock in a blue movie. But you really want to yell and scream and howl, yes I read *Howl*, fucking facety white boy you think just 'cause me black and from the ghetto me can't read? But this is not about ignorant white boy, is about you wanting so bad to howl and bawl but you can't howl and bawl because to howl and bawl is to give it up and you can't give it up, not to another man, not a white man, not any man, ever. As long as you don't bawl out you not the girl. You not born for it.

Come out of prison and say fuck the Bible, a hole is just a hole. Make a deposit or a make withdrawal and leave something in. Either you is the depositor or you is the bank. Either way, in prison you always carrying something in your asshole, and all the battyholes behind bars add up to one trade route. Asshole in the east take goods to asshole in the west, destination: inmate in the south with money or other goods. Bag of cocaine, pack of Wrigley's, Hershey bar, Snickers, Milky Way, ganja, hashish, beeper, toothpaste, diet pill, Xanax, Percocet, sugar, aspirin, cigarette, lighter, tobacco, golf ball with tobacco or cocaine, rolling paper, matches, Lip Smackers, lubricant, syringe with eraser over the needle, fifteen lottery tickets. Three year in prison and a dick is just another thing to put up your ass. Man lying in the bed he didn't sound like a Noo Yawker. Don't think about seeing him again. A cock is just a dick. Rahtid me can't even remember pussy. Not since Miami and fuck Griselda Blanco. I have to go to the airport.

Six-fifteen. In nine hours Josey on a plane from Jamaica. In twelve to thirteen hours he going be here. We going to a house in Brooklyn that he mark out from in Jamaica. Every block in New York have a crack house and a crack house is a crack house, but he want to see this certain crack house. He want to see up front who buying the rock and who selling it, so he can report personally to Medellín. That is what he say on the phone. I ask him if this was a secure line. He laugh for three minutes and say, Do your work and stop watch TV. New York need to be lock tight like Miami, he say, but he didn't say that he really don't believe me can do it. I just want to move in right under this man arm and live there. He said he coming to New York to cool out from Jamaica. But Jamaica need a serious cool-out from Josey Wales. A posse man pass through Brooklyn two week ago and tell me news about what go down in May.

Easter come and gone and Rema, the bump on Copenhagen City backside, acting up as per usual. Nobody know where the Garbagelands end and Rema begin but at least one time per year they puff their chest and declare they want more. More than being Copenhagen City frocktail, and think they can demand and threaten things like go over to the PNP. Garbage to the north and sea to the south but don't eat any fish them get catch. Saturday night, nine p.m, maybe ten and maybe still hot. Man playing domino, woman washing clothes in the back by the standpipe. Girls and boys playing Dandy Shandy. Six car draw down in the middle of the street and fan out, three to the left, three to the right. Josey and five man jump out of the first car. Fifteen more man jump out of the other five, everybody have M16. Josey and him posse sweep down the road, and man, woman and pickney running and screaming. A man and a woman run to they house but Josey follow close and clip the two right by they door. Man open fire and shoot up all playing domino, two man try to run but got trap in the bullet dance. Woman grabbing pickney and running. The posse run from house to house, fence to fence, sticking they hand over the zinc and ratatatat. Where the men be? Nineteen gunmen run and fire, people running mad like ants. Josey Wales walk, he never run. He see a target, consider it, walk up slow and kill. Posse men mark a pattern in the zinc with bullet. Somebody shoot a pickney. The woman screaming too loud and bawling too long so Josey walk up to her and put the gun right the back of her head. Josey and the posse draw away from Rema, twelve people dead. Police draw down on Copenhagen City and take away two gun, but that is all. Nobody can touch the don.

Josey coming to NYC. Don't know he if come here before, he never say. Him brethren in the Bronx take charge of uptown. Two peas, one pod, they go back from 1966. The brethren was selling weed from 1977, but branch to cocaine before it become the white wife. He dealing big as fuck: three hundred thousand pound ganja, twenty thousand pound cocaine. Bronx is the base and from the base he get product to Toronto, Philadelphia and Maryland. Don't know him good and Josey don't need me working for him. Or maybe he tell Josey don't send that man up here. When him posse need a beast, he ship man from Kingston, Montego Bay and St. Ann. A loose cannon is what he call me, but not to me, he say it to Josey.

Josey coming to NYC. This is about me. Is not about me and is not about the man in the bed. As soon as a Jamaican come to New York he vanish. He hitch right beside other yard man in the Bronx so they can build a Jamdown between Boston Road and Gun Hill. Not me. Me want to vanish, that's why me leave Miami for New York. Not coming till night, I don't have nowhere to go. Three and a half line of coke right there on the coffee table. The man right here in bed on him back. Him hands behind him head and he looking at me. Last week in the East Village, a parking lot behind this apartment building. A white boy sprawl out and boasty on a chaise longue like say the beach was one block over. Brown hair, red beard, red scruff all over white chest, and blue shorts he roll up so high me first think him was wearing a bikini. Sunbathing, he say. I ask him if he mean that lying just so in the sun would make him clean. He pull a cigarette from a pack of Newports and give me one.

—Not from around here?

—Huh?

—You're not from around here.

—Uh. No.

—Looking?

—Ah . . . no . . .

—Then how you're gonna know when you found it?

Tristan Phillips

I *see you* just give me the look, Alex Pierce. No, not the look you giving me now, not that owl staring into a flashlight look, the one you give me fifteen seconds ago. I know that look. You been carefully studying me for a while now, how much months, six? Seven maybe? You know how prison is, everybody lose count of days even with a calendar right over the toilet. Or maybe you don't know. Honestly from what I hear from Jimmy the Vietnam vet, prison is just like boot camp. Boring more than anything else. Nothing to do but see and wait. You don't have nothing to wait on, but you realise you don't need to, you just in the middle of wait and once you forget the what for, there's nothing but the wait. You should try it.

Right now I count down days by how long before I going have to shit a crack vial out of my ass and slip into some guard pocket so it will buy me one more month of keeping my locks. A boy said to me only last week, But dready, how you manage to keep your locks in prison so long? They must think you have fifteen shank hiding in there. I tell him, sorry, *told* him—I keep forgetting you're taping this—that it take me years to convince the powers that be that if a Muslim brother can keep his cap and dye his beard red, then I have the right to keep my dread. When that didn't work I tell them what they want to hear; with so many lice and ticks in there, to even touch it might give them Lyme disease. There, you did it again, you and your look. The "if only" look. The "maybe if I had all the breaks"—no, "the opportunities," then I could have been something else, maybe even you. The problem, of course, is if I were you, I'd be waiting all my life to talk to a man like me. No, don't ask me about life in the fucking ghetto, I forget those days long time. You couldn't last two days in Rikers if you didn't learn to forget. Hell, in here you forget you're not supposed to suck dick. So no, I'm the wrong person to ask what it was like in the ghetto. Is not like I was born there.

Nineteen sixty-six? You really goin' ask me 'bout 1966, brethren? No star, me nah talk 'bout no 1966. Nor '67 neither.

But seriously, Alex, prison library serious to fuck. Me go to plenty library in Jamaica and not one have book like the number of books me see in Rikers. One of them is this book *Middle Passage*. Some coolie write it, V. S. Naipaul. Brethren, the man say West Kingston is a place so fucking bad that you can't even take a picture of it, because the beauty of the photographic process lies to you as to just how ugly it really is. Oh you read it? Trust me, even him have it wrong. The beauty of how him write that sentence still lie to you as to how ugly it is. It so ugly it shouldn't produce no pretty sentence, ever.

But how you going know about peace if you don't learn what start the war in the first place? What kind of journalist you be if you don't want to know the backstory? Or maybe you know it already. Either way, you can't know about peace or war or even how Copenhagen City come about the first place unless you learn 'bout a place called Balaclava.

Picture it, white boy. Two standpipe. Two bathroom. Five thousand people. No toilet. No running water. House that hurricane rip apart only for it to come back together like magnet was the thing holding it in place. And then look at what surrounding it. The largest dump at Bumper Hall, the Garbagelands where they now have a high school. The slaughterhouse draining blood down the streets right to the gully. The largest sewage treatment plant so uptown can flush they shit straight down to we. The largest public cemetery in the West Indies. The morgue and two largest maternity hospitals in the West Indies. Coronation Market, the largest market in the Caribbean, almost all of the funeral parlours, the oil, the railway and the bus depot. And . . . but why you come here, Alex Pierce? What you really want to know and why you wasting me time with question that the Jamaica Information Service can answer? Oh. I see. I see your method. When last you go back to Jamaica? No real reason, you just look like somebody who either never been or can't go back. What that look like? Honestly I didn't know until I just said it to see what you would do. Now I know what it look like. All the way to Rikers, how many strings you just pull, eh, Pierce? You know what, don't tell me. I going find out the same way I just find out about you and Jamaica. Ask your question them.

Brethren, you know me come from the Rastafari area, so why you ask a question like that? You really think the JLP was going help the Rasta part or the PNP of Balaclava? You still so dense? Anyway, Uncle Ben's rice tough like fuck anyway. But that day, man. Shit.

You know something though? Balaclava never did so bad depending on where you lived or who you live with. It's not like every day some baby dead or some people get their face eaten off by rats or anything. I mean, things wasn't good. Wasn't good at all. But still me can remember certain morning just going out and laying down in the grass, just pure green grass, and watch hummingbird and butterfly dance over me. Nineteen forty-nine me born. I always feel that when my mother give birth she was already on her way to England and just throw me off the ship. Don't care so much that both Daddy and Mummy check out, but why them have to leave me with this half-coolie face? Even my Rasta brethren laugh 'bout it, saying when the Black Star Liner finally come to take us to Africa, they going have to chop me in half. Man, what you know about the Jamaica runnings? Sometimes I think being a half coolie worse than being a battyman. This brown skin girl look 'pon me one time and say how it sad that after all God go through to give me pretty hair him curse me with that skin. The bitch say to me all my dark skin do is remind her that me forefather was a slave. So me say me have pity for you too. Because all your light skin do is remind me that your great-great-grandmother get rape. Anyway, Balaclava.

Sunday. My little mattress was a hospital bed they throw out. Me was already awake, but it was like the rumble wake me. Don't ask me if I feel it or hear it first. Is like one second there was nothing, then the next second there was the rumble. Then me cup fall off the stool. The rumbling just getting louder and louder, and noise now, like a plane flying really low. It shake all four wall. Me sit up in the bed and as I look to the window the wall just crunch flat. This big iron jaw just chomp 'pon me wall and rip it away.

The jaw just rip into the wall and bite it off. I scream like a girl. Me jump off the bed just before the jaws burst through more zinc and chomp down dirt in the ground, me bed, me stool and part of the roof me build with me own hand. Now that the roof lose two wall to support it start to fall apart. Me run out before the whole thing collapse and still the jaws keep coming back.

No, me don't want to talk about Wareika Hill neither. Where the fuck you get these questions?

Man, what you really care about, '66 or '85? Make up your mind and stop asking question when damn well already know the answer. You come here to talk about Josey Wales. That's all everybody want to talk about after last May. Oh wait, you don't know? Me in Rikers and me know everything and you one of them news-man and you don't know?

I hear me and Wales used to live near each other but it would be another ten years before I meet him. But him was JLP, and after JLP drive me out of Balaclava me never have nothing to do with those people until the peace treaty. Anyway, thanks for Selassie I Jah Rastafari or I don't know what me would a do. Anyway, little after the fall of Balaclava, haha, get it? Anyway, after the fall, Babylon lock me up. Can't even remember which club? Turntable? Neptune Bar? People who know better do better, they always say. The damn thing is all me pocket was five dollars and a bottle of Johnnie Walker. I guess it was a year for each dollar, eh?

So I come out of General Penitentiary in 1972? And is like Jamdown was a different place totally. Or at least a different party running things. Even the music you was hearing was different. Then again maybe it wasn't so different. But 1972 if you were a young man and you wanted anything, a job, a house, shit, even certain kind of woman, you had to go through two people, Buntin-Banton and Dishrag. The two was the top-ranking PNP dons in Kingston, maybe Jamaica. I mean, I come out and me see all these men, Shotta Sherrif may he rest in peace, Scotsman, Tony Flash from S90 posse, all them man dress like top-ranking with plenty girls looking hot and ready and me say is where unu get money from? Them say, You better link up with Buntin-Banton and Dishrag and get a job with the Gully Works Project. At least that was some decent money even if you didn't have to use your head once. I mean, the only thing you had to worry about was the police. That was until the police kill Buntin-Banton and Dishrag. Funny, when the shotters were around I get decent work, but as soon as they kill the shotters I become a shotter. The thing is, though PNP man was vicious, they never really have any ambition. The thing about a thug is he can only think small. Shotta Sherrif take over as the ranking don for the Eight Lanes and him use to have this second-in-command who probably in command now, I think we call him Funnyboy. I can't even remember now. Anyway, all these guys could do was protect territory and make sure they didn't lose any to JLP gunman. But the JLP rudies, man. Them man did have ideas. Josey Wales was talking to the Colombians long before they even realise they would get tired of the Bahamians. Oh and here is something a lot of people don't know. Him can chat Spanish. Me hear him talk it over the phone one time. Only God he knows when the man did learn Spanish.

The two side, PNP and JLP, realise they have one thing in common. Babylon out to kill you whether you was an animal with stripes or spots. After Green Bay everybody did know that, not just gunman.

Them never bother you so much if you was PNP. But them police and soldier would kill anybody. I should tell you 'bout when me run into Rawhide. You no know Rawhide? And you writing book about Jamaica? Rawhide is one inspector in the Jamaica Police Constabulary and the big-time politician personal bodyguard. No me no know him real name. So we down in Two Friends night club downtown, way downtown, on the pier, and everybody just a level the vibes, everybody just cool, no botheration a go on, nobody trying to shoot nobody, everybody just a drink and reason and rub up 'pon a girl 'cause the new Dennis Brown song just a nice up the dance. When who fi burst 'pon the scene but Rawhide? Bad man and rude-boy don't 'fraid of nobody but everybody know Rawhide don't 'fraid of nobody neither. And my boy come in trash out in the latest fashion. Two gun strap to him side like he really name Rawhide and a M16 in him hand.

Now everybody know the rule with Rawhide. If he find you with gun you dead. Just like that. No question, just dead, braps. I just pick out the gun out of me waist with two finger like is baby nappy, put one arm around my girl waist like me dancing with her and push the gun right between her bosom.

Lola! Her name was Lola. She was a . . . Why you laughing? Oh. Right. Anyway, I thought you was asking me about the peace treaty. Boy, you have a way of going off topic. But tell me something, Alex Pierce, why this subject intrigue you? Is that the word? Why this subject intrigue you so much? Honestly now that I look back at it, this peace treaty was a little shit stain that wash 'way in the first laundry.

Shotta Sherrif is the man who approach me about being the chairman of the peace council. First he and Papa-Lo and some other man all go to England to convince the Singer to come back and do a concert to raise some money for the ghetto. Now ask me why with all these politicians in the ghetto every day, we still had to launch a concert to raise money. Anyway, him put up my name to be chairman and nobody object. Shotta Sherrif, man, I never see a man so sad to give me a gun, like me disappoint him or something. Even among the gunmen he always giving me non-gunman things to do, like organize dance and arrange funeral, and even have me talk couple time to whichever politician come through the ghetto. One time some white people with camera come through to do some story about Coronation Market and he just say Tristan, coolie boy, go show them white people the market, and talk you talk. Me don't know what him talking 'bout but when the white woman turn on her camera me see say she don't just expect me to show her Coronation Market, she also expect me to talk about it. Them all give me the mic like me about to host *Soul Train*. Shotta Sherrif, man. Him was something else. Him was . . .

him was . . .

I . . . I . . .

stop the tape.

Just stop the tape. Stop the fucking tape.

Where you going? Sit youself down . . . and make me tell you a story. The Singer readying for the second peace concert. Lighting set up, microphone, stage, everything, the Singer even do one more sound check. Me in the office and get a call from Josey Wales that one of the lighting equipment boxes still at the wharf and they need it onstage now. So me call the Minister of National Security to clear the box. Wales send one of him man from the JLP to go deal with the equipment, this man who call himself Weeper. You spend one minute with this man you smell that he performing, something about him not there, something about him that you just know all you seeing of him is all he set out to show. Him even say yes like he acting in front of audience. So here me was in the meeting when somebody tell me that this box of equipment never reach the concert, even though me have documentation sitting on me desk. When somebody say that plenty man in Copenhagen throwing their old guns to the Wang Gang because brand-new guns show up all of a sudden me look straight at Weeper who didn't even blink. Me end the meeting early and remind them that some of the money from the concert don't come in yet.

—Weeper, one second, me say and he hold back. —What the bombocloth a gwaan?

—What the bombocloth 'bout what? him say.

—What this fuckery 'bout the lighting equipment? You did know it was gun in there?

—Phillips, no you choose me to go pick it up? You ah ask me?

—Don't try play cute, pussyhole, it don't suit you, me say. Him screw up him face like him smelling something bad. Then he say to me,

—Look, brethren, you in ah the peace runnings, gwaan through with that, me not going stop you. Me a deal with peace too, but it don't spell your way.

Then him walk 'way. Funny, I don't think he would have talked like that to any other man in the ghetto. I still don't know if he was trying to show me that him dangerous or him smart. Him definitely didn't like me telling him that he wasn't cute.

But enough of that pussyhole for now. Tell me the truth, Alex Pierce. Why you can't go back to Jamaica?

John-John K

As *for the gig,* batshit crazy Colombian bitch was nothing if not specific. Ice him slow, but let him know though she didn't set up the hit, niggers from Biscayne Bay to Kendal West are gonna learn to respect the mamajama—her words, not mine, since the wetback dyke never learned Yankee-speak too good. That's it, I'm supposed to let that sink in while the motherfucker bleeds out. And she said a whole bunch of other shit too that I didn't understand either, maybe because she couldn't remember the original message. Bitch spent a lot of time acting like the orders came from her, when she was just being the fucking receptionist. But fuck Griselda Blanco. I'm in New York and everything is motherfucking ace.

Dig this, I was back in Chicago, after promising a few goons I would never come back, because this last rubout, five years ago, was kind of a mess. This made man from Southside that grew into a bloated check that the mob wanted cashed. Picked up the tab at Denny's and talked business. They said how's about five hundred bucks and you and your broski Paco rub out this dude named Eustace. Eustace? Him some kinda faggot? Paco said. Mob guy didn't answer. It was simple enough: At nine-ten on Tuesdays his wife stepped out for choir practice while he sat down with his own projector, in the basement, cigar in one hand dick in the other, while he jacked himself silly to Cherry Poppers 1–4. Paco bailed because he said he's a thief, not a killer. Made it halfway down the basement before the guy heard me, but with one hand on his johnson and the other way up somewhere most men don't think about, there was no hand to draw for the gun. I couldn't stop shooting. The noise was so loud at first I didn't hear the wife screaming. She ran away and I ran after, praying she did not reach the door. She reached the door and ran out screaming. So there we were, running down Martin

Street, she in her nightie and bunny slippers screaming like her throat half cut, me behind her. Popped her off in the middle of the road, just as two station wagons passed. One stopped so I fired into the rear windshield and kept firing until they drove off and crashed into a tree seventy yards or so. With shit done I had to leave Chicago.

But then after cooling out in New York for six months, I got a call. Seems word got around. Southside hit was sloppy and messy, but no failure. Collateral damage was hefty is all. I was young but not stupid. Brash but will listen and this one was easy. Kike that cooked the books for the mob for the past ten years suddenly got hit with a nasty case of second thoughts. Who knows, all anybody knew was they've got pics, pics of him heading inside the Fed building and coming out of the Fed building three hours later. Whatever, the Hebrew had cashed in. And I was about to shoot a rat in the bathtub, that's how much I was bored when I got the call.

December 14, four p.m. Two Hundred Seventh Street, Jewish Bronx, but some of those Jamaican niggers who talk funny and never mess with anybody else already started infiltrating uptown. Two floors and an attic. I've been picking locks since I was seven. The real trick was the steps, I was hoping they had all that tacky fur shit, which would mask any creaks. They didn't give me any details, like how many rooms were in the house, so I had to do this the hard way.

First door was the linen closet, like who the fuck has their linen closet right by the stairs, second door was the bathroom, third door looked like a bedroom so I went in, feeling slightly off with the extra weight of the new gun. Empty. I went down the hallway and pushed open the last door. This boy sat upright leaning against the bed head like he was waiting for me. No shit. The boy was looking straight at me and I couldn't shoot. Then I realized he wasn't looking at me or anything at all. Kid was looking straight through me and jacking off. This was fucked up. If I shot now he would wake up the house.

—They sleep in the attic now, the boy said. —You know how old people start to always want everything at fifty degrees?

Within a week, *New York Post* is shitting over a supposed new Son of

Sam. Then Paco called and said to come visit him in Miami. Fuck New York and the rest of suffering America, it was fucking Gomorrah down here. Down here they froze diamonds and used them as ice cubes. I was on the first flight out.

So we're at the Anaconda, and I'm realizing word got around about the New York hit, police reports of a double homicide, husband and wife killed in their sleep, both shot in the head. At the Anaconda I'm checking out the nightlife and there was Donna Summer in the green room and some other people who looked like they were famous. A brother named Baxter who I knew was cool came up to me. You motherfuckers all here catching up on some rays? he laughed then looked at me serious.

—Cleaned up nice in New York.

—My mama, you know I gotta make that bitch proud. Paco knows you're here?

—Fuck that little *putito.*

—So that's a no then.

—Watchu doin' here, John-John? Seriously.

—Chillaxin'. Brother brought me down from New York, too much heat in New York, came to chase some ass, really.

—Yeah, well you might want to take that shit to another club, check out Tropic City down the street.

—What so bad about this one?

—Ancient Chinese secret.

—Huh?

—Look, I'm only telling you this because I like you.

—What? Fucking music so damn loud.

—See those Cubans back there? Big table sitting six?

—Yeah.

—We're gonna wet those motherfuckers.

—How do you know they're Cuban?

—Buddy, look at those jackets. At least Colombians show some class. Anyways, we've been tailing them for a while but they're never together.

Now we got all of them packed in one spot, I swear it's like when your girl sucks your dick and eats out your ass the same night. Two at the table rubbed my boss the wrong way, and she don't put up with that shit. Motherfucker's about to go down like My Lai up in here. You know what's good you better skit. Like now.

—Sure brother, thanks for the tip.

I ran into Paco at the bar with some bitch, his hands cupping her left tit like a bra.

—Dude, we gotta fly, some serious shit's about to blow.

—Funny you should mention blow. Wanna hit it now? We could do two hits off Charlene tits, whayousay?

—Dude, we gotta jet.

—Blow it out of yer ass, JJK. They got Donna Summer. Rumor is Gene Simmons in the back room with Peter Criss and they got some Chinese chick in a sandwich. Dude, chill, just chill, can't you see I'm busy?

—Do I look like I'm fucking with you? Shit's about to blow, so you might wanna quit finger-fucking this pro and listen to me.

—Who you callin'—

—Chill, sweetie, he's one of them queer boys, dunno what to do with a lady.

—Yeah, I dunno what to do with a, Paco, what the fuck?

—Fuck is wrong with you, baby?

—Just ran into Baxter.

—Baxter? That bitch is here? Fuck that bro, man, I—

—He's here on a job, you idiot. Him and about twelve hoods.

—Fuck! Why here? This is a fucking nice club they're gonna ruin.

—Dunno, some shit between the Cubans and Colombians. They're about to wet some table.

—Holy shit, I better warn my boy.

—Do what you gotta do, I'm cutting this place loose.

I went outside leaving Paco, who I guess went around to tell his buddies the place was about to blow up. At first I'm wondering if I'm deaf or something. Less than five minutes later people come running out of the club, but there was still no gunfire. Fire alarm went off, Paco said when he came out.

—You told your buddy to get out?

—Yeah. Good thing too because he came with like five cousins from overseas.

—One? Five? A table with six Cubans?

—Yeah, how did y—

—You fucking idiot. You fucking retarded motherfucker.

I book a flight back to New York the next day. They were waiting for me as soon as I jumped out of the cab at the airport. Four men, one in a brown suit with collars flaring like wings, three in Hawaiian shirts, one red, one yellow and one pink hibiscus. Didn't make any sense to fight. They take me far out to the Gables, past lots with nothing but trees, roads with street signs and light posts still reeling from the last tropical storm, two clubs dead in the day. They passed the empty Coral Gables high school, two stories high with a Mustang parked out front.

—We're supposed to bring you in alive, but that don't mean we gotta bring you all in one piece, Pink Hibiscus said.

—Is this about last night?

—Uh-huh.

—This shit is on my buddy Paco, you know.

—Don't know no Paco. Baxter said he gave you the heads-up.

—So why don't you take this shit up with Baxter?

—Already spoke to him. Spoke to him real good.

—Oh. Your boss, is he going to . . .

—Who knows what that *loca*'s gonna do?

I said she like a loud question mark, but since nobody in the car responded, I guess nobody heard it. I just looked out the window at Florida getting more one color by the second.

—We still in Coral Gables?

—Nope.

—If she's going to kill me, why not have you guys just do that shit now and feed me to some gator or something.

—She's got too much respect for gators, that's why. Now just shut the fuck up. Fucking Noo Yawk accent driving me up the fucking wall.

—Chicago.

—Whatever. We're here.

Here still looked pretty much like Coral Gables. They parked up in the driveway, just as two shirtless boys ran outside, one chasing the other with a water gun. The street was sleepy and empty. Across the road, a blue Chevy was waiting behind a Mustang. I'm from New York and Chi-Town, I could never get with the suburbs and all this shit spread so fucking wide, one house, two cars, three trees all the way down to the end of the road to pick up the exact same shit on the other side. The house was so much like the one before and the one after it that it seemed deliberate, like maybe *chico* or *chica* was trying too hard to be all apple pie. Except these houses were bland and motherfucking big. All one floor up, like going upstairs would mean losing air. They all had Spanish tile roofs and they all had different shades of pastel, this house in blue. You notice this pretty early on in Coral Gables, the difference between a mansion, which just winked a kinda class, and a really big house which popped up extra rooms like a nerd popped up zits. Tacky-ass shit that never stopped screaming yeah muthafuckas, I got me some money, I'ma buy this house right now.

This was one long driveway. Both sides flanked by palm trees like the house was some coconut plantation. Not that this house was so crass. With its stone archway instead of just a front door and wide glass panels all around so you could see the living room from outside, it was downright classy. Brown suit guy pointed to the front door which relieved me a little. Maybe they only wanted to talk, or at least talk first. Civil, refined, maybe there was some kind of class that Colombians got from being on a continent that fucking graceless Cubans never got. Only brown suit guy followed me.

Home cooking. I was hungry. I can't remember when I stopped walking, but Brown Suit pushed me so hard I nearly stumbled.

—Fucking hell.

Brown Suit cut me off with the threat of a gun butt.

—Mistress don't like no swearin' in the house, he said. On the left was another stone archway that led to a living room and little boy with a huge head of black hair, watching *we all live in a capital I* on *Sesame Street.* Bacon and pancakes. We were following the smell of bacon and pancakes.

Josey Wales

B*ad man don't make* note in a book. I tell you something as sure as I know that the sun outside only about to get hotter and heavier. You write it down in your head and you train your head to remember. Forgive and forget not in my book. Not because I don't forgive, if I didn't forgive a river would run red from National Heroes Park all the way down Kingston Harbour. But remember, wait, and move is how I operate. That batty-boy Boy George on the radio just ask *do you deal in black money?* I deal in black everything.

Weeper is in New York telling me he too old to break-dance. He just wasn't the type of brother for Miami, even I know that from when he was in Jamaica. Weeper like to think he's a thinking man, but the man don't think, he just read a few books. Just like how some of these boys think they mature and experienced when they've only been through some fuckery. I give Weeper one thing to do. Maintain the link between Jamdown and Griselda Blanco. She need to get shit quick time to Miami so it can get to New York. We take shit from Kingston to Miami through either North Coast or Cuba.

But Weeper have this thing where he just can't get along with any woman, or rather this thing where no woman can tell him what to do. Then again Griselda is not a woman. She a vampire who cock drop off a hundred years ago. She lose her patience with him and when a madwoman like her lose her patience with you she would make even a hardcore Jamaican rudie go, Bombocloth bitch yuh wicked no fuck. Was just a matter of months before she kill Weeper herself.

But in church they talk about the gift of discernment. Is not just preachers or the spirit filled that have it, it's anybody who think they can jump in these pants and lead for long. The second I meet Blanco I know this was a brute, who don't really have that much sense, but have enough determination to knock down a bull. Like me she realise that right and wrong is just two word some fool invent and what really matter is what I have over you and what you have under me. But she don't figure out what to do with it yet and sometimes an ignorant naigger is an ugly woman from Colombia too blank to know that me deal with both Medellín and Cali and at least boys from Cali been known how to think.

Discernment. I could always look at a man and read him. Like Weeper. Is years now I know the man not only fucking man but is really the one getting fuck, and no matter what he say, he still sorry to leave prison. Is years now I supposed to kill him for that, but why? It move my brain better to watch him fuck pussy after pussy as if battyman behaviour is something pool up in him sperm and if only he shoot out enough he will finally shoot out the need to put a cock in him battyhole. I don't know much 'bout them things and I don't read Bible. But if there is one thing I do know is when a man fooling himself. Is something to watch though. Who knows what him up to in New York. I can't set a man on him tail because that man would find out. And there are some things that only Weeper can do.

Yesterday me woman ask how me get visa to go to America and laugh. She right to laugh. But this year I have things to do. I couldn't tell the last time I care about what happen in a Kingston street. JLP want the country so bad and now they have it. Both of them can choke. Other street want me attention now, and all I have to do is look. Bad man don't take note. Bad man write it down in him head.

Eubie in the Bronx. People can't understand why I check for that brethren, people in this case meaning Weeper who can't stand him. Hard to like a man who cut him hair every two week, talk like he stay in a posh high school for the full seven years and always wear a silk suit no matter the weather. But here is the reasoning nobody catch: If people busy thinking that you is a pimp nobody going think you is a drug dealer. Eubie is a school boy, and that make him think he have class. And him do, a little. Boy all set for Columbia law school but leave because he wise up about the law. Eubie perfectly fine in Queens and the Bronx and I let him take over Miami from Weeper. Didn't tell Weeper, so he call me that week.

—Brethren, what the bombocloth this?

—You look like you need a change. Miami too country for you, you need New York. Plenty book in New York. Plenty nighttime park too.

—What the r'asscloth that mean?

—It mean what it mean, pussyhole. Me stationing you in Manhattan, maybe Brooklyn.

—Me no know them place deh.

—Then buy a bombocloth atlas and learn yourself.

Brethren, you know me have a feeling 'bout them things, and I just don't trust the brother, he say every week in almost the exact same sentence. But Weeper is not a thinking man, he only read a few books, whereas Eubie think far and wide. He leave Columbia to sell weed because there was nothing Columbia could teach him about making money he don't already know. He almost too smart. One hundred thousand pounds of weed and ten thousand pounds of white wife in just one year. I know and he know it and Weeper know it too, which is why he still can't stand him. That man's brain was making us rich. But that man brain need my supply and although me sure he already try to contact Escobar himself, they never going to trust any man that slick. Don't even care that he do it, even expect him to, but I didn't tell Weeper. Weeper call me another time just to say that Eubie must be the only man from Jamdown to get pedicure and he must be a battyman or something which make me laugh so long that Weeper start say that him didn't make joke. I tell Weeper to cool it. I didn't tell him that Eubie, when he was not killing man himself, have two brothers, real relation too, who already take out more than fifty man for him, that I hear about. Me sure there be a name for man like Eubie, but only head doctor know it.

Bad man don't take note. Instead I recall name like how some people recall great men. I make list and remember like a song, like a nursery rhyme. If anybody find out, nobody would take me serious. So I send Weeper and a boy to pick up some equipment in Florida and then put him on another truck to round up some more in Virginia and even Ohio. But the police intercept a truck in West Virginia. Before long gone boys bussing shots in D.C., Detroit, Miami, Chicago and all over New York.

And in all of this the boy still won't leave off Eubie.

—Think him is a cha-cha boy just because he wearing him mother curtain as suit. I tell you, Josey, mark my word, that man going turn 'gainst you.

—I watching him, Weeper.

—Well you better watch him harder. I don't trust him too much. He always have him hand on him chin, like he thinking how he can get over you.

—You serious? He not the only man I watching, Weeper.

—What the fuck that mean?

—It mean what it mean. Why man from Queens telling me that supply spotty between you and Eubie? No link in New York?

—Things not spotty, a man need to learn to bombocloth wait.

—You really think a man going wait? What the fuck wrong with you?

—How you mean?

—Brethren, New York look like a monopoly to you? Ranking Dons, Blood Rose Crew and Hot Steppers all want a piece of each street and that's just the Jamaicans. You don't supply, they find another supplier, simple as that. And then thanks to people who think like you, I have to come to New York and put everything back in its natural order. Jesus Christ, Weeper, you mean I going have to come to New York? Or maybe I should just make Eubie deal with Queens too and bring you back to Jamai—

—No! No, Josey. No, man. Me can't . . . me can do this. Me was just . . .

—You was just what? Don't make man in Queens call me again. Couldn't even understand half of what the fucker was saying.

—Yes, brethren, me will deal with that business, Weeper say. But what he didn't say was that he was over him head, not with low business but because new man from a new posse move in on him turf, the same posse that trying to move in on Miami. People forget that when JLP win election in 1980, plenty man take flight to USA quick. Now they in Blood Rose, Hot Steppers but especially Ranking Dons, and they gunning for territory like everybody still in Kingston. Again this call for thinking and Weeper is not a thinking man, he just read a few book.

Something else. Truth is I don't demand that much, but I say to Weeper, Hey, you remember that pussyhole, Tristan Phillips? The one from the peace council with Papa-Lo, and Shotta Sherrif, and the Singer? The one who just disappear like magic trick even though I send not one but two man to deal with him case? He living in Queens now and me want you to put a case of vanishing cream 'pon that brother. Before he do something like join this PNP gang, although he the same one who go on American TV to talk about the peace movement.

Nineteen eighty-two I dispatch Weeper to deal with that man. Tell him to buy a plane ticket and head to New York, then get a gun and close that Jamaican chapter. One week later I get a call not from Weeper but from Benny, one of Weeper's runner boys, with the message that it was done. I don't bother ask Weeper how high he was when he give this little shit my phone number. Worse, to have somebody who think he can speak to me this way: *Weeper say fi tell you that the vanishing cream done, y'hear? Later.* This is why I don't bother. Because if ask, why the bloodcloth you just do that, he will say *do what*? Not because he is a pussyhole, but because he honest to God wouldn't know. Whatever, I make it roll off me because Phillips was dead and that chapter closed.

Two Thursday ago, one of my men who just get let out of Rikers ask me if I ever know a Tristan Phillips because he say he know everything about me. I say, what you mean by know, don't you mean, *did* know? He say no, Josey, the brethren don't dead, him in Rikers and just serve two out of a five-year sentence for armed robbery. He used to be in Attica but they transfer him to Rikers. And he running with the Ranking Dons now.

Me can send word to take him out, my man say, but I say leave the man be. I call Weeper the Friday.

—You know who me run into what day? Tristan Phillips' baby mother, she come all the way over to the JLP side looking for money, she say Tristan just up and left her so and won't send money for the baby. Funny, eh? I say.

—Yeah that funny, he say.

So now I packing a sports bag for New York City. Don't plan to stay long. Eubie already make all the arrangements. I look and see my boy in school uniform watching me from the doorway.

—Bombocloth, Daddy, is where you just come back from? You look like you high.

—You standing there like you like to watch man. Go to school, my youth.

—School ah fuckery.

—Me look like one of them parent that allow them pickney to cuss in front of me?

—No, Daddy.

—Good. So you better stop screw up you face and get you bombocloth backside to school. You think Wolmer's Boys' School free?

—All education free, Daddy, so no bother come with that.

—You know what also free. A fucking gun-butt in you head for feistiness. So you better stop block me doorway and get you bloodcloth batty to the high school before them lock the gate.

—Daddy, how me going know what to—

—Know? Know what? You mean your education? I thought it was school you going to, so why me still seeing you damn ugly face? Looking more like you r'asscloth mother more and more every day.

I smile with the boy so that he don't feel like I threatening him too much, but he is sixteen now, and I still remember sixteen, so I know hunger growing in him. All this talking back is moving from a little cute to a little threat. Part of it sweet me, seeing this little shit puff him chest out. He turn to leave when I say,

—Next trip, for real.

The boy don't smile or anything, just nod once and leave, and I watch the blue backpack moving away from me. One year, maybe two year from now, I won't have the strength to hold him back.

Tristan Phillips

Is *lie* you a tell me. Two Friends night club never deh 'bout in 1977? It didn't open till '79? Then is which club me run into Rawhide, Turntable? No star, me can't imagine it being Turntable, boy, even the Prime Minister used to go there so. People from the good side of life mingling with middle-class people to feel like them connect to some culture, you know how it go. You sure? How you so sure? For a man who say him don't go to Jamaica since 1978 you know a whole fucking heap about 1979. You same one tell me that is a book 'bout the Singer you writing, but what any of this have to do with the Singer? You know the man check out 1981, right? Or you lock up in a battyhole till now? Me must look like me born behind cow. You writing a ghost story? The Singer duppy haunting Rose Hall? Come to think of it, if you really writing about the Singer, why the fuck you talking to me? You think me is a fucking idiot, Pierce?

You're sorry for wasting my time—what the fuck, sit down, Pierce. Look 'pon you, one little question and you huff and puff and blow your own ass out the room. This might be the first interesting thing you do all day. Look how your face turn red like some choking pig. Sit the fuck down, Alexander Pierce. Fine, how 'bout this: you don't tell me why you want to know about the peace movement and Josey Wales and Papa-Lo and Shotta Sherrif and I won't tell you when I eventually figure it out. How that sound? Deal?

The peace council even had a office. The Singer open up him own house to it, ground floor, around the back. We get along so good people used to think we was brother. In a way, we really was brother. The two of we coming out of ghetto life in Jamdown. Whole heap of people don't know, but me used to be big with the music thing too. Used to play with some boys at the Prime Minister's—sorry, former Prime Minister's—father house. Even grow up with the Singer best friend. Me always think myself smart but I don't know, maybe the Singer smarter. Some people just have this thing 'bout themselves, maybe is a ghetto thing where even if another man don't destroy you, you going destroy yourself. Every man in the ghetto born with it, but somehow the Singer cure it. You look 'pon the two of we in a picture, both of we smarter than the ghetto, but only one really get out. Some people just fated to fuck up even when them smart enough to know better.

So the Singer give me a room to set up office for the peace council. I still figuring out what we going to do, but the first thing to do was collect all the money from the peace concert. One afternoon Papa-Lo send Josey Wales to the house to drop off some money from the west side entrance ticket sales. The Singer outside near the entrance, him just done playing football. Josey Wales park him white Datsun and step out and the Singer look at him as him pass, then look through the office window straight at me. Brethren, lemme tell you, if eyes really did have beams like that boy in X-Men comic, him would have blast me to kingdom come and take the house with him. So as soon as the man leave the Singer march straight into the office. Before me even ask what a gwaan, him say, who was that brother? Me say Josey Wales, man, community activist in Copenhagen City, almost like Papa-Lo deputy. Boy, in that short time me get to know the Singer very well, so me see him lose him temper once or twice. But me never see that man or any man get so furious, that him start shake, he couldn't even talk for a few minutes because every word in him mouth too ragged to come out. Me just sit there and watch the Singer pant and choke, the way he furious. Him say,

—Tristan, me know that brother. Him was here, right here the night I get shot. You want to know when I knew this peace thing wasn't going to last? From right there.

So I fly to Canada to talk to some organizations about the peace council, and go check a brethren in Toronto. Him telling me all this stuff about the concert, so much that me say brethren, is like you was there. Him say no, man, me see it 'pon the TV, the channel that show cultural programming. Me wondering how the hell people in Canada seeing the concert when nobody come talk to me 'bout rights only to hear some company name Copenhagen City Promotions was selling footage to TV stations in Toronto, London and Mississauga. So of course me call Papa-Lo right away and say, brethren, what di fuck a go on? Him say him never know nothing 'bout no footage, since the whole time him was just watching out for Mick Jagger. But why would somebody name them company Copenhagen City Promotions if he didn't come from the area? Then him say, Maybe is from the original Copenhagen in foreign, like me born with the name idiot on me forehead. I didn't bother tell him that no white crew was filming the concert. Look, both him and me know who was behind this. Then him say maybe is Shotta Sherrif. Me laugh and go to hang up the phone, but before he go I say, Pull your leash on Josey Wales or me will do it for you. WLIB New York want me to come back as guest 'pon them talk show, so me tell Papa-Lo me changing my flight from Toronto to JFK. As soon as me hang up me change my mind and go to Miami instead. Plenty Jamaicans in Miami don't even hear about the council yet, plus me can talk to the station 'pon the phone.

Four days later me in Miami. I go check me brethren A-Plus from Balaclava days. When me knock 'pon the man door and he open it, the man scream like a girl. You hear me. Man 'bout fi run since is must duppy did deh 'pon him. Duppy is a ghost, by the way. I tell you, the man couldn't decide to piss or shit himself. He grab me like me was him pickney and you know the rules, bad man don't hug. Definitely not no other man. The man hug me and say, Jesus Christ, Tristan, what you doing here? How you survive that one?

—Survive what? me say.

—How you mean, bredda? Man just done tell everybody say him kill the I.

—What? What the bombocloth you a talk 'bout?

—Josey Wales' four-eye deputy, Weeper. Him tell people only two day ago he just fly to New York and cancel you.

—Cancel me? Then A-Plus, me is a duppy or what?

—You have me a ponder the same thing right now, fi true.

—Brethren, not only did this pussyhole not kill me, but me never go New York.

—What?

—No star, change me mind when me realise me can talk to this radio station by phone. Too much people in Miami wanting to hear 'bout the peace council anyway.

—Boy, brethren, is good thing you show up, 'cause me was just about to grab two man and discipline that pussyhole.

—Hold on, what you mean? Him still in Miami?

—Yeah, man, him deh yah a palaver 'round him friend house on 30th and 46th. You know where Lincoln Memorial Park deh?

—Yeah, man. What kinda hardware you have here?

A-Plus show me a Thompson submachine and a nine. Me take the nine and him control the submachine gun and we drive out to Lincoln Memorial. So we park the car two block away and forward to this friend yard. You ever see that part of Miami? One story house, with verandah to the side and sometimes glass window. Dead grass and dry-up dirt is what them call a lawn. This house with a mash-up car right on the lawn, might as well be East Kingston. Anyway, we draw down on the house, A-Plus taking the front, me skipping 'round the back. Of course the pussyhole them have the door open. Of course me hear Weeper voice loud and clear. Coming from the left side of the hallway. Me take two step and there him be, him back to me pissing in the toilet. I jump the boy, push him past the toilet so that me and him bust through the shower curtain and a ram him into the wall. Him face go right into it, so hard him stunned. Him glasses fall off. Before the boy could do thing me put the gun right to him temple and make him hear the click. Weeper start tremble so hard he nearly shake the gun out of me hand. The man still a piss. Me say,

—Pussyhole, imagine me come off the plane in Miami only to find out say me dead and everybody in the world hear but me. How you imagine that?

—Woi, woi, me nuh know, Tristan, me no know how you fi dead. You, you deh right yah so.

—You no know? But brethren, no you going 'round telling people say you kill me? When you kill me? Last week? Yesterday?

The same time him friend come in the bathroom with him hand up in the air and A-Plus behind him with the machine gun at him neck.

—So Weeper, me brethren, tell me how you kill me, 'cause boy, me have to tell you, me no feel dead at all.

—Who tell you say me kill you, boss? Who a spread lie?

—Me just want to know how you so previous. I mean, brethren, at least kill the I first before you start boast 'bout it?

The pussyhole don't say a thing. He start to cry and the other man start to cry too. Then again is not cry them was crying. Them two was weeping. Of course whoever don't kill I today, will kill I tomorrow so I put the gun to him temple to take him out. The other man bawl out and start beg for him. I mean, him really start beg and plead, all drop to him knees which was too much but still. Me still can't get over how much the man cry and beg, like Weeper was him pickney or something. Before me pull off the gun Weeper glance 'pon the man quick. Me never see a man so furious. We gun-butt the two of them and leave.

You very at ease with all I just say, Alex Pierce. You pissing yourself underneath the desk? Then again, something tell me that you don't frighten too easy.

'Fraid of what? Reprisal? Trust me, Weeper is the last person in the world that would come after me. But in the meantime police kill Copper. Then Papa-Lo. You have to understand something. This peace was between JLP ghetto and PNP ghetto. The police never sign no treaty nor the JLP or PNP. Except police in Jamaica not known for any kind of thinking. You too young to know 'bout old-time movie. You ever see a movie with Keystone Kops? Yes? Well Jamaican police constabulary is a bunch of Keystone Kops. Both Copper and Papa-Lo smart enough to know police have way too much vendetta on the street to be a part of no fucking treaty. But them way too stupid to track down a man like Copper who evade them for ten years. You have some sense, Alex Pierce, surely you must know where I going with this. Anyway, then Jacob Miller crash. Shotta Sherrif soon realize what a gwaan and take one of the five flights to Miami. But then him thief cocaine stash from the brother of a man in the Wang Gang and skip to Brooklyn. But what you know, there in the Starlight ballroom man from Wang Gang New York brethren, track him down and kill him. Shoot him dead right there in the club. Before you know it, everybody involved in the peace council dead but this woman, and me. Whether accident or deliberate, I don't bother wait to find out. Me fly back to Jamaica to bury Copper, then fly out again. And no, me didn't go back.

Dorcas Palmer

S*o I've been* sitting down and watching this man sitting down and watching me for an hour now. I know I'm waiting on instructions from the Mrs. or the Miz or whatever this Colthirst woman choose to call herself, but he's just sitting like he's waiting on instructions too. Back firm, hands in his lap, head straight ahead like C-3PO. I'd say that makes him look like a pet dog, but then being the female would make me the pet bitch. It must be a thing, a whole new level of license to know you can keep people waiting for as long as you feel like it. I always wonder if this was some power tactic bullshit, something to let people know their place. I'm paying the cheque, come kiss my ass. Here's the cheque, now stop the cab and wait four hours. This damn country. Then again, it's her money. If she wants to pay me for doing nothing, I get paid by the hour and it's her tab. Honestly this man really looks like Lyle Waggoner. And I watch Carol Burnett reruns every week. Tall, black hair white at the temples and a chin straight out of a cartoon of a handsome man's chin. Every other minute he looks over at me, but turns quick when he sees my eyes waiting on him.

Maybe I should just say I need to piss so I can get out of this room. Or rather I need to pee. Lord Jesus I can't stand that word pee. No male over ten should use that word. Every time I hear a man use it all I can think is only small cocks pee. He looks at me sudden, probably because I chuckled. God, I hope I didn't say all that out loud. Nothing left to do now but pretend it was a cough all along. The Mrs./Miz just raised her voice from her office, probably with the husband or whatever. Lyle Waggoner looks at her door and laughs, nodding the whole time. What kind of man wears pink pants? Brave? Homo? Well if he was homo there would be no daughters and granddaughters, I guess. White polo shirt with his chest and biceps stretching it in a nice way. Honestly Lyle Waggoner wouldn't get kicked out of the free love orgy if he showed up. I'd bet my next pay that he wear briefs, and a bikini to the pool. You could even say he was a hot silver daddy or fox as American girls call men they have no business fucking. I wish the Mrs./Miz would finish up her r'asscloth call or sooner or later I'm going to start thinking aloud and I won't know until Lyle Waggoner here starts to point at me in shock.

Might as well check out the house. I would get up but something tells me that Lyle Waggoner would blurt out, don't touch that, as soon as I left a foot to move. This just looks like the kind of house where you know there is no penny or lost button in that empty vase on the table. Glass of course, but not a dining table. Both me and him sitting on wooden chairs with a circular back and puffy cushion. Fabric pattern looks like cream and brown paisley. The usual paintings on the wall, three old white women clothed right up to the neck, two white men, all with that sour look white people always have in paintings. Two more chairs on the right and left of the room just like the one we're sitting on. Carpet just like the chairs. Coffee table with *Town & Country* magazines all over it, the one part of the room that looks slightly untidy. Purple love seat with the same animal claw legs as my bathtub back home. One of the living rooms you always see in those ads at the back of the *New York Times Magazine.* On the left wall the paintings just gone mad.

—The one in the middle is a Pollock, he says to me.

—Actually it's a de Kooning, I say.

He glares at me and nods.

—Well, I don't know what the hell my family buys, although that one's been here for a while. Looks like a kid ate all his Crayolas and vomited up the whole thing, if you ask me.

—Okay.

—You don't agree.

—I don't really care what other people think about art, sir. Either you get it or you don't, and it seems pretty stupid waiting on people to get it when you could just as easily enjoy having more museum space to yourself, thanks to one less idiot telling me how his four-year-old daughter could do that.

—Where in blue blazes did they find you?

—Sir?

—Ken.

—Mr. Ken.

—No, just . . . never mind. You think Miz Busy Bee will ever remember to respect people's time and GET THE FUCK OFF THE PHONE?

—I don't think she heard you, sir.

—I told you my name is . . . whatever. You probably have no way of knowing this anyway, but do you know if my daughter-in-law specifically asked for a black maid?

—I'm not privy to that kind of information, sir.

—Ken.

—Mr. Ken.

—I was just wondering, since Consuela, at least I think her name was Consuela, damn near stole everything she could carry out of the house.

—Okay.

I'm pretty sure there was no Jamaican maid named Consuela.

—I thought she was ingenious. Everything she stole, she put underneath the furniture, right? Say today she'll steal bed linen. She stashes it under the bed. The next day it may be soap under the chair near the bedroom door, the next thing by the table right outside, then the armchair in the living room, then the next armchair, and on she goes till she has one item at the console table by the door. That way, every day by just moving each thing over by one space, she always had something right at the door to take away. I said to her, That wetback built a fucking underground railroad right in our home! You know what she says? She says, That kind of talk is unacceptable in the North, Papa, like I wasn't born in fucking Connecticut. So I figured she had had her full of Puerto Ricans.

—Jamaican.

—You don't say. I've been to Jamaica.

And all I could think of is, Oh Lord here it comes, another white man about to tell me about how much he enjoyed Ocho Rios, but would have enjoyed it so much more if it weren't for all the poverty. And the country is so beautiful and the people so friendly and even in all this tragedy everybody still manages a smile especially the bombor'asscloth children. Although he looks like the Negril type.

—Yeah, Treasure Beach.

—Wah?

—Excuse me?

—I'm sorry, Treasure Beach?

—You know it?

—Of course.

The truth was I didn't know it. I barely even heard of it. I wonder if it was in Clarendon or St. Mary, one of those parishes I was never in because we didn't have no granny still living in country. Or one of those other places you have to be a tourist to know about, like Frenchman's Cove or something. Whatever.

—So unspoiled. Granted, that's what everyone says about a place they're busy spoiling. Let's put it this way; nobody there was wearing a Jamaican Me Crazy t-shirt. I asked this one guy because he was in a white shirt and black trousers if he could get me a Coke, and he says, Go get it your bombocloth self. Imagine that. Loved the place right there and then. Anyway, you—

The Miz finally come out of the room clutching her bag and touching her hair.

—Papa, be a dear and show Miss Palmer around, will you? Just don't overexert yourself this time, okay?

—I'm sorry, Miss Palmer, but is there a fucking kid behind you? In the doorway somewhere.

—Papa.

—'Cause I have no idea whose kid she's talking to.

—Oh for heaven's sake, *Papah*. Anyway, your son is going absolutely bonkers over the new apartment just because I want a microwave, saying it's too expensive. So I have to skedaddle. Do show her where kitchen is, Papah, and Miss Palmer, do you mind me calling you Dorcas?

—No, ma'am.

—Peachy. Cleaning supplies are under the sink, be careful with that ammonia business, the odor has a way of sticking around. Dinner is usually at five, but you can order pizza this once, just not Shakey's pizza, they're way too salty. What am I forgetting . . . hmmm. I dunno. Anyway, toodles, bye, Papah.

She closes the door, leaving me and the father in the house. Should I tell him I'm not a maid and God Bless is not a maid agency?

—I think there must be some mistake.

—You're telling me. But my son married her anyway, so that's that.

He stands up and goes over to the window. Tall too. The more I look at this man the more I wonder why I was here. I could pretty much assume there would never come a time when I have to clean this man of his own shit, or put him back to bed after I change out all the pissed-up sheets. He was really tall and now leaning into the window, one leg straight, the other bent like he's trying to push out the glass. I don't think I've ever seen an older man who still had a backside.

—You're the second one in a month. I wonder how long you'll last, he said, still looking out the window.

—I'm sorry, sir, but I don't know why I'm here.

—You don't know why you're here.

—God Bless is not a maid service, sir. That might be why the other employee didn't work out.

He turns around, with his back now leaning into the window.

—I don't know anything about a God Bless and please, please, please stop calling me sir.

—Mr. Ken.

—I guess that is as good as it's going to get. What time is it? You hungry?

I glanced at my watch.

—Twelve fifty-two. And I packed a sandwich, Mr. Ken.

—Know any games?

—What?

—Just kidding. Though I far prefer your wah, to your what. One of the few times I feel like there's a real Jamaican in the room.

I tell myself, This is bait, don't bite, this is bait, don't bite, this is bait, don't bite.

—And what am I if not a real Jamaican, Mr. Ken?

—I dunno. Somebody on the make. Or maybe somebody performing. I'll figure it out soon.

—I don't know about that, sir, since your daughter clearly called the wrong agency. I don't do maid work.

—Oh please relax, that dumb cunt thinks everybody here is the maid. I'm sure it was my son who called your agency, not her. Usually she ignores me, but I've been talking to my lawyer a lot lately so she's probably worried I'm modifying my will. Somehow she convinced my son that I have come to the point where I need to be taken care of.

—Why?

—You're going to have to ask my son. Anyway, I'm bored. Got any jokes?

—No.

—Oh for God's sake, are you really this humorless and dull? Fine. I'll give you a joke. You look like you need one. Okay, here goes. Why do you think sharks never attack black people?

I was just about to say look, this is one Jamaican that can swim when he says,

—Because they always mistake them for whale shit.

Then he laughs. Not a hard laugh, just a chuckle. I wonder if I should get all black American and scream offense, or if I should just let the silence hang until the moment dies out.

—How long does it take white woman to shit? I say.

—Oh whoa. I . . . I dunno.

—Nine months.

He goes red just like that. One long second of silence and then he bursts out laughing. He laughs for so long that he almost having a fit, heaving and coughing and eyes wet. I really didn't think it was that funny.

—Oh my God, oh my dear Lord.

—Anyway, Mr. Ken, I should leave. Your son needs to call a maid service and—

—No no no, hell no. You can't leave now. Quick, why do blacks have white hands and feet?

—I'm not sure I want to know.

—They were on all fours when God spray-painted them.

He laughs again. I try not to laugh, but my body starts shaking even before the laugh comes out. He walks over to me now, laughing so hard his eyes almost disappear.

—On all fours, eh? I say. What do you do if you're being gang raped by a bunch of white men?

—Oh sweet heaven, what?

—Nothing. Unless you worried about being fucked by a pimple.

His hand is on my shoulder now, and he's laughing so hard I think that it's for support.

—Hold on, I've got one for you, and it's a white joke this time. What does a white woman and a tampon have in common?

—I don't know. They both suck blood?

—No! They're both stuck-up cunts.

Now my hand is on his shoulder and I'm the one who cannot stop laughing. We both stop and start again. I don't know at what point my bag fell off my shoulder and landed on the floor. We both sit down in facing armchairs.

—Please don't leave, he says. Please don't.

John-John K

Three doors down the kitchen was all bacon smell, crackle and pop. Dark wood cupboards went all the way around, one of which opened up to show Wheaties, Corn Flakes and Life cereal. A man, not much different from Brown Suit, was at the head of the table like Big Poppa or some shit, reading the newspaper and making lines with a red marker. Two boys on either side of him, one looking older with a moustache he was spending too much time Vaselining. Boy was cute and could've sworn he winked, but his ears were Alfred Neuman *Mad* magazine big. The other boy made me wish I had a dad who didn't call me a fucking fruit every time I tried to grow my hair long back at twelve.

—Yuca! Yuca! Yuca!

—Arturo! How many times I say no shout at the table, she said. Her back seemed to sigh out every word. Her ribbed sweater gave her too many Michelin man curves, but her white slacks pulled it off, that tacky rich feel of men who bought but couldn't sail boats. She had tied her hair tight in a bun, which made her eyebrows seem pulled when she turned around. Dark eyes, plenty mascara this early in the morning, and lips shinier than a teenage girl going down on a Lip Smacker.

—You short.

—Wha? Excuse me.

—Excuse me? Did I utter, mutter or stutter?

The older kid groaned.—You're killing us, Ma, he said. She smiled.

—You like that, Guapo?

—Yeah, Ma, all the groovy cats be digging it.

—Don't be no jiving turkey on my ass.

The older kid groaned again while the other held his plate up for more yuca.

—You, sit down for breakfast, she said, and pointed the frying pan at me.

I kinda stood still. I wasn't sure who she meant, until Brown Suit pushed me, more like double-punched me in the back. Older kid looked at me once then turned away, younger kid sucked up what looked like albino fries and the man said nothing, not once taking his eyes off the paper. Go get him a plate, she said to no one. The man got up and grabbed a plate from the cupboard, then went back to the paper. She spooned out yuca into what I assume was my plate, and chorizo from a red frying pan.

—You the motherfucker who messed up my business, she said.

—Excuse me?

—Again with your excuse, excuse, excuse. Do you need to go potty?

The younger kid laughed.

—How does it hang?

—It's how's it hanging, Ma! Fuck!

—My *muchachos*, don't think I talk English too good. I tell them I am businesswoman in America and I need to sound more American, right? Keep on truckin'.

—Righteous, Ma.

—Anyway, you—yes, I mean you, I'm talking to you. You the bitch who messed up my hit.

—I didn't mean to. Your boy—

—That boy is historical.

—History, Ma!

—History. That boy is history. Got sloppy. Always happen when you give a job to a black-black. No discipline, no nothing, all they do is talk your business yap yap yap yappa-doodle. What he tell you?

—Nothing, really. Said he was going to wipe out a table full of some wetbacks—

—Mind your fucking mouth, *putito.*

—Sorry. Said he and his boys were going to wet some Cubans in the club. Tipped me off to get out of there. Told my buddy Paco that we got to go. He said he was going to warn his friend. Figured it was some bouncer or something, not some—

—Enough talking. Your side of the story is . . . not interesting. You know what's interesting? Them *maricones* haven't been in the same place in six months. Six months, honko.

—Honky, Ma, Jeezus sakes—

—Enough with your disrespect at the table, she said and pointed at the boy. He lipped up quick.

—Back to you. You know what I am? I am American businesswoman. You just cause me a lot of money. Lots and lots of cash. Now what I wanna know is what you plan to do about it.

—Me?

I bit into a yuca. Figured if this was my last meal it makes some sort of sense it would be breakfast. The sound of the TV finally drifted into the room, something about a forty-foot gorilllillillillilaaaa! The man was still deep in the newspaper. I never thought anything interesting happened in Miami that somebody would sit down to read about it. But this was good yuca. Not that I've ever had yuca before, but this was a home-cooked meal and that must mean it was good, even though my ma's food sucked.

She slapped me hard. Said something about me not paying attention, but the slap struck me fucking blind. I reached inside my jacket so quick I forgot I didn't have a gun. Before the sting burned my fucking face, before Griselda pulled back with a hot pan full with oil ready to strike, before I jumped up and the chair fell backward, before I could even call her a motherfucking cunt son of a mangy wetback bitch, I heard the clicks. Five, ten and fifteen all at once. I couldn't remember when the Hawaiian Shirts came into the kitchen but there they were. And the man in the brown suit. And the man at the kitchen table. And the older boy, all looking at me with the same furrowed brow, all pointing guns at me, 9mm's and Glocks and even a six-shooter with a white ivory handle. I raised my hands.

—Sit down, the man at the table said.

—You all better fucking learn to respect this mamajama, she said.

Pink Hawaiian Shirt gave her a manila envelope. She ripped it open and pulled out a photo. Griselda giggled hard and started to wheeze and shake. Fucking thing must have delighted the shit out of her. She handed the photo to the man at the table who looked at it with the same stone face that he read the newspaper. He threw it at me. It spun in the air for a few whirls but landed, almost perfect and straight, right in front of me.

—Looks like el gator prefer to kill his own meat, no? Next time I feed them an alive motherfucker, not a dead one, eh?

It was Baxter. Alligators couldn't figure out what to do with his head. Try not to vomit, say try not to vomit over and over and you won't.

—What was the point to rubbing Baxter out?

—Sending a message. Who have ears let him hear, that's what the sister use to say at the what they call it here? Convent? Uh-huh. Baxter fucked up and you did too. But my boys been doing some checking around, eh? Word is you did a job in New York that even the police thought was clean.

I nearly laughed. Everybody knew I was sloppy. How bad Miami boys had to be where I can come off like a smooth operator?

—This is what you gonna do for me.

I must have blacked out for hours when I hit the sack. Didn't have a clue that somebody was in the bed until,

—No I don't know what I'm gonna do for you.

The greasy-haired trick from last night. God, I hope I didn't take this faggot home only to pass out under him. But he's still here so either he liked it or he couldn't find my wallet and wants to get paid. Or maybe he got nowhere else to go. Well this is one mess, me on the floor with just my t-shirt on, this Colombian bitch jumping in on my dreams with her shitty directions and me not even remembering my flight from Miami to New York City. Let's see, landed at seven p.m. Checked in hotel room in Chelsea at nine (why you wanna go to Chelsea? Pink Hawaiian Shirt asked me. I didn't ask why his eye popped open when I said Chelsea), scoped out this little trick wearing tight running shorts and a Ramones t-shirt like he meant it in the meatpacking district at eleven-twenty.

—Eh? What now?

—You said you want me to do something for you. Unless you paying extra, I gotta go.

—You gotta go? Action on the pier too busy to miss?

—The pier? You old, man. That place you'll fall through the floor and get tetanus or some shit. Besides, nobody really goes there now ever since they start calling that gay cancer shit AIDS. They been closing some of the baths too.

—Oh really? Well how about we do this. You take those pants off, wait, wait, hold the fuck up. First take my fucking wallet out of your fucking back pocket, because this thing I got in my hand, you know this thing I just pulled out from under the bed, don't have no flag saying bang when I pull the trigger.

—Jesus, Daddy.

—No Daddy bullshit. There's a good boy. Next time you pick a guy's wallet don't wait around to make breakfast, you dumb fuck. Now about that something you're gonna do.

I rolled over on my back, legs up in the air. Locked them both in the crook of my arms and spread open like a fucking flower.

—You better make sure you use tons of spit.

Fine, I wasn't expecting a dossier or nothing but she was so sketchy on the Jamaican that he became mysterious by default. First I asked why not just let me take on Baxter's hit and finish the job, but she said no, I gotta earn that shit first (yeah I noticed that she said first, making it clear by just hinting it, that there would be a second and maybe a third and who knows how much more). There was a Jamaican I had to rub out in New York and today was the once-in-a-lifetime chance to get it done right, her dramatic effect, not mine—Jesus I'm a fag. She wasn't one for physical description other than saying he was a black-black and he'd probably have a piece on him. Brown Suit filled in with his address and basic M.O. One day in 1980 he just popped up with a fucking Cuban calling himself Doctor Love and there he was. Griselda didn't work with any fucking Cubans, not when she was trying to kill them all, so orders to work with the Cuban and the Jamaican must have come from Medellín. So here he comes like he owned Miami already with a deal to put Jamaica as the best middle point between Colombia and Miami, especially now, with fucking Bahamians fucking up the link and shooting up their own stuff. Griselda found out the Jamaicans have also been working with the Cali cartel and that was some fucked-up shit. But Medellín was okay with the Jamaicans and even showed their chain of command respect. She had work with them, something she didn't like but couldn't say no to. Just in the way she talked you could tell she didn't like his posse sandwiching her, controlling the shipment from Colombia to the States and moving in on the boys selling crack in packets on the street. He said the Jamaican got his training from the CIA, which was probably bullshit but still something I had to watch out for.

Either way, he is in New York now and somebody wants him gone. She didn't say who but made it clear it wasn't her. I am just message bringer, she said. Didn't matter much to me quite frankly, I never needed to know why anybody wanted anybody gone if they were willing to pay for it. But it was weird, even after giving me the hit she wanted me to stay and talk to her. She kicked everybody out. She lingered on him. Talking about how she heard he could never take a joke, never knew when somebody was bullshitting him or on the make for real, the result being that he once shot a guy because the guy said his fat lips were made for sucking his cock. I dunno, honko, you think Jamaicans laugh at the Jeffersons? *Three's Company*? I tell you, that man never laughed at anything.

Anyway, somebody wanted him dead and it wasn't over business as he was good for business. This was a rub-out ordered by a higher power. The higher up the power, the less sensible the reason. Griselda shut up, her bottom lip trembling, her face opening up to a sentence then cutting off before she said it. Something was not sitting with her right, something she wanted to talk about but couldn't. It was out of her hands. That some ghosts from Jamaica were coming back for this guy in New York City. Whoever wanted him dead didn't really care how, but I had one day, one night—tonight to be specific. Hits were better at home, target's way off guard. She said he would be home until probably late in the night. The house was probably thick with enforcers so set this shit up sniper style.

Whatever, I just wanted to get in, take him out and get gone. This trick was getting antsy, still staring at my wallet and looking over at my pillow. I had put the gun back but now I wasn't sure what the fucker wanted to do.

—You gonna fuck me or what?

Josey Wales

I *was watching* my woman pack my Adidas bag when the phone ring. I was going to leave it but she stare at me with her you-think-you-have-maid-'round-here? look.

—Hello?

—Brethren, me hope you pack at least three breadfruit, ten sprat and a bucket o' rice and peas for the I, zeen?

—Eubie. Wha'gwaan, brethren?

—You know the runnings. Just a take life easy still, you no see it?

—Then no must, man, sometimes you have to control a thing and make it work, till it can't work no more.

—That me ah say. How the brethren?

—Cool, man, cool.

—Mind you know. Me know man like you don't like take plane. You have passport and visa? Is not bus ticket run this thing, you know.

—Eubie, everything kriss.

—Wicked. Then Josey, you ever come New York before?

—No, star, only Miami. Businessman no have time for vacation, star.

—True, true. How the Mrs.?

—She would love to hear you call her Mrs. Damn woman a hound me for month now 'bout when we goin' married like real uptown people and why we have to be so common-law and ghetto. Is you talking to her?

—Haha, no, star. But brethren, the Bible say a man who finds a wife finds a good thing.

—Then you calling me woman a thing, Eubie?

—Me? No. The Bible? You and God going have to take up that one. Although the Bible didn't mean you to take it literal. You under—

—Me understand, Eubie. Don't have to go to Columbia University to understand that.

—Awhoa. Anyway, me living in New York near ten years now and even me still can't understand it. It going be really interesting to see what you make of it. New York, just like I pictured it, with skyscrapers and everything . . .

—Who that, the Jeffersons?

—Stevie Wonder, my man. You Jamaicans know the brethren did more than just "Master Blaster," right?

Two minutes in and this is the second time Eubie trying to tell me that I'm ignorant.

—You Jamaicans? No just last week you jump off the boat in New York 'cause it wouldn't stop?

—Hahaha, good one, Josey Wales, good one.

My woman just give me a who-the-r'asscloth-you-talking-to? look. She can tell how I feel about Eubie even though she never meet him. The thing with Eubie is that unlike everybody here who West Kingston have to raise, Eubie didn't come from the ghetto. He fully form from before I even meet him. He have Bronx and Queens lock down with Medellín before I even think to leave Miami to the pussyhole Griselda Blanco, who prefer to deal with Bahamians anyway. And he take some of the best brothers from Copenhagen City from as early as '77. The funny thing is I can barely remember him. He wasn't from Balaclava, or Country or Gaza, but some good house with two good car and a good education too. I could tell from the one time he come visit and he was looking at everybody like he was at the zoo. And he was sweating right through his silk suit, but wouldn't take the white kerchief out of the pocket to wipe him face. Plenty man in these runnings because this is where you find yourself, so you make do until you make big. But I don't know. If I was him and come from where he come, is no way I would've find meself in this. Eubie is the only man I know who in this game for no other reason than desire. More than that, I think it do for him what chasing down fresh pussy after fresh pussy do for some of these boys. A man with big ambition and small stakes. At the same time, for a man, who in just two minutes set himself up as man 'bout the town, he still sport that white kerchief because nobody in America know it mean the man more scared of Obeah than some people scared of the devil.

—So Eubie, you just couldn't wait to hear me voice even though you soon see me, or you ah check me 'bout something?

—Woi, you sharp, Josey, anybody ever tell you?

—Me mother.

—Hah, well yeah, me call you 'bout something. Something me . . . Well anyway, brethren, the second you say is not my business me would just shut me trap 'bout the whole thing.

—What business, brethren?

—Well I did try to connect with your brethren Weeper 'bout the thing but I couldn't get him and—

—What business?

—So Weeper didn't call you? Me did think you was going tell me that that matter settle up long time. Is just when you all the way on Bronx and hearing 'bout Brooklyn business, you think, that's not my affair, that belong to the man named Weeper. But as me say, me call him house with the number you give me long time and no Weeper. Him change him number?

—What business?

Eubie pause. He certainly not afraid of me so I know he's not nervous. He taking him time, dragging this out. He wants me to know that he have something I want even if I don't think so.

—Well when one of these things happen, it don't mean nothing. Sometimes these basehead will skip from borough to borough to score as much rock as he can get, right? I mean, ah nuh nothing. But when six of them come all the way from Brooklyn to Bronx something must be up.

—You saying you get six customers from Brooklyn today? Maybe they don't know where to go in Brooklyn.

—A where you come from, Josey Wales? A crackhead need him fix, trust me, motherfucker know where to go. He can't afford to not keep that shit local. Close proximity is crucial to success, my brethren, but of course me only telling you what you already know. Anyway, one my boys grab one them heads and ask him what him doing all the way in Queens, and him say he couldn't deal with Bushwick no more.

—What happen in Bushwick?

—No your man Weeper run Bushwick?

—Wha'appen in Bushwick, brethren?

—The man say that two dealer suddenly charge twice what they usually charge, just like that. Me know you know we building a loyalty thing right here and we always looking for new customers but since me no remember you saying anything 'bout price increase, me surprise price just jack up in Brooklyn. I mean, that no make no sense, is because of price fixing why we don't have too much movement from borough to borough?

—Hmmm.

—And another thing, my youth. Seems a couple of your dealers also using. I don't know if that how things work in Miami, but over here that is always, always bad for business. One of them baseheads say he couldn't find your dealer so he go in the crack house thinking somebody would give him a hit only to find the two dealer beaming up. The two of them! I mean, to r'asscloth how you can have your two dealer in the basehouse with line of people outside itching for base? And how the hell you can trust a crackhead to make a business transaction? And where them get it if they not burning out your own supply?

—Josey?

—Yeah, me hearing you.

—Hey my brethren, me just talking it as me see it. And when a man have to skip borough just to get two or three packet that sound like a problem. Make me tell you, in the Bronx me run a tight ship, even from the days when me just 'lowing little weed. Back in 1979 me set things up like any business, better than any shop, because I know from the devil was boy that you can never expand if your core base didn't set right. I don't take kindly to no kind of slackness. Worse if is my brother. You know what me tell the last man who fuck up? Me give him a choice, me say to him, My youth, this is what I going do for you. You get to choice which eye you want to lose, the right or the left. If you car have a loose wheel, it soon fall off and kill everybody. And what go for Bronx also go for Queens.

I still can't believe the man just call me a youth.

—Who hire them, you or Weeper? I mean, Weeper should have seen that and stamp it out quick-quick but then again, Weeper . . . Well you must know what you doing.

—Yeah.

—But I tell you, the last time I have a deputy start using it wasn't long before me have to cancel the bredda. Because here is the thing, Josey, cocaine is not like crack. At least cokehead have some class and even if they didn't have no class at least they have money. You can still manage that like a gentleman. Crack? That man will suck you dick or cut their own baby heart out to beam up. You can't have that kind of fucker selling your shit? No, my youth. No way. But then you and Weeper go way back, right?

—Not that way back.

—Oh.

—Well I don't know. As I say, you must know about Weeper. But you should at least check out what going on at your spot in Bushwick. Me, I go into every situation with a needle and a gun. Either I fixing you or I putting you out of your misery. You need me to go straighten out Bed-Stuy, Bushwick, or wherever, just say the word. I would need some more manpower but still I—

—I already tell you, Eubie, me have them place lock down. You deal with where you know. Anyway, call you when I reach.

—Huh? Oh yeah, sure. Call me.

I hang up. My woman still looking at me. I call Weeper and it ring without answer. I know she watching me because she know when I'm getting mad. I can hear her already saying to no bother show them things in front of the one pure child she have leave. I look at her looking at me.

—Is cool, man, stop look so, I say.

Weeper

Y*ou gonna* answer it?

—No.

—Don't you have some buddy to pick up at the airport?

—I tell you about that? Not till later.

—At least turn the ringer off. It's that thing in—

—I know where to find the fucking ringer. Where's the K-Y?

—Dunno, it's in this bed somewhere.

—Where?

—Said I dunno. Maybe you're lying on it. Or it's under the pillow beneath you. Know what? Roll over. Of course I maintain, I dunno what's so bad about spit. Jamaicans are so weird about saliva.

—Wah kinda remark that? You spit on a man, that's disrespect.

—It's just water. Like would you spit on my ass and lick it?

—Lawks. No.

—Because of the ass or the spit? You realize by licking ass you're licking your spit anyway.

—How you can lick back up your own spit? Once it leave your mouth it gone, it not supposed to come back ever.

—Haha. Roll over.

—What?

—You heard me. Roll over.

—I like it this way. You go deeper.

—Deeper my ass, you just don't want to look at me.

Afternoon in the room. I roll over. The bed too soft and me sinking and he on top pushing me down in the sheet. Sinking. He say inhibited but I don't know what he mean, even though he say it with a smile. Looking at me and not turning away. Today is a Tuesday, a yellow-looking day. He still looking at me—me lips dry? Eye crossed? He thinking I going to be the one to look away first, but I not going look away and I not going to even blink.

—You're beautiful.

—No bother with that.

—I'm telling you, not many men can pull off that glasses thing.

—Boy done with that shit. Man don't tell man them things that is some—

—Batty boy business? I know, I heard you the last seven times. I swear you'd love the Puerto Ricans. They don't think sucking dick or fucking ass makes them gay either. Only if you get fucked, then you're a fucking fag.

—You calling the brethren a bombocloth faggot?

—Oh no, you're crazy about the pussy.

—I like pussy.

—Dude, we fucking or am I supposed to be Harry Hamlin to your Michael Ontkean?

—What the r'asscloth you talking about?

—You want to guess how many times in just two years I just had the previous discussion? It's tired, man, and I'm tired of cocksuckers on the quiet tip. Especially you black guys. I just wanna do this.

I keep my lips shut. I wait on him. But he already sucking my right nipple and then the left one harder, like he going to pull it off. It start to hurt and I about to say what the fuck it hurt but then he lick it. Flick his tongue, flicking and licking. I shudder. I want to beg him to lick the right one just to stop shuddering. I feel a circle of warm spit on my nipple that he blowing dry and cool. He need to stop making me the woman. Not from a fuck but from a blow on the nipple.

—Christ, just let it out, you fucker. You mumble any more you're gonna choke.

—What?

—You can't be cool as fuck and enjoy your own damn body the same time, so give one of them up. Maybe I should leave and you can call me when you make up your mind.

—NO. I mean, no.

He back in my mouth before I can say bad man don't kiss. Sucking my tongue, moving his lips over my lips, tongue on tongue, dancing it and making me do it back. He is making me think like a faggot.

—Aw, look at you. You just giggled like a school girl. There may be hope for you yet.

Lip on top of lip, lip turned on the side licking me in the mouth, tongue on top of tongue, underneath tongue, lips sucking my tongue, and I open my eye and see him two eye close tight. That moan come from him not me. I reach up and squeeze him nipples but not hard, I still don't know hot from hurt. But he moan and now he taking him tongue down my chest to my nipples and my navel leaving a wet trail that feel cold even though him tongue warm. New York spying me do this? I spy what do you spy? B A T T Y with a tight needle-eye. Outside the window is five floor up but I don't know. Too high for the window washer or pigeon or whoever climbing the wall although nobody would be climbing no wall. Nobody can see but the sky. But Air Jamaica going fly right by and Josey going see me. The man tickle my navel with him tongue and I grab him head. He look up for second and smile and the hair pass through my fingers so thin, so soft, so brown. Hair that make you sound white when you describe it.

—Come back, fucker.

I want to say I am here but he just swallowed my cock and that's not what come out of my mouth. Something about foreskin, him saying. Pulling it back, looking at the head, diving down on it and I jump up. *You uncut guys are really sensitive, huh?* Licking, sucking just the head then swallow all the way down until he bump into my crotch hair. Up and down, fucking it, and I feel his lips and his tongue and the top of him throat and the wet and the warm and the vacuum suck and release and suck and release and suck and release and I can't stop grabbing him shoulder every time him pull the foreskin back. And the look, white going down on black then coming up, white going down and coming back up with a twist and lick with pink tongue. The third time I grab him shoulder and squeeze. He stop finally. But then he grab me two ankle and push me ass up and him tongue fucking me. I don't think about how I don't like it so much, don't think that it just feel like something wet is wetting up me asshole. Him leaving me legs up in the air. He roll off the bed and picks up a condom. I still can't tell the difference between covered up and bareback, which is also the name of a condom so I don't understand. I know it's five floors up but what if somebody pass by the window right now and see my leg up in the air? This is really going to happen again. I don't fuck enough yet to not think every time that this is really going to happen. I don't fuck enough yet not to think that there is another hard cock in the room and is not mine. And me just want to grab it and squeeze it and tug it, and maybe suck it one day. And then his fingers now rubbing lube in my asshole, and for once me not thinking prison fuck, though by saying me not going think about prison fuck I do think about prison fuck and he's really rubbing that stuff in me asshole good and fucking me with him finger and he reach something and somewhere that make me jump and no I don't wonder if this is how woman feel when me hit the spot, because fuck women and fuck pussy and fuck trying to fuck the faggot out, at least right here, right now five floors up. And fuck thinking what it going mean the white man on top because I don't think about the white man on top until I think that this is America and if I think like a nigger then it mean something that the white man on top and maybe I should go on top even though he can still ride me. Thank God me not the one who need to have a hard cock.

Phone ring again.

—You gonna let me in at some point, honey?

—What? Oh.

—What are you so uptight about? Gotta say hon, this whole thing about Jamaicans being so chill is turning more and more into a myth. Just sayin'.

—I not uptight.

—Baby, I could probably hang from the ceiling with my thumb stuck up your butt.

—Haha.

—Aha, so the trick is to keep you laughing then. Or to fuck you in the dark. You didn't seem to have a problem then.

—Every movie I ever see them fucking in the dark. Even TV.

—At what point did it hit you that not every man in America looks like Bobby Ewing?

—I like the dark.

—Holy switch the subject, Batman.

—You switch the subject, not me.

—You know the only person who's going to see you out that window is Superman. You can choose to believe it or not. I gotta take a leak, be right back.

Had to slap my hand over my mouth so that I don't say hurry up. I still can't stop thinking that Josey going pop up outside the window like Kilroy was here. And you know what, I going say, This is America and me can do what me want so fuck what any of you want to say, or as Americans would say, Kiss my ass. Lower East Side all lock up and I deal with that business in Bed-Stuy myself and didn't have to call the idiot Eubie either, and if he don't watch I soon take over the Bronx too. In fact I don't need no Bronx and fucking black people, I got white people in Manhattan who will pay three times that much. And when that plane finally land tonight he going see that Weeper run New York and everything that he need done, do better because of me so just fucking leave me alone and don't come to my house and don't look under the sheet but if you do look under the sheet, don't say nothing. How much more fucking things a man must do?

Things just heavy. That's all. Things just heavy.

He come out of the bathroom with him cock hard and bending left and with a rubber on already. White man have lighter skin in the exact shape of the brief they wear. And 'round him cock and balls is firebush. I'm wondering if man supposed to be tender. Is the tender thing that make this feel faggot-like. It never feel that way otherwise. Not at Mineshaft, Eagle's Nest, Spike, New David's Theater, Adonis Theater, West World, Bijou 82, The Jewel, Christopher Street Bookstore, Jay's Hangout, Hellfire Club, Les Hommes, Ann Street Bookstore, Ramrod, or Badlands and not in the Ramble, not with the businessman going home to the wife, or the cyclist, or the hippie long-haired student, or the *guapo* and *muchacho* and *mariconcito*, and church boy, and the clone with all eight inches print out in their jeans, or the man that other man call preppy, or white-hair man walking they dog, or man who look like an ordinary man doing ordinary thing and nothing more. Some come up right behind me when I pull me shorts down, some take me home if they have the white wife, though nobody in America ever know what I mean by white wife so I just say lemon, or yeyo, or weasel dust or big C, or just fucking cocaine. A dealer can pilfer his own stash. Home or park I pull shorts down and they spit or lube and fuck and I wait until the shudder and sometimes they wait until I cum first, then they just jack off on my bottom. But it just feel like man grabbing a man to be a man. In bed and so soft we feel like two faggot. We sound like two faggots. So what? Then we must be faggots.

—You going stand there jerking off all day? I say.

The phone ring right there. He look at it then look at me not looking at it. He go to say something but don't. The phone still ringing. I wait for it to stop and he climb on the bed and grab my ankles. The ringing stop and he have both of my legs in the air. I wait for the phone to start ringing again, because if it was really important he she it would call back. He rubbing my asshole with lube. No phone ring. He rubbing him cock with lube. No phone ring. I almost expect him to say here goes and though he don't I giggle anyway, like some girl. He smile, look at me straight and push himself right in, not fast not slow but he go firm and he don't stop and the one-second hurt just disappear when he fit himself in with that curve cock and just hit it.

Pissing in the bathroom and the fucking phone ring again.

—Hello?

Shit. The man in bed answer the phone.

—Hello? Let's do this again, hello? One sec. I think it's for you.

Five seconds before I take the phone.

—Hello?

—Who the fuck was that?

—Who? What you talking about?

—What the bombocloth you think me talking 'bout? Is duppy just answer the phone?

—No, Eubie.

—Then a who that?

—Is me brethren from down the hall, him come over because him . . . hear me playing some music you . . . you know Phil Collins?

—And you have him answering you business phone?

—Now hold on, Eubie. Me never have him answering nothing. Me come out of the toilet and see that him answer it already. So, wha'gwaan, my youth? What's shaking?

—Don't talk to me with that American lingo.

—And don't talk to me like me is you pickney. Something going on?

—Bet your ass something going on, is three time now I call the brethren.

—Well now you get me.

—I definitely got something.

—What the fuck that mean?

—Anyway, plan change. Me picking up Josey, not you and—

—Fuck that. Josey would tell me if he change him plans.

—Then by all means come to the airport and watch me pick him up. The more the merrier I always say. Another thing. Josey don't want to go to East Village again, he want to see operations in Bushwick.

—Bushwick? Any reason him want to go to Bushwick all of a sudden?

—Any reason you suddenly think me name psychic? You have a problem with Josey talk to Josey.

—I was going take him to Miss Queenie's first. Best Jamaican food in New York City, right in Flatbush, Brooklyn.

—Weeper. Josey Wales look like he leaving Jamaica where he can have Jamaican food all the time to fly up for imitation fuckery? You is a idiot or you just play one on TV?

—Yow, a who you ah call—

—Picking him up nine-thirty. Meet we in Bushwick.

Dorcas Palmer

Maybe some people know something I don't, but I've never come across a man saying "I'm just curious" who didn't have some other motive. *You live alone? I'm just curious*, yes, that was the start of a fabulous night. Granted, I was the idiot from taking him home the first place. Why? Because after going after the man in that loud Jamaican club because he didn't look Jamaican, picking up said man, and giving him a reason in the parking lot to go further, I didn't want to go to his house because what kind of slut does such a thing? the principal of Immaculate Conception High School would have said. Took the man home and he immediately grew seven more hands, one 'round my neck, one already down my panty, and scooping me because he must've thought a clitoris popped out front like a cock. Funny how beer breath smells sexy only in a bar. I said I changed my mind and he grabbed me by the throat and started to squeeze. I grabbed his hands but he only squeezed tighter saying, We not going have any problems are we? I said no baby, me just want to go in the bedroom and put on something more comfortable. You know, like how them do it in movie.

—Then where is the bar so I can fix myself a drink.

—You won't have time for that, babylove.

So I go into the bathroom and I did find something that made me feel much more comfortable. I remembering walking all the way down to near the end of Gun Hill Road just to find one. The shopkeeper looked at me and asked is what me plan to reap with it. The man set himself in one of the dining chairs I had in the living room. No problem, I only needed to walk a block or two and another chair would be waiting for me. Collateral damage. He was bent over, tugging the only clothes left on, socks that didn't match. The cutlass cut through the air so fast I almost couldn't control it. It chop clean through top rail and lodged in the back. The man jumped but not fast enough. He did what men feel they must do, step in closer, nudging and nudging and laughing like he think woman 'fraid. But it wasn't the swinging that frighten the shit out of him. Is was that I could catch myself so quick and swing again, like I was stunt double in a Bruce Lee movie. A girl needed a hobby my mother would say. I slice after him again and start to scream come out of me bombocloth house! He's saying easy baby, easy, and I start screaming rape! Come out of me bombocloth house. I swing to make it look like I missed him and shattered my expensive vase, but the vase wasn't worth shit and I smashed it just to show that this mad bitch mean business. He was still backing away too fucking slow. Can I have my clothes at least? he said but I kept screaming and chasing after him, swinging the fucking cutlass left and right like I was clearing away bush. He ran to the door and slipped out screaming down the hallway about some crazy motherfucking bitch. Don't know who he was talking about. I wonder if I was more Jamaican then and am nothing but some American spazz now. And—

—Fine don't tell me, I don't need to know.

—Know what?

—I swear, my cousin Larry with Alzheimer's has a sharper attention span than you.

—Oh, excuse me.

—No, you're not excused. Now I'm going to have to tell you a joke now.

—Lord, Mr. Ken, not another nigger joke.

—Oh good heavens, no more of those, please. It was about Alzheimer's. Funny, people with the big A joke about people with the big C, as if there something at least about not remembering you're sick that makes that disease better.

—So are you the big A or the big C? The big P? D? My family in Jamaica is all about the big D.

—Big D?

—Diabetes.

—Of course, and P for Parkinson's? Sometimes I wished I had a medieval disease, like consumption, or the bloody flux.

—What do you have?

—Let's not turn this into a movie of the week so soon, shall we? Because then I'll feel like I'm living in my daughter's TV. In fact this whole scene needs to be less *Imitation of Life* and more *Gulliver's Travels.*

He walks over to the doorway and picks up his cap and scarf.

—Let's go.

—What? Go where? Lilliput? The pizza man soon come.

—Oh I never eat that shit. They'll just leave it in the stairway and charge it to our account. Let's cut this place loose, I'm fucking bored.

The truth is, I really wanted to leave. All the slave-era furniture that you just knew was made only a few years ago was getting on my nerves. Somewhere in this house Miz Colthirst was keeping every single issue of *Victoria.* And probably *Redbook* for anytime she felt like making her own icing.

—Where are we going?

—Who the hell knows, maybe you'll take me out for dinner in the Bronx. So I take it you've read Swift.

—Jamaican schoolers read *Gulliver's Travels* by the time they're twelve.

—Oh my. What surprise will she reveal in the next forty minutes? Inquiring minds want to know. Let's go.

This man wasn't joking about the Bronx. I'm not sure why I didn't say anything either when we just jumped out of the cab as soon as it reached Union Square, went to the subway and jumped on the 5, heading right back where we came from. We both sat in a three-seater by the door. I didn't want to look up to see if anybody was looking at me. The graffiti was inside now too. Until we got to 96th, the car was mostly white people, old men and women who probably had nowhere to go and school children in no rush to get home. Between 110th and 125th most of the white people had come off, leaving the Latinos and some of the blacks. By 145th the car was almost all black. None of the groups could resist looking at us. I wished I had dressed like a nurse and he didn't look like Lyle Waggoner. Maybe the black men would think this man must be something special to be able to handle a black woman. Or maybe they were wondering if he's really traveling this far for a call girl. Worse, since we're going to 180th I had to sit and wait till the train ran out of people to look at us.

—You live around here?

—No.

—Was just asking.

—You know it's not safe to be on this train heading to this place this time of day, right?

—What are you talking about? It's barely five in the afternoon.

—It's five in afternoon in the Bronx.

—And?

—You own a TV?

—People decide on what they should fear in this world, Dorcas.

—People who live on Park Avenue can decide if they feel like having some fear today. For the rest of us it means don't go to the Bronx after five.

—So why are we going?

—I'm not going. You're going. I'm just following you.

—Ha, you're the one who told me about the jerk chicken on Boston Road, and I told you I haven't had Jamaican food since 1973.

—And so it goes, every white man must have his own *Heart of Darkness* experience for himself.

—I don't know what I should be more impressed by, the fact that you're so well read, or the fact that the farther we get from Fifth Avenue, the bolder your tone gets with me.

—What next, Mr. Ken? You speak English so well? Americans don't read books in high school? As for tone, since my hiring was a mistake, I think you can rest assured that you won't be seeing me or anybody from the agency tomorrow.

—Wow, that would be a mistake of disastrous proportions, he said, not to me but to whatever he was looking at out the window. I survey the car to see if anybody was looking at that exchange.

—I think I know what you're doing, I say.

—Really? Do tell.

—Whatever it is that you have, clearly it's giving you a death wish. You don't have to be afraid of anything anymore so you can do whatever you want.

—Maybe. Or maybe, Freud, I just want some fucking jerk pork and yam, and rum punch, and don't give a fuck about your fucking dime-store pop psychology. You ever fucking thought about that?

Two men look up.

—Sorry. I just get all of that shit from my son and his wife already. Don't need it, especially from somebody I'm paying for.

Three men and two women look up.

—Well, thanks for letting everybody think that I'm a prostitute, I say.

—What? What are you talking about?

—Everybody heard you.

—Oh. Oh no.

And then he gets up. I open my handbag wide and wonder if my whole head can fit in it.

—Look folks . . . I ah . . . know what you might be thinking.

—Are you serious? They're not thinking anything. Sit down.

—I just want to say, that Dorcas here, she's my wife, not some prostitute.

I know that in my mind I screamed. I don't know if I did it in public but in my mind I sure as hell screamed.

—We've been married for what now, four years, honey? And I gotta say, it's just like the first day, isn't that so, precious?

I can't tell if he's failing badly at protecting my reputation or if he's really enjoying this. Meanwhile I'm looking very hard at people trying hard not to look. An older woman is covering her mouth and laughing. I want to laugh just to make it clear I'm outside this joke too, but the laugh just won't come. The funny thing is I'm not even mad at him. He's holding on to the railing, swinging with the train almost like he's about to dance. The train stops at Morris Park.

—This is our stop.

—Oh? But this is Morris Park. I thought we were coming off at Gun Hill Road?

—This is the stop.

I jump out as soon as the doors open and don't wait for him. I don't even look back. I almost want him to stay on, go the fuck to Gun Hill Road all he wants. But then I hear him breathing behind me.

—God that was fun.

—Embarrassing people is fun?

I stand at the platform, waiting for an apology because I've seen movies, this is what you're supposed to do.

—Maybe you should ask yourself why you're so easily embarrassed.

—Wah?

—I love it when you talk Jamaican.

—You serious?

—Oh for fuck's sake, Dorcas. You don't know a single person on the train, you'll never see any of them again, and even if you do, you won't even remember what they look like, so who gives a shit what they thought?

Jesus sweet Lord, I hate when I'm not the one in the room making sense.

—We should wait for the next train.

—Fuck that. Let's walk.

—You're going to walk. In the Bronx.

—Yep, that's what I'm gonna do.

—You know that they find a body in Haffen Park almost every morning.

—You're gonna talk to a veteran about dead bodies?

—You know crime is not like how you see it on *Police Woman.*

—*Police Woman?* When's the last time you watched TV?

—We can't walk just in the Bronx.

—Don't worry, Dorcas, at worst they'll just think you're helping me to score heroin.

—Did you just say heroin?

This was going to be fabulous, me the questionably documented immigrant walking through a Bronx neighbourhood in the evening with a strange white man clearly out of his element because he's drinking that I'm-a-white-man-I'm-invincible juice.

—Then you not going even call your family?

—Fuck 'em. The wrinkle my daughter will get from frowning over this, especially after her face-lift, will be worth it.

Tristan Phillips

O*h, so you can* go back to Jamaica whenever you want to? Ah so? You sound like man who say they can give up smack whenever they want to. Mind you know, Alex Pierce, Jamaica can shoot through your veins and it become like every dark sweet thing that not good for you. But me done with talking in riddle. The thing is, unless you did know where to look for me, there is no way you could have find me. Yeah, yeah, you're concerned about the fall of the peace process, so tell me something, how you plan to learn anything about it if you not been in the country since 1978? Me surprised you even hear about it, since you never was on the rock when it happen. So you going talk to Lucy? Brethren, you no serious. Lucy is the key. Me and she is the only people from the peace council still alive. You going have to track her down in Jamaica, my youth. You ever wonder how come we two still alive while everybody else dead? Of course not, until right now, you did think it was only one. Remember, you know, on paper me supposed to dead too. Everybody get killed and depending who you talk to, that include the Singer. Tell me something, you ever hear somebody get infected with cancer?

The thing I still can't understand is why this topic sweat you so much. You making it out like The Day Jamaica Gone to Hataclaps, like the place did have somewhere else to go. So what was your favourite spot in Jamaica? Trench Town? What kind of man pick Trench Town as him favourite spot? You lucky you white, eh? Make me ask you something, you think Trench Town is a favourite spot for anybody living in Trench Town? You think any of them sitting on a stoop saying, Now this is the life? Tourist funny, boy.

Oh, you not a tourist. Don't tell me: you know the real Jamaica. You did have a little missus down there? Aisha. Nice name, sound like something you say when you cum. So she a nice girl or she suck your dick? Haha, me no mind, white boy, me is a man of the world. Third World, but still. How much more time we have today? Unlimited? In Rikers? Brethren, is what kinda string you just pull? Still better we get back on topic, no true?

Until the Singer tell me 'bout Josey Wales me never think twice 'bout the boy. But then things and more things happen, and you start to see signs even though you never did like church. I mean, if he did really care about killing the Singer he would have finished the job the very next night. Man must was out to make a different point. I mean, shit, to come straight into the Singer yard two year later like nothing never happen? A man with balls that big? Stay out of him way. Now it easy to say that peace did doom to fail because war is the ghetto man character. Yeah, that sound like something wise, but you have to understand—you know when hope so new and fresh it even have a colour? Like the thing that you save in the back of you head because it never going happen and then all of a sudden it look like it might happen for real? Is like you find out that you can fly for true. We never born behind cow, or naïve as you would put it. None of we was idiot. All of we did know that this peace was a ninety percent chance of fail but, man, ten percent never look so sweet in all we life. You could just grab it. And when Shotta Sherrif say to me that me must chair it this peace council, is like somebody look at me and for the first time see something different from what me even see in meself. I . . .

I . . .

I lost meself again.

And then in a blink: Copper shot, Papa-Lo shot, first me did think that it was just the police settling score now that we guard down. Or worse: political parties which never did want the peace anyway getting rid of it in time for the next election. But we already talk about the intelligence of the police. And even politician wouldn't want it come out that is them kill peace. You have to look deeper. Police kill bad man because them have vendetta. But other than to have a dead body to parade around downtown they don't really get no benefit out of killing nobody. You have think. Who in a better place right now than he was before these killings? Only one man.

Josey Bombocloth Wales.

Papa-Lo dead and now he the ranking don of Copenhagen City. Shotta Sherrif dead and PNP's New York posses scattered ever since, including my owner posse. Every man in New York sniffing, smoking and shooting up the white wife and the Colombian need a man with skill that can get that shit further into the States. And even England now, me hear. Take the peace treaty out of the way, and he just give certain politician a favour so big that they going spend the rest of the life to repay. Kill any movement of Jah people and Americans don't have no reason to be 'fraid anymore that we going turn into Cuba. Me don't know nothing for true, but I'd bet that even some people higher up, maybe people who control coast guard, or immigration or customs or some shit, now all turn a blind eye to certain boat and plane and ship because one man give them Jamaica on a plate in 1980.

Brethren, if me did know why people like me end up in prison, people like me wouldn't end up in prison. Feel free to start your first paragraph that way, call it ghetto wisdom or something, whatever you white people write whenever you get all caught up in shady black people. Yeah, me read too, Alex Pierce, more than you. Man, people like me just excite you, eh? Put a white journalist beside him own "Stagger Lee" and your brain go bananas. Is 'cause you have no story of your own? Right, it's not about you, you're here to tell the story, not be the story. And yet still some part of me tell me that this is your story, not mine. You interested in any year after 1978? How 'bout 1981? Plenty things happen, the Singer get to know this place named Heaven and me get to know this place named Attica. What, you think man get to Rikers because them see a brochure? You graduate to Rikers, brethren.

So anyway, even though me know that batty boy Weeper wasn't going come after me again, that didn't mean Josey Wales wasn't going to. By the way, you ever meet that brother? No? You talking about the peace process and you never meet . . . never mind. I really couldn't know what that man was planning to do, so me start run with the Ranking Dons. It simple: Storm Posse, which is Josey Wales, is Copenhagen City, and Ranking Dons is the

Eight Lanes. And since me was a part of Eight Lanes from the day they bulldoze Balaclava, where else me fi go? No star, political warfare don't end just because you switch battlefield. I needed the safety in numbers, they needed the brains since the stupid little fuckers couldn't even keep track of who selling on what street, or which street you was going get shoot up by Eubie Brown and him Storm Posse.

No problem brother, change you cassette.

Anyway, say this about the Storm Posse and Eubie, even Josey Wales. Them might wipe out an entire line of people at the theater just to get one man, but at least them have some sort of class. Or at least Eubie have some class. Or maybe he just know how to wear silk and not look like a pimp. But my crew? Nothing but dutty, nasty naigger. Like this one time, the bossman hear a man from Jamdown based in Philly just get a huge stash of weed, but though he be part of Copenhagen City he didn't have Storm Posse protection because the fool didn't think he need it. So the bossman send we to Philadelphia.

The man so unaware that we just walk right into him house. Didn't even lock him door. For a man who supposed to have a big stash he didn't act like it. I remember telling Ranking Dons that if this stash is for Eubie there goin' be another war in at least one of the five boroughs. But them convinced this man is an independent, as if man just trip and fall and land on a shipment of weed. Anyway, the man see we and start to run upstairs for the gun because he didn't keep one on him. Me say to meself, Who is this amateur? Ranking Dons sure they send me to the right house, because this man wasn't acting like he have anything valuable to hide. The fucking idiot who was with me then say that maybe is some reverse psychology sinting, you know, if he act like he have nothing to protect then we will think he clean and leave. Hate to say it but that did make a kinda sense. So we tie him up and start slap him around little bit telling him to give up the stash or it only going get worse. Before me even tell him how worse, the fucking idiot clap him with a gun butt straight in the mouth. What the fuck wrong with you? I say to the idiot only to watch him smile at me like an idiot. This man need fi talk now, him say. How him going talk if you mash up the thing he need to speak with, you fucking retarded idiot? I say, and he shut up, but not before he look at me long, as if that kinda shit frighten me.

And if she never scream me wouldn't even know that he have wife. She try to run, but you can't get too far with a baby in your hand. We force her down on a chair while me hold the baby, because this fucking idiot was just going put it down on the cold floor. Three more time I ask the man for the weed stash, and three more time he say he don't have no weed. I know he was lying. Why would he tell the truth? After all, stakes don't raise yet. The fucking idiot all this time looking at the wife and grabbing him crotch. He use him foot to lift her skirt off her legs to see her green panty. Green? How come it nuh pink? he say. Me getting tired of this house, this man and him wife and the fucking idiot, even this baby who sleeping on me shoulder when the fucking idiot say, Yow, my youth, check it, me ah go hoist up the pussyhole and sink down the cock, you see me? Before me even say something him already drop him pants and start grab him crotch through him brief. You one of them nasty American woman who suck buddy? 'Cause you can suck it, just don't make me cum before me fuck you. Oh, and that mean no kissy-kiss.

—You not raping her, me say to the fucking idiot.

—How you mean, who going stop me, you?

Him say to me like he throwing down gauntlet. I thinking, Shit, this fucking idiot going rape this poor gal in front of her own baby and me can't do nothing because everything from car to hotel book under him name. The wife scream and he punch her in the face.

—What the bombocloth wrong with you?

—Nothing wrong with me, me a show the bitch say silence golden.

He pull down him brief and say, You going spread you leg and open up the pussy or me going haffi spread you? The wife start cry and look at either the baby or me, I can't tell.

—Brethren, pull you pants back up.

—Fuck you. It pull back up when me cocky limp again.

—You ah go rape the woman in front of her own man?

—Make him watch and learn what fi do with woman.

—Brethren, me say no raping going on.

Then he aim him gun at me. Shut up, him say. She ask if him have condoms and he say, That condom is plan to kill black people. And, anyway, condom make him lose him nature.

Me looking at him forcing the woman legs open, and the man looking at me and me looking at the baby. Them in the basement behind the bookshelf him say. But me only have five bag, him say. I think he say please after that, but the wife was whimpering as the fucking idiot squeeze her breast. Then he yank her down on the floor.

—Brethren—

—Fuck off.

—You is an idiot? We take the weed and leave. Him can't call the police. But if you rape her police going be here, and them going find we before we even make it to the state line.

—Then we kill them.

He say it just like that. Hey, me no have no problem shooting up a club full of pussyholes, but me not killing no family in cold blood just 'cause them make a wrong move and think them can deal with drugs.

—How much time you go prison, fool?

—A who you ah call fool—

—Me say how much time you go bloodcloth prison?

—One time and me nah go back.

—So if you rape her, them hold you for rape. If you kill her, them hold you for murder. Because maybe you didn't notice, but only one of the two of we wearing gloves and that motherfucker is not you.

He look at me like me lead him into a trap, but you only have yourself to blame for stupid. Especially since he was behaving like the don of dons the whole drive.

—Now why you don't go pull up your pants and go get the weed?

He go down to the basement and come up with only four bag. Bag about the size of the paper you writing notes on. This time I gun-butt him myself. I tell this brethren, Look, don't fucking lie to me or me will leave the room and this man can do with your wife whatever he want. He start cry, the poor man, probably didn't know what he was getting himself into. If the wife stayed with him after that then love not blind, it deaf, dumb and stupid. He say one more bag in the bedroom. The fucking idiot find it under the bed, along with three guns that him was clearly going to keep for himself. I didn't care, I didn't even bother to tell him that gun very easy to track. Besides, something told me that this couple wasn't about to file no police report. Wicked times, eh? But at least with Josey Wales, if he say there was five bags in the house, believe you me there was five bags in the house. Instead you get Ranking Dons who couldn't organize their way out of open door.

You know something though, Alex Pierce? Every single time I mention Josey Wales you jump. Just a little bit, but enough. Nervous tic, eh? Seaga have nervous tic. You jump. I think I figuring it out why you come to see me. Everybody who need to know, know say at one point Josey Wales want me dead, but him clearly not after me no more. The big question is, how did you know there was a contract out on you?

Weeper

I *said I caught* the motherfucking bitch tryna suck my little boy's dick for his pocket money. That same heifer right over there by the doorway. You think I'm motherfucking blind? He's only twelve. All these motherfucking crack hos with they stank-ass pussies all up in this neighbourhood, y'all said you'd keep them away because your biz is almost legit and shit. Well y'all can go kiss my black ass. And another thing . . .

Bushwick. Sunset gone long time but things always fucking hot in Bushwick. Woman standing right in front of me, in me face I can smell garlic on her. Eye shadow but no lipstick, Jheri curl drying out. Belly a muffin spilling over her jeans. We in the street but she keep pointing to the crack ho who start running-walking away.

—And you ain't never said that you was gonna turn that place over there into no crack house. Tired of this shit. The city owns these buildings, not you.

She don't live in this building. She's in one of them house across the street, string of single brick house that make Bushwick look like Bronx. Three black boys and a girl fixing a bicycle right in front of her iron fence, but the fence not protecting no grass lawn, only concrete. Five house on the other side of the road and they all have fence. We in front of my building, three floors up is operations. Patrol car start to roll down the street too much so now we have to stash indoors and give the dealers just enough to sell a little at a time—never enough for police to give a shit. Better this way, at least you can control it. City fix up the building, homeless people move in, and we. They shut the fuck up, I make it worth they while. If they don't shut the fuck up I remind the super that if police get the drop on operations that's the end of fi him cut. Plenty building super in the Brooklyn want a cut of the business that I can bring them. But Bushwick is a piece of shit. East Village never give me a single problem, but Bushwick find a brand-new one every week. And all the way up this street I didn't see a single spotter or runner.

Two near-deserted block over the spotter was sitting on the curb with him boombox booming *the freaks come out at night.* Young boy still trying to grow into too-clean sneakers. He didn't have either the sneakers or the boombox last week. Didn't even see me coming until I was right in front of him.

—Step the fuck off, bitches, I ain't on the clock, he say without even looking up. So I said,

—Look up, pussyhole.

The boy jump out of him fifteen years.

—Yessir! Yessir!

—This look like the army?

—No sir!

—What a go on 'round here?

He look down on the ground, like he afraid to tell me something that I wouldn't like.

—Brethren, your business is to give me the message. I don't shoot the messenger. What going down with the business?

He still looking on the ground, but he mumble something.

—What?

—Nothing, man. Ain't shit going on 'round here for days now.

—Fuckery that. Every basehead wake up and start do heroin instead? No way market just dry up.

—Well . . .

—Well what?

—Well a brother gets tired of sending shit that way only to have them come back and say that I must be down with some wild goose chase or sumth'n cuz ain't nobody with no goods in that alley. I done my job, I can spot a hitter a mile away. I approach them all casual-like and say yo, Bushwick is stupid fresh, you feeling for some heat or some pop rocks or some shit like that, and they nod and before they say some dumb-ass cracker shit I just nod to the alley behind the cut.

—You know where the cut is?

—Everybody knows where to find the fucking cut. They just don't wanna mess with you. Anyways, usually you got two or three runners there to take them to the goods and get that shit sold, but for four days now, people come back this way saying I'm nothing but bullshit because they ain't no runners in the street. And no dealer neither. Your bodyguard got so tired of this shit he gone and got a real job in Flatbush.

—Where the runners go?

—I dunno. They ain't got nobody to steer anymore. Your dealers ain't dealing.

—What the fuck them doing?

—Maybe you should go check the hithouse.

I look at this boy acting like he brave and I think to either gun-butt him or promote him. Josey coming here in less than five hours, to fuck.

—And hey, since I ain't got no buyers to spot, I spot some other shit, yo. Two days now I seen some shit Pontiac cruising and I can just bet them niggers was Ranking Dons. They already sniffing out this place because they know security weak.

—You see plenty for a little shit.

—S'what paid for these kicks, yo.

I looking at this boy and already thinking how me going need him to fix Bushwick before Josey come. I didn't even notice that the damn woman follow me.

—First that stank-ass heifer come all the way through my own motherfucking gate lifting up her dress and no panties and telling my young son that he can hit the pussy for two bucks. Good thing I'm at my window the second I hear any fussin' at my gate. Next thing I know three lowlife goodfernothings come over here thinking this is the fucking crack spot because of some shit going on in your building.

My own building. The cut. The worst-kept secret in New York City. Red brick like red dirt in Jamaica, two window for every room looking out. Fire escape in the middle. Three steps up to dome entryway like the place was posh but the only rich people who ever live in Bushwick used to make beer. Me and Omar outside for almost ten minutes now, and while this woman from clear across the street who live by her window know I was here, no dealer or bodyguard come outside yet. And the boy was right, no runner nowhere.

—Omar, go check inside. Find out if them two bombocloth boy in there.

—Yeah.

Omar look left and right. Habit. Then he dash past the crack ho sitting on the stoop to the front door that open with a little push. Fucking bad sign. I was about to tell him to pull out him gun, but didn't have to. Up the road is a Dodge van resting on four blocks until somebody come with wheels. The kids fixing the bike disappear down the subway station for the L. This woman yelling that while she don't give a hoot if any nigger want to be enterprising and that business is business and if some stupid nigger or cracker wants to blow his money on that shit that's fine, but ain't nobody told her that there was gonna be no crack house. And what kind of dealer sets up a crack house right near where they sell crack? I was about to tell her to go fuck herself because once a junkie get some rock him just itching to smoke that shit right away without delay, so a safe place to light up nearby, with more shit they can buy, means two times the money. Plus now they don't have to worry about police finding any drug paraphernalia 'pon them. But my reason here is not explain things to this bitch like she is my school principal.

Omar is at the door nodding no. Is not until he nod that it hit me that the boy was right and they really abandon the cut for the crack house.

Two blocks west, corner Gates and Central. The only two buildings left on the block that somebody didn't set fire to or that didn't get burn down by accident. There is one on almost every block or street in Bushwick now, a house or apartment or brownstone somebody burn to the ground so that people can collect insurance, since nobody was ever going sell a fucking house in Bushwick. We at the corner Gates and Central. The crack house.

—Fucking Jamaicans acting like you all that. You ain't all that. You can't even control your damn shit. You ain't shit, none of y'all. What you need to do is hire me to run yo biz 'cause you can't run a damn thing. And—

I slap the rest of that sentence out of her mouth so hard she stagger back. She shake her head and almost scream but my punch reach her mouth before anything come out of it. I grab her fucking throat and squeeze till she sound like duck.

—Look, you fucking fat bitch, me done with you a nag-nag in me ears like is bloodcloth mosquito. Don't you get some money every week? So you want money or you want dead, which one you fucking want? Which one? Uh-huh. That's what me was thinking. Now get the fuck out of me face before me use you fucking fat belly for target practice.

She grab herself and run. I start walking to the crack house and Omar and the boy follow me.

Somebody using the Condemned sign as a table. I didn't have to look far. One of my dealers on a mattress right in the front room, just left of the bombocloth doorway. He look like he just take a hit, the pipe dangling off him finger like it about to fall, but he recognize and grab it. I can't see him eye.

—Oi, pussyhole. You a pilfer you own supply?

—Oh, wha'gwaaaaaan, brethren? You come for a hit? A no nothing. Me not selfish, brother, me will share it with you.

—Pussyhole, who a guard the cut if you in here so?

—The cut?

—The cut. The place with the stash that you supposed to watch. The place where you suppose to deal out supply to you fucking runner them. Where them be by the way?

—Runner? Runner . . . what . . . what steer . . . so you want the hit or . . . 'cause me'll take it if you don't want it.

Then he look at me like he know I going take it.

—You understand how you fuck this up, boy? Now me have to find new runner, new dealer, even new bodyguard, and all in just four hour, because the fucking dealer turn user.

—Dealer turn user . . .

He say like he trying to echo but also want to sleep.

I don't bother look into the crack house, but the same woman who try to suck the little boy cock poke her head in the room like she know him. Or me. I wave my gun at her and she don't even jump, just look up and down and gone back into the dark. Omar by the window. The city board it up but the junkies knock it back out. Just my dealer on the mattress with him lighter.

—Where your number two? I say.

—Who?

—You know what? Get the fuck up, before I buss you shit in here.

He look at me. First him eye glaze but then is like it get clear, or maybe he staring at me hard for the first time.

—Don't take no order from some faggot with 'icky 'pon him neck.

I look him in the eye when I lift up me gun and blow a fucking hole straight through him forehead. He still looking at me when he fall right back on the mattress. I grab him left foot and pull him over to the side of the room right under the window. The woman come to the doorway and look again, bend down and go for him pipe. I aim the gun at her.

—Move before me fucking shoot you.

She turn and go back in as slow as she come. I pull him over and set him up that it look like he crouching down. I fold him arms over him knees and push him head down so it look like he either sleeping or coming down from a bad trip. Two rocks fall out of him pocket. I put the pipe, the lighter and the rocks in me pocket. Omar outside waiting on me.

—Omar, find that other dealer. And bring that fucking spotter to me right now.

John-John K

F*uck I wish* this was over. Or at least that I never met that Cuban bitch. Or never ran into Baxter. Or went to that fucking club. Or that fucking boy didn't give me one more reason to head to Miami in the first place. Because then I would be back in Chicago looking for that fucking boy, who I'll just bet hasn't missed me for a minute. *Hey baby I'm sorry and I'm back. Oh yeah, didn't notice that you're gone, did you bring any poppers with you?* And that would be it, wouldn't it? That's the truth like a stone groove. How the fuck did *that* happen? Was this all that it took to need somebody—not have him fucking need you? But there was that one time. That one time when—

—Papi, you gonna slip me some green or not? Also I'ma gonna need some cab money to get back to the meatpacking district.

I gave him fifteen bucks. The boy looked at me funny then shoved the cash in his left front pocket. He pulled his pants up and whispered fucking cheap faggot. If this was only a year ago I would have punched him straight in the face. He would have staggered backways and tripped on his own pants. Landed hard too, head clapping that side table right there on his way down. I would grab him even as he's dazed as shit, drag him out to the fire escape and dangle him off the railing. Fucking cheap faggot, huh? I'll show you who's the fucking cheap faggot. I'd pull him back up, but only after he pissed his jeans. But I chilled and let him go.

There wasn't a book out there about enforcing, but if there was, I'd be fig. 1 in the chapter How to Fuck Up. Ice cool, nah, ice cold, smooth as fuck and just a little psycho. Not me. I'm the sloppy Chicago hoodrat with thin skin and shitty temper that lucked into something he had no business getting into. There was grand theft auto and there was the sloppy hit over on west side, but in between I got black space, a cloud instead of a memory. Before this boy I never even had a reason to remember a phone number. And fuck him for that anyways. That son of a bitch was probably home and ignoring the phone calls.

It's getting late. I know that because Griselda called thirty minutes ago, when I was fucking busy with this trick to say *chico*, it's getting late in between telling her son to turn off that fucking TV and eat his tamale.

The Jamaican. Griselda's Hawaiian Shirt losers were right about the address. I doubted it for a second, mostly because I don't know shit about Flatbush. And those boys are fucking losers. East 18th Street, Apartment 4106, fourth floor of a red brick six-floor walk-up. Studio facing east for a sunrise view. She left it up to me to find out if he was home or not. Good old New York, the whole street was nothing but six floor walk-ups all the way down for two blocks. At least the entrance still had a blue awning. Figured I'd just stand here at the curb on the other side of the street until it was darker because hey, a well-groomed white boy wasn't conspicuous at all. The other buildings just proved that black people in NYC weren't ones for aesthetics. Aesthetics. Listen to me, the fucking faggot.

A reasonably well-groomed white boy with a blond buzz cut in an army surplus jacket. I almost took the heavy-duty suitcase they put out for me, the one with the fucking Uzi supplied by Pink Hawaiian Shirt, no doubt because that's how they do things in Miami. He really took a shining to explaining my job to me. Instructions were to use it then drop it, Mafioso style. But since I was wiping out one man and not an ethnic group, I stuck with my 9. Okay, my 9 and an AMT because a girl needs a backup. Jesus Christ, I wish I could halt this encroaching case of the gay, which seems to get worse the more I stay in this piece o' shit city. The AMT if you need to get close *muchacho*, Pink Hawaiian Shirt said. Maybe this gaydar shit really is a thing because if I stayed just one more night in Miami that *pendejo* would have been balls deep in my ass. You can take that shit to the bank. Back in the hotel when I saw the Uzi, I said who the fuck am I supposed to kill, a Kennedy? Nothing to do now but wait.

Chicago. He was home, wasn't he? Crouched up in a corner somewhere in the apartment and not answering the fucking phone, now there was a kid who hated a bed. Maybe he was crouched like some bird at the foot of his daddy's bed trying to imagine how to kill his dad, *you ever work pro bono?* Look, I know I was sloppy. Sloppy and brash and I didn't think most of the time. And kinda stupid. And people had been warning me for years about my supposedly short fuse, even my pop who didn't think I had the ammo to match the aggro.

That second hit, on Southside to boot, to rub out a goon that cooked the books for the mob on 48th and 8th. Shit did not go as planned, to put it mildly. The man so fucking fat that slugs to his body just came to rest in blubber while the monster just laughed. Took me a while, after the man called me a little pussy meow meow, to figure out that I should just go for the head. But even after the bullet went right through his left eye and the back of his skull sprayed the bed board and wall, the man kept laughing and wouldn't stop.

I kept shooting and shooting, moving in closer and closer until all that was left was the stump of his neck and loose hair. But the laugh followed me all the way up 8th Street, and I couldn't outrun it.

When I got back to my apartment I just felt fucking cold and I was shaking and that laugh was under my skin. Rocky touched me and I grabbed that boy hard and pushed him against the wall. I let him go and let him undress me like I was some kid, and carry me to the bath and rub my hair while the tub filled with warm water. Easy, baby, easy was all he said all night. That fucking boy, that fucking boy, the last thing I need to think of when I'm supposed to be busy.

And now I'm losing my shit in Flatbush. Acting all stupid over this fucking faggot who got the jump on me, this boy colder than fucking midnight for taking up with a guy who kills people because sooner or later he's gonna kill that one, the one where it all started, the one who made him this fucking way. Fuck this. I'm gonna fire a shot and blow a bullet hole in the fucking world and the jocks, and the kids who caught me looking at another kid in the shower, and whoever in the gym yanked my fucking towel and exposed my fucking boner.

If I keep this up I'm not going to make it. There's nothing to do but wait for Griselda to call again. Or maybe one of the Hawaiian Shirts would show up, since she must have sent one to make sure I carried it out, then clean up. Maybe Pink Hawaiian Shirt, who knew too much about clubs, and maybe he would let me go if I sucked him off. I mean, even a bad blow job makes a man close his eyes hoping it'll get better. I only needed a second to grab this gun and blow clear through his head from the chin, and watch blood hit the roof. Sometimes I wish I was back in Chi-Town breaking into cars.

Ten feet away, a phone booth.

—Hello?

—Rocky? Where the hell were you? You gonna answer me goddamnit?

—John-John.

—I called you. More than once.

—I really need to sleep.

—I guess you had a fucking busy day.

—No, not really. Was figuring out what birthday card to send to Dad. I do every year. Why did you call me, John-John?

—What? Huh? What do you mean?

—I'm always pretty clear about what I mean. Why are you calling?

—Well because, because.

—I just watched one depressing episode of *M*A*S*H* and an even more depressing episode of *One Day at a Time.* It was either Lou Grant or bed. Although this episode had to deal with some spazzy suicide chick but then it was only part one, *One Day at a Time*, I mean. What do you want?

—What? What do I want? I don't want anything.

—I really need to get some sleep.

—Then fucking sleep then.

—Huh? You've got a problem, don't you?

—I don't have a problem. It just takes the fucking cake, huh? How somebody who does nothing all day can be so tired.

—And here I thought my stepmother was dead. Turns out she's right here on the phone talking to me.

—Fuck your stepmother.

—You miss me, don't you?

—Don't make me fucking laugh. What a stupid fucking question.

—Yeah stupid. Also makes you sound like a homo if you say yes.

—You're the homo.

—And you're clearly twelve years old. Either way, I don't care.

—You don't care if I'm a faggot?

—No, I don't care enough to have this conversation. Anything else?

—Why are you so fucking . . . ? You know what? No. Fucking no, Rock.

—Well then, good night.

—Good night. Wait! I mean, wait.

—What?

—I . . . um . . . I . . . you . . . you made it with anybody?

—What's it to you?

—Fucking hell, Rock, what the fuck!

—No, the answer is no. I don't see why it matters, we're not together or anything. And you do whatever you like. You made it with anybody?

—No.

—Don't see why not. You are in NYC, faggots, fogies and foreigners and you're still pretty young. Either way, I'm going to my bed.

—It's not your bed.

—Good night.

—Wait.

—What now, Jesus? Would you like some phone sex? You want me to say fuck me Daddy until you beat yourself off. Fuck me, oh fuck me with your big fucking cock Daddy, ooh cum on my face, treat me like a bitch, oh—

—Jesus fucking Christ, can't you say something nice? For once.

—I'm sorry. I'm . . . whoa that was a big yawn. Where were we?

—Good night.

—See you la—

It felt good to hang up on the bitch. Focus. I'm across the street waiting to take this Jamaican out. Except I haven't figured out how exactly yet. I don't even know if this should be a one-man job, in fact it shouldn't when so many things are up for grabs. I don't even know if he'll be alone in his house. Nobody has come or gone for hours, I think but I don't know since it's still too dark for the lights to come on. I'm really walking in there blind and stupid, as if this wasn't part of Griselda's fucked-up plan to begin with. Take the man out, but if he also takes me out that's just a fucking bonus. It's only eight. Even if he's there he couldn't be asleep. The best thing to do was wait until he leaves and take him out in the street. But if he is what she said he is, there's no way he'd be alone on the street, which might be why these Miami boys gave me the Uzi after all. This was getting fucking complicated. Nothing to do but wait till a reasonable hour and move in. Screw on the silencer. Pick the lock, scope out the room, sweep and take him out. Maybe all you need to be a pro is to think like one. All Iceman-like.

Instead all I got is nerves. This isn't supposed to be my fucking hit anyway, I'm just trying to keep myself alive for a few days. Jesus Christ, what kind of hit man's got daddy issues? Ten years ago, at a corner 7-Eleven in Chicago. The day before I walked twenty blocks before I found one. Sweating in my father's fat slob leather jacket. The day before when I was scoping the place, an old man was at the counter listening to talk radio. This time it was a girl in a maroon t-shirt that said Virginia Is For Lubbers, grooving to "Love Train" on the radio. She didn't bother to look up when I came in. At the far end of the mag rack, *Penthouse*, *Oui*, *Penthouse Forum*, *Penthouse Letters*. *Hustler* was fine since they had dicks even though I didn't know that I wanted dick, but behind that, *Honcho*, *Mandate*, *Inches*, *Black Inches*, *Straight To Hell*. But *Blueboy* wasn't sealed and nobody came down the aisle. For a while I wondered who the fuck was breathing like Darth Vader until I realized it was me. Twenty blocks away, nobody would find out, right? This guy was telling her that this Iran thing is really getting out of hand and President Bubba better do something. On the cover the boy's cowboy hat put everything in the shadow but those wet lips kinda kissing a cigarette. *Blueboy* March 1979. OUTLAWS: The Bad Boys Who Love It Anytime.

Sick, was what Pop called me too, one day when the man went through my shit looking for cash so that he could buy cigs and soda and chips to balloon his fat ass even bigger. I wish I coulda been there when he found

Super Nova Cocks, *Super Hung Cocks*, *Cock Tease*, *Cock Hungry* and *Super Surge Cocks*, that one with Al Parker looking like a spurting Jesus. Did he throw up after that one? Did he shake his head and say I knew something was fishy about that boy? Did he sit down and read a few? So I finally come home not ready to take any crap for nobody, least of all that loser, only to see the man hobbling out to the living room, holding the mag with the pink cover, *Super Nova Cocks*, and shouting you fucking dirty little faggot! You fucking dirty little faggot! There's a special part of hell for people like you. Can't believe a fucking son of mine, a son from fucking normal blood, is out there fucking the fudge out o' some fucker's ass. This must be from your mother's side of the fucking family. That's what you do, fag, fuck ass all night long?

—Got it wrong, Pop. Usually it's my ass they're fucking. All night long.

—What the fuck did you say?

—Don't you know, Pop? I'm the hottest piece of ass on the whole east side. They line up around the block to see me, specially them black dudes. This one time this black guy fucked me so raw I couldn't even—

—I oughta—

—You oughta what, man?

Pop stepped to me but I wasn't ten years old. Sure he was bigger, and fatter, but I'd been waiting on this for years.

—I oughta—

—You oughta go back to your fucking room and watch *All in the Family* and stay out my fucking business, Pop. You want two bucks for some Fritos?

I walked right past him to go to my bedroom but Pop grabbed me by the arm and pulled me back.

—I oughta kill you for the disgrace you bring to this family.

—Take your fucking hand off me.

—You're gonna fucking burn, you—

—Take your fucking hand off me.

—I oughta—

I pulled the Beretta out of the holster. Fuck yeah I was carrying a gun by then, just in case one of those cars still had the driver in it and he started to make a fuss. Pop jumped back, holding his two hands stiff, like some bank clerk in a stickup.

—You oughta what, you son of a bitch? Do I look like I'm scared o' you?

—You, you . . .

—I'm one of those men you only pretend to know, talking your shit all the time. I'm going into my fucking room and fucking sleep. Don't ever come in my room again, you hear me?

—I want you out of my fucking house, you're nothing but a two-bit hood.

—And you're a loser who couldn't raise nothing but a faggot. Take that shit to your next bridge game with Mr. Costa. By the way, I suck him off every time he comes upstairs looking for the john.

—You shut your fucking mouth.

—Gag like a fish the way his cock's so big.

—I want you out of my house.

—Oh, I'm gone, old man. I'm fucking gone. Tired of this place and your bullshit. You want some cash?

—I don't want none of your faggot money.

—Your choice then. Maybe I'll take it and buy my own faggot Jim Beam then.

—You're a fucking demon.

—And you're a fucking loser.

I went to my room. The man mumbled something.

—What did you say?

—Leave me alone.

—What the fuck did you say?

—You think you're so smart, don't you? I might be a fucking loser, but you're the one person that everybody'll think is lower scum than even me. Lisa, she had such a rough time with you, nearly killed her when you were born.

Jesus Christ, I don't fucking need this shit. I don't, I really don't. I just want to get out of this city. I didn't even realize I was back at the phone booth until the phone stopped ringing.

—Rocky, it's me. It's ah . . . I'm . . . I'm in New York and I . . . I . . . I want, I want um . . . I . . .—

—Leave a message. *Beep.*

I slammed down the phone.

Dorcas Palmer

N*ow it's too dark* to use it's *getting* dark as an excuse for him to leave. Another Dorcas Palmer, a smarter one, would be wondering how the hell the evening ended up with this man in her apartment. Then again who gives a r'ass. A man can show up in a woman's apartment without wondering what the neighbours think. And besides, I don't know my neighbours. But if he thinks this night is going to end up like some French comedy with me in bed, sheets up to me titties and him with a contented smile as he smokes a cigarette, he just made one sad mistake. He's watching the skyline from my window. Here I thought I had a shitty view.

I know this part, I've watched *Dynasty.* I should ask him if he would like a drink. Except all I have is some cheap vodka because liquor never stopped being bitter and some pineapple juice that I can't say for sure isn't spoiled. And isn't offering a drink just code for would you like to fuck me now? Which isn't going to happen though he really does look like Lyle Waggoner and I heard Lyle posed for *Playgirl.* The sad thing is I really do want to slip into something more comfortable. All this fucking tweed on a summer day was itching the r'asscloth out of me. And my feet have a strict five-hour high heels limit before they start scream bitch what the bombocloth, you trying to kill me? I chuckle too loud and he turns around and looks at me. A smile from a man is a down payment, Dorcas Palmer. Don't sell him nothing.

—I know I promised not to say anything about going home, I say.

—So don't. You have any idea how many people I know that can't keep a promise?

—Sound like rich people problems.

—Sorry?

—You heard me.

—I swear part of the reason why I can't leave—

—Can't?

—Can't, is that you just seem to get bolder by the hour. Who knows what you'll be by ten.

—I'm not really sure if that is a compliment.

—Me neither actually. We'll just have to wait until ten then.

I wanted to say something about the nerve of this man to move into my space, encroach on my time and assume that I have nothing better to do, and then he says,

—But then again, you must have something better to do than humor an old man.

—I've said you're not old two times already. Maybe you should fish for a new compliment.

He laughs.

—The sun's gone. Got anything to drink here?

—Vodka. Some pineapple juice and I dunno.

—Got ice?

—I'm sure I can work up some.

—So you have shit to drink then. I'll have a vodka and some pineapple juice or whatever's in the fridge.

—Your hand sick? Vodka and clean glasses are both on the counter.

He looks at me, nods and laughs. Fucking love this, he says. I'm starting to wonder if this is the movie where the sassy black maid gives the old patriarch reason to live again. Yet still there is no proof that this man is in any way old or need anybody's help for that matter.

—Your son and daughter must be worried by now.

—Maybe. There's club soda in the fridge. Can I use that?

—Yes.

—And it might be time to throw out that slice of pizza. And that half box of ramen.

—Thank you. Any other suggestions for my fridge?

—I'd get rid of the half-eaten burger too. And no self-respecting person should ever be caught drinking Coors.

—I wasn't actually expecting suggestions for my fridge.

—Hmm. Then why ask? You want a vodka soda with a hint of pineapple?

—Yes.

—Coming up.

I watch the man take over my kitchen. Can't remember when I bought lime and it must have been recently because he's using it. He tried three times to cut with my knife before he pulls out another one and strikes them against each other like he's sword fighting himself. Then he chops up the lime. He looks at my glasses on the counter and nods in what looks like pity. I don't remember saving two salsa bottles but he finds them. Chop, crush, squeeze, stir, yes it is something to watch a man work. I don't know if I have ever seen a man in kitchen who wasn't on TV. Actually that's not true. He walks over with both bottles and hands one to me.

—Well? Is it any good?

—It's very good.

—Well thanks for the enthusiasm.

—It's wonderful. Really.

He sits down in the armchair that I had my neighbour help carry up from the street. The neighbour that I have not spoken to since. I hope it don't still smell. He's sipping slow, as if he doesn't want the drink to end, and by extension this stay.

—Aren't you itching in that skirt? I mean, it's summer.

—I'm not taking off my skirt.

—Don't think I asked you to. You wondering how much of a mistake you made inviting me over.

—No.

—So yes then.

—I don't double-talk.

—Good.

It's weird to think it but the only way I can describe how he sits is strong. I noticed it at his home and on the subway as well, him rejecting all these chairs inviting him to slump and sitting straight with his back arched. Must be from his days in the military.

—Shouldn't the police be looking for you by now?

—Can't file a missing persons report until it's been twenty-four hours.

—How soon can you file a kidnapping?

—I'm a little too big to be kidnapped, don't you think?

—Thought size didn't matter.

—Keep this up and you might be having as much fun as me. Don't you have any music?

—You wanna hear what the happening kids are listening to these days?

—Yes, actually. What's the latest? That "Good Times" is quite good, isn't it? Quite good?

—Boy. You've been out of it.

I get up and put a record on, well the one on top of the stack. Funny, back in Jamaica, records were what my father listened to, and it was always dreary instrumental shit like Billy Vaughn "La Paloma" and stuff from the James Last Orchestra. Nineteen eighty-five and I must be the only person to have one of those all-in-one stereo cabinets, or at least one named Telefunken. I still remember the one time my mother brought home a record. It was just a 45 from Millie Jackson called "If You're Not Back in Love by Monday," but I think she waited until we all were out before she would play it.

—Church organs? Good gracious, are you playing church music?

—No.

—That's a preacher, he's talking about the afterworld, and that's most definitely organs.

—Shut up and listen.

He sits back down just as Prince says, *in this life you're on your own.*

—Oh my. Oh my, I do quite like this.

He stands back up, snapping his fingers and nodding his head. I wonder if he was a teenager during Elvis and what he thought of the Beatles. I want to ask him if he likes rock and roll, but the question seems silly for a man finger snapping and tapping like Bill Cosby just taught him jive.

—*Let's go crazy, let's get nuts,* he says. I feel guilty for not dancing. So I get up and dance. And then I do something I never, ever, ever do.

—Doctor Everythingwillbealright, makes everything go wrong, thrills spills and daffodils will kill, hang tough children. He's coming. He's coming. He's coming. He's coming. Whoo hoo hoo-hoo.

I grab the comb on the kitchen counter and it's a microphone for three more whoo hoo hoo-hoos. And then the guitar solo comes and at first I think he's having a heart attack, but he's actually miming the guitar solo with his hands. I'm jumping and yell *Go Crazy, Go Crazy* and the song stretches the moment out so long—I mean, I've listened to the song tenteen million times but it's never been this long, until it just collapses and so do we. I'm on the floor, he's on the couch. He jumps right back up when "Take Me With U" comes on, but I'm still on the floor, panting and laughing.

—That may be the most fun I've had since before the Beatles came on *Ed Sullivan.*

—Is what with you people and the Beatles?

—They're only the greatest rock band of all time.

—The last client had us standing outside John Lennon's hotel all night that night.

—Whatever for? Was he recording with Paul?

—What? I'm not sure that's funny.

He walks over to the stereo and picks up the album jacket.

—Who's the homely looking dyke on the bike?

—That's Prince.

—Prince who?

—Just Prince. The moustache wasn't a giveaway?

—Well my second thought was that this was the hottest bearded lady ever.

—He has a movie showing, named *Purple Rain.*

—Purple Haze?

—Rain. Prince, not Jimi. I should probably take it off. He gets a little explicit.

—Sweetie, I'm the only white man in five boroughs who actually owns Blowfly records. This Prince doesn't scare me. Sorry for calling you sweetie. I understand women aren't into being spoken to that way anymore.

I wanted to tell him that I didn't mind and that it's still the first time anybody—certainly any man—has called me anything nice in a while. But I looked out the window at the skyline turning on its lights.

—Who's the girl on the cover?

—Apollonia. She's supposed to be his girlfriend in real life.

—So he's not gay then.

—You must be hungry. You didn't eat any of the pizza at your house.

—I am kinda. What you got?

—Nachos and ramen.

—Good Lord, not together?

—Prefer week-old Chicken McNuggets?

—Milady doth have a point.

I put the kettle on for the noodles, which means time just sitting and listening to the rest of the album. By the time the kettle is whistling the album is almost over, and I'm thinking of flipping it back to side one because I know I won't be able to sit through the silence and neither will he.

—So where're you from exactly?

—What?

—Where are you . . . Can you turn that off? It's not like Elvis is leaving the building. Where're you from?

—Eat your noodles. Kingston.

—You already said that.

—A place named Havendale.

—Is that in the city?

—Suburbs.

—Like the Midwest?

—Like Queens.

—Ghastly. Why did you leave?

—It was time to go.

—Just like that? Was it Michael Manley and all that communist hoo-hah that was going on a couple years ago?

—I see you're very informed about the Cold War.

—Sweetie, I grew up in the fifties.

—I was being sarcastic.

—I know.

—Anyway, why anything drive me out? Maybe I just wanted to leave. You ever been around family and still feel like you've overstayed your welcome?

—Holy fucking Christ, tell me about it. Worse when it's your own goddamn house that you goddamn paid for.

—You're still going to have to go back eventually.

—Oh you think so, do you? What about you?

—Don't have anything to go back to.

—Really? No family? No sweetheart?

—You really are a child of the fifties. In Jamaica, a sweetheart is the woman you're cheating on your wife with.

—Charming. Speaking of charming, I gotta use your loo.

—Back down the hallway where you came in, second to last door on your right.

—Gotcha.

It would be funny to turn on the TV right now and with Cronkite leading off about the Colthirst big daddy being kidnapped and held for ransom. The wife/daughter-in-law bawling on camera until she realizes that her mascara is running down her cheeks and shouting cut! And the son looking all stoic because he either doesn't want to talk or his wife refuses to shut up. *We thought the place was reputable, but you never know. She seemed so trustworthy—her name was Dorcas, for God's sake. Only God knows how much she will ask for in the ransom note.* I wonder if she will dress up right before the news cameras show up. What's my photo going to look like on TV, though I'm sure the agency doesn't have a photo of me. At least I can't remember. But let's say they have a picture of me, which in just a slight change of context will look like a mug shot. I'll bet from the one day I left the apartment and forgot to get my hair right. The couple will probably hold hands while she begs the kidnapper, meaning me, to have some humanity since her father is not well, not well at all, and—

—What's this?

I didn't hear him come out of the bathroom. No flush, no door squeak, no nothing. Is so my thoughts run away with me that I didn't even notice him until he's right in front of me.

—I said, what's this? Who are you anyway?

He waves it in front of me. I already tell myself that it's not like I was expecting the day to end with people in my house. I mean, this is the house of a woman who never expects company. But goddamn it, I should have checked the bathroom first, if for nothing else to make sure fresh towel was over the sink. And now he's in front of me like he name police, waving the book that is usually safe under my pillow.

How to Disappear Completely and Never Be Found

By Doug Richmond

Cho bombocloth.

Tristan Phillips

B*ullshit, bullshit, bullshit.* You chatting so much shit your tongue probably brown. Oh no? Okay, you know what, let's play it your way. What else you have to ask me. Balaclava? You done ask me that already. Copper? Check your notes, fool. Papa-Lo and Shotta Sherrif, I track the last one from the Eight Lanes right up to Brooklyn, so check your notes.

Oh? Really?

That's not what I think. You want to know what I think? You don't have any notes. Everything you have scribbled down there is doodle and bullshit. For all I know you been writing Mary Have a Little Lamb in Spanish all this time. No? So make me see it. Go on. Yeah right, as you Americans say. Exactly what me did think. White boy, just cut the shit already. Better yet, why you don't stay quiet and I will tell you why you is here? Look at you, man. I mean, it's 1985, you can't get a decent haircut, with this hippie fuckery. Jeans shirt like cowboy, disco jeans pants and don't tell me, cowboy-no, bike boots. Shit. Even man in prison see at least two episode of *Miami Vice.* You get any punaani looking like that? Oh, you know what punaani mean? Really. This is your style or you get stuck in a year and everybody leave you there?

I mean, you come in here telling me that you doing a story about the peace process. For one, that was seven years ago and all now you can't give me a good reason why it's still interesting. You think me stupid? Brethren, there is a thing called context and all now you can't give me one. Don't insult me 'cause I sometimes chat bad. You sure you know what context mean? You know what we was actually doing or you think all we do was put on one concert with the Singer? By the way, everything you ask so far is about the end of the peace process, never the beginning and never even during. Come on, white boy, for a boy who claim to not see the island since 1978, every single thing you bring up so far about happen in 1979 and '80. You ask about Papa-Lo, but only his death. You ask about Copper, but only his death. You never ask about Lucy and even after I bring her up, you just move on like she don't mean nothing.

Oh. You just want to be thorough. Oh. Well you is a journalist, after all.

Uh-huh.

Right, my youth.

You want to know more about when me join Ranking Dons in 1980.

Pierce.

Pierce.

Alex.

Me never say I join the Ranking Dons in 1980, I just said I joined the Ranking Dons. Or maybe you want to know about Josey Wales? He coming to New York, you know. Word in Rikers is that he landing today. Who knows what he coming for. Or who.

Oh.

You quiet now. Look at you. In fact, you quiet every single time I mention Josey Wales. No. Brethren, only minutes ago when I was talking about how Wales fuck up the peace council you immediately change the subject to how me end up in prison when you clearly already know. You don't ask a single thing about me that you couldn't find out in any interview me do for the council, even the one with the New York station me talk about. But is true. Josey Wales coming to New York today. And he definitely not coming to see me.

Look at you. Sitting there like trying to act like you not 'fraid. I give you five minutes to wrap up this interview because you have some pressing matter then run home to your Bed-Stuy apartment and hide under the sink. Oh yeah, Alex Pierce, how long you think it take me to find out what I need to know about you? Thinking that because you live on Bedford and Clifton that you is hardcore. Two-thirty-eight Clifton Place, right? First-floor apartment, no, wait, second-floor—I forget that you Americans don't use ground floor. Haha. Everybody on your street black and dressed like they auditioning for *Thriller* and you one looking like you playing for the Eagles. You is something, Alex Pierce, make me guess, is me comparing you to the Eagles that piss you off. But me wrong 'bout you. You not leaving in five minutes. You not leaving until you get what you come for. Josey Wales coming to New York just make things difficult but you still here for something.

Uh-huh.

Uh-huh.

Yeah.

Huh?

Huh?

Go on.

Just like that? Just sitting there like that?

You know what? Me quiet so talk.

Hmmm.

Hmmm.

Shit, Alex Pierce.

Shit.

Hahahahahaha.

Sorry, didn't mean to laugh. But it kinda funny still. Wake up in your bed and find man sitting beside you. You sure you and him wasn't fucking and him wake first? Calm down, my youth, everybody can see that you not a battyman.

You ever kill a man before? Yes, Alex Pierce, that is what I want to know. You can shut up with the fuck and motherfucker, or I'll call the guard. Answer the question.

Kill anybody since? Haha, I know, just ah run joke with you. What a piece of business is killing a man, eh? Hell of a thing. Everything that him set out to do from sunrise to sunset you just put a stop to it, just like that. It don't matter if it was a good man or bad man, you look at a dead man and wonder if he, if anybody, start a day thinking this going be the last. Weird, eh? You wake up, eat breakfast, lunch, dinner, you work, party, you fuck and you wake up and do it all again. But this one night, this one man not going see a tomorrow ever again. He not going get up, bathe, shit, cross the road, take this bus, play with him children, nothing. And is you do it. You take it from him. I hear you, but that was all there was to it, him was about to take life from you and you just do what called for, or you wouldn't be in front of me right now. What him look like dead? You touch him? Just leave it so? So how you know him was dead?

My youth, you leave the hotel room and nothing happen after that? Interesting. Is not like you book the room under false name. So no news report, no investigation, no police call you, nothing, almost like you dream up the whole thing. Calm down, white boy, me never say you dream it, but somebody clean up after you, somebody clean up good. And . . . hold on, you say blue uniform? Like a blue uniform?

And bald head?

Him kinda red? I mean, light skin, mixed looking?

Bombocloth.

So you telling me that you is the man that kill Tony Pavarotti?

Bombocloth, my youth. Bombocloth.

No, me never know him, but who in the ghetto didn't hear 'bout Tony Pavarotti? That man was Josey Wales' top-ranking enforcer. Hear that the man cold as ice, some people say him mute 'cause nobody ever hear him say anything ever. You ever hear 'bout the place named School for the Americas? You have to be outside of America to ever hear 'bout it. All I know is that Pavarotti is the only boy that for a fact come out of that there place. And the only boy who did know what to do with a gun. Better sniper than police or soldier. And you saying that some scrawny hippie-boy kill Jamaica's number one killing machine? Oh no, brethren, me totally mean to laugh. No, maybe you right, maybe. I mean, you certainly very upset about it, that's for sure. I mean, you sure it was him? Oh wait, you wouldn't know. You just know what him look like. Sorry, brethren, but me have to absorb this some more. Is like me looking at the man who kill Harry Callahan. You remember when this was?

February 1979. So now it come out. You was in Jamaica up to February 1979. You tell me say you was uncovering some shit about Green Bay, too, right? Although that don't mean nothing, even Jamaican newspaper expose the truth behind that long time. But if Tony Pavarotti was coming after you, then the order must did come from Copenhagen City. And since that not Papa-Lo style, the only person who could have send him was Josey Wales. Damn, my youth, is what you do to set off Josey Wales so he would send man to kill you?

You don't know.

Maybe you don't realize that you know. What kind of journalist don't even know him own facts? You must did find out something about Josey Wales that nobody else know. Then again that's not it at all. Josey find out that you have something on him that you didn't even realize that you know. Yes, is six years ago but it clearly haunting you so you must remember something. It must be in your notes or something. Is funny though because Josey not really 'fraid of nothing it seems. He might be what you people call a psychopath. Come, man, think. What out there that only you and him know?

You know a drug connection? A mob link? You do a story about Colombia lately? No, wait, it would be back then. Nineteen seventy-nine nothing really start up yet, certainly nothing that you would know. Green Bay, no. You wasn't covering politics, you was doing stuff on the peace treaty but what draw you into that story? You was following the Singer? Oh. The Singer. Why?

Oh.

Brethren.

You just say it to me, Pierce. You just lay out the whole plan and you still don't see it. We have more in common than you know. Think 'bout it. Right now everybody know that whoever shoot the Singer was aiming for the heart but get the chest and only because he exhale instead of inhale, right? I mean, it even in the book on him. But back in 1978 who would know that instead of the Singer, the gunman and, from the sound of this, you? So him realise him tell you something that he not supposed to know, after all, not even the hospital could say where a killer mean to shoot, only where it hit. I mean, I knew that Josey fire the shot, but I didn't know that till '79. And even then, nobody could have know intention other than who get shot and who try to kill. He didn't look at you a way? He did just cut the interview short right after that? He must. Damn, my youth, you living a movie. The thing is, even though we all know about Green Bay, if I hear you correct, then you find out the truth long before everybody else. What you name, Sherlock? So either he try to kill you because you find out that he try to kill the Singer himself, or he try to kill you because you find out the truth about Green Bay. Although him trying to kill his own people don't make no sense. Now me confused.

You know what, forget Green Bay. Even though you know too much about that too, it say something that is Tony Pavarotti that try to kill you. That means is definitely Josey. No question about it, Josey Wales realize that you know he try to kill the Singer. Or at least you was going to find out, though me don't know if you as smart as he thought you were because for six years none of this ever even strike your mind.

Now this make sense. So this is why you come pay me a visit. I must be the only person in the world who have this kinda something in common with you. What a thing, the only two man Josey Wales try to kill who still living. And any hour now he soon land in New York.

Josey Wales

T*his plane land* twenty-five minutes ago in JFK and we're just leaving customs. Some bird tell me that this only happens when Jamaicans land. I don't know how I know, I just know. Last time I fly to Bahamas the customs pussyhole actually say, Will all the Jamaicans stand to the left of the line. No, I didn't stand to the fucking left and not one idiot say a damn thing when I go straight through customs and give them my passport. Didn't even open my suitcase. Didn't the Singer do that one time? Standing in line when the customs officer start to deal him some customs fuckery. He just grab him bag and walk straight out. Two Jamaicans in this line already get cart off by customs, one of them have three guards escort her. Fucking idiot, I hope she put the coke up her asshole and not up her pussy or worse swallow it, because all that time in there will cost her. Listen to me, thinking all Jamaicans must be drug mules.

Pity they stop the girl who look like she a mule when they should have stop the idiot embarrassing the country in first class. There we are, thirty-two thousand feet in the sky and the air hostess announce dinner service. My girl took one look at what they was offering and say, *No to backside a food you call that? A good ting me bring me owner bickle.* Then I have to watch this damn buttu open her bag and pull out an ice cream bucket with fry fish and rice and peas. Damn fish stink first class so bad that I almost asked if I could move to a seat in the back—I'd even pay for it. Either that or whip out a gun and pistol-whip some class into her, if I brought one.

—Welcome to the United States, Mr. __________

I pass through the door into the baggage area only to glimpse two officers grab the young woman they pull out of line and throw her down to the floor. Outside of customs and we're still inside the airport, one more thing that's different from Jamaica. And there is Eubie. Standing right in front of the crowd of people, a lot of them black, a lot of them Indian looking, waiting on people to come out. Royal blue silk suit with white kerchief in the front pocket like he is the black man in *Miami Vice*. I really need to watch that show. Something tell me that if I call him Tubbs, Eubie would like it, uptown boy trying to play hardcore, except he really hardcore. I spend a lot of time thinking about Weeper too, but not in the same way and not for the same things. And what the hell this man have in his hand?

—Eubie.

—Mah man! Mah main man, he say like an American black man. He's still holding up the sign saying Josey Wales, just like the signs the two chauffeurs beside him are holding up.

—What is this?

—Haha, this? This is a joke that we call a Josey Wales.

—Oh. I not laughing.

—Jesus Christ, Josey, where you sense of humour gone? Or you ain't never have one?

I hate when Jamaicans start to pick up American ways of talking, and when they flip back and forth it put my teeth on edge. I laugh.

—That more like it, although you heart not in it.

Then he flings the paper into the air just like that, grabs my bag and starts to walk out. I'm following him but still watching the paper sail through the air and land near a rent-a-car booth.

—Should be interesting landing in New York at night. Is a totally different city than in the day.

—How soon before we get to Bushwick?

—Just cool, man, Josey. The night young and you just come. You hungry?

—There was food on the plane.

—Which me sure you didn't r'asscloth eat. Boston Jerk Chicken on Boston Road.

—Seriously, you think me leave Jamaica to go eat second-class Jamaican food? That's what you think?

—Fine, you want a Big Mac? A Whopper with Cheese?

In the parking lot, a black minivan pull out and stop in front of we. Maybe is a good thing I didn't have my gun or I would have it out already. But then it's not like this is downtown Kingston. The door open and Eubie point. For some reason I don't move until he get in first. He's nodding him head.

—Good old Josey, still trusting nobody after all these years.

He laugh, but I still don't know what he talking about. I can't remember Eubie from the old days. Outside we seem to be driving through lights, although I thought we would be passing mile-high buildings right away. So far New York looking like Lejeune in Miami, but I thought the streets would have been wider. Nothing but cars speeding past on the highway, which was strange since Eubie himself said nobody drives in New York. Maybe this wasn't New York. I would ask, but Eubie already thinking he too smart. The van slow down and for the first time I realize that another man in the back. Stupid, stupid Josey Wales, you know better than this. No gun, surrounded by a crew from a man I work with but for real don't trust, I should have at least asked for a gun as soon as we step out of the airport. We turn off the big highway and I see a sign saying Queens Boulevard. Strange this boulevard is much wider than the highway. We rolling down this street with brick townhouses, all of them three floors and sometimes four with a verandah and plastic chairs and bicycles outside.

—This is Queens, by the way.

—I know.

—You do?

I don't answer him. We hit a pothole and I jump.

—Betram, what the fuck, man, you just run over a goat?

—Pothole, boss.

—Imagine the don, man, leave Jamdown to run into pothole, what a ting.

—We didn't want him to feel like stranger, Eubie.

—Haha.

I'm hoping that nobody see me jump in the dark, or I might have to do something.

—My boy Josey jump like he hear duppy.

Everybody laugh. I don't like how he's parring with everybody like he and them is size. I don't like when any fucking man disrespect me, even as a joke. This man really thinking me and him is neck and neck. He really think so. I wonder if this would happen if Weeper was managing Manhattan and Brooklyn the way he seem to be managing Queens and the Bronx. We need to talk as soon as we get out of this van. Meanwhile I'm wondering what the man in the back doing. Then we on another highway, and I look over and there is the sea or the river and there is a neon sign of the old Pepsi label, old from when I was a boy.

—So, Josey, I was thinking. I—

—You going talk business in the van?

—What, this? I trust my men implicitly, Josey, meaning—

—You not about to tell me what implicitly mean.

—Woi, Josey check you out, nuh? Man bad like sin! But ah nuh nothing. We can wait until we reach Boston Jerk Chicken. Funny, eh? What are the odds, Boston Jerk Chicken from Portland would land on Boston Road in New York? That is what me son would call irony, from him lit class. They grow up fast, eh? How old you big son be now?

—Fourteen. All this can't wait till we get out of the van?

—Just making convo, but suit yourself.

The van stop. I didn't even notice that we was in the Bronx. I know it was after nine but the street still busy, with people moving up and down in the middle of the road, along the sidewalk and in and out of store like it's still daylight. Cars park on both side of the road and all of them either Buick or Oldsmobile or Chevrolet. Miss Beulah's Hair Technique, Fontaine Brothers shipping, Western Union, another Western Union, Peter's Boutique Men's Clothing, Apple Bank, and then Boston Jerk Chicken. The place look like they was about to close, but somebody must did see Eubie, because a light from the back just go on. So now I'm wondering if Eubie forget that I say no Jamaican food, or if this is another cute disrespect. We sit down, just me and him at an orange plastic booth near the door with him directly in front of me. One of his men by the cashier and two stand up outside.

—How much security you usually need 'round here?

—Not too much, Ranking Dons know better than to try move in on Boston or Gun Hill Road. Last time they try a thing they drop two of me dealers. Now you know this nigger wasn't going take that shit lying down, right? We hear that a party going on in Haffen Park with plenty of Ranking Dons. We just drive down in three car, jump out and shower that whole park with bullet. We didn't even shoot to kill even though one or two man did suck salt that day. All me care 'bout was that at least one of them was going shit in a colostomy bag for the rest of him life. That was the last time them fucking batty boys mess with the Bronx. Pushing smack in Philly is the best move they ever make. Still, them getting bolder in Brooklyn. Too bold, if you ask me.

—Tell me.

—What?

—Tell me how bold.

—Well, your man Weeper can best tell you—

—I didn't ask Weeper, I ask you.

—Okay. Okay. Real talk then. You boy fucking around in more ways than one, while Ranking Dons, driving up and down in a triangle on Broadway, Gates and Myrtle, watching your boy fuck up. Spotters can't find runners, dealers shooting up, meanwhile them boys and they Chevrolets patrolling all over because they know they can't set foot in the Bronx or in Queens. My man report all this to me.

—Your man? How he know so much?

—Don't take this no way, but I have one of Weeper's runners on the lookout for me.

—What the bombocloth, Eubie, you a spy 'pon the man, 'pon me?

—Oh for fuck's sake, Josey, like you don't have man spying on me. Or Bricks run to phone booth every night to make collect call to him woman. Me no care. I actually don't mind at all. It keep me on my toes and remind me not to fuck up. My man report to me twice a week. I mean, I can't imagine he finding out anything you don't already know.

—Like what? Test me.

—Like how your boy Weeper is a user.

—Weeper sniffing coke from as early as '75, that not nothing new.

—But new it is, Josey. Now him smoking crack and you and me know that crack is not coke. Can a man do good business even when him deh 'pon coke? Of course. Every man me know in the music biz a lick coke. Hookers and blow them call it, my youth. Back then the biz did even have a sort of class. But crack is different business. Every single dealer who switch from coke to crack mash up. You can't hold a single thought on crack. You can't do no fucking business. Crack is you business. You can't add number when you on crack. You can't separate what to sell and what to buy. Shit gone to hell and you don't even care. When you see Weeper ask when last he go to Bushwick. Ah smoke up crack and . . . well . . . them other things is fi him business, but the man is a r'asscloth crackhead, and this is a r'asscloth business.

—How you know him smoking crack?

—My man see him do it.

—Fucking lie that, Eubie.

—Brethren, what make you think him hiding it? You no understand. When a man 'pon crack him don't fucking care. Is damn slackness, man. The man a shoot up crack like some crack bitch, and messing up him spots, and when him not doing that, going on with all sorts of nastiness that him must did catch from Miami 'cause there's no way he could be doing that shit in Jamdown—

—Enough.

—And Ranking Dons is nothing but john-crows, before a body even dead they start to hover close.

—Me say enough, Eubie, to r'asscloth.

—Alright, brethren, alright.

—Enough of this bombocloth fuckery, make we go.

—Brethren, the food don't even come yet.

—Me look like me bombocloth hungry? What me want to do is go to Bushwick. Right now, Eubie.

John-John K

So there was this time in Miami way down on Collins in South Beach. I was smoking Parliaments in a Mustang that already smelled like ass, bitching over being given bad info on a pot pickup that was just not going to fucking happen (yeah, the aim was to jack the stash and then sell it), when like moths sniffing out the new chintz, some boys started to come over. A blond one, hair long and curly like he spent most days posing as Farrah Fawcett, glided his way, jeans split at the side and cut like hot pants, so high that white pockets poked out. He was singing too, voice deep enough to kill the Farrah vibe, *more, more, more, how do you like it, how do you like it*. I wanted to say, Faggot, it's nineteen eighty fucking three.

Motherfucker's roller skates stopped somewhere in that girly middle between pink and purple. Lilac maybe, something that fags would know. Rollerbitch never saw him coming, the dirty one, black hair so ashy that it seemed grey, sliding up through the blindside of the car like he's following shadow. I didn't even see him until the rollerbitch glided straight into a kung fu kick to the side from kid's combat boots. Rollerbitch went rolling, teetering, tottering like a drunk dancing queen, trying to regain footing but unable to stop the skates without wiping out on the asphalt. Bitch screamed and cussed and tried to stay up but barreled backways on one foot then the other until he went butt first into a pile a trashbins by the wire fence. Take your clap and your stanky ass to Hialeah, the boy said. Spic of course, but a cute spic, maybe not long from Cuba, not long enough for the dirty *pinguero* to know that *The Wild One* was one fucking old movie and leather wasn't the coolest bet for what was still the tropics.

Spic bent down into the car window smelling like he was smoking only thirty minutes ago. His left canine was missing, but his eyes were black and hungry, his chin strong like Vinnie Barbarino's on *Welcome Back, Kotter.* Kid stuck his hand in the car and I grabbed him—hunter's instinct. Smokes, the kid said, and I let him go. The kid said nothing else, just went around to the right side and got in the car. I would have let him blow me there, but shit I had to jet, these run-down art deco–style hotels were becoming a major downer. Kid said, What the fuck, Papi, I don't travel. I said, Well get the fuck out of my car then. Kid changed his mind and said drive me someplace nice. He took another cig out of the pack and stuck it behind his ear. I'm thinking that hopefully the rifle wasn't on the bed or this kid would get scared. Kid was just staring at my cowboy boots.

—You some ranchero, Papi?

—Take off my fucking hat.

And the fucked-up thing is all I could think about was Rocky. Even with my hand in this kid's dirty hair, as his head bobbed up and down, I thought about Rocky's rules. We had certain rules. Or maybe we thought we did. If you're gonna make it with somebody, fuck guys on the sofa because on the bed is cheating. And only if the guy is really, really cute, because the memory gem said we only pass this way but once and then you just have to make it with him, because we're queers and bullshit rules don't apply. Well, straight rules.

But fucking hell, man, stuff I had put to bed years ago has been staging a fucking reunion in my head these past few days. Fuck if I know why, I've never been to New York. *Here, it's like this, see, suck my finger and suck and suck until you're a vacuum, see, like when you suck on a plastic bag till all the air's gone out? suck so hard. Suck so hard that I can't pull my finger out—I know how to do it.* Nobody told me NYC was a place overrun by ghosts. *You're a fucking freak, John-John.* I never meant to push the boy. Yeah I did. I never meant for the boy to get hurt. Yeah I fucking did. I never meant to kill him. What does meant mean? When he landed facedown on the train track and I pulled him up, just to position his head over the beam so that his loose mouth bit into it and then kicked him hard at the back of his head again and again until I heard the crunch, all I could think about was summer camp. *Is it in? Oh yeah. All the way in? Uh-huh.* Fourteen, back from summer camp and my pop punched me in the stomach once and told me I was a fucking wimp who needed to get hard. Summer camp was all about bad food, calamine lotion and counselors walking around with rulers to stick between dancing couples *to make space for Jesus.* Me and Tommy Mateo, all red-haired whiteboy Afro, sitting on the sidelines hissing that this was bullshit. *Hey, you wanna smoke? Uh, yeah.* Two weeks after camp all I could think of was seeing Tommy again. On the phone he seemed different, busy, like he was talking to somebody else. You know the old train tunnel over by Lincoln? I get there and he's staying far back, like he wasn't the boy whose butt I was stuffing every night in the fucking woods. Tommy blew smoke in my face when I got too close.

Tommy, you wanna, you know?

What? No, you fucking fag.

You're the fucking fag, getting cornholed.

Fuck you, that's because there weren't no fucking girls.

Girls to fuck you in the butt? Camp was full of girls.

Not any girls I would want to fuck, shit, even you were cuter than all of them. But we're back home and girls here are cute.

I don't want fucking girls.

You're supposed to, or else you're a fag. You're a fucking fag and I'm gonna tell your pop.

Fuck, fuck, fuck, fuck, fuck. Why am I thinking all this shit right now? The light in this guy's bedroom went on, then off, the bathroom light went on for half an hour and off. It's been off for half an hour now. Give a man half an hour give or take to fall asleep. He could be fucking some chick with the lights off, but then same rules still apply. He'll either be asleep or distracted. I would climb the fire escape but it's three floors up and that's a pretty fucking tricky thing to tip-toe all the way. Griselda gave me a set of keys but coming through the front door just seemed like a really stupid thing to do. This is New York, he's gotta have locks on that shit. Or maybe he's fucking some chick and don't want her to stay.

Crossed the street and I'm in the building. Every now and then I get some hint that I'm really just a stereotypical fag, for example, who the fuck had the great idea to paint this whole hall area mustard? Ten, fifteen feet and the first stairway still has carpet on the steps. Three floors up I know that's not sweat running down my back. At the door and before I know it I'm sweeping my hands across it like I'm checking if it's real wood or some shit. Given how much I don't trust that Colombian bitch, I'm half expecting the key not to work. I push it in and turn hard, expecting it to break or something, but it works, it works with a fucking bang. Fuck this shit, first I think to abort. Maybe it was louder out here than in there? Either way it'd be wise to take the fucking safety off.

Door creaks and opens and there's no living room, I guess people in NYC don't really need one. Right in front, a dining table and two chairs, or maybe the other chairs are someplace else. Little light's coming out from outside, so all I can see is a couch pushed up against the wall and the bed pushed up against the other side. TV right by the window. Can't tell if it's black sheets or if by the bed is just dark. Either way, I walk up to the bed, look for the slightest lump under the sheet and let rip seven shots from the clip. Three things: the zoop-zoop of the silencer, the slight pop of the bullets bursting the pillow, and the gasp behind me. I swing around to see a naked white man with red hair maybe. Can't tell in the dark since he left the bathroom light off. Bitch gave me the wrong fucking apartment. I raise the gun to get him in the head but he throws something straight into my eye and it's like I'm outside myself hearing myself when I fucking scream. It runs down my face and I taste it. Motherfucking mouthwash. By the time I run into the bathroom and wash out my eye he already pushed up the window and jumped out on the fire escape. And I'm after him, this naked white man running down each step screaming and me trying to get a good shot. I fire and it blasts the metal, shooting off sparks. I'm barely running three steps in the flat before I'm down another staircase, firing at the screaming naked dude, I don't know what he's screaming but it doesn't sound like help. And all I'm shooting is this fucking fire escape. He jumps down the rest of the way instead of taking the ladder.

There we are running down the alley, him screaming like his throat half cut, me behind him, half blind and my right eye still fucking killing me.

Worse, we're kicking up this shit-rot-sour-dead stink with each step. I'm trying to get shots off, but only movie motherfuckers can run and shoot straight, and that's with two working eyes. All my shots keep disappearing in the dark, not ricochet no nothing. He's pretty fast barefoot and hopping and zipping through this dark alley, hot with potholes and trash cans everywhere. I step on something squishy and don't bother to check if it was a rat. We hit a cross street and the sudden headlights and streetlights stop him cold for too long. Pop him off right as he starts running again, just as two cars pass on both sides of him. One stops for a second then peels out, swerving right, almost hitting a light, then left then right again, disappearing down a street. Nobody on the street at all, which was fucking strange for New York, I think. First I thought the wall looked weird, black, bulby and shiny. Then I realized that it was garbage bags, one on top the other making a fucking wall that covered both sides all the way down into total dark. I walk up to the man, grab him by the left ankle and drag him back into the alley.

Dorcas Palmer

S*eriously have you taken* a good look at this shit? At the cover? A pair of thick-rimmed glasses and a big pink nose. Who's it by, Groucho Marx? And my God, look at the other publications from this place. *Improvised Weapons of the American Underground*, and this, *Professional Homemade Cherry Bomb*, and what's destined to be a classic, *How to Lose Your Ex-Wife Forever.* What is this really? I'd think you were militia but you're not in Texas and far as I know militias haven't relaxed their no niggers policy.

Meanwhile I'm trying to figure out why exactly this man has started to think he has the wherewithal to act out in my own house. Yes he's been acting familiar all day, but this shit like he's my father or husband or something is a whole new level. No, he's a bored old man who finally gets a mystery to solve and acting like it is such a hassle. No, he thinks he knows me because I have some obligation to him, and he's so disappointed. Whatever it is this man have some nerve.

—Calm down.

—Whaddya mean calm down? You some kinda fugitive? Why would you need such a book?

—Not that I owe you any explanation, but I saw it in a bookstore and was curious.

—What bookstore, Soldier of Fortune? Those wackos read?

—It's just a book.

—It's a manual, Dorcas, if that's your real name. Nobody buys a manual unless they plan to use it. And judging by the dog ears, you've used it lots.

—I don't have to answer nothing to you.

—Then don't. But come on, surely this book is a crock of crap?

—Yeah, total junk as you would say. That's why I don't use it for—

—I said the book was crap. I didn't say you weren't using it.

Why am I not kicking him out of my house for getting angry with me? It's my fucking house. I pay the rent.

—And nobody gets to speak louder than me.

—What?

—I said it's my house and nobody get to speak louder than me in me damn house.

—Sorry.

—Don't apologize. I'm the one that's sorry.

He sits down.

—It's your house.

Another version of me would say that I really appreciate that he cares, and be even moved that somebody could care about me despite knowing so little. But I don't say any of that.

—I didn't use the book.

—Well thank God.

—Because—

—Because?

—Because most of the stuff in there that it says to do, I already did them. It's not the only book out there.

—What are you saying?

Mr. Colthirst pulls up one of my dining chairs and sits right in front of me. He takes off his jacket and I try to stop reading symbols in everything, at least for one night. This is something I've picked up from American women, this trying to read every single thing a man does as containing a secret message for me. Right now he's the fucking fugitive. He's looking at me with that tilted head like he asked me a question and waiting for the answer. I wish this man would understand that I'm not like all these people he watch on *Donahue.* All these people with their private business that they dying to tell thirteen million people. Tell one of these people a simple hi and they think they must bend down low and tell you what they know. Everybody just want to confess, but they really not telling you nothing. Not revealing nothing.

—Flushing Cemetery. 46th Ave., Flushing, New York.

—Huh?

—Flushing Cemetery. It's where you will find her if you care to look.

—Who?

—Dorcas Palmer. Dorcas Nevrene Palmer, born November 2, 1958, Spauldings, Clarendon, Jamaica. Died June 15, 1979, Astoria, Queens. Cause of death, tragic circumstances, the obituary said, meaning she got hit by a car. Can you imagine, somebody getting lick by a car in New York City?

—Licked?

—Hit by a car.

—And you're using her name just like that?

—Claudette Colbert was starting to sound obvious.

—Not funny.

—I wasn't joking. Claudette Colbert was starting to sound obvious.

—You can't just use a dead person's name. Isn't that pretty easy to trace?

—This might come as a shock, but the department in charge of death certificates is really not the largest in the municipal government.

—I'm more shocked by your consistent use of irony. Not what I remember about Jamaicans. Don't look at me like that. If you insist on dropping bombs every five minutes, I insist on giving this shit some levity when I need it.

—Right. You really want to hear this.

—You sound like you really want to tell this.

—No, not really. I'm not into this confessional fad thing going around at all. You Americans and your "you wanna talk about it?" I mean, Jesus.

—Anyway.

—Anyway, this is New York, because this is New York, not many people who died here, born here. And states don't have some grand national record for everybody. In fact, the department for birth records, and for death records, really don't have nothing to do with each other, they're not even in the same place. So even if there is a death certificate, there is no—

—Birth certificate.

—And if you can get hold of a birth certificate—

—Then you have proof that you are you, without the real you coming after you. What about her family?

—All in Jamaica. They couldn't afford to fly up for the funeral.

—Social Security?

—Oh she's collecting that now.

—She wasn't—

—All you have to do is get a birth certificate. Yes I just called the Registrar in Jamaica and asked for a copy of my, well, her birth certificate. Can't even remember how much I paid for it. People are always ready to believe the worst more than the not so bad, so why not give them the worst? You'd be surprised how many places you can say, I'm sorry but I misplaced my passport, or just say it was stolen. But I do have my birth certificate.

—Guess you'd have a slight issue if your name was still Claudette Colbert.

—Or Kim Clarke.

—Who? When were you her?

—Long time now. She's gone. The next thing I did was contact the census bureau requesting whatever information they had on Dorcas Palmer.

—Oh right, and they handed it over just like that?

—No. They handed it over for $7.50.

—Jesus Christ. How old are you?

—Why you need to know that?

—Oh right, you're keeping that one a secret. Social Security didn't think it a little weird when you applied for a number so late?

—Not if you're an immigrant. Not if you have your birth certificate but can't find your passport. Not if you have a story long enough and boring enough that they will do anything just to get you out of the line. Carry these two with you and you can easily get a state ID. After that thirty-five dollars can get you a passport, but I didn't get one of those. That's in chapter two.

—But you're not an American citizen?

—No.

—Not even a resident?

—Well, I have a Jamaican passport.

—With your real name?

—No.

—Christ. What did you do?

—Me? I didn't do anything.

—Says you. Come on, you must be on the lam. This story is already the most exciting thing I've heard since I can't even remember. What the fuck did you do? Who are you running from? I must say this is quite thrilling.

—Who knew that when you opened your door that your day would come to this? And I'm not on the lam. I'm not the criminal.

—You got a son of a bitch for a husband who used to hit you.

—Yes.

—Really?

—No.

—Dorcas. Or whatever your name is.

—It's Dorcas now.

—I hope you thanked her for her generosity in sharing her name.

He stands up and goes back to the window.

—Since you migrated here under a false name, I'm right to assume that the person you're running from is in Jamaica. But they clearly have the resources to track you here, hence the false names.

—You should be a detective.

—What the hell makes you think you're so damn safe?

—You're blocking the moon. And I'm living here since 1979 and he hasn't found me yet.

—So it's a he you're running from. Did you have to leave kids behind?

—What? No. No kids. Good God.

—They aren't so bad until they start to talk. Who's this guy you're running from?

—Why you want to know?

—Maybe I can—

—What, help? Already helped myself. He's far away from New York City. And probably have no reason to come here.

—You're still hiding though.

—Lots of Jamaican live in New York City. Somebody might know him. This is why I don't live near Jamaicans.

—But why New York at all?

—I wasn't going to spend my life in Maryland, and Arkansas was not going to work out. Besides, a big city is better overall. Public transportation, so you never need a car, you never stand out unless you're with a white man on a train uptown, and jobs where nobody asks anything. And even in between jobs you still have to appear to be working, so leave your home the same time every day, come back around the same time every evening. When I'm not working I just go to the library or MOMA.

—Hence knowing the difference between Pollock and de Kooning.

—R'ass, I didn't have to go to MOMA to know that.

—Don't sound like much of a life if you're still watching your own back. Don't you get tired?

—Tired of what?

—Tired of what indeed.

—Right now life is having a place and establishing credit. Pretty much everything here is on a payment plan even though I could very well have paid for all of it up front. That's from chapter four. Look, if this is the moment where we have the big catharsis, I'm very sorry to disappoint you.

—Oh disappointment is the last word I would think of when I think about you, darling.

I really should have said I'm not your darling. I really should have said so. Instead I said,

—It's getting late. You should go home.

—How do you propose that a distinguished white gentleman of a certain age get himself out of the . . . Where are we?

—The Bronx.

—Huh? Strange, I totally forgot. And how did we . . . Never mind, nature calls.

He closes the door. His jacket had slipped off the chair and I pick it up. Heavy, too heavy for a summer jacket, I'm thinking. It's even lined. I would have sweat off these hips in this jacket. I'm folding it over when I see writing way up in the left shoulder, which does not look like cleaning instructions. It's in handwriting, like somebody wrote it with a Sharpie.

IF YOU ARE READING THIS AND ARE NEAR THE OWNER OF THIS JACKET PLEASE CALL 212 468 7767. URGENT. PLEASE CALL IMMEDIATELY.

The phone rings three times.

—Dad! Dad! Jesus Christ, are you—

—This is Dorcas.

—Dorcas who?

—Dorcas Palmer.

—Who the fuck . . . Hold on, you the woman from the agency? Hon, it's the woman from the agency.

—Yes, from the agency. Mr. Colthirst—

—Oh sweet Jesus, please tell me he's with you.

—Yes, the mister is here. I just want you to know that he was the one who insisted on leaving the house. I mean, he's a grown man who can do what he wants but I couldn't leave him alone and—

—Where are you now? Is he alright?

—In the Bronx and yes. What is—

—I need your address now, right now, you hear me?

—Of course.

I gave him my address and he hung up just like that. No sense beating around the bush as Americans say. I knock on the bathroom door.

—Ken? Ken? Look I, I called your son. He says he's coming to pick you up. Sorry but it was getting late and you can't stay here. Ken? Ken? Mr. Colthirst?

—Who are you?

I press my head to the door because I was sure I didn't hear right.

—Who the fuck are you? Get the fuck away from the door. Get the fuck away I said.

—Mr. Colthirst?

I reach down to grab the doorknob, but he had locked it from the inside.

—Get the fuck away.

Tristan Phillips

Tell me now for real. You really think that Josey Wales fly all the way to New York, six years too late, to deal with you himself? You look like you suffering from a too big view of yourself, my brethren, just a word to the wise. But then again, me pretty sure the reason Josey leave me alone was that what he really wanted to kill was the peace movement. And with that dead he didn't need to kill anything else. Plus, me make a big point to stay out of him way and he stay out of mine, since to take me on would mean directly taking on the Ranking Dons. No, we nowhere as big as Storm Posse, but still he would be wasting a lot of time trying to neutralize we. As for Weeper, he and I know why he'd never make a move on me.

But your case is sorta different though, sorta special. Josey order some vanishing cream for you and you take out him best man. Maybe him respect you, he can be weird 'bout them things. Maybe him all forget you . . . then again no, Josey Wales don't forget nothing. He must think it make no difference whether you living or dead, well the difference being time and money to cancel you. Or maybe him priorities shift.

Still, I don't think he come here for you. People in here only know so much, but Josey not the man you say you didn't meet six years ago. Him and this man named Eubie, who be here since 1979 selling weed and coke, almost turn they dealing into a legit business. Almost. I told you, the one thing about Storm Posse why they will always be bigger than Ranking Dons, is that them boys have ambition. They got plans. Man in here tell me that Storm Posse running things in New York, D.C., Philly and Baltimore. I mean, since I in prison them push all the Cubans back down to Miami. Thanks to them the Medellín cartel don't even think about chatting to Ranking Dons. You know things bad when in all this crack explosion you the one who get stuck with having to move heroin. But that Josey Wales, man, him is a thinker and Eubie even smarter. For one, both of them too smart to trust each other.

You don't seem convinced that he not after you. Listen, brethren, Josey Wales not coming for you unless you give him new reason to. None of them boys in no rush to kill no white people either, because then the Feds would come sniffing. No brother, you gone clear. Unless you going write some article about all this.

A book?

Well some people just asking for it, eh? Brethren, you can't write no book 'bout this. Make me get this straight. You writing book 'bout the Singer, the gangs, the peace treaty. A book on the posses? You know, each one of those is a whole book. What you going write about anyway? You have no proof of anything. Who talk to you other than me?

Listen, you already enjoying God's grace right now. You write anything 'bout this, nobody can protect you. Right now you no longer somebody he need to be concerned about. You have family? No? Why not? Either way, that's good because these boys not 'fraid to lick out 'gainst your family. And by no family you mean no brother, sister or mother? Shit, Pierce, then you have loads of family. Only this year, them boys find two dealers from Spanglers working the Bronx. For once Storm Posse didn't storm the place with bullet. No sah, instead they behead the two boy then switch the heads each on the other body. Why you don't do yourself a favour and wait till everybody dead? Brethren, is gang we talking 'bout, you probably won't have to wait too long. Look 'pon me. Me supposed to be the one who know better. You know me even come 'pon TV? Twice to talk about the warring and the peace. Everybody look 'pon me and think now there is the one man who going graduate out of the ghetto. But . . . yeah, a whole life of fuckery follow that but . . . But even me who know better and can talk better, where you find me? See it deh.

What 'bout Josey?

No, my youth, man like that don't go jail. In fact, I don't think he see a jail since 1975. Which police force, which army bad enough to try take him?

Me don't see Copenhagen City since '79 but me hear 'bout it. Brethren, is like them communist country you see 'pon the news. Poster and mural and painting of Papa-Lo and Josey all over the community. Woman naming them pickney Josey One and Josey Two, even though he not fucking nobody but him wife, no, they not married for real. In him own way, you could call him a classy brother. But still, you want to get Josey you have to mow down the entire Copenhagen City first, and even then. You also have to tear down this government too. What you mean, government? Come, man, Alex Pierce, who you think give this party the 1980 election?

You know what I picking up 'bout you? You is definitely a reporter. No doubt 'bout that. You can go somewhere and just pick up information, especially information that people weren't planning on giving you. I mean, look what you get from me just today. You ask the right question or at least the kind of wrong question that make people want to talk. But you know what wrong with you, or maybe it not wrong at all, it just prove you is a reporter. You don't have no sense of how to put everything together. Or maybe you do but you just don't know how to. Funny, eh? Josey Wales after you for something that you couldn't even do. Oh, you can do it now? That why you writing a book? Because you can figure it out or you still writing to figure it out?

I have a question for you.

I want to know when exactly Jamaica hook you. No, I don't want to know why, you just going give me the same fool-fool bullshit white man always say when they talk about Jamaica, like she's some whore with the sweet pussy you can't give up, or some dumb shit like that. Some one-inch-dick cracker say that one time, but since you have Jamaican woman I going assume you have more than a one-inch dick. So lay it on me, as the Americans say, what is it about Jamaica? The beautiful beaches? Because you know, Pierce, we're more than a beach, we're a country.

Oh.

Thank you for not giving me the same shit. It *is* a shit hole. It's hot like hell, traffic is always slow, and the people not all smiling and shit, and nobody waiting to tell you no problem, man. It is shitty, and sexy and dangerous and also really, really, really boring. Tell the truth I don't like it either. And yet look at the two of we. Change the circumstances and we couldn't wait to go back. It hard though, don't it? Hard for you not to compare her to a woman. Congratulations, that is very non-white of you.

What a non-climax this is! Anti-climax, is that what they call it? You have to admit that if Josey Wales was waiting right outside this prison gate for you it would have been a more interesting story. At least you get to leave, all I get to do is wait.

March 1986, my youth.

What I going do? Me no know, go somewhere in Brooklyn where me can get ackee and saltfish.

Haha. As if me can leave Ranking Dons. My life do stay like yours, Pierce. People like me, our life write out before we, without asking we permission. Nothing much we can do 'bout what God decide he want to drop on you. Oh? Is that them call fatalism? I don't know, brethren, that word seem more connected to fatal than it connected to fate. You know something, maybe you should write this book. I know, I know what I just say, but now me checking things deeper. Maybe somebody should put all of this craziness together, because no Jamaican going do it. No Jamaican can do it, brother, either we too close or somebody going stop we. It don't even have to get that far, just the fear that somebody going come after we going make we stop. But none of we going see that far. I mean, shit.

Shit.

Damn.

People need to know. They need to know I guess that, that there was this one time when we could'a do it, you know? We could'a really do it. People was just hopeful enough and tired enough and fed up enough and dreaming enough that something could'a really happen. You know, sometimes I see the Jamaica *Gleaner* in here and the whole thing in black and white with just one or two headline in red. How long you think it going be before we have a picture in colour, three years? Five years? Ten years? None of them, brother, we already did have colour and lose it. That's kinda like Jamaica. Is not like we never have good times and now have something to look forward to. We did have things going good and then it go to shit. Now is shit for so long that people grow up in shit thinking shit is all they is. But people need to know that. Maybe that too big for you. Maybe that too big for one book, and you should keep things close and narrow. Focused. I mean, to rahtid, watch me asking you to write the whole four-hundred-year reason why my country will always be trying not to fail. You should laugh. If I was you I would laugh. But, man, you did notice it, don't you? That's why this peace thing haunt you for as long as it did haunt me. Even people who usually expect the worst did, if for only two or three month, start to think peace a little then a lot, then peace was all they could think about. Is like how before rain reach you can taste it coming in the breeze. Look 'pon me, me not even forty yet and me already seeing only what behind me, like some old man. But hey, this decade only halfway in, right. Things can go either way. Nostalgia they call it? Must be because me in foreign too long. Or maybe you just can't make new memory in prison. What you think? You should tell me when you have your first sentence. Me would love to know what that would be. Oh, you have it already? No brethren, don't tell me. I want you to write it down first.

Yeah, you can use my real name. Then whose name you was going use? But yeah, man, write the book. Just do me and yourself one favour. Wait till everybody dead before you publish it, alright?

Josey Wales

Still, *me have* to give your boy Weeper some credit.

Bushwick. I still working my brain on how Jamaicans can come to a ghetto five time as big and with tenement three time as high and think they're better off. What, nobody know the difference between a good thing and a bigger bad thing? That must be for some other brother to figure out. So far every single block we pass have at least two house burn down. The last have only two standing and nothing else but stray dogs, stray man and rubble. And everywhere, even the good streets, have this stink that hover in the air then rush you.

—Yeah, man, at least him figure out that—

—Why everywhere smell like the back of a butcher shop?

—Bushwick, me boy. All the meat-processing factories still in Bushwick. Well, one or two. Most of them gone and people around here can't find no work.

—What happen to all the house them?

—Arson, me brethren. Like me say: factory them close. People lose work, property value drop so low that you make more money torching your house for the insurance than trying to sell it. The place so dead that not even a dutty whore would buy a house 'round here.

—Then why set up shop 'round here?

—That is where your friend Weeper smart. As I was saying, this is exactly where you want to set up. Why you think Ranking Dons want it so bad? People who looking for the crack don't want to be seen looking for the crack so where you go? Somewhere that all New York blind to. Look 'round you, man, this is where you go for people to forget you. And then setting up the base house down the road so they don't have to go far. I don't know how me never think 'bout that. If I just buy the crack me no want to wait too long to lick the crack pipe. And me sure as r'ass don't want to take it back where me coming from. No, man, your brethren have me thinking 'bout setting up some shacks in Queens, no lie.

I spin 'round slow to make a sweep of the place. I have to ask myself what was I expecting. The place look like where business must happen, I mean, what else could Bushwick have look like? But still. You don't realize until you come here how much everything you know about America come from TV. The street is wide, but lonely. And worse; all I can think of is that out here is just me and Eubie and Eubie's men.

The van is now two block away and we walking. In front of this house with windows board up, we stop.

—This the place?

—Yeah, man.

—Then make we go in. I goin'—

—Not yet, Josey. You is here to check operations, so make we see how things operate.

He point down the street but I can't see nothing. Not until two people walk out of the shadow into a streetlight. I can't tell from here, but one of them must be the spotter. The other hiding his face in a hoodie. The spotter turn and point down the street in our direction. Hoodie keep walking until the second man stop him or at least try to stop him, but Hoodie don't stop walking. Second man shout something and Hoodie stop and walk over. Further down first man is already talking to somebody new. Hoodie shake hand with second man and stand under the streetlight. Eubie pull me back into the dark. Hoodie cock her hip, a girl. Second man walk about fifteen, maybe twenty feet and shake hand with third man who come out from behind a light post. I pride myself on a sharp eye and even I didn't see him before. Third and second man break hand, and second go back to Hoodie. She start walking and as she pass second man neither of them stop but their hand touch. Hoodie walk past me and go up the street.

—Where?

—The crack house, Eubie says. We can go check it out.

—No. Call that boy over, I say, and point to the boy who was invisible behind the light post.

Eubie call him over and he step to us with that stroll that I'm noticing these black American youths do, as if hand and leg must swing far in opposite direction when they walk. He walk right up to me and don't really stand, just hang off.

—Sup.

—What?

—Him mean what's up, Josey. What's going on, what's happeni—

—Me get it.

—So the young people talk these days, I can't even understand my own boy them, no true?

—How's business, I say.

—It's a Friday night, how the fuck you think business is? People got paid and prowling the street for pussy and dick. Crack hos sucking the D for some chump change and they hit me up. Friday night, yo.

—How long now Weeper have you out here?

—Who?

Eubie laugh quiet, but loud enough for me to hear it.

—Weeper, your boss.

—Oh yeah, Michael Jackson. He's around, at least he was until a couple hours ago. Probably went home to chill, busy day for that motherfucker.

—How you to call your boss motherfucker?

—Josey, it don't mean the same thing over here. Man all call them bonafied brethren, them main motherfucker.

—What kinda fuckery that, Eubie? I don't like that shit.

—Okay, my man, no more motherfucker. Jeez, the boy say.

—You seem to know what you doing out here. How long now Weeper have you as the runner for this spot?

—Gotta watch?

—Yeah?

—What time is it, yo?

—Eleven.

—Five hours now. I's always good at math.

—What? What you just say? Five hours? Him have new man as runner so quick?

—Me could never trust a new boy to be a runner, Eubie say.

—Not new, Pops. Just the new runner. I was a spotter for like two weeks.

—Me see say you control the spot, I say. But how come you get promote so quick?

—Cuz I'm fucking good, that's why. Things're working out fine tonight. Good cuz it was all for shit a week ago.

—Tell we more, Eubie say.

—Mister, I ain't telling your pimp here shit, he says, pointing at Eubie but looking straight at me.

—Pimp? Pimp? Ah who the pussycloth you ah call pimp? You want see me just—

—Eubie, 'low the youth, I say.

I wasn't going to laugh, but I make sure Eubie see me smile. I like this boy. I step to him and put my hand on his shoulder.

—That's good. Good thing, you have sense and you don't take no fuckery from nobody. Good. But understand something. Weeper is paying you because I pay Weeper. Weeper keep you alive because I keep Weeper alive, you understand me?

—Sure thing, Pops. You're the Don Dada.

—But wait, ah where him learn them things deh, Josey?

—Motherfucking Jamaicans be all over the place, yo. Like all them hos your pimp here got working Flatbush.

—Brethren, me say me not no pimp.

—You mean you dress like that on the real? Damn, bro.

I could watch this man get under Eubie skin all night.

—How bad was last week? I say.

—Man, okay. Just know long as I ain't no fucking snitch. But had motherfucker let this shit gone on one more day, this would be Ranking Dons' corner now.

—What?

—Do I look like I'm tripping? Yo, you got spotters sending customers to runners and runners trying to get some shit from the dealers but then you got two dealers and both of them too busy getting high on their own supply, I mean, watchu think's gonna happen?

—See it deh? Same thing me tell you, Josey.

—What did Weeper do?

—Gotta hand it to your boy, he dealt with that shit like a motherfucker. One of them dealers gave him shit right there in the crack house and he popped him just like that, man. Like dude wasn't nothing. Sheeeeet. You Jamaicans don't play and that's a fact. Then he brought me over, promoted me and asked if I got any buddies who looking to make some bucks. I said fuck yeah I got me some buddies. We all working this shit now, Pops. We got this street locked down.

—Who's supplying the dealer?

—Your man Weeper, I guess.

—Where him gone?

—Left him at the crack house hours ago. Figured he got some other spots to check out. Anyway, man, the more I'm here chit-chatting the less money I can make for your ass.

—Good, good. What you name?

—The girls call me Romeo.

—Alright, Romeo.

I watch him swagger back off.

—Everybody on the scene him hire today? Man, him don't even know controlling crucial territory? No, for real, two new boy in the cut right now guarding the stash? We need to check that spot, Josey. It right there in—

—No. Make we just check out this crack house, I say. —Where you boys?

—Them deh 'bout.

—Radio them to hold back, I want to see how this house work without any heavy manners.

We walk two block then turn right. The place look like any other house here with three floor and boarded-up windows missing half of the boards. Like certain house in downtown Kingston where, if you look hard, you can see it used to be posh. Three floor but the steps take you up to the second floor. All sort of shit and garbage and what look like a dog scratching himself at the bottom. That and a fucking fence, as if some family live here and was about to water the lawn. Can't tell from the dark but it's probably brick like every other house on this street. Streetlight like a spotlight on the steps. The rest of the block is rubble. A man sitting at the bottom of the steps like he looking at how the streetlight shape him shadow. Two kind of light inside, the small white one sweeping all over the place like a flashlight, and the flickering light of flame, candle and crack pipe. Only last year I finally make it to Valle del Cauca. Now I'm outside this house.

—You want we go in? Eubie say.

I don't answer. I don't want him to read it like I am afraid to, but I don't want to go in yet. I feel him standing behind me waiting for something to do. Weeper might be inside.

—Well me ah go pee-pee 'round the back. Soon come.

I listen to his footsteps getting farther and farther. If Weeper was inside this long, I don't know. If Weeper inside this long then he . . . If Weeper inside maybe he'll have one of his Weeper-type excuse. If Weeper inside this long, maybe he shouldn't come out. If—

—Motherfucker, you better gimme all o' dat shit! All o' dat shit!

I turn around and smell him first, sweat, shit and vomit. Newspaper chunk popping all over his hair. Black man in a coat and scratching him left leg. The other hand holding a gun at my face. He squint like he in pain, look right and left quick then back at me. Still scratching his leg. I can't tell for sure but it look like he barefoot. He leaning from one foot to the other and squeezing his thigh together like he stopping himself from pissing.

—You think I'm playing, motherfucker? I look like I'm playing? I'ma buss a cap in yo motherfucking ass just like dat! Let go o' all of dat shit!

He wave the gun again. Leggo dat shit, he say. I pull some bill out of my front pocket. I was about to reach for my wallet when he snatch the money out my hand. I look at him as he point the gun at my face. I watch him pull the trigger and before I even brace myself it hit me in the forehead and trickle down my face.

Water.

No.

Piss.

The man laugh and run off, up the stairs past the man and into the crack house. The man on the stairs don't move. Me neither. I wipe the piss off my face. Eubie is coming back to me with another man running from behind him. The man pass him and get to me first.

Weeper.

—Josey! Josey, me brethren, is wah you a do here so by youself? Eubie just leave the I right yah so? Ah what . . . bombocloth, brethren, is what smell so?

—Piss, Weeper. Bombor'asscloth piss.

—But how?

Eubie reach. I don't bother ask him if it was the river Nile he was pissing out. What piece you have on you? I say looking straight at him.

—Nine millimeter.

—Give me. Weeper?

—Same thing and a Glock.

—Give me the Glock.

I take the safety off both gun, the 9mm in my left hand and the Glock in my right, and head for the crack house.

Weeper

Two guns, one in each hand like an outlaw for real. No voice, no sound, no nothing but the stepping. Josey Wales stomp slow into the dark to the crack house, he hear the two of we following and turn 'round and stop and look. We stop, wait till he start walking but Eubie stand still and I follow. Josey walk quick and hunch him shoulders like a beast. I want to ask Eubie what happen, but keep walking. Breeze blowing the smell of piss off him shirt and into my nose. He step right past the man on the step and go through the door. Candles all along the floor over making the house look like church. Candles making slow light, not like Josey moving fast. Plenty beer can on the floor waiting to rock. Paper, board, linoleum shift off and rolling up like skin peeling back. On the wall candlelight making the graffiti jump, a big K and a big S on the right, peeling paint on the left. In the middle another doorway that Josey already step through. He lift the gun on him right and sudden a flash of fire. He kick 'way a whiskey bottle and me right behind him, following him, on the right a man lying flat and him blood creeping out. Bathroom on the right. White man or Latino man, straight hair man on the toilet with him pants down, maybe he taking a shit but he slapping his left arm for his vein to pop. Josey lift the Glock and pop off two. Second bullet lift the man off the toilet and he crash on the floor. He pass the next open door on the right. Flashlight tape to the cupboard, this must be the kitchen. Flashlight shining down on man on him knees like he praying. Cornrow hair, face looking up but eye closed, one little red light, where the crack pipe burning and papapap, gunshot never sound like a pow in the movie, always a papapapap. Still Josey moving and the house don't wake up yet, each step a crunch through beer can and Coke can and pizza box and Chinese takeout and forty-ounce bottle and dry shit, and he still stomping and he pass another doorway with a man lean up slight in the hinge but him back still to we and around him waist two black hands pull him belt, then the button. Her baby holding on to her back, and sucking a pacifier while she sucking the cock. Josey pop him and he slump back on the door but still standing up and she still sucking the cock hard and take it out of her mouth and slap it over and over because he gone soft and if he don't cum he not going pay her. Josey walk off and me walk off leaving her putting the cock back in her mouth. We walk into the living room, who you looking for I think to say but don't and on the right a black woman in a white brassiere, left strap hanging off, smoking. Man behind her with no shirt on only white shorts, or maybe a black shirt since there is not enough light, but him cigarette burning at the tip and papapap and the man slump back in the couch. The black woman turn behind and look, then look at me. Then she turn behind again, and look, and scream. That do it, one scream lead to another scream and in the candle-flashlight a white woman scream but drop her syringe and she dive to the floor but land face-first and the needle stick right through her bottom lip but she flinging garbage left and right looking for it and people all around her coming out of the dark and limping and hopping and crawling and running now. And Josey lift both guns up and let all hell loose, and people running and tripping and falling and one man run straight to Josey but him forehead explode and he fall flat like a tree and a woman run and jump through the window at the back but we one floor up and me sure she scream all the way down and I hope she didn't land headfirst and a man in a baseball cap and plaid shirt with a forty ounce in a brown paper bag come out of a room to the side and say whatdafuck and get two shot in the chest and the bottle fall and shatter and in the room be two, a light-skinned boy with curly hair and a woman with a tam on just about to suck in the first whiff of the crack pipe when the slug burst through her forehead and the pipe drop and muthafucka you dropped the muthafucking pipe you dropped the muthafucking pipe, the curly hair boy say. But Josey moving on and the house clearing out and I want to grab him and say what the fuck you doing but Josey gone dark and he take the stairs and staying on the left side like he in the dark, some of the steps break off on the right and me follow him. A man come right up to the top of the stair and he fire the two gun same time and the man fall over the railing, and a woman grab her pickney and run to a small room and slam the door just in time for Josey to buss three shot in the door. He kick off a doorknob and walk in the room, and a big black man on the mattress on the floor fucking a girl hard and papapap and the man slump down on top of the woman who have to shake her head out of the crack haze before she start to scream. A man run past the door and Josey run out and shout pussyhole! He run out the door and fire at the man with right gun then left and left catch him in the neck near the ear then right in the shoulder left in the back of the head and right in the back and left in the neck and he drop to him knee, and left gun blast a chunk off the top of him head, and right go through a dark area but blood burst through him mouth and him fall and bits of newspaper fly out of him head. Josey walk up to the man and he still firing and firing until both gun click empty. He still pulling the trigger to a click click click. Josey, I say, and he swing around quick, point the gun at me head and click. He stand there with the gun to my head and me stand there looking and me stiffen me back and blow out me breath and tighten me stomach. Give me you other gun, he say. He go over to the man, roll him over and take money out of the man pocket. Then he walk back into the bedroom with the girl whimpering under the man deadweight because he was a big, big man and shoot him again in the head. Then Josey go downstairs and turn into the room and fire one shot and walk out and me look in and the light-skinned boy rubbing the woman pregnant belly and crying. Josey pass the man with the bleeding eye and one-two pap-pap in the head and we pass the white woman in the living room with the syringe stuck in her lip, still on her fours scraping through shit and garbage looking for her syringe. And we pass the bedroom and the woman with the white brassiere gone but the man cigarette still smoking and Josey pump one in him head and we passing the last door and the man still leaning against it and the woman still sucking the cock and the baby still holding on to her sweater and she still pulling at the dick to say get hard baby, just get hard, and she still sucking and we pass her and we pass the man with the cornrow hair and he was still breathing short and gargling through him blood and spit and choking and the flashlight showing blood pumping through him neck Josey put the gun right up to him forehead and fire then he walk into the toilet and pop off one in the white/Latino man and we finally near the doorway and he forget the last man who was shooting up right beside the body of the man me shoot hours ago and walk through the front door and the night swallow him up and I pause for a long time then run through the door and down the steps. The man on the steps gone. I walk over to Josey and Eubie and Josey swing around and point the gun at me again. He hold the gun near me head for a long, long time, long enough for me to start count clicks until the click.

Josey?

Josey?

Is wha this, brethren?

Josey? Is wah this?

Then he don't even give the gun back to me, just drop it and walk off. Eubie turn to walk off too, but then stop, turn back 'round to me. I can't see him face.

Dorcas Palmer

I *don't know* but I'm coming damn close to the conclusion that Heather Locklear's hair looks better in *T. J. Hooker* than it does in *Dynasty.* Or maybe I just don't like that the one woman in *Dynasty* who has to struggle for everything is the bitch, and not even a real bitch like Alexis Carrington, since she doesn't have any money, so she's really just a bitchlet. This is why her hair just don't bloodcloth work on that show. Besides she really makes me want to wear a uniform when she's on *T. J. Hooker.* Maybe become a policewoman for real because trying to wear attractive clothes all day is just too damn expensive, even when you're not trying to look good. Sometimes you just want a shirt that still makes men know that you have breasts.

He's still in the bathroom. It's weird how I have been calling him, he for the past, what, now, fifty-five minutes? I mean, I don't know who the hell is in my bathroom. The thing is, the more I try to figure it out the less sense it makes, so the best thing is to just not think really. Like that man in *Crime and Punishment* where Dostoyevsky says he was beyond thought or something like that. I swear to God sometimes I wish I was still a book-reading woman lost on some bus going somewhere in the city. At some point it just turned into effort like I was trying, which wasn't a problem really until I started to wonder what exactly was I trying to do. I guess everything needs a goal after all. I don't know what the r'ass I'm talking about. Anyway, this man is still in my bathroom like this is *The Shining*, and me out here about to get on like Jack Nicholson. All this time I'm trying to figure what health problem such a strapping man could have and it never occur to me even once that clearly his problem was not physical. It's amazing how I just have a nose for tribulation. I swear to God. At least if he's locking himself in the bathroom he's not about to turn into an ax murderer. From the look of things, I'm the ax murderer in this story.

I mean, this don't make no sense. No, that will lead to thinking again. How about this: There is a man inside my bathroom that needs to come out. I can't get him out so his family is coming to get him. Now I can get some peace from just concentrating on the facts of the situation. I like how that just reduces everything into something I don't need to care about. I like reduction. Boiling down. Editing out. Leaving behind. Enough with the metaphors now for just cutting unnecessary shit from my life. And right now all the unnecessary shit is locked away in the bathroom.

Two sounds that I know. Window sliding up and back down. But there's a grill to keep people out plus we're five floors up, which I guess he didn't remember. He's trying to make an escape. How long before he works up some courage to kick down the door and fight? Would he see that it was a woman in the house all alone and leave? Try to beat me up? I don't know about these ex-soldiers, you know. Everybody in this city look like any minute they might fall apart. You know what? I'm just going to stay sitting on this couch, straighten out the red velvet covering on the arm and watch the end of *T. J. Hooker.* I'm going to sit here and wait until his son or whoever shows up, although given that they called three times to get the address right, who knows when that will be?

Maybe I should ask if he needs anything. That's what people always ask on these TV shows. I'm certainly not going to ask if he wants to talk about it. Maybe I should clean up my apartment since people coming over. Sure, like they coming over to check the place. They won't even notice the bathroom rug that their daddy is sitting on. Maybe he's sitting on the toilet, or maybe the edge of the tub, I don't know. What is he doing in there? Jesus Christ, he was so normal only a few hours ago, so normal and nice and those words that men are just not worth using anymore, dashing, debonair, something else that begins with D. I mean, he was almost . . . I mean, I did everything to not think of him that way since thinking that way about men never ends well, and here it is, things didn't end well anyway. Lesbians must be the most satisfied people on the planet. Maybe I should go over to the door and tell him again that his son is coming, except "fuck you, whoever you are" wasn't very funny the first time I heard it, and it won't be any funnier the second time. I'm wondering which of us just woke up from a bad dream.

Wait and see or see and wait? Never thought about flipping that before. Like we're waiting for action, when more often than not action just seems to make me wait. I seeing the door and waiting for him to come out, maybe armed with my plunger, or hair drier, or curling iron and maybe he will realise I'm a woman and think he can at least beat me up. Funny how the Colthirsts conveniently forgot to mention that I would be dealing with a maniac. Although if I had just said . . .

A knock on the door. There's Miz Colthirst who's wearing a scarf on her head that looks like she's hiding rollers, and a thick camel coat because that makes perfect sense on a summer night. She whispers, For Christ sakes, and walks right past me inside. Since I'm pretty sure I don't have a job anymore and as such don't have to be polite to pushy white people, I was just about to tell this over made up bitch to show some r'asscloth manners in me house when the son make it up the stairs and straight to my door.

—I'm so very sorry for all of this, he says. He doesn't wait for me to invite him in either. Now I feel like the stranger in my house. I'm actually measuring my steps as I walk and hoping I'm not making too much fuss as they gather at my bathroom door.

—Papah, oh Papah, this is just so ridiculous. Get out of there.

—Fuck you, cunt.

—Dad, you know I don't appreciate you speaking to my wife that way.

—I have a name, Gaston, she says.

—One issue at a time, dear. Pop, can you come out now? This isn't home, in case you didn't notice.

—Who the hell put me here?

—Papah, it's because you won't take your pills.

—Why does that shrill bitch keep calling me her papa?

—You were at our wedding, Dad, stop acting like you've forgotten that too.

The son looks at me and mouths, I'm so sorry for all this.

—Anyway, Dad, we really need to give Mrs. Palmer her apartment. She's put up with enough as it is.

—How did I get here?

—You weren't kidnapped, Papah.

—I know I wasn't kidnapped, you stupid bitch, you think that little black woman could have kidnapped me?

Little?

—Dad, we spoke—Dad? We've had this talk about your blackouts, remember?

—Where am I?

—You're in the Bronx, Papah.

—Who the fuck blacks out and ends up in the Bronx?

—Apparently you do, Papah.

—Could somebody shut that bitch up?

—Okay, that's really quite enough, Dad. Stop it and come out.

—You're a joke.

—Okay, Dad. Okay. I'm the joke. Who's the grown man who just realized that he is in some woman's john in the middle of the Bronx and has no idea how he got there? I'm the joke? Listen, Pop, I don't know how you got in this poor woman's apartment and I don't really care either, but unless you want her to call the police for them to drag your ass to jail for breaking and entering, if not worse, then get the fuck out of her bathroom so we can fucking go.

—I'm not going—

—Ken, now!

The wife comes over to me. That armchair, is it Danish Modern? she says. I say no, but I really wanted to say it's so modern it was tossed out on the street only days ago. She's just like rich women everywhere, including Jamaica. If it wasn't for the string of pearls they'd never know what to do with their hands. Ken finally comes out, though nobody has to tell me that I don't get to call him that anymore. He looks the same, except that his hair is not behaving like a movie star's anymore. Some of it is hanging above his left eyebrow. He stands up straight and begins to walk out of my house with his hands in front like somebody cuffed him.

—Gail, darling, could you walk Dad to the car?

—Really, darling, I do think I have a few words to give—

—I'm not walking anywhere with this bitch.

—Both of you get the fuck out of this woman's house and go to the fucking car now.

The wife leaves tugging the pearls and it looks like she's using the necklace to pull herself. Mr. Colthirst stops to look at me, not the up and down summing up that snobs do, but straight in the eyes. I look away first. I don't watch him leave. The son sits down.

—I don't think we've met, he says.

—No. You were gone to work.

—Right. And you're Dorcas, right?

—Yes.

—How did he get here?

I don't know if I should answer him or take in more of how he looks like Lyle Waggoner too. I wonder if he would be happy or angry if I said they looked like brothers.

—Is he that wanted to leave. It's not like I could stop him, all I could do was follow him and make sure he didn't get into trouble.

—But the Bronx. Your house.

—You know I don't have to answer that. You people called the wrong agency—at least that was how it looked. He was the one who wanted to get food in the Bronx. I didn't have to follow him.

—Hey, I'm not judging you, ma'am.

—Not a thing happened.

—Miss Dorcas, I really don't care. So do you know the deal with my pop?

—The Miz never got 'round to explaining anything, but I figured there must be something if you called the agency.

—Every day is a new day for Pop.

—Every day is a new day for everybody.

—Yeah, but everything about it is new for Pop. My father has a condition.

—Not sure I following you.

—He doesn't remember. He's not going to remember yesterday, or today. Not meeting you, what he had for breakfast, by noon tomorrow he won't even remember being in your bathroom.

—That sound like a condition in a movie.

—A very, very long one. He remembers other stuff, like how to tie his tie and shoelaces, where his bank is, his Social Security number, but the president is still Carter.

—And John Lennon is still alive.

—Huh?

—Nothing.

—Doesn't matter if you tell him, doesn't matter what you tell him, by the next day he forgets. He can't remember anything since around April 1980. So he remembers his children, he remembers hating my wife because of an argument they had the same day it happened, but every morning the kids are this surprise we sprung on him. And to him Mom died two years ago, not six. He also doesn't believe it when you explain all this to him and, I mean, why should he? Who wants to be devastated every morning? At least thank God he doesn't remember that either. I mean, you saw how he walked right past you, somebody he just spent the whole day with. In the fucking Bronx.

—What happened to him?

—That's such a long story. Accident, disease. After four years it doesn't matter at all.

—He never remembers that he forgets.

—Nope.

—Is it getting worse?

—I really don't know.

I'm thinking that's not so bad.

—You should know that's why the last one before you quit.

—Really? That's not what . . .

—Huh?

—Never mind. She quit?

—Yeah, I guess it got to her after a few weeks, having to introduce herself every day to a cranky old man who doesn't know why she's there. And even with that she couldn't get past not treating him like he was sick, even though that's what she was there for. You're pretty much waiting for a bomb to go off every day.

—He's not old.

—Huh? No . . . I guess he's not. Anyway, we've got to take him home. We'll call the agency tomorrow and let them know it was no fault of yours that we need a new—

—No.

—Huh?

—Don't call the agency. I want the job.

—You sure?

—Yes I'm sure. I'll take it.

John-John K

C*hrist, what a sloppy* motherfucker. Took him out as soon as he stepped through the door. Well, knocked him out. Maybe he should have switched the light on as soon as he came in. Now I have him sitting on his own stool like a school dunce, hands tied behind his back. I thought about roughing him up a little. But I dunno, maybe it was because he just stepped in, or maybe I just wanted to . . . I dunno.

—You Weeper? I say.

—Who the fuck is you? he says.

I screwed the silencer back on.

—Oh, that is who you be. You look like somebody me know. Me know you?

—Nope.

—You sure? Me no forget people. Once a man enter the room me mark him face, just in case him . . .

—Something funny?

—Just in case him have a gun. What kind o' gun that?

—Nine millimeter.

—Pussyhole gun. That me come to, going get kill with a battyman gun.

—Battyman?

—Samfie business.

—What? Why don't you stop talking?

—Then why you didn't gag me if you didn't want me to talk? I mean, I could bawl out for murder.

—Go ahead, Kitty Genovese.

—Who that?

—Never mind.

—Something you want me to tell you, don't it?

I pull up a chair in front of him.

—Smoke? I said.

—I man rather lick the collieweed, but put a cigarette in me mouth, nuh?

—I'm gonna take that as a yes.

I stick a cig in my mouth, another in his and light them both.

—You must be the first white enforcer me ever see. And me never see you 'round them place. Though me know me see you. Maybe you come to Jamaica as tourist.

—Nope.

—Me know everybody who work for Griselda and me no know you.

—How did you know Griselda sent me?

—Subtract those with a desire from those who have means.

—Hah. What's the skinny on you and Griselda?

—That samfie, stinking cunt, madwoman bitch. She know who she ah fuck with? Long time Jamaica send me to set up the distribution link from Colombia to Miami. I couldn't stand working with the fucking bitch. But I should have known that when I told her to shove her baby foot up her cunt that she would take it personally. Bitch think she could slap me because shipment was late just one time. When word get out that she start bite hand that feed her, them going string her up by her bloodcloth clit, you hear me. She goin' . . . but hold on. She don't fuck with no white man. She don't trust none of them. How come she dealing with you?

He coughs and I pluck out the cig. When he stops and takes two deep breaths, I stick the cig back in, to the side of his mouth, like a movie gangster.

—My mind just don't cater fi that deh bitch, you know.

—Huh?

—Griselda! Me no understand how she move. If it wasn't for me, she would have to deal with Cubans still. I mean, she know what she going bring on herself killing me? What she think going happen to her when Josey Wales hear this? Fucking woman. And who you again?

—Nobody. Somebody doing a favor.

—You can't be nobody and somebody at the same time. Maybe you is some nobody, haha.

—What kind of a name is Weeper?

—Better than four eyes.

—Funny. Want another cig?

—No, them fucking sticks goin' kill you. That bitch. That bitch. How much they paying you?

—Plenty.

—Me'll double it. You want coke? Me can give you two house full o' this. You live like Elvis for the next ten year. You want pussy, me can get you any pussy you want in New York, even pussy that don't turn pussy yet. Or maybe is batty you want.

—Batty?

—Anus. Rectum. Shit hole.

—Oh, I see.

—Me no care what people want to do. Plenty ah chuck badness then spread for man to fuck out the batty. People do what people do, me just want the money. Hear this, a man who run one PNP district? This man they call Funnyboy? Have man suck him cock and eat out him battyhole all the time, then him shoot them dead right after.

—Say what?

—That me say.

—Damn waste of a mouth if one of them eats him out so good, though. You laugh, but that's some serious shit right there.

—How old you be?

—Old enough.

—You a pickney. You just a start. This business here. Me tied up for you to kill me, this don't make no sense. And don't think they goin' make you leave this house alive. After the killing must come the cleanup and you goin' stink like last week garbage.

—I'll live.

—You dead as soon as you pull the trigger. What she paying you? Me will double it, triple it, you know.

—See that's the problem, you could double, triple, quadruple, quintuple, the figure is still the same.

—What? She nah pay you nothing? You doing this for free? You is a sicker cunt than that ugly bitch. The whole of unu crazy. Crazy, crazy. Me kill nuff people and not a single one wasn't business. You people get too used to having endless supply o' bullet. In Jamdown, Jamaica, you make them bullet count, because shipment don't always come on time. Tell me this, eh? Who goin' do the transshipment now that she rubbing out the Jamaican connection? She think she goin' work with them fucking Cubans again? She try to kill six of them in some club two weeks ago.

—You know about that?

—Of course me know 'bout that.

—And you doin' this for free. What them have 'pon you? You catch her eating out pussy?

—Griselda's a dyke?

—Johnny Cash wear black? She chum up to them gogo girl all the time and then when she get tired of them, one bullet, thank you, ma'am. She and Funnyboy should form a singing group.

—That's some funny shit.

—She one crazy cunt, you know. But she never let that get in the way of making bills before.

—That's cuz it's not her hit.

—What?

—She's just setting it up, buddy.

—How you know that?

—You're the same one who just said that a hit from her made no sense. Seems somebody is covering up their tracks to get to you.

—No sah. Fuckery you ah talk. Nobody from Jamdown behind this. Even if is so it go, them wouldn't go 'bout it like this.

—You could say somebody made her an offer that she couldn't refuse. Nothing personal. I hear she has nothing but kind words to say about you.

—She can go fuck herself with a Pepsi bottle.

—No, really. It's probably not my business. Somebody made her an offer she couldn't refuse. Get it? *The Godfather*? No? You're crushing my groove, Pops.

—So is money?

—Fucking Jamaicans. You guys not big on irony, huh?

—Is the money or no?

—Not the money. For her or me. I just got caught in the wrong fucking place at the wrong fucking time. You just ended up with the wrong fucking enemy.

—Bigger than she? Boss in Colombia? Them don't need me dead. Them more 'bout business than she. Josey contact them first years ago, not she.

—Guess they're bigger than Colombia too.

—That only leave God. Is God, don't it? Hah, which angel you be? Gabriel? Michael? Maybe me shoulda put some lamb blood 'pon me door.

—Haha. Wished somebody warned me about this fuckin' city.

—What's so bad about New York? Living the dream here, brethren.

—Lived.

—Pussyhole.

We both laugh.

—Can't wait to jet from this fucking city, I say.

—Who you running back to?

—Huh? Why'd you ask that?

—Pum-pum must be tight like fuck.

—Pum-pum?

—Pussy.

—Oh. I guess you could say that.

—So you love the bitch?

—What? Shit, what a fucking question.

—Look like yes.

—You're stalling.

—Tell me about the girl.

—No.

—What me goin' do? Tell *National Enquirer*?

—You're stalling.

—Tell you before. Me not the only man in here on borrowed time.

—Shut up, you.

—She cute?

—No.

—You like them homely?

—No.

—So she a sweet little thing then. What she name?

—Rocky. Thomas Allen Bernstein, but I call him Rocky. Can you shut up now?

—Oh.

—Yeah, and I don't need your fucking shit.

—So him cute?

—What the f—

—Well if you goin' be a battyman, at least get the best batty.

—Batty? Oh right, you told me. Hah, he does have a cute batty, come to think of it.

—Batty is the first thing you check for? Maybe you really is Jamaican.

—His batty is cute. And his face. Dimples, the boy's got dimples. He always wants to shave but I wish he wouldn't at all. And his hands, they look like he's tough but he's never put in a hard day's work in his life. But he laughs like a fucking weasel. And he snores. And—

—Alright, man, too much of the batty boy business.

—Good stall though. Shame. You're the first man in this fucking city worth talking to.

I get up and go behind him. I push the gun through the hair until it touches his skull.

—Anybody was here when you let yourself in? Anybody was in here?

—No.

—Oh. Oh good. Good.

I'm about to pull the trigger.

—Wait! Wait! Just wait. How unu fi do me like that? Me no get last request? Gimme a hit, nuh? Just one last hit. Have a bag right there behind the TV stand that already cut. One last one. At least make me no care if I get shot or not.

—Fuck, man, I gotta get out of this city.

—You can't cut one fucking bag open and give a man a hit? Give a man a hit nuh, man. Give me a hit.

—That how you Jamaicans roll? In Chicago nobody uses and deals, at least not their own supply. Always the beginning of the end when that happens.

—That why you new whiteys always look so sorry all the time. Unu not having no fun. You not going tell me who take out contract 'pon me if is not she?

—Don't know, buddy. You gonna sniff that?

—You cut me a line? Two hands kinda occupied, if you didn't notice.

I find the bag, actually a sack of bags between the TV stand and the wall. I cut one open with a Swiss Army knife, and throw the pack down. Cocaine spills out.

—Then make a line, no boss, he says.

I scoop out some cocaine with two fingers, and shaped a line the size of a cigar on the desk.

—You have some elephant 'round here you want to kill or something?

—That should get you high.

—That would get all of Flatbush high.

I separate a new line the size of a match.

—This goin' be hard with me hand them tie.

—Improvise.

The Jamaican bends down on the desk and lean his head left trying to sniff through his left nostril. He give up and lean right. —Fucking shit, he said. He tried again, sniffing harder, two, three times.

—Shit, I really need to shoot this up.

—Can't help you there.

—Pussycloth. Still can't believe this bitch. Have a flight coming in only tomorrow night. Tomorrow fucking night. East Village and Bushwick ready, worse, Josey in New York. What going happen tomorrow when there is no me?

—I dunno, Pops.

—Them goin' kill her for this, you know. Is all-out war between the Jamaicans and she over this.

—I told you, I don't think it's her.

—But she tell you 'bout it. Is she you goin' confirm this too. Is alright, everything cool. Who the fuck bigger than Griselda? Must be bigger than Medellín too. Me is just a humble businessman. Is who me piss off so?

Don't know why but I go over to the window to see if anybody was standing by the curb. I need another gun. Then I remember.

—Almost forgot. She wasn't talking to me but she said the guy lived in New York. Some shit about him neutralizing the Ranking Dons in Miami in exchange.

—What, Storm Posse don't have no problem with Ranking Dons in Miami.

—Clearly somebody does, and he lives in New York.

—And? Man who live in New York who have it out for Ranking Dons. Brethren, that is only me. Me and . . .

Shit.

He looks at me but his eyes go blank.

—Eubie. Me and Eubie.

—I was going to say that his name sounded like Tuba.

The Jamaican stares at me his eyes wide open, spooked like Stepin Fetchit, but not funny. Not funny at all. His bottom lip hangs loose like he was about to say something but couldn't. It twitches. His shoulders slump. He looks at me and bows his head.

—Fucking pussyhole want all of New York to himself. And Josey never going know. He never going know because this will look like a Ranking Dons hit.

—Sorry, man.

I go back to the window.

—Yow, my youth, come here.

—Whassup?

—If you going take me out, at least make me go out 'pon the sky, no man?

—Man, I don't know what the fuck you're talking about.

He points with his head at the bag of coke. That didn't work so hot the last time, remember? I say.

—That's why you going help me shoot it up.

—What now?

—Shoot up. Injection. Sniffing is an idiot way to lick coke anyway. A pussyhole hit. Unless you have crack which you should smoke but me no have no rock in here.

—Dude, I ain't got time for . . .

—For what, you boyfriend outside or something?

—Fuck you.

—Fuck yourself and give a dead man his dying wish. Needle in the bathroom cabinet. Bathroom, over by your—

—I know where the bathroom is, I say.

—A new needle.

I open his cabinet and tear one from the wrapper.

—What am I supposed to do with this? I say, heading back to him.

—Just mix up some from the bag and suck it up with the syringe.

—Right, buddy. What am I supposed to use, spit?

—Any water will do. You never do this before?

—Believe it or not, not everybody and his mother does coke.

—Just say no, eh? Good, good. You can just mix some in water.

—I can't believe I'm doing this.

—Just do it.

—Don't get fucking demanding on me, motherfucker.

I grab the bag and walk over by the sink. Coffee cup okay? I say, and he nods.

—How much coke? Dude, you need to talk me through this.

I had the tap on and the coffee cup. He looks my way and says,

—No, use the tablespoon.

—Suck up some water with the syringe, he says. Then press it into tablespoon. Then add like how much would be a line of coke. Then use like your finger and stir it a little, it shouldn't take long since coke dissolve quicker than sugar. Then suck the whole thing back into the syringe.

—Where, buddy? I mean, like, your hands are kinda occupied.

—Batty.

—Fuck you.

—Not like I could stop you.

—Haha. You don't need an arm, brethren. You could go between me toes but that just hurt. Feel for my pulse in my neck and just shoot.

I touch his neck.

—You not going feel much if you touch it like a pussy.

I feel like gun-butting him, but grab his neck like I'm about to strangle it. His pulse pounds under my index finger.

—Just push in and press?

—Yeah, man.

—Okay, if you say so.

I stick in and start to press. Blood pops up in the needle and I jump.

—Dude . . . blood . . . shit . . .

—No, no, blood is a good thing, don't stop. Yeah . . . yeah . . . yesssss.

—That's it, man. Shit. What did they cut it with, B vitamin?

—Haha, no cut, me brethren, this is—

Weeper's eyes change. Something running through him like a pinball hit the wrong sensor and tilt. Motherfucker starts to shake. Small like an electric jolt first, then harder and louder like he was having a fit. His eyes roll back white but don't come back, and foam pools at his mouth, running down his chest. Sounds push out his mouth like breaths, uh uh uh uh uh uh. His head starts to shake so hard that I jump back. His crotch just explodes piss. I grab him, wanting to shout *Son of a bitch you made me give you pure coke*, but his eyes open wide open and scream. He pushes himself off the stool and we both fall backways. Weeper's kicking something awful, as if some monster's grabbing for his legs. I can smell his breath all beer stink and ass and something else. He's still jerking, choking and hissing, like sssssss is the only thing that could come out of his mouth. And me I don't know why, I don't fucking know but I grab him around the chest and clutch him even though he was on top of me. I don't know why but I was hugging and holding him and squeezing him and he was just shaking, man, shaking and shaking some more with the back of his head bumping into my forehead, foam bubbles popping out of his mouth. I grab his neck but don't squeeze. Weeper wheezes three times then quit.

Sir Arthur George Jennings

F*our priests cover* their faces with lightning, speaking a liturgy nobody out in the congregation knows. Every disciple wrote a testament, but not every testament is in the Bible, a man says to a woman who does not understand, ten metal seats down, thirty seats across in the National Arena. The Singer's funeral. Gospel and heresy go in a dog fight over the body. Rastaman chants from Corinthians even though the elders told him to speak from Psalms, and all ten sit while he calls a king, God. Heresy. The Ethiopian archbishop says, *Why go to Africa when it would profit you more to work together for a better life in Jamaica?* The Rastafarians seethe and cuss. The archbishop came with weapons too—every Rastafarian wants to wake up in Shashemaneland, five hundred acres of lands bestowed by a deposed emperor. Defiant Rastas shout Jah Rastafari, only a few asking why is this an Ethiopian Orthodox funeral when the Singer was Rasta. Hundreds sit, stand and watch. The old Prime Minister still beloved by the sufferahs sits still, hunched over in loss. The new Prime Minister sits until called up. He gives a eulogy for a man he barely knew, but closes with a benediction, *May his soul find rest in the arms of Jah Rastafari.* Gospel versus heresy; heresy wins.

How do you bury a man? Put him in the ground or stomp out his fire? They give the Singer an honour on his deathbed, the Order of Merit. The black revolutionary joins the order of British Squires and Knights, Babylon in excelsis deo. A fire that lights up Zimbabwe, Angola, Mozambique and South Africa doused out by two letters, O and M. Now he's one of us. But the Singer is sly. In time people will see that he prophesied over the very thing, singing of the false honour before it was even bestowed. Before the sickness took him. I hear him sing in his sleep, about Negro soldiers in America. Black American soldiers of the 24th and 25th Infantry, and the

9th and 10th Cavalry under the command of the paleface to butcher Comanche, Kiowa, Sioux, Cheyenne, Ute, and Apache. Fourteen black men in dirty boots take the Medal of Honor for killing a people and an idea. The Indians called them Buffalo Soldiers. The Medal of Honor, The Order of Merit, the same sounds flipped. Meanwhile I see the Singer coming in and going out in the top right side of parcels and letters. I'm already out of time.

All this time the man who killed me still will not die. Instead he rots. I watch him as his secretary touches his white scalp, teeming with veins like little blue snakes, and washes his thin hair in black dye. His new wife will not touch the stuff, it ruins her fingertips and blackens her nail polish. *You sure you don't want it a little grey, Mista P? Make it look young but little more natural? Me want it black, you hear me? Me want it black.* The PNP ran his party out of power, but he dresses every morning as if heading to work. Such a strange decade, it looks nothing like the seventies and he's lost with nobody around speaking his language anymore. His party's thugs no longer want him and the thinkers never needed him so now he shouts out against communism and socialism, his jowls swinging like a rooster's. I watch him while he walks to the car, forgetting for the third time this week he is no longer allowed to drive. He trips on the garden hose and falls hard on the concrete. The fall knocks the wind out of him, killing any hope of a scream, shout or sob. He lies there for nearly an hour before the cooking woman sees him from the kitchen window. New hip, new pacemaker, new blue pills to fuck the wife who had gotten used to him flop on top of her, still like a slug. He laughs at death again. At me.

I watch the man who visited him once at night. He's fatter too, and bigger. Too big for both to take up the same space. Flights to New York and Miami. Business bursting out of back pockets, one thousand dead. Money comes out in the wash and buffets up the ghetto. In the ghettos abroad people sniff, cook, boil and inject. Colombia, Jamaica, Bahamas. Miami. *It's an amazing scenario. We see murders everywhere.* D.C., Detroit, New York, Los Angeles, Chicago. Buy guns, sell powder, when building monsters don't be surprised when they become monstrous. New riders, new posse, the likes of which they have never seen. In New York, the headline type is an inch thick: *Jamaican Got City Hooked On Crack.* A juror listens to the Ranking Don on trial, no friend of Josey Wales. Her first time in court.

—Me shot him in the head.

—Where in the head?

—Back.

—How many—

—One time. You only need one.

—What did you do with the body?

—Dump it in a gully. Then tell the driver to burn the car.

—What did you do when you learned he burned all the evidence, sir?

—Me didn't do nothing. I go to me bed.

He looks at her as he says the last line. A juror, dressed like a schoolteacher, doesn't sleep for three days.

Three killers have outlived the Singer. One dies in New York. One sees and waits in Kingston surrounded by money and cocaine, and one vanishes behind the Iron Curtain where he sits knowing, waiting for the bullet to the head. Soon.

Three girls from Kashmir sling on bass, guitar and drums, fresh faces brimming out of burkas, propped up and held together by a backdrop of the Singer streaked in red, green and gold stripes, thick like pillars. They call themselves First Ray of Light, soul sisters to the Singer smiling with the rising sun. Out of a wrapped face comes a melody so fragile it almost vanishes in the air. But it lands on a drum that kicks the groove back up to where the song lingers, sweeps and soothes. Now the Singer is a balm to spread over broken countries. Soon, the men who kill girls issue a holy order and boys all over the valley vow to clean their guns, and stiffen their cocks, to hold down and take away. The Singer is support, but he cannot shield, and the band breaks away.

But in another city, another valley, another ghetto, another slum, another favela, another township, another intifada, another war, another birth, somebody is singing Redemption Song, as if the Singer wrote it for no other reason but for this sufferah to sing, shout, whisper, weep, bawl, and scream right here, right now.

SOUND BOY KILLING

March 22, 1991

One

You think he's napping?

—Me no response for that, boss.

—Huh? Okay, fine, just point me to his cell.

—I point it out two minutes ago. Is not like nobody else down here in the dungeon.

—Dungeon? That's kinda inappropriate.

—When you done see your way out.

—Not escorting me all the way?

—Don't like the dark.

Footsteps echo as I walk and all I can think about is I kinda wished I saw it myself. No kidding. They swooped down on that lil' motherfucker Griselda Blanco style. Such a wicked idea perfected in Jamaica. Give it to the dearly disappeared bitch, if nothing else she did leave us with one great invention. This is how it went down. With his dad Josey counting down the days until he was extradited to the U.S. for murder, racketeering, obstructing justice, narcotics et cetera, et cetera and so forth, it was up to his son, Benjy Wales, all grown up (but fatter, darker and more boring-looking than his dad) to rule as the don of Copenhagen City. Sorta like a regent, or placeholder, or some thing like that. So Benjy was putting together the Papa-Lo Memorial Commemorative Annual Cricket Match. Anyway, somehow this meant a meeting on King Street, which is east of West Kingston. It's always tricky business when a don of the West heads east, worse, heads off by himself on a bike. He gets to the intersection probably just staring ahead, minding his own business, when this other bike pulls up right next to him. By the time he look over to see who it was, two men in black open fire, blasting his heart out of his chest.

Funny, eh? The thing about Benjy, yeah his pops is Josey motherfucking Wales, and he saw gunfire all the time, but he still traveled the world, well the States, went to a posh school and never had to go to bed hungry a single day of his life. What do you get? A fucking gunman who's too used to the good life. He might as well be any fucking brat stepping out his pop's apartment in Central Park West. His father who has brought this country to a standstill at least three times is in prison about to finally get his ass handed back to him, and what does golden boy do? He goes off by himself on a fucking bike? What did he think, that every other gunman would be in church? And a Griselda-style killing doesn't just happen out of dumb luck. That shit was not just set up, but coordinated right down to that particular intersection. These young boys, they really don't think. I'm fucking old. I used to think old was the first time you bent over and grunted *ugh* when you straightened back up. Now old is running into enemies too old to fight, where all you got left from an old war is fucking nostalgia. And any kind of nostalgia is something to drink not shoot over.

Entry wounds to head, chest and exit wounds in head, neck, shoulder and back. Last week I spoke to this Doctor Lopez who was the doc on call in the ER that morning. Bombo r'asscloth, he says, I've never been so scared in all my life. And not just basic fear for himself but fear like it was about to be Armageddon in the ER. By the time Benjy Wales got to the hospital the boy was pretty much a goner, all that was left was to call it. But Benjy's body came with around three thousand party crashers, all spilling in and out of the ER. All that was left was for the doctor to call time of death, but because three thousand people are outside, expecting you to pull a Jesus because that's what doctors do for a don, you go through the most ridiculous theater not named kabuki. Doctor Lopez was telling me all this. They had to transfer him to a bed, which was already a waste of space, but by then the crowd was shouting BRING BACK BENJY so loud you could hear them all the way down in the valley a mile away. First they tried to restore the airway, which is what you're supposed to do, to gain control of catastrophic hemorrhage. Except by the time they brought him in there was nothing in his lungs but blood. Meanwhile the crowd was getting louder, and the doctors had to go through this fucking charade with a corpse. Imagine trying to restore circulation to a body that's just done with circulating. No pulse, no pressure, no level of consciousness whatsoever. It's not that he had stopped, he was fucking done. I asked him at what time were they going to tell the crowd he was just dead, and he said, *No lie, boss, by the time we started to resuscitate him I was hoping for a miracle too.* Outside the crowd was pushing so hard they broke two glass windows.

The worst part was the defib. Every time they shocked Benjy and his body jerked, the whole crowd jerked too, even people outside who weren't even seeing it. Electric shock-body jerk-crowd jump. Electric shock-body jerk-crowd jump. Electric shock-body jerk-crowd jump. After one hour Doctor Lopez finally called what should have been called from the minute they wheeled that body in. And then, whoa. Word then just circled through the crowd that they couldn't save him. Benjy Wales was dead. They kicked down the ER doors first. Three thousand men, women and children, most of them with guns, the rest with the kind of heart that doesn't need guns. *We di bombocloth. We goin' kill the whole ah unu, we goin' murder down this whole bombor'asscloth hospital. Fifty doctor and nurse for killing Benjy.* Some men grabbed a nurse and started slapping her. Doctor Lopez said he jumped in but two men grabbed him and gun-butted him in the head. They turned over the reception desk and the poor security guards did the only thing they could do. They ran. The doc doesn't know how it happened, but just right then a new wave just washed over the crowd and they started shouting that it's not the doctors that killed Benjy, it was the PNP.

By Sunday night they hit Lane Six of the Eight Lanes. They shot every man in sight and raped every woman in reach. Burned down almost a third of the houses and shot some children to seal the deal. Two days later they fucking decimated Lane Three. Then they took that fight to Miami with drive-by shootings, bullet holes in Honda Accords and night clubs. Two of my buddies said they barely made it out of the Rolex Club, the way the Jamaicans were shooting each other up. The Prime Minister had to reach out to the JLP to organize a truce, and even then they had to get the church to organize some peace marches. They only stopped when all this killing was getting in the way of Benjy's funeral plans. I didn't go to the funeral. I'm not even supposed to be here, officially. Okay, I lie. I did go to the funeral, but I think they might have mistaken me for a bodyguard or something. The last time I saw a funeral that big it was the Singer's.

At least twenty thousand people. There's the former Prime Minister, of course. Needless to say, he was opposition in 1976, then Prime Minister in '80 and now back to opposition in '91. First a marching band, almost like in New Orleans, the men in white uniforms, the girls in red minidresses and pom-poms. Then coffin, black with silver handles with the dead boy in a black velvet suit. If you're never gonna sweat why not go out in winter style? The coffin in a motherfucking white-horse-driven glass hearse right up behind the marching band. Then the former Prime Minister walking with Benjy's queen woman in a skintight little black dress, thick gold chain like you see on those rap guys. Big earrings. As soon as you see her you notice every other woman there. Gold lamé minidress, pink minidress, white minidress, fishnet stockings, silver high heels, bird as hats, hats as birds, more cargo chains. One girl had a open back dress that plunged right down into her ass crack. Every woman moving down the street like it was a catwalk.

Josey tried to get leave (which is a weird way of saying it) to go to his son's funeral but they wouldn't allow it. Why would they? Let the don out of prison to twenty thousand of his own people, how the hell would you get him back? U.S. government probably heard that idea and screamed a thousand no's. Funny that for most of the eighties when Josey built his empire—with major help of course—they didn't so much as give a fuck about him. Fucking New York, man, I told him he shouldn't have done that shit. Black boys really gotta learn to control their fucking tempers. That day in 1985 Josey Wales shot out of nowhere to near the top of the DEA and the Feds' list. And as soon as the JLP got kicked out of power he became one hell of a sitting duck.

But before all that, the bigger he got the more untouchable he was. Josey is driving down some street, I can't remember which, but this is in a place called Denham Town. Wales drives straight into a bus. Comes out and he's mad. But the driver is just losing it and drawing a crowd. Don't know what he said but he just going off and off, and shouting and threatening and God knows what. The only time he shut up was when some woman shouted *is Josey Wales* and the whole street scatters leaving the poor bus driver. Josey's not even looking at him when the man makes like Road Runner straight to the police station. Poor guy. About thirty minutes later, Josey Wales shows up at the police station with ten of his boys. They walk right inside, grab the bus driver, and walk right out. Not a single cop even gets up. The man must have shat himself and bawled like a fucking girl when he saw the policemen looking the other way in their own fucking station. Right outside, with cops and people watching, those with guns shoot the bus driver, those without guns stab him. Was like crows upon fresh carcass. They arrested Josey, of course, but the prosecution just couldn't find any witnesses. Not a single one.

Meanwhile Cali is saying this motherfucker is a badass like no other badass has ever been fucking bad. Give him and his posse the U.K.

This was the man who went into Rema with his boys, and killed twelve just like that. Why? Because some of the guys there started to complain that their little community was being neglected. Josey was always one for making his points clear. Police filed a warrant, Josey skips to the USA, but by now he's a Person of Interest so he skips back to Jamaica. They take him to court, but the one witness suddenly she's got amnesia, no wait, she wasn't there, no wait, is a long time now she hasn't changed her glasses prescription so now she's blind as a bat. Really she just can't remember and was so confused by the whole thing, because gunshots were flying everywhere.

But last year, his daughter was outside some club with her boyfriend and some Eight Lanes goons just sprang out of nowhere and opened fire on the two of them. They just Swiss cheesed the dude till he ran out of places to spring holes. Girl was cradling his body when they walked up right to her and shot her clean in the head. All I could think of was at least they didn't rape her first. I still wonder if they knew who she was. I mean, fact is, like with Griselda in Miami, if you keep pushing and pushing too far, sooner or later your enemies are going to push back. And if you keep making enemies, sooner or later they're gonna reach critical mass. Only a matter of time before you make enemies as ruthless as you, after all you're the one raising the bar. Me, I'm never in a place long enough to build a roll call of enemies. That shit is like any other relationship, you nurture it. That's why I never was one for Colombia or Kingston. I'm a facilitator. Speaking of critical mass, by now the Feds had racked up multiple charges against Josey and they wanted him bad. Somebody had to win the war on drugs and it sure as hell wasn't going to be a nigger from a Caribbean shithole who should have stuck to pot. This time, they got him in prison. And this time, he's going to rot.

Yeah, I went to him in prison and it wasn't visitors hours either. As soon as I said hey Josey, he sat up on the bed and took a good while to look up. When he did, he was smiling, but a small one almost like he was shy. And then he said,

—I knew they would send you.

—How's things, *mijo*?

—Looking at you the better one, Doctor Love.

Two

Miss Segree? Miss Segree? Millicent Segree? Miss Segree?

—It's not Miss.

—Oh. I'm sorry.

—No problem, Mrs. Segree.

—It's not Mrs. It's not Miss, it's Millicent Segree.

—Okay, ma'am.

—You know what? Fine. How much is it?

—The entire prescription is fourteen dollars, ma'am.

You know, most of this feminism business was nothing more than white American women telling non-white women what to do and how to do it, with this patronizing if-you-become-just-like-me-you'll-be-free bullshit, but if there's one thing I agree with is damn, I hate when a man feels I'm obligated to disclose my marital status to somebody I don't even know. Even this bullshit about status itself as if married and spinster are the only two choices for defining myself. Or because I'm a woman I'm supposed to have a status at all. Hey big boy, here's my status. Hi, before I tell you my name here's my status. Maybe I should just say I'm a lesbian and throw the problem back in their faces for them to define it.

Xanax for anxiety. Valium for sleep. Prozac for depression. Phenergan for nausea. Tylenol for headaches. Mylanta for bloating. Midol for cramps. I mean, Jesus Christ, menopause come already. Isn't there some fast-track for a hot flash? It's not like I'm ever going to breed, so why keep the damn store door open? I'm at the Rite Aid on Eastchester in the Bronx, just a block from my place on Corsa Avenue. August means I'll be living there two years. Of course despite working at Beth Israel which, it goes without saying, has a pharmacy, I fulfill prescriptions on Eastchester because who wants to see a nurse buying so many pills? Yeah things are confidential but I've never come across anybody who if given the chance wouldn't talk your business. This just make things less complicated and in the past few years I've just gotten allergic to complicated things. Even men. You can't stand a man who's the same yesterday, today and forever? Give him my number. It's always when they start to talk about their feelings and—I love this one—where is this going? that I get so sick I have to reach for the Phenergan.

So I cross the street to the bus stop and pop one. Zantac. I'm going to need a Zantac after wolfing down a muffin for breakfast. I wish Dunkin' Donuts wasn't all the way on Gun Hill Road, I could use some coffee. But I can't stand Gun Hill Road. Especially on these wet days when winter can't decide to leave and spring can't decide to show up. And I'm not ruining one more shoe while they figure it out. Outside the station is always the same old men with nowhere to go and I can't tell if they're looking at me as men, or as Jamaicans. To make it from street to door to turnstile to train would be hard enough if I didn't have to stand there in pigeon shit waiting on the 5. And it never fails, nobody waiting on the train looking like they have anywhere to go. No shopping bag, no knapsack, no briefcase, nobody carrying anything. Me looking like Miss Virgin Mary because I'm going to the hospital. Not a nurse, training to be one.

The school director looked at me and said we don't always get women at your point in life, usually they're just starting out. Who's to say I'm not just beginning life right now? I said to the man who was clearly not buying it, but for some reason didn't feel like telling a woman she was too old. Every day I go to work, I try to figure that one out. But then Lord knows I know everything about knowing people only in the context of them needing something from me. Millicent, it's too early in the morning to be so bitter. You actually like the white stockings and no-sex-here shoes, remember? Meanwhile at Beth Israel you're in triage and find that you like it very much.

But two weeks ago, for like seven days Jamaicans kept coming in with all sorts of gunshot wounds. All of them men, four of them by the time they got here, there was nothing to do. Girlfriends and baby mothers screaming out *woi*! *Wha me a go do with the pickney dem?* As if I knew the answer. Me, I'm putting on an extra-thick American accent and saying shit like *wah-der* instead of water because I don't want anybody to figure I'm Jamaican, which is just fuckery because so far I did like that the hospital thought I was their own Madge Sinclair from *Trapper John, M.D.* One of the doctors even called me Ernie once and even though I said *my name is Millicent, Doctor,* I couldn't stop grinning. But it was just weird, these Jamaicans with gunshot wounds coming from the Bronx, which is not exactly near this hospital. I didn't ask what was going on this week but a doctor did, and one of the men with three bullets in his backside says, *Them kill young Benjy. Is armagideon now, Kingston, Miami, New York, London. Them kill young Benjy.* Who is this Benjy and how did he die? the doctor asks. I'm there squeezing the IV bag in my hand so hard it almost bursts.

—Nurse? the doctor says. I hook it up to the man's arms without looking at him. I didn't want him to give me the eye of recognition. I'm not no kindred spirit. Who's this Benjy? the doctor asks again and I want to say shut the fuck up, but all I can do is start an IV. Thank God, when I finally look at the man he was giving the doctor this stare, eyebrow raised and indignant like he's thinking, What you mean who's Benjy? I certainly didn't want to know.

—Benjy Wales, the son of the don of dons, the man says.

The doctor's face didn't change much, but I had to look away. I just stopped. I don't know—something just went black and I walked away. I could even hear the doctor saying, Nurse? Nurse? But it was like some transistor radio from far off. I just kept walking and walking until I was in the elevator. Spent the next hour in the cafeteria on the ground floor. Told them I was suddenly dizzy and had to tolerate at least three asking me if I was pregnant. I was this close to saying how about me chopping off my pussy and putting it on my forehead. I had to tell them I had a crippling migraine and was botching finding a vein for the IV.

I have this system. It's really only three words: NO MORE DRAMA. Got it from black American women who were sick and tired of men and all their shit. I don't want any fuss, kass-kass, conflict, disagreement or entanglement. I don't even want drama on TV. Ever since the Jamaicans brought their party to the hospital I had to add Tylenol to my list and up the Xanax just so I could go to work. Wales, it's just a name. It's just a goddamn name. Like Millicent Segree.

Waiting on the M10 Express. Ever since then I've had this headache right above my right temple. It never gets better or worse, but just won't go away. Maybe it's a lump. Maybe I need to stop training myself to become a hypochondriac. Honestly only two days ago I got so anxious I couldn't breathe and remembered that people have been known to die from anxiety attacks. Of course this only made me more anxious. The last time it happened I had to start singing "Just Got Paid" out loud for it to pass. At a bus stop in Manhattan. I think a little girl started singing with me. A little black girl is running around the bench at this bus stop. Another is sitting in her father's lap. He's on the bench waiting on the bus. The little girl running is singing something that sounds like "I Know What Boys Like" but there was no way she would have heard that song. The father is trying to balance the daughter, a baby really, and his newspaper. The little girl runs headfirst into his rib cage, and he grunts and laughs. She pushes her bagel to his mouth and he takes a bite like a bear. She squeals. I try to look away but can't, not until they look at me first.

Girls who love their daddies always come at them sideways. I see it all the time in the hospital. Daddies carrying sick baby girls with poor breathing or insect bites. Women supporting sick fathers for just one more MRI or dose of chemo. Maybe fathers are just more narrow on the side. Yesterday, a teenage girl in the ER, after screaming at her father for ten minutes, just came at him sideways, wrapped her hands all around him until her fingers met, and rested her head right in his armpit for him to drape her. It's not like I miss my father. I don't even know if he's dead. But I'm starting to miss not taking Xanax.

I'm waiting at the bus stop with the father and his two daughters. He's just laughing, mumbling, uh-huh-ing and yes sweetie-ing. Still can't tell if he's Jamaican. One just makes assumptions about anywhere between Gun Hill and Boston Road. They don't even notice he's giving them the daddy gaze. This man in the hospital said to me, You just didn't know you could love anybody or anything that much. It frightens you all the time, every time you hear some kid got hit by a bus. The daddy gaze, I wonder when they lose it.

I never hear anything good, so I stop watching news. I don't even want to know what's going on in Jamaica, but if it's spilling into Bronx and Manhattan then the news can't be good. Jamaicans here never tell me anything I want to hear so I don't talk to Jamaicans. I never missed the country, not even once. I hate nostalgia, nostalgia is not memory and my memory is too damn good for it. The thing is, if all of this is true, then why the r'asscloth am I in Jamaican Bronx? Corsa, Fenton, Boston, Girvan, you might as well call the whole place Kingston 21. On Corsa I'm the lonely woman in the house on the corner, the person who is going to die, rot and sprout poppies before anybody even wonders whatever happened to her. The witch at the end of the street, the Boo Radley. Who the r'ass am I kidding, they probably think I'm just the Christian lady who never have no boyfriend. I'm the stuck-up, stoosh nurse who always wears white stockings and sensible shoes who always leaves and returns to her house in uniform so that nobody will know her in any other context and who don't talk to nobody.

I wonder if anybody ever sees me go out at night. I like to think I don't give a shit about what people think, but then I always leave through the back door. I just hope no more Jamaicans with gunshot wounds show up at the hospital. I just hope . . . You know something, Millicent Segree, nothing good ever comes from taking your thoughts down that way. Even thinking about thinking them just makes the headache beat down the side of my head even more. No more damn thinking. Last week a white college boy heard my accent and asked if I ever met the Singer. And it hit me: I'm one of the few who can answer the question with a yes, but it still pissed me off. Then he started to sing the song with the birds, and for a while I could bear it until it made me think about dead years. Shit, thinking about remembering dead years always makes me remember dead years for real and fuck, fuck, fuck, fuck all that. Fuck the dead. I'm still living.

The bus is here.

I'm still living.

Three

N*ah, this is the C.* The A doesn't make stops until 125th.

—Ah.

The man steps back from the doorway as if he saw somebody in the train he didn't want to run into. I watch the door closing him out and sit back down as the train starts to move. New Yorkers, the uptown train has been lying to you. This is what you do, you take the C from 163rd to 145th Street to jump on the express because you're in a fucking hurry and this is uptown, and there're always delays or some drama. I mean, only last week, when I was rushing to JFK to catch a flight back to Minnesota because Mom wasn't doing so hot, a man pulled down his pants and started to shit on the train. He just squatted and dumped, yelling the whole time like he was giving birth. Of course he did this the second the train pulled out of Fulton, which meant it would be forever before it reached High Street all the way in Brooklyn. Six or seven of us, I don't know how many, rushed to the door only to see that it was the one door that didn't open for transfer to the next car. I'm there thinking, begging, please don't start throwing your shit. Please, please don't. When the train finally pulled into High Street we all tumbled out and ran. But that's not my point. My point was, you take the C to 145th and then switch to the A because it's the express. But the A is fucking slower than the C. Come at, say, West 4th Street and wait a minute or two, and there is the same damn C train you jumped off at 145th.

So now I just stick on the C and try to read. That's not true. I stay on the C train to check out people reading *The New Yorker.* I wonder if they're reading IT. An Irish novelist friend of mine told me how once on the train he saw someone reading his book. He asked her, Is it any good? and she said, Some of it but other times it's a slog. For some reason it made his day, and that she didn't even recognize him. So yeah, sometimes I'm on the C looking for that woman, and it's almost always a woman reading *The New Yorker* and hope I can sit beside them and wait for them to turn to IT. I can say, Holy shit, this is like the movies. I mean, this never happens in real life, right? And she'll say what happens? And I'll say that a writer happens to be on the train to see somebody actually reading his stuff. In this version of the story she will also be cute, hopefully black and if not single, then certainly not beholden to a concept as passé as monogamy. Who am I kidding? With all the free-love bullshit I spout I'm the one who sounds old hat. Thanks to Republicans and AIDS, everybody is marrying now, even gay guys are thinking about it.

But one guy's riding the C and he's some kid in torn-off sweatpants and long johns underneath. Leather jacket but I can't see much else because he's reading *Rolling Stone* with what looks like Axl Rose on the cover. Guns N' Roses supposedly saved rock and roll a few years ago, or at least that's what anybody who works at *Rolling Stone* will tell you. I say if this is true, then why am I hearing shitty dance pop from faggy limeys on the radio all the time? A fucking band named Jesus Jones, Christ. And please for God's sake don't play that Black Crowes album again, I heard it the first time when it was called Sticky Fingers. God, maybe the reason why the cab's so empty is that everybody can sense I have grown into such a belligerent motherfucker. It's the weird time after rush hour but before lunch where you can ride an empty car in broad daylight. Cab's covered in new graffiti, on the windows, seats, even the floor, the new ones looking sharp and sci-fi with letters, I think they are letters, that look like molten metal. That and posters for Tang! Non-Invasive Cure for Bunions and Fucking *Miss Saigon*.

Shit, I wish I had a *New Yorker*. Or anything for that matter. Rushed out of the office because I realized I was close to deadline and preferred working from home when under pressure. I handed in part four yesterday. Four of seven. Yeah, a part of me hopes people still read *The New Yorker* or at least pay attention to it the way they did for the Janet Malcolm thing on Jeffrey MacDonald and Joe McGinniss only a few months ago. Not that I'm working on anything so heavy, and besides, who the fuck gives a damn about the Singer or Jamaica now other than frat boys? You, Alex Pierce, are what the kids today call a relic. And it's only March.

I get off at 163rd, climb up the steps hoping the guy who tried to bum a cigarette off me isn't there for another one. Shit, why buy a pack when he can score one or two from me every day? The further I step away from C-Town the more it hits deep that there's nothing good in my fridge. I'm going home to no food, which will only piss me the fuck off, and I'll put this coat back on to walk right back to the C-Town I'm walking away from right now. But fuck it, I'm on 160th already.

It's March, it's still fucking cold and you can't even give these fucking homes away. The brownstone I bought didn't need any work and yet the owner was itching so bad to get out I became convinced something was seriously wrong with it. That only made him drop the price more. He tried to sell me on some shit about Louis Armstrong living here. Only three minutes later he said Cab Calloway. Whatever, I liked a neighborhood that people were trying to get away from, though if you asked me, people are probably skipping because they hate how this part of Washington Heights, pardon me, historic Harlem, had been going to shit since the late seventies, brief eighties fake boom to real bust notwithstanding.

What I'm trying to say is this street, especially at this time of day, is usually pretty empty. So why are there four black guys, all dressed like they just walked out of a rap video, sitting on my stoop? I couldn't turn back, because they had already seen me. If I played it like a scared white guy they would call me out in a second, or smell the fear and chase that shit. Fuck me. One of them, with dreadlocks in fucking pig tails, stands up and looks me over. I'm just twenty feet from my own house and four black guys are on the steps. Two of them just shared a loud joke. I make one little step back and feel like an idiot. They are just black guys sitting on my steps. It could have been anybody's steps and look, fucker, they could be your neighbors and it's your fault you don't know any of them. I tap my ass as if I'm reaching for a wallet that isn't there, and try to fake an oh-shit-I-forgot-my-wallet look, but Pig Tails is still staring at me, glaring even, but that might be me imagining things. I can't just stand there. Maybe I can walk right past and go to the café around the corner. Wait them out for a few minutes, though they look like they've got nowhere to go. Fuck. I can't just stand here. I mean, this is New York City and black boys know better than to jump unsuspecting white guys post Bernie Goetz, right? Except that was a good while ago.

When I get to the steps my door is wide open. Pig Tails shifts to the side and points my way in, as if it's his house. I pause, hoping the police car that circles when it feels like it, creeps up soon. Pig Tails beckons me again, this time with a flourish like he's Jeeves, and I make one step. The other men stare at me. One in a gray hoodie hiding his face, one wearing what looks like stockings on his head, and one with his hair plaited like Jamaicans do before they pull it out into an Afro. Pants so low the crotches are all at the knee and all of them in tan Timberlands. If they're packing, they clearly don't think I'm worth showing it. I don't want Pig Tails to direct me to my own house for a third time, so I step up. I could barely move. Jesus Christ. Only last week a friend of mine, who used to sell coke to Fleetwood Mac, said he got out of the business because the fucking Jamaicans were taking over and they didn't give a shit who and how many they killed. *Bredrin me say ah no so it go*, somebody says outside in a Jamaican accent. This feels like the point where I make a joke about Jamaican mothers teaching them to keep a place clean, but there's nobody to share it with.

I walk down my hallway like it's somebody else's and the floorboards creak and give me away. Pass my own staircase to the second floor and listen for people upstairs. Somebody or bodies are making a fuss in the kitchen. A tall black man in a wife beater and khaki overalls with one strap hanging off is blending yellow juice in what's supposed to be my blender. The other guy walks into my view like somebody yelled action over the noise. He starts talking to me as he sits on the stool by the sink. Black man as well, hair cut low and slightly chubby, but taller than wife beater dude, wearing a royal blue silk suit with a white pocket square like a dying flower popping out of his heart. I don't know this guy. I don't know any of them. I don't think I've ever seen shoes so shiny. Dark red too, almost black in parts. I look up and can tell he's noticed me admiring them.

—Giorgio Brutini.

I want to ask if that's the B-movie version of Giorgio Armani, but then I remembered irony is not always the wisest card to play with a Jamaican.

—Oh, I say.

—So hear this, this man you see here, Ren-Dog? He think me contract him because he good 'pon the trigger. But me really have him 'round because nobody can make a juice like this man right here, Jah know.

—Cho man, boss. Mind me have go to cooking school now.

—You better take a night class, haha.

Silk suit guy holds one finger up to cut off what I was going to say, but I wasn't going to say a thing. He picks up a glass and drinks the whole thing down in five loud gulps.

—Mango, he say.

—What kind? Wife Beater says.

—Julie and . . . hold on . . . me know it . . . East Indian.

—Jah know, boss, you mussi psychic or something.

—Or me is just a country youth who know him mango. Pour out some for the white boy.

—I'm really not thirsty.

—Me ask you if you thirsty?

The smile up and vanishes, just like that. I swear this is something I've only seen Jamaicans do, and they can all do it. A sudden change of face that just runs cold. Eyebrow in a frown, but eyes dead steady. It can make a ten-year-old kid frightening.

—I guess I could drink something.

—Good to hear, my youth. And you're welcome for all the milk, and yogurt, and fresh fruit in your fridge. To r'asscloth, Ren-Dog open the bredda fridge and little most me think you is a serial killer with a body up in there.

—True thing, boss, is a wonder rat don't bore a hole into the fridge bottom yet, Wife Beater says.

—You know you did have milk in there from January?

—Was trying to make my own yogurt.

—The man is a comedian, boss.

—Haha, it sound so. Or maybe he just a joke. Anyway, brethren, come over here so me can take one good look 'pon you.

I take the stool. I can't tell if looking him in the eye would impress or annoy him. Then he starts walking around me like I'm some sort of exhibit. I almost say this museum's closed, I almost do. I don't know why I think joking would bring any sort of levity to a situation because it never fucking does, ever.

—Ren-Dog, me ever tell you 'bout a man named Tony Pavarotti?

—You never tell me but me know 'bout him. Which youth didn't know 'bout Tony Pavarotti when him ah grow up?

—Yow, is near fifteen years, me ah look for you, you know that?

It takes me a good three seconds to realize he was talking to me.

—But Eubie, why you bring up Pavarotti, him nuh dead from seventy-seven? Seventy-eight?

—Seventy-nine. Nineteen seventy-nine. Ren, meet the man who kill him.

Four

What happen to you hair?

—It went white. Prematurely grey then white. The ladies call me a silver fox.

—Premature me r'ass. You greying right on time.

—Funny one, Josey.

—And you living in America too long now, you sounding like one of them.

—Like I living in America?

—No, like you living with Cubans.

—Haha. Nobody ever believes me when I say Josey Wales has a sense of humor.

—Yeah? And who you talking to about me?

—Man, Josey, look at us. You ever think about the past, *muchacho*?

—No. You know I never think about the fucking past. That shit will fuck you up and you can't fuck it back.

—Got yourself a dirty tongue in prison, *mijo.*

—Dirty mouth. When in Rome do as the Romans do.

—Haha. Good one, Josey, good—

—Stop with the bloodcloth patronizing, Luis. How you like that, eh? A big, big word just for you. I don't see the man in seven years and where we end up? Prison. See what I mean about the present too r'ass weird? Especially when the past keep showing up this week. From baby mother I even forget, to relative who worried about money—not me, to Peter Nasser, that one made me wish the cell have hidden camera. That man alone make me start wonder if you really get wiser as you get older.

—Peter Nasser?

—Don't act like you don't know him.

—Haven't spoken to the man since 1980. You forget I was only going through him to get to you.

—Well now that he wanting to become a Sir, he hoping the past don't pull a jim-screechy.

—A what?

—A jim . . . a fast one.

—Ah. But the sir thing, *hombre*. He wants to become a Sir? Don't he already got a dick, *hombre*?

—A knight. A Sir, like Sir Lancelot. Now he want to go down on him knee so the queen can bless him with her sword. Such is the natural things for all black man, that they still want white woman to tell them they arrive, no so?

—Didn't know he was black, Josef.

—Funny, in the five minutes you just call me five different name.

—What can I say, *mijo*? Every time I see you, you're a different man.

—Me is the same man.

—No. You're not. You just say you never think about the past. That's why you can't see what you look like.

—Me don't know what the r'ass you saying. Walking in and running your mouth with all sort of foolishness. Any more of this, a violin going start play.

—Again, the Josey humour nobody seems to know about.

—Brethren, this already tired. And you and me know this is not your last stop.

—Where else would I be going?

—Right back to the son of a bitch who send you.

—What if nobody sent me?

—Doctor Love don't even roll over in bed unless it's for a cheque.

—You know what we are, Josef?

—I know we are chatting total bullshit.

—Relics.

—You hear any fucking thing I just say?

—Something from yesterday. A memento.

—Jesus Christ.

—It means, my friend, that most people will never know. Maybe somebody will find something of value in us, but most of the time we just get thrown out.

—Brethren, if you trying to tell me something with a metaphor you doing a real fuckery job of it.

—Just trying to make merry, *mijo.*

—No. You stalling because you never have to do something close up before. Is a wonder how you ever fuck.

—Phone sex?

—Really?

He laughs.

—It's the thing now, all the porn guys are ripping out their sets and putting in landlines. Some dumpy, never been married dude calls 1-900-WET-TWAT and a five-hundred-pound bitch with a sexy voice says, Hey sailor. He jerks off and it goes right to the phone bill.

—For real?

—Real deal Holyfield.

—Know I should have been a pimp.

—Dunno, drug dealer worked out pretty good. Until you ended up in this place.

—Wanted a change of scenery.

—Now who's using a shitty metaphor?

—All these years I don't hear shit from you. Berlin Wall come down, James Bond run out of story and Doctor Love don't have nothing to do. What, you settle down and go back to being a real doctor? Hold on, for real? You is a doctor for real now? How you do surgery, me brethren, by blowing the body part off?

—Haha.

—Keeping a body alive for a change just seem to be outside your desire. So tell me now, Doctor Love, how this family quarrel reach you all the way in Miami?

—Who said I was in Miami?

—I can see as far as you.

—Hmm. Josef, you're a smart man. The smartest man I've ever met. Surely you expected that if you keep talking long enough all sorts of people would hear you.

—I talking from two years ago. Why now and why you?

—I'm just observing.

—Bombo r'asscloth. You know what? Make we step it up because this just annoying the shit out o' me. You know if anything happen to me, certain files going start showing on certain district attorney desk.

—The word on the street—

—You don't know shit about the street.

—The inspector from the DEA. When did he pay you this visit, last Thursday?

—If you know that the DEA come see me, then you already know the damn day. Jesus Christ, Luis, I wish you was a relic, because no lie—the present version of you is one serious disappointment. How much pounds you put on since me last see you?

—Life has been very agreeable.

—Life turn you into a fat fuck. You sure your trigger finger can even fit?

—You're looking good.

—You used to be able to bullshit better.

—So did you, asshole. Horseshit about files. Everybody knows you never took notes, Josey. DEA wants what's in your head, not in some fucking file. Whatever is living with you, dying with you. You're quiet for once. Nobody gave a shit about you until you decided to clean out that crack house in '85. Around the same time your new best friends at the DEA started to pay attention. I would ask Weeper if it was one of those rare moments of the don man losing his temper, but he seems to have vanished with '85 too.

—Not a damn thing mysterious about what happen to Weeper. Man couldn't keep him hands off him own stash. Was bound to happen sooner or later.

—Injecting himself with pure coke? What kind of dealer makes an accident like that? Even if he's using.

—Maybe it wasn't an accident.

—You saying your boy was suicidal?

—Weeper? Him don't have no reason to kill himself. Just when he start living like how he always want to? You know things bad when before New York the only time he was ever happy was when he was in . . . shit. When he was in here. This very prison.

—Then what are you saying, Josey?

—I not saying a thing. You was the one to bring it up. Fucking Weeper. I knew it was going to happen. Is this what you come for, Luis? Because all you seem to be talking about is shit that long behind me.

—Funny you should talk about people who love to talk. It's really good to see you, Josey. Circumstances notwithstanding.

—I wouldn't see you at all if it wasn't for circumstances.

—Correct. I guess.

—What time you leave?

—Jamaica? No set time.

—What time?

—Tomorrow, six a.m. First flight out.

—Enough time.

—Time for what?

—Time for what you need to do. And to file the news report.

—So you and Mr. DEA talking plea bargain yet?

—Plea bargain? You previous, eh? It have to actually reach court first, Doctor Love.

—Oh, oh really?

—Yes really. You learn plenty when you life revolve around jail and court.

—Speaking about courts, that was fucked up, the appeals court not throwing out the extradition.

—Is a Privy Council, not a court of appeals. And fucked up for who? For me? Way I see it I just making a long overdue visit to America.

—You sound like you're going to Grandma's house.

—Me not the one sweating shit over my going to American jail. That would be whoever send you.

—Nobody sent—

—Alright, my boy. Keep up what you feel you need to keep out. Whatever you going to do, do it in my sleep.

—It was a really nice funeral.

—What?

—Really nice. The loudest funeral I ever been to, but really nice. I don't think I've ever seen a marching band behind a hearse. With baton twirlers. Sexy baton twirlers in miniskirts. At first I thought it was tacky but they were wearing blue panties to class things up. They did your boy good.

—Don't talk about my son.

—There's one thing, though. It was so strange, because, well, I've never seen it before.

—Luis.

—When they lowered Benjy in the grave, a bunch of men and women formed two lines, right? On both sides of the grave and then somebody, his woman maybe? She gave the first man the baby and then they kept passing him back and forth, over the grave, all the way down the line to the end. What does that mean, Josey?

—Don't talk about my boy.

—I mean, I just want to know wh—

—I said don't talk about me bombocloth boy.

Five

T*hen him no suppose* to wake up by now, nurse? Nurse? Nurse? Him no supposed to wake up?

—Ma'am, technically he's not asleep. We have to keep him under sedation for now, for his own benefit.

—Ah the doctor a do this? Why unu don't want him wake up? Ah what unu ah do?

—Ma'am, you'll have to take it up with the doctor, ma'am.

—Ma'am. What a way you stoosh. Is where you come from, Manor Park?

—The Bronx.

She jumps every time the monitor beeps. I'm near the doorway trying to leave this room for five minutes now. Yeah, I know I'm a nurse, but when you work in a hospital the smell gets to you. Not the smell visitors pick up on and not the ones patients pick up either. Other smells. Like that of a man with a serious injury and a man gone so bad you know, even before it is confirmed, he will never come back. A man like that smells like machinery. Like clean plastic. Scrubbed bedpan. Hand sanitizer. So much cleanliness it makes you sick. This man in the bed has a tube going into both arms and his neck, four in a bundle through his mouth, one to take away his piss and another to take away what would have been shit. Last week he needed a tap because there was too much fluid on his brain. Jamaican man, black man under the white sheets in a night-robe with sprinkles as a pattern. I'm not one of the nurses who have to adjust him every few hours, leaning him slightly left, then slightly right a few hours after that. Not the nurse to check his vitals, she left five minutes ago. Not here to check his IV or his nutrients, or to make sure he's under satisfactory levels of sedation. I'm not even supposed to be on this floor for the most part, since my hands are always full in the ER. But here I am, in ICU again, coming so often that this woman, maybe his baby mother—I mean, she is always here with a baby but not today—thinks I'm his nurse. I can't just say I'm not because then she will wonder what I wonder every day. Why am I here?

I don't know.

Most of the Jamaicans who showed up at the ER were treated and sent home including a man who will think twice before he takes a shit for a good six weeks. Two didn't make it out alive, two were dead before they got here. And then here is this man with six gunshot wounds, massive trauma to the head and a cervical spine fracture. Even if he makes it to next week or the one after that, every single thing that made his life a life is probably dead now. I should be hopeful, or pleasantly abstract as they teach you to be with the families of critical patients. But the most I can muster is a kind of indifference, which sooner or later this woman is bound to notice.

I'm gone before she leaves, but most of the time when I visit early she's already here, sitting by the bed and wiping his forehead. Yesterday I reminded her he's also carrying an infection so at least use the sanitizer at the door before picking up the baby, and she looked at me like I was insulting her. It's just a suggestion, ma'am, not hospital policy, I said. I really want to look at him when she's not here. Telling myself I don't know why really works if I don't think about it too much. This man lying in hospital over something that no matter how far a Jamaican can run, it's always inching up behind you. I don't want to know why he is here. Nothing about this warring bullshit is of any interest to me. The only reason I'm in the Bronx still is I can't afford to move to somewhere else, so if Jamaicans want to shoot themselves up over drugs or whatever, it's really their business. I don't want to hear that man's name, not even when they talking about him son. There was a time when hearing it would make me scream. Now when hear it I don't know what happens until I find myself or somebody finds me, staring out the window of the cafeteria as if I'm lost or something. Damn if I can even remember why that name does what it does to me. Damn if despite knowing I could never kid myself, I always, always try.

—So what you know?

—Excuse me?

I hope she wasn't talking to me all along. She's touching his head and not looking at me.

—All unu can talk 'bout is what unu no know. You no the nurse? Him nah improve? You nah go give him no new medicine? Why nobody want chat to me 'bout if him going walk again, I hear 'bout them spine things y'know. Me tired of damn nurse who come in here ah pick up pad and read it, and ah touch him, and ah move him, and doing all sorta thing but can't say nothing but to speak to the damn doctor. And where the damn doctor deh?

—I'm sure the doctor is coming, ma'am.

—The doctor is already here, ladies.

I hope I didn't just say shit out loud. Again. Doctor Stephenson doing his doctor strut right into the room, his blond hair slick this time. Maybe he has somewhere to go after this. Tall, pale and handsome in a British sort of way, meaning he hasn't started using the Bowflex he had shipped to his office two or three months ago but still looks like he just walked out of *Chariots of Fire*. Last week he pulled up his short sleeve to show me his even whiter arm and asked if I thought he could get a tan in Jamaica, because he has failed everywhere else. This damn woman delayed me. I wasn't supposed to be here, certainly not long enough for a doctor to run into me.

—Fancy running into you here, Nurse Segree. ER having a slow afternoon, or they finally transferred you to ICU?

—Uh . . . Doctor, I was just passing by and looked in—

—Why, was something wrong? Did you alert whoever's on call?

—No, nothing was wrong. Nothing was . . . I was just passing by.

—Hmm. ER now sending student nurses up to ICU? I swear you must be the only one I know by name, Nurse Segree.

—Well, I need to be on my way, Doctor—

—No, stay a moment. I just might need you.

I was about to say something but he just closed his eyes and nodded yes once, as if that was all that needed to be said on the matter.

—Hello, ma'am.

—Why everybody a chat to me like me is one old woman?

—Huh? Nurse, what is she . . . well, anyway. And this is your husband?

—Doctor Stephenson, I say. I want to say just talk to the damn woman and stop try to figure out her bloodcloth marital status because if she ever set to start explaining commonlaw marriage to you is another month before you understand, but instead I just say,

—She's listed as the next of kin, Doctor.

—Oh. Well, ma'am, it's still too early to say. He's responding . . . well, he's responding to treatment, but it's early days yet. He's still critical at the moment, but he might be stable in a few days. In the meantime we'll have to run some more tests—

—More test? Test fi wha? You must think him inna school the way unu ah run test. And none of unu test can give me no result.

—Ah . . . uh . . . Millicent?

—Millicent? the woman says. I don't have to look to know she's staring at me hard and frowning right now. The doctor pulls me aside but not far enough. I know she will hear everything he says.

—Millicent . . . ah . . . how do I put this? I'm not exactly following what she's saying. I mean, I think I have the gist but wouldn't want to put one's foot in one's mouth, if you catch my drift. Can you speak to her?

—Ah . . . sure.

—Maybe in your native tongue.

—What?

—You know, that Jamaican lingo. It's so musical it's like listening to Burning Spear and drinking coconut juice.

—Coconut water.

—Whatever. It's so beautiful, good God, I don't have a goddamn clue what you're all saying.

—She wants to know why we're doing so many tests, Doctor.

—Oh? Well, could you tell her—

—She understands English, Doctor.

—But you could tell her in her native—

—It's not a language, Doctor.

—Oh well. Ma'am, as you know, your husband had surgery for gunshot wounds causing serious head trauma and unstable spinal fracture. Sometimes, especially if the patient comes in still conscious, we can tell how it's gonna go. But your husband did not. Also, gunshot wounds have a nasty way of causing more damage where they leave your body than where they entered it. Being that he's not awake and it's too risky to wake him, we're still not sure if either spinal function, or if his mental state is altered in any way. We need to run tests because his status might be changing, maybe even for the better. But there's no way to know for sure without regular testing. We may need to step up a dose, decrease a dose. He might even need more surgery in ways that are just not obvious. That's why we need to test regularly. I hope this makes sense. Ma'am?

—You're fine, doctor, I say, knowing that the remark would irritate the shit out of him. He nods at her first, then me, then leaves. I can hear the patronizing talk he'll give me at the water cooler even now. At least I'm too old now for him to place his hand on mine when he's doing so—a trick which supposedly makes nurses' panties wet. I swear if doctors would get out the way nurses could get on with actually healing people.

—So is where in Jamaica you come from?

—Excuse me?

—Excuse yourself. Is where in Jamaica you come from?

—I don't see how that's your—

—Listen, lady. Me hear you when you tell the doctor how you was just passing by, all of thirteen floor up from the same emergency room me carry him. What him woulda say if me did tell him say is every day you come in me man room like is your man, for no reason? So stop with the damn fuckery because you can't come from no place but Jamaica with a name like Millicent. Millicent Segree? You no just come from Jamaica, you come from Country. So you can go on stoosh with them white people all you want, but you not fooling nobody.

I tell myself I don't have to take this and if I leave right now, this hospital is so huge that she would never see me again. All I had to do was leave. All I need to do is put one foot in front of the other and march out of here before this woman get all ignorant.

—'Cause me sure you never leave Jamaica talking so.

—What if me come from uptown?

—Maybe. You sound flat and dull like them uptown woman for true. But at least you don't look like you live in you battyhole. No, you—

The monitor beeped and she jumped again.

—You want to hear that sound, I say. —Is when you hear one long beep that don't stop that's bad.

—Oh? Oh. Me never know. Nobody never tell me. Why you keep coming up here to look 'pon me husband?

—Me no have nothing to do with your husband.

—Trust me, me love, me never worried 'bout that.

I want to tell her both to fuck off and that I admire her quickness.

—You don't get a lot of Jamaicans in this hospital. Only one old woman who died last year from a stroke. Then suddenly we have whole rash of them, all of them from gunshot wounds. And he is the last one still here. Of course I would be curious.

—Curious me r'ass. If you curious you come in and read the pad by him bed that all the other nurse read. But you come in and look. And if me late you always here, and if me early you quick to leave as soon as me come.

—People shoot people in Jamaica all the time, but me come to New York to see it up close.

—See it up close? You no see nothing. Wait till you see a boy get shot in the club.

—But why they bring it here? Why bring it to America? You'd think if you come here you could brush off all of this crap and start over.

—Is so you do it?

—I didn't say that.

—But is true. You and you stoosh talk.

She gets up for a few seconds then and sits back down. I'm still near the door, wondering if I should back out slow or fast.

—For some man, for plenty man, is that same crap the send them here. Otherwise them wouldn't have no way to come to America.

—I suppose.

—Fact, that. And you not in here just because you never see no Jamaican. You in here for something else. Lady, me is woman too, you know. Me know when a woman want something.

—I really should head back to the ER.

—Then go on. And the next time me can tell the doctor that like you how you just come in here all sort of time when you feel like.

—What you want to know?

—Me husband. Me ever going hear him talk again?

—You really should ask the doctor—

—Talk.

—You don't want to hear it from me, I'm not a doctor.

—Talk, me say.

—Like a four-year-old, maybe. And that's if he recovers. He going have to learn everything over and he still going sound like he's retarded.

—Oh. Him going walk again?

—The way things look, he might not be able to hold a cup again. I hope you know I can be fired for what I just tell you.

—Fired because you is the first one tell the truth?

—Is not my job to tell you the truth. Is my job to tell you what we think you can handle. And nobody here can really predict what might happen to a patient, so nobody want to say something and it don't go so. He could recover or he could—

—Dead.

—That too.

She looking at me as if she's waiting for me to ask that question. Or maybe I'm just reading what I want into her face. The monitor beep but she doesn't jump this time.

—Josey Wales shoot him?

And there I said it. All these years I never said his name once. Could never bring myself to even use it. I know that later I'll start beating myself up over how I let my own mind run wild with me for years over my thinking this man hounding me, when me sure if I walk right past him he wouldn't know me from anybody, even if he stopped to chat me up.

—Josey Wales?

—I don't mean personally. I mean, his gang.

—You don't know no Jamaicans in the Bronx?

—What this have to do with anything?

—Them don't call gang, them call a posse. And Josey not going nowhere since him in prison now for long past two year.

—What?

—So you don't even read one issue of *Gleaner* or watch no Jamaican news? Them going ship him to America for American court this month, me love. Is Josey Wales' posse that shoot up the club. Everybody know Tatters is Ranking Dons' night club. Them don't own it or nothing, but them always in there. You know what funny? Me still remember what song was playing, 'cause me just ask somebody how come "Night Nurse" still sound so sweet. Don't ask me why me didn't see it coming. Josey Wales' son get kill in Jamaica and whoever do it must be connected to Ranking Dons in some way or 'nother. You lucky you manage to run far away from Jamdown, but for the rest of we Jamdown follow right back o' we.

—So your husband was just a bystander?

—No, lady, him was a Ranking Don.

Six

So Jesus Christ kill Tony Pavarotti?

—Jesus is right. Look 'pon the man hair. You woman make you leave the house like that? And here me did understand that all white man shave except the ones who in some cult a breed him sister.

—And is bell-bottom jeans that? To rahtid.

—Brethren, what me want know is, where me can send telegram to tell you that is 1991? You look like you 'bout to sing "Disco Duck."

—Nah, man, Eubie, is "In the Navy."

—The whole a unu can stay. Caw you no know say is this look a carry it now, you no watch the MTV? No, man, my boy just stick to him gun and wait it out till the look come back inna fashion.

—That is one hell of a wait. Then is what you waiting on for the near fourteen years? For one of we to come find you?

I got a hunch these are not the men you ask to get to the point. They've left me on the stool and now I'm in the middle of men circling me like any minute now they're gonna put a dunce cap on my head. Or pounce or knock me over the head with a baseball bat. At first I thought they were circling like sharks but this is a fucking shitty time for a bad metaphor. Fucking idiot, I'm editing my life even as a bunch of big black men with guns take over my house. And we can rule out robbery, though for once I wish it fucking was. Haven't heard the name Tony Pavarotti in years, maybe even seven years or so, and I only heard it once, from Tristan Phillips. I don't think about that day at all. And neither had anybody else since nobody did anything. Even did some checking, as much as I could anyway through microfilm of Jamaican newspapers, and there was nothing. No police report of a murder, or even a body found dead at the hotel. Fuck you, Faulkner, the past really isn't dead. It's not even past. I didn't even know the man's name until I met Tristan Phillips.

—To the neck, I say.

Silk Suit and Pig Tails both look at me like I interrupted them. Ren-Dog, or at least I think that's his name, puts the remaining fruit in the fridge and takes the blender to the sink. I can hear it coming, me telling him not to use the dishwasher for just one blender. But Pig Tails and Silk Suit are still looking at me.

—To the neck's how I did it.

—Did what? Silk Suit says.

I'm sure he said his name was Eubie, but I can't seem to retain anything. Right now there could be seven men in total or six, but I just can't remember.

—Killed him. I mean, stabbed him. I mean, I stabbed him in the neck, probably to the jugular.

—He mean in the neck, boss, Pig Tails says.

Eubie stares him down so hard he winces.

—Which one of we here go to Columbia University? Eh? Which one ah we? You think me don't know where the jugular vein be? How long before him dead, two minutes?

—Almost five.

—Then you hit the wrong jugular, my youth.

—It's not like I had expertise in the area.

—Really? With the questions you love ask and the stuff you like write maybe you should think 'bout that little bit. Especially from what I've been reading in *The New Yorker.*

—Everyone's a critic, I say.

I didn't see the punch coming. Right in the temple. I blink, trying to get the shock out, and shout fuck.

—This look like a movie to you? I look like I have time for the wisecracking white guy?

—I guess you Jamaicans love to carry a grudge, huh?

—I don't think I follow you, young man.

—This Tony Pavarotti dude? Your top man. You guys talk about him like he was the baddest motherfucker there was, and yet some fucking skinny journalist drops him with a fucking letter opener. And then you guys show up fifteen years later—

—Sixteen.

—Like I fucking care. Show up to do what, to finish the job? How *Godfather Part II* of you.

—Boss . . .

—Is cool, Ren-Dog. Brethren think nobody here watch movie.

I'm rubbing my temple and they're still circling. He wait till he's behind me to talk.

—How you think all them man, how Ren-Dog get to be in this room. You think him is here fi make juice?

—Dunno.

—Ren-Dog?

Ren-Dog looks at me and says,

—M60.

—M60. Every man in this posse have to pick a bus and pick a stop. First man or woman off the bus they shoot. Bonus if they dead.

—That supposed to scare me?

—Watch it, boss, look like somebody balls growing in them pants, Pig Tails says.

Me, I'm looking at a man with dreadlocks pig tails, a man in a wife beater making juice and a man in a silk suit that looks like fucking satin with a white handkerchief popping out of the pocket because Momma didn't teach him how to fold a fucking pocket square and it just hits me how absurd this all is. No, not absurd, fucking ridiculous.

—You getting bold, boy, Ren-Dog says.

—No, I'm scared shitless.

—Look here—

—No, you look. I'm fucking sick and tired of you guys acting all big like you on some fucking sitcom. Fucking coming into my house and making juice and trying to have some conversation like you're the intelligent criminal, all complicated and shit in some movie, when you're just a bunch of fucking thugs who shoot women and children. I don't fucking care that you fucking read. I don't fucking care how smart you are. I don't give a shit about your goddamn freshly blended juice. Or how I dropped the baddest gangster you fuckers could produce out of that fucking island. In fact why not just do it, huh? Just do it. The less of your shit I get to hear, the better off I'd be anyways. Just fucking do it, then get out'a my house so the neighbors can call the cops. And take your fucking fruits with you, I don't even like juice.

—You right, Eubie says. —That wasn't supposed to scare you. When I want to scare a man I don't fucking talk. Ren-Dog, deal with this pussyhole.

Seven

S*o what did* Peter Nasser want anyway?

Josey Wales is walking around his cell, without realizing he's pacing I bet. But every time he goes off into the dark corner, I think he's going to emerge with a nasty surprise. Maybe not a gun, but maybe a shank he can throw like a dagger straight for one of my eyes. And it happens every time. He walks past the cell bars slow, looking at me until he's at the corner; turns to head to the back until the slanted shadow sucks him up. Then he goes silent too so you can't follow even the sound of him in the dark. Not even footsteps. Sometimes he stops and you wonder, What is he doing in there? What is he preparing? And then when he comes out of shadow for a quick second your heart jumps. And it jumps every single time he does it. I can't remember which one they said was more dangerous, the wounded lion or the caged one.

—A reason to stop shitting himself. Why you care 'bout Peter Nasser all of a sudden? No you just say you don't see the boy in eleven years? And he's just the sixth man to pay tribute to me this week. Now everybody want to know what am I going to do if I get send to American prison. Well, they should have done more to keep me out of prison in the first place. And funny how everybody seem to think American court going convict me. But check it—when Yankee justice come knocking first, everybody forget Josey and leave it to me to sort it out. And now when things didn't sort out all of a sudden everybody trying to sort it out himself.

—Meaning?

—Meaning certain people still trying to find a good way to kill me. I mean, they tried once or twice. Or three times, no four. My men in here deal with the fourth last week and didn't even tell me until guard find the pussy-hole head in the toilet when one of them go in to piss. All now they can't figure out what an inmate's head doing in the guard's toilet. As for the guards, bunch of fucking 'prentices, them boys. The first guard? Shitting through a tube now and by the time the second reach my cell and burst shots into an empty mattress, him already turn into a widower who find out two days later he would have been a father.

—Damn, *hombre.*

—Some people forget why they're sitting on top and who the fuck put them up there.

—You say that like somebody owes you something.

—They do owe me. Everybody fucking owe me. I give the country to that fucking government.

—That government ain't the government no more and nobody owes you shit, Josef. Nobody forced your hand, nobody stopped you from turning into fucking Tony Montana, and everybody was fine looking the other way until you decided to murder some fucking junkies who weren't worth shit in a fucking crack house for no reason other than maybe somebody stepped on your new shoes, knowing you. You already got what you think you're owed and more. You fucked this up, you hear me? You fucked this up.

He's off in the dark again. I wait for him to come back, listening if his feet are shuffling now. Not Josey. He comes out of the shadow standing tall, almost too tall, like he's bracing his chest for something.

—You want crackhead go to Dumfries Road in New Kingston and get anyone you like. Who to r'ass miss a bombocloth crackhead?

—Nobody. The pregnant girlfriend of a crackhead? Kinda different. There's a whole story about her in *The New Yorker.* Some pattern of yours, Josef? Offing pregnant chicks?

—Fuck off.

—Real classy, don man. Your whole crew of Jamaicans and their why-shoot-one-*hombre*-when-you-can-liquidate-the-whole-block way of thinking. Storm of bullets, eh? Storm Posse. Real classy.

—You are the man who make them, boss, not me. Don't make monster then bawl how them monstrous.

—Dude, when I was running with you some of these boys were still getting breastfed. Not me they're taking after, Pops.

—You know how long it take for me to check my food?

—What? What are you—

—Twenty minutes, three times a day. Ask the rats. Every day me throw piece of the food down and see if they eat it. Every day me expect a rat to drop dead. Every day I have to take each banana and cut it up little, each clump of rice I squash it, each box of juice I suck it through my teeth just to stop any broken glass, or rusty nail or maybe even something with AIDS. You know how long it take before I swallow just a spoonful of food? And me already buy off everybody in the kitchen.

—But nobody would dare, Josey.

—Maybe not, but since everybody outside fucking scared of what they think my mouth going do is only a matter of time, brethren. Only a matter of time before they find a guard or inmate more scared of them than me.

—You've been behind bars too long.

—Maybe I should redecorate, put up a few curtains.

—Never pictured you for gallows humour, *mijo*.

—Not dead yet, Doctor Love.

He sits down on the bed and looks away as if he's done talking for now. It's the first time I'm looking away since I got here, and the first time I notice that the cell, and the entire corridor, is red brick, several of them already fallen out. Figures that Jamaica is where you'd find the exact prison you think of when somebody says prison. At least the floor is now concrete. Seriously it's the kind of prison where you think that all you need is a spoon and some of what these Americans call gumption, and you could dig your way to freedom in a few years.

—Peter Nasser, poor bitch, stumble in here and try to threaten me.

—Oh yeah? How did that go?

—Something like when an impotent man threaten to rape you. He suddenly worrying if the canary going sing. Exact words him say. I would never say such dumb shit.

—I know. But he's not the only one, Josey.

—Which for the two hundredth time leads to why you come here.

—Maybe I'm paying a visit.

—You can visit me in America. Going be there in two days.

—It's a shame they didn't let you out to bury your boy.

—You is a fucking pussyhole, de las Casas. A fucking pussyhole.

—You know what I always found fascinating about you, Josey? Most people I know, man, they can turn it off and turn it back on, but you can keep both going the same time. You can barely bring yourself to talk about your dead son, but can talk about offing two pregnant chicks just like that. You're like what they call a psychopath. What? What's so funny?

He laughed. He laughed so long he started to hiccup, and even then he wouldn't stop laughing. Long enough that I started to hate him a little, I really did, and I've never felt that way about him before.

—That whole sentence, you practice it before you come here?

—Fuck you, Josef.

—No, seriously. What them call the man, you know the man I'm talking about, him even have a show on TV one time. You know the man with the puppet in his lap, the puppet mouth moving but somebody else talking.

—Ventriloquist. You calling me a ventriloquist? For who, the CIA?

—No, I calling you the dummy. So who send you, brethren? Mr. Clark-just-ditch-the-E? Serious now, them man still around?

—Haven't thought about him in years either. I hear he's in Kuwait.

—Your memory too spotty. On the other hand man like me remember everything. Like names. You know how most people forget names? Like Louis Johnson. Mr. Clark-just-ditch-the-E, Peter Nasser, Luis Hernán Rodrigo de las Casas. Sal Resnick? I don't forget names. Certain things like Operation Werewolf? I don't forget things. Even certain dates like October 16, 1968. June 15, 1976. December 6, 1976. May 20, 1980. October 14, 1980? I don't forget dates. What you think? Sound like you run out of talk, *mucha-*

cho.

—I think people are more concerned by what you might say these days.

—Going to say, Luis. Going to say. People dig me this hole. I didn't tell them to make it so big it swallow all of them. I don't know what your boss worried about. All he need to do is make a call to the DEA—the Feds, right? Make a call and part of the story squash.

—DEA aren't Feds. And they don't control either.

—They? So somebody did send you.

—I liked our conversations more when we were on the same side.

—There is the gate and there is the lock. Come over.

—You've gotten all witty in your old age, man.

—Still younger than you. What you want, Doctor Love? You have some stash of money lock 'way to give me when me come out of prison if me keep quiet?

—I didn't say that.

—Well let me say it for you and answer. What make you think I coming out of prison?

—The deal you'll probably sign with the DEA.

—Still don't know what you worried about. Doctor Love is blur, no you tell me that? Most people don't even know him exist. Maybe you die in Bay of Pigs, maybe you blow your own self up on the plane in Barbados, maybe you working for them Sandinistas now.

—Contras.

—Same difference. Or maybe you is just something people make up from scratch when they need a duppy.

—Maybe I'm a ghost talking to you now.

—You might as well be. Man like you the world don't need no more. You know from when I see that? From 1976. Politics don't mean shit. Power don't mean shit. Money mean something. Give people what they want. Peter Nasser think he can send man to talk to me about the error of my ways, but which man in Kingston I don't own?

—You sure about that, Josef? Every man?

—Yes.

—Every single one?

—What, me need microphone in this place or you deaf?

—Every single one?

—Yes, to fuck.

—Even in New York?

—Especially in New York. Must be why them hungry for me over there.

—Who do you think off'd your boy Weeper?

—You mean other than he himself? This argument getting tired, Doctor Love. You don't have to look hard to find out what happen to Weeper.

—Hmm. Before she flew the fuck off the grid I had a nice chat with Mrs. Griselda Blanco.

—Didn't Medellín already sort out that mad cunt business?

—Before, Josey. Listen to me, will you? This was back when she saw the writing on the wall and was looking for friends. She's telling me about this gang, er . . . posse named Ranking Dons, ever heard of them? Most of them are Jamaicans.

—Yes, Luis, I know about the Ranking Dons.

—Oh. Didn't know if you knew them or not. Anyway, so she was telling me how they almost took over the Miami racket at one point. Yet within like a month they all vanished.

—So?

—So, while Griselda certainly had the desire to get rid of them she sure as fuck didn't have the smarts to pull it off. Or the manpower to deal with you Jamaicans. To deal with Jamaicans she needed a guy from the rock. Preferably one already in the States who could mobilize quick and who had a vested interest. And that motherfucker ain't you, Josef. Not like you to underestimate a guy, *mijo.* He gave her back South Miami. She gave him Weeper. And then he just decided to wait out the mighty Josey Wales. Just waiting on you to fuck up. Enter the crack house. Why didn't you just let it go, man?

—Because I hate the taste of piss.

—What?

—Nothing.

—No, you said something.

—Ah never say bombocloth nothing, Doctor Love.

—One man, Josey.

—Eubie?

—Eubie.

Eight

I*'ve just never* been around a, you know, before . . .

—A what?

—A man. I mean, one of these men.

—What a way you facety. Me tell you that me man is one of these man?

—You said he was with those Ranking Dons.

—Not everybody in church ah Christian.

—I'm not sure I get your point.

—You not sure you get my point. For serious, you did always talk so stoosh or is white people you ah take showoff with?

—You think anybody speaking proper English trying to take after white people?

—Trying to take after something.

—Oh so chatting bad must mean you is a real Jamaican then. Well if it make you feel better white people love hear you people talk much more than me.

—You people.

—Yes, you people. Real Jamaicans. All of you so damn real. And you . . . you know what. I'm way out of line here, and this could get me fired. Bad enough I'm talking to next of kin, now I'm getting in an argument. Next thing you know complaints are lodged and I'm reprimanded if not fired. I really hope he recovers.

—What you mean you never see a gunman before? Why you want to see gunman?

She's looking at me like she really wants to know. Her eyebrows raised and her mouth open a little, like she's really curious. I wish I could attack her defensiveness, but it's like she really just wants to know. And I don't have any answer that makes any sense. Mostly because I don't really know either. She gets up from beside him and goes over to the window. This day is going nowhere, and it's March?

—I can't think of anybody else in the whole world who me never want see, she says.

—I understand.

—Where you come from original?

—Havendale.

—Then you don't understand. And you never see one up close.

—No.

—Well . . . hold on. Listen to we nuh, talking like we in zoo and him is gorilla. Me should laugh since it funny. Is long time now this thing boiling up between Ranking Dons and Storm Posse.

—But why it come here?

—How you mean? Where else it fi come? No yah so people want the drugs?

She looks at me like she's some mother who just run out of patience with her kid. I want to tell her I'm not some idiot, but I go over by the window and stand beside her.

—At least it almost done.

—What? That came out so quiet I wonder if she heard me.

—The killing.

—How you know?

—Not too much people leave to kill. And Josey Wales going end up in Yankee prison for a good while. Although me believe it when me see it.

—I didn't know he was in jail.

—Well what 'bout Jamaica you know? News 'bout Josey Wales was all Jamaican newspaper could write 'bout. Yes me read. Every day was a new story about court and trial and witness and delay and privy council. All the people him kill and how America want him bad. Turn on the TV and even American news talking 'bout him like him was movie star. Just Josey Wales,

Josey Wales, Josey Wales and . . . you alright? Jesus Christ, lady . . . hold on . . . me have you . . . me have you.

I nod and realise I'm sitting on the chair beside the Ranking Don. It almost flies out of my head how I got to the chair, but I'm not dizzy enough to forget.

—You alright now?

—I don't need a glass of water.

—Wha?

—In TV show them always ah give people a glass of water.

—Rahtid my girl, you haffi faint fi talk Jamaican? What a ting.

—I didn't faint.

Then she laughs really loud, loud enough I think she might wake up the Ranking Don. Long enough that it turns into a grin, then a cackle, then her chest just heaves. Something tells me that at some point in the laugh she stopped laughing at me.

—When last you talk Jamaican?

—How you mean, I talk Jamaican all the . . . you know what? Last week when this little bloodcloth fatass who run the Rite Aid in the Bronx ask me how far up me legs the white stockings go.

—Rahtid, wha you tell him?

—Further than you ever going reach, you big fat slabba shithouse.

My head has stopped spinning, I think. I don't know. Not sure why it was spinning in the first place. But then she says,

—I wonder if the trial going be 'pon TV?

—What trial?

—You never hear me the first time? Josey Wales.

You know when a woman puts on a show that something's not bothering her? How she straightens a back already straight, and starts to play with her necklace and looks away even though nobody is looking at her, and how she smiles like some ghost gave her a joke? Smile until there is no smile anymore, just her feeling her lips pull back over her teeth? Yeah I'm spying that woman in the mirror on the other side of the Ranking Don's bed.

—That man should hang. Somebody shoulda shoot him inna jail, you hear me.

—For this? I say. I really didn't want to point to the man in the bed, that just seemed too damn dramatic, so I nodded instead. Subtle.

—What, Ranking Dons don't kill anybody? I say.

It's funny, I try to shut all that shit out but I remember, though, not long ago the New York *Post* carried some headline . . . yeah . . . the Jamaican who got New York hooked on crack and it was the head of the Ranking Dons. I remember 'cause it was the last time I picked up a *Post*.

—Ranking Dons don't have no leader.

—Of course not, him in jail.

—No, me mean they don't have no leader like Josey Wales. That man different. One time some man bump him car—no, he bump the man car and chase after him. You believe that? The man run right into police station.

—The police drive him home?

—No. They stand back while Josey march into the station with some other man, pull him out and kill him right in the street, right in front of the police station.

—Oh Lord.

—Oh Lord is right. But you know, you going be so wicked you can't surprise when wickedness come back to you. Both him daughter and his son, the one him was sending to Wolmer's Boys' School 'cause he think he can make him posh, get shot dead. Boy, as mother me sorry when pickney dead. But as me, it serve the fucker right. But is this one start all the kass-kass. Can you imagine, nothing happen when they kill the girl but them kill the boy and Kingston erupt with wildfire. What a thing. And the fire spread all the way to Miami and New York. My man tell me smoke even blow all the way to Kansas. You know where Kansas deh?

—Uh-uh.

—Me neither.

—So he in prison then. And he's not coming out.

—Him can't come out. If he was going to come out he should a come out in Jamaica. But from what me hear, him start chat too much. Too much people scared and stupid. If me was him me would a board plane to 'merica from yesterday.

—So he in prison then? Him not coming out?

—Not for now. Why you business so much 'bout Josey Wales? After ah no ghetto you come from?

—I . . .

Not even Christmas yet, barely December and somebody is already bursting firecrackers but I run and run and run again, then hop, then walk right up to just ten or so feet from the gate 56, walking stiffer, the firecrackers getting louder, especially the rapid ratatatatat ones I don't like so I turn and the gate 56 is already open welcoming me for once open wide like the gate is two arms saying come in daughter only loving and oneness here until firecracker run right past me. Man running backwards nearly knock me over man in mesh sleeveless man almost stumble man with machine gun in two hands and shaking from recoil? Recoil recoil they call it recoil on TV. Machine gun hip shake ratatatattat, no papapapapapapap man run past me then behind me and I follow him with my eyes to the white car like a Cortina bombocloth a man says I look around two more men running one frontways and shouting other man backways with two handguns that firing up and down and pap-pap and my body's jerking with each pap and one man knock me sideways when he run past me and other man knock me on the other side and me spin 'round and 'round and 'round and another man fire two shots and screech white car gone and other car pull up I didn't see that other car it just pull up and I still feel like I'm spinning though I know I just stopped because I stomped my foot in the ground to stop and sirens wake me up or maybe it's mosquitoes and right there near the guardhouse a woman spread flat in the dirt, blood spreading near her head and screaming people screaming too much screaming and I turn and walk into his chest tall man taller than me and thick like a man but thin too and skin dark or maybe is the evening and him eye narrow like a chineyman but he's black no he's dark and right up in me right up to my face right up to my neck and he sniffs sniffs sniffs like a dog Josey get inna the bombocloth car the white car says and he brings the gun right up to my face and it's hole no an O no it's an O with a hole and it smells like matches just as you strike it Josey get inna the bombocloth car the man in the car is shouting but he still in front of me waving the gun closer and closer and right in front of my left eye but the sirens getting louder and he walk away backwards looking at me and pointing the gun and he walking further and further but getting closer and closer and he's in the car but I feel him breathing down my neck and he's driving off but I smell him still here and I can't move the woman is still in the dirt but a bunch of children run to her screaming and some people coming around from the back must be more people to shoot me run and run and run and a car horn blow and a siren and a whoosh and keep running and a bus slow down at stoplight and run and jump and land on the step people looking at me. Reach home have to grab my suitcase no my grip no my handbag damn woman you don't need no damn handbag, grab the small suitcase under the bed the one you took to Negril with Danny, foreign white man grab the suitcase grab the suitcase r'ass bombocloth lizard lizard lizard lizard you r'asscloth so much dust under the bed no time for that now, red dress, blue skirt, blue jeans skirt, Fiorucci jeans, Shelly-Ann jeans, jeans halter top so much jeans but where you going? Calico dress no, purple dress no, velvet skirt no that was a stupid purchase say it just like your mother: purchase panties top drawer, socks who need socks, makeup who need makeup, no lipstick, rouge eye liner Jesus Christ young girl he coming with a O with a bullet in it but where you going? Toothbrush, toothpaste, mouthwash who have time for r'asscloth mouthwash go go go go girl pocketbook—to write what? Bible—to read what? the strapless heels, the Adidas maxi-dress that can wear anywhere, change? I should change, I should change so he can't recognize me he following me he at the door he drive off before me so no no no no too much dress can't run fast in dress need more pants and track shoes no I can't . . . no . . . just stay put. Just stay in your place is not like he know you. Is not like he could ever find you. Where he going to look? But Kingston small. Jamaica small but Kingston smaller him going hunt like a dog that must be why he was sniffing me he's going to hunt me down and shoot me like a dog tonight. Think for God's sake Jesus Christ think. The police going call you a witness and they not going protect you. Take the Bible. No. Yes bitch take the Bible. Don't turn on the radio, don't turn on the TV he will find you through the TV he will smell you out and kill you, that O with a hole and a bullet in it I know. Who don't know about the ghetto, this is why we have state of emergency because man in the ghetto can get anywhere he wants, if man from the ghetto can break into my mother's house and beat my father and rape her then they can find anybody anywhere don't think about them, shut them out, shut them out, shut them out.

Shut everybody out.

Shut everybody down.

Just go.

But I still smell him. I smell him now.

—Nurse? Nurse?

Nine

A *Brief History* of Seven Killings
—*A Crack House, A Massacre and the Making of a Crime Dynasty*
Part 3.
By Alexander Pierce

Monifah Thibodeaux meant it this time. Her mother knew she meant it because there was something final in her voice. Except she had heard that *final* before, and such is the tricky dance of somebody like Monifah, that final is fluid, final means a different thing each week and just when you think a person could not sink any lower, they fall to new depths that a poor mother could never have dreamed of. But this "meant it" somehow felt different from the others even if the stakes didn't seem all that different. She was going to kick her habit tomorrow.

She said so to her mother, Angelina Jenkins. She repeated it to her best friend Carla, who had cut her off three years ago when she found Monifah in her bathroom with a needle stuck between her toes. She even told her ex-boyfriend Larry, who wanted to marry her once, and went as far as picking out a ring at Zales to surprise her. It was as if she had just returned from a twelve-step program and was on a mission to repair the damage done to loved ones hurt.

Monifah was going to kick tomorrow. But kick meant overcoming her self-devouring drug habit and turning back from being what her own mother called a crack ho. And with Monifah tomorrow was always a day away. She was going to kick tomorrow only two months ago. And five months before that. Seven months before that one. Sixteen months before that. But this time, tomorrow, was August 15, 1985.

August 14, 1985, Monifah had been straight for almost a week. A high school dropout from Stuyvesant and pregnant at seventeen, she would have been a cliché's idea of a ghetto cliché had she not complicated her own narrative so much. Dropping out of school after scoring 1900 on her SATs and staying clean for most of her pregnancy. Growing up shuffling between her mother's apartment in Puerto Rican Bushwick and her family in Bed-Stuy and the Bronx, she was, according to her sister, hell-bent on escaping the life that fate had all but drawn up in lines with just numbers left to color.

—With just numbers left to colour? You did feel really cute when you write that, don't?

—Boss, what him mean by straight? Him mean the gal was a fucking sodomite too?

—Ren-Dog, you think any woman not fucking you is a sodomite. One: the proper term is lesbian and two: straight here mean she leggo the coke. So my girl stop licking the crack pipe for a week.

—Zeen.

—What me want to know though, in part one you say is eleven people get kill. So how come you only write 'bout seven?

I don't know if I should answer. Five minutes ago I told them I needed to pee and the Eubie dude said, Me not stopping you. I got up and Ren-Dog punched me square in the face and loosened my left molar. Before that, Pig Tails kicked me on the floor. Before that, Eubie told Ren-Dog to deal with me and he grabbed my shirt and ripped it off. Then somebody behind me hit me in the head and my knees hit the floor. Can't remember when they pulled my pants off or my boots. They dragged me upstairs by my hands, making my head bump into each step, and they were laughing or shouting or screaming, I don't know. Ren-Dog grabbed me by the neck and we're in my bathroom and somebody laughed again and he pushed me and I tripped backways and landed in the tub and I tried to get up but slipped and he's so fucking strong. He grabbed me by the neck again and I punched and scratched and slapped and tore at him, and somebody else just laughed and shoved me right underneath the tap and turned it on full blast. Water hit my forehead and eyes and I tried to remember not to breathe, but water got in my nose anyway and my mouth and every time I tried to scream my mouth would fill up. I felt a boot pinning my chest down and couldn't move my hand and the water was just blasting and punching and slapping my lips and punching my teeth and digging into my eye and in my nose and I started to choke and cough and cry and he still held me by the neck and that's all I remember. I came to on the chair wet and in my brief and choking. Eubie threw *The New Yorker* at me and told me to read.

—I . . . I really need to pee. I really need . . .

They look at me and laugh.

—Please. Please. I need to use the bathroom.

—You just come from the bathroom, little boy.

They all laugh.

—Please. I need to—

—So piss, fool.

I'm on the stool and I'm a fucking man, I want to say I'm a fucking man and you can't treat people like this and I . . . I want to sleep so bad and I want to stand up and I want to hold it, just to show them I can do something, but I can't do so many things, I can't even remember to breathe deep, and my eyes burn and the front of my brief gets wet and yellow.

—Boss, him really a piss up himself?

—What, him be six-year-old? Nasty r'ass.

—Guess him couldn't hold it. Detention for this little boy.

They laugh. All of them but Eubie. I have to rub my eyes every few minutes because they get blurry. And I read this thing slow, because once I get to the end of the article they're going to kill me. I can smell myself and feel my toes in my piss.

—Couldn't find any info on the other four. Besides, seven is a good round number.

—Baby need a nappy, Ren-Dog says.

—Continue, Eubie says.

He's walking to me again and I push back so hard I fall over. He pulls me up and I'm crying again and he says, Collect yourself, boy.

—Now continue.

—But . . . but . . . but . . . but then, but then, but then came a—

—Brethren, from the last sentence. You think we still remember it?

—I'm sor . . . I'm sorry.

—Is alright. Take control of yourself. We not going nowhere.

—She was . . . she was, according to her sister, hell-bent on escaping the life that fate had all but drawn up with just numbers left to color. But then came a boy.

"There's always some f—— boy," her sister says. At Shelly's Diner in Flatbush she has already cried twice in between quiet sips of her ice cream soda. Short, chubby and—

—Why you have to describe her so ghetto?

—Huh? I don't unders—

—Short, chubby, and I remember the rest, "dark with hair that looked like the extensions were just removed." What the fuck, white boy, you think she going like to read that?

—It's what—

—It's what, what?

He was right behind me and I was trying not to shake. My face hurt every single time I opened my mouth.

—How you like if me write "Alexander Pierce step out of the bathroom having shaked the piss from his one-inch penis."

—You . . . you telling me how to write?

—I see the smartass Alexander Pierce finally coming back. I'm telling you I don't know shit about your fucking penis. And you don't know nothing about black woman hair.

His hand is on my neck. He just grasped it. Not soft as I can feel his calluses rub against me, but not firm either and I just don't know. Then he squeezes slight.

—You understand me yet? I want you to understand I not playing. Me is the man who will cut your head off and ship it to your mother. And I not saying that for dramatic effect. You understand me?

—Yes.

—Say it.

—Say it?

—Say I understand you.

—I understand you.

—Good. Continue.

I cough for one minute.

—Ex . . . extensions were just removed. "Money-Luv was just about to get out, you hear me? She look at Bushwick and girl was like, see yah. You could just feel it, you know what I'm saying? I mean, she was just wicked smart—"

—Haha, nothing make a white man sound more white than when he try to sound like a black girl.

—Ah . . . "just wicked smart. And then that mofo just come out of nowhere and ruins her life. I don't even blame the drug dealer for killing her. I blame him." Whether or not she picked up the crack habit from sharing a needle with her old boyfriend or not, by 1984 Monifah was totally hooked on crack and an addict before the drug exploded in popularity by the mid to late eighties. A drug whose light-speed rise in New York City can be traced to a few men. Including the gang that killed her.

It's not uncommon for addicts to have one last score before they go clean. In fact Moni—

—Enough about that sorry bitch. Move down.

—Okay. To where exactly?

—The part where you start to talk about the crack house. You know, like in part two. That was killing number two, right? Part two did more real for true. At least you didn't spend so much time trying to show off how you know pretty word. Move to where she turn into killing number three.

—Ah . . . well . . . ah . . . one second.

—You don't know you own story?

He squeezes my neck.

—Okay, okay. From where?

—The crack house.

—Thanks. There is a Bushwick seen at street level, crack level that all but vanishes as soon as you look up. For all the drug deals, connections, amateur prostitutes, scammers, junkies, hustlers and rap music, Bushwick was still one of those rare places in New York where the Gilded Age stared down on you. Ruined Boss Tweed–style houses of processed-meat millionaires with gaudy pillars and huge front facades ripped from European mansions with imported brick and masonry. The remnants of galley windows and fire escapes outside, dumbwaiters and secret passages inside. It was as if the robber barons had built Bushwick for crack barons.

The crack house on the corner of Gates and Central still had most of its regal, brick-red color. Two stairways led to two doorway arches and a third arch in between, with wide windows to reveal from outside what was once a drawing room. Both doorways still popped with green paint. But the rest of the house was from haunted house central casting, hollow gaps where French windows used to be, holes patched with wood, or stuffed with newspaper, other windows shuttered down with weather-rotten wood, graffiti all over the first floor and stray dogs running in and out of garbage heaps as high as snowdrifts. By 1984, the top floor was so unsafe that an addict fell through the wood and got his neck stuck on a nail. He bled to death and hung there for seven days before somebody called the police. The—

—Jesus Christ, white boy, get to the killing, no man. You no see Ren-Dog almost sleeping?

Ren-Dog yawns big and dramatic.—True that, he says.

I read,

—It's not uncommon for a crack addict or any addict for that matter to score one last time before they get clean, so nobody was surprised when Monifah headed to the crack house. Even with this knowledge her friends still believe she would have gotten herself straight starting the next day. If you scored crack in Brooklyn, the crack house at Gates and Central was your mecca—

The entire kitchen groaned.

—Jesus Christ, white boy, you really write that? he says.

—I wrote what?

—That. You just compare one of the holiest place in the world to a crack house. You want we staple the passage to your chest and dump you off at Nation of Islam.

—I didn't mean to—

—You didn't think. I should make one of them shoot you just for that. Fucking idiot. Fucking irresponsible.

—Didn't think some drug dealer was going to preach to me all of a sudd—

He kicks the stool and I go down.

—Get up.

I get up, but the pain hits me in the stomach again and I fall over. I can't even breathe. He just looks at me, waiting and annoyed. I get up again, just to my knees, fix the stool and sit. Part of me hopes it's spit on my cheek, not tears, and part of me is starting to not care.

—Read the rest. Read.

—Just two blocks down from the dealers, but still on Central Avenue. Nobody can confirm her relationship with G-Money, a former dealer from the area who got kicked out of the ring because he consumed too much of his own stash, but they did share a crack habit. G-Money, half Mexican with thick curly hair and wide smile, had ambitions pre-crack as well. That night his brothers saw him leave at around eight p.m. with someone he assumed was a man, but was Monifah dressed in a hoodie and oversized jeans more to hide her pregnancy than to pass as a man—a pregnant woman would have given even a seasoned crack dealer pause.

An old mansion such as the one on Gates Street had many rooms, corners, passages, and hallways, which is why scoring crack, selling it, smoking it, shooting it, even prostituting for it could all transpire under the same roof. G-Money secured the second-floor bedroom near the staircase, the only one that still had a bed, and Monifah, pulling her hoodie back over her head, scored the crack up the street. Though she preferred to shoot up on her own, she always smoked with G-Money. One floor up in a room all to themselves, they had no idea all hell had broken loose below them. A gang of assailants, men connected with the drug gang that ran most of the streets in Bushwick, had burst into the crack house and started killing everyone in their midst. Preacher Bob, cooking in what was left of the kitchen, and Mr. Cee were both already dead. Addicts on the first floor were in a panic, caught between trying to run for their lives and not wanting to lose their pipes, needles or vials in the dark. On the second floor, a woman jumped through a window at the end of the corridor, breaking both legs when she fell. Right outside their door another man fell from two shots to the chest, from both a Glock and another semiautomatic. The gang kicked down the door, shot Monifah straight in the head, the force knocking her down on the bed, her pregnant belly a dead mound on the mattress. G-Money, before he even knew what was going on, grabbed her pipe and took the hit.

The gang continued. There were more to kill. They called themselves the Storm Posse and police records show they operated the same crack house. The killing might have been a warning. A witness claimed it was not a gang doing the shooting but one member, perhaps the leader. Regardless, this was typical M.O. for the gang: the Storm Posse, a loose alliance of Jamaican thugs bred on Third World violence and Colombian drug money that had become in just a few years the most feared crime syndicate on the East Coast.

Eubie takes *The New Yorker* from me.

—Part four: T-Ray Benitez and the Jamdown Connection. You send this piece in yet?

—Yes.

—Too bad. Because you going to call them right now and make a whole heap o' changes.

Ten

J*osey. Seriously, hombre.* Josey.

I can't even see him. The mattress has been blocking my view ever since he grabbed it with both hands and threw it at me. I jumped back before he pulled up the metal bed frame until it was standing and toppled it over to crash against the cell bars. The mattress took the blow but the bed head struck the bars and sparks were flying everywhere. I jumped backward and fell, even though there was no way he was going to break through those bars. Off in the dark he was grunting and growling and some other beasty shit and trying to pull the damn sink out of the wall when he couldn't knock it over.

—Josey.

Josey.

Josef.

—What the bombocloth you want?

—You're not the first guy in lockdown to try to break the sink or the toilet.

—FUCK.

I'm at the gate. Trying to push away the mattress and the bed with my left hand. Neither would budge. I try to push with my right hand and he grabs it.

—What the fuck, Josey?

—Don't fucking Josey me, pussyhole. If I don't fucking business 'bout shooting some pregnant bitch what you think I would do to you?

He yanks me hard and my temple and right brow slam into the iron.

—Everybody seem to think they can fuck with me all of a sudden.

—Josey.

He yanks me again, pulling my whole shoulder in. The bars crush my chest—he's pulling me through it.

—Josey.

A flash of light and I think it's because I'm blinking.

—Josey, let go. Please.

The flash is a machete, shiny like it's new.

—Want to know what happen to the fourth policeman who comc in here trying to kill me?

—Oh my God, Josey.

—But since me and you bonafied I giving you choice. Above the elbow or below? Choose good, because I hear false arm not cheap.

—Oh my God.

—Uh-huh. Look at Doctor Love, think because he can blow up plane and kill old people who want to die anyway, that he bad. Come strolling in here like me on me knees waiting for whichever bone you want to fucking give me. Huh? You no tired of underestimating me, pussyhole? You no tired of me showing you say me have handle and you have blade? Now, pussyhole, me say to choose.

He swipes the machete above my elbow, cuts through the skin and draws blood.

—Above the elbow . . .

He swipes the machete below my elbow this time deeper and draws blood again.

—Or below? Decide in five seconds or I going choose and I might take the whole shoulder.

—Josey, no.

—Five, four—

—Oh my God.

—Three, two.

—You have another one, Josey.

—Another one what? Another second? Is you who don't.

—You have another son, Josey.

The shiny blade swings up and disappears in the dark.

—You have another son.

The machete reappears right at my throat. He's still pulling my hand through the bars.

—Jesus Christ, Josey.

—What you just say?

—You fucking heard what I just said! You have another son. You think we don't know? Your firstborn dead, your girl dead, you only got one left, Josey, and if you don't think we won't come for him I swear to God I'll take this other hand and gut him like a fucking fish.

—Uh-huh? How you going do that when you bleed to death before you even get to the door?

—Because you're right, Josey. It's not just me. What the fuck d'you think, *hombre*? That I would just waltz in here like a fucking idiot? Like I don't know you? You think Daddy's little thugs can protect him from me? I'm Doctor Love, motherfucker. You seem to forget my motherfucking skill set. So you fucking let me go.

—Me must look like a r'asscloth idiot. Let you go so you can press two wire and blow up me fucking house?

—No, *mijo*, so that I can pull the two wires apart and stop it.

He drops the machete before he lets go. I grab my arm but there's nothing to do but wait until it stops bleeding.

—I don't suppose they gave you a roll of toilet paper in there? I guess no.

—I should have killed you.

—And so what if you kill me, Josef? They'll just send another one. They'll just send another one.

He steps away from me and pulls the bed frame enough for it to fall and shake the whole room. The mattress slides to the ground. He sits on the bedspring but doesn't look at me.

—What Eubie want with my son?

—He doesn't want anything with your damn son. He doesn't even want anything from you. Only that you stay the fuck out of New York, I'm guessing.

—What the CIA want?

—Rasta don't work for the CIA. Sorry, bad joke. I'm not here to tell you who sent me, Josey. Relax, nobody wants your son. He could become another you for all we care, at least that's the status quo, which believe or not, everybody was quite fine with until you fucked it up. You didn't even have the smarts to get caught when your own government was in power.

—I don't want nobody touch my son, Luis.

—I said I'm not after your son, Josey.

—But you wire my house for real?

—Of course I wired your fucking house. You and I both know you can smell a bluff.

He laughs and I laugh too. Wish there was somewhere to sit. He's still laughing when I stoop down to the floor and lean back against the wall facing him.

—All this and you still won't tell me who send you.

—Oh, I figured you'd have guessed by now. I only answer to two or three people.

—You answer to whoever paying the biggest cheque.

—Not so. I have been known to do one or two things pro bono.

—I don't even know what that mean.

—Don't worry about it.

—It funny how nobody come in to check out what going on, specially with all the bangarang going on in here.

—Nobody is coming back tonight, *hombre.*

—Should have guessed that one from the second you walk in. You not going tell me who, don't it?

—Might as well tell you who killed Kennedy. Damn, my jokes are going nowhere today.

—Yeah, your jokes is not what making me laugh today, Doctor Love.

I shrug. He gets up and walks over to the bars right in front of me.

—What if I just don't sing about the important business?

—You mean all the stuff that you've been threatening to sing about?

—Yeah.

—Do you know what's important anymore?

—You really think one little man can bring down anybody?

—Fucking Christ, you Jamaicans love to answer a question with a question. But I dunno, Josey, you were the one who raised the possibility.

—Tell your people we can work something out. Them play their cards right, I can all of sudden forget everything before 1981. I can tell them all roads lead to me. Nineteen seventy-six is not them business, nor is 1979. I mean, is the DEA, they just want a drugs conviction.

—So that TV comedies can stop making very special episodes with Nancy Reagan.

—What?

—Another bombed joke.

—Tell your people that me can sell them a case of amnesia and not even for big money.

—Don't do this, Josey.

—Don't do what?

—Don't beg.

—Bad man don't bombocloth beg.

—Then whatever it is you're doing, don't do it.

—I just making sense, Luis. When you ever know me to not make a sense? You think them DEA people have any witness? My lawyer say the most me get is seven years if that much and only for drugs and racketeering. Them can't make nothing else stick.

—You're conveniently forgetting a whole lot.

—Like what?

—That's not what you said before. You said if they ever made the Yankees catch you, you'd bring down everybody with you. Not exactly those words, but in your own colourful way. Well, *muchacho*, by the looks of things . . .

—And look around you. Babylon fall down yet? What you think all this is, Luis? You really think they have any r'asscloth hold 'pon me? So after they make big show for big newspaper and have them big press conference that them win war 'pon drugs, watch how quick they stop giving a shit when they realise they can't hold me. All this shit is to make Ronald Reagan

George Bush look like they saving precious white gal from turning crack whore. You watch how as soon as I done with this Yankee fuckery I going straight back to Copenhagen City, like nothing happen. And I going remember my friends, Luis. And who leave me here to fucking rot, when them wasn't trying to kill me. I going remember, Luis. Medellín going remember too.

—You so sure Medellín didn't send me, Josef?

As usual you learn nothing if you watch Josey's face. You have to look if he's squeezing his knuckles like he just did, hunching his shoulders a little like he just did, swallowing air and puffing it back out like he just did and standing up straight with his back arched super stiff. Yeah, that one struck him hard. Then he says it so soft I almost asked him to repeat,

—Medellín send you?

—You know I can't tell you that. But seriously, Josef. It really doesn't matter. All of this. You telling me what you can do, you making bargains. You already know how this goes, brother. If they were still interested in making deals they would have sent some other guy. Not me.

—Of course.

—I don't have conversations with them, they don't have conversations with me. I don't carry messages from them, I don't take messages from you. That's how it works. If Doctor Love is in your town, baby, it's already too late.

—I should have chop off you hand.

—Maybe. But I'm still leaving your little dynasty alone, such as it is.

—How I know you not going kill my son anyway?

—You don't. But whoever comes after him, and who're we kidding, Josey, somebody eventually will, it won't be me.

He stares at me for a long time. I'm assuming he's thinking this through while he gives me his best poker face.

—Keep Eubie away from my boy.

—Don't think the man gives a shit about your boy, but I'll send a message. He'll listen to me.

—Why?

—You know why.

—Hey.

—Whassup?

—You think Mr. CIA ever find out that I know Spanish?

—Christ, this is what you're asking me? Nah. Plus they put him on indefinite leave when he beat the shit out of a local girl in Botswana. Louis Johnson was such a piece of shit that his own office let the local police hold on to him for four days before they demanded his release.

—Bombo r'asscloth.

—Fly on the wall, man. Would have given anything.

—I guessing that you didn't bother carry a silencer.

—No guns.

—No?

—They want something far more dramatic than that for Josey Wales.

—Jesus Christ, Doctor Love, that would take down the whole prison.

—Concern. That's sweet. But it's not a bomb either. For one, setting that shit up would be a pain in the ass. And two, well, I don't have a two, but it would still be a horrible idea.

—What is today's date?

—Fuck if I . . . wait. March 22. Yeah March 22.

—Nineteen ninety-one.

—When's your birthday, Josef?

—April 16.

—Aries. Fucking figures.

—You expecting some big statement so they will cry when they make the movie?

—Wouldn't dream of it, old friend.

—So how?

—Don't worry about it.

—How?

I walk over to the bars and hold my hand out.

—Take these.

—What the bombocloth is that?

—Just take them.

—No. Fuck off.

—Josef, pour yourself a cup of water and take the fucking pills.

—What kinda pussyhole way that?

—*Mijo*, listen. They made it quite clear you were to suffer. I'm not a man who usually disobeys orders and I'm disobeying this time.

—You can't just make it quick?

—No.

—And what this pill do, some magic where I won't suffer?

—No. Some magic where you won't care.

—Jesus Christ, Luis. Jesus Christ. Jesus Chr—

—Nah, buddy, none of that sentimental bullshit between us, man. Not now.

He takes the pills and walks back into the dark. Water is gushing from the tap. I hear him fill the cup but I don't hear him drink. He comes back to me, grabs the mattress and puts it back on the bed. He looks at me again, then climbs on the bed, lying on his back. I watch him and listen to him breathe in and out, in and out, staring at the ceiling. He's lying there, his hands on his chest, and I want to say, *mijo*, you don't have to act like you already in a fucking coffin. But I've been talking to this man since 1976 and I've finally run out of things to say.

—How long?

—Not too long. Keep talking.

—Luis.

—Yeah, *mijo*.

—I think about him sometimes.

—Who?

—The Singer. That song that come out after him dead, "Buffalo Soldier." It make me think.

—I'm fifty-two years old, too damn old to think. You sorry you tried to kill him?

—What? No. Me sorry him suffer. A gunshot would have be easier. Sometimes I think the one thing people like me and him have in common, is maybe we must die. That whatever we start, can't finish unless we get out of the way. Don't forget that this ghetto man was an intelligent brother.

—Josef, I'm the one they're gonna forget. Remember, I don't even exist.

—Doctor Love. I wish this was 1976. No, 1978.

—What's so great about 1978?

—Everything, brethren. Everything. You c—

Just one pill would have knocked him out, but I wasn't going to take any chances. I stand there for twenty minutes before I pull the key from my pocket and open the cell door. You know what they say about the wounded lions.

Eleven

S*o here me was,* enjoying the nice little crackhead profile, I mean, somebody have to recognize even scum is people too, you know, them heartwarming sinting that turn them back into "people" so that white woman can talk 'bout how they were so touched and shit. But then you fuck it up because you take it 'pon yourself to play detective.

I don't say anything. I don't look at him or Ren-Dog, this floor and *The New Yorker* about to slip out of my hands.

—For a man who don't know if he going make it through the next ten minutes you must be what white people call cocky.

—You seem interested in white people a whole lot.

—I interested in a lot of things a whole lot. As I was saying, where in this part is killing number four?

—You want me to answer?

—No, I want you to do the running man—what you think I want?

—Well, at some point you gotta cxpand on a story. You can't just give it focus, you gotta give it scope. Shit doesn't just happen in a void, there're ripples and consequences and even with all that there's still a whole fucking world going on, whether you're doing something or not. Or else it's just a report of some shit that happened somewhere and you can get that from nightly news. I mean, while Monifah was getting shot because of one crack hit, somebody just bought a crack vial from somebody, who got it from somebody, whose supply came from somebody.

It's only him and Ren-Dog in the kitchen with me, the others have gotten bored probably. And even Ren-Dog is back in the fridge helping himself to the mango juice he said he left for me. I keep telling myself that this scene is no less dangerous than ten minutes ago, it only looks that way. Bunch of killers gone all domestic in my house and I start to think I'm in a rap video. Until I feel my soaked briefs. Or smile. Or swallow.

—First thing first. All this shit you write about the Storm Posse, most of this shit not even true. For one, Funnyboy is from the Eight Lanes and him still there so there's no way he could be Storm Posse. And who tell you that them call we the Storm Posse because we, what you say? Cut our enemies and innocent bystanders down in a hailstorm of bullets. Anybody here look like the people who would use word like hailstorm? What the fuck wrong with you? And here me did think we pick Storm because hurricane was just too damn long.

—I have a source.

—Your source.

—He's nobody.

—Look how you noble, trying to protect Tristan Phillips. You think he feel the same way 'bout you?

—He tipped you off?

—Not like the man was trying to keep no secret. And who you be that he should keep secret for you? Hell, when your part one come out, two of my men who used to roll with Ranking Dons remember Tristan talking 'bout you and he didn't care who hear. Brethren, seriously you could look 'bout getting a new look. Them take one look at your picture and bam. Anyway, that's how me find out 'bout you.

—Tristan sold me out.

—The only brother Tristan sell out is Tristan. Man licking the crack pipe hard now. Fucking fool, what a waste. But such is life for the Ranking Dons. If a Storm man start smoke him own stash I make haste and done that brother. But if you did go check Phillips in prison that must be at least a few years ago. Why write this something now?

—I knew Josey Wales was in prison.

—And you think he can't touch you now, or you think him so ignorant he would never hear about anything named *The New Yorker*?

I don't know what to say so I just look at the glass of juice Ren-Dog has in his hand and try to remember how many he's downed by now.

—Don't worry, my brother. You right on both counts. But this Eubie person is another story. Look on the front of that magazine and you even see my name and post office box on it. You think 'cause him in prison you safe? Answer.

—Yes, yes I did.

—Them kinda loose thinking get a motherfucker shot.

Eubie grabs a chair by my dining table and carries it over to me. He sits facing me, close enough that I can see the butterfly pattern on his white pocket square.

—This the part where you tell me to abandon my story or you'll do whatever with me? I say.

—You really can't help yourself, don't it? Smart mouth to the end. Or maybe you finally think you have nothing to lose. Well no, my brethren. Even me want to know how it turn out. I mean, I know how it turn out, but me like the sideways thing you ah do. Just stop look too far sideways and rein your r'asscloth self in and me won't have nothing to do with you.

—I don't get it.

He slaps me with *The New Yorker.* It stings but not that much.

—Don't act like you fucking dense. You not my only stop tonight and the other two not going end as nice as you. End of part three you leave the fucking crack house because you gone off on the Jamaican connection, so—

—You want me to take it out.

He slaps me again.

—I want you to stop interrupting me when I r'asscloth talking to you.

—But that's what you want, right? You want me to take out all the Jamaican stuff?

—No, my youth. Not at all. Keep in whatever you fucking want about Jamaica. Keep the Josey Wales part, in fact what you want to know 'bout him? I can tell you one thing, something you wouldn't even dream about. This Monifah woman is not even the first pregnant woman him kill. Keep him, keep Jamaica, burn down the fucking country for all I care. But leave New York out of it.

—I'm sorry?

—You mention here about the Storm Posse with splinter groups in New York. That don't sit good with me.

—But the Storm Posse is in New York.

—Boy, you turn dense again? For one, here's another thing you don't know. No damn gang shoot up that crack house. It was Josey one. One man with two gun. Josey Wales' one kill everybody in the crack house. Me see him do it meself.

—I . . . I . . . that's unbelievable.

—That's Josey. And you're right. The man did want to send a message. But it ain't nothing like them profound shit you write in that story.

—What was the message then, just say no?

—This boy full of joke, eh? Pity we not going be friend.

—Oh.

—All now the white boy can't take joke, Ren. Me look like the kind of idiot who would kill a journalist in the middle of him big story, with my fingerprints all over him fucking house? Me look like me want to become the next Gotti?

—I guess not.

—Don't guess, know.

—What was the message?

—Don't throw piss 'pon the don Gorgon.

—I'm sorry, what?

—That one pass you, white boy. But listen to me now. I don't want no link between this man and any damn borough. If the Fed or the DEA want to prosecute the brethren, let them prosecute. But I don't want nobody come after me because they looking for American links in New York, you hear me?

—Seriously? That's just a matter of time, dude. DEA may be slow and got envy issues with the Feds, but they're not stupid.

—Maybe. But not today. And the dude who going buss me not going be you.

—Look, no agent has ever approached me or anything. You've got nothing to worry about.

—That's because you don't have nothing so far that they can use. But they would with this here part four. Far as you know, them boys in the crack house fly up from Jamaica for a special trip. None of this shit about New York gangs, or Boston, or Kansas City.

—They know you're here. In this city, I mean.

—But they don't know I'm organized, or just how much I have my shit together.

—But that leaves a fucking hole in the story.

—That the hole you worried about? Me not telling you how to write, boss, but your story is about people who get shot. So write 'bout the people who get shot.

—The killings didn't happen in a vacuum. Sir.

—I like how you still seem to think this is a negotiation. I didn't say it did. That's why you can hang Josey Wales out to dry all you want. But cut all that other shit out. Don't want to share Mr. Wales' spotlight, you see me?

—So technically you're blackmailing me?

—Oh no, my brethren. Technically I'm not killing you. You writing a brief history of seven killings, right? Then you have four more killings to write about.

—I see. And what if—

—Don't make this the part of the story where you ask what if I refuse. I don't have the patience and Ren-Dog done play for the day.

Eubie gets up and goes over to Ren-Dog. Whatever they're whispering I don't know but Ren-Dog leaves. Seconds later the front door opens and shuts. He comes back to me and sits down. Closer. Cool Water cologne. I knew I was going to recognize it eventually. He leans over this time, almost whispering but his voice is gravelly.

—So I am here thinking, if Tony Pavarotti was after you, then somebody must send him after you. That could only be Papa-Lo or Josey Wales. And since Papa was on a peace thing till him dead I going just say it was Josey Wales, don't bother confirm it. So why Josey did want to kill you?

—You really expect me to answer?

—Yes, I really expect you to answer that.

—What is this? Some I'm-going-to-die-anyway-so-just-confess fuckery?

—Fuckery? Brethren, me love when you talk the Jamaican still. As for killing you, I don't see why I'm going to do that when I've already made my wishes very clear. And by the way, Josey Wales not going touch anybody for a long time, least of all you.

—Did he tell you about me?

—Somebody like you came up, he couldn't remember your name, just said some white boy from *Rolling Stone* find out too much about a drug thing so he send Tony to straighten him out. Except the years wasn't adding up, and no white man would know anything 'bout any drug deal no matter how he smart. Clearly if you kill him best man he wasn't going send another one. Besides, you disappear after that. Anyway, Josey Wales in prison and he not coming out alive. So I want to know what the fuck you find out to make him try to kill a fucking white man from America. And in 1979? I mean, shit, that was fifteen different taboo him cross right there so.

—You're Storm Posse, though. Don't you work for him?

—Boy, me no work for bloodcloth nobody. Least of all some ghetto mouse in Kingston. Motherfucker can't even read a spreadsheet but think him fucking smart. I not asking you a third time, white boy.

—I . . . I didn't realize until years later that he sent the guy. There was just so much going on in Jamaica, so much bullshit, it could have been anybody, even the fucking government. A guy made me realize . . . shit, shit. I don't know why you asking me this, you work with him so you already know. You probably planned that shit with him.

—What shit? What shit?

—The Singer. Killing the Singer. He's the one who shot the Singer.

—What you just say?

Before I answer he gets up quick and starts walking around me.

—Motherfucker, what you just say?

—He's the one that shot the Singer back in 1976.

—You mean he was in the gang? Boss, even me did know that is must Copenhagen City boys try kill him. Though I would never expect that from—

—I mean, he fired the actual shot. Shots.

—How the fuck you know?

—I interviewed the Singer some months after. Everybody knows he was shot in the chest and the arm, right? Right?

—Right.

—At that time only three people knew that had he inhaled instead of exhaled the bullet would have gone straight through his heart. The doctor, the Singer and me.

—So?

—I went to Copenhagen City to interview the dons about the peace treaty in '79. When I spoke to Wales, the Singer came up. He said it was fucked up that they tried to shoot the Singer right in the heart. He couldn't have known that yet, not unless he was the doctor, the Singer, myself or—

—The shooter.

—Yeah.

—Bombocloth. Bombocloth, my youth. I didn't know.

—Now you're shocking me. I thought everybody connected to Wales knew.

—Who tell you I connected to Wales? When me was building business in the Bronx where the fuck was Wales? You know for the longest while me did think it was somebody else who was behind this thing.

—Who's that?

—Funny, and him is the only one me know that not dead.

—Wales?

—No, not him.

—What do you mean by—

—Did you know, Mr. Pierce, that the Singer did forgive one of them boys? Not only forgive him but take the man 'pon tour, bring him closer than a brother into him inner circle.

—What the fuck, seriously? I think my already considerable admiration for the man just jumped by leaps and bounds. Shit. What happened to him?

—Disappeared right after the Singer died. He knew shit wasn't safe.

—He just vanished. Just like that.

—Well, nobody ever really vanish, Pierce.

—I have some Chilean families to introduce you to.

—What?

—Nothing.

—You good with German?

—I listen to some Kraut rock . . . No.

—Pity. You want a story, there's a story. Every single man but one who go after the Singer end up dead.

—But Josey Wales not—

—The only one who might be alive, disappear in 1981 and nobody seem to know where he gone. But me.

—And where is that?

—You no seem too interested.

—No, I am. Really. Where is he?

—As I said, you not interested.

—And I'm saying I am. How do you know I'm not interested?

—Because I just tell you where him is. But don't fret yourself. This probably too big for you. One day somebody going need to write a book 'bout it.

—Oh. Okay.

—You go back to writing your *Brief History of Seven Killings.*

I almost say thank you but it hits me just as quick that I would be thanking the man for not killing, but merely extorting me. I'm so fucking tired of sitting on this stool like I'm the school dunce but I don't get up. Doesn't matter anyway. I'm about to ask if by writing this shit does it mean I may never get the pleasure of seeing him again, but remember that Jamaicans rarely get sarcasm and fuck knows this is not one of those situations where you want them to misinterpret it as downright hostility. Better to just not think of any of this shit—a day this surreal couldn't have happened anyway. Ren-Dog comes back in and they stand not too far from me mumbling some shit I guess must be kept secret.

—One more thing, white boy.

He turns around. His hand. A gun. Silencer. His hand. A gun silencer. His—

—NOOOOOO! Holy fucking shit! Holy fucking shit! Oh my God. Holy fu— Holy fuck.

—Yes, one more thing.

—You fucking shot me! You motherfucking shot me!

Blood is fucking spurting from my fucking foot like I was just fucking crucified. I grab my foot and know I'm screaming but don't know that I'm off the stool and rolling around on the floor until Eubie grabs me and sticks the gun in my neck.

—Shut the fuck up. Shut the fuck, pussyhole, Ren-Dog says and grabs my hair.

—You fucking shot me! He fucking shot me.

—And the sky blue and water wet.

—Oh my fucking God. Oh God.

—You know it's funny. Nobody ever says anything original after getting shot. It's almost like everybody read a guidebook just in case.

—Fuck you.

—Aw don't cry, big baby. Twelve-year-old boy get shot in Jamaica all the time and they don't bawl like bitch.

—Oh my God.

My foot's fucking screaming and he's stooping down and fucking cradling me like a fucking infant.

—I need to fucking call 911. I need to go to the hospital.

—You also going need your woman to come clean up this mess.

—Oh God.

—Listen, white boy. This is to remind you, because hey, we was getting along so sweet that you probably forget, this is the wrong motherfucker to fuck with, you see me? Josey Wales is the most psychotic son of a bitch I ever come 'cross in my life, and I just fucking kill him. So what you think that make me?

—I don't—

—Is a rhetorical question, pussyhole.

He reaches down and touches my foot. Rubs around the bullet hole in my sock then sticks his finger in. I scream into the palm Ren-Dog just slapped over my mouth.

—As much as I like your present company and much as I love my subscription to *The New Yorker*, make sure you don't give me a reason to fucking come here again. You see me?

He moves his hand but all I can do is cry. Not even weep, fucking cry.

—You see me? he says and reaches for my foot again.

—I see you. Goddamn it, I see.

—Good. Goody goody gumdrops. My woman love to say that one.

Ren-Dog grabs me by the shoulders and pulls me over to the couch. This going hurt like a bitch is all he says before he yanks my socks off. I have to slap my own mouth to keep the scream in my throat. He throws the socks away, rolls my kitchen towel into a ball and places my foot on top. I can't even bear to look. Ren-Dog leaves and Eubie grabs my phone.

—Call 911 when we leave.

—How the fu . . . how the . . . bullet in foot, how do I explain . . . bullet in the foot?

—You're the writer, Alexander Pierce.

I block my balls so it hits my knuckles when he throws the phone in my lap.

—Make something up.

Twelve

Every time I pass on the subway to take the bus I forget that the bus is so much slower. Price I pay for hyperventilating whenever I'm underground. At least I'm awake. Last week I slept past seven stops and woke up to some man in the seat across looking me over, like he was trying to figure out which body part to touch to wake me up. No men on the bus today.

Eastchester is empty too. Maybe the Jamaican football team is losing a game somewhere. It says something about me that even in my own thoughts I'm such a considerable bitch. I'm sure the average person is just as rude, racist, irritable and nasty in their own thoughts too, so I don't know why I'm beating up myself. I just need to get home, make some ramen noodles, throw myself on the couch and watch *America's Funniest Home Videos* or some other no-commitment TV.

I really need to stop thinking about Jamaicans. Or maybe I really need to up the Xanax. I mean, I don't feel bad right now, I really don't, but common cold is not the only thing you can feel coming.

At Corsa. There's no food in my house. I ate the last ramen two days ago, threw out all the Chinese this morning, and those McNuggets were a bad idea, even when they were fresh. I'm looking at my door and the window that looks like I left it open, even though it's March and know there's no food in my house. I really don't want to go to Boston Road, but this is what's going to happen. I'm going to sit inside and watch TV until the hunger I'm not feeling now gets worse, and then end up going anyway.

So I'm walking down Corsa to Boston still hoping for my Mary Tyler Moore moment. The dumbest idea ever on a street packed with people not making it, but I still imagine. This is what happens when your life is work, TV and takeout. It's almost like I'm living like an American, damn it, and screw all of you and your rules. I don't know. But I do know if I had popped a Xanax I wouldn't have been thinking so much already. I like to believe that everything in my house, from towels all the same colour, to the coffee machine where I press one button, is there just to make my life simple, but I'm realizing that they are all there to make sure I don't think. Imagine, my mother thought I could never put my life together.

Boston Jamaica Jerk Chicken. Jamaican Chicken and Food, Hot and Ready. Two rows of orange plastic booths with ketchup, salt and pepper on every table. Eat here? The thought is gone as soon as I think about it. On the counter right beside the cash register, coconut drops are in a cake dish reminding me of country. Never liked going to country—too much coconut drops and pit toilets. Right beside it another cake dish with what looks like potato pudding. I haven't had potato pudding since 1979—no, longer. The more I look at it the more I want it, and the more it feels like I should think it's a sign of something deeper, that what I really want is to taste Jamaica and that just sounds like some psychological bullshit. Funnier to think I just want something Jamaican in my mouth that's not a penis. Damn dirty woman—no, damn dutty gal.

Now me feel like me want chat patois all night, and it's not because I was hanging around that woman and her gunman boyfriend all afternoon. Maybe it's because I'm looking at damn coconut drops and feel like asking if they have any dukunnu, asham or jackass corn.

—What I can get you, ma'am?

Didn't even see him sitting behind the counter, but then I see why he didn't see me. Cricket on the small black-and-white TV on the plastic chair beside his.

—West Indies versus India. Of course we doing nothing but bare fuckery again, he says.

I nod. Never liked cricket, ever. Dark skin, big belly in between two muscular arms and a white goatee. This might be the first Jamaican man I'm speaking to in weeks and his eyebrows are raised—fed up with me already.

—Can I get a roast chicken no fry chicken yes fry chicken and rice and peas if you have rice and peas and some fry plantain and shredded salad and—

—Woi, lady, slow down. The food nah run nowhere.

He's laughing at me. Well, more like grinning and I don't mind except now it making me wonder when last I make a man laugh.

—You have ripe plantain though?

—Yes, lady.

—How ripe?

—Ripe enough.

—Oh.

—Lady, don't worry, it well ripe. The plantain going just mash up in your mouth.

I resist telling him I really mean it when I say that's the most delicious description of food I have ever heard ever, and say,

—Three servings please.

—Three?

—Three. Second thought, you have any oxtail or curry goat?

—Oxtail on the weekend. Curry goat just finish.

—Fry chicken is fine. Leg and thigh thank you.

—What you want to drink?

—Is sorrel that on the menu?

—Yes, ma'am.

—I thought you could only get sorrel at Christmas.

—But wait. Is where you deh the last umpteen years, lady? Everything Jamaican boxed up and on sale.

—It taste good?

—It don't taste bad.

—I'll take one.

Didn't feel like taking all this food back to the house. I don't know but I loved the idea of just sitting in this little restaurant overhearing the announcer on TV get excited over cricket and eating fried chicken. There's a Jamaica *Gleaner* and a *Star* newspaper in the booth right across. Also *Ja-*

maica Observer, which I've never heard of. The man turns on the big TV mounted from the ceiling, and the first thing that comes on is cricket.

—That JBC? I say.

—Nah, some hurry-come-up Caribbean network, maybe Trinidad, the way everybody sound so sing-songy. Is 'cause of them why Jamaica have carnival now.

—Carnival? With soca music?

—Eehi.

—Since when Jamaicans like soca music?

—Since uptown want reason to dance in them brassiere and panty 'pon the street. Then hi, you no hear 'bout carnival?

—No.

—You must no go back too much. Or you no have no family 'pon the rock. You read the newspaper?

—No.

—Is forget you a try forget.

—What?

—Never mind, me love. I hope you raising your children like Jamaica and none of them American slackness, you know.

—I don't have—I mean, yes.

—Good. Good. Just like the Bible say. Train a child how he should grow and—

And I'm already tuning out. I'm in a little Jamaican food shop tuning out a man giving me granny wisdom. But damn this is good fry chicken, light brown and almost chunky and soft inside like he fried it then baked it. And rice and peas together, not the separated shit from Popeyes I have to mix together. I'm already a third of the way through this plate of plantains and was this close to anointing sorrel my favourite processed, possibly toxic, chemical lab re-creation of an original drink.

—Bombo pussy r'asscloth.

Couldn't remember the last time I heard those words coming out a mouth that wasn't mine.

—Bombo pussy r'asscloth.

—What going on?

—Look, me love. R'ass.

All I'm seeing is bad video of a Jamaican crowd, probably the same stock footage they've been using for the past fifteen years whenever anybody does a story on Jamaica. The same black men in t-shirts and tank tops, the same woman jumping up and down, the same placards made out of cardboard from people who can't spell. The same army jeep moving in and out of camera. Seriously.

—Bombo pussy r'ass—

I'm about to ask him what so special about this report when I read the streamer at the bottom of the screen.

JOSEY WALES FOUND BURNED TO DEATH IN PRISON CELL.

The man turns up the volume yet I'm still not hearing a thing. There only the slab on the screen. Some man naked from the waist up, skin shiny like it was melting from all the heat, chunks of his chest and side blackened, large spots white like only his skin was burned off. Skin peeled off his breast like a suckling pig. I really couldn't tell if the photo was out of focus or he really did melt.

—Copenhagen City burning down now. And the same day they go bury him son? Lawd a massy.

It's running across the screen now: JOSEY WALES FOUND BURNED TO DEATH IN PRISON CELL * JOSEY WALES FOUND BURNED TO DEATH IN PRISON CELL * JOSEY WALES FOUND BURNED TO DEATH IN PRISON CELL * JOSEY WALES FOUND BURNED TO DEATH IN PRISON CELL

—No sign of forced entry, no visitors allowed in the cell today, nobody can say how the man get burn up. Maybe him just catch fire 'pon himself. Rahtid me can't believe—

—They sure is him?

—Who else it going be? Some other man in General Penitentiary name Josey Wales? Shit. Fuck. Excuse me y'hear, lady, a nuff people me have to call now. Me can't be— Lady, you alright?

I make it through the door just before the vomit burst my lips open and splatters all over the sidewalk. Somebody across the street must be watching me hack fried chicken while my own belly is contracting the life out of me. Nobody is coming but I still left a mess right near his door. I'm trying to stand up straight but my stomach kicks itself again and I bowl over hacking but no vomit. At least the man is back behind the counter. I go inside, pick up my bag and walk out.

I'm on my couch and the TV has been on for two hours but I still don't know what I'm watching. Don't think I've ever seen a man look cooked. I really should get a cover for this sofa. And maybe a painting or something for the living room. And a good plant, no a fake plant, any living thing would die under me. The phone has been in my lap for minutes now. Just as the credits start to roll it rings.

—Hello?

—Putting you through now, ma'am.

—Thank you, thanks.

My hands are shaking, making the phone rattle against my earring.

—Hello? Hello? Hello, who's speaking?

My hands are shaking and I know if I don't say something now, I'm going to slam down the phone before she speaks again.

—Kimmy?

ACKNOWLEDGMENTS

Even before I knew I had a novel, Colin Williams was doing research for it. Some of that hard work appears in this book, but more of it will appear in the next. By the time Benjamin Voigt took over as researcher I had a narrative, even a few pages, but still not quite a novel. The problem was that I couldn't tell whose story it was. Draft after draft, page after page, character after character, and still no through line, no narrative spine, nothing. Until one Sunday, at W.A. Frost in St. Paul, when I was having dinner with Rachel Perlmeter, she said what if it's not one person's story? Also, when last did I read Faulkner's *As I Lay Dying*? Well maybe not in those exact words, but we also talked about Marguerite Duras, so I went and read *The North China Lover* as well. I had a novel, and it was right in front of me all that time. Half-formed and fully formed characters, scenes out of place, hundreds of pages that needed sequence and purpose. A novel that would be driven only by voice. At the very least I knew what to tell my other researchers, Kenneth Barrett and Jeeson Choi, to look for. In the meantime, thanks to a travel and research grant from Macalester College, where I teach, I was able to do quite a bit of research on my own. Without brilliant and creative students to challenge me all the time, and a strong and supportive English Department, the four years spent on this novel wouldn't have been quite as successful or rewarding. That one-year sabbatical didn't hurt either. Quite of bit of that sabbatical was spent writing at a French café in South Beach, Miami, thanks to awesome support and free room and board from Tom Borrup and Harry Waters Jr., who (knock wood) have yet to charge me rent though I invent reasons to use their place all the time. In fact, the draft that I eventually showed to my wonderful agent, Ellen Levine, and fine editor, Jake Morrissey, was written not far from the actual beach. Before them of course was Robert Mclean, my first-draft reader, and still the only person I trust to read a manuscript even as I am in the process of writing it (though he is still mystified as to why). Jeffrey Bennett, my brilliant last-draft reader, line-edited the whole thing before it went off to the publisher and corrected, among other things, my wildly erroneous depiction of the drive from JFK airport to the Bronx. And thanks to Martha Dickson, who translated my loose English into Cuban Spanish when I made the mistake of thinking Mexican Spanish would do. A writer can go through days of distraction and self-doubt, so thanks to Ingrid Riley and Casey Jarrin for unwavering friendship, support and an occasional kick in the ass. Thanks to my family and friends, and this time around maybe my mother should stay away from part four of the book.